CW01508731

Angus&Robertson

Twenty-seven-year-old Scotsman David Mackenzie Angus stepped ashore in Australia in 1882, hoping that the climate would improve his health. While working for a Sydney bookseller, he managed to save the grand sum of £50 – enough to open his very own second-hand bookshop. He hired fellow-Scot George Robertson and in 1886 Angus & Robertson was born.

They ventured into publishing in 1888 with a collection of poetry by H. Peden Steele, and by 1895 had a bestseller on their hands with A.B. 'Banjo' Paterson's *The Man from Snowy River and Other Verses*. A&R confirmed the existence of Australian talent – and an audience hungry for Australian content. The company went on to add some of the most famous names in Australian literature to its list, including Henry Lawson, Norman Lindsay, C.J. Dennis and May Gibbs. Throughout the twentieth century, authors such as Xavier Herbert, Ruth Park, George Johnston and Peter Goldsworthy continued this tradition.

The A&R Australian Classics series is a celebration of the many authors who have contributed to this rich catalogue of Australian literature and to the cultural identity of a nation.

These classics are our indispensable voices. At a time when our culture was still noisy with foreign chatter and clouded by foreign visions, these writers told us our own stories and allowed us to examine and evaluate both our homeplace and our place in the world. – GERALDINE BROOKS

About the Author

Ernestine Hill was born in 1899 in Rockhampton, Queensland. She consolidated her career as a journalist during the 1930s. When her husband died in 1933 Hill embarked on a life of almost continual travel and writing, from which some of her major published works arose. Hill's first book, *The Great Australian Loneliness*, published in 1937, was a huge success. A strongly visual account of outback travel, it had the added interest of being from a woman's perspective at a time when such publications were rare. It was followed by *Water into Gold*. *My Love Must Wait* was published in 1941. In 1947 she published *Flying Doctor Calling*, followed by *The Territory* in 1951. *Kabbarli,* a personal memoir of Daisy Bates, with whom Hill had a long and turbulent association, was published posthumously in 1973.

A Commonwealth Literary Fund fellowship, awarded to Hill in 1959, provided her with a small pension. Sadly, the last years of Hill's life were dominated by financial hardship and ill-health. She died in Brisbane in 1972.

Also by Ernestine Hill

The Great Australian Loneliness 1937
Water into Gold 1937
Flying Doctor Calling 1947
The Territory 1951
Kabbarli 1973

MY LOVE MUST WAIT

ERNESTINE HILL

AUSTRALIAN CLASSICS

A&R Classics
An imprint of HarperCollins*Publishers*

First published in 1941 by Angus and Robertson Publishers
This edition published in 2013
by HarperCollins*Publishers* Australia Pty Ltd
ABN 36 009 913 517
harpercollins.com.au

HarperCollins*Publishers*
Level 13, 201 Elizabeth Street, Sydney NSW 2000, Australia
31 View Road, Glenfield, Auckland 0627, New Zealand
A 53, Sector 57, Noida, UP, India
77–85 Fulham Palace Road, London, W6 8JB, United Kingdom
2 Bloor Street East, 20th floor, Toronto, Ontario M4W 1A8, Canada
10 East 53rd Street, New York NY 10022, USA

National Library of Australia Cataloguing-in-Publication entry:

Hill, Ernestine, 1899–1972.
  My love must wait / Ernestine Hill.
  978 0 7322 9696 4 (pbk.)
  978 1 7430 9933 9 (ebook)
  Flinders, Matthew, 1774–1814 – Fiction.
  Australia – Discovery and exploration – Fiction.
  Mauritius – Fiction.
A823.2

Cover design by Darren Holt, HarperCollins Design Studio
Cover images by shutterstock.com
Typeset in 10.5/12pt Times Roman by Kirby Jones

for
My Mother

Introduction

Recorded history often avoids the less glorious aspects of its great achievers, but Australian history is full of sad stories. One of its saddest must surely be that of Matthew Flinders. The public remembers the navigator, explorer, cartographer, and the person who gave Australia its name. Popular enduring images of Flinders include his friendship with George Bass, their adventures in the *Tom Thumb*, his cat Trim. From an obscure Lincolnshire family, Flinders went to sea at the age of 16, sailed with Captain Bligh, took command of his own ship at 26, circumnavigated and mapped the continent, survived shipwreck and the numerous other disasters and hardships of a life at sea. If all that wasn't enough for one short lifetime, Flinders was unfairly imprisoned and in exile for six years, and only lived briefly with his wife of ten years before dying — far too young, at the age of 40 — the day before his magnificent life's work saw publication.

Yet these last are the details we tend to forget. The author Ernestine Hill was probably the first to reach into the sadness of Matthew Flinders's life, and she crafted a story of immense tenderness and appeal, a book which has been one of the great successes of Australian publishing. *My Love Must Wait* first appeared amid wartime austerity in late 1941, but its initial print run of 3000 quickly sold out. Subsequent reprints also sold out and despite apparent paper shortages and other production problems due to the war, it was reprinted regularly until the end of that decade, achieving record sales for an Australian novel. Then in the 1960s it saw renewed success with several paperback editions, as well as overseas publications and translations.

Aside from this, and her other popular titles, Ernestine Hill's own story was not such a triumphant one. In many ways hers was also a sad and unusual life and she certainly seemed to have a hunger for travel and adventure that possibly matched Flinders's. She was born in 1899 in Rockhampton, Queensland, and died at the age of 73 in 1972. There is little information about Hill's life, and she liked it that way. A short feature on her written by Mary Durack was published in 1952 in *Walkabout*, one of the magazines for which Hill regularly wrote in her capacity as a freelance journalist. Durack's image of Hill is vivid: 'a slim dark girl in a wideawake straw hat and with no luggage but a small suitcase, a thin swag and a typewriter' who first appeared on the verandah of the Duracks' Ivanhoe station in 1930. And it was no exaggeration: Hill travelled very light, for decades taking the bare necessities and her portable typewriter. Sometimes she was accompanied by trunks of her voluminous notes and manuscripts, at other times she lodged these at temporary headquarters along her journeys across the country.

Hill was cagey about her early years, and may not even have been married, though she claimed to be a young widow, and she had a child. She told Durack that she only wanted the stories of the people and the places she visited to be broadcast, as nothing else about her was relevant. But quite a lot about her endlessly curious personality can be deduced from her books, as they were quite literally her life; she lived the experiences in order to write about them. *The Great Australian Loneliness*, published in 1937, reveals a lone adventurer possessed by the need to explore and experience the land first hand. Writing this book took her five years and 50,000 miles travelling across the country by almost every form of transport available, but if that was not enough, she completed further journeys for more books, notably her other great success, *The Territory*, published in 1951. As her letters to Angus and Robertson's famous editor, Beatrice Davis, show, she oscillated between yearning to settle down and itching to be off, never appearing to reconcile the two; a little about Hill's unusual life appears in Jacqueline Kent's biography of Davis (*A Certain Style*, 2001).

One thing we do know about Hill is her obsession with detail and the facts. A novel *My Love Must Wait* might be, but only in form. Its content was as true as she could make it. She claimed she invented nothing, and the documentary evidence of Flinders's life supports this. 'More than a million words' went into the writing of this book, she told Durack, such was the extent of her note-taking and redrafting.

Hill's final chapter to *My Love Must Wait*, written in non-fiction as a sort of afterword, confirms what Durack also noted in her short article: true to the approach she took for her travel books, she lived, as far as it was possible, Flinders's life. By the time Hill came to write this book she had not only traversed the continent (which doubtless he would have too, if he could) but, like him, sailed all the way around it. She read his logs and journals, she perused his letters and private diaries, so that she can confidently declare at the end of this novel, 'Not in any instance have I played with history' (even the dialogue, much of it in Flinders's native Lancashire dialect, was based on these sources). She also absorbed other writings about the man, particularly Ernest Scott's 1914 *The Life of Matthew Flinders*, which she acknowledges as a source. And then she followed his voyages, sailing in 'strange crafts' (for that, I think we read any vessel that would take her, in these remote places) through the Australian waters that he explored.

In fact it was this that first attracted Hill to the story of Matthew Flinders. In the mid-1930s, when she sailed across the Gulf of Carpentaria during her travels for *The Great Australian Loneliness* she discovered that the skipper was using charts of the Gulf made by Flinders well over one hundred years before — in 1802, to be exact. She was astonished to learn that, such was their accuracy, none had been made since. For her, the seasoned journalist with a nose for a good story, this was the hook, and the rest, particularly the poignancy of Flinders's relationship with his childhood sweetheart, from whom he was to be separated for so long, compounded her fascination. Seven years later, the novel was published.

But why a novel? Hill was a travel writer, and an extremely good one at that, with a special flair for bringing the remote and the unknown to readers yet to be swamped by visual and other forms of media coverage. Somehow, though, beyond her desire for historical accuracy, she sensed that the story of Flinders's life was perfect for fiction. It contained extraordinary dramas and ironies; for instance, the man died just the day before his great work — a handsome three-volume affair in red leather, containing the most exquisite maps and his journal of his discoveries — was published. It was too melodramatic, too tragic. Hill clearly didn't see the need for another biography, instead she saw how the potential for the emotional aspects of Flinders's life, necessarily sidelined in other accounts, could be realised through the form of the historical novel.

My Love Must Wait is not exactly a love story, though this is certainly implied by the flowery title (augmented by equally romantic period cover illustrations throughout its paperback reprints; Hill strongly resisted the title at first, but later when the book proved to be such a success, she conceded its appropriateness). The fact is, Matthew and Ann Flinders spent little time together, and while the idea of their mutual devotion is a strong thematic element of this novel, the actual story contains very little of their relationship. It is certainly a force in the life of Flinders, but what we see surging forward through the narrative are his own adventures and explorations, and the experiences that were so crucial to his destiny, such as his six years of exile on Mauritius — the Ile-de-France — and the destructive weight of Governor Decaen's indifference to his plight.

Hill's Flinders is a poetic figure, grand, tragic and romantic, a man of impulse as well as intelligence, a man caught by the vicissitudes of a fate that swings wildly from benign to hostile, a man whose ultimate destiny should have involved glory not obscurity. By prefacing the book with his end, she establishes the pathos of his early death amid the indignity of poverty and disappointment. And in this sad story surely there is nothing more sad nor so profoundly ironic than the final description of Flinders on his deathbed, his hand laid upon the newly published volumes that represented his entire life's work, but oblivious to them.

These sorts of ironies don't come without some cost. Despite her historical faithfulness Hill does idealise him, glossing over or ignoring certain aspects of his life. She allows us to glimpse his moments of arrogance, misjudgment or pride, for instance in Chapter 18, where he effectively alienates himself from the chance of the French's goodwill by refusing to attend dinner, but these aspects of his personality are generally downplayed; partly this is because she really only writes from his perspective, thus at times ignoring the possibility of other sympathetic viewpoints.

Journalistic excesses and the tendency to over- rather than understate were also features of her writing that often went unchecked (although the American edition of *The Great Australian Loneliness*, entitled *Australian Frontier*, was considerably edited and effectively tightened up from start to finish). Davis, whose editorial hand was restrained when it came to Hill's work, evidently did not interfere in *My Love Must Wait* either; though perhaps a decade or two on, changing tastes might have meant she would. It is a style that is certainly dated now, but even though at times Hill lingers in the depths of her chosen genre, it also allows her to exploit its thrilling heights. Not too far into the novel I think we become seduced by her enthusiasm. By its end we are convinced that this is the way to convey the extent of this singular man's passions and obsessions, elations and miseries.

In this account of thwarted ambition as well as great achievement, two strong souls loom large. I can't help thinking that in writing of Flinders's journeys and adventures, Hill was also writing of herself, of her own intrepid and restless spirit that sought adventure like some kind of addictive drug, and was therefore never satisfied by it.

There is growing information about Flinders as well as the public availability of his letters and diaries and his wife's letters. The sources combine to offer a picture of the 'real' Flinders as a complex man, meticulous, diligent, consumed by conflicting demands, trapped within greater human dramas, possessed of awesome talents. It is a picture of someone increasingly crushed by frustrating events, someone whose achievements never amounted to the great triumphs that they so thoroughly deserved. Ernestine Hill's exceptional historical novel offers us a vital part of that picture.

Debra Adelaide
January 2002

Contents

Prologue

Dawn came to London Street, a creeping old hag, clawing along the tenement railings, peering through the leaden windows at slovenly litter of living.

Leaning brown houses lurched after each other like beggars in a bread-line, nameless and shameless in their poverty, each with a number, 8, 10, 12, 14. A wan light filtered under the doors and welled up the crazy staircases that led to three floors and an attic … to the same stale odours, discoloured walls, humped forms of sleeping humans in merciful anaesthetic still from the cares and cankers of the day, the scrabbling that kept body and soul together. The rented corners where they fed and mated were dark as the holes of mice.

Somewhere a baby fretfully cried, and a sick man stirred. The room was fetid with long illness, and locked from the night air. A hand white as a woman's, pitiably thin in the wide sleeve of the nightshirt, groped for one of the glasses on the low stool by the couch. He raised it to his lips and gulped, a thick and sickening mess of gum arabic and brandy. His gorge rose. He set it down, lay back on the tumbled pillows, watching the paling light. Shabby furniture, soiled curtains, came out of the shades to mock him.

Dawns he had known of leaping flame that kindled sea and

sky; still island dawns with a black frieze of palm-trees; pirate dawns stabbing at the heart of night and routing the wheeling stars, burning the veil on lands unknown. He could feel again the dip of the deck, the swell of the sails above him, the spindrift of early morning on his cheek.

Painfully he turned on one thin shoulder, his eyes seeking, as they sought so often, a mariner's chart on the wall. It was only a shadow-pencilling in the half-light, but he knew it by heart, every fathom. Sixty-four, sixty-two, with a sudden shallow to seventeen, where the coast peaked out like a jester's cap, and swung away to a half-moon bay and the pallid green of shoal. A chalk-white cliff, and on its crest a dwarf clump of pandanus flagging the sky ... there he had anchored, and the wild men crept down to the yellow sands to stare at his ship in wonder.

In the growing light the minute figures of soundings stood out more clearly, dotted line of his ship-track, zigzag and circle, winding black scrawl of the main. He could follow every inch of the way, remembering ... remembering the heart of a boy and the triumphs of long ago.

A wave of giddiness came upon him. The figures and dots of the chart were blended in weird motion of weaving, round and round like threads to a bobbin in spider-web patterns of lace ... the linen geometries of that old Nottingham lace maker who had brought his square pine loom from Flanders to England to weave in his endless webs the destinies of his sons unborn.

He, too, had woven, woven in the weft of the winds ... but now the threads were ravelled and snapped. They lay like a lace of foam on the wave, as soon lost and forgotten. He closed his eyes, and a faint smile of bitterness thinned his lips.

Sun struck the chimney-pots, ghastly as tombstones in a graveyard of the living dead.

The gastric crying of the baby stopped, and a woman came into the room, an old-young woman. A red shawl lent colour to her weary little face. Her autumn-brown hair was tenderly touched with silver—"the first fall of snow on the beech-trees," her lover had said.

For a long moment she bent over him in infinite care and sadness, but he did not move, and she left the room swiftly and silently, in fear lest the sleeper should wake.

He was not sleeping. He was listening now to the ticking of the clock ... the sound of a horse trotting, trotting steadily back across the years to a child that lay huddled under a hedge in a Lincolnshire lane.

I

The Brides of Enderby

The world was bruised and black with rain, the grey cavalry of the rain galloping in across the marshes, wheeling its regiments from the dark rebellion of the sea to the darkening shires.

A mellow morning had turned traitor. Suddenly the little waves, knife-edged with venom, were biting at the sea-wall. The church spires and the fields were lost in melancholy mist, and the hawthorn trailed its bedraggled finery in the mud. Rank upon rank, the gloomy battalions of the enemy swept in, trampling the triumphs of the long victorious summer, its last poor hoarded gold, into defeat.

Under the hedge sat little Matthew Flinders, waiting for the rain to stop and forgetting all about it. For him the dripping briar branches, with their rusted haws, were stalagmite limbs of limestone in some eerie undersea cave, clutching fingers of murderous vines in an Amazonian forest. His scene-painting was sketchy, but his drama very clear. The wet ground soaked his homespun seat and oozed into his stockings. When he noticed it at all, it fitted in as the menace of a rising tide, for all his waking dreams were *Robinson Crusoe*.

A stubby little boy with straight brown eyes, he was not the type for dreaming, and indeed it was a new-found faculty that came with Uncle John. He had never believed *Robinson Crusoe* until he found it true. Uncle John Flinders showed him the island on the map, in a maze of mysterious South American names. He was home on leave from the fleet in the West Indies. Matthew heard his father tell his mother that he was a hobbledehoy. He was not sure what rank that was in the Navy. It could not be very exalted, for his father had sounded sour.

But the big thing was, you could sail on ships if you wanted. Crusoes were not born but made, the lucky ones wrecked on a desert isle where no one had ever landed. When he came to that thought, for some reason, Matthew always sniffed a scent of verbena.

A fresh squall hit like a ramrod, and the hedge rocked about him. He hunched his shoulders with exultation, and chuckled into his neck. Storms he loved. They heralded events. But this was no storm, the bankers could have told him. It was break o' the year. Low clouds were yellow to the east. There was a lot more coming.

In the tumultuous falls of a long hour, the Amazon forest palled. The boy took a backless copy of *Robinson Crusoe* from his pocket and tried to read, but the rain sloshed down in starry spots that made a splurge of the printing, the pages clumped together in sodden blocks. The wind was turning cold, his wet hands growing a little blue. He drew his knees up to his chin, and stared through the whistling thicket of leaves out at the dancing sleet.

That footstep of Friday's would never have frightened him, nor would he have been glad when he found him a friend, only disappointed that somebody else had found the island too. It was queer the way Crusoe let seven and twelve years slip by in a sentence. Still, that was the way in those tropic climes—no clocks, no calendars, nothing to tell the time.

As if in answer to his thoughts came a sound just like the ticking of a clock. He could hear it through the rain, coming closer. It was the steady trotting of a pony, and now the rhythmic scrape of wheels—a fowler coming home from the shores of the Wash. Maybe he was bound for Boston.

With a leap and a slide, Matthew was out from under the hedge, and over the ditch with "Ahoy!" just as a bouncing gig swept round the curve. The horse shied back with white in its eye and snorted. A loud oath came from the driver's seat— "Damnation!"

Heels in air the driver lost his balance. The gig swayed on the rim of the ditch, wheels sliding in the mud and the horse scrambling madly.

Matthew knew about horses. He could manage Nickie at home. Slowly he went forward with a comforting "Wey-y!" grabbed a rein, and led it back to the road. It tossed its head and pawed, then quietened as he patted a rippling shoulder-arched neck and close-shaved glistening coat, no fowler's pony this.

The man in the gig stood up in dudgeon and flourished a whip over Matthew. A shaggy man in shaggy tweeds and leggings, his sandy beard bristling with rage, his blue eyes blazing.

"Ar, belay there young devil! The size of 'ee, comin' at me with thy 'hoy!' to turn me turtle. I'll give 'ee hoy! What be 'ee doing on West Fen of a day like this? Be off, or tha'lt feel the tongue o' ma lash!"

"Thou'st dropped a duck," said Matthew innocently. "Hold, and I'll get it for thee."

He ran back and picked up a dead bird that had fallen. It was not a duck, but a shag.

"These are not good for thy eating," he remarked helpfully.

"I know full well wi'out 'ee telling. Chucken in yon basket."

In the basket were two or three others with their necks wrung, and a bunch or two of the purple-berried samphire from the sandhills by the seashore.

"Thou'lt make a grand dinner!" Matthew grinned.

"One more squeak fra thee, an' I'll thrash 'ee thy mother woan't knaow 'ee. Get 'ee ahaome. Aha, she'll give 'ee hiding enough when 'a sees thee. Where be haome, lad?" He seemed to be cooling.

"Donington, sir. I thought thee might be going to Boston."

'Donington! It's fifteen mile, an' I'm for Revesby."

Fifteen miles! Matthew was frightened that he had come so far.

"Doan't 'ee stand there gawpin' in the rain. Come up, an' I'll give 'ee lift fur as the Cross."

The little boy clambered aboard, and the gig bowled on. They talked in shouts, between gusts.

"What's tha name, son?"

"Matthew Flinders."

"Who braought 'ee aout?"

"Jeb Stulk to Boston. I walked the rest."

"If 'ee live Donington, what 'ee doing here?"

"I came out exploring. It wasn't raining when I came."

"'Ee came out *wha-at*?"

"Exploring. I was following up a stream to see where it came from."

The man gave a loud guffaw. "Well, 'ee faound. Haow did 'ee know to stop the horse?"

"I drive with my father. We have a gig, but not so big and shiny-like as thine."

"Who be faither, laddie?"

"Doctor Flinders."

"Doctor Flinders, eh? Then it's fine dose o' physic tha'lt be getting this night."

All that Matthew could see of his friend was the fringe of beard and the raindrops glistening in it, under a cap pulled down against the weather. The hands that held the reins were not blackened and cut like a flax farmer's, nor wrinkled and whitish like a banker's.

"Art thou a sailor, sir?" he piped in a lull of the wind.

"Why do 'ee ask?" The man seemed pleased.

"Because thee told me belay, like Uncle John."

"Is that where 'ee got the hoy from? Well, I'm a sailor now, lad, an' if 'ee doan't stow thy gaff, woan't never make port by nightfall. Get close in to the lee an' batten down."

"Thou art a sailor—I know thee ..." said Matthew happily.

There was no more talking after that. For nearly an hour they blew along in squalls, soaked to the skin and never a rag above them. Wold and grassland and winding road were lost in steam of fog as they left the marsh behind and threaded the fens. The tide was coming in fast, king tide of September. Already dykes and sluices were brimming in turgid brown pools of flood, and never a banker in sight.

Smartly trotting, they passed a dismal cottage or two, all shut in and dripping from the eaves in their patch of turnips or flax. Not a soul was abroad on the roads, not a ploughman nor a sheep in the hedged fields. Every living thing had raced for shelter in this blinding whirl of sleet. Only the trees stood sentinel in the mist, or the phantom sails of a windmill waved them by.

It was growing dusk when they came to the old Saxon cross that marked the highroad to Boston. The man made no move to pull up, but swung round by the signpost to Revesby.

"If thou'lt set me down here, sir, I'll get a lift on to Boston, and then Jeb Stulk'll take me home, I thank thee."

"Tha'lt be draowned, little fule, ere tha gets a lift. Best come wi' me for a bite o' supper, an' then, if tha be-ha-aves, I'll drive 'ee fur as Boston. I'll wager 'ee ran out o' rations in thy exploring, and feeling peckish, eh, same as I?" He bent down in the twilight to Matthew's grateful smile.

Soon the hoofs were brisker, pounding along under the oaks of a wide and majestic drive.

Revesby!

So it was not the village they were bound for, but the abbey! He strained his eyes through the gloom.

All Boston worshipped from a distance at this shrine of wealth and glory that welcomed kings. Of the abbeys of Lincolnshire, Revesby was the grandest. Mr Lound, their teacher at the Free School, had told them about it—of the parklands where sheep and cattle were so strange you would not know them for sheep and cattle, its hothouses of plants and flowers from all over the earth, that nobody had ever seen before.

The villagers of the whole county were for ever gossiping of the great Revesby parties, when the gentry came from London in coaches with long-tailed horses all the way, with bands of fiddle and haut-boy and flute to play for their May-day revels, and mummers, morris-dancers and jugglers, races and cricket matches, fishing and fowling in gay marquees on the banks of Boston Scorp.

It was whispered that the Big Folk dined on emerald-studded gold plate from the Maharajahs' palaces in India, with blackamoors to wait on them, and that they kept lions and leopards and polar bears instead of dogs and cats. His stepmother had a friend that knew the daughter of the housekeeper at Revesby, and she said that was not true. Now he could tell her, and Betsy and Ann, and all the boys at school, that he had been there!

The abbey was a black bulk of shadow, two or three squares of light in the mullioned windows, nothing to mark the outlines of the old Cistercian pile that for three hundred and forty years had looked benignantly on weald and wold. The wind soughing in the oaks seemed as the chanting of the old-time friars and monks, shaven pates and sandalled feet, telling their beads in chapel, that Henry VIII had whipped out to beg their bread on the highway. Soft breath of a thousand flowers rose on wet night air.

Folk said the squire now had made the chapel a hothouse, and that was blasphemy like as not, but he said that God was more in flowers and the wonders of the earth, even in a swallow's nest, than in the wax candles and the old Latin books.

Matthew wanted to ask which end was the chapel, but now they were rattling across a cobbled courtyard to the stables, and a welcome of bobbing lanterns and baying hounds.

After the cramp and the cold, the warmth of animals and new-mown hay was good. Grooms and ostlers were everywhere, shouting to each other. Splendid horses stamped and champed in their stalls. Doves cooed from the rafters, and soft little cows of grey velvet in the bails were giving buckets of rich, steaming milk. A boy told Matthew they came from the Channel Isles.

"Plainty fowk got'en hereabaout," he said, "but I'll shaow t'someten t'll not see, if t'likes come."

In a low stone tank there was a mottled surface floating, like the upturned keel of a very small boat, but it was paddling itself about with fins in the dim water.

"Amfibby t'calls it, from t'South Seas," said the boy. "T'can swim 'neath water like fish, an' t'can come right aout t'water an' lay eggs like a faowl, an' t'aint neyther. T's maister's," he added proudly, "an' t'll see none like it in England."

Matthew was mystified. He vaulted up on the stone coping and put down a curious hand to touch the creature, but his friend of the gig descended on him, with a grip on his little sodden shoulder.

"Ee'st not wet enough, eh, but 'ee must be diving for turtle?" he growled amicably. "Get 'ee befaore me naow, an' run for yonder gate." He still carried the basket with the shags and pigweed.

The rain was on them in shattering showers as they raced along the path by the kitchen garden, and under thick trellis of leaves to the big house. A bevy of maids in high white caps and aprons gave a concerted shriek of laughter as they passed the scullery door. To Matthew's alarm the shriek was repeated beside him by a grotesque bird chained to an iron stand, that spread fiery wings, and shrieked again, its angry eye upon him. He scuttled faster and, propelled from the rear, found himself in a lofty servants' hall. The long table was set for supper, red rays of a peat fire dancing in the cedarwood beams above. This must be the refectory, where the cowled monks had asked blessing on bowl and spoon.

"Wast frightened by the macaw?" laughed his bearded friend, stamping the wet out of his boots on the flagged stone floor. "Aye. 'Tis savage too. 'Ee must not go too near."

His friend's name was Briscoe, Matthew learned from the jollying of the maids, who found endless amusement in the fact that such a great clerk of the weather should come home half drowned. He was apparently an upper servant of standing, for he ordered supper for himself and "yon little scrimp of a

11

castaway" to be served in his own room, and bade Matthew dry off by the log while he changed his dripping tweeds.

As the child thankfully stood by the fire, regarding with interest his squelching boots and the miniature rivers and tributaries running out of them on to the hearth, there was a slow movement behind him. He turned — and his heart went cold. A huge yellow beast was shuffling out of the shadows. Was it a lion?

He gave a whoop of terror, and bolted for the door, straight into the maid called Mollie, bringing in a smoking-hot dish of potatoes. His voice was gone. He clutched her waist and pointed.

"Thee'st not afeard o' St John?" Mollie laughed. "Why, look'ee here — don't run. Hey! Come, boy!" She flicked her fingers, and the Tawny Thing came ambling. Matthew clutched her frantically and drew in his breath, but she tousled the giant head, and he saw that the big brown eyes were very friendly.

"What is it?" he whispered, still in terror.

"'Tis but a dog," said Mollie. "From Newfaoundl'nd. He'll let thee pat him, boy. Go on."

"Eh, but he's big!" He put out a trembling hand. St John flattened his ears and wagged his tail. He grew bolder, and hugged him round the neck. "He's the biggest dog I've ever seen," he cried in relief.

"He's the biggest dog in the world," said Mollie casually, "and so gentle a' wouldn't hurt the weest little kitten. Out, St John, sir! Brr!"

St John fled from the wave of her cloth, meek as any poodle. Matthew was about to follow, just for the joy of beholding, but Briscoe came and hustled him upstairs.

The fire was already lit in the room, bright welcoming flames. Briscoe stripped him, rubbed him down till he was glowing, wrapped him in a blanket, tucked him in a chair, and spread his clothes to dry.

"What would tha faither the doctor say if we let 'ee go coughin' thyself into tha coffin?" he wanted to know.

As he hung the little coat to the fire, a stream of small white stones poured from the bulging pocket.

"What 'ee got these for? Grave-stones? Or playing supplejacks?"

"No," said Matthew. "They're for my explorations. I mark the bank of a river as I chart it."

"'Ee travelled far?" asked Mr Briscoe politely.

"Fair way. All along the Witham and the Bain, and out across Sleaford Mere, and Moulton Marsh to Fosdyke, along the Boston Deeps. It's wild and lone out there."

"'Tis that."

A little maid came in with a tray, soup and roast mutton, gravy and turnips steaming from under the covers, an appetising pot for starved explorers.

"Red broth!" said Matthew in surprise.

"Love apples. Grow in our garden. Some fowk'll tell 'ee poison. Doan't knaow what they miss."

Little Flinders was hot on the trail of information.

"What hast thou brought the shags and pig-weed for?"

"Aha! 'Ee would knaow that. Well, they're for master."

"Not for his dinner!"

"No. These for the asperiments, for the learned papers he writes, but many a worse dinner he's eaten, when him an' me was out of the world together. Vulture and dog and bat, and weevils atop o' stinking water, an' never turned a hair … but I have seen him sick enough, aye, when he faound some palm-nuts once in the woods o' New Holland 'a thought was good, and vomited his very heart, him as knaows all about palm-nuts too!" Briscoe was vastly amused in retrospect. "But sit 'ee here, boy, an' say thy grace, an' be thankful thou hast not dogs an' weevils for thy supper."

He pulled Matthew up to the table, chair, blanket and all, with a bowl of the good red soup down on his knee. A warm and contented laddie began to look about him.

There was a sea-chest in the corner like Uncle John's, some spears of savages on the wall, crescents of flat curved wood with rough white markings, a snake with legs in a bottle, and some branching flowers of a dead whiteness that seemed to be made of bone. Matthew had seen that before—coral. No doubt about it, this was the room of a sailor.

"My Uncle John's been to the West Indies," he started the ball rolling. "He has maps of the Spanish Main, and the island of Robinson Crusoe."

Briscoe was exasperated. "That's nowt," he said. "Why Drake an' Columbus was that way, an' all the ships in the world go that way since. Why doan't 'ee find a new track, same as we, where's nowt but sea for years an' years, an' then nowt but sea till 'ee find it? Maps? We had no maps. We went an' made 'em."

"Did thee come to an island?" Matthew loved islands best.

"Isles? Trillions of isles. Biggest in the world an' tiddliest, some but a rock an' a cokernut, some bigger'n England, an' one so big 'ee couldn' sail raound it in a year. Crocodiles an' cannibiles too, if 'ee want 'em, an' animiles the like was never seen—big as horses, an' furry like thy cat at haome, an' stands up on their after-legs with their foals in pocket, an' go leapin' fifty feet in a baound right through the woods. Them's the animiles to see. Master says they was on earth before Adam … an' there's ants as builds churches, 'ee wouldn't believe, an' oysters so big a man can lie down in their shell. Daon't 'ee talk me Robinson Crusoe. He didn' see nowt."

"How big was this island?"

"Abaout three thousand mile."

"And how far wide?"

"God knaows. We didn' measure."

"But how far wide on the map?"

"Have I not taold thee, numskull, yon country never was a map? Naobody knaows haow wide she be, she might be wide as Europe or Ameriky."

Matthew was sceptical. "Well, I never heard of that place in geography."

"Jography! … look, lad, when 'ee knaows much as I do o' jography, tha'lt throw thy silly little books in pond, an' go aout an speir with thine own two eyes, an' that's jography, an' that's what man was made for, master says. Quit gawpin' as if 'ee

14

didn' knaow me for liar or loon. Never saw such as 'ee for gawpin'. Eat tha supper!"

Matthew pondered well upon his mutton. Briscoe was no crazy jack, and then there was the sea-chest and the coral. A bright idea struck him, a test question.

"What was thy ship?"

"*Endeavour*."

The boy stopped dead, a mouthful on his fork.

"Thou ... didst ... not ... sail ... with ... Captain Cook?"

"I did. Wi' Cap'n Cook."

Little Flinders drew in his breath. His eyes were homage.

"Then thy master is Captain Cook?"

"Nao! Nao! Cook's dead, ma lad. Slain by the savages at the Sandwich Isles. 'Tis Sir Joseph Banks, my master."

"Sir Joseph Banks! I never heard of him."

"'Ee knaows nowt, little numskull, if hevna heard o' Sir Joseph, an' 'ee a Lincolnshire boy. Well, 'ee will if 'ee goes exploring, for his heart's aye exploring, to the North Pole an' the South, an' east an' west fur as the wind goes. There's no man in this world knaows half so much abaout it, an' fish in the waters, an' all that flies, an' all that grows. 'Twas never Cook took him, 'twas him took Cook, following a star ... aye, following a star to strange adventure."

"This isle thou found, this great isle, could I go there exploring?"

"'Twould take a brawnier man than 'ee to find it, 'ee poor little snape ... rocketing abaout like dice in a box when she's bows under in a black gale off the Horn, or aloft in the shrouds looking for land in the Forties. Master took eight on yon v'yage, an' four of us came back to tell the tale. Tha'lt never make it ... unless tha fill thy belly an' grow big, an' then tha might. Eat up, I tell 'ee."

Matthew tackled his mutton again, but now it was tasteless as hay.

"Mr Briscoe, were there people?"

"A few poor blackamoors, no more ... eh, but will be, for the cap'n put up the flag there, an' 'tis England's. Master says our aown fowk'll live there. 'Twill be their grand new land when England's done. Look, I'll shaow thee."

He rose and rooted in his sea-chest, neat as an old maid's glory box and rich with many a relic, producing, at last, a small gold object from a satin-lined case. It was a medallion.

"Naow who is it, tell me if 'ee can?"

It was not King George. Matthew tried a long shot. "Captain Cook?"

"Aye, that's Cook, an' a good likeness in little, for well I knaow him. This, naow?"

The reverse was easy. "Britannia."

"Aye. Britannia looking to the South Pole, do 'ee see, wi' fairer lands than any she has naow. We faound them. Master an' I an' Cap'n Cook.'

A bell clanged near at hand, and a footman stood at the door, pompous in braided livery and silk stockings.

"T' Maister wants 'ee, Briscoe."

Briscoe carefully put the medal away. "He's waiting for my news," he said. "Well, tide's up, an' dykes full, an' ne'er a banker on guard. The dolts aye wait till the floods are on them. They'll ne'er mend sluices naow in storms like this." He buttoned his collar, pulled himself trim, then took his basket with the shags and hurried off.

Bare limbs in the blanket, Matthew felt miserably small. He could hear the wind howling and the rain still beating—a bad night on the marshes, a worse night at sea. With all his heart he wished he were at sea, bows under in a black gale off the Horn, and swinging to that island years away, the isle that never was on any map. He traced its shores in the firelight, sulphurous blue seas smoking in to flickering alps of flame, sombre valleys and dull red cliffs, and rivers of running gold. There trees of earth and stars of heaven were new—a magic land, a Land Without a Name. Wandering there, he lost himself in dreams.

"Well, 'ee warm naow?"

Briscoe was back again. "Master says I may take 'ee all way over to Donington, in time for thy hiding, eh? Thy cloathes be

16

dry?" ... he felt them carefully.... "Not too, but will see 'ee ahaome. Look sharp, lad, for I've taold Ned make ready."

Reluctantly Matthew climbed into his breeches and jacket. He did not want to go.

"Thy master is here, Mr Briscoe, in this house?"

"Aye, he's at Revesby, nursing his foot wi' the gout, so the King an' his high Lunnon friends must do wi'out him."

An eager face looked up. "I couldn't see him, could I, without his seeing me?—thy master, who has sailed with Captain Cook?"

The lenient Briscoe deliberated. "Naow, if 'ee were very mum, an' creep along behind, perhaps 'ee might."

Matthew thanked him with a radiant smile, and tiptoed in his wake.

They passed through long corridors of many doors, and down a staircase of Italian marble to the wide-flagged monastery hall made bright with Orient rugs and curtains. A cold, wise silence here—you would never know there was a laughing maid in the house. Oil paintings in half-light were a dim fantasy of figures, massive gold frames reaching from floor to ceiling. Knights in burnished armour challenged with pike and lance, gargoyle heads grinned horribly from distant niches. Once the boy gave a startled jump—a hairy black monster was clawing for him with one long arm, the other clutching a tree. Its sharp white fangs were bared, its glass eyes staring ... then he saw that the awful thing was dead, a man-ape. A wonderful house this Revesby, all fascination and fright.

Briscoe motioned him to a great oak door, half open. He tiptoed up, his unlucky boots creaking, and peered through the crack ... a room where the walls were a thousand books, richly bound in leather, the back of a chair, the back of a head, a bandaged foot on a stool. There was a globe of the world in many garish colours. St John, majestic by the fire, raised his lion head.

The grandeur of the room made little impression on the boy, its statuary, its luxury, its wealth. He felt only the power of its quiet thought. This master of Briscoe's, head bent in the light of the branching candles, knew all earth's countries under the sun, its creatures of sea and land and air, its flowers. He had gathered to himself its curious treasures, and travelled in ships beyond it ... .

What manner of man was he? Matthew wondered. Was he strict and methodical, like his father the doctor, a place for everything and everything in its place?—or careless and jolly like Uncle John, with eyes on a far horizon?—or sharp and precise like Mr Lound, their teacher?—or would he talk and talk and talk, like Grandfather Flinders at Spalding?

Hard to imagine him in a dice-box of a ship rocketing round Cape Horn and living on hell-fire stew with the swarthy sailors in their striped caps, a drunken crowd, that Matthew often saw in the streets of Boston when the Baltic trawlers were in. Briscoe, yes, perhaps, and Captain Cook, but Sir Joseph Banks would be different. So still, what was he doing now—reading?

As the child stood watching, not daring to breathe, came a high hollow sound above the rain. Bells were ringing in the night, note after fading note, from far away.

The Brides!

All three raised their eyes.

Someone was trapped on the marshes in the highest tide of the year.

Full well the Fenlands knew the meaning of that mournful peal of bells, "The Brides of Mavis Enderby", crying and dying above the storm, ringing from Boston tower. They were calling the fisherfolk out of their beds till the lanterns would twinkle like fireflies on the beaches and the marshes ... calling to the lost, to guide them ... calling the dead, in slow procession, back home. Too often, through the centuries, had they rung the doom of the sea.

Like an eerie flock of birds, they cried on the wind and were gone.

"Who's there?" said Sir Joseph suddenly, a pleasant voice and deep.

Matthew shrank back, and Briscoe hurried in.

"Oh, it's you, Peter. You heard the Brides?"

"Aye, sir."

"After you've taken the child home, join the searchers. Better wrap up well, and carry food and brandy. We may not see thee back till morning."

"Aye, sir."

Briscoe went for his coat, and strapped on his leggings. Out they went through the servants' hall, where maids and men by the ingle were wondering who had strayed, and gossiping of old tragedies when the bells rang Enderby, past the macaw, now caged and blanketed, and under the dripping vine-leaves. Ned, the groom, was waiting at the garden gate with a chaise. Soon they were out on the highway, the rainy road before them, Revesby and all its wonder a dark blur of trees.

It was a silent journey, jogging along. Ned had to mind his driving by the wavering light of the hanging lamp, Briscoe "had his pipe on", and little Flinders's thoughts were far away.

The Witham was churned into charcoal fog at Boston, a few lozenges of light on the canal dull as stained glass. A fitful sleet swept the cathedral, and its mighty tower, the Boston Stump, was lost in milling cloud. Never a gleam of the peat fire that flamed in the great brazier three hundred feet above them — St Botolph, holding aloft his torch for labouring ships at sea.

The High Street was empty, all its windows shuttered, but a bargeman in the Bull and Crown told Briscoe it was a child that was lost, "some'er Wyberton way". A party had gone out an hour ago.

"Let this be warning to 'ee," Briscoe pointed the moral as he climbed back into the chaise. "'Ee might have easily been caught thyself, for September's aye an evil tide, an' 'ee should knaow it. 'Ee can lean against me if 'ee like, an' sleep."

But Matthew was in no mood for sleeping. For the first time in this adventurous day, he felt uncomfortably guilty. He visioned his home-coming, and his paternal parent's greeting. It was a long way in the wild of the night, between the blowing hedges and over the ditches to Donington, but it was all too short for him. In no time they crossed the bridge by the Corn Exchange, and rang the cobbles of Market Square.

If Boston was sleepy, Donington was wide awake. Shafts of light slanted on the rain from every doorway, a buzz of talk from the townsfolk standing there, curious to see the chaise go by. When it stopped at the doctor's house, Matthew thought he heard a muffled cheer.

The doctor's house was a blaze of light, lamps in every window. Before they could knock at the door, it was flung wide open, and Mrs Flinders, with a sob of relief, clasped the boy in her arms. She held him from her, hugged him to her, and gave a glad little cry.

"Here he is! Matt's home!"

The place seemed full of women, all chirping at once. There was Mrs Flinders's sister, Aunt Franklin from Spilsby, buxom and dark, with baby John in her arms, Cousin Henrietta from Nottinghamshire, and half a dozen of the neighbours, scolding him, kissing him, demanding where he had been. Briscoe, so far unnoticed, twirled his cap, cleared his throat, and nobly came to his aid.

"'Ee'll find him dry, mistress," he said, "an' has had supper. I picked him up beyond the Cross, an' braought him haome wi' me to Revesby. Hoping tha werena feared—'twas further than I thaought, an' raining hard."

There was an avalanche of grateful tears and hand-pressings for the blushing Briscoe, who stoutly denied the heroic rescue they longed to hear about.

"Mattie!"

A shrill little voice called from the stairs.

"Mattie! Thee'd never guess. They rang the Brides for thee!"

"For me?"

Now he was truly frightened, and even Briscoe quailed. "God's love!" he boomed, and thoroughly shocked the ladies.

Excitement grew shriller, every one telling the tale. Yes, when Jeb Stulk came home at nightfall without him his father had feared, and after supper he and Uncle John had gone in the gig to Boston, to call out the bell-ringers and search the Holland Fen.

Briscoe said he would find them at once, and set their minds at rest. Matthew guessed he was glad to escape the racket. He would have liked to go with him ... but the Brides, the Boston bells, ringing for him, for all the Fenlands to hear!

More neighbours were piling in, coming to inspect the culprit. They filled the little sitting-room, and brimmed over into the doctor's surgery, in groups loudly talking. Matthew gathered that they would have been much better satisfied if he had never come home — they could have wept so well for a young life lost. But now Aunt Franklin and Henrietta were carrying trays of cakes and gooseberry wine. Ned was called in from the chaise, and all was clamour till Briscoe impatiently ploughed a way through the crowd.

As Mrs Flinders bobbed her final curtsey, "'Ee needin' be worrited about thy lad, ma'am," he told her confidentially. "He'll aye go roaming, that one, an' aye come haome. 'A's canny. But there's salt water in 'is blood, if I mistake not. Was born for the sea."

Mrs Flinders shook her head uncertainly, but smiled a grateful farewell.

"Matthew, hast thanked thy saviour for bringing thee home?"

The boy's eyes kindled as they clasped hands. How could he thank good Briscoe, not so much for bringing him home as for wafting him worlds away. Briscoe touched his cap and grinned, and was gone in the chaise.

The neighbours were reluctantly leaving now that sensation had fallen flat, when four little curlyheads in nightshirts came racing down the stairs, his sisters Elizabeth and Susanna, their playmate, Ann Chappell from Partney, staying with them for Michaelmas, and, well in the rear, young Sam. They were very self-righteous, all save Ann.

"Ha, Mattie! Now tha'lt catch it!"

"Father's out looking for thee! I wouldn' be thee for a golden crown when father comes home!"

"Did thee go far, Mattie? What did thee see? What kept thee so long away?"

Samuel hoisted his nightshirt, rolled it into a ball, and solemnly croaked, "'Ee got lotht!"

Mrs Flinders was scandalized. "Betsy! Susanna! Back to thy beds with Samuel this instant! In bare feet, too! Thou'lt catch thy death of cold. Ann, I'm surprised at thee!"

Henrietta shepherded them upstairs while his stepmother and Mrs Franklin felt Matthew all over, decided he was a thorough scamp, lectured him and kissed him, and dwelt too long on the thrashing to follow.

"Ah Matthew, thou'st led us a dance this night. Just wait till thy father comes home—and thy father said, if thou didst come home, thou must wait."

It was a bad hour, waiting. He tried to weigh up the joys of the night against its coming sorrows, but Briscoe's island seemed a dream by this, and his father's strap would be real. It was happy respite when Aunt Franklin brought baby John to rock him to sleep by the fire, but she had to take him away again, for the little chap, disturbed by the night's excitement, sat up with bright brown eyes and dimpled outstretched arms, and wanted to play. John loved his big cousin Matthew best. Every one noticed that.

At last, when it was late and quiet, came the jingle of bells and lanterns in the square, the tramping of men and voices. Shout of goodnights, and his father came in, followed by Uncle John. They hung their dripping greatcoats in the hall.

Hearing the news that his son was at home, Doctor Flinders curtly announced that he knew it. He stumped into the room. Matthew rose. Uncle John was behind him, and Uncle John broadly winked, but his father glared.

"Stand there, sir!"

Hands clasped behind him, with a suitable expression of contrition, Matthew obediently stood. The next words were unexpected comfort.

"I've promised Mr Briscoe I'll not thrash thee, but thou richly deservest it. What's that?"

"Yes, sir."

The little doctor was grey and tired. He had been out on the

Fens since daybreak, going his rounds in the gig. The boy was sincerely sorry … even so, he would not have missed that night.

"Thou knowest that Boston bells rang for thee?"

"Yes, sir, but I was not lost. I was—"

"Enough. Thou shouldst be shamed indeed, for giving so much trouble, and now I shall have to pay the bell-ringers and the searchers a pretty penny. Come here and let me feel thee … thou art dry. What is this in thy pocket?"

The precious copy of *Robinson Crusoe* went hurtling into the corner. To Matthew's surprise, his father turned in a fury on Uncle John.

"It's not the boy I blame, John. It's thee. I've had no good of him since thou camest here. An obedient lad he was, and with thy sailors' tales thou'st addled his brain. I'll not have it. He thinks of nought but thy nonsense of the sea. I'll thank thee to have more to do in England than turn my sons against me. Matthew, get thee to thy bed. Thou shalt be punished well enough, never fear. Go, sir!"

With a mute appeal for forgiveness to Uncle John for bringing this upon him, Matthew was thankfully off, but Uncle John was blissfully smoking, his long legs stretched out to the fire. Matthew knew his father's views about smoking. He hoped there would not be what Aunt Franklin referred to as Ructions.

At the top of the stairs a little white figure was sitting, leaning against the banisters sound asleep.

"Ann! Listen, Ann!" He pressed her arm and whispered.

She woke and looked at him, eyes big with dreaming, then remembered.

"Mattie, did thee get terrible hiding?"

He laughed. "No hiding at all, thee silly little wench, but oh, I have a powerful lot to tell thee. I met a man who sailed with Captain Cook! Get thee to bed now, and I'll tell thee about it in the morning."

"Good night and God bless thee, Mattie."

He kissed her gingerly on the cold little cheek, and she went away to bed, smiling vaguely.

"Thee did come back," she said, "because thee were not dead. Even when the Brides rang, I knew thee were not dead."

Cosy in his trundle bed under the sloping walls of the attic, he listened to all the little melodies of the rain, and its deep bass drumming. He hoped Mr Briscoe was home—but he had come home a long way further than that.

"East and west far as the wind goes ...

"Aloft in the shrouds, looking for land in the Forties ... "

As he pulled the patchwork counterpane over his shoulder, and snuggled down in content, he heard again the peal of Boston bells, far in the night away, but this time, in their timeless chiming, the blithe tidings that the lost were found.

They were ringing "The Lincoln Poacher".

Oh 'tis my delight on a shining night in the season of the year.

2

Horizons

Straight as a shepherd's staff above all the clustering villages, the grand old Boston Stump kept its people of the Fenlands safe in fold.

To Matthew the cathedral was Father Time himself. Were there not 7 doors, days of the week, 12 pillars in the nave, 24 steps to the library, 52 windows, 60 steps to the chancel roof, and 365 to the tower? When he was a little boy no bigger than Samuel, his own mother used to tell him that every day in the year should be as one of the steps in Boston Stump, leading to the skies.

Whenever his father had a script to be made up in Boston, and George Bass, his friend in the apothecary's shop, was too busy to talk to him, he loved to slip away into the big grey church on the waterfront, not for its gospels or the prayer books in the pews, but for the chartreuse green and yellow and winey red of its stained windows, the quaint saints in jigsaw with their scrolls and crooks and haloes, above them all St Botolph in his mitre, first Christian of East Anglia. He would kneel in the fourteenth century choir stalls, reverently touching the old grained wood and watching the pulpit brasses shining in that unreal light ... sea light, deep down.

If he had time, he plodded and puffed right up to the top of the tower, the tallest tower in England. From there, being alive seemed different—on a much smaller scale, and a much greater. Lincolnshire was just a coloured map. There was no movement in it, no people working and talking. It was a picture painted, silent and still.

You could look down on the Witham, sluggish as an earthworm, dragging its slow length through the Fens, here and there a ship or a drift of timber, and the roofs of Boston in Euclid far below—Botolph's Town. A whimsical road rambled from village to village, churches snugged down in the trees, the thatched houses and the hay ricks, the mills and the maltings— no sooner had they straggled away to browse in the wind-rippled brown of the flax-farms, the precise green of the potato-fields, than they scurried together again in alarm, for all the world like little flocks of sheep.

You could look out over the ridged wolds to Spilsby, where the Franklins lived, Partney where Ann lived, Aswarby where George Bass lived, Sibsey, Stickney and Revesby, Somersby, Enderby and Tidd, north in a tranquil litany to Louth and the spires of Lincoln, Stamford Mere and Sleaford Mere shining like scraps of broken glass, west over the meadow valleys and the swelling downs to Donington, or east to the Wash and the grey-blue selvedge of the sea. That was where his eyes loved to linger, because the sea led to so much, so far away.

St Botolph was the saint of sailors. His tower, from its first crude heap of stones with a basket of coals glowing, had beaconed Saxon and Dane to invade England when Lincolnshire was Boadicea's Ivanhoe. It had seen carved prows of the Vikings and slave galleys of Rome rowing for haven, and 1200 years later, no more than a day in historical time, it had seen King John, the mean old man, scuttling for his life across country, the barons like bulldogs on his trail. There was the ruined abbey near Swineshead where he had slept the night before he died, fingering in fevered dreams the jewels of his pinchbeck crown lost in the rising tide.

Sometimes St Botolph found wisdom in men. He had seen the Pilgrim Fathers, sober as a congregation of rooks out there on the sandhills, praying together by the flare of a torch, signalling a Dutch ship to take them away to where they would be free to call their God in peace ... and the Dutchmen betrayed them for money, a few poor coins spent in a night at the inn.

Why were men forever obsessed with metal, King John and his jewels, Judas for thirty pieces of silver, the farmers of the Fenlands for the groats and florins their wives hid away in teapots and tins, even his own good father for the guineas of those who could pay? He never troubled the very poor no matter how long and how hard the hours he spent with them, but he did make sure of the others, because he was buying houses and shops in Donington and Boston, to make money for him while he slept, he said, for the sake of the children. He bent over his books at night till the wick of the lamp burnt low, totting up sums in pounds, shillings and pence.

It must be fear of the future, but money had no part in the future or the past. It was never desired nor remembered for its own sake, and you could lose it in a thousand ways for all your counting and scheming. Matthew made up his mind to have as little as he could to do with it. Instead of the sameness of worn coins, passed round from hand to hand, he would collect the varied and beautiful shells of the sea.

The Pilgrim Fathers had no thought of money or invasion. Solemn folk and simple, they visioned earthly peace. God's anger was their only fear. There was the Guildhall beneath him where they had been thrown into prison, and away to the north the lonely sands where they had tried again ... and that time a howling mob, that wanted to keep them only to spy on and torture, came over the sandhills with blunderbusses and pikes, and seized their women and children and destroyed their sacred books.

But the Vision held them. They broke free from the petty vindictiveness of men and braved the blind malevolence of nature, tossing in storms and starvation until they reached the shores of Holland; and there again they went down into the Valley of Humiliation, to be turned adrift in the *Mayflower*, forever seeking, forever steadfast, whether they lived or died.

The grey sea, the cruel sea, had relented in the end, and carried them to a fabulous land of wealth and freedom, to learn among the savages that God was kind. It must be a pleasant good land, for none of them ever came back, but in a gentle spirit of forgiveness they honoured their farewell to England.

Now there was a new and beautiful town they had built and called Boston on the rim of the Massachusetts woodland, looking out on the mighty Atlantic Ocean as this Boston looked on the North Sea.

It still was fighting for freedom. It raised the first American flag in 1773, the year before Matthew was born. A king as silly as John had lost England a continent haggling over the price of a pound of tea. Sons of Lincoln and Nottingham in the feathers and war-paint of Mohawk Red Men had come in canoes by night, and tipped the tea into the harbour, and made King George a joke before the world. Their port was closed to trade and their liberties taken from them, but all the American colonies rallied to their flag, fighting as Hampden fought, fighting for the rights of Britons in Magna Charta. It was a bitter war between nations that were father and son, and they were not Britons any longer, but the best man won. Even Mr Pitt said that—"If I were an American as I am an Englishman, I would never lay down my arms, never, never, never!"

At first Boston had disowned its revolutionary namesake, but now it was learning to be proud of it. The best of us make mistakes, and Matthew would like to find England another continent where she could try again. Was there another one to find? Captain Cook had travelled the globe, and apologized that he had found so little. But Sir Joseph Banks believed, and what was it Briscoe had said?—"Might be wide as Europe or Ameriky."

His own family was especially proud of the Pilgrim Fathers, because there was an ancestor among them, Richard Flinders of Nottingham, a son of the old lace-maker and stocking-weaver of vain Elizabeth's time. Richard Flinders's name was in the American histories with Governor Winthrop, and Bradford and Brewster, Mr Cotton, vicar of St Botolph's, Isaac Johnson, his wife the Lady Arbella, daughter of the Earl of Lincoln, who left her lovely home to die so soon in that Indian land, and all the others.

Richard had led the way ... what a glorious thing it would be if Boston Stump could see his little kinsman following Sir Joseph Banks to another great discovery. He would have a ship of his own and take Samuel, and baby John Franklin when he was old enough, and George Bass, his friend in the apothecary's shop who vowed he was going to sea; maybe Ann Chappell, because her father was a ship's captain drowned in the Baltic, and Ann was the only one of the girls who really liked to listen. But alas, it could not be.

The Flinderses wove no more stockings and lace, sitting at their looms like women. Now they were physicians and surgeons, his own father and Grandfather Flinders at Spalding. Matthew must be a surgeon too, driving round and round in a dog-cart on the Fens, feeling people's pulses and telling them to put out their tongues. No! There was the tilt of a sail in the blue, a collier creeping down from Hull. If the worst came to the worst, he could run away, but he did not want to. His father and the family might not get a letter for years.

That reminded him of Nickie and the gig. Small as a fly they had seemed when he last looked down, and now they were gone from the apothecary's shop. He took the steps two at a time through the square stone tower, and found his father at the Guildhall, busy with birth and death certificates. After some shopping at Mr Prin's, they wound the long road home.

Uncle John was leaving, going back to his fleet in the Indies. So far Matthew dared not ask for *Robinson Crusoe*, letting sleeping dogs lie; but hearing the gig roll out after supper, while the women were putting the little ones to bed with lullabies and laughter, he went to the surgery to see if it were there, and borrow it for an hour. John Flinders was packing his sea-chest. Older than the doctor, he looked much younger, boyish as Matthew. He murmured amusing nothings, and whistled as he packed.

"Now, let's see, a dictionary in case we have to write the Navy Board asking for a pension, and the *Materia Medica* in case we meet the enemy. That just leaves space for a cake and a bottle o' rye. Hullo young Matthew, what's the quest?"

"Thou'rt not going, Uncle John? Not on account of me?"

"On account of thee! Admiral Gardner'd like that. My boy, my nation needs me, strange as it may seem. I've dallied long in country lanes. My barque is on the sea."

"Thou couldst not take me with thee? Not a hope?"

"Matthew Flinders the Third or Fourth, I wouldn't if I could. Follow thy father and hug the shore. Stick to thy Nickie and let the white horses alone. Thou art a Matthew, not a luckless John, a spendthrift and a roamer. Thou wilt bank thy savings, and be a man of consequence on the Fens."

Matthew looked uncertain. Was there a satire in this?

"Oh please be with me, Uncle John. I want to go to sea."

John Flinders left his packing and took up his pipe.

"No. Be a surgeon," he advised. "At sea thou'lt throw thy life away, and gain nothing, not even wife and children, at least not that thou knowest." He smiled at that, and Matthew could not follow.

"I don't want children," the little boy said solemnly. "I want to be captain of a ship."

John looked him up and down reflectively. "One never knows," he said. "It may be written. But thou'lt never be captain of a ship unless thou art a Nelson with powerful influence. Look at me. Eleven years a sub-lieutenant, and a sub-lieutenant till I die, a nasty smash-up on the deck of blood and powder, or tossed over the side to the fishes, 'and may the Lord ha' mercy'. I don't know. What dost thou want of me? I cannot take thee."

"How can I learn to steer by the stars?"

"Ha, there's knowledge will not hurt thee. Thy father cannot blame me for that. Why, thou mightst be lost in thy gig, and find thy way home by't." He smiled again, and then said very kindly. "Here, laddie, take these. Time was when I studied them myself, thinking I might be captain, but never will be. There's dribbling greybeards in the service midshipmen still, and lucky I am to draw a sub-lieutenant's pay."

Delving in the bottom of his sea-chest, he brought out two well-annotated books, frayed at the spine. They were

Robertson's *Elements of Navigation* and Hamilton Moore's *Principles of Trigonometry*. Matthew was delighted with the first, crestfallen at the second. Already he was learning that at school. He had taken it this year with Latin.

"Latin for thy doctorin'," said John. "There's not a sawbones in the Seven Seas swilling in his cabin, will call a wooden leg a leg. But this other will give thee distance of shores, height of mountains and width of rivers. Study it well if thou wouldst tie threads to the constellations and shoot the sun.

"But stay clear of the sea, I tell thee, a thankless mistress, a lone, mad thing, a gipsy. 'Twill twist thy soul and make thee but a manikin of a man, up in the yards dancing to the fiddle of the winds. The green combers will be thy hills and valleys, changing and gone. Every port in the world with lights a-glitter in the evening will be thy homecoming, with home in none. Thou'lt sweat in a cockpit with lice and 'roaches for thy bedfellows, and turn from linen and lavender to crawl to it again, hungry for salt air and rotten pork, and the swell of a thousand fathoms swinging thee on to God knows what but the slavery thou wilt call freedom. Thou'lt lose count of the years, like a Tom o' Bedlam, and the faces of thy fellows and thy friends, aye, even those thou lovest best, will seem less real to thee than faces in the clouds. Thou'lt stand watch with ghosts in the starlight and with the devils of hell in storms ... and thou'lt drown at last, nothing surer, with a blinding light in thine eyes and thy head bursting, and not even a stone in the graveyard to tell that thou hast lived. It will not matter, for thy friends will have all forgotten thee. No. Play with the village maids, and pay them, with trinkets and with fairings, and take a lady for thy wife, and plant thy patch and hold it, and laugh at fools like me, forever adrift."

At the bitterness of his uncle's words, Matthew was taken aback, but John Flinders had turned with tight lips to his packing. The boy, discomfited, took the books and loitered up the stairs.

Next morning his uncle seemed merry enough, as he left on the Cambridge coach, resplendent in tabs and gold buttons, a last wave of his hand towards the Wash to Matthew.

"I'll see thee yonder?" he called, and Matthew nodded.

The holidays were long and empty without him, and his tales of war in the Indies, where a dapper little French army captain named Napoleon Bonaparte was snatching all he could for the empire of France, and a dapper little English sea-captain named Horatio Nelson was all that was holding him back.

The next best thing was Cousin Henrietta. A gay and efficient redhead, Henrietta was governess to Captain Pasley's girls—Flag-Captain Pasley of H.M.S. *Bellerophon*. Sometimes she went with the family down to Chatham, where the big dogs of the British fleet lay guarding England's threshold. She could, when she chose, speak a little of the language the boy so loved to hear. But nowadays Henrietta had the family dining-table filled with bits and pieces of frills and frocks unending, from plans and specifications of the latest fashions from Bath. She spent most of her time on patrol with her mouth full of pins.

Sing-song and doll games of the nursery fry, with Betsy a shrill little mistress of ceremonies, were far too infantile for a patriarch of twelve; so in long days of wet weather Matthew introduced himself to Ptolemy in his temple at Canopus, learned to divide the earth into 360 circles, to measure a ship's rate with log and line, and time and tide by altitudes of moon and sun. Better than all, he learned to chart imaginary lands, and from his garret window fixed his gaze on the fixed stars.

By the time the holidays were over, he was filling his slate with hieroglyphs, prattling of lunars and logarithms and "great circle sailing"—glorious words—daring to differ on the subject of the newfangled time-keepers with Mr Maskelyne, Astronomer-Royal. Cook had charted his way by time-keepers, and that was enough for him.

In the first term of the new year, out of patience with his nautical obsession, Dr Flinders drove his son over to Horbling Grammar School, and put him in charge of the Reverend John Shinglar, a stooped young dominie of lantern jaw and moth-eaten gown, whose passion in life was Virgil. Mr Shinglar received the strictest instructions to head Matthew off into Latin, but though he did his level best with thousand-line detentions, trigonometry topped the school report, and Ptolemy always won.

"Why teach him so much of this overgrown geometry?" asked the doctor testily one day, calling as he passed on his rounds. "Night after night he fills his notebooks with this abracadabra of sums that he calls physics. There's nothing of physics about it. I should not object if there were."

Mr Shinglar, with rueful smile, pressed his finger-tips together. "It shames me, sir, to admit it, but in this subject thy son enlightens the rest of the class and me. I can't understand the infatuation, unless we have another Archimedes, in which case, my dear Mr Flinders, would it not be wrong of us to obstruct the way of genius?"

"I'll obstruct it with a willow cane if his Latin doesn't improve."

But he clucked his Nickie along the lane with an afterglow of pride. Teaching his teacher, eh? After all, a good mathematics paper would stand a budding surgeon in good stead. The boy was ambitious and conscientious. He would go further than he himself had gone, and that was the aim of human life, each generation one step higher.

Not that he, Matthew Flinders III, was utterly insignificant. There was so little for a man to do in a sleepy county like this—boils, rabies, a fit, a tooth to pull or a broken arm to set. When they had anything complicated they pined away and died. But a singular case had come his way quite recently, the child of a hemp-farmer near Brothertoft, born with variolar pustules.

Now a cure in variolar pustules well written up for the Medical Society might give a man some standing as a specialist. It was a great thing to be known to the Medical Society. Who knows, it might even lead to a practice, with a house in a terrace, in London, when he had enough money to buy it from his rents, either for himself or for the boy. The little doctor, grey at the temples, with four children from one wife and another one coming from the new—he, too, cherished his dreams.

But when he reached the farm at Brothertoft, and hurried in with his black bag, business-like and brisk, he found a bow of black crepe on the door-handle, and the farmer met him with down-bent head. The child—that precious child with variolar pustules—had developed the croup since his last visit, and died but yesternight. He looked at the poor little wizened shape almost with animosity. Instead of writing a treatise of triumph, he must write a certificate of death.

"Now my deductions are worthless," he told the flabbily-weeping mother. "Learn to take reasonable care of thy children, for science's sake if not for thine own!"

He drove home disheartened, sat down to supper with a weary sigh, and told his wife Elizabeth about it.

"There is no opportunity for a man of intellect in these parts. The Fens are flat, and ever will be."

"True indeed, father." His eldest son at his right hand surprised him. "To make my mark, I must go out in the great world."

"So thou art a man of intellect, Matthew!" He suppressed the boy with an acid smile of irony. "And the great world—or so thou tellest me—is round, and brings thee back to where thou has started. Never again dare to mention the sea in my presence, sir! I am sick unto death of thy eternal song. Cut up thy little brother's meat, and kindly hold thy tongue."

Matthew mutely turned to his little brother's plate, but Samuel screamed and kicked so hard he had to be carried away. Samuel never seemed to have an intelligent grip of the fact that you were trying to help him. With stubborn intensity of purpose, he wanted to do everything himself, until he got in a hopeless mess and cried.

They were full and busy days for young Flinders at Horbling—three miles to school every morning, shivering through the winter, but what joy of the hedgerows and the ditchwater reflections of flag-lilies and meadow-sweet when spring was in the air! The Reverend John was rather a drone, but a kind one, and his schoolfellows slow to catch the meaning of things. But they liked him and he liked them, and in the play-hour they could be happy fighting.

Holidays were the best times, out with his father or grandfather to the windy Lincoln heights, or the gloomy seas and brown sands around Fosdyke, or spanking along behind the pony over the silver dykes and the marshes. There men were turning the silt of centuries into ploughlands, holding back the land that was ever slipping from them, stolen away in quicksands. Grandfather Flinders had been reared on a farm. A hundred and fifty years before, his fathers had worked with the Dutchman Vermuyden, draining the fertile fen pastures and building the dykes to make this part of Lincolnshire a little Holland, the windmills with their slow sails turning in a green patchwork of wheat and potatoes and clover.

Or perhaps he would be off with the Franklin boys, Willingham and James, tickling trout in the stream near Partney Mill, fishing for bream in the South Footy Drain and the Hob Hole, teasing gipsies at the horse-fairs, and following the sheep-walks for miles across the wolds and open moors, to ramble the ruined abbeys where bees were building in the fallen stones. You could find buried coins and potteries of Caesar's legions out by the old Roman road of Cliff Row. One day they unearthed some bones in a sandhill that Mr Shinglar said were of the labyrinthodon, a great sloth-lizard that roamed in forests submerged for a thousand thousand years.

Matthew, if he could help it, never was far from the sea. He loved to watch the fishing-smacks and the Baltic traders come by to the Skalp and the Haven, the sun-blackened sailor-men shouting a strange language, or just to lie still by the grey North Sea and listen to its voices.

Never a word in these days he heard of Briscoe and Revesby, save that Sir Joseph Banks was away in London, and that in a terrible winter, when the Wash tides had risen over their fields too often, he renounced the rents of his tenants. They spoke of it in awed whispers—£9000 all told. Nine thousand pounds in one year—he must be rolling in money! Either that, thought Matthew, or he cared little for it, knowing it did not matter so much in the long run. But of course you must have it for happiness, for yourself and for your fellows.

In his second long vacation, Henrietta came back, Henrietta, harbinger of fate. Many a time she had told the tale of her young cousin's incorrigible exploring, of his astronomical vigils and his passion for the sea. Now Captain Pasley wanted to meet him. The Pasleys were at their country home at Radcliffe, near Nottingham, and his father had said he might go. A flag-captain of His Majesty's Navy was not to be ignored.

On a soft summer afternoon, white clouds drifting beyond the skyline of the elms and the honey-yellow of the flax, they crossed the border by coach, Matthew scrubbed up and shining from his new boots to his nose, Henrietta the glass of mode in poke bonnet and mittens. Radcliffe Hall was a pretty old manor tucked away among the larches. Pink with anticipation and tongue-tied with nervousness, he clumped up the drive.

Though Mrs Pasley and the girls were charmingly natural and informal, he sat on the edge of his chair with an awkward "Yes, ma'am" and "No, ma'am" and so painfully minded his P's and Q's that Henrietta despaired.

Captain Pasley was a round man, hearty, round head on a portly foundation, round chin, round bushy eyebrows jutting from a reddish complexion, round bushy mop of white hair. His breezy manner and quick twinkle of a jest recalled Uncle John. He talked with Matthew on the moonlit lawn after dinner, while the girls were playing the piano, a glass of port on the clipped green sward beside him, a glint of amusement in his eye.

A few leading questions and, no longer self-conscious, Matthew discoursed at large of Vasco da Gama, Drake, Magellan, Columbus and Ptolemy, of compass steering and Cook's journeys and Briscoe's island, how to reef a royal in a southerly gale, and why the tides rose on the Fens. He knew Robertson's *Elements* from tattered cover to cover, with all the fo'c'sle fallacies and the deep-water wisdom of the ancient salts that hung about the quays at Boston. In pointing out the constellations, Pasley could not fault him.

The captain stretched his silken calves, and raised his brows, and smiled. This boy would do. In point of fact, he would like to keep him with him. This boy would do quite well.

"If thou'rt interested in Cook's voyages," he said, "thou'st missed a chance by being born ten years too late. Phillip has gone to that island with a pack of felons, and a man I know well, Lieutenant Bligh, sailed last year for Otaheite, following Cook's track. He was his master on the *Resolution*, a bluff customer but a man of mettle. Has gone to transplant the breadfruit from the Pacific to Jamaica. It's an idea of Banks to feed our negroes of the plantations. Banks commissioned the ship and fitted her out for him—some old trader they patched up and christened the *Bounty*, after her job. That's a long enough voyage for thee, and if I know Bligh a lively one, with not too much bounty. But thou couldst learn much from him, as he from Cook."

Matthew fretted with restlessness, to think that he had missed it. "Thou hast spoken of Banks, sir. Didst thou mean Sir Joseph? He that lives at Revesby Abbey?"

"Lives mostly at Soho Square, where he can keep an eye on the doings; but aye, that's the one. Thou knowest him?"

"Oh no, sir. At least he knows not me. But has Sir Joseph the power, sir, to commission ships to travel?"

"With the Royal Society and the Admiralty and the King behind him has power enough for every fad and fancy. I'll tell thee what, lad,"—the crow's feet of laughter showed at the corners of his eyes—"if thou wouldst have a ship, go to Sir Joseph. Tell him thou'lt bring him moss from the hob of hell or orchids from the Arctic, and thou'lt get thy ship, though the Frenchmen should blow the rest of us out of the water. Brush up thy botany, and dangle a sprout in front of him, or thou'lt never have a hope. And bring him back sprouts, and more sprouts, the more outrageous the better. Thou couldst come with a cargo of rubies, but without the sprouts he'd never forgive thee. I believe he'd sell India to China for the slip of a mulberry-tree. But hark, I hear the chink o' cups and supper."

It was a homely supper party in the big drawing-room, with its gold-mounted mirrors, its carpets and curios such gracious, spacious contrast to the prim little sitting-room at home, but it was just as friendly. A glass of lemon punch balanced on his silver-buckled knee, his belaced right hand commanding thrilling signals or lunging an imaginary sword, the captain entertained them with gruesome tales of war in the Americas and Quebec. The girls smiled dutifully at the climax — they had heard most of dear papa's stories before. Matthew was flushed with admiration, pop-eyed with longing to share.

"If only I were older, sir!" he cried.

"Thou'dst fight the Frenchman too, like our Maria!" laughed Mrs Pasley, handing round plum cake. "Tell him, Maria, about thy battle, the Battle of Eddystone Light."

Mute Maria dimpled sweetly into her curls.

"Then I shall!" announced her father. "By the Lord Harry, there's a little game-cock, a chip of the old block! I'm commander at Plymouth, d'ye see, and this daughter of mine takes the Admiral's cutter for a bit of a sail on a fine day. When she gets out beyond the Light, what does she sight? — she sights the Frenchman, or the Frenchman sights her, which was it, Maria? He gives chase, a cruiser, if you please. And what does our Maria do? Turn tail and run for it? Not she. She gives the order to fire. Two little brass cannon that wouldn't pot a sitting partridge, but the marines take that order from a chit of a girl — they take that order and fire! She can thank her stars there was one of our frigates on the lookout — chased her in and chased the Frenchman back. But what I say is this — while England's women are made of stuff like that, what about it, young Flinders? Art thou and I to fail them? No sir!"

He beamed at his blushing little girl, and put a hand on her curls. Matthew led a family cheer for Maria.

It was after supper, when the captain had called him into his study to show him how to read the marine barometer and plot by sextant, that they heard the Lincoln coach go trundling by. A wild scamper down the garden, with shouts from the servants to stop it. Too late. It turned the corner of the lane. They must spend the night at Radcliffe.

Never mind, said Mrs Pasley. Henrietta was at home. Maria could sleep with Jane and Bess, and Matthew could have her room. So there was time for more of the mysteries of the sextant, more tales of war and wreck, and, in a trance, he was off upstairs to bed.

Maria's little room wide and cool and dainty—so different from his cramped attic at home. Long shadows of the poplars in the moonlight were straight as the masts of ships, lawns smooth and green as a river-calm. Lucky people, and so kindly. They had forgotten nothing for his comfort—a crystal jar of water on the mantel, a cushion at his bedside for night prayers, even a nightshirt underneath his pillow. He blew out the light, clambered in, and slept like a top with a slant from the moon across the foot of his bed. What heaven to be a lord of the wave like Pasley—to come back to his loved ones in a home he had earned for them like this.

He woke in he morning with the bright sun streaming in, leapt out of bed—and doubled up with laughter. Pretty pink bows were tied under his chin, and laced up his scrawny elbows, his scrawny feet swimming under waterfalls of lace. It was Maria's nightshirt they had left him!

The girls gave a shrill squeaks and pips of delight when he told them, very shyly, at breakfast. Nothing would do but he must give a performance in full dress. Up and down the breakfast room, prancing and prinking in Maria's pretty fallals above his raw new boots, Matthew was moved to give them a hornpipe. Henrietta strummed, he clumped, the children and Mrs Pasley collapsed in hysterics, and the captain gave such hearty gusts of laughter he voewed he must loose canvas or founder.

"Aha, young rascal! We'll have thee aboard the *Billy Ruff'n*!" he promised at parting. "A great ship for play-acting she is, and piping all hands to dance."

Bellerophon! It was a jest. A chuck under the chin from the captain, a kiss on both cheeks from Mrs Pasley, affectionate wave of good-bye from the girls, and Matthew was off with Henrietta on the morning coach. The greatest event of his life was over.

"Was I too forward?" he asked with sudden misgiving.

"Not at all, Matt. Thou wert splendid, and how they enjoyed it. I am glad thou hast met the captain in his home. 'Twill do thee more good than a thousand recommendations to have made a friend of the children. He is pleased with thy nautical knowledge too. He told me it surprised him. Something good will come of it, never fear."

"Dear Henrietta. Thou art so kind, for this is all thy doing."

She brushed away his thanks.

A few days later, when he was making his bed, for Mrs Flinders was ill and they kept no servant, Henrietta came with the smile of a conspirator, and roguishly closed the door.

"A secret, Matt! There's a letter from Captain Pasley on thy father's table. That can mean only one thing—a post for thee!"

He blankly stared.

"Now is the time to see thy father," Henrietta went on eagerly. "Plead with him to let thee go, and promise him thou wilt do well."

"Oh Henrietta, he'll not listen. Has forbidden me to speak to him of the sea. 'Tis my life's chance, I know, yet what can I do? My father is there now?"

"No. He's driven over to Sibsey. There was a message on the slate, and he left early."

"Hold! I have it! I have it, Henrietta!" He rose with shining eyes and hugged her. "A dearer cousin than thee I never had. He has never forbidden me to write of the sea. I, too, shall write a message on the slate by the surgery door." He was off like a whirlwind down the stairs.

Three times he filled the doctor's slate with agitated pleading, three times cleaned it off and began again. What could he say? His thoughts were all astray. The message he finally left was brief and simple:

DEAR FATHER,
I promise that thou shalt ever be proud if thou wilt let me go to sea.

Thy son,
MATTHEW FLINDERS.

The livelong day he was a-prickle with suspense, longing for the hours to be gone, listening for the gig, in the end flying from the sound of it, waiting to be called, waiting to be lectured, or thrashed—or set free. He came in to supper with scarlet cheeks. His father's face was remote as the Sphinx to his expectant gaze, and never a word his father had to say, then or for many days after. The message had been rubbed from the slate. Could they have dreamed the Pasley letter?

He was more restless than ever now. The house in Market Square was depressing. Its dormer windows no longer commanded the stars. They looked out on moss-grown tiles and monotony, and Matthew mooned his misery. Ptolemy had lost his power to wile away the hours. He belonged to the Land of the Blue and White Nile, and Matthew would never follow. He would be chained to this market square all his born days. Had it not been for Henrietta, he would have given up hope.

"Patient a little longer," she said. "I'm sure there is something in the wind. If I hear any news, be sure I'll let thee know."

She went back to Radcliffe, *en route* for Chatham with the family. School term began again. He took his satchel gloomily, and humped the books off on his shoulder. Dux of the school for the past year now, he wanted new worlds to conquer. His feet had worn a groove deep in the Horbling road. Collecting sprigs along the way, he tried to teach himself botany, but his heart was not in it, and except for a few old women out on the Fens gathering simples, nobody knew the science of leaves and flowers.

On a burnt-gold October day, when he came home dispirited and threw his schoolbag in the corner, Betsy announced that his father wanted to see him. Some trouble. He faced the music, to find the little doctor bright and bland.

He handed Matthew an envelope, heavy with the official seal of the Navy Board in London, that he had already opened. Inside was a brief communication in copper-plate.

Matthew Flinders, aged fifteen years, of Donington, Lincolnshire, was appointed to a berth as lieutenant's servant on H.M.S. *Alert*. He was to report forthwith on board the ship at Chatham.

The boy was speechless with excitement.

"Sit down, Matt," his father suggested smiling. Vaguely, by rearguard action, he found a chair.

"I have opposed thy desire for the sea for two reasons," his father was saying—he might have known, but his face grew pale and sullen. "One is that I felt thou couldst do best for thyself and thy fellows in the profession to which thou wert born, and in which I can guide thee."

"Yes, sir"—perfunctorily. He was not impressed.

"The other that I had no wish to see thee tossed helter-skelter round the world in danger and in bad company, in a life that can give thee little even at best. You know my views."

"Yes, sir."

"But since Captain Pasley has made himself thy friend, the position is somewhat changed. The captain has written me that a chance may come to take thee in hand himself, and in any case that he will keep an eye upon thee, and put thee in the way of advancement."

"What, father? You mean I can go?" The air was electric.

"Well my boy, thy heart is set upon it. We get no good of thee else, I can plainly see."

Matthew was dumbfounded. A slow grin spread itself over his earnest freckled face.

"Father! How can I thank thee?"

"By remembering our name, and doing it honour."

"I'll try, sir. Oh believe me, I'll try." He pounced on the letter again, and scoured it with his eyes. "Chatham! The *Alert*! Lieutenant's servant!"

"Heaven help the lieutenant!" said his father dryly. "Look at thy boots, sir. They've not been blacked for a month, I'll swear! Thou'lt catch it hot from thy lieutenant. Well, if thou art a misfit, as I strongly suspect, come back and begin again. Thy home is here for thee always."

"Oh never fear, father, thou'lt never see me back!"

"What, never?"

"I mean, thou'lt never have to make me a doctor because I

42

failed—Oh father, forgive me! I'm sorry to the heart I should disappoint thee, but I'm so glad—I cannot tell thee."

"I understand, my son. I only trust thou wilt make me proud—as thou hast written on my slate." He smiled, and Matthew smiled, in recollection. For the first time they were friends, father and son.

"As for the doctor," he went on, "I still have thy brother. It means only that I must wait a little longer. Samuel, I trust, will take kindlier to physics, the real physics and not thy hanky-panky. Go now. We'll talk of it to-night. There will be much to plan."

Matthew wandered off bewitched.

He was going to sea. All Donington knew it by morning, and Boston by the end of that week. Mr Prin was to make his uniform, a blue cloth coat with stand-up collar, white cloth waistcoat, white breeches. What glory! On the day it was finished, he paraded in state to the apothecary's shop to show his friend George Bass, but George was gone!

He has passed his preliminary examination with first-class honours, Mr Francis told him, and was away in Lincoln, walking the hospital boards and studying for his finals.

"A penetrating young man," said Doctor Flinders when he heard it. "He, at least, will go far in the profession."

"Not so far as I in mine," suggested Matthew. "When thou seest him in Boston, father, tell him I missed him to say good-bye. I wish he were sailing with me. He loves the sea as I do."

"We of the Fenlands have no cause to love the sea," answered the doctor sadly. "It robs us of our sons and our soil."

Purchasing, packing and planning were over. The day came when he boarded the south-bound stage-coach, his father with him as far as Cambridge. Henrietta would meet him in London, and Captain Pasley had offered to see him safely aboard the ship. While they strapped his trunk on top, there was a hasty farewell kiss to the family, Betsy, Susanna and Samuel, irrationally wistful at being left behind, Mrs Flinders with the new little step-sister in her arms.

The bells jingled warning, the postilion whipped up the horses, and Market Square shouted good-bye.

It was a keen autumn morning. The drift of white mist on the Fens lifted before they reached Spalding, where Grandfather Flinders met them to add his gift to the stack, a neat small medicine chest he had specially selected, bound in calf's leather.

"The main thing for a happy life," announced Grandfather Flinders, "is to take a dose of calomel after thy bath on Saturday night, and always read a verse of the Bible before retiring. Clean in mind and clean in body, thou'lt come to no serious harm unless it be shipwreck, and that is the good God's will."

He stood at the cross-roads waving them out of sight, his long white beard a landmark.

Now they were in country new to Matthew, bound for Charteris and St Ives, strange rivers and villages, an inn painted blue all over, the goose girls driving their quaint flocks—some of them all the way to London.

High hills came into view, the first Matthew had seen. His heart, like David's, leapt, and he lifted up his eyes. His father sat quietly by, pondering a parting sermon. Cloud-races over the valleys provided him with his text.

"Shadow and light, Matthew, dark days and bright, evil and good," he said that night as they lay in the inn at Ely, "will be thy lot, as every man's. Be not dismayed by the one, dazzled by the other. Keep thou the path. Life's achievement, and not its pleasures, will bring thee lasting happiness. God bless thee, my son. To sleep now, for thou must be astir before daybreak."

Hurried good-bye in the dark of the morning, a last reassurance that all was safe, and Matthew was off, into the dawn alone.

London was sorry disappointment to one who had visioned fairy towers—endless round of carriages and carts through an endless round of shops and houses dismal in the rain. Cousin Henrietta and the Pasleys took him everywhere, from penny peep-shows to the singing concerts in Vauxhall Gardens, from Punch and Judy to the Tower. He was vastly amused and interested, but his heart was already aboard ship, and glad when the time came for Chatham—a forest of masts, the smell of bad oysters, pageant of ships and sailors.

Captain Pasley was a different man at Chatham, curt and unapproachable, of great importance and little time. He briskly shepherded Matthew up the gangway of the *Alert*, handed him over to the tender mercies of the master, strode aft for a word with the commander, and left him to his fate.

The *Alert* was a worm-eaten hulk that never moved from her moorings. That was a blow. She was mostly used as a training-ship, and a home for disabled heroes and officers out of work who showed the youngsters the ropes. Aboard her he learned seamanship and philosophy—learned to gulp down vertigo at the maintop, to splice a knot and take in a skysail, to blacken boots and take a kick from them, and run with hot toast and skilly between decks sheltering it from the rain with his hands. He learned to eat and sleep with seven others of his age, or younger, in a fetid hole three decks down, among the slime and rats and cables, where there was scarcely reasonable room and not enough air for two, to wake to the slash of a wet towel across his face, and fight for the right to read at night, and fight for his shirt in the morning.

He scarcely knew which lieutenant's servant he was. The commanders were constantly changing, the lieutenants usually drunk. He soon learned that human nature is not what the parsons preach. He learned the fundamental facts of life in good set terms—incidentally, that such vermin as he had no right to be born.

If there were days when he felt miserable and dirty and hungry, butt of all the bullies aboard, victim of his own ambition, he was careful to say nothing in home letters. He dreamed of a life on the white-winged ships that slipped past him down the river in the moonlight, heard in an anchor chain running out the music of the spheres. The smell of a ship—and God knows it smelt—would keep him a willing slave for ever.

It was a pinched and bitter winter, of broken sleep in the shivering cold and dreary waking to dreary days of kicks and no ha'pence, but at least he escaped without a flogging. Reward came with the spring, when Pasley asked for his report.

What the report was he never knew, but the captain sent for him to join the *Scipio* for a trip through the Downs, by way of Beachy Head—his first swing of blue water.

The Channel was swarming with shipping, schooners, barques and smugglers to every port on the south coast bringing refugees in thousands, aristocrats of France flying from the Terror. War had been strangled by the red hands of revolution.

Hardly was he back at Chatham than he was summoned to take his place as junior midshipman on H.M.S. *Bellerophon*, the great, the noble "*Billy Ruff'n*", ship of the line.

One hundred and eighty-six feet long by fifty feet wide and fifty deep, she was a giant of the Grand Fleet, newly built at fabulous cost of £30,000. Two thousand British oaks, each a century old, had gone to her making. She bristled with guns, spoke in a voice of thunder, could throw a cannon-ball three miles. Bellerophon was her figurehead, in cloak of scarlet and gold, mounted on a snow-white Pegasus, the snow-white plumes of his helmet flying like the white caps of the wave, and in his right fist, upraised, a silver javelin.

So far she had never moved out of the stream at Chatham. God help the Frenchmen when she did go out to meet them! A ship that launched herself as she did, no damage and no loss of life, had some triumphant destiny, they said.

To Matthew, after the pig-sty of the *Alert*, *Bellerophon* was heaven. Sleeve buttons and cocked hat, a dirk in the leather belt over his right shoulder, he walked on air—one of the young gentlemen, R.N.

Home for the Christmas holidays in Donington, the family scarcely knew him. So tall and so resolute, he was a son for the little doctor to be proud of, driving round in his gig. Chosen friends at Saturday night socials delighted in his tales of the press-gangs, or gay impersonations of Earl St Vincent in all his iron severity, and Black Dick Howe, with poker as staff and table-napkin cravat.

At Chatham the Navy was seething with a new kind of scandal. Bligh was back from the Pacific without the *Bounty*, without his master's mate, one Fletcher Christian, without his crew, save for a few odd men out. Tales of bloodlust and hell afloat were rife. Bligh was a devil incarnate. They had set him adrift in an open boat to die for his misdeeds, with eighteen of his men, not faithful but unwanted. They had rowed for 3600 miles to find a ship at Timor, for England—and revenge. H.M.S. *Pandora* was gone to the South Seas, to bring the mutineers to justice.

Pasley was troubled. Heywood, his wife's nephew, was on the *Bounty*—and missing. His mother was grieving. The boy was young, fifteen when he sailed, and whether Bligh was right or wrong, Pasley had promised to save him. All those who had gone with the ship Bligh denounced as guilty of his murder. Otaheite was not so far as they thought, and he would see them hanged—aye, flogged to pieces and hanged.

It was a quiet year for young Flinders, while a second fleet set out for Cook's New South Wales, with men and women chained. He studied, and stood his watch, and made good friendships. The *Bellerophon*, a tall ship, was his religion and his pride.

The future brought of the *Bounty* mutineers, ten miserable stragglers, but not in the *Pandora*. She had been wrecked in Cook's Endeavour Straits. Heywood came home, in irons. He had known nothing of the mutiny, he swore to Pasley, until the boat had been cast off and gone. God knows how they had lived through the cruelty and the wreck of the *Pandora*.

There was a grim court martial in London—they heard of it in rumour. Six men and boys swung at the yard-arm of the *Brunswick* at Portsmouth. At the appointed hour the ships of Chatham drummed requiem in warning.

Bligh was morally to blame, the seamen said. The goad of his vicious tyrannies, his petty persecutions, had perverted men of worth, set them longing for the palms and the reefs, the bright, dark women of Otaheite with peace and contentment and laughter in the circle of their arms. But Bligh or no Bligh, there would never again be mutiny like this aboard His Majesty's ships.

Poor little Heywood was among the doomed, hounded down by Bligh to the end, till Pasley, by sheer weight of his friendship with Howe and St Vincent, at the eleventh hour took his neck out of the rope.

"The boy is of fine spirit," he said to Flinders when the first news of the outrage on the high seas came to them in England. "Will be an admiral yet, as Fletcher Christian might have been, for I know him. God knows where he is now. We shall hear in time. But this man Bligh kills spirit, unless thou hast the wisdom to see through him, young Flinders, and let him rant, and let him filch small perquisites from thy wages, and pare thy cheese, and steal thy pigs and coco-nuts."

"I hope, sir," said Matthew smiling, "that I shall never be near him. My loyalty is to the *Bellerophon* and thee."

Pasley turned to him, deliberating, the old twinkle in his eye.

"Wouldst thou have war?" he asked, "or exploration?"

"Thou knowest, sir. Thou knowest my heart is on the far horizon."

"Post-Captain Bligh," said Pasley, "leaves again for the Pacific, and the breadfruit. Two ships, the *Providence* and *Assistant*. In the new time-keepers thou art especially skilled. I have thought that if I nominated thee, thou mightst find a berth aboard. Will journey to Van Diemen's Land and Otaheite, survey some Fiji Isles he has discovered, then back through the Straits of Torres and the Endeavour, to the Cape Colony, to Jamaica, St Helena, and so home. A voyage round the world. Does it call thee?"

3

Bounty Bligh

The news was received in Lincolnshire with something of alarm. Matthew to sail round the world with Bligh, the bogy of the Navy! Fantastic tales of starvation and torture aboard the *Bounty* were rife in all the sea-coast towns where pig-tailed sailormen wander.

"Thou'lt hang at the yard-arm yet, my boy," laughed his father.

"Come what may, I'll never be among mutineers, sir. It would kill all my chances of command."

"Never mind thy chances of command. It would kill thee. Do what thou'rt told, and keep quiet, to save thy precious skin. Strange as it may seem, Matthew, we'd like to see thee again some day. Thou'lt be a long time away, taking the chances of the sea in company that is not the best for a lad of thy age, but I think I can trust thee to be sensible. Thou'lt have a lot to do with this Captain Bligh as time-keeper midshipman, probably more than any one else on the ship. Remember that he is a brave man, and if he is a bully, be blind and deaf and dumb."

"I'll do all that for the voyage, Sir. It's the chance I've been wanting above all others, to follow Cook through the Pacific seas"—his young voice quickened in eagerness—"and we'll touch upon Terra Australis, at Van Diemen's Land on the way out, and coming back through the Straits of the Endeavour, where Captain Bligh sailed in the boat."

"Yes, but Cook has more or less charted that, my son. It seems to me thou art somewhat late. Why, the place is New South Wales, and a convict station."

"They don't know where the coast begins, or where it ends, father. I'd start where Cook left off."

"Thou'dst start! What in? A wherry? Thou'rt only a midshipman yet, Matthew. Don't play at command, I warn thee, when Mr Bligh's about."

"Believe me, father, meekness is my name."

Mrs Flinders was just as full of misgivings for the eldest son of the family. A full-fledged sailorman, he scorned her loving attentions, but not the good Lincoln hams and plum cakes she packed away deep in his sea-chest in sealed tins.

"Don't let any one know thou hast these, Matt. There's a separate hamper to share with thy friends, and I want thee to keep these, in case."

"Of what, mother? Another boat journey? Oh, we'll stock up for that with little pigs and plantains in Otaheite, where the girls are so pretty. I'll smuggle one of them home to thee to be a May-day queen."

"Such talk, Matt Flinders! The naked heathen women! I'm shamed of thee." She whisked him out of the kitchen with her baking cloth.

His sisters and young Samuel were casual about it. They were used to his comings and goings by this, and he lived on another planet. His school friends had become apprentices, or scriveners, or bankers on the Fens, their vision confined to the gaieties and gossip of the village green. George Bass was still in Lincoln. Ann Chappell might have listened with wide-eyed wonder to all that he was going to see and do, but in the hasty week of his home leave the doctor's gig was not called over to Partney, and he did not care to suggest a special visit to seek the admiration of a girl.

Anticipations were dimmed in apprehension when the order came to board the ship at Debtford. The world did seem a long way round as he waved the family good-bye from the

Cambridge coach. Not for two years, or three, or four—perhaps never—would he see Donington again.

But his spirits soon lightened as they bowled along through hedgerows, villages and towns to London. High summer clothed the shires with mellow gold.

In the city he met a fellow-midshipman from the *Bellerophon*, a fat, cheery boy named Bob Ogilvie. They rattled down to Debtford together, hiding their misgivings in lighthearted mimicry of all possible and probable Blighs, thinking out daring repartee for exciting situations. When the crisis came, they invariably relented at the last moment, and, either with conspicuous heroism or impassioned appeals to the crew, saved the captain from the dire results of his own brutality, gallantly rowed him home again across the roaring foam. "Stow thy gratitude, Bully Bligh! What we have done we have done for the honour of England!"

"Jests aside," said Matthew, "I think we need have no fear. Lightning never strikes in the same place twice. Bligh knows that all England is watching him this time. To please him may be impossible, but a record of no complaints with such a man is worth more than the praise of others. Our commanders hold our future in their hands. Let's try, Bob, just for the fun of it, to see if we can make him smile upon us. Let's draw the old serpent's fangs, and tame the lion."

"Provided," said Ogilvie, lowering, "he does not go too far!"—but on his rosy-apple face a frown was only comic.

The *Providence* was an easy quest in the shabby shipping of Debtford, a brand-new West Indiaman, 420 tons and impressive, swarming with carpenters, painters, and sailors stitching sails. She was mounted with twelve carriage guns and fourteen swivels. The *Assistant*, a 100-ton tender, was moored alongside, Lieutenant Portlock in command. Ruth to Naomi, whither the *Providence* went she would go, and she also was armed. One hundred and thirty tried and trusted men had been selected from His Majesty's ships at Portsmouth, and they were to take on a small army of marines from Chatham. There would be no mutiny this time.

Post-Captain Bligh was in his cabin, checking over a list of stores. He growled them in, and scowled them to attention, while he totted up totals, cursed the chandlers, sniffed at snuff, and spat. An unkind slant of sun showed up the grease and dust of long wearing on the stocky blue shoulders of his uniform, the drifts of powder in his untidy pigtail.

"Hangman's noose!" whispered Ogilvie, slanting his eyes to the pigtail. Matthew swallowed a smile in time. The commander swung round on them.

"Silence!" He was like an angry turtle, except that his eyes were clever and keen beneath that receding brow.

Mumbling rapidly, he checked his addition then dealt with the boys briefly. In Flinders he showed a flicker of critical interest slightly aggressive.

"Captain Pasley has spoken well of you. That means nothing. I judge you by your work." His tone soured. "You doubtless know that Captain Pasley by his intervention, I shall not say interference, has saved from the gallows and his just deserts a midshipman of my former company. He will have the good grace to leave my affairs, and my men, wholly to me in future. I shall examine you later. Report to the master, Mr Nicholls."

Ogilvie pulled a wry face when they were safely outside.

"I think I like him," said Matthew. "A lot of pepper, but good red meat beneath." He was to like old Bligh, with the usual reservations, to the end of his days.

Through June and July the ships were tied up at Debtford, refitting and taking in stores. The commander was in London most of the time, in close touch with the Admiralty and that almost legendary power behind the throne, Sir Joseph Banks. Lieutenant Portlock, who had been master's mate of Cook's *Discovery*, was a crisp and efficient deputy. First-Lieutenant Bond, who filled the place of the shadow of Fletcher Christian, was Bligh's younger cousin, a bit of a martinet, but kindly. Lieutenants Tobin and Guthrie were likeable fellows, both young, Tobin artistic and literary, Guthrie lean and lank and energetic. They kept order in brisk good humour. There was a tight naval regime about the *Providence* that the *Bounty* had never known.

The breadfruit had become as the quest of the Holy Grail, staff of Imperial life. It seemed that the West Indian colonies would no longer exist without it—the truth was that England was paying heavy duties to America for flour to feed her slaves, and wanted a cheap substitute that would grow there.

The botanists, when they came aboard, were received with the utmost deference. James Wiles and Christopher Smith from Kew Gardens, they were regarded as the high priests in a sort of sylvan worship, the mysteries known only to themselves, and the ceremonies to begin when they reached Otaheite, to which the sailors referred with a knowing wink. Happy days! Happier nights!

With nine midshipmen, the ship was ratehr overrun by young gentlemen anxious to distinguish themselves under the eagle eye of authority, good rebels in private, but models of circumspection on watch. There was one, William Day, an overgrown lad with a hare-lip, frankly nervous. He had not sought a berth aboard the *Providence*. It had been thrust upon him by an ambitious father. He collected all the fables of Bligh's devilry in circulation along the waterfront—eyes lashed out of their sockets, nicked ears, and dead men hanging in the rigging. So he became the butt of their practical jokes, and blood and horror tales. The captain's voice, or a good imitation of it, could startle him like the crack of a whip. Sometimes he whimpered in his sleep.

Two or three convict ships were anchored in the channel, rotted old castled hulks where the chained brutes waited for transportation, wolfish eyes watching through the bars. Now that the sluggish tide divided, for the first time in their squalid lives they loved their native England, hung their matted heads in bitter weeping for the reeking alley-ways and thieves' kitchens that were all they knew of home.

The purring of the cat and the shrieks of its victims were a daily commonplace, the ear-splitting screams of women condemned to three dozen at the bulkhead. As the boys drew past in the ship's boats, closer than need be in the morbid curiosity of youth, they might catch a glimpse of a shaven head in a neck-yoke on the quarter-deck, or be greeted with obscenities or entreaties from caged wild beasts unseen. Bound for the Land of the Holy Spirit, those beings seemed demons in hell.

All the time Matthew could spare from his nautical and mathematical studies he spent in reading discovery, "peering in maps and charts", tracing the evolution of exploration from Ptolemy again down to Cook. He took the soundings, in fancy, of a myriad islands sprawled on seas of unruffled blue. He kept imaginary journals with scrupulous exactness, assimilated the various styles of the great English navigators, and grieved that he did not know Dutch.

For light relief, propped beside him at mess, or beneath a ship's lamp in his hammock at night, he read Dampier's *Voyages*, in thirteen sea-stained volumes lent him by Portlock, finding within those yellowed pages entertainment and inspiration.

This William Dampier was a man after his own heart, a farmer's boy who loved the blue furrows of the sea better than the brown of earth, and became a pilgrim of the winds and high adventure. Free-booter, slave-trader, pirate from the West Indies to the East, he raked the world, and robbed it, and set it on fire to see it. There was no Royal Society in Dampier's day, and a man aboard a ship must earn his keep.

In death and danger all his life, here was your true scientist. He would sink a fleet and sack a city in a sentence, to devote two pages, with illustrations in the margin, to a catfish, a catamaran, or the sapadillo-tree. He made maps of the wind and wave for his fellow-pirates, and hungered for the knowledge of new lands.

That precious journal of "Observables" he carried across the torrent of the oceans and the raging of rivers in a "joynte of bambo well stopped at both ends". He tucked it into his girdle in shipwreck and rapine, more precious than his cutlass, and dried off the scrawled pages, blood-spattered or wave-sodden as the case may be, in the blazing suns of tropic beaches, while his comrades caroused around him in rum and revelry.

Dampier was the man who twice marooned his old friend Robinson Crusoe on John Fernando's Isle, and had so much of far greater value to write that he lightly bestowed the story on a tavern copy-writer. And how the old pirate could write! He would have made a much better job of it than Defoe, for no romance Matthew had read was half so rich as this.

Under the Jolly Roger, in a stolen sloop from Mindanao, he was the first Englishman to set foot on the shores of New Holland, to write of that slowly-wakening land as none would ever write of it again—but when he was sent back in command of a king's ship to see if the last of the continents were worth owning, he had forgotten to hoist the British flag. So Cook, a century after him, was reaping the honours. That is, if New Holland and New South Wales were one. Many thought they were two islands or thousands.

Some day Matthew would follow him along that western coast, to learn whether those swirling tides, of five and six fathoms rise and fall, did funnel through a passage to the south. Another intriguing problem was that of the variation of the compass, noted by the old sea-dog with much mystification, and never yet solved. Here was something to bite on in the cause of nautical science.

In mid-July the *Providence* and *Assistant* sailed through the Downs, took on the marines under Lieutenant Pearce at Little Nore, and loaded ballast at Sheerness. From Spithead, on 3 August, they weighed anchor, bound for the blue.

The low land about the Start merged into the tumbled horizon. The lights of Portland winked them farewell. To Matthew Flinders the wind in the rigging was a massed orchestra of 'cellos. He had crossed the threshold of his homeland and his youth to become a citizen of the sea. Creak of the cordage, jibe of a sail, were solos in a symphony.

He woke in the morning to a minor commotion amidships. William Day was missing on his first watch. He had answered the roll-call at Spithead and then run for it. An abandoned kit and a folded hammock told of a last-minute flitting. Those nicked ears had been too much for him.

Ships of all nations passed them as they swung down the Channel in fair weather and a fair wind, Swede, and Dutchman, the Frenchman in the distance. An English frigate, *Winchelsea*, carried their first letters and their last farewells to London. A few days out, there was the thrill of firing a gun at a little Portuguese trader, but she was putting in to Cork, her mission legitimate and peaceful enough, a cargo of Oporto wine.

With a lofty reserve quite newly acquired, the commander kept to his cabin and his charts. One brief order of "three watches every man, to make 'em look alive and keep 'em out of mischief", and he was content to leave discipline to his officers, the best the Navy could give him.

A capricious task-master Matthew found him, but not unbearable. His splenetic rages over trifles were appeased by respectful silence. The truth was that Mr Bligh was not well. He was suffering the reaction of a two years' typhoon of mental and physical emotion, strain of the boat journey, suspense of the courts martial, and the triumph of his vindication and promotion. His enemies had been completely routed. In frequent and savage headaches, with a wet pack on his brow and a smile on his thin lips, he liked to lie still and gloat.

The clockwork order of the *Providence*, the little *Assistant* trimly sailing in her wake, the redcoats grouped about the decks, gave him a security and a standing he had never known. The botanists at their studies, and young Flinders and Ogilvie under his thumb, busy with their nautical tables and cross-bearings and seven-point logarithms, bolstered his self-importance as the leader of a first-class scientific expedition. The *Bounty* had been a blessing in disguise, redeemed him from the limbo of odd jobs to an honourable and enviable command. No longer a manikin of war and whim, he was an emissary of empire.

So he chewed over the satisfying cud of his thoughts. At times he was almost benevolent, though benevolence ill fitted the set of that bull neck. When Day's kit was sold at the masthead, the master showing contempt of a quitter by gingerly handling the boy's possessions, those who were hoping for a volcanic display were disappointed.

"Yellow in the guts. We can do without him," remarked Mr Bligh conversationally, and stumped aft.

Matthew had promised Pasley to send his impressions from every port of call, and it was now that he began to put into writing the highlights of every day's events in his life. Always methodical, he stowed away the rough drafts. In the grey after-years, when the letters were lost, the angular schoolboy calligraphy of those early copying-books faceted many bright memories, brought back the swing of the sea and the scent of a shrub to torture and bless a man grown old in sorrow.

One morning, in dense fog, he was called up from his time-keepers to see a fantasy in the clouds, an island in the sky. Seething spume of white mist was breaking on its sombre headlands. The crest was crowned with sun.

Shades of Columbus! It was the peak of Teneriffe.

When the fog cleared they entered the roadstead of Santa Cruz, and hove to in a glass calm completely hemmed in by the hills. A few Spanish merchantmen were mirrored in steel. The breath of the land was hot as a furnace.

Matthew and Christopher Smith—quiet, whimsical Christopher—took shore leave together. They scoffed oranges and limes in the market-place, where Our Lady of Candelaria holds sway in marble over the cannibal chiefs of the Canaries, with human shin-bones in their sculptured hands. They climbed the dirty cobbled streets, where half-breed senoritas smiled to them from bird-cage balconies, proffering delights of Tenerifa that to two such ascetic souls made no appeal.

Three mellow notes of the Angelus at noon, and a chanting of *Aves* rising and falling like the wind among the palms, drew them to an old Spanish belfry in a byway.

There was an iron grille almost on a level with the paving stones. On hands and knees the boys bent to peer. It was an underground chapel of hooded nuns at prayer, before a blue and gilt statue of the Virgin. With eyes downcast, their lips to their folded hands, they murmured the responses. Most of them were young, and some were very pretty.

Suddenly they rose from their prie-dieux with a starched rustle of veils, genuflected to the high altar, and went billowing out of the chapel. One of them chanced to look upward—flash of dark eyes beneath a snowy coif. Seeing the laughing boyish faces at the grating, she hastily made the Sign of the Cross and fled. That fluttered the dove-cote. Reproachful glances, an undignified scuffle, and all were gone.

In mischief, Christopher rang the convent bell. He was greeted by a hawk-nosed old portress, a square-rigged ship, broad as she was long. They innocently asked in Latin that they might come in to say a prayer, but she wagged a fat forefinger, and in shrill Castilian bade them begone... then, because they were so youthful and clear-eyed, she relented, delved into her capacious pockets for some candy that she called *dulce*, and gave them with it a paper flower that Our Lady of Candelaria had blessed. From the world, the flesh and the devil—young scamps that they were—she would do the praying for their redemption, and for their safety on the stormy sea. Christopher slipped a silver dollar into her alms-box, neatly in evidence, and she closed her grille on a beaming motherly smile.

Back at the ship they found Portlock in command, and the commander in a high temperature of Koepang fever. He kept to his bunk on the way south to Porto Praya, and sent a boat in to see if a sick captain could find sanctuary ashore. But those bald rocks and glaring hills showed no clemency of coolness or peace.

Pearce and Tobin returned poste-haste with a few wizened oranges, all skin and fibre, and the news that plague was raging. The natives were dying in dozens. They would do well to get out. They were just in time. The season of Buonavista rollers was at hand. Even as the *Providence* cleared the bay, she lost her bow anchor.

A few days of refreshing breeze brought Bligh on deck in his normal cranky humour, finding fault everywhere, demanding explanations, snapping them short with abuse. In sickness or adversity, he was possessed of angelic strength and patience. When heaven smiled, he was a fiend incarnate. Bob Ogilvie christened him "Sweet William", and "Sweet" he was to them for the rest of the voyage.

For two days they kept company with a French brig bound out for Gambia. When they parted she courteously carried their dispatches to the Admiralty, to be sent to England from France on her return in six months' time.

A school of dolphins playing ushered them into the south. Danny Dree, an old quartermaster who had been a whaler, gave some lively demonstrations of the art of harpooning, but his hand had lost its cunning, and all his harpoons were broken reeds. On a calm blue Sabbath they crossed the Line, and Bligh, for the first time, read the morning service. His head bent in an obviously sincere piety, he kept one eye on the men and the other on a frigate bird wheeling.

No one but Matthew noticed the keen delight of Bully Bligh, now that he was writing sea-birds in his log. Never a noddy passed unnoticed—"Good eating, Mr Guthrie, sir, extraordinary good eating to dying men, you'd not believe it." A flight of fairy tern could put him in good humour for the day. When two big albatrosses adopted the ship, serenely sailing, his gratification was nearly superstitious. Peter and Paul the seamen dubbed them, and when Paul, with curious eye and gaping beak, flew on board and broke a big boat-hook, the captain showed the genial asperity he would have accorded to the misdoings of a favourite child.

"God bless m'soul! There's power for you!" He beamed upon the damage. For all his faults, Bligh dearly loved the sea-birds.

Taking advantage of a beneficent mood in beneficent weather, John Letby, one of the quartermasters, after a roaring night in the fo'c'sle, challenged the mate of the hold, knocked down the bosun, and was sentenced to thirty lashes.

Where, if ever, they wondered, was Bounty Bligh? Matthew could have enlightened them. One evening the captain discovered him writing.

"A journal, eh?" he grunted. "There's too many bloody journals on this ship. Tumble up and earn your stew!"

Spring had spread a gay carpet of green from the Sugarloaf Hill to the Lion's Rump when they came in to Cape Town, with a welcoming bark of the guns from the old Dutch fort. For Matthew, the ghost of Francis Drake looked out from Table Mountain, there was only one ship in the crowded port, the wraith of the *Golden Hind*.

Walking miles in his shore leave, he marvelled at the chequer-work of cultivation over the hills, the traffic of ox-carts on the sandy roads to the villages in the valleys, the fat and freakish colonial Dutchmen smoking their long pipes, and women and girls five times normal weight.

Bligh made friends with the governor, and took young Flinders on his health trip to Stellenbosch in the uplands. While Lincolnshire was deep in sleet and snow, here he was feasting on grapes and almonds in the leafy orchards, riding in a carriage drawn by four zebras, or swallowing the dust of eight galloping oxen, shooting deer and ostriches from a covered cart—at least, the captain did the shooting while Matthew primed the breech-loaders. Gorillas sprawled in the sun on Paarl Hill, and beautiful little quaggas skipped for the rocky heights at their approach.

Before they said good-bye to their host, Mynheer Breddau—twenty-five stone of wheezing geniality and the best garden in the Cape—Bligh had collected 240 different plants for his botanists, and had presented in return thirty nectarine cuttings, the first to be planted in South Africa.

Ships came and went about them in the harbour, whalers and slavers, French brigantines and convict transports for New South Wales. One windy afternoon a small Dutch snow showed up at the entrance, flying English colours and barking for help. The *Providence* sent boats to tow her in—the *Waaksamheyd*, with Captain Hunter from Port Jackson, and the crew of the *Sirius* wrecked on Norfolk Island. They had borrowed this bit of a yacht from Batavia, because there was nothing else in the South Seas to bring them home.

In an English colony of tents rigged on the shore they spent a week together. Hunter, a godly Scotsman with a sagacious eye, would come and yarn to the captain for hours, about his surveys and the jails he had helped Phillip to build in this new place, Port Jackson—"a gr-rand place for a prison, Bligh, betwixt the impr-regnable mountains and the etairnal sea, but yon's a str-range, secret lahnd, and I'm thinking it might be moorre than a prison some day."

Industriously copying a chart, the time-keeper midshipman was his most interested listener.

On Christmas Eve—fair weather and light breezes—the *Providence* and *Assistant* swung out of Table Bay for Van Diemen's Land, ten thousand miles across the Roaring Forties, and nothing in between except the isles of Amsterdam and St Paul—sinister sentinels in illimitable seas.

The silver gulls and the gannets were their only living companions, and for three long months they scarcely sighted each other.

Under Magellan's Clouds and the swinging lamps of the half-deck at night, where the sailors were dealing out cards and fables, Danny Dree taught Matthew to play the flute, and full-throated the chanties rose on the wind. Sea-mews screamed about them all day long, and dark myriads of petrels followed their wake, skimming between the surges. Now and again they saw a whale blowing. For the rest, the routine of blue water. Sauerkraut and sweetwort kept the men from scurvy—not for nothing had Bligh sailed with Cook. One night he told them the tale of his death in Kealakakura Bay, for as they neared Van Diemen's Land came memories of the master.

Long green weeds floating—like the lashes of coachwhips to county-bred Matthew—and a grampus on the port bow, brought them at last, under scowling skies, to a melancholy land.

Broken pillars of blackened rock guarded the sea-gates, with funeral plumes of smoke on the cliffs from the camp-fires of the Indians. It was Flinders's first glimpse of Tasman's Isle, that Bligh had seen three times. Heavy swell broke on the bomboora in a white fury of spray, and the little *Assistant* was nearly swamped as she rounded the head. They were making for Adventure Bay, that Furneaux named for his ship.

No sooner had they cast anchor than Bligh was off in a boat, with Bond, Portlock, Tobin, Guthrie, Flinders and Tom Walker, and the botanists, bound for the woods. Straight as a die, he made for the landing-place of Cook's *Resolution*, where the *Bounty* had wooded four years ago.

The curious blue gloom of the bush depressed Matthew at first, the sepulchral columns of mighty trees, thirty feet in circumference, boughs twining like serpents. The captain was in voluble mood, trotting round looking for landmarks, finding them, and rejoicing—the blazed trees of the *Resolution* that he, as her master, had fired, the well he put down when he was captain of the *Bounty*, of which the cross-logs still remained in place, even a scrap of red cloth he had left there for the natives. It was quite new and fresh in colour. The poor benighted souls had never touched it.

"I tell you, Mr Bond," he said, "the only honest men on earth are cannibals. Now come with me. There's something else I want to see… ."

Scent of the gum-tree leaves after rain was keen and rarely enjoyable as they trooped in his wake, sea-boots trampling the wet grasses. They passed a deserted bee-hive hut with crayfish shells and bones littered about it, and whitish stones carefully wrapped in a soft and pliable bark.

Tobin said these stones were the fire-flints of Stone Age man, and Bligh tried to demonstrate to them just how the thing was done, but he failed to strike a light, skinned his hands and cursed, and in impatience threw the things away. Inside the hut was nothing but a rank smell of human habitation, and a rough basket woven of sea-rushes. Guthrie picked it up, and put the fire-stones in it, to carry back to the ship as a curio.

"Put those back, Mr Guthrie!" snapped the captain. "What did I tell you, sir? The cannibal for honesty every time!"

In a little open space, he surveyed the bush closely, as though for something lost.

"Now somewhere here … wait a minute … ha!"

He bent above a diminutive shrub not more than a foot high.

"Look at that, Mr Portlock. Examine it well. What is it?"

Portlock went down on his hands and knees, and showed the required surprise.

"Not apple-trees here, Mr Bligh, surely?"

The captain beamed. "Apple-trees here, Mr Portlock, sure enough," he mimicked, and then proudly, "because I planted 'em. It's a poor little specimen for a three-year-old, but, by God, it's held its own, and there ought to be others about.... I tell you this land is better than that at the Cape. If they don't grow apples in it, I'm a Dutchman." But though they wasted nearly an hour, they could find no trace of the others.

"Never mind. The time will come," Bligh told them, as they sauntered away. "Look at the rainfall. Look at the vegetation. Look at the soil. There's no more fertile earth in the South Seas"—he bent down and ran some of it through his fingers— "a heavy chocolate loam it is, and I've seen no better in Kent. Some day, this'll be another England, mark my words. It's a pity Phillip couldn't come here instead of that damned God-forsaken spot he's got to. And talking of England, we'll plant out those oak-trees here, Mr Wiles. This is the place I brought 'em for, so get 'em across to-morrow or the day after, and we'll see them well started before we go. Another England ..." He savoured the idea. "Why do you grin like a cat, Mr Bond?"

"Well, to be frank, sir, I can't for the life of me picture the hop-fields of Kent, the apple-orchards of Devon, and shall we say the church spires of a Christian land in this ungodly spot. We won't live to see it, at any rate."

The captain concertina-ed his thick neck. His eyes glinted anger.

"You won't live to see it, ha! What's that to do with it? I won't live to see these oak-trees grow. If our forefathers were all like you, Mr Bond, there'd have been no England at all. You have as much vision as a louse."

With a truculent sermon on living for posterity, he led them back to the beach, so pleased with the success of his apple-tree that he ordered shore leave for the crews.

Summer in the antipodes was snare and delusion—a daily deluge fell, and the temperature down to fifty-three degrees. The crews were all heavily coated during the three weeks in Adventure Bay. Wiles and Smith came down from the hills, their bags laden with rich botanical booty. Wood and water parties scoured the forests, ring of axes and white men's voices echoing strangely through those silent sylvan aisles. In brief glances of sunshine, the midshipmen off duty bathed and did their washing in the creeks, polluting the pools with soap, hanging shirts to dry on the virgin scrub. No Indians were in evidence, only their smokes in the distance.

But the unseen were watching. Bob Ogilvie and George Killsha left two tin cups and a linen bag by a deserted hut on the bank of a stream, and came out of the water to find them gone. Next day they had been put back, in a very conspicuous place on a fallen trunk. Somebody else was making scientific investigations.

Flinders attended the captain, forsaking jollier company because those gimlet eyes missed so little, and because Bligh was the one that knew the country best. They saw kangaroos, a blur of brown, leaping away up the hillside, a pig with an evil eye that was not a pig, but a Van Diemen's Land devil. Friendly little birds like robins played about their camps bringing thoughts of England in snow-time, and parrots of bright-winged plumage flew above.

One day they shot a black cockatoo, and measured its wings, three feet eight inches from tip to tip. Bligh spread the tail, and pointed out that the yellow speckle, in flight, would make a yellow circle.

Flattered by the youngster's keen attention, he gave him many a paragraph for his journal, and advice that was worth a good deal to an aspiring scientific writer.

"Don't miss anything. You never know its value till it's lost."

"To hell with sunsets. I want facts. Sunsets fade. They don't count, but a bird's feathers do."

"Never mind what you deduced. Tell us what you saw."

These were only a few of the pearls of wisdom he gathered up in their rambles, none the less valuable for their setting of good round oaths. If he was gaining from Bligh's companionship, so was Bligh from his, for the boy's delight in new impressions quickened his own, made him feel ten years younger. Sometimes their party of plodding marines was amazed to hear that throaty baritone, hoarse as a seagull's call, let loose in a stave of song.

They had pastured out the ship's goats on a little Isle of Penguins, and as sure as "Old Sweet" landed there, they followed him around bleating. A hoary billy in the lead blankly defied the captain's shouts and curses, and countered his attacks with an offensive from the rear.

In later years, when Bligh's mutinies were under discussion on the quarter-decks and in the mess-rooms, Matthew could always show the other side of the picture, finishing it off with kindly laughter and a skipping imitation of Sweet William and the *Providence* goats.

A good gardener was lost when Bligh put out to sea. Wherever he found a patch of rich soil he planted apricots and peaches, strawberries, some more apple-trees, and even rosemary. He freed a cock and two hens from the crate with great expectations—"Next time you come round here my boys, you'll be feasting on omelettes and fruit."

One day he sent Guthrie and Flinders with some watercress to set in a creek. As Guthrie scraped the earth just under the water, something sleek and slaty swam through his fingers, and burrowed into the bank. By hasty digging he unearthed the creature.

Here was a puzzle—animal, bird, reptile or fish? It had the bill of a duck, like the tongue of a boot, four legs, webbed feet, a furry tail and spurs and bristles. Blind in daylight, it fought furiously with claws. Strangest of all, it had teats like a cat, and they found an egg in its burrow!

No one on board had seen such an atrocity. Tobin thought it was probably new to natural history, and he and Bligh spent the rest of the day sketching it. Even then, they were afraid that nobody would believe them.

Sailing orders were posted. The last water-parties reported a camp of natives at the head of the gully. Heavily bearded and wearing kangaroo skins, the men carried ten-foot spears, but they had been shy enough. The only interest they showed in the sailors was to try to snatch their caps.

Anchors were up when Portlock reported a man missing. Boom of the guns and a fire at the masthead all night brought no answering call, though the blacks lit fires up and down the shore that twinkled like the lights of London. In the morning Wiles and Smith caught the fellow in hiding. Bligh was merely facetious.

"So you're the first immigrant for Van Diemen's Land? Well, I'd rather it was you, you fool, than me. Get back to your ship and behave yourself, or we'll put you ashore at Port Jackson. It's where you belong."

In the afternoon they cleared the bay, but a smashing gale drove them in again at night. By dawn it abated and the fluted black cliffs of Van Diemen's Land fell behind, lost in the mill of the clouds.

Bligh gave the order to swing far to the south of New Zealand. If Cook had missed anything down there, he might as well find it.

But the Bounty Isles were the only break in reeling horizons of storm, as under topsails and t'gansails the two ships raced south-east before the wind.

4

The Drowned Continent

The 16 March was Sunday and Matthew's eighteenth birthday. He woke to the croon of the trades and the sway of the long Pacific swell, the first blithe day in many weeks. The turquoise blue of the sea was a gift, and the crest of the sparkling wave. Dolphins were back again, those jolly troupes of tumblers in the deep, and a skipjack pirouetted past on its tail. The men sang as they trimmed sails for sheer joy of the morning, and ship's washing, festooned in the rigging, fluttered gaily as bunting.

After service, marines and officers spent the forenoon sitting round on the sunny decks, cleaning their guns and yarning. The *Assistant* was in the lead—she had kept up with the *Providence* through all the wild weather—and Portlock put back in a boat with a treat for the commander's table, a little salading he had been growing in tubs all the way from the Cape. There were a few lettuces and chives, etiolated and undersized, but welcome strangers for all that, horseradish for the salt junk, and a festive contribution of Cape figs from his own private locker.

"And that's not all," smiled the grizzled lieutenant when they praised his diminutive garden. "We'll be having potatoes before we reach Timor. I've planted some in Adventure Bay soil, and so far they're doing well."

Bligh thumped the table with exasperation. "Oh, damme, I forgot! I planted potatoes there myself three years ago, Mr Portlock, and now I've forgot to collect 'em. I saw no traces above ground, and I never thought of digging. Blow me down for a mullet-headed fool!"

Sunday dinner was pleasant enough for all, but Tom Walker broke one of the time-keepers in the afternoon, and the captain was furious. His best had already crashed in a gale, and he had only one left. He savagely locked it away.

"What about our reckoning, sir?" Matthew asked him.

"Reckoning to hell! Get back to the lunars. I've vital work to do with this, and I'll not trust it with such careless mongrels."

He sulked off to bed with a headache again, but not for very long. The trade-wind brought poignant memories to Captain Bligh. The trade-wind had seen his humiliation, his travail and his triumph. It had carried him four thousand miles to salvation and success. It made him restless.

As Matthew and James Wiles stood at the taffrail watching their first south-easter sunset, a cockleshell of ruffled gold with a sea-rim of vivid rose and blue, Sweet William stopped in his stride and stood beside them. A hundred leagues out there to the east lay Pitcairn's Isle, and the sunken ribs of the *Bounty*, though they were never to know it.

By some strange telepathy he spoke for the first time of her mutiny and her men. There was vicious hatred still in his heart. His face darkened to an ugly red as he called on a just God to scourge them, wherever they might be hiding—"Aye, and I'll live to see it, never fear."

They were bored with the rights and wrongs of the *Bounty*, ragged to death in the fo'c'sles of every one of His Majesty's ships for the past two years.

"Unprecedented, sir!" was Wiles's non-committal observation, and Matthew made none. It was not required of him. It may have been the tender beauty of the evening sky, but he thought he sensed an underlying sadness when Bligh railed at Fletcher Christian, monster of ingratitude who once had been his friend.

Now they understood the order of the morning, that the men should make ready their guns. They were nearing the islands, Bligh's dream was to see the three tall masts of the outlaw in some quiet cove.

There was a phenomenal display of marine pyrotechnics that night, the glittering heavens far less bright than the phosphorescent sea. The prow of the *Providence* split the waves in long knives of fire. Her wake was a sparkling shawl of coruscations. Yellow lamps hung in the soft dark of the water. Young moons bobbed gently in the wash of the ship, and serpents of living light writhed and coiled along her side.

The child in Matthew was jubilant—he would tell them at home that the Pacific had staged a pageant for his birthday— but the budding scientist wanted to know why.

Danny Dree was in his element of loud expatiation. The sailors hauled a net that shone like Solomon's Tabernacle, piling a million million crabs, jellyfish and cuttles in scintillating pyramids on deck. The boys wore them as fiery eyebrows and moustaches, skipping about in devil-dances and posing ludicrously as statues, with luminous legs and arms. Someone discovered that, when they faded, a touch would bring them to light. Matthew wrote his name with his finger on a man-of-war two feet across. The letters shone for a brief moment, then waned, and glowed again—an omen, and a prophecy.

At the pipe down, they slung their hammocks on deck in a warm wind. After all her roystering, the ship seemed scarcely moving, whispering along, her sails a ghostly twilight. In such a night, it was sacrilege to be sleeping. His hands crossed behind his head, young Flinders lay awake exulting, in his own contentment, in the splendour of the stars.

Day after day was a lullaby rhythm, fair winds and tranquil skies. On 5 April, they thrilled to the lookout's "Land Ho!"

A ravelled thread of the horizon became a sandy shore, with the paler blue of lagoon beyond, and seven tall coco-nut trees tilted on a rocky point. For twenty miles along the coast they ran, and would have sent a boat in for turtle, but a heavy surf was running. The only inhabitants were a few brown noddies, and indeed the drowned island was but a wide hollow circle of sand.

A day or two later, Bligh called all hands on deck to read many rules and regulations for conduct and barter at Otaheite. He nailed them to the mast with brass-bound mallet and brass-bound language. God help the man who made trouble for him there this time. They were to speak no word to the natives of the mutiny, nor of the murder of Cook in the Sandwich Islands.

At the high round isle of Maitea, the two ships hauled in the lee and anchored a couple of miles from shore. Four canoes came off to trade, bringing coco-nuts and plantains. Matthew and Bob had expected bronze gods, but these pedlars were grey-heads and stripling boys, wrinkled and lean as dried olives. One of them wore a ragged shirt.

Bligh spoke to them in their own language and threw them a packet of nails. He learned that the men of their island had all gone to war, and that the shirt had belonged to Patini, Martin, one of the men of the *Bounty*.

The reason of the war they did not know, for they were but *tautau,* of the slave class, but look!—they pointed north-west— you could see the smoke of the burning, and sometimes you could hear the crack of the guns. Yes, they had white men's guns in Otaheite.

Bligh's chin was rigid. The wind was freshening, and he clapped on sail to catch it.

In the morning light they neared the island of dreams, the island of all in the world so beautiful that the Frenchman Bougainville had called it Venus rising from the sea, L'Ile Cythère. With all her sensuous loveliness, playing with the glittering necklace of her reefs, Otaheite smiled them welcome in the lazy, hazy noon.

In one of her rarest poetic fancies, Nature had drawn the island in the perfect form of a woman's hand-mirror. It reflected all the nuances of love. High above them, in sun-gold air, were the twin peaks of Orohena, seven thousand feet, citadel of Mau-i, god of the sun … and beyond, the fantastic turrets of Mouaputa and Moorea, "eye of the needle", the mountain with a hole clear through.

From those passionate peaks fell gorges and canyons of sable gloom, clean as a knife-cut and thousands of feet sheer, swiftly lightened to the laughter of mountain streams, cascades and shimmering palm-groves, here and there a blissful little river, sea-shell beaches, blue lagoons brimming the reefs. The cliffs were wreathed in vines and veiled in flowers. Breath of the land-breeze was fulfilment, and desire.

They skirted the north-west coast to ever more luring and more intimate glimpses, fiords of dreaming colour and light, and silver-gleaming bays. Smoke of the war was still to the west, but no fishing-canoes were in sight. The grass-huts by the shore was deserted. The Matavai people had fled. Bligh was quite mournful. His little heaven was now a heaven forsaken.

Coco-nut palms were black flags against a vermilion sunset when they dropped anchor in Matavai Bay, within sight of Cook's Point Venus and Vaiete, "the water-basket", in the sharp twilight shadow of Mount Aorai. The big village of grass-huts was silent, but a double royal canoe put off from shore piled high with coco-nuts and squealing hogs. As the sails were furled, like a theatre curtain, on the Otaheitian moonrise, Iddea, Queen of Matavai, came aboard. The bosun's mate, in sudden doubt, played the pipes for George III!

In ecstasy of soft words and softer laughter, Iddea greeted Berai. She threw her olive-tinted arms about him, and drew his bullet head to hers. The rows of seamen in their striped guernseys gave a whoop of hilarity, Tobin, Bond and young Flinders broadly smiled. Bligh scowled, then very tenderly captain and queen rubbed noses. He turned and embraced with the same gentle affection a toothless old man behind her, clad in white robes of rare weaving, two noble statues in living bronze, and after them a stripling, ceremonious and solemn. He presented them to his officers, with dignity and pomp—Tootaha, high priest of Otaheite, Oripia and Whaidoa, the king's brothers, and Otoo, Iddea's eldest son, heir-apparent.

"These people are necessary to my well-being," he muttered hastily. "You will now present your respects in turn, and in the same manner."

To the stifled guffaws of the crew, and here and there a cheeky whistle, white noses rubbed on brown, cross eyes grew clear in mutual laughter.

"So the Great White Bird has a chicken!"

Iddea pointed to the *Assistant*, her golden body, in rolls of fat, shaking all over in jollity. "Tooti's ship was its father, eh, as Tooti was father to Berai?"

It was hard to imagine gruff, nuggety Bligh as the son of suave, middle-class Cook, but Sweet William encouraged the fiction for its value, and nobody had ever denied it—unless perhaps the mutineers. There might have been satire in Iddea's smile.

The fulsome breasts of the island queen fascinated the seamen, and the voluptuous swing of her grass skirts as she walked on flat, noiseless feet with an anklet of flowers. Never before had they seen a woman aboard the *Providence*, and what a woman was this!

"Where is Taina?" Bligh spoke sharply in the island tongue. "I would have speech with the Pomare. When Berai's ships come to Otaheite, Taina, the king, must greet him."

"Ah, Taina!" The sidelong glances were forgotten, and the note in her voice was urgent. "With the fighting-men of Matavai, Taina is gone to Oparre. There have come white men in shipwreck, with treasure of iron and guns, and little yellow shells to pay that we do not know. They have sailed away in a stolen canoe, but Matavai is glad, for those men are not as Tooti and Berai. They are evil. Oparre has come then, with many canoes and fighting songs, saying we have kept the white man's treasure, burning our villages. But we have the guns and we drive them away, and now we go to burn. Look westward, O Berai, to the red feathers of fire! All is well, for now Berai goes to Oparre. The big dogs bark on his great canoes, and Oparre is no more! They shall see!"

Her voice was a deep brown colour, sweet as honey.

"What men are these? You have seen them before?"

"Never. They are come drowned out of the sunrise. We gave them life, and food, and our women, and so they repay."

"There is no foolish talk of war, Iddea, when Berai comes to Otaheite. You will send to tell Taina that I am here, and he will bring me the white men's guns. If the Oparre men follow, Berai will be friend to Matavai, but Berai has work to do for King Gargo. He comes again for the breadfruit. So you will go and tell Taina."

"Why not Berai go? He has many small canoes, many warriors. Iddea has but old men, now, and babies ... "

"Enough. Berai has spoken."

She rolled her eyes, shrugged her golden shoulders, and with a lingering envy of the "big dogs", promised she would go.

The captain was not troubled about the war. He knew these island skirmishes, a little spear-throwing, a lot of noise, and an orgy of peace-making under the palms—but he must get hold of the guns. White men were still across at Oparre, living with the women and inflaming the men to fight. Tootaha produced a letter they left for an English ship. They belonged to the little schooner *Matilda* scavenging her way from Peru to Port Jackson, ripped up on a reef outside. Two of them had gone on, looking for Port Jackson, in a boat with mat sails. A motley lot, negroes and Indians among them, they had played fast and loose in Matavai, and been turned out with nothing but their shirts. At first Bligh refused to take them to England, and told them to wait for a whaler, but later he relented, and let them join the crew.

The marines of the *Providence* set up a camp by a pretty river near Point Venus, a thirty-foot compound and a row of grass huts that they called Breadfruit Walk.

Whenever he came ashore, Sweet William with a *lei* round his neck, was the pivot of a circle of beautiful females. Babies in arms tugged lovingly at his pig-tail, and little naked toddlers hugged his knees. Canoes of the petty chiefs of all islands swarmed in like bees, till the captain's nose was skinned with rubbing, his right arm limp from handing out gifts.

"An old man of the sea," he said, "works hard for his living, and by God, I've been at it since I was seven."

The sailors were living like peers of the realm on sucking-pig, oysters and chicken, but shore leave and liquor were niggardly, and the patrols were armed. Crews were rigidly kept to duty aboard, caulking and scraping, mending sails, salting pork, hammering up boxes for the breadfruit out of Van Diemen's Land timber. At sunset on the first day, there were thirty-two plants in the boat. No dallying!

The first fair wind brought Taina, in a covered canoe, with both wives, Iddea, and Whairedi her younger sister, much more alluring and dewy-eyed and slim, but all friendly. When the *Providence* saluted with ten guns, Taina wept for joy. King Gargo was his ally. Let Oparre put that in its kava-bowl and swallow it.

He knew quite well of the *Bounty* affair, and raised his tattooed arms to heaven, thanking the shark-shadow gods of the sea for Berai's deliverance. But when Sweet William rated him for his friendship with Christian, he swore a good round English oath that that was a bloody lie.

The audience ended with the commander decking him up in a scarlet coat with gold lace, and handing out cheap print frocks and beads for the whole of the royal family. Readily Taina promised to give back the stolen goods to the *Matilda's* men, and the muskets, when he could call them in, to Berai. He was so glad that his skin was safe, he was happy to "render unto Caesar". In the sequined moonlight of Otaheite, now let there be feasting. White men's kava was better than white men's guns.

Already the captain noticed a sad degeneration in these too willing children of the south. The corruption of civilization was upon them, in trickery and vice. Hospitality was given now with an eye on the main chance. They hung about the ships, begging and thieving. Bond in his bunk one night was awakened by a twitching of the sheet, and sat up to see it vanish through the port-hole. They caught the thief, and put him in irons, and gave him thirty lashes, with Taina's loud approval. He never winced, and they put him in irons again.

Taina was drunk on board most of the time, mixing rum and kava, singing the endless sagas of the Pomare, with both wives holding him up. In all stages of drunkenness, and with many a cunning trap, Bligh led him to talk of the *Bounty*. He learned all he knew, and no more. She had gone east, west, the gods knew where, and what did Taina care?

To diapason of the trade-wind in the palms, the three months in Otaheite passed as a happy dream. Bligh had his own house ashore. The mutineers' long-deserted dwellings were given over to the botanists and scientists as observatories and conservatories.

Tobin and young Flinders, now captain's off-sider, shared the cot of the ill-fated Ellison. Green-thatched, within sound of the sea, it was garlanded with tekoma bells and the purple creeper of Bougainville. Poor little Tom Ellison. Once he had served with Tobin, a willing lad, and Tobin had seen him hanged because of his love for this spot.

The lieutenant sketched all day in the softly-diffused green light of the open shutter, with a too-appreciative gallery of laughing island beauties. Matthew set up his quadrants and made observations for the sole-remaining time-keeper, and copied the new charts of Adventure Bay. One of them was his own, his first.

In the glamour of afternoon, white radiance over the bay, they went down to the beach where all Otaheite noisily supervised the boats putting off with the breadfruit.

With crowds of olive-skinned friends, they dived in the crystal pools of the rivers and swam in the lagoons, brown and white together, gay as children. They rambled the waterfall valleys, and the crests of the cliffs falling sheer to ocean, eating mangoes, bananas and sweet figs that they plucked as they passed. Sun-browned as the Otaheitians, they went surf-riding on planks of pandanus in the tumble of foam on the reefs, and tuna-fishing with hooks of pearlshell.

They saw the little *itae* birds, like flocks of white butterflies, hovering round the coco-nut blossoms, and the sacred *ito* trees bending above the tombs of the dead. Sometimes they found carved wooden gods, age-old, in the jungle, and once the corpse of a chief who had been dead four months, sitting up in a spirit-house, his eyeless sockets regarding his own dried entrails.

Five thousand feet above the villages and the sea, they crossed the dark stillness of Lake Vauhiria on a raft of palm-logs, and challenged Orohena the unconquerable.

There was a legend of a hidden lake between the peaks, where swam the red ducks, their feathers the insignia of the chief of the land through generations—but the summits were shaly and sliding and treacherous, with no foothold and such dizzying drops that the giant palms in the valley looked like ferns.

Every night there was an island feast, with dancing, and chanting, and love... so they drank deep of the perfume of the *tiare* flowers.

Authority kept an eagle eye on those *tiare* flowers when they were wreathed round beguiling smiles and gestures, and dusky hair. If human nature was just nature in this enchanted land, the older men were discreet. Matthew, for his part, was all idealist, and shy of tar-brush charms. Bob Ogilvie christened him "the marble bust of Cook".

One day Bob, who had been doing some scientific scouting on his own account, cajoled him over to Tautira village, ostensibly to see a wall of skulls. On the way back, in a grass house squalid with pigs and loud with their squealing, he introduced him to a recumbent beauty, obese to obscenity, reeking with rum and coco-nut oil. She could, so Bob informed him, furnish some intimate biographical details, not yet published, of his idol. She had known Captain Cook very well.

Scandalized and annoyed, Matthew refused to speak to the lady. He treated it all as a joke. Such feet of clay were not for the world's appointed. Their hearts were ever set on higher things. He was very young.

For him, the blanks of the ocean map, with two or three dots on the sea-routes. Voyagers had written that the isles of the south were legion, stepping-stones across the Pacific from Australia Incognita to the Americas—high peaks of a drowned continent, the continent of Mu.

He talked much with the old men of Otaheite, heard the legend of Uiterangiora and the dark sea-rovers who had sailed with him to the ice-rim of the south and the ice-rim of the north. In their outrigger argosies, steering by the sun and stars, and making a sextant out of a gourd, they had seen many gods and far too many people. Before they sank beneath the wave, all those gods and people were one. Now the sharks swam in their temples, and the coral insects were building above that old lost world.

The boy Matthew sniffed at the breeze with the zest of a hunter. If only—but their way led back to the east.

On King's Birthday they decked ships and fired six hundred sky-rockets. Taina, in compliment, gave a *heiva*, with two hundred dancers, fire-walkers, and a mighty feast. That was a page for the journal.

A child of the royal family died from cold through being out so late. Iddea wailed a good deal, Taina showed no emotion. He resented his children. They were his superiors in rank, and he had to address them politely from a distance of ten yards. Besides, there were too many, and always obvious prospect of more, one way or the other.... That was another page, and so was the human sacrifice to Etaui, the Hog God of Matavai.

It was a man of Raiatea, clubbed to his death unaware, and brought to Matavai in procession by sea—white-draped canoes mirrored in silver water, tattoo of drums, chanting of the white-robed priests.

They carried the body, trussed like a mummy, to the Great Marai. With bamboo knives they neatly severed the head. A high reedy singing, brown bodies swinging, it was offered to the flat-faced wooden god.

Riding on a man's shoulders, Otoo came forward, Otoo, who would reign in Otaheite when Taina died. One eye from the dead man was cut out, and given to him to eat. The other was laid on the altar.

Then Otoo, slim in the thighs, standing naked, with arms upraised and facing sunrise, was girdled by the high priest Tootaha with the sacred feather belt.

Bligh noticed some strands of curly auburn hair in that belt, and made reverent inquiries. Poetic justice. It had been torn from the scalp of Skinner, barber of the Bounty, slaughtered for his aesthetic contribution to imperial glory. Sweet William secured a lock as souvenir. He already had Martin's shirt and Thompson's skull, for a nice little museum of the mills of God in his house at Lambeth.

On 19 July, a day to be significant in Matthew Flinders's life, the ships were ready to leave.

Two thousand breadfruit were stacked in tiers on quarter-deck and galleries. Every inch the *Assistant* could spare was filled. There were about five hundred other tropical plants for His Majesty's Gardens at Kew, and three dozen or so botanical freaks for Sir Joseph's hothouse at Revesby. Matthew had his doubts. These treasures of a southern heaven would never survive a winter in gloomy Lincolnshire. Even Sir Joseph could not commission the sun.

The commander was mightily pleased. Hands clasped behind his back and cocked hat atilt, he dearly loved to promenade in that green shade.

"All the plants are now in charming order, and spread their leaves delightfully," he wrote in his journal. Once Bully Bligh would have flogged a man who talked to him like that.

Fair exchange, no robbery. On the slopes of Aorai he had planted oranges and citrus, a gift to Taina's people for all time, but the silly old man was much better pleased with the muskets and grape-shot.

Laden with hogs, chickens and fruit, in a guard of honour of a hundred canoes, and showering cheap gifts into outstretched hands, they cleared the harbour to shouts of "*Maira Eree!* — Long Live the King!" Silken scarves in the dawn, Otaheite waved them farewell.

Matthew was in his cabin, stowing in his sea-chest speckled cowries, branching coral, and bizarre weaving of Polynesian mats to cheer the little sitting-room in Donington, with pearl and nautilus shells for Betsy and Susanna, and tortoise-shell fish-hooks for Samuel, when he felt the swing of deep water.

All sail set, a pageant of winged ships, they threaded the pageant of the islands.

The first hour or two they spent in throwing the stowaways overboard. Five miles—or ten—were nothing to such swimmers. They had already had one Otaheitian boy, Maidudi, as ambassador from King Taina to his fellow-monarch King Gargo, but when, after five hours' sail, the trusting smile of another turned up in a basket of yams, Sweet William let him stay. Sixty miles was a little too much, and he could be useful with the breadfruit in Jamaica. His name was Bobbo, and the botanists took him in charge.

On seas of limpid, lazy blue, they steered south-west for Aitutaki and Tonga—more sucking-pigs, more nose-rubbing, and glory—and then north-west. Islands beckoned in the dawn, dreamed in the sunset, annotated, every one, with the bright green asterisk of the coco-nut palm, heavens of delight guarded by sooty black devils, the bones in their noses a foot long, and pearlshells strung round their neck by human hair.

To send a boat ashore here would be murder. Bligh had found that out himself when he passed in the open boat. Signal fires reddened the night skies, and canoes came off by day, but the men with the ochred faces and the raised scars of battle on their breasts were best kept at a distance—not like the loving beauties of Otaheite. Beads and baubles they threw away. They wanted only iron, cold iron of war.

The Tongans called them Feejee, and said that they ate saltwater men. Bligh in his open boat, had been first to sail the islands. Now he was making a running survey—in more ways than one. In these unsounded waters, Matthew worked as never before. Checking the chronometer by Jupiter's satellites and the moon, taking his sights by the islands at night, he was helping to fill an empty map.

The two ships made their way feeling for every fathom. Knife-edged reefs kept them on the brink of disaster. Each day new lands of loveliness swam into view, as though God had suddenly split his world into kaleidoscopic fragments, each one crowned with the majesty of palms—Viti Levu, Vata Varu,

Ngairai, Kandavu, the paradise of Ngau, Taviuni of the golden doves—another Indies for England.

Stepping-stones across the Pacific, they passed to the New Hebrides, and the Isles of the Holy Cross, King Solomon and King Louis, threading, deviating, forever watching, for what? Bligh knew.

One day one of the *Assistant's* men saw an old grey sail in the water. He forgot to tell Portlock till nightfall, and was flogged for gross neglect of duty.

"All ships in these waters," Portlock explained, "are looking for relics of Lapérouse."

"Lapérouse be damned!" said Bligh. "It might have been the *Bounty*!"

On another day they sighted a waterspout, like a broken column of antique Greece, holding up the sky.

A month of halcyon sailing brought them to the gap in the great reef that shelters the coast of New Holland for a thousand miles, and the straits of which Cook had written "no sensible seaman will sail".

Bligh, to his sorrow, had already done it, with men who were dying of hunger and thirst, rowing, rowing, rowing.

A maze of reefs and islands and shelving sands, they were the nastiest ship-trap in the world, and the islanders head-hunters. Edwards, taking back the mutineers a year ago, had lost the *Pandora* there, with thirty-one of her crew, and nearly lost the mutineers. Bligh would never have forgiven him that.

"We'll find a way through," he said. "God's mercy if we miss it!"

Beyond the gateway of the Coral Sea, the islands crowded in, two hundred and more between New Holland and New Guinea, small, but volcanic and rich. They could support, with little cultivation, thousands upon thousands of blacks.

Now they proceeded steps and stairs, first the boats, then the *Assistant* finding the deep channels, then the *Providence,* very slowly, groping her way with the lead.

Adventure did not keep them waiting long.

All through the first day the man at the masthead had sighted canoes out fishing from the two great islands of the gateway, Mur and Erub. With the sunset and a score of small islets, they came closer.

Tobin was in the leading boat, looking for an anchorage for the night, when a big outrigger a couple of cables' lengths ahead shot across his bows and swung alongside. There must have been fifteen men in her. They held out green coco-nuts and grinned.

Hideous were those betel-nut grins with a tooth or two missing. Tobin gave the order to pull away. The blacks pulled after him with long easy sweeps of the pole. He made signal for the *Providence* to stand by, ready for action, and ordered the men to load muskets. There were seven beside his own.

Matthew had been patrolling the stern-walk between the wilting breadfruit, thinking out problems of these erratic, irrational tides, when a shout from Tom Walker brought him to the rail. The natives were stringing arrows.

He was about to remark to Tom that it was a curious thing these savages should share the art and skill of Robin Hood when a shower of arrows peppered the boat—declaration of war! Everybody ran for'ard.

Tobin's men set up a shout, levelled their muskets and fired. The blacks fell flat. As the smoke cleared, they saw one innocent still sitting on the bamboo hatch. The coxswain took deliberate aim, and he fell.

The boys of the *Providence* cried shame, and Bligh was shouting mad. He was not looking for trouble in seas like this. The canoes fell swiftly astern. Three others joined them to cut the cutter off, but the pinnace of the *Providence* was on their trail, and they skimmed away to the islands. The ships found deep water as the tropic night came down. After that, a "nigger-watch" was kept.

Through milky seas thick with plankton and marine life, straining their eyes for colour of shoal, the purple and pale green patches of coral and sand that encircled them as a net, they came to blind ends and tangles, and zigzagged and retreated, a mile ahead in four. In these mad tides and uncertain currents, nature was in league with the cannibals. A dead calm meant helplessness; a gale a shipwreck—and the pot for those who escaped drowning.

Coral clawed their anchors in foul ground. There were breathtaking shoals from forty fathoms to three. Many a time they close-hauled with a shout, and went on their way rejoicing. They had to find deep water at dusk, and tack there all night through, but the worst ordeal was the dazzle of afternoon sun on the sea that made them all "reef-blind".

Some of the islands they shaved so closely that they could speak to the natives. Once or twice the blackfellows ventured aboard. Whistling amazement at this and that, and giving away the rings in their noses for hatchets, they were quite friendly … but it was an armed truce, both sides ready to hit and run.

Sometimes, on those blinding white beaches, only a dog and a child came down to see them through. On others, the painted warriors were thick as angry bees. There were villages of houses with doorways, but no doors, well thatched and fenced, and set in small patches of taro. Woollyheaded beauties swung their grass skirts and lured with the betel-nut smiles. The men, with their seared, angry faces, wore nothing but a pearlshell. With the inferiority of the human race since time began, they covered only what was creative of their own human kind.

Even when the population waved palm-branches and pointed to piles of green coco-nuts—sweet milk for his thirsting men—Bligh was cynical. Too many of the picket fences were hung with skulls.

Anchored near shore at night, the hump of the islands blotting out the stars, they could hear above the haunted howl of wild dogs the curlews and chanting of some savage psalm, and see skeleton figures wheeling in the firelight to the gorilla grunt of the drums.

Portlock reported grey shadows in the water, legged animals twenty feet long. Bligh knew them. Crocodiles. Taking them by and large, the straits of the pious Torres and the gallant little *Endeavour* were not a good place to be wrecked.

Matthew was fascinated by the seventy-foot war canoes with their grotesque carved prows, like big black centipedes crawling on the water, and by the grace and skill of their navigation when they curiously skimmed past the ships and sheered away to windward. He was to see a naval engagement, his first taste of war, and it depressed him.

A few of the islands Bligh had named—Darnley, the noble Erub of Tobin's battle, and Stephens; Tuesday, Wednesday and Friday for days of the week, close to Cook's Prince of Wales; Warrior, where the men lined up in files like guardsmen at a military review, and an isle with a cape like Dungeness. There nine canoes with a hundred natives came out with water and nuts, a gay flotilla in the blue of the morning.

The *Providence* was striking a cheerful bargain, axes and nails for currency, and trying to coax the natives to come aboard by a rope, when the *Assistant* unexpectedly put up a signal for help. The enemy was round her like crows round a dead sheep. Bone-tipped arrows were flying. Three of her men were already fatally wounded, the light rain of her musketry futile as a volley against mosquitoes.

As Bligh shouted the order to load the swivel guns, "Shoal water!" screamed the man at the masthead, and "Hard aport!" yelled Bond. They swung her about in time, scraping the reef with a churn of coral and foam. Her broadside of round and grape shattered the nearest canoe.

In an instant the island skiffs were tossing like walnut shells on the tide. The blacks were doubling and diving like porpoises, swimming to windward with long powerful strokes, returning to help their wounded, some of them showing fight. A second volley of grape over their heads sent them off, under water, for the shore.

One lone figure remained, sitting upright in a canoe. To the surprise of everyone on board, a dozen of the strongest swimmers came back. Danger forgotten they crowded about him, with gestures to the shore of hopelessness and shrill cries of grief. A sad insight into the heart of the savage. That still figure held for young Flinders all the majesty of death. Whoever the black man was, he was beloved.

That night the singing was a dirge. The fires of hate glowed red.

Wiles and Smith made haphazard botanical collections in hasty journeys ashore, under guard. From Dalrymple's Isle they brought back some dark red plums that grew on a gnarled old gnome of a tree peculiar to this archipelago. Bligh remembered that the natives called it the *wonghi*. They worshipped it as an island god, and believed that those who ate of the fruit would somehow, some day, come back. He had eaten of it gladly enough, and here he was, surely. Matthew promptly tasted, and found the *wonghi* sweet.

"You want to come back to this gridiron of hell?" Tobin asked him.

"Just give me the chance, sir. It's a rare bit of surveying, and now we're through I'd like to try it again by other channels."

"Don't halloo till you're out of the wood," warned Tobin. "For such surveying, once in a lifetime is quite enough for me."

They landed for a constitutional on Cook's Possession Island, the only isle in the group that seemed safely uninhabited, though even here were tracks of bare feet, and deep holes in the sand where the natives had been digging out turtle eggs. The commander held a brief memorial ceremony in Cook's honour, and Tobin unfurled the Union, to flutter where the *Endeavour*'s had flown twenty years before, when she laid claim to the title deeds of a Terra Incognita.

A hasty "Amen" to the thanksgiving prayer, and Midshipman Flinders went bounding over the hill, the spear-grasses tearing at his hose and his right hand whipping back the branches as he ran, to stand on a desolate half-moon of beach looking south to the blur of New Holland.

There it was, vague enough, illusion, dreams come true! Surely Briscoe's island. A thousand leagues … from these tepid tropic seas to the icy Southern Ocean, and somewhere between a solitary nest of jail-birds. What else? Nobody knew.

A year to sail right round it ... he would gladly give ten, would give his whole life's sailing to know its secrets. Archipelago or continent, a hundred isles or one? Would it prove to be an Indies of gold and spices and silver—or shallows of sea-birds and sand? So near, so far! How could Bligh pass it by? Austrialia del Espiritu Santo, South Land of the Holy Spirit ... a veiled, mysterious land, not yet awakened. He shaded his eyes to the distance, but those low shores faded away in mirage, and his wistful thoughts followed.

There was a shout from the other boys coming after him through the woods. George Killsha, with no clothes on, was dancing a fandango, prancing and yelling like a savage, whirling his trousers round his head and belting them on a rock, while Bob and Walker and little John Busby were doubled up with laughter. George fled through the forest like a startled nymph, down the beach with a shriek to Matthew, and disappeared in the breakers.

They told him the story, helpless with glee. George had found a little green pouch hanging to a branch, cunningly woven of sticks and leaves filamented together. He thought it was a black-fellow's purse, and prized it open, to be covered with millions of swarming green ants, their bodies transparent as glass and with bright black eyes. Their stings were as lively as they were, so exit George to play with the crocodiles.

"I know," said Matthew. "The green tree-ants. You'll find them in Sir Joseph Banks's journal."

"You'll find them closer than that!" yelled young Busby, and the broken nest came flying straight for his head. Four happy boys together, they chased each other through the sunlit bush, bell-flowers and butterfly legumes at every step. Under a tree, Matthew picked up a pound's weight and more of tiny attractive berry-beads, hard as ivory but glossy, and pied red and black. He carried them home in his cap, to thread a necklace from the wild Torres Strait for dark-eyed, dark-haired Ann.

Next morning the *Assistant* stepped from four fathoms to eighty. Everybody heaved a sigh of relief. They called the passage Bligh's Farewell, and beyond a snow-white dot in the sea that Cook and Bligh had both named for its nursery of boobies, the way was clear to Timor. In nineteen days they had climbed the stairs from the Pacific into the Indian Ocean.

It was late in September, the fag end of the year. Water was foul and the heat was sour. There was thunder in the air, and in the commander's temper. The men were sickening one by one of dysentery and fever. Worse than all, the sacred breadfruit were drooping. There was not a thousand plants alive.

A whitish scum in the soil roused Bligh's suspicions. At odd times he stood in the shade of the deckhouse, craftily watching while the men were watering, saw them licking the drops from the water-bags, and cursed them. One rank copper morning, he tasted the water-bags, every one of thirty. In one he found salt water. He was livid.

"I'll flog the whole ship's company!" he bawled. "No jack of any crew alive will beat me now!" He raised his fist to the glazed horizon and shouted for the master-at-arms, but before the man arrived he turned in with malaria, and in his delirium forgot it.

Crawling along in a flat calm, watching at night the whiplash of the lightning mustering up the dark clouds of monsoon, they came at last into the little Dutch settlement at Timor—a European roof or two, a dirty scatter of compounds sweating under an unnatural, yellow sun, and the companionship of three white men, the only white men other than those at Port Jackson in the Great South Seas.

In full vice-regal regalia, Mynheer Wanjon, the governor, with his two off-siders, was on the landing stage to meet them, a straggle of coal-black slaves behind them in vari-coloured sarongs.

A sallow little man with a flaxen down of beard, eyes streaked and faded like the *operculi* you pick up on the seashore, he greeted Bligh with effusive honours and sincere admiration.

"Dees time a better velcome ees, myn commodore!" he beamed. With a pudgy wave of a ringed hand, he extended to

the ships the freedom of Koepang, as he called his bedraggled
kampong. More brightly still he beamed to see the sailors carry
ashore a cask of rarest Madeira, Bligh's remembrance of one
who had been a friend in dire need.

That night there was a gala feast for the gentlemen in the old
white Residency under the palms, a row of slaves pulling the
punkah above them—shellfish soup, pickled geese eggs,
scraggy but sweet Malayan chickens curried with young
bamboo shoots and *blachan* in snowy piles of rice, wild duck
roasted with *taro* and *guava*, ruddy-gold *papayas* steeped in
Oporto wine, the squareface gin of Holland with the juice of
island limes. Beneath crossed flags they clinked their glasses to
the Houses of Hanover and Orange, to Abel Tasman and James
Cook, pathfinders in a trackless world of waters, to the empires
to be of Britain and the Netherlands—always to be, friends.

In the rank breath of the tropic night they sat out on the
white-anted balcony, under the *allamanda* creeper, thick and
glossy as ivy, hearing the gourd-music of Timor, like the heavy
breathing of a sleeper, watching the feverish flicker of its
lightnings, listening to strange reminiscences of the sea.

This miserable native trading-post was the last strand in the
drag-net of commerce far-flung from Batavia. Queer flotsam
drifted in on the tides from the unknown. Bligh's was not the
only crew of starving men that Timothy Wanjon had saved.

Before the stricken company of the *Pandora* had made
haven, a six-oared cutter came in with eight men, and, strangest
of all, a woman and two young children. Her name was Mary
Bryant, a fine woman and fair. They told a tale of shipwreck on
a whaler, and Wanjon believed them, for honest they seemed
and brave, but, maddened with arrack and jealousy on a
drinking bout in the village, one of them was jailed and spoke
the truth. They were convicts from New South Wales, who had
stolen the boat from Phillip and made away north for freedom.

All they had was two muskets, a fish-net, flour, salt pork,
grapnel and nails. For three months along the coast of New
Holland they lived on fish and wild green things, and they
carried a kind of shale that, burning with driftwood on their rag

of a cutter, served them for cooking their fish and kept them warm through gales of winter. Would it be coal, perhaps? The clerk produced a lump of it from under a pile of papers in the bare and dusty office. They had picked it up, the woman told Wanjon, on the shore of an island at the mouth of Hunter's River, and there was much of it there.

Bligh had little knowledge of coal. He passed it on to Portlock, Bond, and even young Flinders, who came from Newcastle way. It was not peat — Matthew knew peat — and it certainly glittered black; but James Watt was still boiling his tea-kettle, and silver and gold were the only metals men knew.

At any rate, the governor assured the captain he need have no fear. Their boat journey could never challenge his, a mere 2000 miles. Edwards had taken them with him to Batavia, and so back to prison in England. Wanjon was sorry for the woman. She deserved a better fate. With an absent air he regarded his squat ebony wife.

They spent a fortnight in the bay, refitting. Wiles and Smith, from excursions in the hill forests, brought unheard-of treasures, calladiums with fleshy leaves spotted like toads, crotons splashed with shadow and sun and rainbow, crimson cock's feathers of amaranthus, coiled snake-vines and gossamer lilies that bloomed but one night in the year, betel-nut, perfume-trees and cinnamon for the King's gardens at Kew. The *Providence* loaded two live buffaloes for beef, and crates of the glowing mangoes and *papayas*.

On the day they were ready to sail, an old seaman, Tom Lickmann, died in the horrors of arrack. They buried him in the jungle beside Nelson, the botanist of the *Bounty* — another pang of memory for Captain Bligh. Mynheer Wanjon came aboard, bringing a packet of letters in square Dutch script, all "i's" and "j's" and "k's" and double "a's", for his friends and relations in Dordrecht. He had not seen them now in seventeen years.

The peaky little Dutchman waved them "*Tot zien!*" from the stern of his catamaran, and the ships weighed anchor for Madagascar.

Time-keeper Midshipman Flinders watched the small white figure ashore, saw it hustling the slaves to run up the flag, the red, white and blue of the Netherlands, heard the crack of the weak salute that answered the *Providence* guns. He looked down at the budget of letters in his hand... and saw in fancy the lindens and the cathedrals, the barges tied up in the still canals, the cobbles, clogs and shining kitchens, the patchwork of old-world wisdom and beauty that is Holland. An ordered music of flute and viol, a faultless design for living, but a long way across the world for poor little Timothy Wanjon, who had not seen his loved ones in seventeen years—seventeen years of trading cheap cloth and knives for dyes and spices, haggling with the head-hunters, hearing the maniac throbbing of the drums, keeping accounts in hell.

"A penny, Matt," said Bob Ogilvie, passing by.

"I was but thinking... there was one toast of empire we missed at that dinner of ours with the governor. Such men as Timothy Wanjon... and William Bligh."

"Oh, perish the thought!" scoffed Ogilvie, and skipped as Sweet William, with an angry red scowl, came pounding along the deck, looking for the midshipman in charge of the boats, or any other fool that got in his way. Philosopher Flinders himself neatly side-stepped behind the pinnace. He could hear Tobin shouting from the quarter-deck to the topmen in the shrouds, and Bligh disclosing an unsuspected personal knowledge of the ancestry of the steersman. The tall pine masts swayed above him as the *Providence* quivered to life. Tier upon tier, the sails filled out, curved like magnolia petals to catch an obedient wind.

To Madagascar—seven thousand miles! To find their way by compass and sextant, miracles of the mind of man, across the great diagonal of the Indian Ocean, a mighty hollow in the side of earth, womb of the world that, as old geographers told, had thrown off into stellar space earth's only child, the moon.

No islands here, no continent drowned, no peaks of dream in roseate light to call one on with promise of palms and glory ... day after day a golden monotony of sun and cloudless sky and vacant sea. Sometimes they sighted whales spouting, spouting like the old salts of Boston, world-travellers with a roving eye, winking at the ships...

Three watches every man, and round the Cape of Good Hope again—they would never have known it except for Bligh's log in that waste of windy waters. A week before Christmas they anchored in St Helena, an isle of burnt-up cliffs after the pageantry of the Pacific, but the village, such as it was, in a pleasant valley. A British whaler and a French merchantman were anchored alongside. It was good to be back on the sea-tracks, and hear their comrades singing.

Picturesque in lava-lavas where every one wore trousers, Maidudi and Bobbo went along with the commander to prepare a dish of Otaheitian *pia* root for Lieutenant-Colonel Broke. He very blandly shook hands with them, and dressed them, too, in trousers. They were not sure that they appreciated either.

A wizened negro piloted them into the harbour of St Vincent, Kingstown Bay, to learn that England and Revolutionary France were at death-grips again. The Cross of St George was flying victory everywhere, thanks to Horatio Nelson. African slaves, on their stiff, frizzed heads, carried the breadfruit, solemnly as though it were a Sacred Host, up to the botanic gardens.

Now they threaded the West Indies, so different from the East with their spired cathedrals and squalid dungeons, the whining of the *Aves* and the shrieking of the doomed, crucifix and gibbet in silhouette against the blood-red sunsets, vicious wealth and abject slavery, the dirty drinking-houses and the rotten pirate hulks of the water-front—so different, to those who had heard the song of the waves on the Otaheitian shore.

Here ships of all nations were a flight of moths on the sea, proud galleons with their scarlet beading and gold leaf, their tinted Virgins and weather-beaten saints that looked on rapine and murder with chiselled, expressionless eyes. Sleek black and white frigates, with their raked masts, alighted like swallows on the bay, with sloop and barque and brigantine, Spaniard, Dutchman, Portuguese and Dane, and crippled French prizes, to be auctioned to the highest bidder, the White Ensign flying above the Tricolour.

Scarred and tattooed sailors of the Seven Seas, with evil, mottled faces, thronged the taverns to fight by day and lust by night where harlots writhed their polished bodies, whirling in veils of flame, to the obscene screaming of the Congo pipes and fandango of tambourines. The West Indies were a painted veil of cruelty and greed. Here faith was blasphemy, the sea polluted with filth, and God and man defiled.

Among all the faces, on all the ships, Matthew looked for Sub-Lieutenant Flinders of H.M.S. *Cygnet*; but at the clarion call of war, Nelson had gone back to the Mediterranean, and Uncle John with him. In the hills and valleys of the big green combers, where would their pathways cross?

On 10 June, from Port Royal in Jamaica, the *Providence* was standing out for the cobalt blue of the Caribbean—and the wild old Atlantic, shouting beyond the reefs.

Sweet William was very pleased with himself. Eight hundred and thirty breadfruit plants, sprouting in West Indian gardens, would keep his memory green to His Majesty's honour. There was a nice little pile of silver plate and golden guineas from the grateful planters about which His Majesty, at present, need know nothing. The *Bounty* was forgotten. Now he was Breadfruit Bligh.

James Wiles and Bobbo had stayed behind to help the wonder grow, but Christopher Smith was doubtful of its future.

"Even should it flourish," he said, "will those negroes eat it? Their meat, it is easy to see, would be Otaheite's poison. So will they thrive on Otaheite's bread? Men have been starved and flogged and hanged, they have fled the world in exile for this insipid stuff. What if Bligh's voyages should be in vain? In my belief, Matthew, my boy, that little apple-tree he planted in Tasman's Isle will bear a richer harvest."

5

War's Alarms

Homeward bound!

The captain's servant was running from the galley with red-hot flat-irons, pressing tails and gophering cravats for the pomp and circumstance of London. Hoarse voices in the fo'c'sle were croaking of Devon and Dee and Seven Dials, while in the neat clipped accents of the officers' mess came anecdotes of Kensington and Cambridge. Even Sweet William, whose father was a cake of salt, was showing intelligent interest in old copies of the *London Gazette*, and the *Providence* was either Whig or Tory.

There was plenty of rum left in the casks, so now a more generous ration. Scot-free of mutiny, the breadfruit venturing its tender fronds in Jamaica, who was to care if Bligh was proud of his men?

> A capital ship, O a capital ship,
> With a walloping window-blind!

Only Maidudi was haunted. The winds that were lilting them all to home were shuddering cold to him. The fog was a nightmare of gauze, and in it he saw devils. At every breath a white spirit leapt into his nostrils. At Otaheite the waves were laughing and sparkling, for ever friends, but here they were like the ominous thunder-clouds that loomed over Aorai when the gods were angry. The sailors coiling their ropes with a song reminded him sadly of the women weaving palm-leaves for the matting that had been his roof and his floor. The creaking of the cordage was the laugh of the old witch-doctors. Thin and silent, he sickened of his pease. They would see him standing for long hours of the pale Atlantic sunlights, watching the wake of the ship.

War. In the world of wonder that had been theirs, how could there be war, a malignant hatred of nations of men, blind animals fighting? And yet they were glad to be fighting, fighting the Frenchman, the arch-enemy, Royalist or Republican. Blood and powder were the condiments that flavoured the dish of life.

In the mist off the coast of Ireland they picked up the convoy, *Charon* and *Scorpion*, His Majesty's frigates, taut fibres in the whipcord that held Britain's empire together. Clipped squares of canvas and slim raked masts, they skimmed to meet them like a couple of gulls, swooped round and took up positions, flags whipped to the top as precisely as on review day at Spithead.

Charon and *Scorpion* guarded them past the Needles and through the Downs. On 7 August, two years almost to the day since they left England, they cast anchor in the stream at Debtford, where Maidudi was found in his hammock dead. The ambassador to King Gargo, they buried him in St Paul's churchyard, alone by an old grey spirit-house in a land he never knew.

London River was a forest in winter, a forest of leafless oaks. There were twelve miles of ships from the Tower to the Nore, 48 ships of the line, giant three-deckers of 90 guns in command of the quays, beyond them the gallant 74's. The Thames and the Medway were choked with shipping—frigates, two-deckers, sloops of war, gun-brigs, the captains' gigs and the cutters, barges deep in the water with spars and loading, press-gang tenders flocking in from every English seaport from Liverpool to Lowestoft, from Grimsby to St Ives.

The Three Towns were swarming with sailors, tailors, farmers, scriveners, butcher, baker, candlestick-maker, hatter, beggar and thief, dragged into the Navy. They were packed hundreds together in the chandlers' stores and the warehouses of Chatham, Debtford and Sheerness, drunk as lords on their sixpence a day in the streets, stamping and swearing to the housewives' horror in every cottage in Kent.

Officers were sleeping five to seven in a room in the inns, post-chaises and the stage-coaches rattling down from London at all hours, bringing captains and lieutenants back from leave.

Smoke and sawdust thickened the day in bedlam of hammers ringing on copper and steel. White acres of canvas littered the decks and the wharves, where the sail-makers sang at their sewing to shrill cries and whistles from the powder-hoys, as kegs of shot and powder and crates of the blue-black cannon-balls were stowed. By night the fiery vomit of the furnaces made Hades of Chatham dockyard.

Jews, pedlars, bumboat women and motley of humanity herded the ships at anchor. In rumour, rush and sensation Matthew and Bob drew in the hot breath of Moloch.

"It'll be lucky for *La France*," said Bob, "if she *vives* long after this."

If they had any ideas that they were off on leave to play Sinbad the Sailor at home, they were quickly disillusioned. With their pay-cheques from the *Providence* came Navy orders to rejoin H.M.S. *Bellerophon*.

Briefly they paid their respects to Sweet William, deep in a ring of his cronies. There were hand-shakes of "*Tot zien*" to their good friends, grave Lieutenant Portlock, Pearce of the Marines, Tobin "R.A." with his folio of sketches under his arm—and excellent sketches, too—and Christopher Smith, labelling his collections for consignment to Kew. With great expectations they were off in a boat to find their alma mater, the *Billy Ruff'n*.

Kitbags on shoulder along the noisy quays, they looked for that dashing figurehead in vain. Everybody knew the *Billy Ruff'n*, but nobody knew where she was berthed. In the crowded Debtford dusk, with all the trafficking to the taverns, they failed to find a lodging in two hours of trudging. There was nothing for it but the Mitre Inn on the waterfront, expensive, but they had their pay intact.

The big coffee-room was a din of Navy officers, endless salutes left and right as they sat them down in two vacant chairs at a long table set for sixteen others, captains, lieutenants and masters' mates. It was sailing close to the wind in naval etiquette, they knew, but they got through with a few inimical stares and scarifying remarks on the subject of "wood-bugs".

The French in the Channel, they heard, were stinging like hornets. Great Britain was out to smash the nest. After fifty years of salt water and shot, Lord Howe was coming down to take the fleet to war.

"Give us Black Dick," they had cried, "and we fear nothing!"

Through an avenue of powdered wigs, holding his sirloin high on a silver dish above them, the landlord took his place, whetted his knife on the steel, and with a wink to the company plunged it in the air.

"That for the Froggies!" shouted Bob.

Questioning stares subdued him.

"Whence the rabble?" inquired a supercilious voice, silencing Matthew's feeble cheer.

The landlord, bland as ever, was serving the prime cut to a lean bronzed captain at his right hand, small, even frail of stature, full lips and keen eyes, kindly but commanding. Busy hum of talk, gusty laughter and flagons of ale passing. The boys were relishing once again the roast beef of Old England.

A ruddy commander with a row of medals rose to his feet.

"Gentleman!"

The room fell silent.

"We are honoured to have with us to-night"—he paused, and bowed extravagantly to the little bronzed officer—"Captain Nelson of the *Agamemnon*." There was a buzz of interest and applause. "You all know the signal work of Captain Nelson, with Admirals Hood and Rodney, keeping our flag high in the

Americas and the West Indies." (Cheers.) "Proud we are to welcome him in this gathering of British sailors. We have no doubt that greater deeds are ahead of him, nearer home and in our nation's need. Such men as Captain Horatio Nelson will lead us to victory!"

The men stood, and turning to the head of the table, raised their glasses.

"To victory!"

They sat down, and the little captain stood. He wore no wig, but his own hair, fluffed and whitened. His voice was crisp with purpose, his expression whimsical, even sad.

"Gentlemen—There is no doubt that we shall acquit ourselves well should the Frenchmen give us a hearing, but I doubt the Frenchmen will." He raised a humorous eyebrow, to laughter and cheers. "The enemy can build good ships." (A cold silence.) "They cannot, however, make good men." (Loud cheers.) "I am no mathematician. I know more of guns than of figures, but to my way of reckoning, three Frenchmen are equal to one Englishman." (Cheers and stamping.) "I have no doubt that the time will come when the scribes will write our story, no more than a sentence, gentlemen, in England's transcendent history. For me, I hate your pen-and-ink men. A fleet of British ships are the best negotiators in Europe." (Cheers, stamping and whistles, that threatened to bring down the house.) "With you I pray that the great God we worship may grant to our country victory, and may no misconduct in any one tarnish it, and may humanity after victory be the ruling spirit of the British fleet." (Ringing cheers, raucous cheers, and cheers that split the rafter.)

The quaint little captain sat down, and they filled his glass.

Matthew nudged Bob. The fork was in the beam. Small fry must leave.

The middies scuttled to their garret. All through the night cheers and laughter shook the Mitre Tavern. In the dawn hours they heard the landlord and his servants helping the gentlemen to bed.

They breakfasted alone on eggs and ale, and set off again to find *Billy Ruff'n*. They were still on the trail at midday, abreast of the *Invincible*, hailing the quartermaster, the man who weaves a cat's cradle of ropes to enslave the wind.

"*Billy Ruff'n?* Aye!" he cried down to them. "She's here. Coming now."

He pointed at a ship, limping in on the tide... but what a ship! At first they thought it was a barge struck by lightning, and the quartermaster jesting at their expense.

Her hull was cracked and battered, her maintop no more than a t'gallant mast, and her foretop a t'gallant. She had a jib-boom for her bowsprit, her figurehead was a gaping hole as though a tooth had been drawn, and the sails, three of four sizes too large and bent to fit, were foolishly draped about her. Strange to see, a white ensign was flying at her mizzen.

The boys glared at the quartermaster, and Bob was about to jolly him when, brisk of step, two captains hurried past them. They stopped to survey the hulk with pitying interest.

"Gad!" said one, "the *Bellerophon* did catch it!"

"Excuse me, sir!" Matthew saluted. "Yon ship is never the *Bellerophon*!"

"Yon ship is the *Bellerophon*, young man!"

The boyish faces fell in abject sorrow.

"She has been crippled by the French! What then, sir, of Captain Pasley?"

"If I knew my flags, sir, I would say that Rear-Admiral Pasley is aboard." They strutted off with a sniff.

As soon as the derelict was within rowing distance, they were off to her in a wherry, and waiting on a splintered deck for an audience with Rear-Admiral Pasley.

Two years and gold lace epaulettes notwithstanding, he was the same jovial Pasley with the twinkle in his eye.

"Well, if it isn't little Flinders and young Ogilvie! Safe back with that breadfruit I hope, or whose neck do I take out of the rope this time? I'm gald to have you, lads. Welcome home!"

"But you, sir? And where's our ship? Has there been a battle?"

"Our ship is right here, make no mistake, and plenty of fight in her yet, in spite of His Majesty's valiant efforts to sink her.

Aye, me hearties, a battle, but with H.M.S. *Majestic*. Bore down on me in a gale, fell right across me bows, smashed away me bowsprit, d'ye see? And me figurehead and cut-water, then, God love ye, as if that wasn't enough, boarded me alongside and ripped out me foremast and maintop. Not a life lost, as it happened, but I had to come in in jury rig, as though the damned Frenchmen had given me a hiding. The *Ramillies* took us in tow for Plymouth, but we left her chasing our wake, and after a bit of patching, here we are!"

"You outsailed the *Ramillies*, sir, in this condition!"

"Outsailed the *Ramillies*? We're the Flyer of the Fleet! I'll back the *Billy Ruff'n* on my pocket-handkerchief against a frigate in full rig. Aye! We're a sailer! We've left the Fleet behind whenever we've put out. Dick Howe's been setting us races on the road to Finisterre, and nothing's caught up with us yet, and never will. Why, if I hoisted skysails we'd take off for Kingdom Come. But come now, for a glass of Oporto, and tell me all about it!"

He led the way into the great cabin, under the beak of the poop, where between sword and spy-glass hanging on the oaken beams, Maria and the family smiled remembrance. One hand playing with his laurel-wreathed gold buttons, he heard their reports with interest and satisfaction, but his time was brief... an admiral of the van.

So the Flyer of the Fleet had come home on broken wings! *Billy Ruff'n* in splints was the joke and admiration of the dockyard... but scarcely a month had passed before *Bellerophon* was galloping on Pegasus again, his white plumes flying, and the tall masts unfurled their white plumes to the skies.

She was a red ship now, from poop and prow to the orlop deck, capstans, gun-carriages, hatchway gratings, even gangway-ladders, all of the red of blood, and for that grim reason—that none of it would show. She bristled like a hedgehog with the iron spikes of her guns—twenty-five heavy 32-pounders, for six-inch balls, on the lower deck, the gun-carriages of the wood of elm, that never shatters into splinters.

On the upper deck were the long eighteens, filling them up to the ports; on the quarter-deck, the sturdy nine-pounders; on the fo'c'sle deck the carronades, the "smashers", guns everywhere, in the captain's cabin and in the officers' mess.

Six hundred and fifteen men aboard her swung their hammocks above the guns, slept between them, ate between them. Midshipmen's quarters were down in the cockpit on the orlop, below the water-line, a safe place, but they would give it up to the surgeon when the fun began, their mess-table for operations and amputations.

Above him all day Matthew Flinders would hear the trucks rumbling, the bare-footed powder-monkeys padding round and round at practice, each gun-crew ramming down the shot as though it were for the very heart of Robespierre.

In November, *Billy Ruff'n* was ready to take her place in the Grand Fleet when it sailed to Black Dick Howe at Spithead. Flying Pasley's colours, and with Captain William Hope, one of Nelson's lieutenants, as flag-captain, she was to lead the van.

In a storm of cheers she cast off ropes and was away downriver. After the wallowing of the *Providence*, to Matthew she seemed to swift and sheer as a sea-eagle, spreading her wings to the wind.

He had sent away excited letters to Lincolnshire. He would be with them when he could. The pageant of the Royal Navy he crammed into seventeen pages, with panegyrics of friendships old and new, and glad news of his own advancement. Captain Bligh's report of him had been very nearly praise, and Admiral Pasley had made him his aide-de-camp. Captain John Hunter, Phillip's second-in-command to New South Wales, whom he had met at the Cape, was with Howe in the *Queen Charlotte*, and Henry Waterhouse, who had sailed with him in the *Sirius* when they founded Port Jackson in New Holland, was fifth out of seven lieutenants in the *Bellerophon*, a splendid fellow with great tales and an odd sense of humour. They could imagine the joys of association, in the hours off watch, comparing notes of their travels in the Pacific.

While they were at Spithead, the spies brought news of a reign of terror in the French fleet after mutiny at Belleisle. L'Amiral Morand de Galles was in the Bastille with all his fine connections, half his captains paying court to Madame Guillotine in purge and purification. A youngster, Villaret-Joyeuse, had been appointed to a high command of scratch lieutenants, pilots, and merchant-captains, good citizens of the Republic if not sons of the sea.

On 18 November, Howe and the British were off on a "catch-as-catch-can" to the Bay of Biscay and back, after "Channel-gropers". The frigate *Latona* was their sentinel ahead.

On a squally morning with a big slaty sea running, the *Latona's* t'gallants fluttered free, and the crack of her gun signalled "Enemy in sight".

Blue-and-yellow of "General chase" flew to Black Dick's masthead, *Bellerophon* first to carry it on, the Tricolour underneath.

Ten French sail were swinging right for them, in resolute battle array. By noon they could see the mainsails clearly, and after dinner the hulls. These ten bold Frogs were asking for punishment.

If they had known it, the Frenchmen were more surprised than they were. Lying in wait for a merchant fleet leaving Plymouth for the Indies, they were amazed at the bravado of a convoy of four or five, and amused to see the red flag "Engage".

With a horrible shock they realized their heroics. "Engage" it was, and with the British Grand Fleet!

Hysterical signals flew to every halliard. With the first of the *Billy Ruff'n's* balls to speed them on their way, they turned like a flock of pigeons and fled before a rising gale.

Bellerophon and *Russell* crammed on sail, *Vanguard* and *Montagu* following, but sea and sky were with the Tricolour, and heaven scowled on the Union.

Mountainous waves broke over in welter of yellow foam.

As the men rushed aloft to shorten sail, the shrouds snapped and frayed out in a howler. From a nightmare of wet, stinging ropes on the *Bellerophon's* mainsail, young Flinders looked down on the *Russell*, flapping and floundering astern. Her fore-topsail and her main and topmasts were gone. Then there was a rending crash as the *Bellerophon* herself struck a sea, her jib-boom shattered.

Squalls were growing in fury. Dusk came down in chaos and ruin, and the Frenchmen were lost in it. By morning light, never a fleck on the grey.

In a silence too eloquent they came back to Torbay. The next week London papers were vicious with lampoons and cartoons of "Lord Torbay" on a bucking horse in the rain, shying from a Tricolour scarecrow. The old man laughed at the ridicule. There was a bigger bird in the bush.

France was starving. War and revolution together had soaked her soil with blood. The fields yielded nothing but hunger and hate.

Robespierre that year spent 5,000,000 francs to buy American grain. A squadron had sailed in September under Rear-Admiral Vanstabel to bring French and American vessels of the mercantile marine–117 ships all told—safely back from Virginia. A spy came running to Whitehall. Villaret-Joyeuse, with the greatest fleet in French history, would meet them off Cape Finisterre, and see the corn into the granaries of France. Villaret-Joyeuse was doomed if he failed.

"Fight if you must," were his orders from the National Convention, "but only if you must ... and if you do fight, conquer the eternal enemies of our nation. Failing that, M. l'Amiral Villaret-Joyeuse, your head, and not the words of your mouth, will make the explanation. If any ship of yours strikes colours, flagship or corvette, that ship is traitor to the Republic!"

So the French would meet the corn-ships ... the British would meet the French.

On the bright spring morning after May-day the Grand Fleet sailed from Spithead, the grandest fleet that England had ever known, a sight to take the nation's breath away.

The oaks had spread their leaves full foliage, 158 sail.

There were 49 men-of-war, 38 of them ships of the line, and three great merchant convoys bound for Newfoundland and the West Indies.

Like huge May-day floats they swayed out into the stream, pinions free and pennants flying. Castellated towers of ivory in the blue, the cords cutting shodows into the canvas, sunlights glinting on brass, and the red and black chequer-board of the bulging hulls—to Matthew Flinders on the *Billy Ruff'n* it was the most beautiful sight that human eyes ever beheld. Bob Ogilvie said it was "washing-day in Valhalla".

*Audacious … Caesar … Culloden … Ramillies … Invincible … Gibraltar … Orion … Thunderer … Russell … Marlborough … Glory …*in stately array they led the way for 2000 guns and 16,000 men, with cheers from a thousand thousand throats, the frigates and the little corvettes trimly sailing beside them.

Never was such a procession of the peerage of the sea. *Royal George* dipped the flag of Admiral of the Blue Lord Hood as she passed the masts of her ill-fated namesake, sunken memorial to Kempenfelt and his pen and the twice six hundred. Followed the *Barfleur* under Sir George Bowyer, Rear-Admiral of the Red, "Cold" Collingwood his captain; *Royal Sovereign*, Sir Thomas Graves, Admiral of the Blue; *Montagu*, Rear-Admiral of the White Sir James Montagu; *Queen*, Rear-Admiral of the Red Sir Benjamin Caldwell; Lord Hugh Seymour with the *Leviathan*; Captain Sir Chales Cotton with the *Majestic*; Dismal Jimmy Gambier with the *Defence*; and the *Queen Charlotte*, flagship, 90 guns, the Union flying at her masthead, tallest stick in the fleet, above the Red Ensign of Earl Howe.

At the Isle of Wight they divided in a grand march of Britain's majesty, a rhythmic procession of white banners in massed formation, and fluttering above them all the Cross of St George—St George of Merry England, St George of Fighting England! A myriad craft trailed in their wake, streamers flying and women crying. Holiday crowds at Cowes waved them away with martial music of bands.

Uniting at Portland Bill, down the Channel they went, a shears to nip the corn of France in the bud.

Two days' sail, and off the Lizard their ways again divided. Montague led the convoys south-west to the cross-roads of the trade-routes. The Grand Fleet turned south to Brest.

For Brest was the hornet's nest.

They neared the harbour in morning light on 5 May. The frigates *Latona* and *Phaeton* were out round the island to reconnoitre, crouching like Indian braves behind the headlands, topsails reefed, for the feathers must not show.

The French fleet was there. Twenty-six ships of the line they counted, and frigates and corvettes. Howe had twenty-six sail. He showed no intention of taking them in under the frown of the fortresses and the fire of the land-batteries.

"But that's the Nelson touch, sir," Matthew overheard Hope say to Pasley. "His idea is to run right for them, and give them hell's delight where they least expect it. He believes no captain can do wrong if he places his ship alongside that of an enemy."

Rear-Admiral Pasley snorted.

"Lord Howe is a sea-veteran of seventy years, the other a whipper-snapper of thirty!"

The Grand Fleet was off along the track the corn-ships must take on the road to Finisterre.

For days they saw nothing but grey water, not even the scraggy coast of Spain. The milk-white summer fog came over. Lost to each other in a curd of mist they were sailing between earth and sky, faint sails and phantom spars and shadowy shapes. The men, groping in thick wet vapours, could but dimly make out the fo'c'sle from the poop. Villaret-Joyeuse might have taken his twenty-six men-of-war right through them unseen—and Villaret-Joyeuse did! ... heard their drums beating and their fog-bells ringing, and silently slipped by.

Four hundred miles of sailing blind, and Howe gave the order to turn back.

"Now you see 'em and now you don't." *Phaeton* and *Latona* reported that Brest harbour was empty. The Frenchmen were gone. Montagu and his few sentinels south of the Bay of Biscay would be at their mercy. Again the squadrons hurried south.

At two in the morning on 21 May, they saw lights strung out on the sea.

Drums beat to quarters, decks cleared for action, and every ship made sail ... but a shot across bows disclosed a Dutch-Lisbon convoy captured by the French a few days before, and dutifully sailing, with prize crews, for Brest. Howe took his prisoners and his prizes. On board the *Queen Charlotte* the Dutch skippers gave him the knowledge he wanted. The French Grand Fleet was two days westward.

Only forty-eight hours' sailing, but by the time they were there the French were forty-eight hours south-west. Black Dick would chse them, if he had to, over the rim of the world. The next night *Audacious* met *L'Audacieuse*, with an American ship in tow, like an ant taking home its booty. *L'Audacieuse* cast her prize adrift and fled. Where?

For five days they battled wind and sea. On the sixth, the fortunes of war were kind.

The rising sun lit a grey weltering world of waters as Humphrey Andrew, signal midshipman of *Bellerophon*, reported "Frigate *Latona* signalling. Strange sail south-south-west."

At nine o'clock the sails were thirty-three. The time had come! Villaret-Joyeuse, the boy admiral, must fight for his convoy and his head.

By noon, three leagues of ocean tossed between them. The Frenchmen swept round on the larboard tack, and held away to the wind. As they made in a ragged line for the crescent coast of France, a rumble of drums through the British fleet beat "Clear for action!"

Matthew neatly blotted his books, packed them in his trunk, latched his lockers, and joined the rush on deck.

The ship was a nest of ants disturbed. Men poured out of the hatches. Whipped on by the curses of the redheaded bosun, Bill Chapman, they were swinging aloft, hand over hand like apes ... sanding the red decks ... tearing down bulkheads ... stowing gear ... pegging down and belaying ... dousing the galley fires in spouts of steam ... hanging wet felt fire-screens at the hatches and companions … unlashing the guns and chocking them as they thrust their iron muzzles through the ports, cannon and shot stowed in the crummets beside them. The gun-crews, fourteen men to each, took up their posts, powder-monkeys running with firelock and flint, filling the tubs with slow-match. It was a miracle of concerted action.

Billy Ruff'n was stripped for the fight in five short minutes, and black holes gaped in the sides of all the ships as their gunports swung wide open. The sentries, taking their posts at the open hatches, were quickly dismissed by Pasley.

"None of my crew," he said, "will run from a damned Frenchman. No man can be a coward on the *Bellerophon*."

Hubbub died down. They were ready, waiting—redcoats drawn up under the poop, every man at quarters. The admiral, with Hope and his lieutenants, was standing on the quarter-deck. They talked together in low tones of the wind and the enemy.

"Flagship signalling all ships!" called Humphrey Andrew.

Now they waited breathless … an elaborate hoist of flags on the *Queen Charlotte*.

"All … ships … to … ?"

Andrew crossed to Captain Hope with a bewildered frown. The familiar twinkle was in Pasley's eye, and Hope was smiling.

"All ships to—dinner, sir?" Humphrey quavered.

"Look it up!" rapped Hope.

Andrew fumbled the pages of his signal-book as they flipped over in the wind.

"All ships to dinner!" he declared.

A shout of laughter swept the decks, and echoed through the van.

"Just like Dick Howe!" growled Pasley. "Sends us off to dinner when he knows we've got the fire out! Well, I'm not one to let my broth go cold!"

The admiral went back to his hole in the oak with Matthew at his heels.

Crews were fed, guns were fed. Black Dick was ready for the French.

At two o'clock young Andrew was rewarded. Pasley's colours were at the *Queen Charlotte's* yard-arm, with signal "Attack and harass the enemy's rear."

H.M.S. *Bellerophon* was away at the wind of the word, *Russell*, *Marlborough* and *Thunderer* ploughing along behind her. As she left the Grand Fleet to leeward, up went the blue-and-yellow of "General chase".

At six bells she was clawing up wind after a huge French three-decker loitering in the enemy's rear. In a slant of storm light they read the name on her stern, *La Revolutionnaire*. That meant 110 guns and a thousand men. Now, if ever, must *Billy Ruff'n* be Flyer. Every yard of her canvas grappled for power.

As she shot across the Frenchman's stern, Bellerophon reared on his white horse from the whirlpool of the waters. His javelin shone yellow in the rays of a drowning sun. He plunged, and drove it at his foe in a Valkyrie's ride to slaughter ... and on the downward roll the *Billy Ruff'n* fired, first full broadside of the battle, sweep of a scythe along the enemy's decks, cutting down Frenchmen left and right.

Iron rang and screeched on brass as the great guns leapt at the lanyards. A searing hail of shot slit open the side of the giant *Revolutionnaire*, with a splintering, smashing, screaming, as the 32-pounders thudded home. The Frenchman lurched and swayed, her tall masts staggering above them. As Bellerophon and his flying plumes rose from the waves, the echoes of his vengeful laughter racketed away in the clouds.

Seventy-four guns fighting 110, 615 men fighting a thousand. France had learned nothing from the clumsy armadas of Spain. The race was to the swift, and *Billy Ruff'n* was playing hit-and-run.

The Britisher tacked to leeward, pouring in shot and shell. *La Revolutionnaire* doggedly stumbled on, to pick up her lost position in the fleet. Only her stern guns could answer, and the eager little mercenaries of the Republic, with their gaudy cockades and cocked hats and sashes, were poor marksmen. Firing on the upward roll, they shot into *Billy Ruff'n's* shrouds.

Time and again they were mown down by a merciless broadside that shattered the masts at their roots, the men in the rigging falling like birds in a storm.

For *Billy Ruff'n* fired on the downard roll, dropping iron into the big ship's vitals.

Once as they raced astern with a salvo into the castled hull, Matthew saw the glass of the poop-windows shattered out and pelting like rain on the sea, the beautiful antique filigree of balustrades ornate with gold leaf and red beading, that had cost the old Breton craftsmen generations of toil and love, floating in wreckage.

Another broadside pounded with the hammer of Thor. Timbers parted. Sails were spattered with blood. Above the clamour of war and storm, they could hear the shrieks of the dying.

Still the French captain was running away, not from cowardice but to cover the Frenchman's rear. If he fell, the wolves would follow. He was keeping the Britisher at bay. Only once, by a trick of the wind, did she come within full range.

Three rows of angry guns raked her from stem to stern, the enemy crying for revenge in blood. Hope shouted to back topsails to get out of that deadly vortex. Matthew, looking upwards, saw the mizzen topmast drunkenly sway outward. Grimed seamen with hatchets ran aloft to cut it away. There were a few shrill screams as Sawbones Fargher got his first customers for the day.

Sails herding black on the sunset ... *Leviathan* and *Thunderer* were alongside, *Marlborough* and *Russell* to lee, *Audacious* a mile to windward.

Howe had been impatiently signalling the van to make all sail for aid, but *Billy Ruff'n's* speed was her undoing, and even the flagship could not help. Except for a reassuring salvo or two, the battle had been hers alone.

La Revolutionnaire was fighting them off two at a time, now, but her masts were gone, and already she was drifting. Where were her colours?—perhaps they were shot away. *Audacious* came up and engaged her in mortal combat, while the van made sail in the twilight to catch the next.

All save *Billy Ruff'n*. Her work for the day was over. Howe called her back with "Abandon chase". Pasley's men had done well, and of those 615 men he had lost—not one.

Through the night the lights of ships see-sawed in the storm, British triangle and French arrow. Enemies in sleep, French and British lay down beside their guns.

In a temperstuous daybreak, Signal Midshipman Andrew announced: "Signal No. 39. Admiral intends to pass through enemy's lines to obtain the weather-gauge."

Bellerophon was behind *Queen Charlotte*. Howe was proud of his terrier, but he could not keep up with it, and ordered it to his heels. During the night they had drawn abreast of the French line of battle, a league to west, stubbornly standing.

H.M.S. *Caesar*, 80 guns, was leading the van, *Valiant, Queen, Invincible, Royal George, Russell, Defence, Marlborough, Royal Sovereign, Impregnable* and *Tremendous*.

Squat in the water, they swung out their gun-ports and fired at a great range. Venomous little spurts of flame answered from the French ships, and rose in rolling wads of smoke grey as the clouds above. The squadrons were stringing out, to strike head for head.

Queen Charlotte hoisted the Union, Admiral's flag and colours, St Andrew's cross above the Blue-and-yellow.

Then "No. 78", read Humphrey. "Leading ship to tack first, others in succession."

No answering ripple stirred H.M.S. *Caesar's* sails.

Her pennant called her smartly to attention from the masthead of the flagship, with Signal No. 34: "Engage the enemy's centre." Then three times No. 39, "Break through the enemy's lines."

The *Caesar* was holding a straight course. Under close scrutiny of French and British spy-glasses, she remained preoccupied and serene.

Again her pennant flew to *Queen Charlotte's* masthead. Lord High Admiral Howe was commanding in good set flags.

"H.M.S. *Caesar*. No. 74. Leading ship to tack."

To the blank amazement of every officer in the fleet, the

Caesar spilled the wind from her sails and wore away to leeward, a straggle of ships after her, breaking the van.

On *Bellerophon's* quarter-deck, his captain and lieutenants about him, Pasley was scarlet with anger and shame.

"A blind man, a madman, or a coward!" he said to Hope.

"Who's in command of the *Caesar*, sir?" Matthew asked Waterhouse.

"A James II Irishman — Molloy."

French sails were slipping to windward, growing smaller on the sea.

H.M.S. *Queen* snatched the lead, *Valiant, Invincible, Russell* and *Royal George* tacking for the enemy's lines. The Frenchman's rearguard turned back to cut off the *Queen*. For the scattering of British they were proving too strong. *Queen* was in for heavy weather. The psychological moment would be gone, and Black Dick's strategy with it.

"Tack *Queen Charlotte*, Mr Bowen, sir!" he said to his master. "We'll show the fleet what we mean."

Queen Charlotte led the squadrons on, her flags flying courage. *Bellerophon* fell into line behind her, *Leviathan* and all the ships following, but the French were in full flight. All they could do now was to cut through the rearguard, and try to engage them from the windward.

Heavy three-deckers loomed before them, the Tricolour a challenge in the grey.

Hot cannonade and racking fire, *Queen Charlotte* battered her way past the prows of *L'Aéole*, sixth ship from the rear. *Bellerophon*, jostling between *L'Aéole's* stern and the prow of *Le Terrible*, leapt to a double broadside with rip and tear of her lightnings and thunder of point-blank range. *Leviathan* raked *Mont Blanc* so closely that she unrigged her topmasts, and British van and Frenchmen's rear were a jungle of ships and slaughter.

Into the deepening twilight they fought, like tigers in the jungle, until two of the Frenchmen limped away. The rest were battered wrecks. They had suffered a dreadful carnage ... but still they held the road to Finisterre.

The fleet that night was a maze of barges and lanterns. It was a warm night, sails scarcely stirring, triangles burning bright, on the near horizon the faint constellations of the French.

Midshipman Flinders sat with Pasley in the oak-beamed cabin, stuffy with smoke and powder. In his neat slanted caligraphy, he was writing the admiral's dispatches. Pasley had discarded his wig. His bald head shone in the lamplight as he dictated, his round face beamed with pride of his ship.

By two bells the report was complete. Matthew rose, dried the copper-plate pages, and heated the seal.

"Come, lad," said Pasley, "and we'll hear what's to know."

They rowed away from the *Billy Ruff'n*, a clack of hammers and a cobweb of new ropes—and still no dead men, Fargher told them, laughing—the admiral smiling from the stern-sheets on the striving bargemen in their coloured jerseys, on the wooden-faced marines.

Ten minutes later they bumped against the wracked and wrecked *Queen Charlotte*. Crews were all at supper, but bosuns' whistles were piping, side-boys and quartermasters helping the captains and admirals aboard to make their reports and receive orders.

The quarter-deck was hung with horn lanterns, here and there a little group of officers.

In the very shadow of the guns sat My Lord Howe.

His dead white hair and snowy ruffles at his throat accentuated the blackness of his deep-set piercing eyes. His face was adamantine with the iron rigidity of the guns. Matthew remembered that they said of him, "He never made a friendship except at the cannon's mouth."

There was a rough wooden table in front of him, a map, with crude drawings of ships ... beneath it his lean partrician calves in silk, his long flat shoes buckled in dull silver. The decks were spattered in dark brown stains—of blood.

A weary old man in an arm-chair, he had written Britain's history in three continents, had helped to make Canada British when it was French.

He was in conclave with three of his admirals, Hood, Graves and Gardner. Senior captains of the fleet, Sir Roger Curtis, Douglas, and Cuthbert Collingwood, were standing thoughtfully by.

"Well, Tom!" Howe stretched out a veined and sinuous hand. His dark face grew bright with a surprisingly pleasant smile. "A hard dog to beat thirty years ago, and a hard dog to beat to-day! The *Bellerophon* behaved most nobly."

Pasley flustered, and drew up his chair with a scrape.

"But you, Dick! You're looking worn. How about a turn below?"

"I've sat in this chair for forty-eight hours, and I swear by God I'll not leave it until we've got 'em beaten. I've been whipping the French all my life, and they'll not get away from me now ... "

Their voices lowered. The five were deep in plans, five admirals of England ... Hood, with his glass-cold eyes and Roman nose, erect, remote, an aristocrat; Graves, the county gentleman; Gardner, bluff old sea-dog from the Barbadoes; Pasley, his wig atilt, as it always was in moments of enthusiasm; Howe, listening, with the impassive chiselled calm of a Red Indian.

In the smoky orange light of the horn lanterns, *Queen Charlotte's* shrouds hung limp, her leaning masts and ragged canvas a ghostly frame to the scene.

The captains waited in respectful silence, but a chattering group of lieutenants, who blissfully believed themselves out of earshot, was engaged in lively discussion of the *Caesar*. Her officer had presented Molloy's report and gone.

"Gad, sir," said Larcom, "how could the man show his face here? What cock-and-bull yarn Molloy will tell I don't know, but he's shamed us before the enemy, and we can't shut our eyes to that."

Howe turned. His profile was sharp as his voice.

"I desire you to hold your tongue, sir! I don't desire you to shut your eyes, but I desire you to hold your tongue until I call upon you, as I probably shall do hereafter, for your observations!"

Larcom froze to the salute. The group faded away.

The moon rose milky on a milky sea. Now this weird etching of a ship broke silence. From the lower deck came the sound of her carpenters at work, the murmur of her thousand men.

In an hour Pasley was ready to return.

"Take care of yourself, Tom," Howe said kindly. "A good night's rest, for by Heaven, my friend, you've earned it. There'll be no action to-night. I need daylight to keep an eye on my captains."

They rowed back to the *Bellerophon* in thin veil of mist. It was a heavy fog at daybreak, and the French were almost out of sight. As the British moved, they moved, like reflections in a mirror, trending north-west.

In two long days they had travelled 130 miles, following shadows beyond their reach, and never a sailor in the british fleet that did not curse his luck and curse the *Caesar*. Pasley was apprehensive. Was there going to be another Torbay? That night the *Phaeton* frigate came whispering down the line. In the wan moonlight they sailed in skeleton rig.

"Now you see 'em and now you don't!" The sun rose on 1 June—and the French fleet was there.

"They're not a fleet," laughed Waterhouse. "They're an optical illusion. We crippled four of the blacguards, and they're still twenty-six!" Villaret-Joyeuse had apparently picked up four of the Rochefort convoy, looking out for the corn-ships.

The fog might have been a dream, and nothing more. For the French ships were standing away in line ahead, a league to windward, exactly as on 29 May. God had turned back a page of time, and given them yesterday. Howe's strategy would serve.

Signal No. 39 flew straight to the flagship's yard-arm.

"Admiral intends to break through the enemy's lines and engage them to leeward." Then, in characteristic manner, before flags for action came flags for breakfast.

Troubridge had a French captain prisoner on his ship. M. le capitaine was contemptuous.

"Your 'Owe," he remarked, "desire no more to fight than our Villaret-Joyeuse."

"An English tar, monseer," Troubridge informed him loftily, "fights best on his belly. A Frenchman has little of that to fight on."

His prisoner described a particularly charming bow. "Ah, monsieur, when the corn-ships arrive, *nous aussi!*"

At half-past eight the mutter of drums and signal—"Each ship to steer for her opponent in the enemy's lines."

Black Dick sent up the blue-and-yellow. It was to be a duel of the sea.

Now they advanced under crowding sail on the stately caravan of the French, waiting like Arab tents in the desert the attack of the wheeling Bedouins. A trickle of fire ran down the enemy's line, with warning thunder of the broadsides.

Bellerophon was away on his winged horse again, second ship in the van, and making for *L'Aéole*. Ahead of her, *Caesar* was to engage *L'Orient*, behind her *Leviathan* was running for *Le Trajan, Royal Sovereign* for *L'Amérique, Marlborough* for *L'Impétueuse, Defence* for *L'Indomitable*.

Already *Bellerophon* was so close that the *francs tireurs* in the rigging were levelling muskets—but Pasley had no time for engagement now. Every second was vital. Howe wanted the weather-gauge to make the wind his ally. Into a rising gale of shot, they beat their way across the Frenchmen's prows. The vicious hail of his cannonades might have been a swarm of gnats. "Fire as you will but get us across," he shouted. His eyes were on his van, Hope's on his ship, all hands at the braces.

Midshipman Flinders on the quarter-deck looked down the white rank of the British, saw them advancing undaunted, watched them slipping through the gaps in that moving wall of smoke. It was magnificent, and it was war!

Bellerophon was nearly through. A massive shadow was creeping along the deck. It was the huge castled stern of *L'Orient*, blotting out the morning sun ... a splendid chance for the gun-crews here, but the guns were all deserted.

Then Matthew saw that they were shotted and primed. The spark of a match would set them barking and biting. He raced across the swaying deck to the slow-match kindled in the tub. As each gun bore on that towered hull, he fired the priming. With a flame and a roar, the stream of shot poured through the cabin windows, tearing a jagged hole.

His heart beat faster, with fierce exultation. He was struggling to bear the last gun round when he was swept off his feet. He could feel no pain but the world was swimming … there was no deck beneath him. He had a choking sensation—then he felt the iron knuckles of a strong right hand digging deep into his collarbone, a hefty body swinging him left and right. The admiral's round face, ruddy with vexation, was glaring into his. The admiral's voice, like the bark of the guns, cut short his martial rapture.

"How dare you do that, youngster, without my orders?"

"I heard the general order to fire, sir, and I thought it a good chance to have a shot at 'em."

"I gave a general order to fire, but not to a strip like you. Get up there, and take this signal to Andrew." Matthew was off with a flying start.

Now *Bellerophon* was through, and swinging round on *L'Aéole*. For the third time that morning the signal going to her masthead called *Caesar* … *Caesar* was still to leeward of the French, three cables' lengths to leeward. *L'Orient* was doubling, *Le Trajan* coming up astern, *L'Aéole* was bearing down.

These unexpected odds of three to one suited the French captains. They closed on little *Bellerophon*. She answered them, every one. In furious fire, wood and canvas were falling, cannonballs scorching across the decks and screaming into her timbers. The poop balustrade shot up in flying splinters. There was a hoarse cry. Men were falling.

A busy group was gathered about a figure on the deck. Matthew's heart turned to stone. A twitching arm showed many liens of braid, and there was a glint of gold epaulettes. They were lifting hm on to a stretcher. Pasley! Was he gone? The ship was an inferno as in terror he ran, and bent above his friend, his beloved commander.

A low groan reassured him—the admiral was alive. They were mopping his sweating brow. With straining eyes and swollen lips he tried to rise, but his right leg lay in a red mess on the deck.

Harry Waterhouse, Matthew and Smith, the sergeant of marines, lifted the stretcher to carry him down. Anxious faces surged about them, disappearing as Hope came striding up.

"My God! Get Fargher here! He's bleeding to death!"

Pasley looked at them through a haze of coming unconsciousness.

"No. Take me below," he said. "Never you mind me leg, Mr Hope. You look after me flag."

Limp and heavy, they carried him below, the ship pitching and rolling in convulsions of bombardment and the shock of her own broadsides ... down into the reeking cockpit where Fargher and his mates, sleeves rolled up and hands dyed red to the elbows, with a quiet preoccupation were fighting blood and death.

The mangled body of a dead gunner was taken from the table. Gently they laid the admiral there. His eyes were closed, and he was scarcely breathing.

Up the companion like monkeys they ran, and out on to the quarter-deck where spars were shattering down, and *Bellerophon* firing like clockwork, but firing at three at a time as the guns bore! With a sound like the twanging of a harp, the foremast of *L'Aéole*, the nearest, came slowly splintering down.

"Chop off their wings, boys! Cut out their guts! Slash 'em!" Burlton, the first lieutenant, was shrieking. Blackened gunners flung themselves upon the burning guns, broadsides raved and smashed from ship to ship. With a split and a roar *Bellerophon's* mainmast came thundering about their ears and fell over the side. A fountain of water shot inboard and swept the sanded deck. There was a yell of triumph as *Le Trajan's* main-topsail-yard crumpled under a heap of lifeless canvas. Now *Leviathan* was on her, pumping lead into her hull.

The mutilated Frenchmen were drawing off, bearing right for *Caesar*, 500 yards to leeward, well in their track. She would have done well to get through when the chance was with her. Hope signalled her to attack, and now she went in with her guns wildly blazing. Some of her shots struck the British ships and ripped away their rigging.

Faithful little *Latona* led *Bellerophon* out of the fray. Her main- and fore-topmasts were gone, the shrouds nothing but rags. From smoke and stench of the main deck, lusty throats were bawling songs and obscenities at the French. The pitiful limp forms were very few.

The van was victorious, but between *Bellerophon* and *Queen Charlotte* now was a long line of fighting ships in full blare, Tricolour and St George jerking and striking above the mad pandemonium of battle. *Barfleur* led the centre squadron, the gallant little *Queen* the rear.

On the quarter-deck of the flagship Lord Howe had shut his signal-book.

"No more book, gentlemen. No more signals. Each captain, every man, fights as best can for his country."

With *Gibraltar* ahead of her, *Brunswick* and *Valiant* astern, *Queen Charlotte* challenged *La Montagne*, sinister mountain of guns and men, the largest war-ship in the world.

Admiral to admiral, Union to Fleur-de-lis, they spoke in sullen thunder. Villaret-Joyeuse was a stripling, winning his spurs. In his plumage of Chanticler, glossy sea-boots and great cocked hat, he hopped about with a shrill crowing of orders. Strings of flags at every mast and yard-arm flapped questions, answers, requests, demands, commands and new decisions. "Fight if you must!"—he was not afraid to fight. Victory or Madame Guillotine! In they lurched together.

Howe sat in his chair unmoving. He could see but a quarter of a circle, but that was enough. Sometimes he frowned, sometimes he smiled, a grim unnatural smile. He was hearing again the music he loved, the music of the broadsides, peering through the powder-smoke with those inscrutable eyes. The two black guns beside him were his fortress. Now they alone, of the guns of his fleet, were silent.

Curtis sheered the ship so close under the Frenchman's stern that the Tricolour tangled in his shrouds and he scraped the jib-boom of *Le Jacobin* following. The old man timed the steady boom as each gun bore, sweeping the enemy's decks with death and destruction. When *Queen Charlotte* tacked, there was hell to pay.

Now they were to windward. At last the British held the whip to last the Frenchmen back.

Cutting away wreckage and clearing the red decks, men of the *Bellerophon*, watching, knew many an anxious moment. *Brunswick* was locked with *La Vengeur* in death-grips. They saw the colours of *Royal George* shot down, and a man climbing the mast to nail them back. Alongside *Invincible* drifted a hopeless wreck. Eleven ships they counted with their masts torn out, *Marlborough* and *Defence* among them. Eight of the enemy were hulks, but with colours still flying from their battered stumps they growled defiance at the foe.

Leviathan and crippled *L'Aéole* were at each other still. Away to leeward, *Queen* was floundering, nothing left her but the shattered trunk of a foremast. She was running the gauntlet of a line of enemy ships, in a terrible punishment returning shot for shot.

At half-past eleven the smoke and thunder were gradually dying away. Blue seas were a litter of broken ships and their dead. In the shadow of the guillotine, few of the Frenchmen had dared to strike colours.

At noon, Villaret-Joyeuse hastily shepherded his ships worth taking home, and made away down wind for Brest, leaving eight cripples to their ate. The British were swift to pounce.

It was a grim aftermath, victors and vanquished in equally sorry plight, except that the frenchmen, in their crowded ships, had lost nearly seven thousand men, the English less than a thousand, with two thousand wounded.

Down in the cockpit surgeons' saws were busy. The sailors were sweeping up the clotted red sand from the decks, and grey cocoons of canvas, weighed down with cannon-balls, slid into the sea. The French used more cannon-balls to bury their dead than they ever had fired at the British. Hundreds of prisoners came on board, sullen men and sallow, speaking shrill jibberish, herded like wild beasts into the caverns of the orlop, and battened down.

Many a strange and tragic tale was told on the trestle-benches at dinner—

Of the cock that flew out of a crate to the stump of the *Marlborough's* mainmast, and crowed them on to victory.

Of Harvey of the *Brunswick*, mortally wounded, dragging himself to the companionway with both legs gone. "My legs," he jested, "even yet refuse to take me below. Never strike the flag of the *Brunswick!*"

Of the two seamen of the *Culloden*, flogged for fighting in the very height of the battle.

On the *Barfleur* Rear-Admiral Bowyer had also lost a leg, and Captain Hutt of the *Queen*, with her ghastly death-roll of 200, whereas *Bellerophon* had lost but four, among them her redheaded bosun, Bill Chapman, and the sergeant of marines ... and last, remembering, the *Caesar*.

Where was the *Caesar* in the battle off Brest? Molloy would tell them at the court martial. All they did know was that she had been well thrashed.

"Hearts of oak," grinned Bob, "have palpitations."

"If Caesar hide himself, shall they not whisper, 'Lo, Caesar is afraid?'" young Flinders capped it.

A shout from the side. The boys went running. *Thunderer* was passing with a prize, dragging the mutilated hulk. Someone said it was *La Vengeur*, that the *Brunswick* had thrashed to pieces.

It was drunkenly rolling along in her wake, a gaping wound in the side, no masts, no colours. A single officer was clinging to the rail of the quarter-deck, a pitifully bent figure in the big cocked hat. Inert forms were stretched in rows upon her slanted decks.

She fell, and rose, and fell again, bows under ... and this time she did not rise. They gave a gasp of horror. Then "*Vive la*

République!" — it came from three hundred throats in one vindictive dying scream as *La Vengeur* heeled over, the bright sun blazing a funeral pyre on her copper. Her tow-cable parted with the sound of a gong. The waves grew smooth above her stricken timbers as the seething waters took her down.

"The French have fought well this day," said Hope, "and they know how to die!" He sent Matthew forthwith to the *Queen Charlotte* with his dispatches. Admiral Pasley was drugged with laudanum, but not in grave danger.

My Lord Howe sent up the signal for his ships to re-form line.

The old man rose stiffly from the arm-chair where he had sat for five long days. His swarthy face still set in grim lines, but his dark eyes were bright. Two or three steps, from weakness and loss of sleep he tottered.

Sir Roger Curtis was at his side.

"Why do you hold me up, Sir Roger?" he said gently. "You are treating me as a child."

As he stumbled for the companionway, his officers followed in silent admiration. He paused, and turned to them, sensitive of his weakness.

"Signal my salutations to the fleet," he said. "Good work, gentlemen. Quick work, gentlemen! I am proud. It seems a year since this morning. Pray tell me, what is the date?"

"'Tis the firrst o' Jewn, m'Lord!" said methodical Captain Hunter.

The old man bowed his leonine white head, reflecting. Then, with his rare smile, "The first of June, so it is," he said ... "A Glorious First of June!"

6

Under the Southern Stars

The glorious first of June! It was the toast in every tavern, castle
and court in the kingdom of England—in good English ale, in
fine Madeira, in the rare old vintages of the province of
Champagne, the sailors' rum, and Lincolnshire's gooseberry
wine.

The Grand Fleet at Spithead, licking its wounds with pride,
was the eighth wonder of the world. George III shed the light of
his countenance upon it, Queen Charlotte herself beside him
and three of his fifteen children, fat little German princesses in
their mittens and plumed hats. They left the royal coach at
Portsmouth, surrounded by cheering multitudes, and rowed out
through avenues of gaily-decked ships to Spithead, where
H.M.S. *Queen Charlotte*, transformed from a wreck to a palace,
lay at anchor.

Again her decks were red, but with the piled carpets of
Mechlin and Axminster. Flags that had flown so urgently in
command were now a rainbow festoon. After her ordeal by fire,
she was stage-setting of a gigantic patriotic tableau, H.M.S.
Bellerophon ahead of her, H.M.S. *Queen Charlotte* astern.

The quarter-deck was a pavilion of flags, draped, scrolled
and curtained, the lion rampant of royalty, red on a yellow
ground, and in full majesty the Union. On a Jacobean table of

polished mahogany were piled the congratulations of empires, a resplendent array of orders, ribbons, medals and jewelled swords encased in embossed shagreen. There stood the admirals and captains of the fleet—those who were able to stand.

Young Flinders pondered the honours of England. He knew how they were won.

At three o'clock the drums of parade were silent. The hot June sun beat down on the heads of twelve thousand men, redcoats and blue, lined up in painted ranks on the painted ships.

Obese, and with his vacant smile, His Majesty ambled through the lines, attended by Lord Spencer and Earl St Vincent. The black 32-pounders of the *Queen Charlotte*, unreal in bunting, brayed the royal salute of twenty-one guns.

Earl Howe stood under the flags in the peacock splendour of his orders—"my trusty Lord Admiral", figurehead of England victorious.

Echo of the last gun died away over men and ships unmoving, save for a flutter of flags all down the line. It was the sacred moment of ceremonial honours. The sea-gulls dipping seemed a breach of discipline.

My Lord Howe received the Order of the Garter and a diamond-studded sword. Graves and Hood were exalted to the peerage. Curtis, Gardner, Bowyer and Pasley were created baronets, Bowyer and Pasley with pensions of £1000 a year. Admirals returned to their ships in chains of solid gold. There was promotion for every officer in the battle—save Captain Molloy of the *Caesar*—with bounty and a medal to every man.

At four o'clock His Majesty ambled away. Fifes set up their paean of triumph, the drums beat the British fleet into a roaring night of revelry.

As they filed past the paymasters of the Navy Board at Portsmouth—an epic chapter, the King had said, in England's history behind them, and all England, and home leave, ahead— Matthew and Bob lightheartedly signed for their medals.

"Full legal names and full addresses?"

Bob looked uncertain. His secret would have to come out.

"Ogilvie, Primrose. Sheepwash, Devon," he wrote.

Matthew inscribed below him, with a whoop of unholy joy.

"Come along, Buttercup from Bilgewater!" he shouted. "You lamb in wolf's clothing, come on!"

An hour of rejoicing in the madly milling throng, and they bade each other a hilarious good-bye.

As Matthew ran up the steps of the Royal Naval Hospital, a carriage emblazoned with the arms of Earl Howe drove away. The wards were full of suffering and dying, a ghastly sight in the light of the dimmed lanterns. There was choking smell of quick-lime and the sickening odours of gangrene. A coarse male attendant led the way to the admiral's private room.

Pasley lay back on his pillows, that well-loved face now yellow and drawn.

"Greetings, Sir Thomas!" Matthew shyly put out his hand. The admiral clasped it with a pleasant nod.

"Going home, Flinders? Don't forget to tell them that you started the Battle of Brest."

"I thought I might wait here, sir, while you have need of me."

"I'll not have need of an aide-de-camp again"—he turned away his head.

Heavy gold chain in its nest of purple silk, red cedarwood box with royal crest.

"Well, Sir Thomas, surely to-night you have the glow of life's achievement?"

"Aye. His Majesty gives me a noble send-off, a generous parting gift for the old wooden-legged sailor."

"Ah, sir!" Young Flinders laughed outright. "I can't see you sitting on the Radcliffe green, watching the players at cricket and telling the veteran's tale."

The admiral visibly brightened. "Well, now, talking of Radcliffe," he said. "Sawbones is letting me go from this hell tomorrow. His Majesty sends a carriage, d'ye see? If you'll lend a hand and work your passage, you can come home with me. Go across to the ship betimes for me sword and me belongings, and say good-bye for me to *Billy Ruff'n*." His voice faltered. "I've started her on her way ... it's up to her now."

Matthew glanced at the hollow in the sheets, and quickly looked away, with a thought for the sacrifice that had launched *Billy Ruff'n* into her glorious career.

The journey home was a triumphal procession. Every village, every town, turned out to welcome a hero of Brest. They brought choice wines from every cellar, dressed turkeys, seasoned hams, venison and veal, laurel wreaths and flowers to fill a graveyard, weighty gold watches inscribed and hung with seals, and models of the *Bellerophon* in scores, some small enough to be the jollyboat of the biggest. At Cambridge a wood-carver brought along a blocky effigy of the British bulldog carrying off French Chanticleer in a splinter of flying feathers.

By Nottinghamshire, they were laden like a pedlar's wagon, two coaches to follow. The admiral was more each day his rosy, jovial self, signing contracts for a wooden leg in every hamlet they passed. Radcliffe, and the Manor gates—Lady Pasley and the family in tears of joy and sorrow.

Matthew was to travel on home by one of the carriages, but while they sat at luncheon under the trees in revel of reunion, he heard the rumble of the Boston coach and flew for his kit-bag, Lady Pasley after him pleading at least one parcel for the homefolk. A long-distance salute to the laughing admiral, and under his arm a turkey in paper pantalettes, he raced down the lane and climbed aloft on the coach. The uniform was enough. The Pasleys, settling to their lunch again, heard loud throaty cheers.

Mid-afternoon, and Donington was quiet—Bodycoat, Odling, Hopper, Blanchard, Tagg, Hiley, Cawkwell, the shop-signs of the High Street just the same.

The ivy was a little thicker on the house in Market Square. The doctor's slate still hung by the surgery door.

He rapped. No answer.

He peered through the casement window—a place for everything, and everything in its place.

The front door was open. He looked in at the sitting-room, so familiar and so strange, then went into the kitchen. Everything shining neat, a fire burning brightly in the blackened grate, but not a soul. He put down his turkey on the scrubbed deal table and his kit-bag on the floor. Then he heard the whirr of a spinning-wheel in the girls' room upstairs.

Betsy or Sue—perhaps his stepmother. He would surprise them. He tiptoed up, and with his back flat to the wall, he cautiously peeped in.

The spinning-wheel was by the window, merrily turning, a foot in a neat little slipper tapping away, the thread flying through two coral-white hands. She wore a frock of soft white muslin lightly sprigged in green. It was neither Betsy nor Sue. It was a stranger.

A sudden panic came over him—the family might have gone. But no!—the surgery, and the old worn carpet on the stair.

The spindle was thinning out. The whirring stopped, and she turned to wind the bobbin. He saw it was Ann Chappell, but what a different Ann since last they met. Lips pursed in thought, the sun glinting on her wood-brown hair, Ann had grown quite pretty. Came a sound of voices from the alcove. Betsy and Sue were there. He slipped back.

Ann snapped a thread and spoke.

"Did thy Cousin Willingham admire my new rose bonnet?"

It was Matthew's cue. He stepped from the wings.

"No, but his cousin Matthew thinks it adorable!"

She stared at him with frightened eyes that widened into wonder.

"Mattie!"

Two dark heads popped from the alcove, with little squeaks of joy.

"Matt!"

With a flutter of skirts they ran. The spinning-wheel went over. Three pairs of arms were round his neck.

"Mattie, O dearest!"

"But how thou hast grown!"

"Hast fought in the Battle of Brest?... Oh, art thou wounded?"

"How didst thou come? We were watching the Cambridge coach!"

"Down, little lubbers, and give me room to breathe!"

He sat on the cushioned window-ledge, a splendid figure in their hero-worship. Sea-tanned, bright-eyed, a wilful black crop of hair, he was so gallantly erect and sturdy in his blue, square-shouldered coat. One arm round Betsy and Susanna on his knee, Ann nestling in beside, he lived for them over again the Battle of Brest, carefully veiling his too vivid memories of the slaughter, but unable to keep tragedy from his voice when he told of the sinking *Vengeur*.

"They're wicked, ruthless men, and they deserved it," said comforting Sue.

"They but fight for their flag, Sue, and they have sweet little sisters like you." He tousled her curls.

Merrily they clattered till the doctor's gig turned in to Market Square, Mrs Flinders and no less than two baby girls on her knee.

Matthew stood in the hall in shadow, the girls twittering behind the door. He coughed as Doctor Flinders strode briskly through from the stable.

"Yes, sir. What can I do for thee?"

Matthew saluted, his face alight with glee.

"Canst fill a hungry heart, father, and a hungrier man!"

The doctor peered in the twilight. "It's the boy!" He seemed uncertain. "Light the lamp!... Matthew!" He quavered with pride and emotion. His son's shoulders were higher than his own as he turned him round to take stock. "So thou art alive, with never a scratch nor a scrape! God be thanked! Elizabeth! See who's here!"

Ann and Betsy ran to take the babies, and Matthew was enfolded in his stepmother's arms.

There was a covert shuffling in the kitchen.

"Avast!" said Matthew. "I know who this will be ... Samuel Ward Flinders, if I mistake not, and a scrubbier little biscuit-weevil ne'er played hookey on the Fens! Quit looting the galley-cupboards, sir! Stand to attention! Let us see thee... aye, brawny enough to run aloft and splice a rope with the next man."

"I thought it was callers," Samuel grinned.

"And who is it, Sam?"

"It's Matt." He turned aside to hide his shyness.

Matthew caught him under the arms and hoisted him to the ceiling.

"Thy mother is troubled," announced the doctor. "We did not know when to expect thee, prodigal, and have killed no fatted calf. Thou wilt share our supper as thou hast found us."

"In finding thee," said Matthew, "I find what I love most."

As he tried to circle them with his arms, Ann shrank away, feeling herself the stranger, but Betsy affectionately drew her into that warm circle. The little doctor, overwhelmed by the exuberance, cleared his throat and set his spectacles straight. Matthew noted the spectacles. His father was growing older.

It was a happy dining-table that night in the opal shade of the big lamp, with the cruet for *Queen Charlotte*, a teaspoon for H.M.S. *Bellerophon*, the familiar knives and forks for the big French three-deckers ... until they remembered that he had been round the world.

"Begin at the beginning," they cried.

His voice grew husky, trying to cram three radiant years into three radiant hours for those dear, eager, listening faces. Ann Chappell's eyes were grey, and that surprised him. He would have said they were brown. He was reminded of the pearl-shells and the mats from Otaheite, the tortoise shell fish-hooks for Samuel, the wicker-covered flask of Jamaica—purely medicinal—for his father, and the red-and-black berry beads from Torres Strait.

Like a conjurer manipulating magics in a hat, he produced them out of his kit-bag, Sam joyously rooting beside him, piping with excitement. This big brother of his was an unexpected asset. Just wait till the Horbling Grammar boys saw Matthew riding by.

"How are Thomas and Willingham, and James and all the others, not forgetting Baby John?" he asked his stepmother, beaming at her mats in the lamplight.

"Baby John!" she laughed. "Thou'llt never know him. Going to Louth Grammar School, all the way by himself, and top of his class, but gracious goodness, Matthew, such an untidy little rascal. Will ne'er be proficient as his brothers, I fear."

How happily Matthew slipped back into the "thees" and "thous" of Lincolnshire, as they talked of old friends and new worlds till the watchman called midnight. "Full circle sailing," he slept in his own old corner under the eaves.

The handsome young midshipman was Donington's hero of Brest, greatest naval battle of a century. So proudly the little doctor drove him round on the Fens behind his new chestnut, to Grandfather Flinders at Spalding, the Franklins at Spilsby, to Grantham, Bicker, Bolingbroke, Sibsey, Stickney, Dalby, Surfleet, Louth, Tumby, Hareby, Kirton, Lusby, Langton, and Boston every day of the week. Never was a country doctor with a more comprehensive practice needing such wide detours.

Could this strapping young Ulysses be the little stubby boy who once sat so meekly beside him? The glittering gold medal was a lodestar, bringing grey-headed gaffers and schoolgirls and squires to stop the gig. Lord Howe on one side, a British ship in glorious sail and a French ship foundering on the other, "*Non Sorte Sed Virtute*"—"No other sort but us has virtues," translated the gaffers.

One afternoon they called at Revesby Abbey, with a message from James Wiles in Jamaica regarding botanical specimens, but the white-haired, black-clad housekeeper told them that Sir Joseph Banks, now a Knight of the Bath, was in London, and Briscoe in his train—Oh for a handshake with Briscoe!

Flushed with pride were the Reverend John Shinglar at Horbling, who asked him to address the scholars; Goody Cawkwell, the sweetshop marm of Market Square, who nursed him when he was a baby, and Mr Prin of Boston, who fitted him with his first uniform. Nobly he had acquitted it. Proudest of all was Cousin Henrietta, living with her family at Spalding now, and teaching a little dame school.

"Spinster of this parish," she laughed, "but have I an eye for a sailor?"

"I have much to inspire me, dear Cousin Henrietta, when I remember thee."

On Sunday the Franklins, in two drags, drove over to join them at morning service and spend the day. It was an embarrassing procession to Matthew, cramped in with his sisters and his cousins and his aunts, submerged in frills and babies, pink and blue parasols unfurled in full rig above. Endless greetings and salutations, they came to the stately old church deep in the elms at Donington, where he had prayed through all his childhood, St Mary's of the Holy Rood.

Those solemn grey stones had been laid by the Knights Templar in the twelfth century, even before Boston Stump reared its bluff head to the sea-wind. The mossy dampness of the sunlit walls, the shafts of saintly colour sloping across the blood-red pews and the fretted marble font, were a wine of benediction. How well he knew it, the same stocks and phlox on the high altar, those rough stone steps in the chancel leading to nothing but the leaden lights of other years.

The villagers came bustling in, starched, combed and humble, hushing their coarse Flemish voices to a suitable reverence. They disposed themselves in fidgeting files, mopped their brows, and looked round to see who was absent. Their eyes stopped automatically at Matthew's blue coat and gold medal. Graown fine young lad, young Matt, haome from t'wars.

Flinderses and Franklins filled two of the longer pews, their dark heads in tiers, nine-year-old John, the chubbiest, creating a mild commotion with his hassock, and ostentatiously ranging his prayer-books on the stand. A mock frown from Matthew, and he subsided.

Diapason of the organ swelled to the sunlit beams. The curved door of the vestry opened, and into that hall of wavering sound paced an angelic Samuel leading the choristers, and gentle Mr Tebbutt, the vicar, austere in priestly robes.

The organ, in a melodious chord, chanted out the key. The choir led, and the people followed.

> Now thank we all our God
>> With hearts, and hands, and voices,
> Who wondrous things has done,
>> In Whom His world rejoices;
> Who from our mothers' arms
>> Hath blessed us on our way
> With countless gifts of love,
>> And still is ours to-day.

Ann glanced at Matthew, and lost the place.

"Almighty God, the Father of Our Lord Jesus Christ, who desireth not the death of the sinner but rather that he may turn from his wickedness... "

"Thee and the Frenchmen!" stage-whispered Susanna, turning round. The doctor tapped her on the hat.

Mr Tebbutt's reedy tenor pronounced the absolution, and from the bent heads of the kneeling throng came the long-drawn "Amen". Then "Our Father... Which art in Heaven... Hallowed be Thy Name ..." the murmur of the palms in Otaheite.

Exultant, the organ led the Benedicite.

O ye seas and floods, bless ye the Lord, praise and magnify Him for ever;
O ye whales and all that move in the waters, bless ye the Lord...

They looked at Matthew with meaning glances. He buried his nose in his hymn-book.

But there was worse to come. A pest on Mr Tebbutt, he chose his text from the 109th Psalm:

They that go down to the sea in ships and occupy their business in great waters,
These men see the works of the Lord, and His wonders in the deep.

The whole congragation was smiling his way, old women nodding. He bowed his head—and remembered the phosphorus that night in the Pacific.

Better if Mr Tebbutt had left it to King David. His sermon droned on and on, Firstly, Secondly, Thirdly, Lastly, a soulless saga of the ships of Tarshish in all their manoeuvres, a rambling monotone, dull as the bees in the laburnum blossoms yellow by the vestry door.

At last Hymn No. 592, 592nd Hymn.

> O Lord be with us when we sail
> Upon the lonely deep,
> Our guard when on the silent deck
> Our midnight watch we keep.

Samuel led in his clear treble, the little doctor boomed and Grandfather Flinders bleated, but Ann's girlish voice rose high above all.

Out of those filtered sunlights into the bright summer day they gathered in happy groups, waved hail and farewell from their drags under the trees.

The Franklin girls were so many and so pretty that Matthew could scarcely keep count of them, Elizabeth, Lucy, Sarah, Mary, Hannah, Isabella, Henrietta, with Betsy, Sue and his stepsisters like petunias in rows. Ann Chappell was most flowerlike of all, dear little Ann whose father was lost at sea.

"Is this the famous rose bonnet?" he teased her. "Tt, tt. And I don't see Willingham here."

She bobbed and dimpled. "Perhaps he was afraid, Matthew, of being o'ershadowed by thee. Alas, my poor Willingham has only an Oxford scholar's gown instead of a medal of Brest." She clasped her mittened hands and sighed... mischievous grey eyes smiling.

With a twirl he undid the bonnet-strings under her chin, and laughed at her precious exasperation.

"Ah, Matthew!" she almost cried. "After twenty minutes' trying!" Her lashes sweeping her cheek as she surveyed the disaster, her pout of annoyance as she wound and unwound the ribbons made her sweeter still.

"I'm truly sorry, Ann. Here, let me do it. I'm a great hand with a reefer."

"Midshipman Matthew Flinders. Can it be? Well, well!"

He turned—to face a stalwart gallant of six feet two, in ribboned top hat and immaculate stock, crimped brown hair as neat into its bow as any fashionable wig. Fine hazel eyes laughed into Matthew's. The well-cut brown suit would grace a Nottingham squire. He flicked his boots with his riding whip and acknowledged Miss Chappell with a sweeping bow, at which Miss Chappell was amused. There seemed some understanding between them. Who could this long-legged stranger be?

"I see plainly," the intruder sighed in mock sorrow, "that I am long forgotten. He who hobnobs with Collingwood and Howe would scarce remember an apothecary's boy compounding a balsam to rub his manly chest."

"George Bass!"

With a shout of laughter, Matthew gripped his hand.

"Thou'rt such an Adonis, George, how could I know thee? I hear thou art a surgeon, and making well!"

Ann beamed. "Indeed, all Lincoln swears by Doctor George."

The family was about them, imploring them to dinner.

The lanes rang with laughter as they jogged along home. The big dining-table crowded to its utmost, Matthew was in for the Battle of Brest once more. Through that tranquil summer afternoon, he and Doctor George were out over the Fens for miles together.

Haytime in Lincolnshire, sun-gold stooks in the fields, flocks of sheep in the shade of the elms, and in all the villages the old men sitting outside the inns like Toby jugs.

In drags and dog-carts, the younger Flinderses and Franklins were off through the fragrant lanes of hawthorn to the flax-fairs and the harvest homes, a gay crowd at the smock-races and the ducking-matches, and rowing on the Witham in the long calm evenings under the bows of the queer ships pulled in at the silent quays.

Always within sight of the old church towers, within sound of their gentle bells, they wandered a poet's England, about them the richest tapestries of summer so soon evanishing, and sermons of the life of man written in stone. There were pleasure-parties to Grantham and St Ives, bonfire parties in the ivied Saxon ruins, moonlight picnics in the hay singing rounds—Paul's Steeple, Sweet Kate, and Oyle of Barley—lads and lasses joining the dances as far as Mablethorpe and Scrivelsby and Clee.

Merry it was when Mr John Sparrow, the fiddler, bow legs jigging and his bow sawing away, took his place at the end of the rows for "Left Hand and Right".

Hey! And they were off, all the boys with bells to their garters and a feather to each cap. Clap hands, clap knees, clap left and right, clap under your partner's dimpled chin, then down and through and up the middle, face partners, cross and clap again, round in a spiral follow-my-leader, then dancing all in a ring—the swishing skirts, the jingling bells, with a jump and a clap, and hey!

Or perhaps it would be "Greensleeves" with its joyous bass and dreamy treble, or "Bluff King Hal", a courtly bowing and twining, "Joan Sanderson" the hilarious finale.

Doctor George would start off with the cushion, gaily curvetting round till the music stopped. Then,

> "This dance it will no further go!" he sang.
> "I pray you, good sir, why say you so?" they chanted.
> "Because Joan Sanderson will not come too!"
> "She must come too, and she shall come too,
> And she must come whether she will or no."

they all sang in chorus.

George laid the cushion, his hand on his heart, at the feet of Sarah Franklin. Sarah and the cushion and he swung to the trill of the fiddle, and finished with a kiss to loud applause.

Now it was her turn. Alone in the circle she wilted.

"This dance it will no further go!"
"I pray you, Madame, why say you so?"

The cushion at the feet of solemn Henry Sellwood, the vicar's son from Somersby, and they were off again, to Hannah and young John Booth, Jean Churchill and Tom Franklin, Mary Hudson and Willingham, Betsy and James Harvey, and inevitably Matthew and Ann, till all were kissed and teased, and blushing. "Joan Sanderson" was everybody's favourite.

Willow rivers of the Fenlands and ghosts that haunted many an old abbey heard their holiday laughter till church spires were dreaming in autumn mist, and rooks homing early.

A friendship far deeper than that of boyish years had sprung up between Matthew and Doctor George, who was by no means sure that the boards of Lincoln Hospital were his allotted path in life. Most nights in the house in Market Square, though the little doctor was ever waylaying him into the surgery to view atrocities in bottles, would find George Bass for hours on end in the attic, poring over "the world in folio". He was never tired of listening, of learning … of longing.

After maelstrom of battle and revels on the flowery mead, Matthew was surveying again his own path in life, back to his squares and his circles, a studious candle burning in the garret window long after Market Square was asleep. From his torn scribbled notes and spattered *Bellerophon* journal, he had compiled in faultless miniature sketch, the three episodes of Brest, a fair copy for Admiral Pasley. On the first chill day of September, he rode over to Radcliffe, and Doctor George came with him to meet his hero and his friend.

Pasley was sitting in a wheel-chair by the fire in the library, Lieutenant Henry Waterhouse with him, to Matthew's pleasant surprise.

"Ah, what I wanted!" The admiral pounced on the sketch. They had compiled in full the *Bellerophon's* report, with special reference to the conduct of the *Caesar*. At a court martial on the *Glory*, Molloy had been dismissed the service. His only defence was that his rudder had jammed.

"So his future in the Navy," said the admiral, "and his past, are now oblivion. An extraordinary affair it was, for the man is not without courage. You knew, of course, that the corn-ships reached France?"

Matthew was amazed. "Then what, sir, was the purpose of the battle?"

"One asks no such questions of king and country."

"Nelson," said Harry Waterhouse, smiling, "calls it 'a Lord Howe victory'."

The admiral was nettled. "Let your precious little Captain Nelson show what he can do. If the corn-ships did get in, it was through a Sargasso weed of the dead."

"A pitiful sight indeed, sir," ventured Matthew sadly, "and for what reason, after all? You distress me... but what does war ever achieve save woe?"

"As a British campaigner of thirty years, I would have you know, Midshipman Flinders, that without war there would be no empire."

Matthew stood rebuked. "I meant, sir, that my ideal is a world in which the affairs of nations might be decided in wise deliberation and mutual agreement, or by buying and selling if you will, but without violence and the hatred of our brother man. Then would our hands be free for great achievement in science and discovery. Surely there is some dominion that can be ours without destruction and slaughter."

"If you can find it, my boy, by all means try," said the admiral loftily, "but I cannot see that the ideals of a junior midshipman are likely to change the face of earth."

Deftly Harry Waterhouse turned the subject to the *Billy Ruff'n's* exploits, and the exciting moments the three had shared together.

Doctor George was at a loss whether to show most interest in the knitting of the leg, duly examined, or in the deeds of derring-do recited, with baffling "luff" and "larboard". But now the Pasley girls returned from their morning walk, Bess Waterhouse, Harry's sister, among them, all ringlets and bewitching smiles. Gay introductions, and he was no longer in doubt as to his interests. They bore him off to show him the garden.

Taking leave of his senior officers rather abruptly, with apologies for having interrupted, Matthew was about to follow.

"Not so fast, young man! Despite your exalted ideals, I perceive you are as ardent a fisherman of the ribboned fry as your handsome friend, but we have news for you." Under the admiral's lowering brows the old-time friendly twinkle, but ... "Sit down, sir, and hear the worst!"

Matthew was apprehensive. Was he discharged? He waited with grave misgivings.

The admiral took snuff. Frowning, he conned some papers. He looked at Matthew speculatively, then cleared his throat.

"You have the mind for a voyage to New South Wales."

"Sir!"

"Captain John Hunter is known to you?"

"I met him at the Cape, sir, and saw him again aboard the *Queen Charlotte*."

"He has been appointed governor of our prison colony in New South Wales in place of Governor Arthur Phillip, resigned. Will leave on a five years' commission, Harry Waterhouse here in command of his ship, the *Reliance*, and his nephew William Kent, with H.M.S. *Supply*. For some inexplicable reason"—the admiral became facetious—"my friend Captain Hunter and your friend Waterhouse think they can make use of you. Now, sir. What of it?"

"Sir!" It was scarcely audible.

"Hard work, Mr Flinders, and a long way from home leave. From what I learn you will be expected to devote at least part of your time to"—there was a dramatic pause—"marine surveying and exploring."

Matthew looked into the fire ... sulphurous blue seas smoking it to flickering alps of flame, sombre valleys and dull red cliffs, and rivers of running gold. There trees of earth and stars of heaven were new....

"Well, Midshipman Flinders, I asked you what of it? Does it please you?"

The boy's face was transfigured. He was incoherent with joy, with thanks, with plans, breathless at his own good fortune. New South Wales, with Hunter whom he respected, and Waterhouse, his friend! Marine surveying! He grinned at Harry, and realized that he must not grin at his captain. He dared not thank his admiral—the world was gloriously awry. With scarlet face and shining eyes, he stuttered.

Doctor George came back with the girls.

"Here, sir!" the admiral called him. "Your friend, it seems, is in need of your attention. Take his pulse."

George seized him by the wrist and solemnly drew out his watch.

"He should have been dead ten minutes ago!" he announced in consternation.

They cantered back together through a light refreshing rain, Matthew delivering an impassioned soliloquy, Doctor George answering in monosyllable.

"To New South Wales! Exploring! For this was I born. I knew it! I tell you, George, the place is unknown, a vacant space in the map. 'Tis the most elusive of all the ocean's secrets. For centuries it has been fable. Tasman sailed right round it, and did not find it. Cook never thought of it till it was there, before his eyes! In all his explorations, he girdled the earth, but he scarce alighted in this great island—if be it an island. When I was in Van Diemen's Land, I looked north to it and visioned it. When I was in the Torres Strait, I looked south and beheld it. I longed to go. Now the wish of my heart is answered. While I have life I shall seek. Oh George Bass, what shall I find?"

"This fiery fervour," said Doctor George, "is deuced contagious—worse than any fever I ever knew. I envy you! For two pins I'd throw my pills and potions to the winds, and ship before the mast as an A.B. Surgeon turned sailor—surely with the two I could earn my keep."

"Stop!"

Matthew reined in his chestnut so sharply that Doctor George's roan reared back in fright.

"What was it?"

"An idea! Have they a surgeon for the *Reliance*?"

"Ha! How could we know?"

"Come. We'll go back and see."

They wheeled in the twilight, and back over the border made it a race to Radcliffe. The rain in their hair and breathing hard, they put the proposition to the admiral. The admiral was amused. He knew little of the appointments. He called Captain Waterhouse. There had been no appointment of a surgeon yet, so far as Harry knew.

"At any rate," Pasley suggested, "put in an application to the Navy Board with copies of your credentials."

"In all probability," said Waterhouse aside, "they will refer it to me."

The family begged them to stay to dinner, but they were eager to be off. Lightsome farewells again on the porch, Maria, Sabina, Jane and Lady Pasley, in their silks and satins a gracious group in the rainy lamplight, and Miss Bess Waterhouse, tall and divinely dark, with a last lingering smile for Doctor George.

"Do you believe in love at first sight?" that young man asked Matthew, as they trotted down the drive in the wet breath of the dusk and scent of the larches.

Matthew reflected.

"I'm afraid I'm not an authority," he said.

"What! Nineteen! And you've never been in love!"

"I didn't say that. No indeed, sir. I said I was not an authority on love at first sight. I've been in love so long that I can't remember."

But was he in love? That was the question he asked himself, galloping through the mud next morning fifteen miles to Partney, to the little old rectory deep in the grove where Ann Chappell lived with her mother and stepfather, and one small step-sister, Isabel Tyler. He knew he loved Ann most dearly, had always loved her, much as he loved Betsy and Sue … but was he what the poets call "in love"? Romeo and Juliet died for each other—he wanted to live. He wanted New South Wales. Wheeling, he cleared a hedge in exultation.

The deep-thatched rectory under the elms seemed desolate, swept by the falling leaves. Ann, in gingham pinafore dusting the parlour, herself answered his knock. He could hear the slow uncertain strumming of Isabel's music practice.

"Canst come out for a moment? I have great good news to tell thee!"

She put off her pinafore and took her bonnet. They strolled through the low white picket gate, past St Andrews, the modest brown church where Mr Tyler was arguing with the verger, and into the shadow of the mighty oak, far-famed in Lincolnshire, a thousand years old. Planted by Venerable Bede, it had seen the tree-worship of the Druids, thunder-worship of the Vikings, moon-worship of the Romans. Now it sheltered a little Christian church from the bitter east wind. Its roots were deep in the grave-mould of many generations of men. In those brown aisles, not a leaf stirring—a cool, damp silence that defied time through centuries of struggle and storm.

Ann sat on a great arched root, and clasped her knee in her hands.

"Well now, thy news?"

"I sail with Captain Hunter for New South Wales."

"There will be war?"

He smiled, and shook his head. "Twenty thousand miles away from war—in seas where no ship of the line has ever sailed, by coasts unknown to man."

There was a pause.

"How long?"

"Five years."

"Five years!" Her face went white.

Swiftly he was beside her, holding her very close, muslin and ribbons and all their fragrance against the smooth blue tunic.

He stilled the quivering of her lips with a determined kiss, the first real kiss of his life, that sent a man's strength and a man's tenderness into his arms, and a hot heedlessness throbbing in his brow. Her eyes were laughing and crying as he kissed her again and again, long, deep, thirsting kisses that stirred a rustle of apprehension, as a wandering breeze, in the old oak itself.

Flushed and trembling, he drew away, then Ann slipped her hand into his with the dear familiar trust of their childhood. The first passion quieted, he put a resolute braided arm about her, and with warm kisses of infinite gentleness brushed away her tears.

Together they turned the picture-book pages of the past, all the way from babyhood and schooldays.... Ann sitting on a rung of the millwheel dangling bare legs in the pool while he sailed his boat through the dark lagoon to the cresses ... Ann, pushing her earnest little face into his maps when he was poring over his homework.... Mattie, making Ann and Betsy black up for pirates. What a scouring it was for them, and what a trouncing for him! "Do you remember ... ?" "Yes, but the day... ."

"Ann. My little Annette. We always knew."

His lips slipped from the kindness of hers to the pulsing of her throat. Her light hands touched the wave of his hair in the light of the withered leaves.

Dreaming a thousand dreams, planning a thousand plans, they sat there, clasped in their joy and sorrow, until the noon sun shadowed the oak at late angles. The twanging of the harpsichord had ceased long ago.

Ann freed herself from his enfolding arms.

"I must go, Matthew ... my dearest."

A wild thrill swept through him again, and he took her in another crushing kiss, but this time they drew apart laughing. Between more kisses—would he never make end? but now so whimsical and so sweet—he tucked her curls into her bonnet, and straightened her creased shawl.

"Mr Tyler," he said, "will never approve of such goings-on in the graveyard. My own little Ann, are you glad? Are you glad it's me? What can I do to be worthy?" Such serious questioning eyes, such wilful hair, such sad drooped lips.

For answer, she took his hands and held them to her heart.

So there was yet another last kiss, a kiss of closed eyes and deep fulfilment and walking together in blissful abstraction, as those who have just awakened, they came out into the sunlight.

Reverend Mr Tyler, and Mrs Tyler and Isabel were much impressed with his news, and that he should be chosen for exploration.

"But what exploring," asked Mr Tyler blandly, "is there still to do in South Wales?"

"*New* South Wales!" they enlightened him. "There's all the world between."

A swift promise of swift return to Ann at the little white gate, eyes that held longer and closer than kisses, and he was off to the Franklins for dinner. The dear good Franklins, bless them that they lived so close.

Far down the road, a lazy road where nothing ever hurried, Ann watched him galloping, watched him through her smiles and her tears. Never once he looked back ... but Matthew would not look back. She knew, as lovers know, that his thoughts were hers.

When the rector came home from the village, she was still watching the road, the table not set. Blushing, she bustled to do it.

Came a most exasperating time, then, for the little doctor at Donington. His chestnut would be gone from the stable at odd moments, and his eldest son was always "at the Franklins", to borrow a book or return one, a Latin lesson with Willingham, a pound borrowed from Thomas to pay back, or what not.

"Why this sudden excess of affection for our kinsmen at Spilsby?" he demanded of Mrs Flinders.

"He's very fond of little John," she explained.

"Mmn. I have an idea he stops short of the Franklins. He's very fond of little Ann," observed the doctor dryly.

"Well Matthew, they're only children playing games."

"For children of that age, my dear, the game is falling in love. I've played it myself. I know. Send Sam to hire me a hack."

On 1 October the blow fell, the dreaded letter, the longed-for letter, from the Navy Board.

Midshipman Matthew Flinders must report on board H.M.S. *Reliance* at Spithead.

The chestnut was gone from the stable very early. It was still missing very late.

Doctor George called several times that day to disappointment. For Doctor George had his commission as the surgeon of the *Reliance*, to sail with his friend to the Unknown Land.

Matthew arrived next morning with the unfailing Franklins, no less than four of them—Willingham, long-haired, aesthetic; Thomas, the eldest, his head screwed on the right way; James, an enterprising schoolboy; and John on his brown pony. Matthew heard the news of Doctor George with a glow of gratification, but, strangely, he seemed an older man.

"I'm going to sea," announced John in the light of the lamp that evening.

"Oh so, young man?" said Thomas. "What dost thou know about it? Thou hast not seen it."

"Have I not? 'Tis grey, and blue, and far-away—a path to follow."

Matthew looked at him quickly. Cousin Matthew, so quiet to-day, seemed reassured and glad.

"Where didst see it then?" Thomas persisted.

"Willie Cust and I. We saw it. Played hookey from Louth when Cousin Matthew first came home. Walked out twelve miles across the dunes to Saltfleet, and the sea. 'Twas grand and far-away. I'm going there to find things."

"And didst not get a scrounging from thy master?"

"Thought we were sick of the sneezes, but even if a scrounging, we were ready for that. 'Twas worth it."

How Matthew liked him, a sturdy little man, with his laughing black eyes and dark chestnut curls, his broad English cheekbones and high forehead. Willingham was the poet, Thomas a magician in money mathematics, and James a promising boy. What was the knot that bound him to John, so much his junior, with a deeper affection than for all the others?

He turned to his brother, Samuel, always sensitive and silent.

"You, Sam. What are you going to be? A surgeon?"

Scratching at homework for Horbling, Sam looked up.

"I suppose so." He bit the end of his pencil. "But best, I'd like to go to sea."

"Is it true?"

"I'd sail with thee tomorrow if I could."

"Then wilt thou come?"

Matthew's urgency surprised him. He paused.

"For Captain Waterhouse would take thee, I feel sure, if I should ask for a berth. There's always room aboard for an extra boy. Tell me, Samuel, art thou in earnest? 'Tis hard travelling, and high climbing, but I could help thee."

"There's a chance," said James Franklin, envious.

"I would come, but I doubt my father will let me."

"Shall I ask?" Matthew rose.

John's eyes sparkled with expectation. "How old are thy boys aboard?" They laughed him down.

"I'd give the world!" said Sam.

"I'll ask him now." Light, resolute step, Matthew ran down the stair.

The doctor was totting up accounts in the surgery. He raised a furrowed brow. Matthew sat on the edge of the table.

"Financial troubles, father? How is the practice?"

"With my son wearing out my only horse on the Fens, it might be better," he countered.

"'Tis not easy, father. I have seen. A long upward pull. The four girls, heavy levies in war, and Samuel's school fees. I have a plan for Samuel. It will be many years before he qualifies as a surgeon, but he has already reached the stage where he might serve his country at sea. He himself is eager. If I can find him a berth, wilt thou give consent? George Bass and I will promise to take a father's care. He would no longer be incumbrance on thee, and would be making his career. The Navy needs men as never before, and when war is depleting the ranks, promotion is swift. With me, he would be assured of a training reasonably safe. Thou knowest I have powerful friends who may help him. May we consider it, sir? The decision must quickly be made."

The little doctor covered his eyes with his hand. "I had hoped," he said slowly, "to send Samuel to Oxford, even as thy cousin Willingham, but it seems that the drapery and grocery business is ever a more profitable investment than ills of the inner man. I cannot pretend to keep up with the folk at Spilsby, nor even to hope for Samuel a successful practice here. The war is killing commerce, and our little towns are dwindling. He is a clever boy, Matthew, but lacks thy application."

"The discipline of the sea, father, will soon remedy that. We'll make him a good sailor, a good officer, and a good man, which last is the foundation of the other two, and the foundation of all happiness." Next day it was decided.

A gallop of farewell to the admiral at Radcliffe, a word to Waterhouse, setting out on his southward journey, and Samuel, too, packed a kit for the South Seas.

Those last days were dismal in the house in Market Square. New Holland had lost its glamour. The future stretched before them—a vacant sea, and five years wide. No Flinders son now in Donington, to follow in the profession, and Matthew's brief sweet love was laid aside—who knows, perhaps forever. Father and son put a brave face on their melancholy, but the clock was their enemy. The relentless little scythes of time were cutting away the hours.

By Michaelmas, good-byes were over. If there was a night when the old oak at Partney heard all the sighs, the passionate kisses and promises, the dreams of lovers' making, they were but the memories of one passing year, blown away with the falling leaves.

Doctor George, Matthew and Samuel travelled south together. To the watching eyes of the young explorers, Boston Stump faded blue down into the shires.

H.M.S. *Reliance* and H.M.S. *Supply* were anti-climax, the one a naval bygone, the other a dejected little tub. England had use in war for every ship worthy of the name. The farther the others had to sail, the less she cared how soon they fell to pieces. But quarters, food and company were good.

Midshipman Flinders found himself on the list as senior, sharing a cabin with the surgeon!

The crew was well chosen, officers few. There was Kent of the *Supply*, a whip-lash of a man, sailor to his spatulate finger-tips; Harry Waterhouse, hiding his youth in his new-found dignity, and Shortland, first-lieutenant, a likeable madcap. Shortland had been to Port Jackson with the *Sirius*, and piled up with her on the reef at Norfolk Island. His father was agent for the convict ships, and he had a rollicking repertoire of hair-raising tales. If the *Reliance* was to be their home for five years, these were the type to make it home.

Hunter, the new governor of New South Wales, was an albino lion, of mental and physical magnitude, an imaginative Scotsman, benevolent and exact. White hair flowed back from a broad white forehead above the clear eyes of a visionary. His pace was slow, his judgment sound. He wrote vigorous English, and spoke vigorous Scots.

Born to be a pillar of the Presbyterian Church, a shipwreck on the coast of Norway in youth had given him a taste for salt water. He ran away from the cloisters of Aberdeen University to the Heights of Abraham and the taking of Quebec. Lieutenant for twenty-six years, he had burned his first command, the fireship *Spitfire*, and as flag-captain to Lord Howe, had fought the vain fight against American Independence. Thirteen of those years he spent on the coasts of Canada and Newfoundland, mapping them for Britain, and then Howe sent him as second captain of the First Fleet to the Terra Incognita. Commander of the *Sirius*, a flagship of the felons, he was Phillip's right-hand man in New South Wales when he transplanted his thankless thousand from the prison hulks into a prison whose walls were the forest trees.

Well he remembered young Flinders with Bligh at the Cape, knew his record with the *Providence* and the *Bellerophon*, and showed a lively interest in the surveying.

"I hear ye're a hand wi' a spurrit-level, wi' a sagacious eye for furrin shoores, an' fine lines for a map. I ha'e a map for ye to draw. There's 188 miles o' fooreshoore i' Port Jackson alone, an' God an' the de'il know whut's beyond it. I made a survey masel' o' that, an' Broken Bay an' Botany Bay, but mickle moore than an eye-stretch. Ye micht begin from there, an' read the riddle."

"Aye, sir. George Bass here shares my love of exploration. If we can take one of the ships for a time, we might chart the whole island."

Hunter grunted. "One o' the ships! Where ye travel now, laddie, a ship's a rarer sight than an honest man. Not e'en a boat can I gi'e ye, for these o' oors will be in sairvice to fish for my starving people. An' I'm theenkin' it's an ambeetious undertaking to chart yon island. Cook made the east coast twa thousand mile, an' that's the *east* coast."

"Has Cook established that there is never a break, sir?"

"Now, queer ye should say that." The governor put down his napkin, sketched a coastline with his finger on the cloth, and tapped a spot near the base of it. "There's a wee whusperin' in ma mind that there micht be a break. In '89, when I took the *Sirius* to the Cape for wheat, there was ane stretch noorth o' Van Diemen's Land where I could sight no shoores to west'ard, wi' an easterly set o' current an' a strong noorth-west wind, the verra breath o' ocean. It's a point we might get a chance to clear. Keep it in mind, for I can do mickle aboot it. I'm His Majesty's jailer, Lord High Panjandrum of the gallows tree."

Doctor George that night disposed of the problem of a boat. He bumped alongside in the infant sister of a wherry, eight feet by five, reeking to high heaven of bad mackerel. They gave him an ironic cheer as he climbed aboard, and drew it up by the painter.

"Less levity there!" he warned them. "This is H.M.S. *Tom Thumb*, my first command." He carefully put the baby to bed in a corner of the long-boat.

Kent was as lightly satirical about his first command. A little old American sloop, 170 tons, of worm-eaten birch, the *Supply* was nothing but a tender. "She's a museum piece," Kent said, "but I'll make her swim."

"A museum piece i' verra trewth," ruminated Governor Hunter. "Yon wee *Supply*, wi' Phillip abooard, was first ship in to one o' the grandest harrbours i' the univairse. William, ye have a historic command."

"She has a past," laughed Kent. "God help us in her future."

"We'll take her back to the scene of her triumph, and let her die in peace," suggested Shortland.

"She'll not be retirin' yet awhile," said Hunter. "Cherish her well, Willie, my boy, for she desairves it, an' I've wurruk for her to do."

A few hurried weeks at Spithead, and they sailed for Plymouth, to wait for the Admiralty's store-ships. It was a long wait. The Admiralty thought of nothing but guns.

Hunter fretted and Kent cursed as the months went by. Miss Bess Waterhouse came down for a few days to see to her brother's comfort before he went away. Doctor George thought it a shining example of rare sisterly affection. He spent so much time telling her so while he showed her the sights of Plymouth from a dog cart that she forgot what she came for.

Matthew put in the time teaching himself all the sciences through the alphabet from biology and geology to zoology, and teaching Doctor George navigation. They scoured the hills of Drake's Devon and the governor's library for every scrap of knowledge under the sun. George was an apt pupil. Matthew acclaimed him in his father's words—"the penetrating Bass". Samuel had settled down well as the servant of Shortland's servant, a good little "fetch-and-carry", learning the ropes.

One bleak windy afternoon, a precise county gentleman appeared on board with a dark companion. He strode the quarter-deck with authority, obviously a man of mark. A perpetual frown of concentration lent power to his cold, large eyes, his intensity of purpose belied his frail physique.

He was briefly announced. Captain Phillip.

He spent a long time in conclave with Governor Hunter, while the black man waited, clothes flapping on a scarecrow frame, gibbering in the chill wind, convulsed by a racking cough. He was Bennelong, one of Phillip's two souvenirs of a newly-discovered black race. The other had died in his first English winter. If Bennelong could last the distance, they were to carry him home. When Phillip had gone, the poor creature crawled under one of the gun-carriages, and stayed there like a sick dog.

Four months my Lords of the Admiralty kept them waiting at Plymouth. When the first of the store-ships did arrive, it was blown inshore in a gale, and cargoes lost. Hunter, in dudgeon, decided to sail without it. The black man was visibly dying on his hands, and his colony at Port Jackson drifting on the rocks. He refused to be pigeon-holed till "crack o' doom".

"If only they *cared*," he cried, "there's hope abounding! Phillip believes that yon colony will yet be one o' the brightest jewels in the crown. Blind they are, that wilna see!"

At last they sailed in full convoy on 15 February, *Queen Charlotte* and Lord Howe remote and regal in the lead. Hunter received strict instructions to keep clear of the Cape of Good Hope—French influence had made it enemy ground. He promptly suggested to Howe that the British should buy it.

"It's not likely they'll sell," the admiral laughed.

"Did ye ever ken a Dutchman wouldna sell his wife for guid gold guilders? Think it over," Hunter advised. "Try them."

Safe through the seaways of warring Europe once they passed Finisterre, the guardian angels folded their wings and left them to cross the windy sea. It was May when they reached the River of January.

While the Portuguese viceroy, an offensive little yellow man, kept Hunter cooling his heels in that panoramic harbour, Matthew was off in the whaleboat, marking and charting the dark blue shores of Brazil as far as Cape Frio. Movement and the sea-wind kept his heart from hungering for Ann. Aboard again, he learned the native language from Bennelong. The black boy grew stouter and brighter, more like a human being every day.

Fourteen weeks, if fates were kind, would bring them to New South Wales.

South of the Line, lying together on the quarter-deck at nights, they lifted their eyes to a new vault of heaven.

If the old Greeks made poetries of the cold northern stars, what legends of the immortals here to trace, what canticles to sing. They sailed under Magellan's Clouds into Magellan's ocean.

Magellan's Clouds—the very name was music—glittering drift of a maze of suns, whirling universes flung by the hand of

God into unmeasured and immeasurable space. In this pure southern air, these southern seas, untarnished by the breath and the trade of men, even the night had colour … faint spume of stars to sounding bell, low smouldering red and burning orange, a flame of yellow, smoky green, and blinding white, and cold metallic blue.

To Matthew they brought the mathematician's delight of new calculations, new courses to trace, new vectors. Old friends. He had solved a few of their secrets, but how many more, to lead him on forever.

Sirius hung like a masthead light in the spars of the *Reliance*, as her weird geometry of ropes, in luminous arcs and circles rose and fell to the rhythm of the waves. The two little faithful ships were sailing down to the feet of Orion, Orion the Hunter, striding across the hemispheres with his hounds in full cry at his heels, Saiph in his right thigh, that jewelled hilt of his sword, lodestar of the Arabs, first sailors of the south. Betelgeuse sparkled red in the giant's shoulder.

"He's a trew Scot," said Governor Hunter. "'Tis a fine cairngorm he has there."

By Fomalhaut, the peacock's feather of Dorado in its 180 degrees sweep of the skies, those Arab caravels had planned their lunar distances and groped their way through chaos. A million light years away, the Great Spiral of Andromeda lifted its countless star-cities out of time. The Sickle of Leo mowed a silver harvest. Volans, the Flying Fish, skimmed phosphorescent seas. Caelum, the Sculptor's Tools, chiselled columns of luminous dust. Rigel burned perpetual, a pin-point of blue heat, piercing with the intensity of 15,000 suns.

Away down to the western heaven Scorpio clung, his claws serrated with sharp tongues of light, a poisonous twist to his curving tail—Antares, that could dwarf the heavens themselves in the arch of his scaly back. Even to the blind untutored mind of the aboriginal, that king constellation of the skies suggested the stinging serpent. Bennelong and his people called it Gudda, the Lizard.

To Bennelong the Pleiades, those spinning sisters with the fates of men in their luminous web, were the simple "bees' nest", whirring of a myriad wings. To him the Milky Way—the Ghost Walk of the Indians, the Silver River of China, Al Lahn, the Highway, to the Arabs—was only the honey trail. Two small stars flying across it near Scorpio were Gijiriga, Green Parrots. Red Mars was Gumba, fat. The tail of the Great Bear was Ngungu-gu, the Night Owls.

At the foot of the Cross, the mighty nebula of dark worlds was Gao-ergo, the Emu, and Crux Australis itself was Ngu-u, the Tea-tree ... that glittering pendant of the Southern Cross hung round the zone of the Pole, south of Alpha and Beta Centauri and their dark brother, Proxima, nearest of all to this lonely little spinning top of water and sand, the Earth, where man is as a grain of salt consumed in a candle-flame.

"Those are the distances," said Doctor George, "that hold God's interest."

The aeons between the eternal stars made short work of fourteen weeks of sailing. They swept through the forties in gales, and by August were skimming the east coast of New Holland. As they neared Port Jackson, Bennelong sent up the smoke signals that would tell his coming to his people. Night after night he was prancing round the gun-carriage, whining the songs of his country till the bosun's belaying pin put him to bed.

As his spirits went up, Governor Hunter's went down. He was bracing himself to the grim ordeal before him.

"So I take my throne," he said, "in a kingdom of rogues and wretches. England's outcast. Ishmael. His hand against every man's, and every man's hand against him."

"Have you forgotten, sir?" said Matthew Flinders quietly. "And God said 'Arise, lift up the lad, and hold him in thine hand, for I will make of him a great nation.'"

On 7 September they entered Sydney Heads, the north a sphinx of the sea, its lion paws in supplication of the mighty Pacific, the lion's head of the south defying its anger and its foam.

7

Hell in Heaven

Those majestic sea-gates led to the most dreaded prison in the world, a dead end of exile, and misery, and starvation. "All Hope Abandon Ye Who Enter Here."

Low down to the rim of the hills a crescent of moon was setting—"like a slice of ripe melon," said Doctor George, with his flair for unusual simile.

The wind had fallen. The harbour, eerily lonely, reflected clouds and stars. Shadowy headlands circled many a pale silver bay. Officers and marines and men stood in little groups on the half-deck and quarter-deck, enjoying a pipe of peace in sheltered waters. All along the north shore twinkled the corroboree fires of the blacks, and Bennelong was gibbering with joy. He leaned far out over the bulwarks, and emitted an ear-piercing tremolo of greeting to his people. A long-drawn wail, like the cry of a curlew, came from a moonlit beach.

The governor stumped on deck with a deep Scots sigh of satisfaction for journey's ending. In the half dark he pointed out the Manly Cove, where Phillip had been speared by its dusky defenders; Rose's Bay; Lieutenant Bradley's Head; the bay where two rushcutters had been murdered by the blacks, and his garden island, where the men of the *Sirius* planted "the firrst wee plot".

"Aye, 'tis a bonny harrbour we found for His Majesty, but mickle he'll mak' oot o't, for a moore wicked, moore urraleegious pack o' hewmans ha' ne'er been gathered thegither in ony cranny o' the airth. A sink o' infamy, an' the white de'ils worrse than the black de'ils. Ye can whup their buddies to ribbons, but ye canna save their etairnal souls i' this heathen, hopeless lahnd."

Curfew had rung some hours before, and the settlement would be sleeping. A shame to wake them to its sin and sorrow. They anchored in a cove near by till morning. Bennelong called it Woolloomooloo, a swift liquid ripple in the throat. When he heard there were no boats for the shore, he slipped off his jacket to swim, but they promised him a bang of the big guns at landing, and he turned in with the rest.

In the first pallor of dawn, Flinders was awakened by a distant peal of laughter, the heartiest and most infectious laughter he had heard in his life. Probably a tribe of natives heralding the ships. He sat up and listened. The stars were fading, but the breeze was cold, and day was still far off.

He was settling down in his hammock when it came again — a low throaty chuckle bubbling up in crescendo until it broke in strident cackles of uncontrollable mirth, over and over, louder and louder, then dwindled away to a chuckle again, and gasps of helpless exhaustion. He imagined those blackfellows holding their sides, their eyes streaming with tears.

The next time it split the welkin, he woke George Bass.

"What merry fools, whoever they are!" he said, then "Hunter's wrong. No land could be forever accursed when its people can laugh like that."

"There's something satirical about it," George observed sleepily. "It gives me an unpleasant feeling that we are the butt of the jest."

They were. When Waterhouse told them they had been listening to the bald-headed mocking bird, the demon genius of New Holland, they refused to believe it.

"Cap'n talk tru," Bennelong cut in. "Kookaburra all right, bird alonga tree. You hearem plenty bimeby."

Day broke in a tender radiance of colour soft as a dove's breast on one of the loveliest harbours in the Seven Seas, scarcely less splendid than Rio. Earth, sky and sea were closed in a glittering crystal of pure ethereal light. As far as eye could see, the wooded hills swept down to the wide shining water, headlands and havens in sparkling spider-web, gleaming lanes of waterway cutting the virgin forest. Half a dozen islands were jewels in the blue.

There was a sharp crag of rock in the centre of the harbour, and on the crest they saw a man waving. That solitary figure gave a weird dancing impression. Curious, they went for the glass.

It was a dead man prancing on a gibbet, in flapping rags and creaking chains a Ballad of the Hanged. The crows were wheeling above him. A fearful shadow fell over the brightness of the day. The seamen pointed and laughed.

The rock, Hunter told them, was the Pinch Gut. There Phillip had starved his rebels into submission. Seventy-five feet high, a broken tooth of stone, it had been the natives' Wattamanyi, a little fishing-heaven of happy legend; but since the white man had made it a place of horror the black would never go back.

As the ships swung round into Sydney Cove, the guns of the battery at Lieutenant Dawes's Point brayed welcome, scattering the parrots from the trees in shrill clamour of fright. The straggled huts in the clearing woke to ecstatic life. The people flocked to the foreshores shouting and screaming like the parrots, and like the parrots a motley of soldier red and convict grey. They had seen no English ship for over a year at Port Jackson, and the poor ravening wolves went raving mad. As the governor's long-boat pulled inshore, they cheered till their throats were raw.

The settlers were drawn up in two straight lines, and Hunter walked stiffly between them, attended by Shortland and Waterhouse, to the white log hut on the rise.

Scarcely had he passed than the mob closed in, madly embracing the men of the ships, crying for news of London. They whooped and hugged their children in hysteria, and danced with each other and sang. A bundle of letters was snatched from Kent's hand and scrabbled to pieces, for few could read and write.

Matthew looked upon a sea of faces ... evil, half-witted faces with black, decayed teeth and shifty eyes ... clear, good faces that turned away in perpetual fear of recognition or reproach ... young faces, old wizened, crooked faces; highwaymen, reckless; prostitutes, slyly defiant and ashamed; pickpockets, furtive; forgers, poachers, rebels, children not yet in their teens. Near him stood a white-haired blind man, with head bent, listening, and a barefooted woman with strangely well-kept hands.

When they heard there were no store-ships, the racket deepened to a roar. For months they had lived on moulded pease and blacks' offal.

"Are we rats," the blind man cried, "to be trapped in slow starvation?"

Others were baying for "Meat! Meat!"—the baying of hungry hounds. "In the name of the living God," they cried, "give us meat and bread!"

Ruffians in kangaroo pelts threatened with their fists. Women in ragged shifts pressed forward, and brazenly showed their nakedness with ribald jokes and curses. The redcoats brandished their muskets and bludgeoned them back, but now they were shrieking with laughter again as Bennelong came on the scene.

Bennelong, the dude of St James, Beau Brummel of Botany Bay!

Twirling his gold-headed stick, he minced along the landing-stage in a claret-coloured tail-coat most elegant to see. Between a top-hat and a sprigged silk waistcoat, his always vague black countenance was lost in a wide white grin. The smoke signals he sent up from the *Reliance* had brought all his friends and relations, a bedraggled little tribe on the outskirts making for him in a welter of yelping dogs.

In unearthly wailing of love and pride, a skinny old witch was clutching that dazzling figure in her arms. Bennelong mingled his genteel tears with hers. The mud ran down and stained his velvet shoulder, but he did not care. It was his mother, Metty. That anguished pride of hers was pitiful.

While she hugged her swaggering son, his brothers snatched at his hat, dragged his cravat, tried to borrow his shoe-buckles. He smacked them away with his Vauxhall cane.

"Odd bodikin!" he yelled, "begone! Hab at thee, wretch! Ye bloody blackfella, belay!"

Three years the darling of London and Bath society, friend of the Prince of Wales no less, his family appalled him. He lifted his nosegay of painted flowers to his nose, and turned aside and spat, but his modish Chippendale bow only sent them into hysterics, and at his limp and flabby handshake they recoiled. A pot-bellied piccaninny who had lost his pocket-handkerchief and swallowed the full moon offended those delicate sensibilities badly, and his sister Garrangarrang was the last straw. With breathless affection and her baby on her back, Garrangarrang had come from Botany Bay in such a hurry that she left her clothes behind.

"Which way Gooroobarrabooloo?" Bennelong wanted to know. The wife of his heart was missing.

"A-wai-yee!" they wailed. Gooroobarrabooloo was his no longer. She had made off with Karrina, that the whites called Carney, long long time ago. Life was short. This Penelope had no time to lose in waiting for Ulysses.

Bennelong was crestfallen, but wise in the ways of women. He drew out of his pack a rose-coloured petticoat, a pink silk jacket, and gay gipsy bonnet with pink silk streamers. The faces of the convict women grew sharp with envy. Then he carefully rolled them away again, the fit of Governor Phillip to Gooroobarrabooloo from a haberdasher's shop at Bath, but she was not going to get them till she had the grace to show up.

A loud tattoo of the drums at the fort called the convicts to order and toil. The doors of the log prisons opened and the chain-gaings came out, a hang-dog skeleton crew between their redcoat warders. Morose groups went off to their work in the

154

fields. Fields! A few tilled patches of rocky ground that yielded little but heart-break.

In a very few days Matthew knew Port Jackson. There was shamefully little of it to know. It was seven years since Phillip and his First Fleet of eleven ships, all silent and all damned, had sailed for Botany Bay and found a fitter setting for Gethsemane. He freed his thankless thousand in the wilderness, limping from the weight of their chains, shrinking away from the sun. Shimmering bush and sparkling harbour lay all about them, sanctuary of forgiveness and forgetfulness, heritage for their children in the happy years to come. A Providence more merciful than men had brought the prodigals from the Valley of Humiliation into the light, but their hearts were still in darkness and they could not see. They hid themselves in hollow trees, and cried for their far-away England, and the crime and the grime of old years.

If Phillip had visions of a future, they had all dissolved in degradation and despair. His Government House was a spectre, the white log hut falling to decay. There were drab little colonies of hovels of a sickly terra-cotta clay, like beavers' lodges, on the banks of the Tank Stream. The tanks were holes in the rocks.

There were a mill and a government store, crude as a child's drawing, a scar of road over the hill to the brickfields. Human teams harnessed to carts went plodding along it all day, eighteen miles to Parramatta where the gentry had their homes, out of earshot of the screams of the tortured and the fighting of the free, and thirty or forty miles to a poor scattering of half-hearted farms along Lord Hawkesbury's River. There man's inhumanity stopped short.

On the west side of Sydney Cove was the hospital, a rambling village of tents always overcrowded, and a little thatched church of wattle and daub. For the rest, log jails. Smithies, saddlers, shoemakers, bakers and plasterers had their forges and benches under the trees ... and beyond the rim of the hut lights at night the camp-fires of the Indians, dancing and wailing in their *yoolong* ceremonies.

The settlement was a dirty litter of fowls and pigs, streeling women, drunkenness and vice. There were hangings and floggings every day—crowds gaping by the gallows, craning their necks and crowing to the music of the triangles, here and there the chimney-pot hat of a gentleman, rejoicing that the rogues got their deserts. Too many of the brutes had the impertinence to hang themselves, to deprive His Majesty of the pleasure. A lively sight was a thief in the pillory, ears nailed to the board, a gang of idlers pelting mud.

The officers of the *Reliance* ashore gave the festering place a wide berth. Happy were the hours young Flinders spent in the bush, with Doctor George and Samuel, sometimes alone with his thoughts and his love, to lose in its sunny silences the shame and viciousness of men.

Acacias in blossom in the distance, a field of the cloth of gold; goblin shrubs of honey-scented brush; a brown snake gliding and gone; the curious smouldering blue of the deep gullies; leafy stipple of light and shade on the leaves, vivid flowers and bitter little fruits, and the waratah, like a blackfellow's firestick, red as a glowing coal. Spreading fig-trees framed the harbour in slaty silver etchings, with black swans sailing and silhouette of blacks in their canoes. A fascinating land, its fauna and its foliage, its scents and sounds, so new. The very grass beneath his feet was different.

Or they would be off in *Tom Thumb* together, paddling about in her, fishing in the pretty nameless bays, swimming in the pale green shallows, browning on the warm brown rocks in the afternoon sun. Away to the west on a clear day you could see the vague blue line of the mountains, the prison walls, watch-towers of the unknown. The convicts believed there was a lost white race out there.

In a few weeks they had the mazes of Port Jackson by heart, and on a fine day in October *Tom Thumb* made it a race through the Heads for Botany Bay. She weathered well. Samuel was on duty at the fort, totting up sums for the master-at-arms, so they picked up a boy, chewing a straw on the waterfront, to bail—a spare boy, with drain-pipe trousers, an idiotic stare that belied his native intelligence, and a gnawed straw hat. He said his name was Martin. Christian or surname? Bond or free? They never knew. His sailing rig was a clay pipe and a tin, and all he had in the world was lots of time. Matthew envied Martin.

Through the wide sandy reaches of Botany Bay there was little to admire or inspire, except that Cook had been there. They rowed twenty miles farther than Hunter had gone, along his insignificant George III's River, and found in its monotony some hopeful patches of green. That was all. They duly reported to Hunter. He decided to put a little settlement there, and name it Bankstown, in honour of Sir Joseph.

With a gun on his shoulder, and redcoats in the rear, the governor was monarch of all he surveyed, and he conscientiously surveyed it—rode all round his little domain with an eye for secret stills and fertile spots. He found enough of one, few of the other.

In November George Bass rode out with him to cross the Nepean River. In the party was Collins, judge-advocate, soldier turned lawyer, as tanned as his boots, with no knowledge of law but plenty of common sense and a flair for memoirs.

By a camp-fire in the lonely dark they heard a distant bellow.

"The lowing herd," said Doctor George, "winds slowly o'er the lea."

"Lord, I could have sworn it was cattle," remarked Collins.

"Ye'll hear nae cattle i' this colony," said Governor Hunter, "an' ye'll find no lea. Ane solitary cow we had, an' shot her, for she went bad like the hewman haird. O' the four cows an' twa bulls I brocht for Phillip, all else got away an' died i' the bush, or were speared by the blacks, for a' I know. A man was hanged for that, an' he desairved it."

In the morning light they were over the hill to discovery. For cattle were there, the homely red and white of cattle in a sweep of downland brushed silver with sun and dew. Could it be that the convicts were right? A lost civilization?

But when they rode closer, it was plain to see that these cattle had never known man. They sniffed the wind in panic, and wheeled, heads down, for the scrub. As Hunter raced out in the lead to ring them back, a great black bull brandished its long horns, pawed the ground and lumbered at him. He stood and fired—a heavyweight brute, six balls before it fell.

Sixty-one they counted, young and old, Cape of Good Hope breed, progeny of those that had escaped from Phillip's shiftless hungering people. They had found for themselves the pastures that men could not find. The carcass of the black bull was carried back for meat. It was tough, but meat. Hunter declared the downland valley a sanctuary till he could add to the herd.

"Now I ha'e the pastures for the beef," he said, "if I can get beef for the pastures."

"In this Ultima Thule of ours," Doctor George observed to Matthew, "human flesh is whipped into bloody rags and kicked into earth pits, but the flesh and blood of animals is sacred."

Rum ships and women ships came into the harbour, and Port Jackson was hell let loose. In righteous Presbyterian wrath, Hunter tried to stamp down this iniquitous traffic in rum, but, a Canute of antipodean shores, he was powerless, with the redcoats against him, to hold back its inflammatory tide. The New South Wales Corps, the Rum Corps, laughed in his face.

"A set o' the most atrocious characters that ever disgraced hewman nature!" he thundered, "superior in every species o' infamy to the most experrt in wickedness o' the convicts."

Most of them had been kicked out of all the reputable regiments in England, Scotland and Ireland, or convicted themselves, and let loose on condition they flogged their fellows to the ends of the earth. They did their work well— maimed the poor devils in body and mind, goaded them on with liquor, and flayed them to their vicious hearts' content. A "Botany Bay dozen" was a mild beginning—twenty-five lashes. Three hundred with the right and left cat left a mass of quivering pulp.

Since Phillip left, Major Grose had let his soldiers have their own sweet way, with land, with slaves, in the women's huts, in the jails. Grose had the grace to get out when he heard Hunter was coming. He refused to sit down and be meek under naval authority. Weak, pleasant Paterson had taken his place to hand over, more interested in the flax plants and the pepper plants he thought he had discovered here for Sir Joseph Banks than in the scrag-ends of humanity in his care.

Macarthur, paymaster of the New South Wales Corps and inspector of public works—ironic phrase—was cock of the walk in the straggled streets of Sydney, a strikingly handsome busybody, according to Hunter, a clever bully, a firebrand.

His redcoats boarded the ships and bought the rum—at 1s. 6d. a gallon, and sold it at £2 a gallon. It was the anaesthetic for living, and worth ten times the price to deaden pain. The convicts gave their grain and their labour, and thieved and murdered and even prayed, to get it. The first trade route of the colony came direct from Jamaica, but Cape brandy and Bengal wine, mountain dew and arrack and kava, anything from anywhere was just plain rum, so long as it induced dull stupor. A man would sell his wife for four gallons.

The *Reliance* had brought out a boat-builder Tom Moore, but the heavy green woods of the bushland merely sank; a printer, George Hughes, but few could read; a windmill and a town clock, but there were no granaries, no tools, nothing to grind, and the waking hours were best forgotten. The mice in the government store were dying of malnutrition; the white settlers were as naked as the black. There was not a needle and thread, not a bowl and spoon to be bought for love or money. That mattered little, for there was nothing to sew and nothing to eat. The convicts' hour for breakfast was cut out, because they had no breakfast.

Week after week, and still no store-ships, but to add to the general depravity the *Indispensable* came in with 130 female felons, the sweepings of the brothels and jails of London.

On duty with the *Reliance*, a cable's length from shore, Matthew saw the demented creatures, matted hair and scarred shoulders, eyes blinded by a long darkness, slung out in slings, or crawling on hands and knees, too weak to stand. Down in the cesspits of the ship they had hidden the dead among them, to steal the food of the dead. When the hatches were open, came the filthy reek of typhus.

Always the convicts died in scores when the transports came in. They could live in the gloom and the slime down there like the rats that shared their beds, but they could not face the cleansing breath of the sun. Its vital heat burned their diseased bodies, the antiseptic scent of the eucalypt pierced their raddled lungs. In hovels and prisons all their lives, they could not survive the ordeal of fresh air.

More mouths there were to feed, and soon still more. It was alarming how quickly the women concieved in this warm southern land. Practically the whole female population was pregnant or just delivered. Hags that had never had children in their lives before aspired to the halo of motherhood; the others achieved it easily enough, to the girls in their earliest teens. They welcomed the prospect—a stroke of good luck that got them out of work. They sat at the hut doors gossiping and fighting, with babies forever at their breasts ... and those babies were truly beautiful. Born in the shadow of the gallows and the whipping-post, they were healthy and happy and sweet. The children rambled the paths of the bush. Hungry they may have been, but the crime and the grime had missed them.

For all its woe and wickedness, there was an occasional green isle in Port Jackson's sea of misery. In January Sydney saw its first play, when a pack of rakes put on a merry show in a tumble-down store. Matthew and George sat in the pit, and that was a rollicking night. The play was The *Revenge*, with props somehow smuggled—one did not ask how—"From the York Theatre, London". Prices of admission were paid at the door in little bags of shelled corn and covert flasks of rum. Actors and audience alike were warned that if they did not behave themselves they would all be transported in a body next day to Norfolk Island—but that made no difference to the fun.

When a celebrated Barrington stepped down to the bottle-brush and mutton-fat footlights to rant an immortal prologue, that misbegotten theatre, innocent and guilty, howled in unholy glee.

> From distant climes, o'er widespread seas we come,
> Though not with much éclat or beat of drum;
> True patriots all; for be it understood
> We left our country for our country's good... .
> And none will doubt but that our immigration
> Has proved most useful to the British nation.

He got no further. They cheered him to the echo and brought down the ramshackle house. Even the occupant of the vice-regal box permitted himself a dour smile.

Next day Matthew was off a thousand miles across the Pacific with the *Reliance* to Norfolk Island, Cook's queer little isle of funeral pines. Those pines, like the plumes of a hearse, foreshadowed strange and lonely history, yet Lieutenant King had created there a happier Sydney Town, the white stone huts snugged down in a carpet of yellow flax.

Perched on a fertile pinnacle of the drowned continent, undaunted by the great arcs of ocean about him, King had made his patch of black mould as nearly a Utopia as the baleful eye of Port Jackson would let him. Phillip had sent him out there with nine convicts and six women. A kindly, capable man with a belief in human nature, he made a moral of the devil. Now he had a thousand settlers, well-housed. They could at least feed themselves, and keep the island British.

He waved his hand to the legions of the pine-trees marching over the hills, the sea-wind sweeping those dark harp-strings in minor harmonies.

"Our Black Watch against the enemy," he laughed. "Masts for the ships of all the world."

Of his four-square Government House facing the bay, his contented English wife had made a contented English home, her six-year-old boy playing about its lawns with little William Charles Wentworth in petticoats, the toddler son of the doctor. They were the first cherished children of the south that Matthew had seen.

"What are you going to be, little man?" he asked of bright-eyed Phillip Parker King.

"I shall be a sailor like my papa, and find islands of my own."

"That's the spirit!" Matthew patted his dark head. "You'd better follow me."

A number of officers came back with the *Reliance* to Port Jackson, among them D'Arcy Wentworth, to replace the drunken surgeon, Leeds.

The settlement was more than ever stagnation and starvation after a breath of the blue. Death was their daily familiar, and sometimes it seemed that the land was indeed accursed.

Floods rising thirty feet in a day had drowned the farms at the Hawkesbury River, and some of their people. At Parramatta hailstones three inches across whipped the wheat from the ear just as it was ripe. At Toongabbie a Pharaoh's plague of locusts came in a cloud and devoured every blade of green. The game had been driven far away by seven years of hunting, and the watch at South Head looked in vain for an English sail.

There was pitiably little need, now, to choke a man in the rope. The wretches fell dead in the chain-gangs, in the queues waiting for rations at the store, in the bush aimlessly wandering … fell dead in the streets for lack of the heart to live. The heat of summer was fatal to moles of the London slums. Doctor George, assisting the surgeon Balmain at the hospital, its tents spreading like an evil white fungus, rowed home each night in *Tom Thumb*, not caring to speak of the day.

On Sunday the men of the ships went on parade to service at the wattle and daub church, to hear Mr Johnson preach. They were the congregation. The convicts never dared to come past the redcoats gaming and lounging under the trees, where they ran the gauntlet of taunts and sneers, and maybe a playful whip-cut. The texts were all of the anger of God, and to them the anger of men was the day's sufficient evil.

"Repent ye, and be converted, for ye know not when the hour of judgment shall strike!" ranted Mr Johnson, glaring at the bare bark walls above the blue-jackets' blameless heads, where a fierce sun slanted like an avenging sword … and little Barrow, a midshipman of the *Supply* went for a swim in the heat of the day after dinner, and died of cramp on deck before their eyes! That week, a boat that the *Reliance* sent down to fish, turned turtle in Botany Bay, and five men drowned.

Senior Midshipman Flinders was in charge of the search party. He found no traces of either boat or men, but good company in a knowledgeable greybeard camped in a seaside glade. He was Henry Hacking, waiting for the ships to pass to pilot them in to Port Jackson, and meantime hunting kangaroos for his pot. He said there was a river away to the south that was not on Cook's chart.

"We'll take *Tom Thumb* and find it!" announced Matthew to Doctor George when he came back.

Kent condemned the voyage as madcap. Shortland said no eight-foot tub could live through it, and Waterhouse washed his hands of the whole affair. The governor gave them grudging leave, wagging his finger in warning, but when they suggested that Samuel would be a handy boy, he was adamant. The Flinders family was not going to lose two of its sons at once. So George went in search of Martin. He found him still by the waterfront, chewing the same straw. Martin was willing, and *Tom Thumb's* crew was complete.

They stocked her that evening with a couple of muskets, a few bags of food, and a bucket to bail. As she was off down the harbour in the track of the setting sun, the *Reliance* wickedly answered Doctor George's pennant of farewell, fluttering a foot above his head, with an ensign at half mast! That night they slept on a rock in the bay for an early start in the morning.

Three boys in a boat on a sunlit sea—they cleared the Heads at daybreak on 25 March, and stood out for a wakening breeze, by dawn swinging south.

Under the frowning brow of the cliffs, the cockleshell danced along. Her petal of sail was a challenge to fate in the rough and tumble Pacific.

Now they had started there could be no turning back ... on the one hand those sinister broken cliffs hundreds of feet sheer, ramparts against the ocean, the great green tides crashing in at their feet in futile fury of foam, on the other hand for hundreds of miles a waste of waters tossing, tossing to that far-away land that the Maoris called the Long White Cloud.

All day *Tom Thumb* went spanking down in the arms of a boisterous norther. When the shadow of the cliffs slanted black on the sea, they were level with Cook's Hat Hill, and bowling on past it, no hope of landing, still sprinting before the wind. The sharp teeth of the rocks inshore were certain destruction. There was nothing for it but to spend the night in the boat.

They cheerfully gnawed their salt junk and quaffed cold water, and through the long darkness tossed in the vague. Doctor George's six feet two folded into sections. Martin curled up like a cat in the prow, and Matthew nodding at the tiller—a tight fit and a lively lullaby.

Two or three pleasant little isles smiled them welcome in the morning. Islands were young Flinders's weakness, and for these they decided to steer; but water was low in the casks, so at the first sign of a break in the cliffs *Tom Thumb* turned its nose for the shore, to buffet beyond the barricades in a roaring Niagara of surf. A game little scout, she ran up and down the line, but no picket gate could she find in these foaming defences. At last the valiant George stripped off and swam a cask ashore. By a rill in the woodland he filled it to the ninth rung, and pushed it before him through the waves till he reached the *Tom Thumb's* side.

Matthew was swinging her clear of the breakers with one hand, lending the other to Martin to haul the cask aboard while George hoisted and clung to the gunwale, when a South Coast comber caught them all amidships. George, Matthew, Martin, *Tom Thumb* and the cask went hurtling head over turkey a hundred somersaulting yards in for the shore. They landed well in on the beach.

Matthew had enjoyed this sort of thing with a coco-nut palm-leaf for a surf-board among the laughing brown people of Otaheite, but here he was not so sure, for all their powder and stores were swamped. For hours they battled their tiny tub back against the breakers, George scarlet as a crayfish all over, his fair skin peeling like a peach. It was late in the afternoon when they got her off.

Those smiling islands were a snare and a delusion, and a long way farther than they seemed. By the time they arrived the sun had set, and not a landing could they find. They dropped the stone anchor off the point and huddled down together, to cramp and toss through another chilly night.

Early next morning they zigzagged back to the main, and landed at last in the lee of a saddled hill. A southerly buster came romping in—no hope to show sail against it—so they decided to make the best of their forced leisure in drying off the powder and catching a fish or two.

Bracken for a fire—Matthew was off to the woods. With his arms full of brown fern, he started up with a jerk ... a bush was leering at him with a horrible, painted stare, nose-bones a foot long and a tiara of sharks' teeth.

"Indians!"

He gave a shout of warning, and skittled for the beach. The bush stood up and stalked him on long black legs, another bush striding in the rear.

"Indians!" echoed the boy Martin in weak, shrill treble.

"Indians?" said Doctor George. "The deuce! So they are."

Matthew stood. The Indians stood. Doctor Bass strode slowly in from his fishing on the rocks. All five stood, stock still.

"Hunter said these blacks are cannibals," Matthew muttered to George.

"They look like cannibals. They smell like cannibals. My God, Matt, if they are we shall never know!"

The Indians stood like statues, green branches in their hands. Those straight black bodies were rank with fish oil. The offal of years was festooned in their beards and clogged in their matted hair. They had the hunter's trick of glancing suspiciously left and right under bushy brows without moving the head. It conveyed the impression of craft and ferocity ... and the muskets were clogged with sea-rust.

The silence was awkward. Who would be first to move ... war or peace?

Matthew tried a hail in Bennelong's language, the only native language he knew, a few words learned when the

Reliance first sailed under the southern stars. They were a hundred miles south of Botany Bay, but it worked like a charm. The Indians each showed a missing tooth in surprise and friendly smiles.

"Dilba!" shouted the first man, smiting his hairy chest. He waved his hand to his comrade. "Jeri-jeri."

This called for etiquette.

"Flinders!" reciprocated Matthew, tapping himself on the shirt button, and "Doctor George!" with a graceful sweep of his arm.

"Belinda" was easy, but Doctor George wore an old red coat, so they let him go as "Sojer". He indignantly denied the charge, but "Sojer" he must be.

They showed a keen sartorial interest in the white boys' beardless chins, and tried to pull off their own odorous whiskers. Ever obliging, George got out the shears. Dilba first, then Jeri-jeri submitted with witching smiles. They tossed their beards with disgust in the sea, and trotted round with hairbrush heads and scrubby, happy faces, occasionally wiping their clammy hands on whiskers no longer there.

These new friends were very helpful. Jeri-jeri speared their breakfast from the rocks in less time than Doctor George could bait the hooks, and Dilba offered to pilot them round to a river with ducks and fish—he made the motion of flying things, and pointed with his lips. Matthew was hot on the trail of that river. After the meal together the five piled on board *Tom Thumb*. Manfully she carried them round the point with no other mishap than a cracked oar.

The river was not much more than a creek, but its banks were a place of arresting beauty. Leafy filigree of carboniferous ferns had stored the heat of the sun in cold brown clay centuries deep. Rounding a curve, they found a camp of blacks' gunyahs under the forest trees, the blue incense of their eucalypt fires drifting in filmy veils through sun-flecked boughs. An army of sullen warriors crowded down to the water. In silence they watched the boat come by, and ground in the shallows.

"This looks like an ambush. Keep near the boat," George murmured. "I'll mend the oar, and you get the powder dry."

Boy Martin rowed with his heart in his boots.

Another band of hunters strolled into the scene. All looked distrustfully at "Sojer's" red coat. When Flinders pointed to the richly-fertile hills, they answered "Illawarra".

He turned to spread the powder in the sun. They tasted it and spat it out. He took up a musket to clean it, and there was instant commotion — a sudden scatter for spears.

"Drop that gun!" shouted George in consternation.

Matthew already had dropped it, with sheepish smiles and pantomime of innocence and peace. They scowled and muttered together. These natives had heard of the white man's death-stick. Things looked black.

It was a critical moment, but Dilba was their saviour. He was strutting from group to group demonstrating his hair-cut — stroking his cool chaps, rubbing his stubble, brandishing the sail shears and showing how easily the job was done. With a flash of inspiration Matthew, by gesture, offered to barber the lot. One old hirsute Job was game to try it. Amused, the others crowded round, keeping an eye on the gun.

Bally white eyes in ebony black followed the shining steel with awe as it swept away the beards of their generation. At every snip of the blades the customer jumped and the audience jabbered. Ill-humour had vanished. The unshaven were eager and the shaven comparing clips. It was a tall order playing Delilah to so many Samsons, but while Martin filled up with water and George mended the oar, Midshipman Flinders shaved for dear life. When the blades flashed under their noses, those savages shivered with fright. Matthew in boyish mischief was tempted to a snip.

"Shall I?" he asked George.

"We're dead men if you do!" boomed George.

The barber's chair was empty, the oar mended, the powder dry, and *Tom Thumb* ready to go. But now there was a crafty move to souvenir those entertaining devils. Dilba tried to cajole them farther up the river with promise of good times and high living, conveyed in gesture of big fish and fat belly. They smiled and nodded, but pointed out to sea, graciously retiring, as from royalty, without turning their backs. They felt safer when the little skiff swung into mid-stream. In the end, the blacks came with them, shouting and singing, pushing them down to the sea.

"Phew!" whistled Matthew as they waved a glad farewell to the shorn black sheep of Illawarra. *Tom Thumb* took up the running to the south.

By twilight a shadowed cove showed up in the lee of the cliffs, and gratefully they pulled in—their first night ashore in three. Too weary for a night-watch they threw themselves down, and slept on the cool sand. After nights and days of cramp and toss, it was soft as a bed of roses.

In morning light they explored. There were black lumps of shale about that looked like coal. Matthew remembered Mynheer Wanjon in Koepang, and his shale that the convicts had found along these coasts. Now that he knew a little geology, he was fairly certain it was coal.

"I wonder," said Doctor George, turning it over with his foot. But *Tom Thumb* had no room for ballast, and they threw the specimens away.

The weather was breaking now, and seas were rough. It would be madness to go farther against the wind. They started back.

A day's hard rowing had brought them only four leagues nearer home, and dusk came in black clouds to the southward. Snakes of lightning writhed on the horizon.

A seventy-mile gale burst above them in the darkness. *Tom Thumb* was riding a switchback of rollers ten feet high, up to the crest and down to the trough, flooding as the hissing foam came inboard. Straining their eyes in the blackened night, they could see no shelter. The squall had blotted out the stars.

Matthew steered by the shadow of the cliffs, and the roar of the surf at their feet—George clung to the bellying sail—boy Martin bailed doggedly. They ran for an hour in the teeth of the storm, but their little ship was giving up the ghost. She could not survive that maelstrom of sea for ten minutes longer.

High breakers ahead!—and no outline of cliffs beyond them. There was time for only one mistake, and were they going to make it? Screaming to each other above the wind, they dragged down the mast and sail, grappled the oars, and shot her straight for the reefs. Her nose went under in the creaming smother of spray.

Like a gallant little hunter to the hurdle, the *Tom Thumb* cleared the barrier.

Quiet water ... but another white blur ahead! All right! They'd chance it! ... False alarm! It was a ghostly curve of beach. They were safe in the crescent of a snug little cove, and all the peril past.

Shoulder-high they carried *Tom Thumb* through the waves, lit a fire and sat around it laughing, boys together. Life was a grand adventure, even the stormy sea their friend.

The rest of the journey was calm seas and smiling weather. They found the little river that Cook had missed, with sleepy lagoons and a glorious beach in a paradise of bushland. For two days they fished and explored there, naming the place Port Hacking. The islands where they tossed offshore they gave to their little comrade, Martin, the beach of their deliverance was Providential Cove, and Dilba's home-country Illawarra.

A bouncing breeze bowled them home, and after her nine days' buffeting *Tom Thumb* nestled in under the wing of the *Reliance*.

The governor was dryly pleased to see the truants—he had doubted that he ever would again. Thanks to these two young daredevils, his domain was growing. He invited them up to Government House, to a dinner of Nepean beef cooked by a convict lassie, and the roast beef of Old England could not have been better.

Thoughtfully chewing a cow-heel at the vice-regal board, a fellow-guest was Bennelong with a badly broken jaw.

Bennelong, his fine feathers moulted, had fallen on evil days. First of the New Hollanders to submit to civilization, he was killed by kindness and wrecked in rum. The whites called him a black man, and the blacks called him a white man. Nobody wanted him now.

Whimpering, he told his tale of woe. Gooroobarrabooloo had come back, grabbed the rose-coloured petticoat, and then showed him her heels. For two glorious days she had been the belle of Port Jackson, then she traded away her glory for a bottle of fire-water and went bush to Carney with nothing on. Bennelong threw away his rifle, and took a spear and went after her... but *a-wai-hee!* The hand of the hunter had lost its cunning. He missed Carney every time, and Carney beat him to a pulp. When he went down to Coogee, and pirated Boorea's woman, Boorea said "That all same white-fella!" and knocked his teeth out with a nulla-nulla. Bennelong was cynical. White-fella talk of loving a brudder was gammon. Now they were all at the brick-fields, waiting to spear him. He dare not go out without a bodyguard of soldiers. Gubnor was his only friend.

Blubbering like a baby, he left the table, and came back in a hurry for his after-dinner port.

Schemes for further excursions were cut short. Hunter wanted cattle to feed his starving people. They had not tasted meat in seven years. The *Reliance* and *Supply* were to be patched up for a journey to the Cape. Doctor George's spare time was at his own disposal, but Midshipman Flinders must return to duty on board.

As they walked down in the bright moonlight to Paterson's house in George Row, the settlement was smoking with rebellion, a double guard on duty. The *Marquis of Cornwallis* had come in with Irish rebels, and a madness of mutiny on board. The soldiers shot down the mutineers like dogs, and women were hanged and flogged to death for putting ground glass in the officers' porridge and stealing the table knives.

"As if we hadn't hell enough," said Collins, "without importing the Irish."

Paterson's house was a hot-bed of libel and intrigue. The governor and Macarthur were fighting like wild-cats, the soldiers were brazenly flouting the law, there were rumours that a French fleet was about to seize the place. There were thefts and murders every night, and hangings every day.

"These ragged brutes had the temerity," said Grimes, the surveyor-general, "to steal the geese from my back door. They will follow the dictates of their vicious inclinations!"

"The dictates of their starving stomachs," corrected Doctor George.

Back in their cabin on the *Reliance*, in the moonlit stillness of the harbour, they shared a night's good work on a chart together. Matthew's quill scratched its jubilation. At last he could write a new name in the map.

8

A Map Without a Name

Great Britain had bought The Cape. The Dutch, as Hunter had said, would sell for good gold guilders—£600,000 cash down the price of a protectorate. Port Jackson, for the time being, was reasonably safe from the French. It might even get some salt pork when the Admiralty remembered it, and could travel ten thousand miles to buy its beef.

But all through the southern winter the forties were roaring. No ship could live against "the brave west winds". To arrive dead west, they must sail due east for sixteen thousand miles— under the eagle beak of the Horn, where the Atlantic and the Pacific fight their eternal battle in clash of winds and waters, on past the ragged Falklands with their ice-rivers of quartz, across a desert of sea to the rocky caravanserai of Tristan da Cunha, then two thousand five hundred blank sea-miles to Africa. That was the route Hunter had taken in the *Sirius* for bread. Now Kent and Waterhouse would follow. The world was round, and they would go backwards round the world.

The old war-horses lay rotting in the harbour. They must have new armour. H.M.S. *Reliance* was a xylophone of hammers all day. H.M.S. *Supply* was beyond redemption.

"Don't drive a tack," Kent warned them, "or she'll come asunder. Leave her to me. I'll keep her together by faith."

Hunter mourned his museum piece, his fort, his flagship, his link with Phillip's dream and civilization, but he wanted every hoof for the cow pastures, and so the *Supply* must go.

While Matthew was tethered aboard the *Reliance*, shouting himself hoarse to Whitechapel dolts and Epsom touts who could not tell a boom from a belaying pin, Doctor George was off, in June, to find a pass through the mountains. To him that zigzag of blue seemed a simple crossing.

Colonel Paterson withered his airy nonchalance. With Commissary Palmer, he had been there, following one of the rivers. All normal rivers he had known, from the Tweed to the Limpopo, diligently plodded to the highlands and the hills, but in this weird country—"Nature reversed" as Major Ross had called it—they disappeared in sand, or leapt like he-goats from crag to crag. Five waterfalls had damped their stores and their ardour. The sixth sent them ignominiously back, with no more than a few botanical freaks for Sir Joseph. Watkin Tench of Phillip's fleet before him had been baffled by static cliffs and earthquake chasms. Matthew's old friend at Botany Bay, Henry Hacking, had climbed those broken peaks to never-ending ridges.

George blithely loaded his packhorses, and with two convict bearers, whistled away west. He was back in a month, a ravenous and rueful man, his clothes in tatters.

Fifteen days and nights in rain and sun, he had rambled a delirium of scrubby gullies to where the iron cliffs thrust their buttresses to the sky. He scaled the broken heights with his climbing irons, let himself down into black ravines with his ropes and his grappling-hooks, staggered on through horizontal jungle, scratched and clung, crawled on hands and knees, and dangled down in space till he reached the crest ... and covered his eyes and shuddered, for the earth was hacked from beneath his feet in dizzying miles of air to the tufted tops of the gum-trees.

Goliath shadows sprawled across a madman's maze of valleys. Beyond, there rose another range ... moon-mountains and moon-craters, skeleton ribs of earth veiled in a thousand shades of filmy blue.

Doctor George had seen red water flowing, red prehistoric beasts, and two crows flying that must have lost their way. He had seen one solitary native wandering like a damned soul in one of Dante's pits.

"Those peaks!" he cried to Matthew. "Sublime! Appalling! You feel you're falling from the hand of God, with all hell yawning underneath. The spiked stone walls, Matt ... no escape!"

"A landsman's job!" laughed Matthew. "I'd sooner take a header from the maintop down to Davy's locker. A league inland, and I'm all at sea."

A week later he was at sea. In trappings of tar and varnish, H.M.S. *Reliance* and H.M.S. *Supply* were off down the harbour together, swinging to the south of the Long White Cloud, following the straight curves of their geodetic course.

The first thousand miles to Norfolk Island were the first few strokes of the brush on a gigantic mural that might never be finished. Week after week, month after month, they watched the spirit-level of the horizon rise and fall, the swollen sails booming in the prevailing wind like marble boulders. Shrouds sang in the E flat harmonies of the forties. The fluttering pennant at the masthead was an arrow, pointing to the Cape. The only realities were the clouds and the storm petrels, and the bergs glistening blue and grumbling deep.

Weaving concentric circles with the latitudes, they were blown round the globe. They clung to the wind, and the world turned above them.

Eagle's claws of the Horn stretched out for them where they climbed the Himalayan slopes of ocean crested in perpetual foam, and tossed like toys into the hollows. Ghost fiords of the Falklands faded away in that welling of the waters. Tristan da Cunha was no more than a spray on the wave.

The neat little farms at the Cape seemed petty and unreal to those who had come from the freehold of the deep. Between Sugarloaf and Lion's Rump, they furled sails in the fold.

Kent, Shortland and Waterhouse were off to the cattle market. They knew nothing about cattle, but the crafty, too-courteous Dutch dealers would teach them to be wary.

Matthew watched them trundling away in the dust in an old Cape cart.... His Majesty's factotums. How many he had known ... shabby lieutenants on a few pounds a week fighting for their lives all their lives in the war and on the waves in rotten ships ... ambassadors to the foreigner and the cannibal, trading for wheat, gold, pearls, pepper, territory ... diplomats, chancellors and high financiers to the feathered savage, walking encyclopaedias of wide-world knowledge, vegetable, animal and mineral.

He thought of Bligh, planting his oranges and his apple-trees in odd corners of earth; of Tobin, with never a lesson in his life, picturing unnamed harbours ... homeless men, nameless men, their wave-washed journals the first pages in the chronicles of empire, their future at the worst a watery grave, at the best an old age of cards, prating to their families on Navy half-pay ... and here he was aspiring to be one of them. Why? "I gave my heart to know wisdom."

While he was at the Cape of Good Hope, he passed his lieutenant's examination, and was appointed to H.M.S. *Supply*. Lieutenant Matthew Flinders, R.N.—at twenty-one. What would the little doctor and Sub-Lieutenant John Flinders say to that?

"Hold your horses!" said Kent. "I've been a lieutenant, Mr Flinders, for seventeen years. There's a long life, I hope and pray, before ye!"

Kent was inordinately interested in a small flock of sheep, two dozen Spanish merinos, bearded in wool to the ground, from royal herds guarded by the insane Philippes even as the silkworms of China. Property of a Dutch government official bankrupt to an English trader, they might be sold to pay the lawyers' fees.

Hunter said sheep could not live in the rank scrub of New South Wales, but Paymaster Macarthur had a mongrel dozen or so, ridiculous creatures from the Cape and Calcutta, with Roman noses and coarse useless wool. Guarded from the blacks by convict shepherds, they were fending for themselves well enough on his grant-of-land farm at Parramatta. If Hunter would not buy these merinos for the government, perhaps Macarthur would take them. Kent staked his few pounds a week against their shaggy fleeces. He gave up his cabin to be their fold.

Waterhouse had given up his cabin to a herd of black Cape cattle. Samuel, with a bright smile, was standing a watch as cow-herd, never ailing, never complaining, studying his lunar tables with his officer brother, and giving the brightest promise. Many a happy excursion they shared from the trim Cape Town to the tumbled heights of Table Mountain.

Every hoof and horn, every bale of hay they could pack aboard was slung down the hatchways and corralled on the decks by hulking, naked negroes till the ships were floating barns.

Smelling like a byre on a rainy night, the *Supply* in August lay in the lee of Smits van Winkel, warned by the Dutch and British skippers that she would never make the crossing, but stubbornly waiting for the *Reliance* and a favourable wind.

Suddenly her slack sails filled in a gale. No argument, no beating back to haven—she was off, two days before her time, pelting across the Indian whether she liked it or not.

Typhoons took her in their teeth and shook her like a rat. Day after day the rising peaks of water slapped at the clouds. When darkness fell, the terrified lowing of the cattle was as the moaning of the sea. God knows how the creatures lived—their hay was floating in salt water. "It's those fat-bellied, lean-livered Boer farmers," Kent explained. "They cross them with chameleons so they can feed on air."

Whiplash Kent, at sea since he was twelve, the sea was his enemy and his friend. Thin lips set in a relentless smile, blue-grey eyes for far sight from his Highland mother, "I'll make her swim!" he said. The *Supply* was falling to pieces about his ears. Night and day by the wheel he lashed her on. When her timber-heads fell off, he was first to hear it. When her stern worked loose, he hauled it in and bound it round with chains. Her sides opened and gushed in water, her rotten bulwarks and her beams caved in … he cobbled them with canvas and tar. When she reeled to drown, he cut away her t'-gallant mast, and cried on God in curses that were prayers, and with his own hands straining dragged her back.

In months of whirling foam and storm, they scarcely knew where they were, nor cared, so long as they made New Holland. There was nothing but New Holland, in six thousand miles, to make. "I hope there's enough of it there," said Kent, "to catch us when we break."

Kent, with a black stubble of beard and eyes red with watching ... screaming above the tumult to the men in the shrouds, to the men at the pumps, who never dared to leave them ... snatching a mouthful as he ran aloft himself to swing and sway in the braces ... snatching an hour's doze, wet through, on a coil of rope, and listening, even in his sleep.

Kent was the ship. She woke when he woke, and battled. She went down if he gave up. Flinders learned from him to make a dead thing live—to fight the sea. He learned from Kent that a man can defy the fates.

Port Jackson Heads at last. They felt foolish in calm water—felt foolish in the narrow, dirty streets where men were philandering and whipping each other.

Kent went ashore to sleep. His command was a bag of bones.

"A museum piece for ye now, sir," he grinned to Hunter, "if she never was before. Cherish her well, but she'll do ye no more work."

"I'll no see a guid ship go waste, Wullie. She rides well in dead water. We'll juist keep her by against the time the colony micht ha'e a wee bit to stoore."

Thirty-five sheep the convicts landed, and twenty-seven of the cows. Hunter was grateful for the cattle, indifferent to the sheep. Macarthur bought the thirteen merinos still alive for fifteen guineas each. That meant £195 to Kent, more than a year's salary. He spent it to buy a house.

Forty-one days after them the *Reliance* arrived, but only just. Gales had shivered her timbers, and set her masts awry. Her pumps were working all the way up the glass-calm harbour.

Waterhouse and Shortland said they were surely born to be hanged.

About a third of their stock had died on the journey. They brought thirty-three sheep and forty-nine cattle, a few for private citizens, three lambs for King at Norfolk Island—but King, they learned, had been invalided home. Harry Waterhouse invested in a tiny little farm, that he bought near the house of Doctor Balmain. Farms were more encouraging now. While they were away, George Bass had walked from the cow pastures to the south coast near Illawarra—good meadows all the way.

Sails of a windmill were turning on Port Jackson's humble skyline, with a half-built tower for the clock to tell the wretches the time. A new Government House of white brick was impressive on the rise, a camp of blacks and a redcoat sentry in front of it, not forgetting a new log jail. When Matthew came up from the foreshore, he would stop for a word with Tom Moore, the boat-builder, hammering at the hull of a schooner on the beach … the *Cumberland*, a sleuth to chase the convicts that escaped.

"Once you get a nail through them, these hard timbers make her tight, Mr Flinders," Tom said. "If you're taking her yourself at any time, sir, I guarantee safe sailing."

"It may be, Tom," smiled Matthew. "Indeed, I wish I could."

The convicts were still wandering, wandering anywhere, wandering mad. Matthew and George met them miles away in the bush, old men and their granddaughters, fainting mothers and their eager sons, men absconded from the woodcutters' gangs carrying their axes, desperadoes dragging the ball and chain. Most of them were of the Irish rebels and the Scotch Martyrs, following the visions that had made them exiles, visions of a different world and the brotherhood of man. With a bag of offal or a sack of sago, they asked the way to China. Others were stealing the fishing-boats, and steering along the path of the moon out into the Pacific.

"'Tis pitifu'," said Governor Hunter. "They'll mak' nane ither but the Heavenly Shoore, an' if we suffer them to escape into the Hielands they are lost, not only to us but to a' the wurruld, for perish they must."

The governor, alone in his white house, grieved for his demented, tormented people. Lacking the instinct of cattle, they could never find a way out. Many of the flogging sentences he commuted to work for the public good, but the public good was an ironic phrase in dealing with these cringing inferior wretches. They whined, and wept, and coughed in squalor, and drank themselves into horrors and crimes with the rubbish they fermented in filth. They would steal, and they would not work, giving the soldiers every excuse to cut them to strips in the triangles.

Hunter made a magnanimous gesture. He told them to select four men, and he would equip them, to find a path to freedom … but the infamy of the convicts knew no bounds. An ambush lay in wait to kill the men for their stores and their guns, so a guard was sent with them. They found good pastures for a hundred miles south of Parramatta, and the wild cattle increased to 170. Then, as on all the others, the prison walls closed in.

Port Jackson provided its usual grim diversions, the dogleg streets sordid as ever. The transport *Britannia* arrived with rumours of fiendish floggings, women's bodies thrown over the side and no questions asked. The *Jane Shore* never arrived at all. There was a witch hunt at Parramatta that year, and a rising of the Irish at Toongabbie. Either the rebels or their enemies set ablaze the wide acres of corn that were the only food for the hungry.

Hunter and Macarthur were fighting like tigers now. Two redcoats sacked and burnt the house of one of Hunter's servants. The governor put them in irons … and anonymous letters blew about in the mud, accusing him of graft and corruption, and of running the traffic in rum. Vile slanders, he learned, were in circulation in high places in London. He swore it was the paymaster's doing.

In a fine flourish of ink and feathers, he referred the Secretary of State, for his character, to two-thirds of the flag-officers of the Royal Navy, head of the list Earl Howe, whom he had served for twenty-five years.

"I need only add further, my lord," he wrote to the Duke of Portland, "that if the sacred person of the Saviour were to appear in this colony in its present state, there are people who would readily prepare for him another crown of thorns, and erect a second cross for his Crucifixion—and none, I am persuaded, more readily than the person of whom I have complained."

On a crystal clear morning, the Pacific a gentle tumble of blue to the far horizon, two *Reliance* sailors, clambering the cliffs at South Head, found the headless body of the watch thrown down, butchered with a white man's knife, and two days dead. The troopers arrested a convict who had quarrelled with the man. For lack of better proof of his guilt, they set him to bury the body. The corpse did not shrink nor bleed at his touch … a sure proof of his innocence, so they had to let him go free.

The next day, John Fenlow, a colonist, found guilty of the murder of his servant in a rage, was strung up to the gallows. The hanged were always thrown to the surgeon, for dissection in the cause of medical science. Balmain called Doctor George to assist at the postmortem. Licking their lips and shouting, a mob of two or three hundred followed the horrible thing to the hospital morgue, to jostle within its lime-washed walls and gape. Shrill women with babies in their arms and children tugging at their skirts, louts and old lags, they pressed as close to the surgeon's bench as the guard would let them, fascinated to see the inside of a man, squeaking and shrieking at every cut of the scalpel.

The redcoat took the gall-stones from Balmain's hand, and held them up to the crowd to show the bile that had brought about the murderer's evil temper … and those leering faces, young and old, were a frieze of devils to Doctor George.

"Let me out of this!" he muttered to Balmain, and paddled off in *Tom Thumb* for the *Reliance*, where Matthew was second lieutenant now, helping to build her again.

"'Tis only human ignorance and hate," he said, "that make this country hell. Out of the nightmare, the air is pure, the mind wholesome, the land a dream of heaven. George, we must get away and find it."

That evening, as they watched the harbour sunset stippling a westward lane of cove with gold, one of the ship's boats that had been fishing down the coast came back with two bearded, famished strangers. In a ring of Turks' caps on the half-deck, John Thistle, the cox, was telling a stirring story. John was a particular friend of George and Matthew, a fine type of Scottish seaman, forever whistling "Bonnie Dundee". Amused at his eloquence, they wandered up to hear him.

"A stream o' smewk," he was telling, "black as the de'il an' blacker! Ah kenned, d'ye see, 'twas no a negro's fire, so ah hove ashoore, an' there yon puir gewks, nakked as the day they were boorn, an' keenin' juist like bairnies. The last twa callants o' a sheep-wreckit crew ... a crew o' seventeen, wull ye believe it?... creepin' twa hunder leagues on bluidy feet, devourin' shellfish frae the rocks an' weeds frae the wood. The ithers a' perished, crows reivin' their bones. Why, juist i' the nick o' time we were for these, or yon black stream o' smewk wad be their fewneral plewm!"

"About this smoke, John—" Matthew asked him, "why should you think it was more than an Indians' fire?"

"Och! 'twas nae moore than a bittie o' shale, Mr Matthew, sirr, a wee scrap o' rotted shale they pickit up on the sand."

"I'll swear that shale of ours is coal," said Doctor George to Matthew.

Thistle was off with Waterhouse to take the tidings and the castaways to the governor. The last survivors of the wreck were sorry remnants of humanity. Clarke, the supercargo, told a tale of fighting endless leagues of scrub, where hill and valley fell to beach and cliff in fold on fold of rugged grandeur glorious to behold, heart-breaking to climb; of the silver blades of many rivers ripping the fabric of the valleys to where the crest of distant alps gleamed white in quartz or snow. He told of cannibals stealthily following through the jungle, painted faces and upraised spears; of kindly tribes who fed them and forded them on to take up their terrible journey, of the dwindling of their comrades left behind to wander and die.

Their ship was the *Sydney Cove*, Calcutta to Port Jackson, with 7000 gallons of rum. Flung away on an uncharted isle in the Furneaux, Captain Hamilton had sent his crew for help. Four white men and thirteen Lascars, they were tossed up in a gale on a ribbon of strand that runs for ninety miles. With no food and no guns they braved the frowning forests and scaled the battlemented rocks, for four months and 600 miles of fear and hunger to the splash of water and the termite hovels of Port Jackson, the only civilization in the south. Two of them had lived the ordeal through. The fate of the others was a mystery. Hamilton was living on rice and rum at the Furneaux Isles.

Hunter sent down his pretences of ships, the 40-ton *Francis* that he kept as a link with Norfolk Island, and the little 10-ton *Eliza* under Archie Armstrong, master of the *Supply*. A month later, the *Francis* came back with Hamilton and half his fiery cargo. The *Eliza*, in a gale, had gone down with all hands.

Doctor Bass took John Thistle, with a whaleboat and crew, and went down the coast to find news, or relics, of Clarke's party. They picked up a pocket compass, and saw a native running in a ragged shirt—a doleful circumstantial evidence.

Back in the cabin on the *Reliance*, George threw a glittering black nugget on the desk. "It's coal, Matt. Seven leagues south of Cape Solander, and practically all the way we travelled in *Tom Thumb*. I traced a scar of it seven feet deep and running for six unbroken miles, plain as day—or I should say night—in the cliffs. On the upward swing of the wave, you can touch it with your hand from a boat. It runs down in about two miles further into the sea … the surf swings back with every tide on coal! But you can't land there for miles, except on the little sandy beach between Saddle Point and the Providential Cove, under the inland cliffs the natives call Bulli. Lend me your *Tom Thumb* chart. I want to attach it to this report to Hunter. A good discovery, Matthew, my lad. At least it keeps these homeless beggars from freezing, and you never know, it might be worth more some day. I've seen Lancashire coal that gives out a regular candle-flame, and in Whitby they make the stuff into jewellery."

"Anything more of the new coast?" Matthew wanted to know.

"New! It's as old as Lucifer. Here in this brittle black rock is a lost world, where the savage sea-beasts with rows of teeth came out of the slime of creation, where the tail-less pterodactyl flew, the brontosauri lumbered in the smoking mud, and the spiny palms raised their green fronds under a steaming sun. They at least remain. O Matt, if we could but read the age of this ageless prehistoric land!"

"Here! Here!" Matthew laughed at him. "The penetrating Bass. You seem to have caught fire with your coal, George, but a rare discovery it is, and I congratulate you. I wish it were gold or silver."

In his ranger coat of kangaroo-skin as tanned as his tanned forehead, hazel eyes bright with humour and ambition, George dusted the Bulli sand from his leggings.

"Silver would do. Can you not see me, a Pizarro of the south, carrying it home in *Tom Thumb* to mint into George III florins?"

One night a shot rang out, echoing down the harbour. A gang of broad-arrow buccaneers had made off with Tom Moore's *Cumberland* on her maiden trip to the Hawkesbury. Shortland chased them in an armed boat, sixty miles to the north. He came back a month later with a fairy-tale of coal — serpentine reefs and humps and islands of coal at the mouth of a new river he had named for Governor Hunter.

"Jewellery!" said Shortland. "There's enough up there for a city of jet in the Arabian Nights. It's another Newcastle."

When he heard of the river, Matthew began to fret. Exploring and surveying were his special commission. He asked the governor was there any chance.

Hunter, chin in hand, thought the matter out.

"The trouble is a boat, lad. God or the de'il couldna charter us a ship when they're a' carryin' rum. Hoots! I hae it! This

Hamilton here o' the *Sydney Cove*, a Glasgie Scot an' a rascal trader, he's our man. He's brocht up nae moore than half his carrgo, an' pesterin' me but yester-eve for a ship to collect the rest ... me that has nocht but the *Francis*, an' her a walnut fu' o' wurrums. But I'll send her. Aye, I'll send her, an' I'll mak' him pay for it, an' I'll send you wi' her. Look aroun', laddie, an' write whut ye find, an mak' us a charrt o' the Furneaux."

Matthew went down to the foreshore walking on air, to pick up George and *Tom Thumb* near the big brass lantern at the circular quay. George was a little crestfallen that he should be out of the picture.

"Why not see him to-night?" Matthew urged. "I found him in fine good humour for expansion. The cattle are thriving, there's a store-ship sighted from the Head, and they've just found a new little animal, a furry sloth of a small grey bear that lives in the tops of the trees. It climbs with its baby on its back, and cries with its doubled-up fists in its eyes, exactly like a baby. The natives call it *koala,* and 'tis surely a quaint citizen to send to Sir Joseph in London. The governor will show you. Go along up. I'll wait."

George came back exultant. He could take the *Reliance* whaleboat and, no hang-dog crew, but six of His Majesty's men.

"Which way are you going?"

"South—to look for the gap in the wall."

The rushlights of the squalid huts were lost in the glory of full moon.

On a sultry December evening, Doctor George was away in the big 28-footer with his blue-jackets, John Thistle in the stern whistling "Bonnie Dundee". Bound south in the teeth of the wind, they sheered the corner of the Head, striding the diminutive track of *Tom Thumb*.

New Year '98 had come and gone before the *Reliance* was a ship again, and Lieutenant Flinders could be off in the *Francis* with Guy Hamilton for the rum and the wreck. Six hundred serrated miles, and they swung away from the green wooded capes of Cook's landfall, in a flowing tide for the islands of the marooned—black scoriated cliffs in a rebellious sea. The first group of three, a dark stubble of trees valiantly facing the gale, he wrote down for the indomitable Kent, his friend.

Windy smudge of smoke beckoned them to the rock of preservation, where the rotted planks of the *Sydney Cove* were littered high on the strand. Guardian imps of a pirate's lair, a few lean Lascars had kept themselves alive there for a year. While Hamilton shipped his precious casks of Port Jackson's elixir of life, Matthew with his sextant in a little skiff went drifting through the maze, sighting and sounding by changing hills in the changing sea.

Every jagged coastline was a moving blur of seals, from their wave-washed ledges chanting deep-throated their anthems of the deep. They surveyed men with no amazement in their blurred blue eyes, but raised themselves on their powerful flippers and gazed into the guns of death ... slaty legions, fearless in their own domain.

One proud old Plato from his tribune of stone raised his venerable head to the sun. Matthew crouched in a cleft of the rocks. He fired point-blank into that wet sleek breast.

At the third ball the majestic creature gave up his contemplation of the infinite, and as one who turns to urgencies of action dived into the sea, a dark shadow swimming down. Half an hour later he was back on his pedestal, quivering nostrils questioning the wind.

Again Matthew crouched and fired ... a gush of red, and the old philosopher fell. Six balls they found in that bullock body, to be roasted on driftwood, a camp-fire feast for the sailors.

Through all the channel-races the smaller, blacker fur-seals flocked like pilgrims. The human invaders landed at Passage Point. While Matthew marked his lonely station by lines of sun and sea, a Glencoe massacre stained the snow-white sand. Whiskered cubs whimpered from their lichened rookeries, impotent mothers floundered in their anguish, and hoary apostles defended the rocky heights. They slaughtered, skinned, and filled the boat ... and so they left the poor affrighted multitude.

Dusk was split into myriad wings, millions upon millions of petrels, "the wee Mr Pitt birrds", as Captain Hunter called them, homing to their nests in the sands. The islands were a honeycomb of burrows. Each night those leathery brown wings were a fat, fishy supper. Hamilton said he had lived on them for six months, with an occasional goose or seal for Sunday dinner, and a noddy of his own rum—"dreenkin' the profits". He dubbed them mutton-birds, for they came like lambs to the slaughter. They even burrowed underneath the tents. To Matthew's unvitiated taste, the flesh of the aculeated ant-eater was more palatable. Thousands of penguins passed by his skiff, treading water like little squads of blue-jackets on parade.

He saw pallid isles of whitish granite, studded with what might be tin; trees creeping away from the wind like bent and wizened beggars; a valley filled with the sulphurous ash of infinitesimal bones, and goblin swamps salt and red as blood. He threaded the channel where Armstrong sailed to his death, and from the crest of a hill saw the smokes of Van Diemen's Land.

Before the month of February was out, Hamilton had his rum aboard, the last 3000 gallons. Turning north, they sailed back into their century from that Silurian archipelago.

Doctor George was awaiting his friend with epic news to tell … George, dark as an Otaheitian chief, jolly as a hunting squire with two greyhound dogs at heel. His rough charts were spread out on the desk they shared in the cabin. Two months ahead of the *Francis*, in his surgeon's phrase, he had "tapped the arteries of the ocean".

"The swing and crash of a big strait down there, I'm assured, Matt, but here's my map, such as it is. I'll tell you the whole story."

He dangled a leg from the table, more eloquent than ever before.

"From *Tom Thumb's* farthest south, 'tis the same capricious coastline of smiling beach and frowning cliff, the white dragoons of Pacific surf driven back in confusion. Then there's a curious circumstance of a waterspout on land. In burnt basalt rocks like old iron pots, the sea fumes underground to a thirty-foot crater, where every wave breaks high in a column of spray. The natives call it a salt-water devil, Kyamma.

"I came to a haven with outpost shoals, and a river as grand as the Hawkesbury, fertility of silt centuries deep, a Witham of the south. There's the bay where the transport sheltered, named for Sir John Jervis, and a bay of two folds, 'tis marked by a cape"—Doctor George smiled—"the peculiar bluish hue of a drunkard's nose.

"Past a dromedary hill, we rounded Cape Howe to new sea-country and wild weather. 'Twas Christmas week, so westward singing carols. We ran all night by moonlight into New Year, and found that silver boomerang of beach that runs for ninety miles, then out across a vault of water that should be land according to Tasman.

"There was a stiff gale and heavy punishment on New Year's night. One of our planks started. We were half full of water! Four hours we fought. A false flick of the tiller would have sent us under. Moby Dick himself couldn't have lashed us harder, but she's a fine whaleboat. She brought us through to the dawn, and some faint wisps of smoke on a far-off isle. I thought it was an Indians' fire, and made across for water.

"They were white men, Matt, gone black with sun and scurvy!" George's eyes widened as he remembered. "Seven convicts who had fled right out of the world, down to loot the rum of the *Sydney Cove*, but their comrades had stolen the boat and left them there, waving like scarecrows to the empty sea. I gave them a few stores and promised to call back.

"When we swung over to the main again, *it still ran west*.

"From there, we limped into a great discovery." He bent over his chart, carefully drawn as a surgeon's stitches. "This is a fine harbour, with shores of soft dark soil and cool ferns. I've called it Western Port, and that's Phillip Island." He had drawn a rough diamond at the entrance. "The trees are monstrous, there's plenty of water, and black swans in thousands. This swan song legend is poetic and untrue. Their dying cry exactly resembled the creaking of a rusty ale-house sign on a windy day. The birds have a far sweeter call there than those we hear at Port Jackson. There are green mites with a tinkling of bells, and one musician, but you'll not believe it, with a remarkable tail exactly like a lyre.

"All the way round we found our world to live in. At night we looked for shelter, by day we hunted food. The limp bags of flour were frightening me—'tis queer that civilized man cannot live without milled flour! Why can't this country, with all its rich vegetation, give us wheat? At any rate, by those dwindling bags, I judged the time to turn. We battled back to the seven convicts, but no hope of taking them with us. An old man and an ailing man we managed to board.... I put it to the crew, and they agreed to divide the daily bannock. The others we ferried across to the main, with a musket and shot, a kettle, and a pocket compass to make Port Jackson. Think of it? They haven't come in. I doubt they ever will.

"On the way round we struck a citadel of rock, a huge bearded promontory in a twenty-mile rampart of defiant granite. 'Tis the foundation stone of the continent, if continent it be. I named it for Tom Wilson, who coached me through degrees and was kind to me on my lonely nights in London, and it sheltered us from the venom of the strait, in a sealers' cove.

"The southerly bowled us home. I had those convicts forever in my mind. Once I put ashore—you'll laugh—seeing a tall dead tree. I thought it was a mast of despair. I came back through the Heads on the night of the twenty-fourth. Whenever it shall be decided that those westward-setting tides and high winds, as Hunter said, are 'verra breath o' ocean', Van Diemen's Land may prove to be an archipelago."

Matthew sat back in his chair, his eyes kindled bright with excitement.

"George Bass, thou hast said it! I've written in my own journal the significant strength of those westward-setting tides, that long south-west swell hammering in on the coast.... A passage from the Pacific to the South Indian! Thou hast written a sentence, to quote Captain Nelson, in England's transcendant history."

"Alas, you'll have to write it for me, for how can I be sure? And here,"—he threw his childish drawings aside—"this is no map for a new kingdom on earth. Be my cartographer, Matt, make me a proper chart."

Bass talked and Flinders wrote till sunrise wakened the harbour to jade and silver.

The tedious Port Jackson days dragged on. Constructing his own charts and the young doctor's, Matthew sent in to Hunter his reports of the *Francis* journey, a faultless copperplate of cartography and calligraphy, geometric to the dotting of i's and the crossing of t's. In the work of his hands, the work of his brain, he would have no compromise with perfection. His fair copies were fair indeed.

From May to July, the *Reliance* snatched him away from hope of exploration, over to Norfolk Island, taking the surgeon, D'Arcy Wentworth, back. The transport *Barwell* was in harbour when they returned—mutiny and misery as usual, Rum Corps soldiers in irons aboard, accused of high treason and plotting to seize the ship. It appeared they had fired their rifles and shouted "Damnation to king and country!" Waterhouse, Kent and Flinders, as senior officer in port—and two of them on the sunny side of thirty—were called to constitute a Vice-Admiralty Court, and sit in solemn judgment. They found that high treason was only low mentality, and let the soldiers go free.

In September, Bass and Flinders had another interview with the governor. Hunter bethought him of an out-of-work ship in port that might serve their purpose and his—the *Norfolk*, built by the Crusoes of that sombre isle to battle the Pacific to Port Jackson when there was nothing else to do it. Wormy now, with a list and a leak, glad they were to get her! Thistle and the whaleboat crew were "ready, aye, ready", and Waterhouse stocked them up with everything he could spare.

As they were about to leave, a patch of sail in the blue brought a woe-begone tale of Otaheite and its first doleful missionaries, with tattered haloes and tattered hymn-books, driven out by a drunken king.

Taina the Pomare, at first mildly amused, had wearied of their dirges and prognostications of hell. When a hurricane came, he thought they had brought it. In one fell swoop he threw them to the shark-gods, and ordered a heathen *heiva*. Nineteen men, women and children, self-righteous and ragged, they wailed and bailed across four thousand miles of sea, from the godlessness of kava to a malevolence of rum. With them in the little snow *Nautilus* came an enterprising gentleman named Bishop, who scouted beaches of paradise with an eye to the main chance. He showed a sprightly interest in those seal-herds of the south, and offered the *Nautilus* as consort to the *Norfolk*.

On the first day of October, Lieutenant M. Flinders received his first commission, to sail from Furneaux Islands westward, and if a strait be found to sail right through it, returning by the south of Van Diemen's Land.

A week later he boarded his first command, twenty-five tons of tarred pine from one of the loneliest islands in the ocean. With a home-made quadrant and no time-keeper, he was to measure new latitudes by moon-time, under the cold blue eye of Fomalhaut in Pisces. Doctor George was by his side, and eight *Reliance* volunteers who wanted to be with them in the van. Bass in his kangaroo-skin vest, Flinders in his penguin cap, and John Thistle, hard-bitten, in moth-eaten guernsey, they might have been fishermen of Dee. Pearly light of dawn in her sail, the *Nautilus* blithely followed.

Two Folds Bay—on a breezy morning they landed, George and his hounds for the woods, looking for rivers and grasslands, Matthew with his theodolite, cutting the coast in squares. Suddenly from a hollow in the sandhills rose a shrill chorus of feminine squeals. A bevy of nymphs in glossiest bronze pelted for the woodland, and a grizzled warrior emerged, officiously waving a waddy. Matthew's ingenuous smile made him a friend. With the true Neanderthal courtesy that never failed to amaze and amuse these young explorers, he accepted a couple of ships' biscuits and returned the gift in kind, producing from his belt of human hair a blob of sickly grey blubber.

Toujours la politesse! Matthew obligingly tried a bite, but his gorge rose. The slimy stuff refused to go down. He gulped. His friend was blowing off like a porpoise, finding the biscuit dry as beach sand. Finesse to the winds—the diplomats grinned at each other and spat.

The old man admired the theodolite as a novel arrangement of spears until its mysterious discs and dividers were brought into play, when he gave the thing up as hopeless. With wrinkled brow and comical stare, he watched this inexplicable blue being bowing to arrange the plumb bob, clinking and squinting as he paced the beach with oblong nets of chain, skewering his head into a complicated boomerang to take a straight eye on the sun. He decided it was a harmless devil, and, bored, wandered away.

"To him," suggested Doctor George, "'tis doubtless some new totem worship."

"As it is," Matthew smiled, "to me."

Later in the morning, a band of kangaroo-tail kilties came over the sandhills from the wild duck lagoons to pay their respects to the strange visitors, and finger their freakish dress. Big, good-humoured fellows, the boys sat among them laughing till the sun at the meridian called Matthew to his final calculations. He wrote in the journal that Two Folds Bay should make a good whaling station.

In the rough weeks of early November, they threaded the Furneaux Isles, the young leader sounding from his ship, or out over the cliffs, theodolite on shoulder by day—at night, by rush-light in the rickety cabin, with myriad figures and many names, marking every fathom, every mile.

Patriarch hills, a Babel tower of sea-birds, a Judgment Seat of rock, a point like a battery of guns, and a cape of barren mountains like a giant's cup set in a saucer twelve hundred feet high, he had much of strange adventuring for his journal, of intricate design for his chart. It was heavy work, but the pride of it left him no time for fatigue. "The indefatigable Flinders," said George, "in every sense of the word."

"Ah, Mr Matthew, sirr, there's a hot hell awaitin' ye," warned Thistle. "Whit wey will ye run on Sunday, an' no be keepin' the sabbath?"

Clear eyes above a determined chin, Flinders looked beyond the horizon.

"The stars still shine on the sabbath. How could we keep it better, John, than in telling the glory of creation?"

Nevertheless, came a sabbath sundown when he stood alone in the doorway of Hamilton's gaunt old hut on Preservation Island, far out of the world of church bells, sharing the benediction of far islands and far seas. The hand that held the sextant fell to his side, and the tender light of evening dreamed in his dreaming eyes.

A V of swans on lazy wings, went crying to the west. Rain-washed granite of the nearer islands sparkled into crystal. In yellow radiance of the setting sun, haze lifted from the high mountains of a greater isle beyond, their white pure peaks, bathed in late showers, reflecting the fading splendour. Beauty in sterility ... serenity after storm. Altair twinkled in the twilight blue.

That night he wrote in his chart "Mount Chappell ... the Chappell Isles."

They parted from the *Nautilus* at the Furneaux, and left her to her grisly work. Now they skirted the north coast of Van Diemen's Land, Matthew and John Thistle surveying, George with his dogs beating the wildwood. Everything that grew, flew, crept, slunk and climbed was new to him. One day he found a pouched pig, goggle-eyed and shuffling, hissing its clumsy way, snout to the ground. He nursed it as you would a baby.

"Its countenance was placid and undisturbed," he said, "as if I had nursed it from its infancy. I carried it a while, then threw it over my shoulder, but when I tied its legs together while I gathered specimens, the trouble began. Look, it bit the elbow out of my jacket!" He pointed to it kicking in the boat. "I think it will be easily tamed—we might even make it domestic."

"I think not," said Matthew. "'Tis a wombat."

On 3 November a deep bay narrowed into a shining gauntlet of estuaries and a wide noble river, its shores an Eden of fertility ... now and again they saw Adam and Eve in fur-skin cloak. Duck and teal were in thousands in the lagoons, black swans so thick about them in the channels that they were caught by their Grecian necks and hauled into the boat—an excellent dark meat. After four years of ships' biscuits and salt pork, who could blame them if explorations in that captivating spot kept them for a month? They put to sea in early December, the journal as full of healthy enthusiasm as Matthew's inner man.

Now the coast swung up, completing an arc of over a hundred miles. A circular head reminded George of the Christmas cake he was missing. Dawn brought the long south-west swell of unfettered, unbounded ocean, breaking in ruffled plumes of spray on a low reef ahead. Hands clasped together, they whooped and danced with each other on deck. George Bass was right. They had opened the strait.

At nightfall they anchored in the lee of scattered isles where the reddish hair-seals wallowed and barked, and sooty petrels were homing in cubic millions, one long dark cloud that passed for an hour and a half. Flinders, in ecstatic mood, totted them up in massive mensuration.

"'Tis easy, George. Taking the stream to have been 50 yards deep by 300 in width, and that it moved at the rate of 30 miles per hour, and allowing 9 cubic yards of space to each bird, the number would amount to 151,000,000. The burrows required to lodge this quantity of birds would be 75,750,000, and allowing a square yard to each burrow, they would cover something more than 18½ geographic square miles of ground."

"Good Lord!" said Doctor George. "What Matthew-matics are these!"

Morning light disclosed an albatross island, a snowfall of birds. Bass had to fight his way up the cliffs, challenged by angry seals. Two square miles of feathered white, the albatross mothers were brooding. Right and left with his club he swept himself a path, the angry birds unmoving save to drive at him with their shovel beaks and to batter him with their great arched wings. In the hour he was ashore there the *Norfolk*, in tremendous tides, had been swept five miles away, past another little isle that Flinders had called Trefoil, because its outline reminded him of Fenlands clover. The whole group, for the "wee whusperin'" in his mind that had led to their discovery, he wrote into the map for Governor Hunter.

A grim cape was omen of the gloomy days to follow. Through tumultuous leagues of storm the *Norfolk*, with her men from the north, beat bravely south, to the cold zones where men were unwelcome and unknown.

The melancholy of that brow-beaten shore preyed on Flinders's mind. Those lowering ranges were stupendous works of nature … awful effigies of peak and pylon defied in diabolical majesty the siege of wind and sea. To the boy from the Fens they were astonishment and horror. He kept well out from that ferocious coast, clapped on sail and frankly fled from its black despair, naming no more than two stark monoliths in memory of Abel Tasman's hero ships, *Heemskirk* and *Zeehan*, that mapped the track of the globe through nothing. Glad they were to swing round into the path of the *Resolution*, where James Cook had doggedly followed, and to happy remembrances of the *Providence* in Furneaux's Adventure Bay.

They sailed into that glorious harbour and river discovered by Sir John Hayes in his merry-go-round of the world for fame and fortune. Flinders named the pillar cape at its entrance, a Herdsman's Cove that was a paradise for cattle. He sounded a bay for the little *Norfolk* there, and scaled the heights of a venerable mountain that Hayes had called Skiddaw.

Looking down on heavenly panorama of earth and river and sea, with its tall gum-trees and richly-bearing soil, glens and gullies of waterfalls and ferns, he recalled Bligh's vision of this tangle of green land … an England of the south.

A human voice hailed them from the timeless hills. It was a quaint little blackamoor in fur sporran and cap of clay, representing the landlords.

Their solitary host in Van Diemen's Land, and the first of its people Matthew had seen, he was cheerful and obliging, much admiring their red silk neckerchiefs, and trailing them round through the scrub on a wild goose chase to hunt for his abode. He had forgotten the way home … doubtless, with these glamorous albinos, he feared for his charming wives.

Matthew tried him in Otaheitian and the language of Port Jackson, but they got no further than smiles and the gift of a swan as they made back to their boat in the beautiful Derwent River. The prettiest of its islands Matthew named for Betsy.

The east coast of Tasman's isle was perilous in storm. Past Maria Island, that the bristled Dutchman dedicated to his far-off sweetheart, and past his colourful Schouten Island farther north, they swung out on the ship-track for Port Jackson.

Home letters were awaiting the Argonauts there.

Lieutenant M. Flinders, R.N.,
Navy Board, Portsmouth,
For *H.M.S. Reliance*,
New South Wales.

Hastily he scanned his budget through—Betsy's schoolgirl scrawl; the admiral's leonine flourish; ... ah, the small, flowing, deliberate hand of Ann; James Wiles in Jamaica; his father's prim, straightforward lettering; Henrietta's friendly slant; Willingham Franklin from Oxford; Christopher Smith, gone botanizing out in Pulo Penang; and again the small, flowing, deliberate hand of Ann.

What hours of joy ahead after months of wandering and wondering! The English mail was the keenest pleasure Port Jackson ever knew. It cured them of their homesickness, and brought it again, a thousand times more poignant. He carefully stored Ann's letters by, and started on the others.

The house in Market Square was tranquil as ever,... there seemed a listlessness between his father's lines. Grandfather Flinders was still making the pace in his gig round Spalding, but Uncle John was dead—of yellow fever in the Indies—after receiving his commission.

Matthew stopped to remember him. Uncle John on the Cambridge coach, "I'll see thee yonder?" ... "The faces of thy loved ones shall be no more than faces in the clouds" . . and now, "Not even a stone in the graveyard to tell that thou hast lived."

Sadly he turned to the next. Admiral Pasley, wooden leg and all, was commander-in-chief at Plymouth. His Majesty had need of the old sea-dog still.

Great news! Nelson victorious at the Battle of the Nile.

The admiral wrote in grand style:

France has become a vampire that lives by the blood of the nations. This upstart Napoleon a Charlemagne, a juggernaut, a fiend in human shape. He has ravished Europe in invasions of wholesale massacre for his vanity of empire. Because Austria, the Netherlands and Spain tamely wear his yoke, he dared to challenge Britain, set out for Egypt to take the road to India, his armies parading roundt he Pyramids, his ships in the delta of the Nile.

Nelson crept in over the sandbanks in the night and battered them into bloody wrecks, burnt them to ashes, one of the greatest battles of all time. Our Bellerophon has made a magnificent showing. She engaged your old friend, L'Orient, the flagship, 120 guns against her 70, but her anchor dragged and she drifted into hell. As before, she tackled them three at a time, but with appalling slaughter. Darby, her captain, and five lieutenants were carried below in the first half-hour, either dead or dying. A boy of fourteen took command of the quarterdeck, a midshipman named John Hindmarsh. He gave the order to cut the ropes that saved her. With the ship on fire and the dead piled deep, they fought for an hour and a half, and thrashed the Frenchmen. They got away in the darkness in rags, not a stump over two feet standing, but in forty-eight hours they had her a ship in full rig, ready to take the fleet home. For a week the bells of victory have been ringing. This one-eyed little scout of a Nelson is an Alexander of the sea.

There has been a made mutiny of our seamen at the Nore, having the damned impertinence to demand better rations and more than sixpence a day, but Bligh was in the thick of it, to some extent the cause. Wherever this man is, there shall mutiny be.

I have heard at the Admiralty of your fine work in exploration. I am proud to claim you as my pupil and my friend. I have need of an aide-de-camp again if you are coming home.

Coming home!

No longer could he resist Ann's letters. With careful fingers he broke her dainty seal, a little French fancy of hers, to honour her Huguenot ancestors of Aix-la-Chapelle, the dark blue wax imprinted with a "Vue Prise du Pont Neuf ".

"My dear Matthew," — so quiet, so restrained, but "My" was a little blacker than it need be.

Ann was become a most active-minded person. She discoursed at length of this and that, *au fait* with the war and the world, with news and philosophies of all their friends and cuttings from the London papers. She had been studying science and art, from miniature painting to botany. Now she had taken up Latin and geography.

I find this last most necessary to keep in touch with thee, but indeed thou art beyond geography.

Thy descriptions of the new land are enthralling. I read them over and over again with gladness. Thou hast asked me if I would ever be willing that we should make our home there. Believe me, dear Matthew, I should be more than willing, for if thou canst find happiness and beauty in that wild strand, so shall I. But, as thou sayest, this is but a dream. We know not what the future will bring.

With thee, I have but one prayer — that we may be together. Oh if I could but see thee this instant, as thou art, reading my letter, in that far-off country where thou tellest me the sun so generously shines. Alas, here in Lincolnshire 'tis all blizzard and snow, and the most longing thoughts of thee. God guard thee in perils, and bring thee safely home.

Thy most affectionate, thine own
ANNETTE.

For minutes he sat there, the swing of the sea forgotten, grave as Governor Hunter when he pondered the hanging of half a dozen at a time. Home. He must go home. The years were flying, and he was twenty-five. He looked out on the dazzling harbour, and saw only the shadows of an oak.

George Johnston, the governor's secretary, tapped him on the shoulder. His Excellency would see Lieutenant Flinders.

As he rowed across with Waterhouse to the landing-steps, he learned with amazement that Hunter was to be recalled. King, of Norfolk Island, had been appointed in his stead.

In the curtained study of his crude Government House, Hunter sat at his desk. If he knew of his deposition, he gave no sign, welcomed Matthew as warmly as ever, praised his *Norfolk* charts.

"'Tis a craftsman's wurruk ye do now, laddie, an' whut grand news ye brocht! Yew an' I an' the young doctor will celebrate this nicht, wi' our friends frae the *Reliance*, an' wan or tew. I thank ye for the fine grewp o' isles ye've gi'en me, but why, tell me, hae ye nae christened the bonnie harrbour ye found, an' grandest o' a', the strait?"

"In discoveries of magnitude, sir, I needed your authority. May I suggest that we write it down together—and that we write it down Bass Strait?"

"Ye may. Wi' a' my hairt, Mr Flinders, I concur. A laddie no a seaman who can mak' twelve hundred miles o' uncharrted shoore in an open boat like yon desairves his name written i' big letters i' the map."

"The harbour, sir, we might make a gift of grace to the hydrographer at the Admiralty, our good friend, Mr Alexander Dalrymple, for his constructive interest in our colony and the south."

"Dalrymple it is. An Edinboro' Scot and a brain. Aye. Poort Dalrymple, 'tis euphonious. An' now I hae letters frae England, an' wan that concairns yew. Ye may read it, Mr Flinders. 'Tis from Sir Joseph Banks."

Matthew's eyes widened. "I did not know Sir Joseph knew I existed."

"Sir Joseph, Mr Flinders, sir, knows most things aboot this colony. Since he, wi' his influence in high places, sent the prison-ships that were plague ships oot across the wurruld to the land he discovered wi' Cook, has kept a patairnal eye upon us moore than ye micht think. A remarrkable man. Hae ye no met him?"

"Unfortunately, not."

"'Twill be fortunate for yew the day ye do, for, as ye'll see, ye're a man he values."

Matthew read—a fair, free handwriting, confident, almost careless. Sir Joseph was sending a plant-cabin and two botanists, Cayley and Suttor aboard H.M.S. *Porpoise*, to transplant English fruit-trees to New Holland, and particularly hops to brew beer, "diminishing the consummation of unwholesome spirits".

He suddenly went off on another tack.

We have now possessed the country of New South Wales more than ten years, and know nothing of the interior. It is impossible to conceive that such a body of land as large as all Europe does not produce vast rivers, and situated in a most fruitful climate does not produce some native raw material of value for manufacture in England.

Mr Mungo Park, lately returned from a journey to Africa, where he ventured further inland than any European before him had done by several hundred miles, discovered immense navigable rivers running westward, penetrating the centre of that vast continent and monopolizing trade for our settlement at Senegambia, offers himself to be employed as a volunteer in exploring the interior of New Holland, by its rivers or otherwise.

His moral character is unblemished, his temper mild and his patience inexhaustible. He has knowledge of astronomy to calculate latitude and longitude, geography to make a map, draws a little, has a competent knowledge of botany and zoology, and has been educated in the medical line. He is very moderate in his terms, will be contented with 10s. a day and his rations, £100 for instruments and arms.

He will want a decked vessel about 30 tons under the command of a lieutenant with orders to follow his advice in all matters of exploring, such a vessel to be built in the country, and Lieutenant Flinders, a countryman of mine, a man of activity and information, who is already there, will I am sure be happy if he is entrusted with the command, and will enter into the spirit of his orders, and agree perfectly with Park.

I should suggest a crew of ten men, four for boatkeepers and six to proceed into the country with one or both of the commanders for inland journeys. Park will embark with King on the Porpoise.

As for me, Pitt rules, Fox grumbles. I would willingly remove myself to your quarters, and ask for a grant of land on the banks of the Hawkesbury... .

Matthew was silent. Discovery. His love. Six years. And he must stay.

"Well now, there's a chance for ye, laddie, eh?"

"Yes, sir."

"'Tis honour ye've won for ye'sel, to be chosen by Sir Joseph."

"Yes, indeed, sir. My gratitude is unbounding."

"By a' accounts, this Mungo Parrk is God's guid man, an expedeetion in himsel'. Ye don't seem so set up as I thocht ye'd be ... in fact, ye seem doonhairted ... "

"Indeed no, your excellency." Matthew smiled his brightest. "'Tis English mail day. My thoughts have been of home. As you have said, 'tis an honour, a magnificent chance."

"If ye'll tak' my advice, Matthew, ye'll tak' note o' Sir Joseph. The power behind the throne i' trewth, an' not far behind the throne—the managing-director of New Holland. I'll see ye at eight o'clock then, for a richt guid dinner."

As Matthew went down the hill deep in meditation, the chain-gangs clanked past him in the dust on their way to the log jails. Port Jackson must needs be home for a long time yet ... he stopped with a glad exclamation. Ann had said she would come! He wheeled and crossed the rough wooden bridge over the Tank Stream for Colonel Paterson's house, the only home he knew with a woman in it, where the men of the *Reliance* were mothered, and scolded, and entertained on many a happy night.

Mild-eyed and classic of feature, Mrs Paterson was a gentle Scotswoman, cheery and gay though starved of all companionship. She and Mrs Macarthur were the only "gentry" in the colony, deprived of each other's friendship by husbands forever fighting. Mrs Macarthur, a remarkable young woman very rarely seen, graceful, sweet-tempered and wise, was a striking contrast to the irascible John. Those who knew her marvelled at their union. None valued her more than Macarthur himself, none knew so little of her lonely life. At Elizabeth Farm at Parramatta she cared for his babies, cared for his garden—the only orchard in New South Wales—reared his merino lambs, and found her respite twenty thousand miles away, in letters to friends in England. On the rare occasions when she did visit the settlement, sitting erect with much dignity in a rickety shay, her bonnets were the envy of the town. Matthew was of the few who shared her smiles. It did not do to mention her in the presence of Mrs Paterson.

"Why will you ladies meddle with politics?" he ruefully asked one day.

Making him a cup of precious Bohea tea, Mrs Paterson rejoiced at the thought that he should bring Ann to the colony. She visioned a naval wedding in the little bark church.

"She may live with me as long as she likes," she told him. "'Twill be a wonderful uplift to society."

That night his letters to

> Miss A. Chappell,
> The Rectory,
> Partney,
> Near Spilsby, Lincs.

were feverish with plans.

A sordid scene was enacted in the courthouse. Isaac Nichols, overseer of the government work-gangs, an emancipated convict who had led an exemplary life for ten years, was charged with receiving stolen goods—£60 kegs of Cuban tobacco—from a thief already hanged for the crime.

Hunter swore it was a plot of Macarthur in revenge for opposition, and of his henchmen to get a man of integrity out of their way. Kent, Flinders and Waterhouse were duly called up on the Bench, with three of the Rum Corps officers and Judge-Advocate Dore, to listen to perjured evidence by men of evil reputation, men that Phillip had spread-eagled and branded with searing irons writing "Rogue" in living flesh.

A Port Jackson sensation, Army versus Navy—Macarthur himself gave evidence there, and the parson and the hangman, a precedent in British law. Nichols made a despairing cry from the dock—by industry he had found happiness and respect, therefore he was hated and hounded down. The case dragged on for days. The judge-advocate's verdict sent the Rum Corps off triumphant, and Nichols to fourteen years in the jail-gangs of Norfolk Island, in iron fetters.

Another sensation! Hunter refused to condemn an honourable servant. Using the governor's prerogative, he referred the case to England, and called the members of the Bench to state reasons for their verdicts in writing.

Young Flinders's keen analysis was Isaac Nichols's salvation. He sketched the characters of witnesses as they appeared before him, he sounded every scrap of evidence, and charted all its snags. He rose to Machiavellian heights when he deduced, in a liar's sworn statement, two Sundays in one week.

"'Twill tak' a year, or mebbe tew, to free the prisoner," said Hunter, "but Mr Flinders, ye've saved an honest man."

"You have the makings of a fine lawyer," laughed George.

"Perish the thought!" said Matthew.

Doctor George was going home. He told the news awkwardly in their one unhappy hour together.

"Bishop has a cargo of 9000 seal-skins from the Furneaux. Do you realize what that means, Matt, at fifty guineas apiece? When we are in at the making of a country, we should be making our fortunes."

Matthew fixed him with a questioning stare.

"So I'm going home to buy a trader—floating another South Sea Bubble, you'll say—but in pearls, in pigs, in endless ways there are thousands to be made. Waterhouse is in it. Why not you? All we need is a ship."

"It makes no appeal to me," said Matthew briefly. "I thought we were twin souls in exploration."

"Well, now that you're going with Mungo Park, what's to become of me? You're a Navy officer. I'm only a stray surgeon. Besides, I'm marrying Bess Waterhouse. I have to think of the future, you know, and this is the place to make it. I'm truly sorry, but you'll understand."

A moment's troubled thought. "Perhaps you are right, George."

A month or two later when Hunter gave him the little *Norfolk* to relieve the tedium of waiting for Mungo Park by filling in Cook's sketchy chart to northward, Doctor George was waiting for a ship. Samuel would go with Matthew, the first excursion that the brothers shared.

Doctor George came with them as far as Sydney Heads—a handshake, a promise of meeting some day, somewhere ... *Tom Thumb* was slung over the side, and the wave widened between them.

There was a last hail of "Fair wind and farewell!" George standing up in his diminutive skiff, "like a candle in a candlestick" as he had so often said. His vigour, his humour, his bright mind, his valour and his comradeship had made him a friend of friends.

The *Norfolk* was silent and empty as she sheered for the lion's paws. The tall, beloved figure of George Bass faded in to the headland and the night.

Banished by fear of the rope and the cat, there were white men living with the Indians at Broken Bay, convicts who had crossed the Rubicon of the Hawkesbury. To go farther was death. To turn back was death. They must live in the sharp scrub with the savages. They heartened Flinders with legends of great rivers and deep forests to the north. From one of those rhinoceros headlands he commissioned his lieutenant, an intelligent, jolly black boy who signed on as Bongree. He nodded and grinned when offered a trip on the bird canoe.

They sailed out by the little palm beach with Bongree an ambassador to his race, his retainer paid daily in grey pork and flour, and a mug of sweet tea.

The *Endeavour* had swept on her course by night. They filled in her dotted lines. "Cook reaped the harvest of discovery," said Matthew to Samuel, "but with a broad sickle. The gleanings of the field remain for me."

He named a Shoal Bay and a Sugarloaf Point, but the next were Cook's Three Brothers. To his Solitary Isles he added no less than five, and checking up the master's latitudes, swung round into his Moreton Bay, wide, calm and impressive. Its mangrove shores attracted him, he threaded them for many days, off in the boat ahead with Bongree and Sam to sound.

Sunset reddened the sandy flats, and off the point a crowd of blackamoors was hauling in the seine, the red smoke of their fires spiralling upward. Without any thought of danger, they backed the boat in.

The cheerful Bongree went ashore unarmed, Matthew, in his cabbage-tree hat, wading along behind him. There was a pleasant little parley on the foreshore. Bongree exchanged a tasselled cap for a fillet of kangaroo hair, but the Indians gazed speculatively at Matthew's cabbage-tree hat.

One tried to hook it with a wommera. Matthew wheeled and caught him, to a general display of white teeth in a laugh. But the blacks were pressing forward too eagerly now, and they all converged on the boat.

As they pulled to deep water, a spear flicked past leaving ripples in the bay. Flinders raised his gun and fired in warning. The powder was wet, and the trigger feebly snapped. Another shaft fell short. He fired again. This time a man fell flat in the water, and staggered ashore mystified, feeling for the unseen spear. Back at the *Norfolk*, an etching in the moonlight, they named the point for the skirmish, and meandered on up the bay, with a seven-mile walk through the woodland to the foot of Cook's Glasshouse Peaks.

The eternal calculation of a never-ending coastline took Flinders ashore again and again. His antics with level and quadrant amused a hearty audience of the blue-quilled kookaburras. Reproachfully he dotted their leafy home on to the chart, and steered due east past a terracotta cliff and out along the sandy flats. Six miles beyond the place of the encounter two dark aides-de-camp of the distant hills beckoned him ashore.

The power of his death-stick was terrible, he made them understand, and to make sure of respect he fired at two red-billed birds. They flew into the forest screeching. The black deputies followed. They soon reappeared, lured by the woolly caps presented, which they promptly adopted as sporrans for their hair-belts, their women chattering like Debtford wives behind the brambles.

Again the numbers alarmingly increased. They crowded in on Flinders, intent on that cabbage-tree hat as a pack of fops round Brummell in the Strand. To embrace these natives was to embrace death. Matthew was determined to demonstrate his shooting-stick. A carven hawk, like one of heraldry, sat on a tree near by. He squinted, and fired the pan.

There was a blast and clouds of smoke ... but when the suffocating fog of war cleared away, that coat-of-arms hawk still sat in stony reverie, its buzzard eye unblinking.

A blow to British prestige, but the acrid smell of powder and the devil's wink of flame had certainly made an impression. The natives thinned out a little, looking askance at the musket and its gleaming shot-balls.

Eager for negotiation, Flinders let Thistle and another Highlander of his crew dance them a reel, but the reedy skirl and the whirling tartans were missing, and their sanguine battle-whoops mingled feebly with the catarrhal cries of the scandalized seagulls. Next item in the jamboree was a solo by Bongree, but Bongree was an indifferent songster, and try as he would he could not make both ends meet.

"I've hearrd an' auld herrin' wumman squawkin' a dom sight better I' the fish-marrkets o' Dundee," grinned John Thistle, puffing from his haggis dance at Matthew's elbow.

Now their hosts came to Bongree's rescue, bolstered up his fading octaves with a harsh madrigal that wavered and jarred on their ears. With bouquets of blankets and caps they left the gorilla men engrossed in their harmony and counterpoint, and rowed to the little *Norfolk* sleeping at anchor. That clamouring *Missa Solemnis* was lost in a volatile evening sky.

As the skiff cantered out of Cook's Moreton Bay past a new Moreton Island, Matthew was puzzled, as often before, by the little brass compass. The needle would swing and lean without any change in that curling wake. Sights of the sun showed the course as erratic and suddenly curving. When John Thistle was at the helm, they sailed right off the chart.

"Yon wee compass has nae time fur me," was his excuse. "It skips like a fresh-caught trout when ah gae near it."

"Let's have a look in your pocket, John.... Ah!" The young captain had solved the mystery. He drew out a battered claspknife. "That's the trouble, I'll wager. A magnet here to pull us all over the ocean!"

"But whit wey, sorr? Ye're no tellin' me ma wee poke-knife can wurruk the ship agley?"

"I have a theory it does, John—that every piece of iron in the *Norfolk* is bending the compass from due north."

"Weel, noo, yon's a thing to ken ... an' whit wey did nae ither callant theenk o't befoore?"

"I'm not quite sure of it myself. I'll need a real ship to prove it, and I mean to have that some day."

The insidious piece of metal was stuck in disgrace into the creaking gudgeon, where the pinewood rudder clocked and rattled under the cold shoulder of the Pacific tide that rolled them home. One night there was a magnificent shower of shooting stars from Leo—the mane of the Lion falling red. Lying on the rocking deck, they watched it for an hour in wonder.

"Ah tak' it for a sign," said John solemnly. "'Tis grrand guid forchin, Mr Matthew. See, the verra heaven o' God reign glory on yere heid!"

On the way in to Port Jackson, they passed the first little boat of men and women chained, bound north to the Coal River. Four or five ships were in the harbour now, traders bringing all the trumpery sweepings of the bazaars at Bengal. There were stores here and there in the dog-leg streets, dandies parading in top-hats and check waistcoats, the women with bonnets and parasols, frills and feathers—and to the log jails were added debtors' yards. The whaler *Albion* had arrived, Captain Ebor Bunker, three years from Brazil across the southern oceans, a fortune in her holds in spermaceti blubber and bone to bolster the busts of London beauties.

News was awaiting young Flinders at the whitewashed Government House. He was a feudal lord, he learned, with ticket-of-leave men for serfs if he desired it. Hunter had planned the new colony at Bankstown, on George III's River, the first three hundred acres of bottle-brush and cockle-shells for him. H.M.S. *Porpoise* was on the way with Sir Joseph Banks's gift of fruit-trees, and New South Wales was making a quaint return. The outlandish little "duck-bill" that Matthew had seen in Van Diemen's Land with Guthrie was going home to Sir Joseph in pickle. Seeing was believing the queerest creature in the history of the world, all the missing links of the animal kingdom in one.

There was yet another item of interest. My lords of the Admiralty were sending the *Lady Nelson*, a brig of sixty tons, for purposes of survey, under Lieutenant Grant.

"Frae whut I hear, he's a fair seaman," said Hunter, "but no artist above the usual trot. Weel, we've gi'en him summat to build on." He glanced at Matthew's maps with gratification, "the profile o' this country for three or four thousan' miles, an' twa islands i' place of one." A bitterness came into his voice. "They've passed me oot, d'ye ken? Aye. Captain King is named to supersede me, to show whut he can dew wi' Macarthur an' his thrice-damned rum. To tell ye trewth, he's welcome to it, but he'll wait ma will. I'll go when I'm reidy, an' no befoore, wi' Wullie Kent on the *Buffalo*. Oh, an' I'm near forgettin'. This young man Mungo Park will not be coming. They wilna pay his ten shilling fee. Ye've lost yere expedeetion after a'."

"Then I rejoin the *Reliance*, sir?"

Hunter's eye twinkled upon him. "Aye, laddie. She can tak' ye home."

9

The Lincoln Poacher

The door of 32 Soho Square, with its polished stone pillars, was the threshold of fame and fortune, portal of the wide wide world.

Would it open—or would it remain closed?

In his painfully new lieutenant's uniform from a sailor's tailor at Debtford, cocked hat rigidly straight, gold buttons twinkling bright, Matthew stood for twelve long seconds before he dared to ring. To steady his nervousness, he studied those Atlas pillars.

"Porphyritic granite," he muttered, and pulled the bell-cord.

The panels slanted a fraction of an inch, and a parrot eye observed him … the door swung open.

"Sir Joseph Banks?" His voice sounded hollow and meek as he added "Lieutenant Flinders."

Louis XIV in lard gave him a frozen stare, motioned him to a Rajah's throne of pearl-inlaid ebony, then paced an imperial minuet adown the broad marble hall to realms beyond his ken.

A Queen Anne clock in Campeachy mahogany clucked in cold disdain. A leopard rug grinned at his temerity. He brushed imaginary dust from his shoes, and coughed to break the cathedral chill.

Hogarth, Holbein, Gainsborough, Reynolds … he raised his eyes aloft.

The day before yesterday he had received Sir Joseph's note. Had he left it ungraciously late before putting in an appearance, or had he materialized with undue haste? He really must invest in a book of etiquette.

Dear Lieutenant Flinders—

I thank you exceedingly for the proposed dedication of your "Observations" to me, and shall be very happy if you will call when in this vicinity.

Yours sincerely—Jos. Banks.

In this vicinity! For such a call he would take a trip to China.

The lackey came back, deigned to impart that Sir Joseph would not keep him waiting long, then stood inhumanly still, a life-size Dresden statue. From regions above came the yearning sweetness of a violoncello ... he had heard no music save fo'c'sle chanties in the past six years.

Scrolled doors flew open. A quaint cavalcade appeared. First came a portly dame of quality, deep-bosomed and consequential in plum-coloured brocades, the feather of her velvet hat sweeping low on one shoulder, a hairy poodle peering from the hollow of her arm. Behind her a tall flunkey, Gold Stick in Waiting, paced with stately step, and behind him ambled a blackamoor, a squat African ape of a creature, white eyes, gold ear-rings, red trousers and frizzy hair. Louis Quatorze unbent to open the door. They sailed serenely through it.

The violoncello played on ... deep thrilling harmonies shattered by the clang of the bell. Again the parrot eye. Louis held converse with a beery, bearded sailor.

He returned in sour displeasure with a weird little beast in a cage, its eyes expanding and contracting like glassy black moons. Matthew knew it, the Amazonian cuscus. He watched its antics absently, listening to the 'cello above. A bent old gnome of a scholar in a skull-cap crept out of the library with some coveted tome, and under the Winged Victory slunk away.

Matthew smiled up at the Hogarth. Sir Joseph Banks's household was worthy of that brush.

In sober black, with waved white hair, a gentleman emerged, a slender, kindly, thoughtful man, detached as one who dwelt in other worlds. Profusely he thanked the footman for tendering his forgotten hat. Another bell jingled. Louis beckoned Matthew in his ceremonial wake.

Sir Joseph rose.

"Lieutenant Flinders? From Boston way? And how is Botany Bay?"

Matthew had the impression of bright eyes and a warm hand.

The bewigged and venerable "power behind the throne" of his imagining faded into thin air. Sir Joseph Banks was alive, and young, vitally dark and in the vigorous fifties.

He rummaged in amber-handled drawers.

"Your charts were a pleasant surprise to me. I see we stand corrected, Cook and I." Sir Joseph's smile was something to remember. He drew out the charts, of the Furneaux, Bass Strait and Van Diemen's Land, and laid aside those on his desk. "Mountains of the moon," he laughed. "Sir William Herschel, whom you might have seen, has brought them. Epic work, but I doubt they'll mean as much to posterity as yours. Well now, tell me, what do you propose to do?"

"Sir Joseph,"—serious Matthew took his cue—"I have too much ambition to rest in the unnoticed middle order of mankind. Since neither birth nor fortune has favoured me, my actions shall speak to the world. In the regular service of the Navy there are too many competitors for fame. I have therefore chosen a branch that though less rewarded in rank and fortune is little less in celebrity. In this the candidates are fewer, and if adverse fortune does not oppose me I will succeed. Although I cannot rival the immortalized name of Cook, yet if persevering industry, joined to what ability I may possess, can accomplish it, then will I … that is if you, Sir Joseph, or any guardian genius will but conduct me into a place of probation. The hitherto obscure name of Flinders may thus become a light by which even the illustrious name of Sir Joseph Banks may some day receive an additional ray of glory."

"So—?" inquired Sir Joseph.

"I hear that the *Lady Nelson* has gone to New Holland to survey. New Holland is mightier than we thought, sir. It may be, as you say, a continent the size of Europe. A 60-ton ship is child's play. We need two ships, one to survey the coasts, the other to explore the rivers. I am prepared to take the command of one. If I could make a map of that country, I should not have lived in vain. But I apologize for the informality of thus addressing you, on the ground that constant employment abroad and education amongst the unpolished inhabitants of the Lincolnshire Fens have prevented me from learning better."

"The Fenlands, Mr Flinders, are very dear to me."

Sir Joseph Banks sat back in his chair, shrewdly appraised his man. Broad brow, living eyes, arms folded, he was of the world, and it had given him most things he wanted. No Hogarth rake, no worshipper of wealth for all his money, the splendid vitality of his early years, evidenced in his fine physique, was now full tide of thought—the mentality of Oxford, the physique of Otaheite, yet was he content to light the way to others. As "the Sun of Science" the London papers lampooned him, prancing with a foot on each hemisphere, a butterfly net in his hand.

Baronet, Privy Councillor, Knight of the Bath, President of the Royal Society, D.C.L. of Oxford, founder of the Royal Agricultural, the Linnean, the Antiquarian societies, as a boy he scoured the village lanes round Harrow and Eton for treasures of leaf and tendril, drained the Serpentine with young Earl Sandwich to study its fish, lay out in the fields of Chelsea at night listing the stars. As a youth he followed Cabot to Newfoundland, sailed the spheres with Cook to the discovery of two dominions, and with Solander, pupil of Linnaeus, challenged the North Pole.

An occasional attack of hereditary gout had numbed his flair for foreign travel, but £6000 a year to play with, vast estates in three counties, even the idiotic court life of London and the favour of an indulgent king, could never numb that boyish zest for knowledge.

A gay story went the round of the clubs that Sir Joseph once entertained the idea that fleas were of the genus of lobsters. He boiled the crustacean creatures to see if they turned red.

"Fleas are not lobsters, damn their eyes!" he snorted—or so the jesters had it.

"The Butterfly of Bath" they called him—but he alighted on the flowers of philosophy.

He transformed the stiff Royal Gardens at Kew into a Hesperides. He sent George Vancouver, one of Cook's midshipmen, in the track of Drake to write Britain's name round the globe. His influence financed Herschel's great telescope that had mapped the skies for Britain. He endowed the Chair of Natural History at Oxford, sent Mungo Park to Africa, backed Jeffries in his first balloon flight across the English Channel, believing it a feasible thing that man should take to himself wings. The enemy acclaimed him scientist and *savant*. They made him an honoured member of *L'Institut*. He believed in humanity. Even the felons of New South Wales he claimed as fellowmen.

Straight brows above penetrating eyes, Sir Joseph was deep in thought.

"New Holland," he said slowly, "is a star of the first magnitude on Great Britain's horizon. I see the future prospect of empires and dominions. Who knows but that England may revive in New South Wales when she is sunk in Europe ... but you know, perhaps, that the French are there before us?"

Flinders started.

"Baudin, a merchant captain with a large expedition of twenty-three scientists, set out from Calais to survey and examine those shores in good ships a month ago—the *Geographe* and the *Naturaliste*. We gave them a passport."

Flinders winced. "Then I am too late."

"I have lived long enough, Mr Flinders, to know we need never take anything for granted. Would you race the Frenchmen to New Holland?"

For one anguished moment, Matthew thought of Ann—home leave.

Discovery! "I would, sir."

Sir Joseph placed his finger-tips together.

"This, of course, as the enemy has it, is all *en l'air*. We must take time to think, there is much to plan, but you are a man of knowledge and achievement in that country, and your offer comes at a critical time in its history. If my Lords Commissioners approve the scheme, as I think it probable they may, you would be prepared to leave at the earliest, I take it, for summer sailing in the antipodes?"

Alas for Matthew's sacred dreams—the old oak at Partney was farther away than the fig-trees at Port Jackson.

"Aye, sir," he said.

"Thank you, Mr Flinders. I'll see what I can do. Keep in close touch with me. In the meantime, I hope to see you one day at breakfast for our scientific lectures, or more particularly on Sunday nights, when I gather a few friends from the Seven Seas. I hear you were with Bligh in Otaheite, and sailed the Horn as I did long ago... ."

Louis Quatorze stood at the door, announcing in wooden tones:

"Mr and Mrs Brinsley Sheridan. Hall-so a stoodent, sir, Mr 'Umphrey Davy. The person with the cuss cuss is still waiting."

"Show Mr and Mrs Sheridan in. Ask Mr Davy to wait. Give 'the person with the cuss cuss' a guinea, and tell him to come back."

As Matthew followed through the hall, a courtly gentleman and a rarely beautiful woman passed him by. He recalled stories of duels, an elopement, a nunnery, and a roguish play of the day, *The School for Scandal*.

Lucky Samuel had gone home, but now he must wait for a hurried leave that would be only hail and farewell—perhaps none.

From his dingy room in the Fountain Inn looking out on the drab shipping, he hid his heart-ache between the lines in his first home letter to Ann.

My imagination has flown after you often and many a time, but the Lords of the Admiralty still keep me in confinement at the Nore. You must know, and your tender feelings have often anticipated for me the rapturous pleasure I promised myself on returning from this antipodean voyage, and an absence of six years.

It is a shock to my spirits and the ardency of my hopes that will not easily be done away. Thy meekness and benevolence, thy resignation to the will of fate in the great hour of dissolution, only show how much greater is the loss of thee than before we were sensible of.

Ann, he knew, went visiting at this time of year.

I should be glad to have some little account of your movements, where you reside and with whom, that my motions may be regulated accordingly … indeed, my dearest friend, this seems to be a very critical period of my life.

I have done services abroad that were not expected, but that seem to be thought a great deal of. I may now perhaps make a bold dash forward, or may remain a poor lieutenant all my life.

A crescendo of cheering and a music of bands drew him to the window. A carriage drawn by four white horses was making slow progress through braying, horraying crowds. It was hung with garlands and flags, and showered with roses. The roads were lined with yelling thousands. They swarmed the sloping roofs, leaned out of the houses like cuckoos out of clocks, waving their aprons, pelting flowers and screaming.

The carriage swung round for Bluetown in the milling square below him, postilions whipping a way, the mob delirious with joy, and the occupants gaily saluting. There was a wrinkled ancient in ambassadorial robes, a lady of fashion so magnificent that she must be the Princess of Wales, and a sparrow of a man in admiral's plumed hat, shyly saluting—and with the left hand! The Star of the Garter blazoned on his breast. Nelson!

Nelson for the first time in England since the Battle of the Nile, the noblest hero of all time, the darling of their hearts come home. Saviour of Italy, saviour of England. Hail! Hail! Hail!

Matthew caught one glimpse of his face as he chanced to look upward in mechanical salute with a fixed but pleasant smile... a shrunken face from that he had remembered, an eye gone, teeth missing, an arm gone, physique frailer than ever, racked by victory after victory. For all his glory Nelson paid the price. But who were these others that shared it? He called to a stevedore below.

"Hit's the Heye-telian embessador, sir, Lord 'Emilton an' 'is lidy. Gaw sive Nelson!" he bellowed. "Give it ter Boney, Nelson! *Gaw sive the King!*"

They passed on their way to London by a road feet deep in flowers, and London River rang that night in revelry and rejoicing.

Next morning the serving-man came to announce "a young gentleman".

"Show him up," said Matthew—probably one of the *Reliance* boys on a message from Waterhouse—but a fat, rosy youngster ran into his arms.

"Cousin Matthew! It's me! It's John!"

Little John Franklin in middy's rig, dirk, cocked hat and all!

Matthew hugged him to him, then held him at arm's length.

"John! You're in the Navy! Never!"

"Aye. H.M.S. *Polyphemus*. In the end papa had to let me go. He sent me a trip on a trader to Lisbon, thinking it would cure me. After that I would die for the sea, so Thomas brought me down and bought my outfit, and put me aboard ship, and we're just come back from a cruise of the north. The first thing I saw was the *Reliance*, and asked them there for thee, and here I am!"

"My little John! How tall thou'rt grown, and how spruce and genteel. Thou'llt sail within three points of the wind, and run nine knots under close-reefed topsails." Matthew caught him by the shoulders and looked into his laughing dark eyes. "Now listen, but don't breathe a word ... if thou art a good boy, there's just a chance that thou might'st sail with me. Work hard with thy tutors, and come to me on Sundays. We'll see. But now we'll have some coffee, and thou'llt talk to me of home."

Brimful of news and hilarity, John clattered before him down the stairs. By his plate was a letter. Sir Joseph had recommended him to the Admiralty. His presence was required in London.

Enchanted days they were for Matthew now. My Lords Commissioners, Earl Spencer, Earl St Vincent and Yorke spoke highly of his work. They thought it should receive instant encouragement in the urgent need of Britain in the south. Now in the matter of a ship, what would he suggest?

He thought of *Tom Thumb* and the *Norfolk*, and suppressed an exultant smile. Their lordships' weighty patronage was pleasant to the taste. He was commissioned immediately to seek a suitable vessel, and refer the matter to Sir Joseph.

That meant day after day of scouring the docks from the Tower to the Nore with Sir Isaac Coffin, Resident Naval Commissioner at Sheerness, and Whidby, the Master Attendant, who had fitted out Vancouver. Most left-overs from the war were fit for nothing but firewood, but one sloop, H.M.S. *Xenophon* was found to fill the bill. A veteran of convoy, recently re-coppered and repaired, she was still a fair sailor—and 334 tons of Flinders's dreams came true. He had asked for the command of one ship—he was given the command of two. The *Lady Nelson* would join him in New Holland, flat-bottomed for the rivers and bays.

Sir Joseph's Sunday nights—the house in Soho Square aglitter, carriages rolling up in the rain, gilded cornucopias pouring out silks and velvets, stars and laurel wreaths, coronet and ribands and decorations. Sir Joseph was a benign host, his brown hair dressed with powder and pomatum, square-cut, gold-laced frock-coat, scintillating silken hose, the Order of the Bath ... but Matthew liked him better in his home-spun tweed jacket and leggings.

Warmly he welcomed his motley of guests, that ranged from a poltroon Prince of Wales—a bespangled rosebud in diamonds and pink silk, shoe-bows, knee-bows, neck-bows, feathers and lace—to a grizzled whaler. Sir Joseph's invitations netted them all. He put the new word "lion" into London's social language.

They said that at any moment a lion might appear, and "Who was the lion?" the news-sheet scribblers asked them. Aristocrats and *hoi polloi*, they came to laugh at each other.

There you would see the grave and hoary Astronomer-Royal, Dr Maskelyne, in deep converse with a Pennine ploughman who had seen a shower of meteors and reported a volcano in the moon; Fannie Burney, the garrulous *Evelina*, gossip of a century, ogling "Old Q" for the latest scandal at Almack's; benevolent and witty James Watt who had invented a pumping-engine with steam-driven pistons to clear the flood-waters of the Cornish mines, and was suing Hornblower for his rights; Lady Hester Stanhope, stately and beautiful young niece of Prime Minister Chatham, learning the geography of Palesitne from a bearded pilgrim Jew; fat and jolly old Dr Erasmus Darwin, proclaiming in impassioned poetry his prediction of

> A flying chariot through fields of air,

and

> Sea ballons beneath the tossing tide,
> The diving castles roofed with spheric blass...

One night George Romney, the artist, was there, face to face with the model who made his fame, the slavey-goddess Emma Hamilton, most talked-of woman in England, Nelson's love.

That scandal had burst above their heads like a fireball in the sky. It rocked the ships at sea and all the salons and saloons. They whispered she was about to bear his child. If that were so, she was a matchless actress. Her "Attitudes", to Matthew's unsophisticated eyes, were a marvel of classic beauty, and none acclaimed them more blatantly than the withered old diplomat, in snow-white satin from top to toe, who was her adoring husband.

In those luxurious rooms where the great gilt mirrors reflected the flash of jewelled snuff-boxes and the restless flutter of fans, where flute and hautboy and harpsichord were drowned in clatter of tongues, Matthew would slip away to a quiet corner ... to compare notes with a Navy officer, to sniff the pungent fragrance of the conservatory near by, to study the graphs of an earthquake machine. It was no use. He was swooped upon by a watchful Sir Joseph, who foisted him willy-nilly into the fashionable world—sat him down with Earl St Vincent, landed him into a time-keeper argument with the Astronomer-Royal, Dr Maskelyne (who told him that his calculation of the latitude of Lieutenant Dawes's little observatory at Port Jackson was only one point out), and insisted that he plod through long descriptions of New Holland for that silver-tongue, Mr Burke.

"My countryman, Lieutenant Flinders, who is about to survey the unknown coasts of our continent down south. His name as an explorer is known to you, Edmund—or it should be."

The son of the little Donington doctor, stiffly returning the effusive bow of the illustrious Mr Burke!

He was more at ease with a gentle, stammering Mr Lamb of the East India Company, who told him his father came from Lincolnshire, and showed him an eerie poem that a friend had written of "The Ancient Mariner". It recalled vivid memories of slack sails in the doldrums, and the Albatross Island in Bass Strait. The friend, said Mr Lamb, had never been to sea.

Matthew was happier when those Sunday nights merged into Monday mornings.

Sir Joseph had undertaken to fit and equip the ship, generally to direct her, to engage the scientific staff, superintend the erection of "the largest possible greenhouse"—in short, to make the expedition his own. In confident anticipation he christened the old *Xenophon* "H.M.S. *Investigator*" and, eager as a child with a new toy, gave her all his valuable thought, the power behind the throne that so blandly, so blindly, would sign the commission. Sir Joseph's bouquets of Chinese myrtle camellias to Her Majesty Queen Charlotte, a kennel of Newfoundland pups to one of the fifteen children, his barrels of oysters and live turtles for soup to the kitchens at Buckingham Court, evoked royal smiles of destiny on empires yet to be.

"Is my proposal for the alteration in the undertaking of the *Investigator* approved? J.B." he once wrote to Evan Nepean, secretary to the Admiralty.

"Any proposal you make will be approved; the whole is left entirely to your decision. E.N." was the affable return memo.

Sir Joseph, the childless, treated Flinders as a son. The parrot eye of Louis Quatorze no longer bent his way. So much to plan, so brief the time, he was welcome whenever he came. One of the finest scientific libraries in the civilized world was his to command, Miss Sara Sophia Banks, in her Barcelona quilled petticoat, its librarian—the portly dame of his first appearance; but her Gold Stick in Waiting was only in commission when she went calling on the Princesses at Kew.

A remarkable woman, deep bass voice and dry humour, she was Sir Joseph's keeper of the keys, his secretary, his ready reckoner, his second self, an authority on natural history, on heraldry, on coins, with collections of curiosities unique, even as the store of her cosmopolitan mind. Very downright, even forbidding. Miss Sophia could, if she would, unfold treasures on earth. The lucky lieutenant was one of her favourites.

On quieter evenings the Herschels came from Richmond, tiny Caroline, "the lady of the comets", the tall Sir William and his brother John, explorers of the heavens, who made the empyrean Britain's empire, multiplied the thousand stars of Tycho Brahe's tabulation into shining legions wheeling to time-table out of time. Those were memorable nights, for Matthew spoke their language.

Through the "seven-foot Herschel" in the conservatory, he went a-sailing into inter-stellar space, past the guiding lights of Sirius and Canopus, by lunar lands forlorn, through phosphorescent seas of nebulae to island universes more dazzling, more glamorous than the earth constellations of the Pacific. A cold blue moon of blinding light far down in the southern circle, he met his old friend Fomalhaut, that had guarded his little skiff from antipodean reefs.

The Herschels encouraged him with the most delightful stories of their early struggles through travail to the stars—

Caroline barking her shins over pulleys and gear, taking William's notes in the black dark of the barn … sweeping the floors for William, then sweeping the skies for her comets, timing them by a metronome on the stable roof … William walking round a post for hours polishing his lenses … Caroline caught on a butcher's hook that held aloft the brilliant little "seven-foot" that found for them Uranus and fame. They invited him down to Richmond to meet the Great Nebula in Andromeda and all his celestial friends through the giant "forty-foot" that was itself one of the sights of England.

They did more—they swept him from the divine music of the spheres to the spheres of divine music. Caroline at the harpsichord, John with his singing viola, and white-haired William brooding in the deeper chords of his 'cello, they carried him away on waves and whimsies of harmony into the new world of Haydn, Handel, Mozart, and this young rebel whose sonatas and symphonies were taking Vienna by storm, Ludvig van Beethoven.

When he grieved that such a world was for ever closed to him, they showed him the glory that the masters had made of Danny Dree's old flute, and of their great kindliness gave him many a lesson.

Then there was Lady Banks herself, pleasingly plump and gracious in her chiffons and slab curls, her cupboards filled with priceless old china, her walls with miniatures and etchings. She served him tea from her new Japan cups, transparent as eggshell, the first to be seen in Europe.

"Koo Cheong, Pekoe, Soo Chang, Bohea, gunpowder, or Russian?" she would beam upon him … and he told them of the Port Jackson convict women, out in the scrub, gathering their poor little weeds that they called "sweet tea".

At that, Sir Joseph would bear him off to the study to see Port Jackson's sickly yellow clay that his crony Josiah Wedgwood had made into plaques and medallions. There was an allegorical group of Hope, attended by Peace, Art and Labour, sent out to the colony to stimulate the poor brutes to endeavour, and a more cynical Slave in Chains that had inspired one of Erasmus

Darwin's bravura sonnets—"Hail. O Britannia, potent queen of isles."

Sir Joseph had always a thousand questions to ask him, a thousand droll stories to tell of the days when he sailed with Cook, of "my pretty little girl in Otaheite", and the natives that stole the quadrant, of all things, just before the transit of Venus; of Cook's murder of the Maoris—"the most disagreeable day of my life, black be the mark for it!"—of the frozen death of Tierra del Fuego and the fever of Koepang; of the endless, barren hills of New South Wales, "like the back of a lean cow, covered with long hairs, and where her scraggy hip-bones have stuck out further than they ought, accidental rubs and knocks have entirely bared them. At first glance I doubted the country would support a shipwrecked crew."

At their second meeting Matthew had asked for Briscoe—to learn that Briscoe had given his life at the Battle of the Nile— "the last of my old retainers to make the journey with Cook, always hankering for ships, and so he enlisted with Nelson, as so many of our best men do. Where did you meet him? At Revesby?"

"Aye, sir, and longing to meet him ever since, for it was Peter Briscoe's tales of Cook and thee, and my uncle, John Flinders, first gave me my love of the sea. So Briscoe, too, has gone." He told the story of a little boy from the wind and the rain, hearing of unknown lands by a Revesby fireside in a simple sailor's telling—a lad who peered through a door at a globe of the world. The door had opened.

"I recall the night." Sir Joseph's smile was kindlier than ever. "If I mistake not, they rang the Brides of Enderby for thee."

All through that hurried November, under the grey of London skies, Matthew remembered the cloudless crystal of the days in New South Wales, its rollers and its romping surf, smouldering blue of the mountains, the limpid green of harbours.

He hated this imbecile social round, the "drums", the "routs", the "riots", cards in the candle-light from dawn till drunken dawn, racket of the Auction Rooms, snuff and scandal of the coffee-houses, the "Gazettes Extraordinary" that lived like rats on offal. He hated the bucks and the beaux, high heels and pasty faces, perfumes, powderings, posturings of the mincing creatures who called themselves men. Ranelagh and Vauxhall, with their sculptured shrubs and masquerades of smirking immorality for immorality's sake, meant nothing to him, whose eyes had seen the glory.

The cock-fighting and the women's prize-fights, with bets on Bruising Peg, were revolting as the floggings in New Holland—and in the spiderweb of London, no escape. It injected its money-poison and kept them slaves and half-wits. He steered clear of George III's levees, with the painted faces and the pomp, and longed to be away on his three hundred acres of nothing at George III's River. In many ways he would be glad to be back … if he could only take his love.

Hurrying up and down from the Nore, he corrected the proofs of his "Observations", and spent hours over the charts with Aaron Arrowsmith, who had just challenged Ptolemy with a new map of the world on Mercator's projection.

On 12 December, my Lords of the Admiralty inspected the *Xenophon*. On the eighteenth, her commission as H.M.S. *Investigator* was approved by Earl Spencer, and referred to a king no longer sane. Matthew patiently waited His Majesty's pleasure.

Waterhouse and Shortland were back into the war. Doctor George had married Miss Bess, floated his £10,000 company in a fine fanfare of optimism, and in a gay little brig, the *Venus*, 140 tons, 12 guns, had gone back to the South Seas for a fortune in pearls and pork. It was a lonely Christmas in the noisy river. Matthew wrote to Ann in hopeless yearning—how would they pass the years?

Study music, French, geography, astronomy, even metaphysics, sooner than have thy mind unoccupied. Soar, my Annette, aspire to the heights of science. Write a great deal, work with thy needle, and read every book that comes thy way, save trifling novels. It seems promotion will not come with my appointment… .

Even so, he had his ship.

New Year was a good three weeks old before my lords returned from the Yuletide junketing that was denied their underlings, and remembered the Frenchmen in New Holland. On 25 January, Lieutenant Flinders's commission was delivered. From that day began the haste and fret that were to eat away his life.

H.M.S. *Investigator* lay at the docks at Sheerness, north-country built, elderly now, but her mission was exalted as that of Columbus, and her young commander had chosen her as the nearest he could find to Cook's plans and specifications of the ideal ship of discovery. To him her rigging presented theorems in Euclid unending. In her furled canvas he saw the charts of virgin shores, the scroll of fame.

Captain Martin formally handed over with good grace, and volunteers were called for. The entire crew, led by bosun Charles Douglas, offered themselves as one man. First of them all, from the north country, was her first lieutenant, Robert Fowler, fair, frank and efficient.

"I believe she's an enterprise of Sir Joseph Banks's sir? My father, a Horncastle boy, went to school with Sir Joseph. Needing a lieutenant, sir? If so, I'll gladly apply for the post."

"From Lincolnshire?" said Matthew. "I think I can speak for Sir Joseph. Welcome home."

With Samuel as second, as the powers had already promised, except for a master, his officers' list was complete. Among the six ambitious "young gentlemen" who had sent in their names, a bunk was reserved for John Franklin, and for the son of Matthew's old schoolmaster, Sherrard Lound.

They had decided she was to be a ship of youth for three good reasons. Old sea-dogs of the service would make it a hard going for "a strip from God knows where"; a voyage round the world called for health and virility—a long, strong pull in a boat, and miles to walk ashore in no land for weaklings; and beards in the fo'c'sle, as Sir Joseph knew them, were rum-sodden nests of sedition and sin.

There was no lack of young men to answer the call. A fine crew was chosen in a week from a roll-up of hundreds, the last eleven from Vice-Admiral Graeme's big *Zealand* lying alongside. When Flinders read out the purpose of his voyage and called for the eleven, 250 out of her company of 300 crossed to his side.

The next few weeks were pandemonium of preparation, settling the crew in quarters, sealing the gun-ports with stench of burning oakum, the shipwrights' hammers singing a song of gladness as they took the copper two streaks higher for tropic sailing, reconditioned the holds, built jolly-boats, long-boats and cutters, and a greenhouse on the quarter-deck. Stevedores and chandlers staggered up the gangways in swearing procession all day, with eighteen months of salt provision and twelve months of dry.

A comfortable ship. Flinders decided to cut the commander's cabin in two, making space for a natural history museum. Two of the gentlemen could mess with him, and even then she was roomy. Doctors Bell and Purdie arrived. He duly installed them, with a pang at the heart for Doctor George.

Sir Joseph had selected his scientists, all young men save Bauer, a gentle Austrian who was to serve as draughtsman to the botanist. The botanist was Robert Brown, a reserved intellectual Scot who in boyhood had won Sir Joseph's undying regard by sending him an unknown moss from Ireland. "This young man will make his name," he wrote in introduction. "He works with a warm interest and a cold mind." The artist, William Westall, of no less promise, was a boy in his teens, and the astronomer, Mr Crossley, was of Dr Maskelyne's best.

On 16 February came an envelope heavy with Admiralty seals.

"Captain Matthew Flinders." A radiant surprise! Promotion!

That day he hoisted his pennant, the youngest captain in naval history with one exception, Horatio Nelson—and Nelson only because his senior officers in the Indies had died of yellow fever.

At the beginning of March, Samuel was back for duty, bringing all the news of the home-folk—but little Franklin, with a long face, came to forfeit his bunk. With Admiral Hyde Parker and thirty-five sail of the line he was off to Copenhagen, Nelson in H.M.S. *Elephant* leading the van, to fire a salute to Elsinore Castle, and teach the Dane to be polite to Britain in the Baltic.

A few days later the Grand Fleet was on the wing, the *Investigator* slipping down to the Nore to board her marines and await the passport from France.

Hostilities with England were wearing thin while Napoleon was mowing fields of men at Hohenlinden and Marengo. Nevertheless, the nations were still at war, and if the ship had to fight her way to discovery, Sir Joseph's greenhouse must go overboard.

Oh dear no. Sir Joseph spoke to Lord Hawkesbury, who spoke to Citizen Otto, the French commissary in London. In return for the courtesy extended to Baudin, a passport could not be refused.

On 6 April it arrived. Flinders studied it in his cabin, Mr Brown translating—a document so brief and simple that he could almost read it himself. Through M. Jurien, his Minister of the Marine and Colonies, Napoleon graciously extended the freedom of the seas.

"*La corvette* Investigator, *sous le commandement de Captain Matthew Flinders*" was beyond the reach of national grab. Her expedition "*sur la Mer Pacifique*" to extend human knolwedge and promote the progress of nautical and geographical science was lovingly nestled under the Eagle's protective wing. She might pass right under the prows of ships of war, take refuge and find assistance in need in ports of the Republic, in Europe and throughout the world, a pre-arranged signal her safeguard.

"*Il est bien entendu cependant*" ... that she would not voluntarily leave her allotted course, that she would not engage in commerce or contraband, and above all, that she would not identify herself with any hostility to the Republic, nor in any way further the interests of its enemies.

He sat over the passport late that night. Through its starry accents, flourishes and scrolls inscribed on immortal parchment, he looked deep into the clear grey of a waiting woman's eyes. His ship was safe, a haven for his love.

He wrote at once to Ann.

H.M.S. Investigator at the Nore,
April 6, 1801.

My dearest friend,

Thou hast asked me if there is a possibility of our living together. I think I see a probability of living with a moderate share of comfort. Till now I was not certain of being able to fit myself out clear of the world. I have now done it, and have accommodation on board the Investigator, in which as my wife a woman may, with love to assist her, make herself happy.

This prospect has recalled all the tenderness which I have so sedulously endeavoured to banish.

I am sent for to London, where I shall be from the 9th to the 19th, or perhaps longer. If thou wilt meet me there, this hand shall be thine for ever.

If thou hast sufficient love and courage, say to Mr and Mrs Tyler that I require nothing more with thee than a sufficient stock of clothes and a small sum to answer the increased expenses that will necessarily and immediately come upon me, as well for living on board as for providing it at Port Jackson, for whilst I am employed in the most dangerous part of my duty, thou shalt be placed under some friendly roof there.

I need not, nor at this time have I time to enter into detail of my income and prospects. It will, I trust, be sufficient for me to say that I see a fortunate growing under me to meet increasing expenses. I only want a fair start, and my life for it, we will do well and be happy.

I will write further to-morrow, but shall most anxiously expect thy answer at 86 Fleet Street, London, on my visit on Friday; and I trust, thy presence immediately afterwards. I have only time to add that most anxiously I am,

Most sincerely thine,
MATTHEW FLINDERS.

P.S. It will be much better to keep this matter entirely secret. There are many reasons for it yet, and I have also a powerful one. I do not know how my great friends might like it.

Next morning he gave the order to jettison guns for an extra fifty tons of water—away with the long eighteens of slaughter and destruction. Twenty-six-pound carronades would be enough to frighten away pirates and inspire respect in the Indians.

Much was awaiting his attention. He applied to Vice-Admiral Graeme for ten days' leave. The first morning he spent at the Admiralty, taking delivery of all existing charts that Dalrymple had copied for his guidance, the stray threads of old Dutch and Spanish fable, straggled lines of west and east drawn by Dampier and Cook, a bay or an island that had sheltered a shipwrecked crew—those mysterious coasts that loomed out of the blue once in a century, to fade away again like a forgotten dream.

There were the quadrants and compasses to be collected, checked and forwarded, with Arnold's and Earnshaw's time-keepers, and the letters from the Admiralty to the Governor of New South Wales with instructions regarding the *Lady Nelson*. Then there was the commander's scientific library to select, and all books and journals of South Sea travelling to be conned over at India House, the British Museum, and various booksellers.

There was a bizarre order to place with the hardware merchants and haberdashers—

500	pocket-knives
500	mirrors
100	combs
100	red caps
200	strings of white, red and yellow beads
100	pairs of ear-rings
1000	yards of blue and red gartering
100	yards of brightly coloured linen
300	pairs of scissors
200	finger-rings
1000	needles
200	files
100	shoemakers' knives
5 lbs	of red thread
100	hatchets
50	axes

and any other engaging ironmongery they happened to have around, with trumpery King George medals made to order, and a couple of bags of new copper coins. In gewgaws and gimcrack such as this a handful of mariners from antiquity onward had paid for the peace of a hemisphere.

The East India Company selected for him an adventurous ship's clerk, John Olive, and the Navy Board a captain's servant, Elder, a staid fellow with excellent recommendations. Then nothing would do but Sir Joseph must bear him off to the terra-cotta and gilt windows of his own tailors Messrs Schweitzer and Davidson, the pride of Old Bond Street, personally to supervise cloth and cut of a Navy captain's uniform, special order, to be ready by the end of the week.

"I will have you take particular care of this uniform, Elder," Sir Joseph admonished the waiting servant. "See that it returns to England in good condition, worthy of His Majesty's decorations, and with contents well cared for, safe and sound."

"I'll do my best, sir," Elder promised with his wan smile. Matthew chuckled to see the supercilious Mr Schweitzer, creator of Beau Brummell, instantly and literally grovelling at his feet.

It was a most impressive person that rang for Louis at Soho Square on the following Monday evening—a dashing young captain in Navy blue, gold braid, gold anchor buttons, gold epaulettes gleaming, three-cornered hat with a debonair tilt, the sword of His Majesty's commission buckled to his side.

With an appreciative nod for Schweitzer's part in the fitting out of the *Investigator*, Sir Joseph led him into the study. In the candle-light of the desk were eighteen dun-coloured, leather-bound volumes.

"This," said Sir Joseph, "is a modest manual that you will find of value. It aspires to be a compendium of the knowledge of the world, compiled by a friend of mine, Dr Andrew Bell of Edinburgh—it needs must be a Scotsman for such an undertaking, the book of a thousand centuries, with no beginning and no end. He calls it *Encyclopaedia Britannica*, and this is his third edition. For patience and enterprise alone, 'tis worthy of an honoured place on the bookshelf in your cabin, but I think you will find it as nearly a mirror of truth as the human mind can make one."

Matthew fingered the uncut pages and was lost in Volume I. Before he could express his thanks, Sir Joseph had opened a satin-lined case, old and discoloured, where minute mechanisms nodded and swung, marking off sidereal seconds. The precise little footsteps were lost in his deep and vibrant voice.

"This guided the *Endeavour* round the world. May it bring you safely home."

Cook's time-keeper!

"For me!"

Matthew was almost startled. Reverently he cradled the dark wooden joinery in his hands. Star-time. Sun-time. The steady clitter was heard again, marking sidereal seconds ... and these were of the greatest of Flinders's life.

"I go to survey the coasts," he said, "of the continent the master found. With the help of God, there will be no need for any man to follow after me."

He looked into Banks's living brown eyes. The moment was sacred between the two as a profession of faith.

"But come," said Sir Joseph, "dinner waits."

In the morning Troughton told him that the nautical time-tables, those dove-tailed arcs of the stars neatly recorded in recurring decimals, would not be ready for a week.

He stood on the corner of Whitehall, his dark eyes darker with dreams. Three days to Lincolnshire, and three days back. Ten minutes oblivious while London wheeled about him ... and then he was off to the White Horse Inn, running, to catch the coach.

North, through the pageant of the English spring, and spring was in his heart.

Outside the city boundaries the hawthorn lanes, the harebells and scent of the dusk began. As they rattled along through Epping Forest, a wizardry of moonlight, the horses' hoofs were keeping time to the old rollicking tune:

When I was bound apprentice in famous Lincolnshire,
Full well I served my master for more than seven year,
Till I took up to poaching, as you shall quickly hear,
Oh, 'tis my delight on a shining night in the season of the year!

Harlow, Saffron Walden, Cambridge, Ely, cracking whips and creaking leather, plunging through bog and quagmire, they left the miles behind, past sleepy inns in the small hours, cathedral towers in the dawn, and over the border to March. The Fenlands were a sea of blue flaxflowers, with flung spray of the apple-orchards and sails of windmills slanted silver in the sun.

From Spalding he greeted Boston Stump with its coronet of spires, passed the bridges and the quays of the Witham in the gloaming, and came in time for late supper to the White Hart Inn at Spilsby, smocked shepherds and whiskered gaffers, the slow speech and the simple thoughts of his own people.

Partney at sun-up.

The Tylers were at breakfast in the little brown rectory with its deep thatch and gay garden like a poke-bonneted dame. Mrs Tyler sat at the coffee urn, Ann with bread-knife on board, ready to saw away, the Reverend with head bent while Isabel said grace.

A quick step on the gravel path, a shadow in the doorway, then something between a laugh and a cry as Ann and the bread-knife were folded in two blue arms. Ever decorous, he kissed them all.

He had changed much—keen wide eyes that could fathom shoal and sound a man's character; dark hair waved back from a mathematical brow and fluffed to his braided collar; the round hard chin of command; bottom lip curved and full, the top rather a despot. In profile he was a stern realist, full face something of a dreamer, but that sea-tanned face was quick to laughter. Sturdy and rigidly erect, though he thought, and spoke, and acted swiftly, no nervous movement ever betrayed an endless mental activity. When he smiled, he seemed a boy of seventeen, when he frowned, a man of forty.

"I've come for Ann," he said, his arm about her—Ann blushing and tremulous with joy, her head nestling into the broad shoulder of His Majesty's and Mr Schweitzer's highly exclusive coat, her frail white hand on the hilt of the sword.

"Have some coffee," mildly suggested the Reverend. The girls bustled about him, and breakfast went joyously on.

"Well now"—Matthew pushed his plate aside, so business-like he might have been engaging a bosun. "You have my letter, Mr Tyler, sir. Am I to take it that my proposal is approved?"

The Reverend stroked his shaven chin in heavy deliberation.

"Father!" Ann pleaded, and he melted into a smile.

"We shall talk it over. How long is your leave?" he countered.

"To-day with you, to-morrow at Donington, Sunday night in London. I'm truly sorry to hurry you, sir, but the marriage must be to-day."

"Marriage!" Mrs Tyler gasped. "No banns? No gown? No posies?"

"Do I gather," it was Mr Tyler's last stand, "that you are taking our daughter directly to live among the cannibals and convicts of New Holland?"

"At once!" said Matthew briskly. "We sail within the month, God and the Admiralty willing, but a happier home we could never find than the one I shall make for her there, sir. A land of rare beauty in eternal summer—and I have dear friends among its women who will care for her and keep her happy until I have completed my survey." He thought of Mrs Paterson and Mrs King, and longed to multiply them by forty. "Trust me, Mr Tyler. Believe that I shall never take her into peril. Annette is dearer to me than all the world. But come—our marriage, sir. Tell me what is needful."

"Well!" The Reverend scratched his head. "I can perform the ceremony, but there are witnesses to find."

"Dear child!" protested Mrs Tyler feebly. "Will she have no wedding gown, no posies at all?"

Ann solved both problems in one—no backward bride.

"Hannah Franklin will most surely lend me her new white brocaded silk for dancing, and Mary Hudson from the Hall will come with her to be witness. We'll keep it a secret from every one beside. Father! To Spilsby, for Hannah and the gown!"

All three Tylers were away in the gig. The little brown rectory was quiet ... the lovers alone ...

At noon, one bell ringing. Hannah, Isabel and Mary Hudson twittering in frills and thrills, Matthew at the altar-rails, rigid as Cold Collingwood on the quarter-deck, Mr Tyler saintly and solemn in his vestments ... and Ann in her lace bonnet and white brocaded silk, wood-brown curls falling to dimpled shoulders, grey eyes clear and serene, a spring posy in her trembling hands.

Dearly beloved, we are gathered together here in the sight of God and in the face of this congregation ...

Mrs Tyler bowed her head. She was the congregation.

"Wilt thou have this woman to thy wedded wife ... ?"

"I will."

A slant of sun set his gold epaulettes shining.

Drowse over the village—nobody knowing. While Mrs Tyler and the girls prepared the wedding feast, the lovers were lost in the young green shade of the old old Partney oak.

Mrs Flinders ... so quaint, so elderly it sounded when he drove her back to the White Hart at Spilsby, but not in the moonlight of their wainscotted inn room, daring to dream together all they had dreamed when the seas of the world divided.

"My wife ... "

The Donington coach was early next morning and the Flinderses late. When they were up and off, a gig came after them at full tilt, Mr Tyler shouting.

"The money!"

"The money?"

The money for Ann's board. Matthew grabbed it in handfuls from breathless Mr Tyler, and for safe keeping from highwaymen or being lost in ectasy, stuffed it down in his boot. A last family kiss for the rosy bride, and they turned the corner of the white-blossoming lane.

The coach set them down at the doctor's door for a few precious hours at home before they caught the south-bound to Cambridge. Matthew spent most of them with his father in the surgery, but how could they hope to span the years? They talked of the future rather than the past. Grey little Doctor Flinders, his spectacles dewy with emotion! After the first shock of surprise, he gave them his loving blessing.

So much to say, and so little said. There was a festive dinner round the big dining-table, Betsy and Sue prouder and prettier than ever, the small step-sisters gazing at this unknown blue and gold brother with shy, childish smiles, his stepmother beaming. Betsy was to be wed herself in summer to William Dodd, and they would live in Boston—black-haired Betsy, of Betsy Island, losing Annette, her friend.

"Thou wilt to-day pardon me if I say but little, beloved Betsy," cried Ann, in tears in her arms. "I am scarce able to coin one sentence, but now I am a part, though a distant one, of thy family, dear Betsy. It pains me to agony when I remember I must leave all I value on earth, save one—alas, perhaps forever. Ah, my Betsy, but I must not, dare not, think. Farewell! Farewell! May the great God of Heaven preserve thee and those thou lovest, oh everlastingly. Adieu, dear darling girl. Remember your poor Annette."

God's blessing! In farewell to his father, the first shadow of parting fell upon Matthew's heart.

A hail to Henrietta as they passed through Spalding, that night they slept at Huntingdon, the next at the Norfolk Hotel in the Strand. On Monday morning, he presented himself to Sir Joseph, "with grave face," he laughingly told Ann, "as though nothing had happened."

Busy days—and evenings—that were heaven, Ann in the rocking-chair by the window, wide-eyed with wonder at London, showing him all she had bought for their comfort on board, their home in New South Wales, while he knelt beside her, holding her in his arms. One night she brought a stray grey kitten she had found in the street, a purring blue-eyed mite. She called it Trim.

"Born to fame, Mr Trim!" she held it up, its furry paws helpless. "Thou art H.M.S. *Investigator's* specially-commissioned ship's cat."

It cast an anguished glance at Matthew, and protested in soundless meow.

At the end of the week they were down to the Nore, the ship like a gull in the moonlight.

Discovery and his love!

He still had no master, had tried as far as Portsmouth, but experienced men were hard to find with all the fleets at sea. The East India Company, in return for services to be rendered in opening up the sealed book of commerce with New Holland, had voted £1200 for captain's and officers' mess, £600 paid in advance.

The controller of the Navy office had selected a good cook. Russell Mart, the carpenter, was guaranteed in proficiency from stepping a 100-foot mast to carving models in a bottle. Bob Colpitts, gunner, was looking forward to a holiday. A Derbyshire miner, John Allen, was the Royal Society's nearest approach to a geologist. A conscientious stone-cutter, little more, but in a new country, he informed Captain Flinders, the reefs were naked to the eye. You just picked up the gold and silver, if any. Sagacious and likeable was the quaint little redhead, Peter Good, gardener from Kew, in his sylvan glade under the guns.

Apples, oranges, peaches, pears, apricots and grapes were already thriving in Mrs Macarthur's starved acres at Parramatta. Matthew wrote to Sir Joseph suggesting God's good berries. There were no gooseberries in New Holland yet, no cherries, currants, raspberries, no plums, no nectarines, so they were sentenced to transportation with Peter as warder. Now that Captain Hunter had introduced cream to the colony, Matthew visioned a dinner for his friends, the Kings, at the whitewashed Government House, with dessert of Devonshire's cherry pie and Lincolnshire's gooseberry fool. His Majesty's ships, thanks to Captain Bligh, were becoming floating orchards.

They were waiting for the Admiralty seal that would set them sailing. Drowsing and browsing in their inimitable way, my lords had not given them a thought. He plaintively wrote drawing attention to the fact that summer was over in the antipodes—that somewhere on the coast of New Holland, perhaps, the Tricolour was flying.

Ann was as much at home as Trim. To a county girl the ships at the Nore were sensation and delight. So different from the haughty captains' wives and the bumboat gypsies of the docks, the sailors all liked her, shouted with laughter at her innocent questions, told her tales as tall as the masts, donned clean shirts and shaved every day just to pass her by. In the light of the latticed windows of the Commander's cabin, she worked at her embroideries, or gaily sewed on buttons for Samuel and little Taylor, the midshipmite. She leaned rapt on the rail to hear some stirring story of battle, sweetly presided at dinner with Matthew and the scientists and bluff Doctor Bell. She even stormed the bread-room with Mrs Tyler's recipe for yeast that never failed to set.

On May-day the lovers slipped away in a boat for a halcyon day on the Essex side of the Thames and the revels at Southend, Matthew and Ann dancing the maypole together, an unforgettable May-day of young blue skies and laughter, the twining ribbons, the phantom faces of smiling strangers to an unknown fiddler's tune.

Glorious days of do-little—he was longing to be gone. Well into the middle of May the *Investigator* lay at anchor in the stream, ready to sail for Spithead. The astronomical instruments from Troughton, fireworks for distress and toys for barter, and the private signals from Admiral Graeme were delivered, and still no word from Whitehall. Stagnation brought unnecessary troubles and cares, too much time for inspection showed up too dearly the ship's age. Her gun-ports were low on the water. How long would the jig-saw planks and oakum keep them sealed from the southern ocean? With a third of their pay in advance, it was hard to keep the crew aboard. Two of his men deserted from the *Advice* brig tendering alongside—went ashore carousing and were lost in the taverns.

Then again, Samuel had let a prisoner escape, a man they were guarding for Vice-Admiral Graeme. He dived overboard and swam off when there was no one on the quarter-deck, and it was Samuel's watch. He said he had left Midshipman Sinclair in charge. Ken Sinclair looked at him in surprise, but did not contradict him.

A sailor's troubles are over at sea. The commander engrossed himself in researches of compass variations, and watched for the Admiralty barge.

He did not see it when it came.

It was an afternoon of honey-gold over the hop-fields of Kent and the dreaming river, a few sea-birds and a few wherries wheeling in the lazy blue. Ann was reading in the cabin, sea-light rippling in the beams above her, when Matthew hurried in, as he managed to do at least once in the hour.

"A hair of thy head, Annette," he said, "one single shining strand."

"But surely thou art growing sentimental."

"Could I be otherwise when I think of thee? But no. I need it for the sextant, an artificial horizon."

"Artificial, sir!"

He kissed her mimic frown, her laughing lips, and then, as ever, she was in his arms, and he was telling her the thousand happy secrets, closing her eyes with kisses, her light hands caressing the wave in his hair.

He felt her grow rigid, and blushing scarlet she rose.

He turned.

Nobility in plumed hat and gold-laced coat was standing in the doorway, eyebrows up and thin lips down in grimace of sour surprise. Behind, two others were peering.

Earl St Vincent!

Lord Spencer!

Mr Yorke!

"Hr-r-rm!"

With flash of buckles and swagger of swords, the peers stalked in.

St Vincent glared at Matthew, and took up a solid stance—Anubis, the dog-faced god, cast in terra-cotta.

Lord Spencer raised a jewelled lorgnette, and scarified Ann.

Bland Mr Yorke studied the captain's bookshelf.

"My lords, I had no idea—" Matthew bowed.

Lord Spencer swung on his scarlet heels, and focused the lorgnette upon him. "Obviouslay!" snapped Lord Spencer.

"I am exceeding sorry, Captain Flinders," St Vincent's accents were sharp as the axes for the Indians, "that we should select this moment to intrude upon your—ah—privacy. We happened to be at the Nore, and thought we might inspect the *Investigatah*."

"Most certainly, my lords. May I present you to my wife? Mrs Flinders."

They bowed. Two jerks and a convulsion.

St Vincent was outraged. Spencer frigid. Mr Yorke turned from the bookshelf, acidly amused.

"We understand from Sir Joseph Banks that you are not a married man."

"I was married in Lincolnshire a month ago, my lords, to Miss Chappell, who has always been my friend."

Ann stood, very pale, clasping and unclasping her hands.

"Our apologies, madam, for intruding."

She dropped a little curtsey. Mr Yorke, with critical eye, approved.

"If your Lordships will excuse me—" breathless, she vanished.

"And may I ask, is Mrs Flinders making the voyage with you?"

"It was my intention, my lords, to take her to New Holland."

"Oh." A weighty silence. "Howevah. Would it be convenient for us to see the ship?"

Matthew led the way on deck, his dignity as scattered as his crew.

My lords seemed satisfied, even pleased. He gave a sigh of relief when they had gone. There was another jubilant love-scene in the cabin, boy and girl kisses of mischief and mimicry of might.

On a morning in May the ship of science shook the sailmaker's creases from her courses, and slid down to the broad wash of the Thames Estuary. The white horses bit and slapped at her black-tarred bow as she tacked and stood into the Downs. Ramparts of the enemy, the coast of Napoleon's domain, loomed through Channel haze.

To starboard the coast of Kent was engraved on the parchment grey of the sky in tawdry pigments. A black breakwater framed the huddled terraces of a Kentish town, Folkestone, perhaps, for there was a tall spire blown into clarity by the desiccating wind.

The grey scuttling waves were beating a merry pattern of sound on her slight timbers, when the dawning came to her captain of a jarring through the ship. There seemed to be a mammoth crew scrubbing a mammoth deck. It grew until it scratched his tense nerves with its harshness, then with the jolt of a hackney coach striking the kerb, the *Investigator's* keel bit into solid ground.

The captain, with a word to Ann, fled up the companion, his ship grinding from rudder to counter.

Slaty waters dyed white around him. She was aground, object of pity for the Kentish fisher-folk. Anguished, he cried to Fowler: "Back topsails! Grab the breeze, or we're here for a week."

The topsails swung around, and tugged at the rooted masts, then—was it the clouds that were moving, or was it the masthead?... the keel was scraping free. With a lurch the ship was off, and sliding into deep water, the seamen cheering in the shrouds.

On the hardest-sailed seas of the world, here was an uncharted shoal. Discovery was beginning before they were out of sight of the smoke of London. They threaded the Needles into Spithead, where the harbour-master gave them a clean bill. From her trip ashore, the *Investigator* had suffered not an atom of damage. Flinders put the shoal on the chart of the Channel— marked it down as the Roar, and gleefully forwarded the amended chart straight to the Admiralty.

Four days later came a letter from Sir Joseph. It requested his presence in London. Sailing orders! Admiralty instructions! Blithely he ran for the coach.

Sir Joseph was grave. His manner was brief. He flicked at a clipping.

"The notice of your marriage from a Lincolnshire paper," he said.

"Yes, Sir Joseph. That is true."

"I understand from the Admiralty that Mrs Flinders is aboard the *Investigator*, and that you have some thought of carrying her to New Holland. If that is the case, I am very sorry to hear it. I beg to give you my advice. By no means venture to a regulation so contrary to that of the Navy."

"But Sir Joseph, I was not aware of any such regulation. There are many captains whose wives travel aboard their ships, as you doubtless know, and without the protection of a passport."

"Regulation 21. You will find it recently listed. I conjecture that it has been necessary by the fact that our fleet in the Mediterranean has been made a laughing-stock of lanterns and levity, by the—er—friend of one who is a genius in naval warfare, but in private life human. In future, the ships of His Majesty's service will not carry women to sea. There is another matter. On going to the Admiralty, I was mortified indeed to learn that you had been ashore in Hythe Bay, still more mortified to hear that several of your men had deserted, and also that you had lost a prisoner entrusted to your care, a midshipman being in charge of the quarter-deck at that time."

A Hogarth quack on the wall leered down on Matthew's misery.

"The chart of the Channel, sir, supplied me by Arrowsmith was the cause of my misfortune. Instead of a shoal in the chart, four to sixteen fathoms are marked. Finding so material a thing as a sandbank three or four miles from shore not laid down, I thought it my duty to prevent a like happening to others. Giving the most exact bearings, I wrote myself to the Admiralty. It would have been easy for me to suppress the whole circumstance, for we have suffered no particle of injury, not even from the carpenter's report. I have no master aboard, there was no pilot, and having constantly been employed in foreign voyages, I cannot have much personal knowledge of the Channel."

"Mm. And the deserters?"

"Left, not our ship, but the *Advice* brig. They went ashore with money in their pockets, and stayed so long they were afraid to come back. Our ship was moored in an English roadstead, which accounted for a midshipman being in charge on the quarter-deck."

Sir Joseph was cold and unimpressed.

"These reports have pained me, Commander Flinders. I could only say in defence that as you were a sensible man and a good seaman"—his voice grew crisper—"such matters could only be attributed to the lack of discipline that takes place when the captain's wife is aboard."

Matthew flushed.

"Lieutenant Fowler will tell you, I think, sir, that discipline is improved. It is true that I had the intention of taking Mrs Flinders to Port Jackson, to remain there till I should have completed the purpose of the voyage, and then to have brought her home again in the ship. I trust that the service would not suffer in the least by such a step. The Admiralty have probably thought I intended to keep her on board during the voyage."

Sir Joseph looked very directly into Flinders's troubled eyes.

"I am convinced, from what I have heard, that if they hear of her being in New South Wales, they will immediately order you to be superseded, whatever may be the consequence, and in all likelihood order Mr Grant to finish the survey."

Matthew drew in his breath sharply. Sir Joseph's eyes were of a garnet hardness he had never seen before. Was there no memory of his own impetuous loving ... of Lady Banks in her unimaginable but doubtless distracting slenderness and tenderness of youth, of "my pretty little girl in Otaheite"? Had the Sun of Science lost its warm human ray?

"It would be too presumptuous of me," he ventured in earnest undertone, "to beg of Sir Joseph Banks, my powerful friend, to set this matter in its proper light?"

Sir Joseph took snuff, very remote.

"I thought I might have conveyed to you that I do not approve. If you care to take the risk, I shall present your case, as it stands, to the Lords of the Admiralty. I promise you no success."

An awkward silence. The world turned cold.

Matthew picked up his cocked hat. The Hogarth quack was openly laughing.

Sir Joseph rummaged in amber-handled drawers and produced his map of the moon.

"You may need a little time, Flinders, to think the matter over. It would not be wise to delay too long." He took up his quill, and wrote a note in a margin.

Matthew stood facing the light, chin high, cheeks strained and white, his right hand on the hilt of a virgin sword. He saw sulphurous tides smoking in to alps of vague white sand ... he saw a woman's closed eyes and eager lips, and felt the quick hunger to take her ... he saw minute mechanisms that nodded and swung, marking sidereal seconds, precise little scythes of a ticking clock that measured the passionate, passionless waves of the sea.

"I shall give up the wife for the voyage of discovery," he said very clearly.

Sir Joseph rose.

The Sun of Science was shining in benevolence again. "I knew," he said, "that would be your decision. I also know that you will be a credit to yourself as an able investigator, and to me for having recommended you. You have my sincere esteem and real regard."

He held out a warm, human hand ... but the scrolled doors closed with a chill finality.

For the first time in his life, Matthew Flinders stood irresolute, his heart crying to him to turn back while there still was time. And he knew there could be no turning back. The way is the way, and there is an end. Pattern of a man's fate, ravelled as threads of the foam ... the old Nottingham lacemaker had woven it in his strand long ago. With rapid steps, unseen, a pale young captain of His Majesty's Navy was lost in the throng of London streets in the blue of a June day.

He kissed Ann in silent greeting, and hastened to many duties—he dared not take her in his arms.

Perplexed, she watched him shyly as he sat at the top of the table at mess, so young, so old, his lips set in too straight a line, his dark eyes brooding. Brown's prim exactitude, Fowler's gusty sailor laughter, bluff Doctor Bell's endless twitting of his bride, could not rouse him to attention, to the quizzical little smile she knew so well and expected.

Together in their cabin, she lifted his hand from the page of his writing, and held it.

"What is it?" she asked, afraid.

He tried to control the twitching of his cheek that would betray emotion ... then slowly drew her fragrance to him, nearer, closer, brokenly whispering that so he must hold her for ever. He buried his face in the laces at her breast with a deep sobbing breath.

She trembled. "I know!" she cried. "They will not let me go."

Through the quiet of the night he held her, hearing the little voices of his ship and the lapping of an idle tide. A lover's eloquence, a lover's vows, were the stuff of dreams and heartbreak. In grief and love, she was passionately, pitiably, his. Her fingers sought his profile, the ruffled brows, hollow of the eyes, full lips a little grim, the sharp masculine curve of throat and shoulder ... she was feeling as a blind man feels, so that she might remember. His eyes and hands in the darkness burned memory of her beauty in his brain.

Together they faced the melancholy daybreak, grey above the masts of ships—ghost-ships sailing out of the world. The chanties of the sailors were a mournful wailing of farewell, a dirge of the division of the sea.

"How shall I renounce thee?" he said in solemn sadness. "They ask of me more than is human."

"Thou wilt go—to the unknown land, my dear, to find there honour and fame that I may share it. Think of the honour that is already thine, to be chosen for this truly glorious project. Ah never fear, the years will be gone before we know it, years no more than a dream, and thy name will live for ever. I have no fear of the sea—it cannot take thee from me, for God has kept thee and ever will. Matthew, I know thou wilt come back."

He slipped to his knees beside her, hearing the beating of her heart.

"Thou art my dark star," he said, "the dim companion of Sirius. How can I shine, without thee ever near me? How shall the light of ambition burn in the dark of the loveless years? Stay with me in thy thoughts, my love, or I shall indeed be drifting. Write to me constantly, write me pages and volumes. Tell me the dress thou wearest, tell me thy dreams, anything so do but talk to me, and of thyself. When thou art sitting at thy needle and alone, then think of me, my love, and write me thy thoughts. Think of me as I read the letters of this dear hand, fifty times over—let it write me something for every day. Thou art my happiness. Oh dearest, kindest, best of women! Thou art the end of all my actions. If I loved thee before our marriage, how much dearer now. When the long watch is over, know that I am thine alone in the last thoughts of each day, near to thee, with thee, living in our looks, our thoughts, our words, our kisses, our everything of love!"

Elder, with the morning coffee, knocked twice unheard.

It was an abrupt young captain that came again to command. Ann, the darling of the ship, had become a nervous stranger. She worked all day at her embroideries in the cabin, fashioning a little "forget-me-not" of fine silken threads. They were afraid of the night now, lest parting should be to-morrow. They were afraid of the dawning, lest it should be to-day.

My Lords were piling on the agony of suspense. At the end of June, directions had not arrived. Flinders wrote plaintively that the French must already be landing on the coast of New Holland.

On 1 July the fleet came home from Copenhagen, bells ringing madly for another Nelson victory, the taverns of

England ringing with the tale of the glass to the blind eye. The signal was popular badinage in the streets. You would hear them shouting "Cease action!" and the hilarious "Now damme if I do!" That was England.

In a war-stained uniform, little John Franklin told stories of heroes and horror. The salute to Elsinore Castle would echo through the aisles of history.

Captain Matthew listened with a smile, remembering Brest.

"What's it to be, John? War or peace? Honour in arms or discovery? Killing Frenchmen, or south with me?"

"South with you!" John Franklin fairly shouted.

To the crowded shipping at Spithead came a lone old ship from Port Jackson—H.M.S. *Buffalo* with Hunter and Kent aboard. One night they heard the throaty whistle of an approaching "Bonnie Dundee". John Thistle!

The *Investigator*'s master—just in time. Thistle was promptly promoted to blue cap and gold buttons. Six years in New South Wales—and he was ready to go right back. The *Investigator* was truly a ship of friends.

Shore leave till they were weary of it. Day after day they waited. My Lords of the Admiralty, in summer weather, were inspecting the feet at Torbay.

The commander sat for his miniature to the nineteen-year-old Westall, but so much haunted by the sadness of its dedication that he pressed it into Ann's hands at last—the yearning shadow of a shade.

In a musty corner of a dockside tavern, the Sign of the Prancing Mare, Thistle found a cunning man, a soothsayer named Pine, who conjured visions of the future from a crystal ball. He told Thistle many boding things—of a ship that sailed to distant climes to join another, of voyages in the unknown and voyagers lost. Thistle would drown, and then there would be shipwreck, not one ship, but two, fading down into the sea together. The credulous among the crew went to consult the seer, came back with whisperings of the shipwreck but no foreshadowing of death. They laughed about it in the fo'c'sle.

One day Ann slipped in to the Sign of the Prancing Mare, turning a deaf ear to its language as ripe as its rum. She sought Mr Pine in his garret, and for an eerie hour gazed at that lean face, grotesquely ballooned in the translucent ball of fate.

She came back to the ship puzzled.

"What did he tell thee?" Matthew, laughing, chided her in kisses.

"It was a curious thing, Matthew." She was thoughtful. "He could not see us at all. Two lovers, man and wife, he saw, but they were old—a grey-haired man, he said, forever fretting."

"The charlatans of the waterfront, my dear, have cost us a good half crown!"

On 17 July came sailing orders at last, ponderous parchments richly dight with signatures and seals.

King George III—who knew nothing whatever of it—commissioned Captain Matthew Flinders to investigate the new continent of New Holland, to circle its shores and span them, to bring information, vegetable, animal and mineral—in trite fact, to set another jewel in that jeweller's masterpiece, the British Crown.

Captain Flinders was to sail to the Leeuwin, where the Dutchmen's old sloops had drifted north from knowledge. He was to circumnavigate the whole zone of the continent or archipelago, and thoroughly survey it, returning to Port Jackson for his stores. Then he was to make a detailed examination of the north coast and west, and other unknown shores he might have discovered, and again returning to Port Jackson, engage in exploration of Bligh's Isles of Feejee. After that, he was free to return to England.

The Admiralty estimated the duration of the voyage as a possible four years. They suggested that Captain Flinders might be gone with the first fair wind.

Four years. Farewell.

Summer moonlight slanting in the commander's cabin, slanting through the oaks of a ghostly fantasia of ships....

Ann left the *Investigator* next morning, a forlorn little figure in muff and tippet, down to the waiting hackney coach where friends would take her to London to await Mr Tyler's coming. John Franklin, standing by the coach, seeing the tragedy of their eyes, wondered at their silent good-bye.

The ship was ready to sail that evening with the land-breeze. It was a Sunday, 19 July. The docks were quiet. The men chanting in step to the whirling of the capstan, the last strand was broken as the anchor, caked with slime, clattered into the ropes and tackle that would hold her up round the world.

Cries and jeers of the bumboat women faded astern. Fresh canvas booming, fresh hemp squeaking, fresh cedar groaning, and fresh hearts beating, the marble-smooth wake lengthened to the docks. Fiddles of ocean, with a sweeping of strings, swung under the steersman's song.

Flinders looked up to her swelling sails, the tall masts swaying. Light of the great adventure was in his eyes. With a hand on Franklin's shoulder, "For this was I born!" he said. "If the plan of a voyage of discovery were to be read over my grave, I would rise up, awakened from the dead!"

10

Investigators

"*Fine weather and light breezes.*"

All sails set, the *Investigator* put to sea flying the White Ensign, a silver gull of peace among the war-dogs of the Channel.

Not for Matthew the welling tears of slowly-fading horizons. As soon as she was well under way, he called his officers into the cabin to receive standing orders.

"You all know your duties," he said. "I need not detail them again. Alertness is the watchword. This ship is consecrated to science, and she must look the part. Ropes belayed and coiled fair, sails in perfect trim, no slovenly afterthought of weather-lifts, braces and back-stays. Each officer must be in a position to correct mistakes in the log, and none may alter sail without my knowledge.

"Cleanliness is godliness in any ship, and more than any in this. Seven bells—hammocks piped up and the between decks washed and swept, the lower deck after breakfast. I shall inspect at noon. There are to be hourly reliefs for the lookout by night, four-hourly by day. Although I am approachable at any moment in any matter, I am not going to belittle you with martinet interference. Every man to his own responsibility. But remember, lenience is not laxity. Indulgences are not to be abused."

Turning to the juniors, he quelled with a glance of stern surprise John Franklin twirling his cap.

"From the master's mates and the midshipmen I expect much. You must not only supervise, you must share the work, up in the top with the men—seniors in charge of topsails, younger gentlemen mizzen-top. Each one of you must know the ship's position from the astronomer's daily observations, and submit to me your journals once a month. If you show interest and aptitude, I shall allow you to stand watch in the cabin, and learn navigation and marine survey, both for the purposes of this expedition, and for your own future advancement. Remember that youth is the time when knowledge, reputation and fortune must be laid in to make age respectable. Thank you, gentlemen. That is all for the present." They trooped out.

He took off his three-cornered hat, and looked absurdly boyish.

Samuel smiled a crooked smile. "Quite the commander!" he observed.

Matthew's expression hardened. So aloof and abrupt was his manner that he might have been old man Hunter. "I am the commander!" he said briefly. Samuel smiled again, and sauntered off. A curious boy with a streak of resentment hard to understand.

He dined alone in his state-room that night, and his watch was a long one. Lights of the men-of-war about him, faint crinkle of moonlight on the sea, his thoughts and his heart were with Ann. The Great Purpose was launched. His ship was travelling south, in the tracks of Lapérouse and Cook, to survey the last of the continents, but the wind in the rigging was an elegy, and the triumph was hollow without the woman he loved. Two years, or three, of aching loneliness, of constant need, but "this, too, shall pass away", and the rewards were deathless. In the time between, a new world was his kingdom. The stars were setting when he went to rest.

In the first day's run the *Investigator* gave warning of sinister things to come. Midshipman Sinclair leaned on the spanker boom, and it carried away, rotten through. Mart, the carpenter, looked for other faulty timbers, and found plenty to do.

Free of the eternal war-talk, and rumour, and alarms, the commander's table at dinner that day was a pleasant one. On his right hand was Fowler, telling tales out of school of Sir Joseph in his boyhood, and on his left, Brown, of the gently sardonic Scots humour and the steady blue eyes. Next to Brown sat bluff Doctor Bell, and directly opposite, Bauer, an untidy eater exuding geniality and enthusiasm. Westall was shyly attentive, Dr Purdie full of vim, and good John Thistle frankly nervous. This was John's first experience up among the gentlemen. With a wary eye, he was making a note of the order of spoons and forks. Lound and Sinclair and Taylor and little Franklin and the others down at the end of the table shared a subdued hilarity all their own, and Samuel sat in Fowler's place on the first lieutenant's watch.

One chair was vacant all the way to Madeira. John Crossley, the astronomer, was the world's worst sailor.

Off the coast of Spain there was a mild sensation—out of the mist at midnight a brig on the starboard bow. She refused to show colours till a shot woke her up—a Swede, in sullen mood, remembering Copenhagen.

The main-royals bellied to heavy wind, and sleety storms swept over. They dried the ship out below with stoves. Already she was making three inches of water in the hour, but Fowler said that was her normal gait. The leak was below the waterline, and the pumps were good. Before they put in to Funchal, the cutter was away to explore the cliffy isle of Bugio in the Dezertas, and picked up a hawksbill turtle, Item No. 1 in the natural history collections. The tiny green linnets called canaries were wheeling and singing in the caves, and puffins skimming about the boat. One of the seven that Matthew shot as specimens had an exact fathom of brass wire binding on its wing—"A story here, my lads, if we could only read it. What Crusoe of what lost isle sends us a messenger?"

Funchal was swarming with Englishmen, three British ships in the harbour under Commander Bowen, with the 85th

Regiment on board. The Frenchmen were expected at any moment, and they were going to catch it hot. For the rest, the population of the quaint white town scaling the hills seemed to consist mainly of nuns and priests, the church and convent bells for ever ringing. While the ship loaded water, the British consul, Mr Pringle, invited Matthew to take up his quarters at the prettiest little mountain villa he had ever seen. He fared better than the botanists. They put up at an inn in the town kept by an Irishman, and were nightly devoured by armies of Portuguese fleas. By day they scoured the peaks of Puica Ruiva.

Fruit harvest was late that year, grapes, pears and peaches green and tasteless, but the water-boatmen loaded them up with strings of pungent Spanish onions that shouted their popularity a cable's length. As Fowler remarked on the night they sailed, "We can shift those carronades now, mister. We won't need any guns to keep the Froggies away." The only misadventure was a harsh one. When Brown and Bauer and Westall were coming off, the boat with their sketches and collections capsized in the surf, and everything was lost. With the first asperity he had shown, the captain punished a couple of drunken seamen— twelve lashes. Men on duty with the scientists were forbidden liquor ashore.

On the long run now to the Cape, Matthew studied dietetics for his crew whether they liked it or not—plenty of fresh meat, oranges and lemons, hot breakfast four times a week with all the porridge they could eat, barley broth with Spanish onions, and when these gave out, lime-juice by the gallon, sweetwort, and a potable soup that they detested. They revolted from it in liquid form, so he made them eat it in cubes for the vegetable value. Every fine day their bedding was shaken out and sunned, and both decks sprinkled with vinegar to freshen them, and every wet one they were aired in front of the stoves.

On Sundays and Thursdays, wet or fine, throughout the voyage, the commander mustered the company and personally saw them clean. A resplendent little figure in blue, strutting up and down the lines meticulous as a maiden aunt, he frowned on stubble and humorously levelled a spy-glass at the polychromatic patches of a brawny sailor's pants. "A shining example!" It was his favourite expression. "That's what I want my men to be, at sea or ashore."

Crossley was pathetically under the weather, his intentions good but his complexion chronic green. He managed to crawl up to take the latitude at noon, then staggered below again with gulps and mute apology. The captain and the second lieutenant shouldered the work together.

A solitary swallow circled the ship as she rolled south to the Line, an incongruous visitor among the albatrosses, skimming the scuttles and ports for flies, alighting on the boats and sometimes on the cabin. Each morning Matthew watched for that friendly speck in the blue—a last message from England. On the fifth day it was missing. They found it dead in the captain's state-room underneath a bureau. John Thistle didna like it. "A bird in the ship's aye lucky, but no when it dies abooard." They laughed at him for an auld Scots wife.

They passed San Antonio, a twinkle of lights fifteen leagues to the west. Sails on the morning horizon, and two little luggers came posting up, apparently privateers, for they fired a shot to leeward and came right on with English colours flying. The *Investigator* had hoisted her ensign and pennant. Now she cleared for action, but kept her course in lofty dignity. The small dogs decided not to worry the big, hauled to the wind and made off. It was just one of the chance encounters of the sea.

"*Hoisted topsails in fine weather*." The trade wind runed in the shrouds. Gleaming shoals of flying fish pelted like summer rain. On the eve of crossing the equator, the sailors hooked a giant bonita that gave a pound and a half of fresh fish to every man, and six gallons of oil. The commander was so pleased that Midshipman Franklin was primed by the crew to ask for a celebration. He stood at Matthew's right hand after dinner, and waited very politely.

"Well, John?"

"Please, sir, may we have the ceremony to-morrow, when we cross the Line?"

Matthew brushed away a smile, and scowled in mock severity.

"I see no Line, and to-morrow is not in the calendar. Explained precisely what you mean."

The company laughed at the youngster, and he laughed back.

"The shaving, sir, and the ducking," he pleaded.

"Don't tell me you're going to start shaving, John—an old war veteran of your age!" Matthew chucked him under the chin, and poked a playful finger in his dimples. "Right! Here's a bargain. You tell me when we will cross the equator, and I'll allow the ceremony, but on one condition only—in full latitude. We can't have the *Investigator* wrong in her calculations, playing the fool with old Father Neptune."

John scrabbled at figures all the evening, and finally won them the day, a fine little boy and doing well. Ship's biscuit agreed with him. He was hourly growing taller and rounder, filling out his uniform and threatening to leave it behind, a favourite from the fo'c'sle to the quarter-deck. Matthew was very proud of his young kinsman. He wished that Sam were blessed with that contagiously merry nature. Some day, if he had a son, he hoped he might be like John.

The day that never was was uproarious. The commander played Neptune in a hempen beard with the cook's pitchfork, Sam and Thistle helping him out with the shaving, for very few had crossed the Line before. At night they put the ship under snug sail and served out grog to all aboard, with dancing to drum and fife on the half-deck in the moonlight, while the gentlemen celebrated in the cabin with walnuts and wine. When Dr Bell congratulated him on his prowess with a razor, "Oh, I'm an adept at that," laughed Matthew, and he told them of the tale of the barber of Illawarra, and of Thistle dancing the Highland Fling in the wilds of Moreton Bay.

"Prancing cannibals, those New South Welshmen," he said. "I was afraid of them once, until I learned that our common

252

bond was laughter. Show fear, and your life is in deadly peril. Laugh, and they all laugh with you. Madmen and fools are safe in the South Seas."

As he talked of New South Wales, his dark eyes glowed interest, and he held his young listeners spellbound, keen to be there. Ship's bell tolled midnight, with them still clamouring for more, but "It grows late, boys, let us dismiss"—he gave the order smiling.

They rose as one man and left him to his log-books, and the last thoughts of the happy day to be written to the grey-eyed girl in England. The fo'c'sle sang the sirens down till sunrise.

Two or three times they veered from their course, trying to track up lost islands, those almost mythical isles of the old-time mariners that had the knack of disappearing for a hundred years or so, and turning up in the same place when they were forgotten. Faulty compasses were to blame. Fifty men cannot land on a beach, and light a fire and eat a seal all in the same dream. The islands were there, he was sure. Ile Sable or San Paula was one of them, the alleged latitude a little south of the Line. In two days' cruising around, it failed to show up. "I have a shrewd suspicion that we've come too far," he told Fowler. "I'd like to go back across the equator and look for it there, but there's nothing about these will o' the wisps in Admiralty instructions, so we'd better not waste more time." A stolen day for Saxembourg further south was just as futile, and later on the quest of Bligh's St Paul, half-way across the Indian Ocean.

The *Investigator* was constantly reminding him that she was the old *Xenophon*. He could never go farther to the wind than abeam without a copious leaking, and every sea that struck her broadside gave her St Vitus's dance. Her spirit was willing, but her battle-wracked frame was weak. They shifted the ten-pound carronades into the after-hold to steady her, and made ready for re-caulking at the Cape.

The English fleet was in when he arrived there in October, six formidable battleships, their guns trained on the fort. War in every port of the world that men had made worth owning! His crew was in first-rate health. There was nothing to do but caulk and refit. While the men picked oakum, Brown followed in the sacred footsteps of Linnaeus, his master, on Table Mountain, and Mr Crossley thankfully hurried ashore, to set up his tents for the time-keeper observations on the road to Simon's Bay. It was a great site for scenery but a bad place for work. Naval officers on promenade turned in for a yarn at all hours, drunken sailors caroused about it on Sundays, and Dutch peasants and African slaves came for a peepshow at the sun—through the theodolite!

Flinders called on the commander of the English fleet, Sir Roger Curtis, and changed the two men who were giving him trouble for two of more sober habits. He had no stomach for floggings. A drone of a midshipman was shipped back to England, and in his place he managed to get Denis Lacey of the *Lancaster*, who longed for the chance to come with him.

A fortnight was more than enough in Cape Town. They were hoisting boats to go, and Matthew hastily scratching the last passionate postscripts to Ann. "I am as one half of a pair of scissors," he was telling her sadly and quaintly, when Mr Crossley, an hour aboard, knocked at the state-room door.

"May I see you at once, Mr Flinders? An urgent, a most regrettable business."

Matthew motioned him in to sit down. He was very ill at ease.

"I am afraid, sir, I must leave you." He spoke spasmodically. "Much as I have wished that my name should go down with your own—to posterity in the grand achievement of the *Investigator*'s …explorations I feel … I feel, Mr Flinders… ." He cleared his throat twice, put his handkerchief to his mouth and swallowed.

"You feel seasick!" said Matthew conclusively. "Not already, surely?"

"It seems I'm one of those people, sir, who can't … stand it. Most unfortunate, but there you are. It's the smell … it's the smell of the bilge. Excuse me! I'll be back in a minute." He finished in a rush and fled.

Thus Mr Crossley tendered his resignation. In a little while he was back, pale but relieved, to make it formal, and for a more ceremonious farewell. He had put off the evil day till the last possible moment, hoping against hope. "But it's no use. I can't face it. I see so many spots on the sun, sir, I'll be losing my reputation. I'm not afraid of cannibals, and I don't mind shipwreck, but I *can't stand that*!" He pointed with a groan through the port-hole to the shimmer of the dancing wave. "One solid acre of England, and I'll never lift my foot from it again."

"How are you going to get there?" asked Matthew mischievously.

"If it's humanly possible, Mr Flinders, to walk up through Africa, I'll walk."

They spent an hour on the astronomical books together, and shared a parting glass. Then Mr Crossley, in regret and relief, packed his trunk for the shore. Matthew sent for Second Lieutenant Flinders. "

"Crossley's leaving us," he said. "A life on the ocean wave is not for him, so he has very wisely put in his resignation."

"But what a squib to wait till the last moment! What luck have you now of getting one from the fleet?"

"There's better luck than that, Sam—for you. Will you take over the astronomical work?"

"Oh heavens, I couldn't take the responsibility for a job like that—not at twenty, they wouldn't allow it."

"What has your age to do with it? It's the quality of the work. Under the circumstances, I have the power to appoint you."

"Yes, perhaps ... but how would I know that the work is up to standard?"

"I would."

"Well, if you'll stand behind it, that's a different matter. Yes, I'll take it on." He showed a kind of hidden exultation, and Matthew was glad. Fate had turned up a magnificent chance, and Sam had the sense to see it.

"How is Franklin with the time-keepers?"

"Oh, they're all lazy beggars, they don't do any more than they should."

"Make them want to. I'd like to see John get on."

"This ship," remarked Samuel dryly, "is turning into a sort of family party. It's all friends and relations, showing the world what we can do."

"Which is not a bad basis," Matthew suggested, "provided we do."

From that time on, Sam was official astronomer, with a brilliant brother to help him out, and John Franklin an offsider with the time-keepers. They were becalmed for a day under the frowning brow of Great Smits Van Winkel, then the breeze came in from the west, and they were off across the Indian Ocean.

Now the ship travelled on wings of the wind. A thousand miles a week she put behind her, in "the gull's way and the whale's way", where the only events were sunset and dawn and the stars of the summer night.

On the tranquil sabbath evening of 7 December, the lookout sighted land, the Leeuwin, Land of the Lioness in the old Dutch charts. The commander called him down, and went aloft, Vancouver's sketch, and that of Beautemps-Beaupré in his hand.

He saw far-away shores, like wisps of smoke, with wisps of smoke above them, a maze of islands dreaming in the dazzle of afternoon sea. The shabby green coast of the main was strangely like the coasts of New South Wales. If New Holland and New South Wales were two islands, they were very close kin.

Glamour of sunset in her sails, and her captain at the masthead, the Ship of Youth drew in to the Land of Age. Eighty fathoms of chain ran out as they slipped the anchor through the apple-green waters down to the coral sand. From far away they could hear the Lioness growling.

The days were alight with interest now, every man and boy on the ship keen to be first to find it, investigators all. John Thistle in a boat ahead, Samuel taking his azimuths by two compasses on the binnacle, they proved the Isle of St Alouarn to be but a curve in the coast, hauled round Vancouver's Eclipse and Seal and Breaksea, and came by moonlight into King George's Sound ... about them the dusky stillness of the bush, above them the silver stillness of the stars. In the red dawn the boats were off to the shore, wood and water and exploring parties, oars dipping and flashing in the early morning sun.

A grey land, silent, waiting. Its own people, whoever they were, had vanished, nothing to show their being save a few wurlies deserted and the ashes of fires still warm.

The big bell tent and the marquee were rigged for the botanists by a rill in Princess Royal Harbour. The men put down a well close by, and a saw-pit for the carpenters, cutting the forest primeval to knock up dozens of new plant-boxes for the insatiable Mr Peter Good. The cooper mending his casks, the sailmakers mending the sails, there was soon a busy village in the eucalypts' light shade.

In a halcyon fortnight of soft breezes and sunshine, Westall set up his easel and canvas on a convenient headland, sketching in the feathery outlines of the Sound, and Mr Brown, with Bauer in tow, wandered in seventh heaven. A botanical Columbus, he had discovered a new world, a rich vegetation quite unknown, yet old as the rolling globe.

Here the antique fossil ferns were still blowing green, that no other eyes had seen save in traceries of stone. There were prehistoric treasures at every step, living relics of the cretaceous and carboniferous ages, millions of years before man. The fecundity of these seemingly sterile sands was amazing, and the drab grey of the bush, on closer acquaintance, a glittering prism of colour, from frailest pink and mauve to rabid scarlet and burnt gold, everything a riot of bloom from the forest trees to the dainty scarlet legumes. He found orchids, earth's rarest, growing in lavish profusion and rubbing gossamer shoulders with sweet little plebeians on the ground; blossomy carpets of blue and dreamy purple; a flower brown as the habit of a nun, of poignant and beautiful fragrance; carnivorous small atrocities, their hairy cups full of dead ants; climbing vines, ground-creepers, honey-scented shrubs in numberless novel varieties, and one ridiculous stick of a stalk that bore a perfect replica in green and crimson, or green and black, of a kangaroo's paw.

The Tyrol in spring was a commonplace to summer in King George's Sound. Mr Brown was never to be found—not lost, but gone before in paradise.

Matthew was checking up on Vancouver's charts, rowing from beach to beach taking his angles, surveying Princess Royal Harbour and Oyster Harbour with Sam, trudging for miles alone through the sand and the tussocks of wire-grass, climbing the highest hills for panorama. The only break in the line of the coast was a far sparkling lagoon that he marked down for later attention. Fold after fold, those sleepy hills faded away to the north in a veil of haze.

Homing boats at twilight were laden with fish and oysters, a nightly feast for ship's company. They found low humped islands of sand and scrub, pitted all over with the nests of the little black "Mr Pitt birds", or alive with the small brown and grey kangaroos that the blacks at Port Jackson called "wallabi". They found craggy isles of micaceous granite studded with garnets, scintillating in the evening sun like Hindu temples, and isles white as gypsum with the guano deposits of thousands of years. They found roseate lakes, set hard as alabaster—crystallized salt— river-courses without water, fresh-water lagoons black with geese and wild duck, seals with red fur sunning themselves on sea- swept ledges, yellow snakes in the brushwood, and the tracks of Dampier's yellow dogs.

On one crag of a rock there was a wide circle of driftwood and evil-smelling offal of bones and feathers and fish—a ceremonial haunt, a blackfellows' feast?—but there were no human tracks, and they had seen no canoes. More probably it was the nest of some gigantic bird of prey, a condor's aerie.

There were trees scarred by axes and saws, and a sheet of copper eight feet square engraven "August 27. 1800. Chr. Dixson. Ship Elligood", showing recent visitation of white men, too recent for Flinders to be pleased—but no trace of Vancouver's bottle and parchment, nor of the vines and fruits he planted in that dry, crackling bush of midsummer drought.

Once they inadvertently set an island ablaze—a pillar of fire in the sea.

Smokes at the head of the bay—the natives were losing their fear of the strange visitors, curious to know what they were up to. The commander gave orders that they were not to be molested, nor, indeed, noticed.

"They're as shy as the wild birds," he said. "Follow them, and they'll fly in fright. Leave them alone, and they'll make friends. It's quite natural. If we were living in a state of nature, frequently at war with our neighbours and ignorant of the existence of any other nation, we would watch extraordinary people from our retreats in the woods, and if we were sought and pursued, hide ourselves. But if they continued peacefully employed in their own occupations, curiosity would get the better of our fear, and we ourselves would seek communication. Now when they do, I want you to remember that familiarity breeds contempt very quickly with these Indians, and before we know where we are there'll be a shower of spears and gunfire. Leave them to us. To the man who interferes with them, one way or the other, I shall show no mercy."

One day two sable figures appeared about thirty yards from the tents, stock still. How long they had been there, nobody knew. They were not, and then they were. One was an old man of knowledgeable head and courageously casual bearing. A kangaroo skin flung over his shoulders lent to his upper half a "noblest Roman" dignity, but his left toe resting on his right knee transformed him into a ludicrous human figure 4. The other was a stocky warrior with thick curly hair and heavy features.

The captain was out on the crest of some isle, the botanists away in the woods, but Dr Purdie, who was trying out some taxidermy, put down his scalpel on the rough wooden bench and ambled across with amiable greeting.

The wild men neither scowled nor smiled.

He motioned them to a nearer view of the doings of the camp. They stood their ground, unimpressed. The ship at anchor in the bay failed to interest, and even when Purdie brought a hatchet and some beads and laid them on the ground they remained sphinxes. After watching for an hour or so, they vanished into thin air as mysteriously as they came.

Purdie thought them dull, but next morning they were back again, a vociferous crowd of braves behind them, all peaceable, though some carried spears. Proud of his social success, the doctor trotted fearlessly among them, handing out various small toys and jotting down words of their language, the old man master of ceremonies, now very voluble. He mortally offended Midshipmen Taylor and Franklin by inquiring, in unmistakeable gestures, if they were "womany".

"Womany yourself, old Boko!" shouted little John, with a mimic punch in playfulness at a feature sufficiently flat. The boy's antics were rewarded by shrill shrieks of laughter, and a general friendliness from that moment on. When Matthew came back he found a big camp in contentment on the creek, and all the wurlies in the woods were showing signs of life.

On a cloudless day, the trees dancing in a bright wind, a party of the gentlemen set out for the distant lagoon, carrying stores and water. Boko ran after them, predicting swamps and devils, and pointing them a long way round.

"There's a camp with the women somewhere near. Tell them all to follow me." Matthew gave the order, and obligingly made a turn-off towards the forest. Boko came with him a little of the way, hallooing reassurances to friends unseen. Matthew shot a parakeet for the old man, who, with never a wink of surprise at the gun or the explosion, ran off home with the bird. Extraordinary the aloofness of these crude people from civilization, and all its works and pomps. Like the natives of New South Wales, they accepted the white man and his doings without any envy or emulation—neither inferior nor superior, quite content with their simple life as the good God made it, unconcerned with yesterday or to-morrow. He reflected that no doubt they were wiser than he.

At the foot of the dune John Thistle caught him up.

"Hae ye coonted the pairty, Mr Flinders, sir? Did ye ken we were thirteen?"

Matthew stopped and totted up the men straggling down the sandhill.

"Thirteen. So we are. Bad luck! Do you think I'd better send one of them back, John, before the fatality?"

"Eh, it micht be as weel. It's no that I'm fearfu', but we needna fly I' the face of Providence."

"Oh nonsense, man. What's come over you with your omens and prognostications? That quack of a soothsayer in Spithead has frightened you out of your wits. I'd get you a rabblit's foot to carry about, but there's never a rabbit in the length and breadth of New Holland. Perhaps a kangaroo paw might prove a lucky charm."

He pleasantly frowned on his own friend, "Bonnie Dundee". "That one of the men who sailed with Bass should be tied to a witch's broomstick!"

Thistle grinned. His guernsey open on his hairy chest, his jeans tucked up on his hairy Highland legs, he was as sturdy a seaman as ever sailed the sea.

"Am I as bad as that, sir? Weel, I'll say no more ... but there's a wee voice tellin' me to be wary, no' for masel, it's no the sooth-sayer, but for yew! When things is going too weel, I'm aye uncairtin." His blue eyes looked straight into Flinders's with wisdom and warm affection. "Ye've got yere grand chance, Mr Matthew, juist as ye tauld me when a laddie, and ye've got it easy and bonnie. We canna see it pile up on the rocks, or go down in fifty fathom. No' that it will, but I mind an auld sayin' ma grandmither had—'Beware o' the day when your dreams come trew!' Aye. Yon's the time to be watchfu'."

Matthew's eyes flew to his ship, a pencil-sketch in the bay in the blue of the morning.

"Not much chance of her going down in fifty fathoms to-day, John." He bent his head in reverie for a moment, and his thoughts were with his love. "There is no armour against fate," he quoted softly.

"Maybe not, sir, but we can be canny."

"I wonder." He plucked the leaf of a shrub, crushed it in his fingers, pleasurably sniffed the scent, and passed it on to

Thistle. "Do you smell lemon in that gum-leaf? Better keep it for Mr Brown. Well, we're not afraid of unlucky thirteen. Come on, we'll try it out."

They travelled through shining valleys of eucalypt and goblin groves of a giant bottle-brush, writhing like the suicides in Dante's seventh hell. They circled the shores of the big lagoon, and camped there in a night haunted by screech-owls and wild dogs. The water was brackish and bitter, their flasks at a low ebb on the long trek back. In the burnished copper heat of afternoon, Bauer, puffing purple, suffered a touch of the sun. He lay down in the shade exhausted, the veins standing out on his brow. Bell and Brown and a few of the others stayed with him, to come on in the cool of the dusk.

All was well at the camp by the rill when the captain led his party in after sundown, but by midnight, when the belated ones had not returned, he was very restless. He paced up and down in the firelight, listening for every stir in the bush. At last the sound of white men's voices and footsteps.

"Here they are, Thistle!" he shouted, in a self-revealing relief. John Thistle, "aye watchfu'", turned over in his hammock and smiled dryly into his pillow.

A lazy golden Christmas under the gum-trees, and corroboree for carols at night. The riding light of the *Investigator* glowed red as a planet low down on the bay. Shore leave for the crew—the camp-fires of white and black glowed red in the woodland. Deep-sea chanties were blown on the wind with the eerie wailing of the wild.

Flinders lay in the cool sand, his head pillowed on crossed arms, gazing contentedly at the starry litter of the skies and Dr Bell's broad back. Brown sat hugging his knees beside him, with Ken Sinclair and Lacey and Westall beyond. When he turned, he could see Sam's sharp profile in silhouette on the phantom white of the beach, where a long wave curled crisply in every little while.

The others were scattered round within hearing. Sometimes the talk was general, Franklin's high pipe of excitement and a gust of laughter from Thistle, but for the most part they spoke quietly together, telling over memories of Christmas in England and contrasting the Christmas on this sun-browned, faraway shore. Who would believe that they had been swimming in the sea in December, hiding away from the sun, sharing their wild goose and plum duff with a procession of naked savages?

Brown was enthralled with his collections. Everything was so incredible, so upside-down, so new. Peter's garden, when they got it home to Kew, would be the envy of the scientific world. The country, as they had seen it, was a grid-iron of bony ridges—Sir Joseph's lean cow, a barren, sloping land, poor soil.

"It's remarkable," Brown said, in his slow, incisive way, "that this insignificant, this almost invisible vegetation, should be so valuable, so fascinating ... abundant plants, yet not a blade of grass for cattle, not a square yard of earth worth cultivating. It being granted that the Frenchmen don't snatch it from us, what can England do with this New Holland, or New South Wales, or whatever you call it? You think it's one island, a continent?"

"Not a bit of it!" replied Matthew. "I'm almost convinced that we'll find a channel, and sail straight through. But the islands, no matter how many, are one big family. If it's not a continent, it's the archipelago of a continent submerged. Terra Australis ... New Holland ... New South Wales ... Java la Grande and all the rest, old names, outworn." He sat up in sudden eagerness. "No. They won't do. This is a young land, a kingdom of the sun, a world for youth to conquer. The Spaniards called it Terra del Oro, the Land of Gold—that was better—or Austrialia del Espiritu Santo, that was better still. The Great South Land of the Holy Spirit. There's music, a benediction in the name. Out of these misty scraps of maps, we're going to make a true one. Whatever we find, I call the whole land Australia!"

"And verra fittin'!" cried thirsty Mr Thistle. "Here! Fill the glasses, lads, and we'll mak' a toast o' the christenin'. To the New Year in a new land—Australia!"

Guggling of good Madeira wine from the stone jar, they stood on the sands and raised their glasses to the sleeping continent. From the glittering fires in the gully, the plaintive singing of its own dark people rose and fell, and rose clamorous on the wind.

"Bonnie Dundee" wiped his big blonde beard with a sigh of satisfaction. "But if yon's the national anthem," he added, "my bagpipe's a dom sight more speeritin'."

"Oot wi' it, Thistle!" called Purdie, "an' gi'e us a reel!"

By the end of the week and the year, the survey of the Sound was finished. Peter's plant-boxes packed with Australian earth and stacked in the ship's greenhouse, and the botanists and the astronomers ready to leave. When tents were struck, the vacant place of the village and the blacks standing listless about it looked so dejected that Matthew decided on a parting gesture to liven things up.

"We'll drill the marines," he said to Fowler. "Get them in and put them through their paces. It will give these poor benighted wretches something to remember."

Peal of the fife and pulse of the drum, the redcoats marched ashore. Whooping in ecstasy, the natives flocked around them like children. They mobbed the line of march, and manhandled the drummer, tracing the white cross-bands with their fingers, trying to snatch the drum.

"Halt! Shoulder-r-r arms!"

Fifteen men moving as one, rhythm and flash of muskets in the sun.

"Atten ... shun!"

Wooden soldiers. Manoeuvres had begun.

The blacks were mesmerized into dead silence, watching every move. As the drill became familiar, they mirrored the motions with their hands, "as in a glass, darkly". Old Boko hopped to the end of the line with a stick to use as his musket, grounded, presented, shouldered with the best.

Before the order to fire, Purdie came out from the group of officers standing under the trees, and pantomimed a crack of thunder and nobody hurt. The final volley was the signal for wilder leaping and laughter, and yelps of congratulation as the marines marched back to the boats. At last the white men had shown them something worth while.

That night, in the New Year revelries of last shore leave, the aisles of the forest rang to a new corroboree, red coats and white cross-bands of His Majesty's Marines painted in ochre and pipe-clay on shiny black bodies, squeal of a reed fife and drumming on bare flanks, with Boko hopping and popping as master-at-arms.

It was the dance of the Ghost Brothers, who now must go back in a ghost canoe, to Kurannup, their heaven in the sea.

II

Yellow Sands of Lilliput

On New Year's Day, in a light breeze, they sailed from the glory of King George's Sound, through a tangle of islands east-north-east to follow the hazy main. In d'Entrecasteaux's Group alone, Flinders counted fifty-six isles. Tracing the profile of that sandy shore, he ran the ship so close that they could see beaches and breakers from the decks. Less than a mile out all day, at night he hauled to the wind and deepened the water to anchor, and was back to the land at daybreak, faultlessly following monotonous miles inch by inch in his charts. Many a fair wind he missed for the sake of his botanists, while he scoured the heights, theodolite on shoulder, up over the boulders to the crest.

Coasts of illusion, the watcher at the masthead was fooled again and again. Peninsulas and capes of trees proved to be only trees, island studded bays mirage, and mountains merely refraction. Wine-jellies, the red *medusae*, undulated about them in millions and an oily scum, that they tried to analyse, reddened the wave. Fins of monsters slit the blue. A shark they caught was twelve feet long with a seal bitten in half in its belly, one half skinned and in it the barb of a broken spear.

Sometimes they tacked in the nick of time from the sinister ripple of a deep reef, but Beautemps-Beaupré's charts were good, Vancouver's even better, and with Thistle in a boat ahead always their John the Baptist, they gave the breakers a wide berth and neatly skimmed the shoals.

On the fifteenth day the land rounded away to the north from a bold headland that Flinders named for his first friend in the Navy—Cape Pasley. In a hand as bold he marked it down in the virginal white of the chart. The old man would chuckle to see his name at the ends of the earth. Goose Island commemorated a ship's dinner, a sand-drift chalk-white the cliffs of Dover.

"*Strong breeze and cloudy.*" By the end of January they were skirting the cliffs of Nuyts Land, unseen for two hundred years, a mighty arc of over a thousand miles. Vague ramparts of a vague country, those immutable walls kept siege against the southern ocean, league after baffling league with never a breach nor a landing-place.

The *Investigator* plunged in a head swell, her old bones creaking, her old leaks weeping. Her main t'gallant mast was sprung. Again she was making four inches in the hour. Where it was not madness to try it, he let the reefs out of her courses and bore in to the land, but the seared red walls towered above her six hundred feet sheer. Nuyts Land had nothing more to give him than it had given to the Dutchmen—trend of the coast, drift of the winds, and set of ocean currents. It was a vizor on the face of nature. That huge half moon of weltering seas he named the Great Australian Bight.

In his first month of sailing, he had covered 2000 miles with a magnificent record of work, each night his charts and journals completed before he went to rest, the line of the map, in perfection, creeping a little bit further.

On 28 January they sighted a bay, and the Isles of St Peter and St Francis, the Dutchman's farthest east.

"Eureka, Robert!" he said to Fowler. "Now our voyage begins. The riddle to read, and the secret's ours … unless——"

"Unless those thrice-damned Frenchmen have been along here before us," Mr Fowler finished for him. He nodded ruefully. "I know."

"Well, I'll tell you something that perhaps you don't know. You're looking at the coast of Lilliput."

Mr Fowler elevated an eyebrow. "I thought that was in the moon."

"According to Gulliver's latitude, we're right on top of it now—north-west of Van Diemen's Land, about thirty degrees two. Swift tacked the satire of his little men on to Van Diemen's Land because it was the most outlandish place he had heard of, but he reckoned without us. It shows that you can't be too careful. If he made any researches, which I doubt, it is possible that one of the old Dutch mariners might have seen a gunyah on the shore, and imagined the size of the inhabitants from that, just as Tasman and his men prattled of giants from the notches in the trees."

"You don't expect any pygmy tribes then?"

"I expect nothing, I want facts." His thoughts flashed to Bligh. "The only thing I do expect is to turn the corner any day, and run across to Java. There's a sea, or there used to be, in this part of the world. We might be seeing the Frenchmen on the north instead of the south, or anywhere between the Pole and Java."

"Where I'd like to see them," said Mr Fowler hopefully, "is at the bottom of that sea."

The bay shoaled rapidly to three fathoms, and Thistle was off to sound. Smokes were everywhere, but the natives, giants or gnats, were out of sight. Poor scenery but fair shelter, the captain, with a smile for his first lieutenant, wrote down "Fowler's Bay".

"Blessed are the meek," twinkled Mr Fowler, "for they shall inherit the earth. But should I take precedence, sir, of the Lords of the Admiralty. Honour to whom honour is due."

"Exactly," said Matthew. "To the men who came with me to find it. Don't be troubled. My Lords Commissioners are not forgotten. There is plenty to go round in this country. I'm a poor man rich as Croesus," he laughed, "with kingdoms to bestow."

The vacant spaces of the map!—Flinders worked like a man possessed, by day charting the islands and by night giving them away. In twenty-five miles of sailing, Midshipman Kenneth Sinclair, for all-round proficiency, and Dr Bell and Dr Purdie had a headland each, Lound, Lacey, Evans and Franklin shared an archipelago between them. The youngsters were all excitement on the lookout.

"Play up, and I'll put you in the log," Matthew told them. "Play fair, and I'll put you in the map."

If Swift were looking for fantasy in Lilliput, he might have written truth. Surveying was a navigator's nightmare.

From three leagues the yellowy shore merged into the horizon. Glass-calms of windless days were as a hall of mirrors, islands, islands everywhere, and most of them mirage. Form and colour and distance were lost in a midsummer haze so low on the sea that the real islands loomed out of it and very nearly wrecked them. Clouds of locusts circled the ship, a typhoon of whirring wings, and the bush birds flew crying about it at night, seeking coolness from the furnace of the land. Smokes spiralled into the sky all day, with never sight nor sound of the men who made them.

Bare to the waist and burnt scarlet, the boatmen bent to the oar in a bath of sweat. Exploring ashore was to take a walk in Hades. The spike-grass tortured their blistered feet, and the scorching sands were honeycombed knee-deep with the nests of millions of petrels.

Half-blind in glare, and falling into bird-holes all the way, two miles at a time in that heavy heat was all Matthew could manage. They caught a few lean kangaroos, a poor meal for eighty men weary of pork and sweetwort. Dark clouds of the mutton-birds flew in to the beaches at night, but no boat's crew was early enough to catch them at home in the morning.

The main was a maze of dead ends. The first "great gulf that led to Carpentaria" ran them aground in an hour. They called it Denial Bay, for St Peter near by and their own blighted hopes. Then the trend of the coast was south for a hundred miserable miles, and though the *Investigator* danced a fandango after every speck in the sea, she found little of geographical note—a Smoky Bay, a Streaky Bay, a cape each for Brown, Bauer and

Peter Good, the only optimists in the ship. Their store was daily growing, plant-boxes springing green with sprouts that to their eyes, and theirs alone, were miraculous. One island, Brown said, was remarkable in that it was the first in thousands of miles that contributed nothing new to the collections.

Herring-boning and zigzagging, they found another archipelago, the Investigator's Group (the largest of its islands named Flinders for Samuel), a Coffin's Bay and a goodly headland for Sir Isaac, in appreciation of his interest at Sheerness. Then a flight of albatrosses promised better things. The coast took an easterly swing—to Cape Wiles, for James in Jamaica, old friend of the *Providence*, and Sleaford Bay, memories of Lincolnshire.

It was a sweltering Sunday morning in the middle of February. The ship was lazing along in crisper, bluer seas. Her commander had snatched an hour's rest in his state-room. Sun-blistered feet up on the table, he was reading the *Letters of Junius*, when a shout brought him anxiously on deck—a cliffy island on the starboard bow, land falling away dead north.

River, gulf, strait—or sea? Now, perhaps, they were for it. All boredom and torpor of heat were gone.

Fowler found an anchorage and swung out the boats—the captain and the master for the island.

"It's the grandest yet, sir, and the loftiest," said Mr Thistle as they neared the beach. "Why, ye'd ca' it a moontain i' these pairts, a guid twa hunder feet."

"Take it, John. That's Thistle's Isle you see before you, so make good use of it."

"Weel now, lewk at that!" Mr Thistle roared with laughter. "It's no whut ye'd describe as a Gairden o' Eden, sir, an' ah canna theenk whut ah micht dew wi' it, but it's a bonnier patch o' naught than ony o' the ithers. Thank ye verra kindly, Mr Matthew, sorr. Eh, but it feels fine to be a laird."

The boat's crew grinned as he tweaked his cap, and sat with arms akimbo, admiring his new possession. All liked Thistle, good-humoured as a dancing bear, even when he was on the rampage.

But Thistle's Isle was a different proposition, and grimly hostile to its new administrator. The air ashore was dry as sulphur, the place deathly still. As Matthew and John climbed through the raddled scrub, a yellow snake lay asleep in the path, its yellow eyes half open. It slid through the sand a second too late. Matthew had the butt of his musket on its throat, and John, a walking hold-all, produced a sail needle and twine from his "poke". They bent over the writhing thing to sew up its mouth and take it back for the botanists. It measured seven feet nine.

They were half-way through the ticklish job when a flying shadow warned them. A pallid eagle was wheeling for them on evilly silent wings. They stood erect, and beat the air and shouted. It swerved within twenty yards, flew into a tree, and sat there watching, so uncannily still it seemed a sculptured bird.

Keeping a wary eye on it, they were moving on when a second white vulture swooped from a bough above—fierce creatures these, outstretched wings ten feet from tip to tip, viciously hooked beak and steel talons. The island was alive with them, motionless in the trees, in the blue sky. They preyed on the kangaroos, stealthily waiting till they came out to feed, then pouncing and tearing. Of man they knew no fear. Matthew and John kept their guns at full cock during the rest of the exploration, and though tracks and skeletons were everywhere, never a living kangaroo did they see.

From the crown of the hill Matthew named three little dots of isles for Spilsby, Sibsey and Stickney at home. Six leagues to sea, easily visible in that clear air, a cluster of inaccessible rocks he dedicated Neptune's Isles. None but the seals and the mermaids would ever scale them.

The ship's tanks were low, but no water could they find. Flinders intended after dinner to take the *Investigator* over to the main, and search for water while making the survey, but there was unexpected trouble. Samuel's longitudes and his did not agree. The time-keepers were at variance, and one of them had run down. That meant repeating sights on shore, and waiting that night for lunar observations.

"Yours are sure to be right," said Sam carelessly. "Why not let them go."

"Nothing is 'sure to be right' in navigation. To-day our bearings are vitally important, and you're in charge of the work."

Sam was sulky and Matthew terse. The time-keeper midshipmen were logged. When the commander came back from the island with his sights, Thistle took a water-party in the cutter to the main.

"May I go with the master, sir?" It was Franklin, pleading for a trip.

"No."

"I haven't been ashore for a week, sir."

"I said no. Attend to your duty with the time-keepers, and earn your trips ashore."

"I wasn't the only one, sir, and I didn't know."

"You should have known, and reported to the second lieutenant. That will do."

As John went back to his logarithms, he shot such a glance of fierce resentment at his cousin the second lieutenant that his cousin the captain was amused. He knew there was no love lost between them.

It was a tranquil evening with light breezes from the south. Matthew stood on the poop-deck, looking to the shore. A single heavy fleece of cloud was flung in the western sky, and, as he watched, the setting sun deckled its upper rim with gold … fiery coastline of a fairy land, a running pencil of living light tracing the shores of dream.

Where would it lead him, to Java, or Cook's Cape York? Were the French before him, or would he solve the riddle, for Britain, for Sir Joseph, for Ann? Discovery and his love—more than one man's share, perhaps, of happiness. He had been restless of late, needing her, longing for it all to be over. Four years … and only six months gone. But since the coast turned northward, all had changed, the mood had passed. To follow knowledge … breath of life … he could not give it up. He saw the cutter coming off with sunset in her sails. There was thrum of a banjo in the fo'c'sle where the men were all at tea.

Fowler was ten minutes early off watch that evening.

"Did Mr Thistle find a creek?" Matthew asked him, as he put his head in at the state-room door.

"That's what I came to see you about, sir. Mr Thistle has not come back."

"But I saw them an hour ago, and they were coming off then."

"Aye, sir. I saw them myself. They haven't returned."

"Who is with Thistle?"

"Taylor, and a crew of six."

"Where have they gone then?"

"That's the question."

"Wave a light, Robert."

"I've already done that, sir."

A moment's puzzled silence, and Matthew spoke in lower tones, urgent.

"You'd better go yourself, and see what's happened. Take the long-boat and go now. The tide's turning, but there's little wind."

"Aye, sir."

The boat was manned, and Fowler's lantern bobbed away on the wave. All hands on deck stood peering into the darkness towards the shore. They heard a faint hallooing, and the distant crack of muskets. Then there was silence ... too long.

Eight bells. Two ... nine o'clock. Anxiety ran like wild fire through the ship. What menace was in the quiet dark? Where had they all gone? The captain ordered Colpitts to fire a gun.

It was nearing ten when they heard the sound of oars, and Fowler's shout. No sign of the missing cutter. He climbed on board, his face white and tired.

They had scoured the shore, and seen nothing, and called, and received no answer.

"I'm afraid they've been caught in a tide-rip, sir, and turned over. There's a big rip running from the head. We were caught off guard, and nearly swamped ourselves."

Thistle gone! And busy little Taylor! Six men! Matthew's heart grew cold. The crew was crowding round them, whispering.

"Perhaps they've gone farther north," he said, "and can't beat off against the wind." But he knew the wind was too light to hold them, and he knew that the men knew.

All night the ship was awake, flares burning at her masthead. No sign of life on the pale seas at daybreak, no figures on the far-away shore. In the first grey of dawn the boats were out, all who could leave ordered out with the search-parties.

As John Franklin clambered down, Matthew remembered with a start that he might easily have been with them. Had it not been for the neglected time-keepers, the boy would certainly have gone, but had it not been for the neglected time-keepers, they would have left the unlucky place by mid-day. How can we unravel by reason the twisted skeins of fate?

"Put the younger midshipmen out on the headlands," he called to Samuel, "and give them each a flag to wave in case they see wreckage or"—he hesitated—"any other traces."

Some of the boats spread out to the north and others to the south, while Fowler moved the ship across to the main. The beauty of the morning and the rollicking breeze calmed their fears. Surely at any moment they would hear Thistle's throaty "Hoy!" by the smoke of a camp-fire in the woods, and see the cutter beached in the shallows.

An hour passed, two … and nothing happened.

Midshipman Franklin, on his headland, grew weary of watching the white-caps tumbling by. He was examining the Union in his hand from sheer boyish fidgets when a guilty ambition stirred in his curly pate. Nobody had planted a flag in the new land yet. To wave it was to write his name in history. What happened to cadets who stole a march on the commander?

None of the boats was in sight, and the ship so still that she seemed deserted, no one at the masthead. With a wicked little chuckle, he unrolled the pennant, held it aloft for one mad moment, then let it flutter free.

"I take possession of this land of the south of Australia for His Majesty King George III of England," he hurriedly informed a passing seagull, then propped the flag in a cleft of the rocks and solemnly stood to the salute.

A moment later his whistling stopped abruptly. A boat was putting off from the ship, the captain in the prow, making straight for him. Now he was for it. What would he say?

A hundred yards off, they cupped hands and shouted.

"What have you seen?"

To John's credit, let it be said, he blushed. He wagged his head violently.

"Only weed," he piped.

"Which way?"

He pointed to the south, and they pulled down.

With a sigh of relief he folded up the Jack, took a little diary out of his pocket, and wrote in a round childish hand, "Flag planting south Australia." He would show that to cousin Matthew some day.

The crews gathered at the ship at noon. One had picked up a floating oar, another the bottom of the missing cutter, stove in and dashed to pieces on the rocks. Brown's shore party in the afternoon found white men's tracks but no fire, and the captain's from the south brought in a little water-keg that Thistle carried with him on all his excursions. Fowler was right. They must have upturned in the rip, and the tide had drifted them to sea.

It was tragic writing of that night's log. The place was Memory Cove, the headland Cape Catastrophe, with the group of islands for Taylor and each of the men.

John Thistle gone ... his friend. Never again the whistle of "Bonnie Dundee".

Anchored in the cove, her flag at half-mast, the *Investigator* was a ship of mourning.

There was slow procession of her sailors through the sandhills to set up a post of stone with a graven sheet of copper, a monument in the lonely scrub to Thistle and his men, with the warning *Nautici Cavete*.

No hope now, but Flinders could not leave. For twelve miles in and out the coast, he was searching the islands, and forever scanning the empty sea in his melancholy quest of the dead. In his long explorations, he preferred to be alone. One morning he climbed a hill—to a pageant of wonder. A magnificent far harbour was glittering blue to horizons, a second Port Jackson in the south.

Discovery lightened the gloom. Now there was worth-while work. They moved the ship round, and set up tents on the shore, collecting, sounding, surveying. At last they had something on a grand scale to redeem a monotonous map.

The new harbour was Port Lincoln.

Day by day the well-loved names of the Fenlands filled the vacant chart—Cape Donington, Boston Isles, Spalding Cove and Grantham, Stamford Hill and Kirton Point, Lusby, Tumby, Kirkby, and a wide shining lagoon, in honour of Doctor George, a second Sleaford Mere. There was Revesby Isle for Sir Joseph, the Partney Isles for Ann.

Flinders's energy electrified the men. The grief that had numbed the ship was gone. No time for misery, he hastened them from one task to another. When they could find no river, he showed them how to dig soaks in the manner of the New Hollanders, on the rim of the milky Sleaford Mere that they believed to be salt. Its brackish waters deepened under their shovels, and filtered through the sands to fresh. Sixty tons they carried off to fill the ship's tanks.

One day he ordered three guns to be fired at given intervals, then made off to Boston Island to dangle a musket-ball on a piece of twine. The midshipmen thought he was water-divining, but he waved them away with a smile and went on counting. Three times, as the guns barked, he practised the mystic art, then brought out a notebook and worked a sum.

"Now I can tell you," he said. "This bay is too remote from the meridian to use the false horizon. Very well. I had to think out a scheme. From the flash of the gun till I heard the shot, there were 85 pendulum vibrations. Sound travels, as you know, at 1142 feet a second, and 6060 feet make a geographical mile—so that the length of our base line is exactly 8.01 geographical miles, simple reckoning. Never be beaten, my lads. There's always a way."

There were native pads and native huts all round Sleaford Mere, and natives were sensed but not sighted. They had the knack, as he well knew, of falling flat in the landscape, or "freezing" into the shape of a dead tree. He would not allow them to be harried or hunted. Toys, beads and tomahawks were left on stumps in the woods.

"For the sake of those who come after us, we must make a good impression with these Australians," he explained, "just as Vancouver's ship and the *Elligood* paved the way for us at King George's sound."

Australians. He liked the word for its euphony—the first time he had used it.

At the head of the bay a boat's sail and yard drifted in, a sad reminder. Fowler went back to Memory Cove—in vain.

On 6 March the work was done. From that sunny new Lincolnshire in the south they eagerly followed the coast on north—to another disillusion. The waters grew more shallow and more sheltered every day. This was not a sea, but a rapidly narrowing gulf, shelving shores that dwindled away in mud.

There was a majestic range at the head of it, barren red peaks like rusty knives jagging the pale sky, and a low range of crouching hills to the west. The fortress walls again. The *Investigator* anchored in the deep channel. Brown, Bauer and Westall, the adventurous three, started for the peaks, which seemed but a stone's throw away, while Matthew led his party west.

There was another anxious night with flares at the masthead when the scientists did not return. They hove in sight next morning, boots cut to pieces, with boxes of seeds and curious plants. The range was an optical illusion like all else, a good fifteen miles away. Camped by a fire on the summit, blackfellows' fires all round them, they had looked north to desolation. Daybreak unveiled a forbidding land. The botanist accepted the mount with a deprecating smile—Mount Brown.

So the inland sea was a fable, and Australia was not two islands but one.

In the fag end of a fagging summer they followed the east coast down. For four months they had had no fresh meat. Now and again a haul of the seine gave them a dinner of fish, or a stray wallaby flavoured the soup and dumplings. What would they give for a bone to pick! They conversed of beef-steaks they had known, and fat lambs frisking on the downs.

Every morning they dressed the ship to catch the lightest airs. The graph of her course was as a streak of lightning, here, there, everywhere, grateful for any event—but little enough did they find in those seemingly sterile sands.

One night she embedded her nose in a sandbank. They hoisted out the cutter and hauled her astern with a kedge into deep water. On another, there was an impromptu celebration. The Madeira wine was turning acid, so it was served out to the company on the old man's birthday, the "old man" a beardless twenty-eight. Sitting on the quarter-deck in the budding green of Peter's garden, they toasted the moonlit gulf in the name of Earl Spencer, rendering to Caesar.

The weather broke in gales. Once again the old ship took a bone in her teeth, and breasted blue water for a swift sixty leagues to the south. On 21 March, under close-reefed topsails, she was skirting a glorious isle in latitudes much cooler, the cliffs sheer to five hundred feet, green hills blessing their heat-glazed eyes.

All day they ran the gauntlet between cliffs and reefs, where huge seas were pounding in thousands of tons to a break. For seventy miles they could see no smokes nor signs of habitation. The southward skies were black with menace of storm.

Towards evening a lucky little landlocked bay showed up on the starboard beam. They hurried in for shelter, and dropped anchor in a tranquil nine fathoms.

Long rays of a copper sun lit up the deeply-wooded slopes, and a lawny space of parklands—crystal vales of enchantment in the flying showers. It was the prettiest country they had seen since leaving King George's Sound. Too late to send a boat ashore, every glass in the ship was levelled there.

Lacey and Lound announced that the rocks in the valley

were moving. The joke went round against them. Not even New Holland, Land of Illusion, could manage that.

By morning the gale had blown itself out, and early sunlight proved them right—or very nearly. Those dark brown rocks, that slowly moved, were old men kangaroos in scores, feeding on the grassy flats. Out with the boats! Tally Ho!

It was a heaven-sent morning, the land-breeze cool and fragrant with the scent of eucalypts, the waves of the bay whipped silver. Flinders led the huntsmen with a double-barrelled gun, some carrying bowie knives and muskets, on the trail of those kangaroo-tail patties that Mr Thistle had so often praised at mess.

A parliament of pelicans on a sandbank watched them go by in petrified amazement, never a spread wing of panic, but an Indian Army major of an old man sea-lion, doubling and diving about the boat, challenged their right to land. His whiskers bristled in outraged dignity when they grounded in the shallows and leapt ashore. Dew on their boots in the lush grass was the first they had seen since they left England.

Hundreds of kangaroos were feeding on the lawns, like deer in an English park. The captain was ahead of the rest in his brisk, short stride, and as he came over the rise, a furry giant eight feet high looked up with quizzical interest, paws folded, sensitive nostrils sniffing the wind. There was no fear in those brown eyes, only a friendly surprise.

Within five yards he fired. The kangaroo fell, its powerful hind legs kicking in futile agony till he came up and shot it through the head. Guns were cracking all round him, shattering the peace of the morning. Every bray of a gun brought out bellowing seals from under the bushes, ludicrously flapping through the sea-grass and slithering over the rocks into the waves. Poor gentle creatures, the kangaroos showed no terror. They stood, bewildered by the noise, to be peppered between the eyes with small shot, beaten to death with sticks. Before the dew was gone, that grassy flat was a shambles.

But oh, the stew to come! The captain had ten to his bag, and the others brought the tally up to thirty-one. He called a halt to the slaughter. As the sun grew warm, the lucky survivors casually bounded for the woods.

They were heavier and darker than the kangaroos of New South Wales, with richer and glossier fur and plenty of fat, weighing from a succulent 60 to 125 pounds. All hands to the butcher's shop, rich red steaks were rich brown grills for breakfast, the cook ranting as the ravenous sailors snatched them from the coals. Throughout the day the ship's coppers were bubbling and simmering with forequarters, hindquarters, heads, tails, and the last of the Portuguese onions, platters emptied as soon as they were full, and the meat-hungry mob passing them up for more. There were no regular meals that day. It was one long dinner.

The commander was away with his theodolite to the crest of the little hills, through vegetation so dense that he could not see above it. As a rule, in this flat land, horizons were his bane, the long, vague, colourless levels—but here he was closed in a hedge.

He doubted that black or white man had landed before him upon this island realm in turbulent seas, dominion of the kangaroos, where they lived with seals and the sea-birds, unafraid and friendly. If his were the first footsteps on these unmemoried sands, he had brought death by violence and shattered faith. He was ashamed.

He wondered idly if the seals were more intelligent than the kangaroos, for they had repulsed his landing, and fled from the sound of shot. The seals were travellers, and they remembered. On southward coasts of ice translucent, once they had trusted, and been betrayed.

Of the blue ridge of hills across the strait, the highest he named Mount Lofty, the bay of their anchorage for Sir Evan Nepean, and the Strait for his ship. The isle belonged to their hosts—Kangaroo Island. He hurried down to the landing-place with thoughts of 'roo-tail soup. There he met Brown's party, rejoicing in a remarkable growth of the carboniferous age.

It was a resinous grass-tree with blackened trunk of close-packed yellow cells, green tufts like a Fijian's head-dress, a seed-stalk eight feet long and straight as a lance. Brown computed its age as about 900 years—it had begun to sprout in this island when the Conqueror was a boy. Slow as a stalagmite, while empires rose and fell, it grew to its maturity, with a few more patient centuries to wither it. All over the isle it grew in such profusion that the shimmering bush was a prehistoric forest, its treasures uncounted for a botanist. Brown said he might spend a lifetime here, a southern Prospero.

The sailors told of a pale, strutting bird, a dwarf emu smaller than those of the mainland. The ship's museum must have specimens. Across the roseate sunset bay, the boats pulled with a will, hot on the trail of the best hot dinner Australia had given them yet.

On 25 March they cleared Nepean Bay, crossed Investigator Strait, and tacked east along the main, where many smokes were writing in the sky. From sand-ridges and poor land they came to hills and forest, and a worthy gulf that Flinders named for Earl St Vincent. The map of the peninsula between the two gulfs, as he drew it, was a buskined leg, reminiscent of Italy. That went down for the Right Honourable Charles Philip Yorke.

"A land of vines and olives," Matthew laughed. "If only we could prove that true." But though plains in the lee of the range promised green fertility, on closer acquaintance they were the usual jaded brown. On All Fool's Night a blackfellow's fire glowed red on the crest of Mount Lofty, and before she solved the riddle further, the *Investigator* was off back across her strait for a refresher and refitting at the island of kangaroos.

Mending the sails with seal-skin, stepping a new topmast of the island pine, checking the time-keepers, sketching, collecting and surveying, they spent five days of gales there, regaling themselves on good thick sea-pie, roasts, ragouts and rissoles.

Already the kangaroos were shy. Thirty of the pygmy emus were seen in one day by various people, but, wise in their generation, never when guns were at hand. They remained a mystery of the impenetrable scrub.

That scrub gave Flinders an afterthought of uneasiness. He noted that the bush was young, striplings and saplings, with undergrowth of brilliant glossy green. Great trees fallen in his path seemed not to have crashed from senile decay, but all at the same size and time. Could someone have kindled a fire here many years ago? Lapérouse? When the fate of Lapérouse was known, his journals would tell. He hoped not. He wanted to be first to claim this far-flung isle—a Robinson Crusoe island of his childhood dreams.

It was on the eve of their leaving that he found the great Valhalla of the pelicans, a vast lagoon on the east coast where myriads of living birds, and their babies learning to fly, had communed for thousands of years with their own dead. Their nesting-place was their graveyard, the young ones fluttering white in the white of their ancestors' bones.

Westall was with him, his picture just completed, his easel under his arm.

"Think of it, William," said Matthew in one of his whimsical flights of fancy, "for ages these islets and inlets have seen the twilight of the pelican gods. Where could they find more perfect peace than in this lagoon of an unknown land in the antipodes? It is quite in keeping with the feelings of pelicans—that is, if pelicans have any—to resign their breath surrounded by their progeny, and in the very spot where they first drew it. Alas, for the pelicans! Their golden age is past. It has much exceeded in duration that of man."

Back at the ship, they found one of the sailors nursing an angry wound from the bite of an angry seal. For no good reason, he had attacked the creature with a stick, and come off second best.

"My sympathies are with the seal," said the commander dryly.

The last sights were taken and the time-keepers set. On 7 March they sailed away from the dominion of kangaroos.

The spiral of strait that led to the wide ocean again reminded him of a private entrance in one of the old manor halls. He called it the Backstairs Passage, with a cosy corner in the island shore as Antechamber Bay.

12

Fleur-de-lis

From the lost island where time stood still they dreamed along the main—red rounded cliffs, scored by ravines and gullies, bristled with a low scrub, like the rumps of mammoth and mastodon in weird ambulatory motion of mirage. Loping away to the north, where were they going?—to the salt shores of a secret sea glittering to an Indies of ebony and spices?—to a Sahara?

Never had white man penetrated thirty leagues from the coast, and the mind of the black man was vague and silent as the land. Had some dark Cortés lifted that sun-gold veil? Were there not rivers here, clemency of hills and forests, running brooks? What wrinkles in the face of earth would tell the stories of that timeless past, of civilizations lost, and buried cities? Or was that earth, as it seemed, a withered parchment, the eyeless mask of a mummy, ages dead? An old, old continent Major Ross had said of it, rotting back into the sand.

So Flinders mused at the masthead, sunburnt, wind-burnt, keen dark eyes under his cabbage-tree hat. He sat in his cut-away cask, a board nailed across it as table for the rough charts, his sextant, quadrant and compasses hanging in a case by his side.

Down below him the deck rose and fell, no more than a gentle breathing to lullaby of fair weather. A light wind in the cirrus clouds of her sails, his ship seemed half asleep in the cobalt blue of lazy waves crested with sun and flecked with ravel of foam. Now and again she dipped for the pleasure of it, her prow playfully tossing back a silver hail of spray.

The men had caught a dolphin. He could see it plunging on the half-deck in a little ring of sailors, Charlie Douglas, the bosun, trying to harpoon the slithering thing with his knife. Away to the east, there was a faint white nick in the sea.

Eight bells—a cup of gunpowder tea with the gentlemen. He clambered down from the maintop, and the lookout went up in his stead.

He was with Brown, inspecting Peter's garden, when the lookout called "White rock ahead, sir!" He crossed to the side and levelled the glass. The white rock was conspicuous, a pallid smudge of quartz a league from shore. It moved. It was a sail! A sail in these uncharted realms where ships were never known? The *Lady Nelson*, thousands of miles to meet him?—or the French?

"Clear for action!" He gave the order sharply.

There was chaos in the greenhouse, chaos in the ship as the guns were trundled up.

One bell. The stranger came slowly on. They could see her hull, no 60-tonner but a heavy-castled galleon, half-dressed—in calm.

Two bells. The *Investigator* hoisted colours. The Tricolour was the reply.

Three bells. They hove alongside.

Tall as a tenement, the foreigner lunged to leeward with a free wind. She carried a Union Jack and a flag of truce forward. *Le Géographe* they read on the scroll of her stern—one of the ships of Baudin's expedition.

England and France, at war through the centuries, were meeting out of the world, on the undefended frontiers of science. Like a fighting cock the Englishman swung round to keep the broadside.

The Frenchmen were ten months out before Flinders sailed from Spithead. What had they charted, where had they planted their Tricolour, what did they know? Was their white flag in good faith? Behind closed ports the *Investigator's* guns were ready to blaze on treachery. Her captain, in full-dress uniform, ordered out the cutter, and Brown came with him to interpret. He would have no twice-told tales.

Sallow faces looked curiously down as the cutter pulled to.

The deck of the ship was grimy, and she stank. There was a half-watch only, men covered with scurvy sores, swarthy men with matted hair and ragged clothing. Some of the sailors were cutting up dolphins. They argued in a shrill nasal whining. So hungry they were for the dolphins, they scarce took note of his coming.

A carelessly-dressed officer saluted.

"*Monsieur le commandant? Mais certainement. Par ici.*"

He led them to the quarter-deck, to a grave elderly man, grey hair greasy on his brow, a face like a very old and very benevolent bloodhound, with the same bloodshot eyes. His uniform was stained and shabby, and apparently water was short. A pale young person in a Polish cap, one eye sharply appraising them, the other a twitching socket, moved away.

"Ha! *messieurs les anglais*! Good efening, gentilmen."

The commodore took a slightly oblique course to usher them into his cabin, a litter of cones, charts, journals, books, dividers, his clothing hanging from half-closed drawers and chairs, smells and stains of wine, and some shrivelled plants in broken pots—a joyful glance between Brown and Flinders in pride of Peter's floating Eden.

Baudin motioned his visitors to sit down. "You will excuse not tidy," he said. "I think, on seeing sail, it is my consort ship, *Le Naturaliste*. Always we lose her, gentilmen, but always we find her." He smiled, and poured them a glass of very old *vin de Champagne*.

"To La France and Britain!" he said pleasantly.

"To Great Britain and La France!" they solemnly raised their glasses.

"You have a passport from our government, Commodore Baudin. May I see it?" There was no need for Brown's Edinburgh French.

With a reproachful glance for the inquisition, Baudin began to root. He unearthed the passport from the bottom of a drawer with a sigh of satisfaction.

Flinders examined it and handed it back with his own, so precise in its case with a gilt *fleur-de-lis* cut in mottled morocco.

The commodore waved it away. "Are we not friends in this so unexpected place? You go to the east, gentilmen? I lose my geographer in a boat and eight of my men. If you meet her, will you be kind to pick her up for me?"

"Wrecked on the coast, sir?" Flinders showed concern.

"No. Jus' lef' be'ind."

A surprising statement. "Having suffered the loss of a boat and eight men myself, I shall keep a close lookout. Which way have you come?"

"From the south and east of Van Diemen's Land. We lose the boat on the north."

"You travelled through Bass Strait, then? Along its northern shores?"

Commodore Baudin nodded and poured another glass of wine. He tossed his down at a gulp. His eyes gave the impression of having been stewed.

"What have you found between this and Westernport?"

"Nossings," said Captain Baudin tranquilly.

"No inlet, river, or shelter of any kind?"

"Nossings of any kind."

"The sealers say there is a large island at the western entrance of the strait."

"We see no isle, monsieur, but the chart!" he shrugged, "it is so *bad*. I show you." His handkerchief hanging out of his coat-tail pocket, he started another uncertain search, and finally emerged triumphant with a copy of Doctor George's pen-and-ink.

"Oh, this is not the chart, sir. 'Tis but a drawing from an open boat—see here, this note, 'From Mr Bass's Eye-Sketch'."

"Oh so! This I not look before."

"I have the new Admiralty charts that I shall be happy to

give you. But what of the south coast of the continent—between this and the Land of the Leeuwin?"

"We go there now," announced Captain Baudin.

Flinders shot a glance at Brown of bare-faced jubilation. He could not resist the question, "But where have you been, may I ask, sir?"

The commodore proffered snuff—declined.

"*Hélas,* we suffer much misfortunes of sick. We leave Le Havre in Octobre, we stay forty days at Ile-de-France, then, monsieur, we make this coast of the Leeuwin you speak, but it is time of storm. We take the course of north. *Quel stérilité! Quel horreur!* I am most sick, we all are sick, my men die with no water. I go to Koepang, and there we have fever and trouble. Six of my scientists not come, ten men are dead, me, I am for the most part dead. Ah messieurs, this is to France a land *fatale.* St Alouarn, d'Entrecasteaux, Huon de Kermadec, Lapérouse, look you, our people perish. Sixty of my men I have now no good of *scorbutique.* There is times, messieurs, I think I too see La Belle France not again."

He blew his nose in a violent emotion, and his eyes seemed more than ever stewed.

Flinders rose with an audible sigh of relief. In the nick of time he had filled in the last vacant space in the map of the earth for Britain.

"In your journey along the north-west coast, Captain Baudin, at about the Rosemary Isles of Dampier or elsewhere, you have found no great strait, no sweeping tides, no traces of a sea?"

"I cannot go near. It is too much isles and reefs ... but there, monsieur"—he puffed his snuff-stained vest in pride—"we write the marks of our nation for *éternité*, the glory, the history of France!"

"I congratulate you, captain. I am sure you have followed the track of the Dutch with the greatest national credit. Good!—I mean I am glad you are safe. If you care to stand company for the night, I shall bring you charts in the morning that I hope may be helpful." Flinders could scarcely repress the twinkle in his eye.

"It is *plaisir, monsieur le capitaine*. You are most kind."

Through the night, the two ships of warring France and England burned friendly lights together in that unknown sea. The big *Géographe* was a clumsy sailer, helplessly drifting in no tide, no doubt from her lack of able-bodied men. The *Investigator* backed topsails to keep her abreast. She had thirty guns, and the Englishman six carronades.

At six in the morning Flinders and Brown were aboard her. The commodore was much more brisk and business-like—and much more inquisitive. His men had learned from the boat's crew that their purpose was exploration. He had not known that the British were on his track, and did not seem particularly pleased.

Was there a patronage in the English captain's manner when he gave him the rough sailing directions to Kangaroo Island— water and meat in plenty, and good skin caps for his men—and to Port Lincoln, a haven two hundred miles on? The charts of Bass Strait and Van Diemen's Land, "Compiled by M. Flinders, 1798", he accepted with admiration, and invited his visitors to breakfast.

A merchant-captain of long and strange experience, a well-read man and a most gracious host, Commodore Baudin was a *savant* run to seed. Several times the one-eyed person intruded on the scene—apparently not an officer, though of a certain authority. He was neither referred to, nor introduced.

Fetid ship and scurvy crew were more repulsive in broad daylight, a horror of slow-motion and disease. A hundred out of 170 men were below. The watch had scarcely strength to heave the sails. The rosy-cheeked boat's crew waiting below was striking contrast to those listless, famished faces.

At eight o'clock the Englishmen rose to go. Baudin came with them to the gangway.

"It is happy we are met. If you find my people, you will care of them, messieurs? And if you meet *Le Naturaliste* will you please to tell that in the cold and wind beginning I am to Port Jackson?"

"Certainly, Captain Baudin. Who, may I ask, is in command of the *Naturaliste*?"

"Hamelin. But permit me, *monsieur le capitaine*, what is your name please?"

A glance to Brown of incredulous amazement. Had he not known before?

"Flinders, sir. Captain Matthew Flinders."

"Oh so!" The commodore was impressed. "Then you are *auteur* of these charts you give! *Superbe!*" He admired them again. "I am of honour to meet you. Wait, there is rocks." On Flinders's chart, he indicated a reefy trap. "Guard you!" he warned. "*Trés dangereux! Adieu, messieurs. Bon voyage!*"

Flinders went down the gangway with a chuckle. The foeman, after all, was not worthy of his steel. News for Sir Joseph! He had raced the French to New Holland.

H.M.S. *Investigator* blithely dipped her white ensign and winged away eastward, leaving *Le Géographe*, with mournful sails, to moon along the main.

Guns on the quarter-deck by the binnacle were a splendid opportunity for compass deviation research. Matthew spent the morning taking bearings by azimuth and amplitude, and writing his observations. He had a good use for guns as masses of magnetic iron, but always the swing of the ship's head varied his calculations. This was a problem that demanded thought and time. They stretched off upon the wind till noon, and then brought to with the main-topsail and went on with the surveying. At dusk, when the wind freshened, they were far from the encounter bay in a long rolling swell.

"Breakers to west'ard!"—in the cloudy dawn, the man at the lookout crying.

The commander was up and aloft, scouring the horizon with his glass as the ship heaved and swung. After two thousand five hundred miles, he was hoping against hope for a river. He sighted nothing but tumbled waves to a monotony of sand. It must have been but a break of foam on the wave.

They ran into squalls. Through fitful gleams of sunshine the coast steadily mounted higher, but Baudin had skirted these shores and they had lost their appeal for Flinders. He made a big swing for the sea-gates of Bass Strait, the clap of waters declaring war in gales, the Pyrrhic victory in which both sides retreated.

Storms cleared. A covenant rainbow framed the sealers' isle that Baudin had denied. Were the Frenchmen lying or lazy? Cautious now, the investigators turned back to the main.

On 25 April they sighted the bluff pillars of a magnificent bay. Between those heads a two-mile tide rose in a roaring rip, beyond them the spiny tidal waters rushed over mackerel sandbanks. George's description was wide of the mark, but no doubt this was his Westernport, for the Frenchmen could never have missed it.

The ship whirled in the mill-race between Scylla and Charybdis to a vast quadrant of tossing water. From the masthead aerie, no margin of land could they see. The commander and the botanists were away in the boat to a leonine station peak, seven miles of heavy climbing for anxious observation.

It was a bay to shelter a grander fleet of ships than ever sailed the sea. The peak looked out on paradise. Majestic prairies rolled away to the west and the south-west, to the north were the black spurs of never-ending ranges—yet still no binding coastline. Here in this southern Baltic the soil was dark and loamy, the tree-ferns damp with eternal dews, the native camps cold and deserted. In tidal waters they gathered oysters salt and delicious. The artist mixed pigment of misty grey and blue. The naturalists made havoc in the greenwood, where snowy cockatoos, their under-wings stained crimson, shrieked at the trespassers from the tall forest trees.

Lithe black inhabitants appeared and disappeared, dappled into invisibility in that leafy chiaroscuro of light and shade. Sometimes these soft-voiced people of the woods came near in laughter to exchange their weapons of death for toys. They seemed to know the lethal secret of the flint-lock. When the sailors were abroad with muskets, they vanished as the watery sun into the clouds.

The investigators pitched their tents on the Hebridean shore, hearing the grey waves lapping and gathering Scotch heather in the hills. Flinders rose in the early dawn to cross the harbour, and with Brown and Westall set off on a ten-mile walk. There was invigoration in the cool spicy air. From the top of the hill they saw the plains again, in all their fertile beauty, treasures of a rich earth starring the concave valleys with a Persian pattern. The wealthiest land of all he had seen in Australia—day-dreaming, he visioned a noble city, of homes and harvest and trade, its cathedral spires against those guardian blue hills, three-deckers of England at the quays.

He turned to the east—freehand curve of a coast smiling for miles, and Bass's Westernport below him! George's drawing was true—the discovery was new! Had the French blind men at the masthead?

They plodded down to the seashore and rowed across to the glade. The natives were gone, but the grassy dwellings were still furnished with signs of habitation. When the boats made off to the *Investigator* through a flotilla of black swans, the black men reappeared to sing a Neanderthal farewell.

On a fair wind they made the open sea.

Wilson's bluff promontory was a fine balance to the disc of water northward. They sheered its frowning rocks to Flinders's old trail, worn familiar now with the wakes of the whalers. Up the ever-besieged coast to Port Jackson, they stood off those shadowy columned Heads in the starlight of 9 May. Flinders was so much at home in that harbour that he tacked to run up in the night, but H.M.S. *Investigator* was no *Tom Thumb* and a stubborn wind held her. The noon gun had frightened the parrots before she swung to anchor. Elder polished buckles and boots, the cutter was swung overside to clatter of block and tackle, and in Sir Joseph's immaculate uniform, still warm from the iron, the young commander stepped ashore to call upon old friends.

Port Jackson was drab and dejected as of yore, the chain-gangs hobbling through the dust. The Union fluttered from the flagstaff above the whitewashed Government House, dog-leg slums now filling the sunny bushland, a few more privateers and whalers in the cove, and the lost sheep *Naturaliste* tethered in Neutral Bay.

If shades of Governor Hunter stalked the straggling garden, Government House, for the first time, was home. Mrs King had made it cheerful as her four-square cot on Norfolk Island, and the blacks' camp no longer festooned the front door. The boy Phillip was at school in England, but a little daughter Elizabeth played on the strip of grass trying to be a lawn.

Most of the best friends were missing. Doctor George had come and gone—taken his *Venus* to Point Venus, to trade with Otoo in Otaheite for the little pigs of the Pomare, and turn them into Port Jackson's salt pork. Shortland was with Nelson, Waterhouse out of their ken, Kent with H.M.S. *Buffalo*, fighting his old enemy, the sea. He had given his house to Mrs King to be an orphanage for the broad-arrow babies they found every day in the bush. There were over a thousand abandoned in the settlement, "the most neglected and the finest children in the world," King said.

A consequential man, King, but a good fellow. He and Macarthur were Montague and Capulet now, with brawls of their henchmen in the street. The colony was still steeped in rum and aflame with hatred. The convict ships still brought a ghastly fruit for the gallows tree.

But no longer was Matthew a naval officer pinioned in the port. He was guest of honour, a captain calling, pathfinder of empire, the substantial shadow of James Cook.

Moored near Bennelong Point—where was Bennelong, bedraggled and forgotten, last seen begging about the slums?— the *Investigator* set up her tents on shore for theodolite and time-keepers, Samuel in charge with John Franklin as offsider—"little Mr Tycho Brahe", King christened that popular young man. The ship worked hard at anchor, carpenters, coopers, copperers and sail-makers refitting.

After nearly a year at sea they could get no fresh meat, though Macarthur's Spanish rams were doing well and growing wool for blankets. The governor sent them an occasional basket of vegetables from the vice-regal garden; the fowls flying wild in the settlement they caught—otherwise Port Jackson's cupboard was bare. There was no sauerkraut against scurvy, no limejuice in the store. Ship's biscuit, tobacco and rum were easy buying.

To replace Thistle and the seven men lost, Flinders asked for convicts—free pardon and a trip to England if they served him well. He soon filled up the gaps in his crew with good men gone astray, but none could be trusted as master. The *Atlas* transport came in with sixty dead, a charnel-pit limping up the harbour, and the *Hercules*, a charge of wholesale murder, in the usual mutiny, against her captain, Luckyn Betts.

Once again Flinders was called to the Admiralty court—that fined Captain Luckyn Betts £500 for Mrs King's orphanage. The next day a sturdy, good-natured man named Aken, master's mate of the *Hercules*, sickened of life on the transports and all that he had seen, applied for the post of master, and swung his hammock in Thistle's berth.

The green in the greenhouse was growing beyond the *Investigator's* strength—and half Australia still to find. They built her a bigger one, sawing and hammering on board the old *Supply*, for Hunter's museum piece and the veteran of the Horn had become a carpenter's shop. Angular panes of glass, flashing back the sun, were new facets of science on the main-deck, and Peter Good was very proud. Sir Joseph would be pleased with his sprouts.

One day a familiar black grin showed up in the greenery.

"You savee me, cap'n? Bongree. Fella been talk you walkabout long way, might I lookout blackfella belong you allsame that time behind?"

With a hearty clap on the back, and a ragged old lieutenant's uniform to strut in, Bongree was installed as ambassador again, with a friend of his named Nanbaree for company.

When he could snatch an hour, Matthew spent it at Mrs Paterson's—where the meek little colonel was savagely threatening to shoot Macarthur like a dog—and at Commissary Palmer's new mansion over the hill in Woolloomooloo Bay. Palmer had the best cook in Port Jackson, a saddened woman, Margaret Catchpole, transported for a dashing ride on a stolen horse to save her smuggler lover. Caley, Sir Joseph's botanist, had fallen in love with the woman and offered her marriage, but, weary of life's emotions, she kept her quiet way.

On 20 June a call for help came from the signaller at South Head. A ship was floundering off the point, too feeble to make her way in—*Le Géographe*, Commodore Baudin. Flinders's boats were first off down the harbour. They dragged the paralysed Frenchmen through the Heads, four men of her 170 able to climb the shrouds.

For them King, in his kindness, killed the few fatted lambs, and the limewashed mill belched all day the dust of the grinding grain. The crying invalids he sent to the cool wards of the hospital, and the locked storehouse was laid open to the voyagers in their distress.

They had come round the snarling south coast of Tasman's Isle, for Baudin was fearful of the millstone waters of Bass Strait. *Le Géographe*, a ship of science, had drifted north with falling men to guide her, a rag on the sea.

Two days, and a peregrine whaler brought news. A treaty was made at Amiens—England and France in a national kiss of peace.

Revanche! The swarthy, smiling *matelots* were given the freedom of the prison port. Latin and temperamental, they squabbled in the drawing-rooms of Government House, and filled the grog-shops with fresh-made politics to suit the situation.

The two expeditions were one in science. Tents together, all day broken English and shattered French mingled in discussion of longitude and strata, and topics of turtle and toadstool. Young John Franklin tried to converse about chronometers with M. Boullanger in Latin, and when Commodore Baudin dined on H.M.S. *Investigator*, eleven guns boomed welcome.

One-eyed François Péron was naturalist. Somebody laughed. "That eye of his sees more than stalks and shoots."

King was horrified. So charmingly sincere, so well-informed, so friendly, Monsieur Péron could never be a spy.

Louis Freycinet, maker of good charts, was acid with disappointment.

"Ha, Captain Flinders, if we had not been kept so long picking up shells and chasing butterflies in Van Diemen's Land, you would not have discovered the South Coast before us."

Commodore Baudin was gravely sorry that they could not reciprocate with charts. His method was to send all soundings and drawings to Paris, and get the maps made there, to plans and specifications. A remarkable method! All Flinders's foundations were done at the masthead.

The *Lady Nelson* was due for duty from the dumps of the Coal River. With three sliding keels, "His Majesty's Tinderbox" was built as a fantastic experiment so she could tuck up her skirts and wade into rivers. Lieutenant Grant, who had blown out from England in her, knew when he was nearing land by a horse-fly on the sails. First to follow through Bass Strait, he had named a dead volcano for Dismal Jimmy Gambier, and scattered a few honourable names around it. So Matthew light-heartedly erased the name of Baudin from that coast—the French could claim no more than a barren fifty leagues. Again, the English were there before them.

Grant had resigned as soon as he reached Port Jackson, to till port and starboard plots of greens on Garden Island. He had left Murray to his mule command.

"Wait till you see her. You won't blame Nelson for walking out," laughed Grant.

In the winds of July she bundled through the Heads. A keen young man was Murray, but not at surveying. Scouting the southern coasts a few months before, he had pulled out a plum of discovery from under Flinders's prow. The sealers' isle in Bass Strait he had marked down for Captain King, the Hebridean harbour of the heather hills he had claimed and named Port Phillip.

"The only things I ever put on the map," he said, "and I expect, sir, you've done it a good deal better."

"You've done it first, John," said Matthew. "That is the big achievement."

The rum and corruption of Port Jackson were infesting his ship, and now he was ready. A year from England, the whole of the south coast an established fact in Admiralty charts, his guns shouted farewell and he was off, twelve months' pork and pease heavy in his hold, and Cook's coast before him.

For two thousand miles that strand wavered away to the north. The *Investigator* was as a shuttle in its shed of water and sky and earth, leaving a trail of light—weft of the longitudes, web of the winds, threaded capes, threaded bays and the filigree of the soundings.

All that Cook had missed in his running survey she found, with wonder and adventure in every bay, marking the great ranges and glorious forests beyond. The wildwood was a harvest to her botanists, the shy black people always helpful and friendly, the natural history museum in the commander's cabin filled with curious treasures of land and sea.

The days lengthened into months, the miles into thousands. Her sails a shimmering reflection in glass-calm tropic seas, her commander at the masthead, H.M.S. *Investigator* seemed a ship of destiny, white-winged courier of a nation yet to be.

Her little consort flapped along behind her, always in trouble, always a drag-anchor. *Lady Nelson* lost her anchors and her sliding keels in the coral, she ripped herself open on the reefs, settled like a seagull on the sandbanks, and even with her best step forward feebly beat the breeze. The *Investigator* waited for her for days at a time—and she was supposed to lead the way. Always she arrived with a tale of woe … and the sailors whispered, remembering the soothsayer of Spithead and Thistle's curse. In wreck she would be worse than useless, she was a wreck already. When she tied her guns together to throw over as anchors, Flinders, in pity, sent her back. He made straight ahead for Torres Strait, where the thousand miles of the Great Barrier Reef were lost in puzzle of shoals.

Where the ribs of the reef met the spine of the coast, they entered the seething shoals, the shuttle winding slowly, hook and thread of line and lead, that still figure in vigil at the main-top, his voice calling down halls of canvas and echoing back in gruff obedience from the steersman bent at the helm.

His eyes were strained to the viridian of the sea, watching for the dorsal ripple of the big reefs under, and the brown tumble of spinning sand and sparkling shell where the rising ramps of massed animal life rose in cliffs on the seashore.

Point to starboard ... point to port ... deftly the thread was cast till the pattern straggled for miles, in its scale on the parchment chart. Pillow of blue water under her keel, blue water ahead, and the passage was complete.

Dark flocks of islands in the sea crowded to the crest of Cape York—the straits that he had sailed with Bligh in nineteen days of torture. He entered the Pandora's Passage, the canoes of the head-hunters about him, bringing coco-nuts and water to trade for iron, as of old—then, with a navigator's inspiration—"Guessin' be God," Fowler called it—he challenged fate, forgot the old sailing directions, and made a southward course.

Eyes straining for colour of shoal, sounding bells ringing and the leadsman chanting all day long, they crept round Cook's Cape York, where the islands crowded even closer. At the fourth dawn he saw the white-capped rock of boobies that marked the western gateway—he had found the channel and threaded the strait in three swift days!

The coast fell away in a smoky blur for 600 straight miles—land of the *Duyfken*, where the little Dutch Dove had alighted two centuries before him. The *Investigator* turned for the great gulf named for Carpentier by Tasman.

Haze without horizons, sweat and sorrow and thirst. She was lagging along the main in a flat calm, her commander seeking in the vague the landmarks he never found. His men were sickening of the dreaded scurvy, and he himself was painfully lame. His tired eyes were colourless and shallow as the sea.

In this featureless land he was mapping by what he could find, white drifts of sand, a belt of greener mangroves, red cones of the ant colonies, columns of fleeting smoke in the sky—that might mark the Indian villages, if these were not restless nomads like the rest—even the aeries of the pallid eagles, the carrion nests that remain for thirty years.

So he named the nothings of the shore, took soundings that the growing coral would alter in sea-change, marked the erratic tides that knew no law, and charted the sandbanks drifting. Vanity of vanities, but the work must be done.

The old Dutchman who had travelled here he honoured all the way. A bountiful island gave them a feast of turtle. Sometimes he found a fire alight, and saw the natives running. They peered through the scrub and paddled away on their crude cane rafts. Wherever the botanists landed, the wild men fled in suspicion, and from the grim old Dutch histories, he knew he was on dangerous ground. The men were armed now, and never out of sight.

The coast turned north-west for another 600 miles. His ship was rotting in these tepid tropic seas. Heavy with barnacles, bored with toredos, her copper peeling and her wood falling away, she was making ten inches in the hour!

The livid red clouds of the coming monsoon were danger signals in the sky at dusk, so to the weird bristled islands of these shallow seas he took the ship to careen her. When Aken and Mart ripped off the rotten planks, the timbers of the hull came with them.

The *Investigator* was falling to pieces. Would she complete the voyage? Would she carry them home? The mad season of cyclones would break at any moment.

A thick night of thunder and venomous tongues of lightning in the west. The ship was an inferno of sandflies as she lay offshore, and Flinders sat with bowed head in his cabin. The sweat, in little steady drips, ran out of his hair. He was sick, his men were sick, and the world all trouble. The time-keepers had run down, for the third time on the voyage. That meant he would have to take twenty-four sets of distances, an added labour to his long travail ashore.

He had logged the culprits once again and dealt with Samuel, and Samuel was defiant. Always there was a barrier between them—that open resentment that Matthew could never fathom. Samuel worked for his Navy pay, and no more. Worse than that, he evaded work if he could. He blamed others, and excused himself ... he had even passed John Franklin's laborious and quite inadequate reckonings on to Matthew as his own ... and in the presence of the crew he had laughed him aside as brother and not commander.

Samuel sat at the other side of the table, apparently deaf to reproof, idly sketching with a pencil.

"The log," said Matthew, "will be dealt with by the Navy Board. You are in charge of the time-keeper midshipmen. Make them do their duty, and do your own. Far too much you refer to me in the astronomical work. I want to see two Captain Flinderses in the Navy, but at this rate you'll have no hope of promotion when we get back."

"If we get back," said Samuel with a sneer. "The ship's rotten through—a lovely command they gave you. With the cyclones coming, the way you hug the shore and the reefs, we'll finish up at the bottom, and where's your promotion then—the bloody promotion you live for, keeping us all in hell. You talk about the French with scurvy—look at that! and that! and that!" He showed his ulcerous sores. "You've got it yourself, and you won't give in. Bell says it's murder. The ship won't last, and the men won't last, till you get this decoration you're after."

Matthew was silent ... distrait. He felt very young and alone, afraid for his ship. Aken had said when the gales came down she would crack like a raddled egg. Fowler was reassuring, but Fowler had no responsibility for a derelict or a ship of the dead. He took little note of his brother's ill-humour. It was a maddening night.

"I promised Sir Joseph"—was he speaking to his brother or himself—"that I would not fail. The wish of my heart is to survey this great continent so that none will need to follow ... but we are indeed in dreadful condition. I doubt that I can do it. With the blessing of God, I would have left nothing to be discovered. I know there is risk. For my men I dare not face it."

"You've done nine thousand miles of it, and God knows that's enough. Run for Koepang while you're alive, and let's get a ship to England, and give up this groping in the mud. Consider yourself lucky you've quit."

Captain Flinders rose, and if his shirt sagged in sweat on his chest, he was very much the commander.

"You will be ready, sir, at six in the morning to take a boat to the island. We go on with the surveying."

He turned back to his chart, its pattern. Nine thousand miles … another three thousand before him.

Ashore on one of the red raddled islands he found an India rope and the rim of an earthen jar, and on another one a small wooden anchor of Chinese framework, a straggle of houses half-built, a pair of the blue coolie trousers worn by the Chinese. There were stumps of trees sliced by European axes … the mystery of the Asiatics again.

The next island was a fantasy of chasms, rifts in the rocks thirty feet deep, where shrubs crawled up in serpent growth, thirsting for sun. Some paleolithic Rembrandt had smeared the rocky walls with clay of the seashore in crude conception of his totem gods of kangaroo and turtle, and Westall copied the oldest of the masters in oils.

Each day brought food for thought abounding, but little food for debilitated men. The hogs were dying. In hurricanes fish were few. Electric storms split the sky. Torrents of rain steeped sea and land in a poisonous green light. Breath of earth was bitter with the reek of the mangrove creeks, and the slimy roots of the mangroves writhed and reared like snakes.

They came to a wide mainland bay of grisly blue mud. Tasman's Groote Eylandt, that Flinders had explored, was a haze twelve miles to westward. Nearer the bay lay a tongue of land shaped like a waddy, or "woodah" in Bongree's language. The beaches were covered with human tracks.

Unlike the gentle shadows of the woods of New Holland, the natives here were six feet of sullenness and savagery, circumcised in some ruthless Stone Age rite. Their gods were rounded stones of Phallic symbol. Guarding their cretaceous coasts, where the rakish pandanus was their flag, they reconnoitred in their canoes in those sluggish tides for miles. They would accept no overtures from alien Bongree, nor trade their poor possessions with the ship.

Limping under a steaming sun, and coughing upon hordes of flies, Flinders had checked his angles. He motioned the boat, to take him back to the ship. On a point shimmering like tempered steel, he passed Westall, sketching, and the clap of axes came over the water, a party with Whitewood, the master's mate. The canoe that landed from Woodah Island he did not see. Slipping between the trees, the blacks closed in on Westall. With the valour of discretion, he packed up his paints and joined the wooding party. The blacks ran after him, slipping between the trees. Whitewood and his men faced them on the brow of a little hill.

Glistening bodies and gorilla brows, they stopped and stood their ground. Each of the seven carried a hunting spear.

Whitewood, smiling, held out a tomahawk and some beads. The nearest offered his spear, and the mate went forward to get it. In a flash, the spear was through his breast.

He raised his musket and snapped the firelock, but a shower of spears came over and he fell. The muskets cracked behind him. The savages snatched his hat and ran.

Flinders heard the shots, saw the canoe madly paddled to sea. A sharp fire from the shore—one of the blacks leapt and fell overboard ... and then his men, in a little procession, came out of the woods carrying dead or dying.

Aken was sent with two boats. He brought off Whitewood, four barbs in his body, and a seaman, Morgan, fallen in a stroke of the sun. Foaming at the mouth and raving, Morgan died that night. Bell, a taciturn man, growled that Whitewood would not live. In the heat and fetor of the mangroves, to the weird wailing of corroboree in the scrub, the silver moonlight seemed an evil dream.

They found the dead native on the beach, his head, in a last agony, pillowed on his arm. It was pathos to Flinders. Till now no ship of his had killed, nor needed to kill, one of these poor wild creatures. When Brown was lost that night, through lack of a compass, the commander, with a boat ready, watched for his flare till daylight, when Brown made sign. He had thought it safer to camp in the rocks than to light a fire.

The ship moved northward to another haze of bay. Here, where the old Dutch *Arnhem* had drifted out of ken, was endless trouble with the blacks. In cunning they smiled—to snatch muskets and axes—pleasantly beckoned the botanists into the woods. For the first time in ten years on the coasts of New Holland, Flinders had found treachery and craft, the design of deliberate murder.

Fowler caught a boy as hostage for the return of an axe, and brought him on board, an intelligent stripling named Woga. He gaped at the sheep and the hogs, and collapsed in hysterics of laughter at little Trim washing his face. The cat and the cannibal—even melancholy Matthew smiled. He would have adopted Woga, but that Baudin was following, and the blacks would have their revenge.

From where the *Arnhem* disappeared, the coast elbowed west.

Clouds and islands, bays and their reflections swimming in deceitful seas ... the watcher at the masthead was dizzy with fever and blind with glare, but the chart followed its relentless line of mathematical precision. Delirious, he sometimes wondered if he were charting his dreams. Below him his ship was laboured and slow. He goaded her on ... and on... .

Beyond the vague islands that he named for the English Company in India, he met the Vikings of the Timor Sea—the glassy sweep of a tropic bay was a harbour with ships in port.

H.M.S. *Investigator* backed topsails with a jerk, and hoisted colours. No ensign flew to the masthead of the queer little flagship, a cross between a Torres Strait war canoe and one of the clumsy junks of China. They put up a white flag, symbol of peace in the signal books of the polychromatic world.

The Britisher tacked and came on, a swan among snipe. Her second lieutenant was sent in a boat well-armed.

The men were coloured, Samuel reported to Matthew—two moons from Macassar, bound down into the Gulf.

As Flinders, Brown and a Javanese cook-boy rowed to the prau that carried the white flag, five others joined the six at anchor.

A squat little admiral of the Celebes, his regalia a loincloth, smiled them aboard the rackety flag-ship. The Javanese boy translated.

Sixty praus and a thousand men were scattered along the coast under Salu, Rajah of Boni. Pobassoo, this captain of the van, had but two small brass cannon lent them by the Dutch—little he knew of the *Investigator's* carronades, puny in the Channel, but ready to blow them out of the water. Theirs was the strangest commerce of the earth, and the only export from Australia.

"*Tre-pang*," said Pobassoo, when asked why he had come.

Flinders did not understand.

"*Beche-de-mer*," translated the cook-boy, who had come to him from Hamelin's *Naturaliste*.

He shook his head.

Pobassoo led him along the deck, and held up a sea-cucumber. This half-living thing was a trade. Slant-eyed Chinese merchants in sleeves of coloured silks, counting their *cash* under the swaying lanterns of Banjermasin, paid 20 dollars a *picol* for the white, 40 dollars for the black—with sharks' fins and birds' nest soup, it was a gourmet's delicacy for the mandarins of Peking.

Pobassoo showed how they dived for the slug in the shallows, boiled it and dried it in mangrove smoke and sun. He had come to these shores for the past twenty years, blown by the winds of monsoon for a thousand miles, and blown back in the wind. These tattooed men admitted that the naked savage was their foe. There was burning and slaughter, and stealth lay in wait for their praus ... so they had left the legacy of hatred, and taught the honest cannibal to be a killer and a thief.

Westall sketched the ships at anchor, Flinders copied the Arabic writing, and gave them a note for Baudin if he should come that way. They left these Argonauts of the unknown south, outlined in stereoscopic storm light.

Capes, bays and islands ... days into months ... in March, at the Wessel Islands, the surgeon Bell called ending. H.M.S. *Investigator* was a scurvy ship, her men with spongy gums and livid sores. In the first fair wind she must run for Koepang, if her rotting hulk could make it.

They entered that forlorn haven, its coco-nut palms rags on the sunset of 16 March ... the little Dutch houses under the bougainvillea vines, shades of Timothy Wanjon.

But Timothy Wanjon, and Baudin's Frenchmen, and Nelson, the botanist of Bligh's old *Bounty*, were a row of leaning crosses in the rank jungle under the palms together.

13

A Village in the Sea

Full circle sailing.

On 9 June the *Investigator* was at Sydney Heads again, the old familiar gateway, but a shadowed ship, a sandy grave and a sea-grave behind her. In a race with death round the continent, she was losing.

Charlie Douglas, the stalwart bosun, they buried at Goose Island Bay in the lonely west. Seaman Smith had gone to the deep at sundown. Eighteen men were dangerously ill, and for eight there was no hope.

Koepang had saved them from scurvy and given them fever. The tropic fruits of its wet season brought violent dysentery. That Dutch outpost was more degraded than ever, no hope of a ship there in many months, no food to share. There was nothing for it but Port Jackson, the only other light in the South Sea— five thousand miles to run. With God and the wind behind them, pump forever croaking, they had made it in forty-eight days.

The tiered cliffs were grey in rain as they ran the old track.

Port Jackson was dull and cold. The launch went ashore with the dying.

Peter Good was too ill to be moved, good little Peter, with his cutty pipe, furrow of concentration in his brow, the crows' feet of good humour at the corners of his eyes. For love of the work, he had added more than 500 plants to the botanists' collection of thousands in the rarest garden that the world would ever see. The greenhouse was Peter's home, his plants his children ... he could not care about them now.

There were three ships in harbour, big East India traders, *Bridgewater*, *Cato* and *Rolla*. As the *Investigator* swung to anchor, the *Lady Nelson* hailed her going out. With John Bowen and a cargo of convicts, she was off to found a settlement on the Derwent River in Van Diemen's Land—their tubby friend "Tinderbox" writing a chapter of empire.

Mr Schweitzer's uniform had lost something of its pristine freshness when Captain Flinders limped up the hill to call on Governor King. The governor hailed the discoveries as the most inspiring page in the history of New South Wales. The channel through the Torres Strait was a new road to India—he published Flinders's journal in full in his news-sheet, *Sydney Gazette*, printed under a gum-tree by a creole from St Kitts. He delivered to Captain Flinders a pile of English mail. Ann, he learned, had been gravely ill after he sailed from England—but that was a year ago.

No letter from his father . . with misgivings, Matthew opened the one in his stepmother's writing.

The little doctor was dead.

Slowly he went back to his ship. The brothers were together in grief.

"I had hoped to make his latter days the most delightful of his life," said Matthew sadly. "I thought that time was coming. You chide me for ambition, Sam, but I promised my father that he should be proud. How much I cared he will never know.... Our mother and the girls, they need us, and here we are at the end of the world."

Samuel's unfriendliness was forgotten. The death of the little doctor brought them closer than ever before—a younger Matthew he seemed, with all the energy and ambition, the kindness of heart, but with fuller lips and lighter eyes.

"On 12 June departed this life Mr Peter Good, gardener ..."

a word of regret and honour in the *Investigator*'s log, bluejackets filing to the graveyard in the bush—and Peter's name made immortal that night on the high green island, a dot in the chart, beyond Cape York, where the coast of the continent swung down for the great Gulf. The neat little sea-chest was opened and auctioned at the mast. Five that belonged to the *Investigator*'s dead were sold within the week. Drooping her sails to dry in an ill wind, she was a funeral ship.

Her commander was crippled with a painful affection of the bladder. The valiant Brown was lame. King sent them away to one of the glory-corners of the world, the broad silver reaches, the little brown farms of Hawkesbury River. There Matthew found health and happiness again, rambling in the sunny bush, sailing his skiff among the blackfellows' canoes, reading the adoring letters from Ann, and writing to her:

If I could laugh at the effusion of thy tenderness, it would be to see the idolatrous language thou frequently usest to me. Thou makest me an idol and then worshippest it, and, like some of the inhabitants of the East, thou also bestowest a little castigation occasionally, just to let the ugly deity know the value of thy devotion. Mindest thou not, my dearest love, that I shall be spoiled by thy endearing flatteries? I fear it, and yet can hardly part with one, so dear to me is thy affection in whatever way expressed.

Alas, like Trim, I am becoming grey... .

He gave her news of the ship and all its people, of Mrs Paterson and Mrs King,

who would have made thee so happy here. Two better or more agreeable women are not easily found. These would have been thy constant friends, and for visiting acquaintances there are now five or six ladies very agreeable for short periods and perhaps longer.

The little schooner *Cumberland* came along on her pilgrimage of the farms, with a diverting tale of derring-do and the French.

After six months' most gracious acceptance of King's hospitality, Commodore Baudin had made a charming gift of Sèvres china to Mrs King, with £50 for her orphanage. Then his two ships sailed, not north, but south. Hardly were they out of the harbour than rumours rose in a cloud.

England and France were sparring at each other again, and it was said that Louis Freycinet had mapped the harbour for the landing of French troops, that François Péron, touring the colony as the honoured guest of the settlers, was engineering a rising of the Irish. Now they were gone to Van Diemen's Land, that Bass and Flinders had proved another island. What if they should unfurl the Tricolour, and plant a colony there to storm Port Jackson?

"God bless me!" said King. "Why didn't I hear it before?"

The *Cumberland* was his only ship—he sent her on a flag-planting race, a diplomatic mission, and young Robbins, in command, knew as much diplomacy as a Nepean bull. He found the Frenchmen at King Island in Bass Strait, peacefully chasing butterflies and picking up shells ... but he raced in and hoisted the Union, upside down in haste, and set two marines strutting on guard.

The Frenchmen were mildly amazed. Baudin dispatched a self-righteous and cynical letter to Governor King. So little could he credit King's distrust that he thought the Union was a flag used for straining water and hung out to dry. His artists had sketched the hilarious incident—Port Jackson on guard, of a rock and a seagull—and Baudin sketched the history of Port Jackson. It was a clever letter, the velvet paw, a satire of a *savant* run to seed. His was, in all sincerity, he said, an expedition of science.

"If you ask me," said Flinders, laughing, "it's even too peaceful for that."

For all Baudin's barbs, Port Jackson was proving worth owning after all. Bright fields of wheat were shining in the sun as far as the Emu Plains, here and there a mill to mark a village. There were plenty of cattle and sheep for meat, vineyards and fruit-gardens, but still none so rich as Mrs Macarthur's.

The urchins that Flinders had known grubbing naked in the bed of the Tank Stream had become a generation of strapping young farmers and, emptied by the buckets of a thirsty ten thousand, the Tank Stream was rapidly fading away. The settlement was still a sorry motley of soldier red and convict grey, and the triangles made even shriller music, but there was a lull in vendettas. Macarthur had gone to England under arrest. Meek little Colonel Paterson had challenged him to a duel—masks, cloaks and pistols under the placid gums by Parramatta River. Macarthur was the better shot. Paterson was convalescent—a serious wound in the shoulder, a more serious wound to his pride.

In the web of events, Matthew again had missed Doctor George.

Bass and the *Venus* had come and gone, for pork, fish, seals, salvage, anything they could find in the Pacific, including the shaggy llamas of Peru to challenge Macarthur's sheep.

"We are sick of civilization," George said, in one of those light-hearted letters of his he left for Flinders with Bishop. "I shall sail on another pork voyage, but it combines circumstances of a different nature also."

He was making no fortune, but following the sun and the sea as far as the Sandwich Islands and beyond. He told of comic adventures with Taina in Otaheite, and made a facetious reference to "digging gold in Peru".

Bishop had curious suggestions to make about those "circumstances"—Bishop had gone mad. Even so, Matthew felt misgiving.

He wrote in his letter, to leave with King:

This fishing and pork-carrying business may pay your expenses, but the only other advantage you get by it is experience for a future voyage, and this, I take to be the purport of your Peruvian expedition.

The Spaniards were tougher customers than his cannibals. He did not like Peru. However, he told George of his own journey, and of the journey to come.

For H.M.S. *Investigator* had been declared unseaworthy, and he was off to England for a new ship.

Governor King had sent his inspectors on board. They ripped off sodden planks, and pushed their canes through her worm-eaten timbers. Eleven out of ninety on one side would hold out the sea, and on the other five out of eighty-nine. Her bows were rotten through, the stemson riddled and yellow with decay. The only sound wood was in her stern.

"Not worth repairing in any country in the world, and a menace to her company" was the verdict of Palmer of the *Bridgewater*, Park of the *Cato*, and Tom Moore, colony boat-builder.

King, as senior naval officer in the south, condemned her. The ship of science, ship of dreams, was a hollow shell.

On a day in July the governor came aboard to lunch and talk it over.

"I have no ship to give you," he told Flinders. "There's H.M.S. *Porpoise*, this misfit they've sent me out for protection and peddling—decayed, her copper gone, and far too small to carry stores and men for two and a half years on an uninhabited coast. *Lady Nelson*—out of the question. We could buy the *Rolla*, but £11,500 they want for her, and then she would have to be fitted—a six months' undertaking with bush timber. What else? H.M.S. *Buffalo*, away with Kent for heaven knows how long, and too small in any case."

It was King who made the suggestion nearest to Flinders's heart. "I'll tell you. Take the *Porpoise*. Get the crew to England for a new ship. I intended to send her in any case, for the summer passage of Cape Horn."

"I scarcely like to appear in England before the voyage is completed, sir——"

"Oh nonsense! What wisdom in waiting here? Far better to take the big garden and the finished charts, and start again."

England! Ann in his arms! The governor was flattered at Matthew's exultant smile.

"But why travel the old ways, sir, across hemispheres of storm? My passage through the Torres Strait is summer all the way in the swing of the trade. We hug the shores as close as Vasco da Gama, and thread the needle of the reefs with ease. You know my route—trade route to the Spice Islands and India, a short cut to England."

"Well, it's your picnic!" King was pleased. "But Flinders, don't tie yourself to the quarter-deck all day. I'll give you the ship, let Fowler take her. You go as passenger, on deck when you're needed, and for the rest, make charts. That's the best, my lad, that you can do for England."

"I thank you, sir. With all my heart I shall follow your directions."

So the *Porpoise* was decked with the hanging gardens of Babylon, and the crew clumped into new quarters, leaving the *Investigator* a derelict on the shore, Colpitts, the gunner, on guard to keep the convicts out. He was a ghost of better days, haunting her silent decks. Brown and Bauer decided to wait in New South Wales, growing another garden for the new ship.

When sailing orders were posted, Palmer of the *Bridgewater*, Park of the *Cato*, presented their compliments to Captain Flinders aboard. Might they keep company in the Torres Strait trade route? They had decided to try it in any case, from the excellence of his charts, but with the pathfinder to lead them, why not travel in convoy? If he would wait a day or two, they might all sail, together.

Stores aboard, men ashore, the Indiamen and H.M.S. *Porpoise* spread petals of canvas on 10 August 1803. It was a great day in Harbour history when three big ships put out together. The governor came with them to the Heads, and swung overside under flying flags to a little regatta of sightseers. A boom of farewell—they rounded the head to the north.

Reefs out of topsails, stunsails and royals set, ships of the line of commerce, white shields to the winds, they sailed for India—and England!

Fresh breeze and cloudy. A week to sea.

The *Porpoise* was a wayward sailer, but always in the lead—was Flinders ever behind? Now the Great Barrier Reef lay a hundred miles north-east, to curve for a thousand miles, closing them in calm.

Flinders and Fowler were in the gun-room, in after-dinner jollity with the little band of passengers, a Rum Corps major on hearty furlough, and varied adventurers of the sea.

Once Matthew held up his hand to hush the laughter. He thought he heard a drumming ... low and far away ... but no, the cordage in the freshening trades. The hearty major sang a ribald song.

There was a growing undertone against the swish and sway, and again that eerie drumming ... like the drumming of the redcoats when a man was hanged.

"Helm alee!" Aken's shout.

Close-hauled, the *Porpoise* jibbed and swerved.

"At her old tricks again," said Flinders to her captain. And then, in the course of his thoughts, with his whimsical smile, "She wants as much tiller-rope as a young wife."

Samuel went past him, running.

The major went on singing, the others listening with sly laughter.

"Breakers ahead!"—the cry of the lookout in the minarets of the shrouds, weak in the wind as a heron's call.

"A reef! Here we come!"

Fowler knocked over his chair. His boots vanished up the swaying companion.

"Stand by to the braces to bring her about!"

His voice from above was strident with apprehension.

There was rip and creak of straining timbers, and the ship leaned over, leaned till the horn lanterns were insanely vertical out from the slanted walls.

Rush of sailors from the fo'c'sle. As Flinders lurched and crawled up the crazy companion he heard a crash of chairs and crockery. The major, with five men after him, raced downhill. They fell in a foolish heap.

A witches' oil of black volatile water was seething along the decks, seamen calling and caterwauling in the shrouds. The surf was a deafening boom boiling to the rim of the hatches.

A last anguished yelp from Fowler, a grinding of timbers and a paralysing shock as the ship heeled over. The three masts came down with the crack of guns, the hawsers parted and flew wide like the flying web of a smashed loom, and the drumming rose in a roaring crescendo.

The blade of the coral reef drove deep ... they were down, in a welter of ghostly foam.

Catherine-wheeling lights and phantom sails, the other ships came after.

"Fire a gun!" bawled Fowler. "For Christ's sake, fire a gun!"

But the guns were choked with flurry of spray. A shout went up from fifty throats, men's voices above the wind.

White chargers rearing at the bit, the ships clawed back and curvetted, but the wind of fate in their stunsails was dragging them on to their doom, and the reef sucked them in.

Blind in the mosaic of the dark, men swarming in the rigging, they tacked—tacked madly—and plunged for each other's bows. The men on the wreck screamed as lights and sails swung together. With a clamour of bells they reeled to strike, a thousand tons of impact.

Then with a superhuman wrench the *Cato* went about. She missed stays, canted for the reef, staggered and fell in a horrible cracking chaos, and was lost from sight.

The *Bridgewater* by a miracle shaved reef and ship, and stood away swiftly to southward.

H.M.S. *Porpoise* lay like a dead whale in a swirling mass of flotsam, her precious garden a ruin of drifting green weed, her men, like half-drowned flies, crawling out of the water. Somewhere among them, Flinders crawled to Fowler—Fowler, sitting like a surprised child, bracing his heels against the gunwale.

"We're fast. It's a shelf. Pray God we're all alive."

"Aye, aye, sir!" said Fowler in a daze, touching his cap to his passenger.

"The *Cato's* a deuce of a wreck, but the *Bridgewater's* pulled clear"—he pointed to the steady lights, shouting above the waves that were thundering in on the keel in terrible rhythm, breaking and retreating. "Sam! There you are, thank God. Call the roll and tally our people. Most of our boats are smashed flat, but Fowler, swing out the cutter. I'll get the charts and the log-books and make the *Bridgewater* for the rescue. Midshipman Franklin! Franklin there? Hoy!"

"Aye, sir." A weak but reassuring chirp from a pile of wreckage aft.

"To the time-keepers and the charts. Come with me."

They swung out the cutter. It stove and went down in the hammering surf. All they had now was the gig.

Clambering through the horizontal cabins awash in every wave, Flinders snatched his charts from the locker, wrapped them in waterproof sailcloth, strapped them to the seat of the gig, and with six men pushed off, rocketing through welter of foam and rocks.

A midget boat in a mighty sea of blackness, they followed the *Bridgewater*'s lights, and the *Bridgewater*'s lights grew dimmer—she still was standing on. An hour of hopeless, frenzied rowing—they tried to get back to the wreck, but the surf-tide defied them. All that night, wet through and shivering in the wind, bailing with the cook's boots, they spent rowing in the lee of the reef, battling up and down.

On the *Porpoise*, Second-Lieutenant Flinders, after an hour of pandemonium, managed to call the roll—gruff bass and shrill tenor answering from the havoc, all safe and unhurt to the last man. Of the ship's proud masts they built a raft, and burned blue lights to call the *Bridgewater* back. Some said she answered, but in the small hours her twinkle of lights was gone.

"*Wind fresh from the east and a little squally.*" In the creeping grey of dawn Flinders swam and scrambled aboard along the drifting spars. The ship was high on the reef, and beyond, a blessing to their eyes, was a wide shoal island of snow-white sand.

The *Cato* was an abject wreck, still bullied by the breakers. Head on to the raging sea she had fallen, all night scoured by its surf. As yet every soul was safe, but her people were clinging to each other in the bows, a rope of living men.

That windy morning they spent in landing the companies on the island. All stores and gear in the *Porpoise* were intact, even the sheep still living, but of that rarest garden in the world, Brown's achievement, Peter's loving labour, nearly all was lost.

By noon, ninety-four half-naked men were cheering on the strand, and except for three boys of the *Cato*, drowned from floating spars in crossing, every one on the ships' lists answered to his name. Their sea-chests scattered about them, they strained their eyes for the *Bridgewater*, and saw her, hull and courses. Flinders hoisted two handkerchiefs on an oar.

In the ebb of afternoon, they began to land stores and clear the rapidly-breaking ship. Mended boats and handy-Andy rafts swarmed like noisy sea-gulls around a dead whale, the waves hissing over the ribbed sands with the murmur of a conch shell, a funnel of lowering cloud above. Casks of beef and kegs of rum were floated in in dozens, flour, water, pork, pease, ropes, oatmeal, sauerkraut, molasses, hogs, spars, canvas, enough to feed and shelter a hundred men for three months. The castaways might be drowned, but they would not starve. The *Cato's* people had nothing to eat and nothing to wear, so they were welcome to the messes, and blankets and clothes. Raw hairy sailors strutted in the clipped braids and navy cut of His Majesty's lieutenants.

By nightfall sheep were running among the fluffy flocks of noddies in waving fields of the sea-grass. A fire of driftwood beaconed the dusk, with torchlight processions of Roman rite, the green saline flame of the tarred ropes throwing chill shadows across the deckled dunes.

Ninety-four men and boys high and dry in the middle of the Great South Sea, they crept under each other's coats to sleep in the crisp cold sand, many a lively tale of the wreck but never a sorry heart among them, the minor symphony of the surf their lullaby.

At dawn they hoisted the Union, canton downward, flag of distress. Shy of the shoals, the *Bridgewater* would return with the first calm weather.

They waited, through two long days of squall.

Under slapping eaves of canvas Captain Flinders, senior officer and elected to command, sat and planned as governor— governor of a Fenland shore in the wide Pacific.

That sandy flaw in the sea became as a disciplined three-decker. The ensign flew into the sunrise, and fluttered down at sunset. Beneath its rippling shadow, a busy village grew, tents, docks and taverns. All day the ecstatic cries of the sea-gulls mingled with the rusty croaking of the tars, able seamen, stable seamen, in strange situation. All day, all night, the soft steady billows lapped in rise and fall of the tides about their home.

"*Wind more moderate, with finer weather.*" Still the *Bridgewater* did not come—nor the next blue day, nor the next.

It was clear as the sky above that Palmer was not coming back.

They were marooned—but no coward captain of an Indiaman could baffle ninety-four British seamen.

In canvas walls on a seashell floor, the village held a parliament and passed a bill for its future—Flinders and Park would take a boat for help. A captain of two years seniority and a barnacled skipper of the merchant marine would stand on the quarter-deck of the 16-foot cutter, and with a bireme of twelve rowers set a course of 800 miles to the only lights of the south.

Rigged and fitted to play her part, the cutter was christened H.M.S. *Hope*. On 27 August she slid away from a cheering crowd, and through the hills and valleys of the big green combers left the lapping lagoons behind her.... As she sailed the castaways hauled down their flag of distress, and hoisted the Union canton up, a flag of courage and faith.

Two hundred miles of open sea they sailed in sixty hours, then herring-boning the coast made down. The wind failed. Oars rose and fell in ceaseless rhythm for seven days without it. Sandy Head—Indian Head—the Glasshouse and Cape Moreton—the Solitary Isles and Smoky Head were milestones on the way, two hundred leagues of tossing sea between them. Sometimes they stopped for a meal of noddies or oysters on the rocks, but mostly salt pork and ships' biscuits, with cold water, was a hand to mouth grab. On 9 September they crept round the bomboora of the lion's paws.

Governor King had just sealed a letter to Lord Hobart, a very complacent letter stressing the colony's progress, announcing the Van Diemen's Land settlement to be named in his lordship's honour, and those white-winged heralds of imperial wealth fluttering through Torres Strait ... when a bearded crew with a rag-tag boat bumped in at his private steps. The governor emerged in righteous dudgeon to scout them out of his garden. By that time the ringleader was on the mat.

His Excellency was about to shout for the guard when he recognized the overgrown countenance of Captain Matthew Flinders, weather-beaten and the worse for wear. Mr Schweitzer's uniform was conspicuous by its absence.

"Great Heavens!" cried Governor King, "the ships are back!"

"Unfortunately no, your excellency. We came without them. The *Porpoise* and the *Cato* are where the *Bridgewater* left them, piled up on a coral reef nearly a thousand miles from here."

He told his story for the rest of the afternoon.

It was a difficult moment when Brown came for tidings of the garden—a whole year's work and endless trudging, the death-blow to years of research ahead. It was kindly King that braced the botanist with the philosophies of a sailor.

That night they decided what to do. Luckily for the castaways, the *Rolla* was still in harbour. Passages paid, she would take them to China, where they would wait a good six months till the convoys sailed.

"I can face anything in the world save waiting," said Matthew ruefully. "If I had a ship of any kind, I would beat them home."

Sitting out on his patch of lawn that was growing steadily greener, King blew Cuban tobacco at the Port Jackson stars.

"I could give you the *Cumberland*," he laughed.

Flinders sat up, eager and gay. "You mean it?"

"Well, I scarcely expected you did."

"She's bigger than the *Norfolk*, sir, and hardier than the *Investigator*. I'm well inured to cranky ships—so I can take the *Cumberland*?"

"If you'll take the risk, why not. You could start in her, in any case, and pick up a ship on the way."

"Round the world in a 29-tonner with God and the wind, I'll do it! I'll go back to the reef with the *Rolla*, see them aboard, and be off through the Torres Strait to try Koepang for a ship—if not, the Cape.

"Or Ile-de-France. You have your passport, we've made these Frenchmen friends. We could do with some knowledge of that place that might be of use to Port Jackson, not necessarily in war, but in general commerce and foodstuffs."

"Aye, sir."

So King sent a courier to the Hawkesbury River for the *Cumberland*, booked a passenger-list of ninety-four on the China-going *Rolla*, and prepared a bundle of dispatches for Whitehall.

Ebor Bunker's whaler had galloped in with startling news of bother in Bengal. When the bailiff French had come to claim Pondicherry, under the Treaty of Amiens, they found the Union nailed to the fort, and a Bombay garrison showing fight. The French Governor-General Decaen, arriving in state, was scouted out of the port. Not even allowed to land there, he turned his Tricolour tail to the wind and fled, vowing vengeance in the name of Napoleon. Captain Kidd corsairs of Surcouf officially under the Jolly Roger, but unofficially under Bonaparte's red star, were foxes lying in wait for Britain's fleets in the Indian Ocean. In Europe, the old bad feeling was smouldering again to flame. Nelson was back with the fleet in the Mediterranean. That signified sinister things to come.

Under the circumstances, King was of the opinion that a transport of troops instead of troopers would do Port Jackson no harm. He knew there was a clause in Admiralty instructions forbidding Flinders to carry dispatches, but that applied to wartime. With luck the *Cumberland* would beat the China convoy by half a year, and if Captain Flinders would be so kind——

He handed over his budget. Captain Flinders was delighted.

When the *Cumberland* was not in from the Hawkesbury at the end of the week, impatient Matthew thrashed the north-easter to find her. They met off the little palm beach and hurried back. The *Francis* was to go up with them, to bring tidings and sundries back to King in Port Jackson.

A week and two days from the landing in the cutter they were ready to sail for the wreck, but now the skipper of the *Rolla* wanted another night with his fancy girl ashore. When Flinders fired a gun at daybreak, he was not aboard. By ten o'clock a wild north-easter had lost them all hope of sailing. It raged for two days. When they did get away, the ships were so slow that the *Cumberland*, in exasperation, was running circles round them.

Wreck Reef was a colony under the British Crown, its myriad sea-birds vanished before the invader. Hammers were ringing, the seamen singing, and shacks lined the shore. H.M.S. *Resource*, a trim little 20-ton schooner they had built, was lying in the anchorage, and beside her the keel of a second was laid.

On 7 October a gull on the horizon changed by magic into a sail, t'gallants rising into courses over the curve of the world. The sandbank was delirious with joy. A great shout rose from the sea-grass.

Lieutenant Samuel Flinders went on winding his clocks with the coolness of Francis Drake.

"Look !" they cried to him, "the ships of our salvation!"

"So I see," said Samuel quietly. "'Tis my brother back again." In a lifetime's family trust, he had never known Matthew fail.

Surely enough it was the *Cumberland*, *Francis* and *Rolla*, in that order, steps of stairs. They hove to in the tiny port—the strangest port in the world's directory—and a puffing half-moon of guns barked greeting.

In the two busy days of taking off stores and people, Flinders was round the rocks and sandbanks, sketching them in to the map where waves had been. He gathered treasure of radiant shells, the secret of the Pacific, and rare collections of birds' eggs and grasses for Sir Joseph's glass cases in Soho. When little John Franklin, faithful shepherd of the surviving sheep, came shamefaced to report that he had driven a horny-footed crew over Westall's delicate drawings, and when Peter Good's once-glorious garden reduced itself, in the bitter end, to a solitary box of seeds — well, he consoled himself with the philosophies of a sailor.

He called for volunteers for the *Cumberland's* crew — eleven men, captain included, was all she could hope to carry. With Aken and Elder first to answer, the best sailors crossed ever. They were willing, with him, to go round the world in twenty-nine tons. Samuel handed over to him Cook's time-keeper and its rate — Franklin and Sam he sent with the *Rolla* to China. The charts of the new world packed in casks, and his trunks and sea-chests for seats in the cramped cabin, on the evening of 11 October they were ready to set out on the long, lone adventure.

There was a grand farewell on the *Rolla* that night that set the reefs ringing, with glasses raised to the humped old wrecks black in the swirling tide.

A last grip of good luck to Fowler and Sam in the morning, a hand on John Franklin's curly head with "Keep thou the path", and a white feather leapt to the *Cumberland's* counter. She was away on the leeward tack, close-hauled.

12 October. Fresh breeze and cloudy. We returned their three cheers, and at 25 past nine bore away on our course to the Torres Strait.

Under mackerel clouds and cumulus, a silhouette against the moon or a silver gull in the sunlight, they clawed along coasts familiar.

In a letter to Ann to post at Koepang — or carry on himself — Matthew wrote:

I very much wish the Cumberland were broader. In 1½ hour's cessation from pumping, the water washed over the cabin floor.

Writing here is like writing on horseback on a rainy day, and much worse than writing in the *Norfolk* sloop. We are dry only when at anchor. I am sitting on the lee locker with my knees up to my chin for a table to write on, and in momentary expectation of the seas coming down the skylight, for they have broken me two panes of glass already.

I get some speed out of her, but of all the filthy little things I ever saw, this schooner, for bugs, lice, weavils, mosquitoes, cockroaches (large and small) and mice, rises superior to them all.

We have almost got the better of the fleas, lice and mosquitoes, but in spite of boiling water and daily destruction among them, the bugs still keep their ground. Before this vile bug-like smell will leave me, I and my clothes must undergo a good boiling in a large kettle.

I shall set my old friend Trim to work on the mice.

Where the islands crowd in to Cape York, Flinders found another swift passage and checked his old charts—no figure at the masthead this time, no proud perspective of thirty feet up as from the *Investigator's* maintop. The waterline was hissing at his feet.

The *Cumberland* was a hovel of heat in the sea as she made across the Gulf to Cape Arnhem, where a cheery savage, remembering his ensign, hailed him with a rag on a pole. There he made a sorry discovery. Rooting in the casks, he found that his charts of this unknown part of earth were gone. He was working on them on the night of the wreck, and so they were forgotten, to be a mess of ink and water. The best he could do was to fill the gap with conjectures of log and bearings. The minute accuracy of shores and islands, that had cost a sick man so much labour and anxiety were lost.

Light airs, the mirror-birds wheeling, trickle and cluck of water under the pintles, the schooner slid by on the glass of tropic seas. On 9 November, the mountains of Timor loomed out of twenty leagues of sparkling haze.

In the humid shade of the great peaks, a bone-white shack of tropic timber sheltered another ambassador of the House of Orange, who accorded the hospitality of the Hague Palace on piles of rattan matting in halls of bamboo. Looking out on the Indies and their sickly-sweet wealth, Flinders was offered a home, a sea captain's home on a headland, where, framed in splashes of pandanus, the calm leagues stretched to infinity.

But he must go, back into the *Cumberland*, a melting-pot of ambition and achievement. He was anchored to her by the brassy braid of Mr Schweitzer's salt-stained, shipwrecked uniform. He must sail those infinite leagues and empty days to Sir Joseph and a new *Investigator* ...to Ann.

The wheel of the horizon, wheel of fate, was turning.

Yellow sails in a yellow sky, the grey peaks of Timor went down into the north-east, and over the curve of the world the grey peaks of Ile-de-France rose in the south-west.

14

Clipped Wings

The smudge on the horizon gradually resolved itself into a patchwork of brown and green.

All his life he had known a thrill of pleasure and expectation in the approach to islands—it might have been the echoes of Robinson Crusoe from his mind's awakening to the wonder of the sea—but no tropic paradise was ever so welcome as this. He looked at the skin of his bare legs, dry and flaky with scurvy. He ran his fingers round inside the collar of his shirt, and shuddered at the sickening smell of vermin. Whatever it was, he had killed it. The reek from the water-butt, when he went to wash his hands, was nearly as vile.

Ile-de-France was a riddle, a rocky maze. A wall of serrated cliffs fell sheer for miles, with no inkling of a landing-place. Beating along the coast, he was keeping a lively lookout for a trader, to give him a lead in. There were slave-ships, he knew, constantly plying backwards and forwards to Madagascar. He must strike the luck of a guide sooner or later.

Towards noon, Aken reported a flag on one of the hills.

"Hoist colours!"

Up went the White Ensign, and a French jack at the foretop-masthead, Baudin's signal for the pilot when he came in to Port Jackson. On went the *Cumberland* under easy sail. A scattering of sea-shells on velvet, the white roofs of a little town showed up in the greenery two or three miles off, cleverly tucked away in a cleft of the cliffs.

As they turned for the roadstead, a schooner was just making out. They tacked to greet her. With no answering flags she hauled inshore to let them pass, and then swung round in their wake. This was mysterious, and scarcely friendly. Flinders gave the order to heave to, and wait for her to come up. Whereupon she doubled, clapped on sail, and fairly raced back for the roadstead. Again the snub direct.

"After her, boys!" he shouted. "Take all her motions. We must make the passage through the reefs."

The steep brown cliffs came nearer. Looking through the spy-glass, at the little town enclosed in its circle of stereoscopic light, he was mildly amused at a Lilliputian pantomime of panic. Flitting before him, translucent in the sun as a dragon-fly, the schooner dropped anchor without furling sails. Over the side, hot-foot into a canoe, two or three men in uniform were unloading a heavy chest. They pulled for the shore for dear life.

A crowd had gathered on the waterfront, negroes mostly, and a pompous little colonel with an armed guard was marching it about in a bees' nest of shouting and gesticulation. All sorts of small craft were putting in to shore from the shipping, and the sailors climbing the cliffs with sticks in their hands ... no—but surely not—muskets! The officers of the schooner handed over their box to the military man, and the guard hustled it in to a little beehive fort, while the crowd surged closer to hear some exciting tale.

"Treasure trove!" laughed Matthew to Aken. "I wager they think we're pirates. Mr Surcouf and his corsairs must have struck trouble of late. You'd better go and explain it, Aken. Take the letter to General Magallon, and the passport. That will work the oracle. Here's a jest!"

He stood at the rail with his glass, watching Aken ashore. There was, undoubtedly, tension. The military man examined the papers, but made no salute of greeting, and the figures on the landing-stage, as they waved this way and that—now to the *Cumberland*, now to the schooner, suggested an altercation.

The boat pulled back. Aken's expression, as he neared the ship, was not reassuring.

"Trouble for us here, sir!" he shouted. "The war's on again."

So that was it. The Treaty of Amiens, as so many had said, was not worth the paper it was written on. But two boats were coming off. He hurried into the cabin, to make himself presentable.

A suave grey-haired Frenchman, graceful in black knee-breeches and lace cravat and ruffles, was waiting on deck when he came out.

He bowed elaborately while the equerry presented his card—"M. d'Unienville. Major de Savane."

By the time Flinders had made his acknowledgments, and learned that he did not speak English, the second boat had pulled alongside, and a second Frenchman, the military cock-sparrow in his flambuoyant Republican uniform, was scowling upon the first.

His aide-de-camp presented his card—"M. Etienne Bolger. Major de Savane."

So the Major de Savane was twins!

In a high nasal whine and a guttural bark, they began to discuss some problem. When one gave an order to his men, it was loftily vetoed by the other. When the other made some suggestion, it was loudly laughed to scorn.

Matthew suppressed a smile. Like Pilate, he washed his hands of the argument in a gesture, and waited very politely for enlightenment. None of his men knew a word of French, and none of these knew English.

But now the schooner was heaving across, and as she came alongside there was a call for Bonnefoy. A seedy but affable person, obviously a clerk of sorts, emerged from her nether regions, and, assiduously wiping a rat's tail of whisker with a large and loud check handkerchief, in due course appeared on the *Cumberland*. He "knew ze Angliss, monsieur, to making explanations, but first we proceed you to safer anchorage, more near the shore."

Safer for whom, thought Matthew, but he gave the order to follow the schooner in. The Majors of Savane stood rigidly alert, aloof from each other and him.

As they sailed, he learned from Bonnefoy that this was Baie du Cap. The governor lived in the capital, Port Louis, north-west.

"Why, pleasse, has monsieur le capitaine chased French trading ship?"

"I chased nothing. I merely sought the entrance. I have letters to your governor, General Magallon, that will explain my case."

"But General Magallon is not now governor. He is gone. M. Bonaparte, First Consul, has appoint great man of his own army, le Capitaine-Général Decaen to rule in Ile-de-France. He, in turn, has appoint M. Bolger, who is just arrive, in place of M. d'Unienville, who has not yet his papers and will not go." That explained the dual personality.

When the ships were at anchor, Flinders submitted through Bonnefoy his passport and his purpose—the great need of water and food, and clothing and repairs.

The Frenchmen held another angry colloquy. They agreed on one point only, that nothing could be done. M. le capitaine must make application to His Excellency the Governor.

Flinders thought not. "When I put in to your island," he said, "I had no knowledge of war. Under the circumstances, I think I shall make for the Cape. You will not refuse me supplies, and I shall not trouble you further."

d'Unienville seemed agreeable, Bolger hotly opposed it. He had new regulations. All strangers calling at this island must now report to the governor.

Very well. Matthew agreed. He had his passport.

Bolger offered him horses and guides to go overland. d'Uienville proposed that he should take the schooner round by sea.

Naturally. There was no other course. He would not leave his ship.

The upshot of it was that Bolger dispatched a courier post-haste with the news to Port Louis, and d'Unienville usurped the Residential honours by inviting him to dine.

"I shall be very happy," Matthew accepted readily, and then, with a diffident smile, "if your excellency will first grant me the favour of a bath."

One glimpse of Bolger's infuriated countenance, and he realized his tactical blunder.

"And it may be that *your* excellency will be good enough to grant me supplies of water and food to my ship, for which, of course, payment will be made."

The luxury of striding full length again, the clear spring water, of which he drank nearly a gallon before lunch, M. d'Unienville's delicate veal and *confits*, the pleasant French people he met, and the bright fertility about him were the happy respite of an hour or two, but there was so little conversational contact, and so much flat contradiction in Savane that he was glad to get the *Cumberland* under way.

With a gift of fresh meat from the courtly d'Unienville, at dusk they followed the schooner out. She was detailed to pilot them round—no doubt with her guns primed. As they turned west with a following wind, Matthew was half inclined to give her the slip, and make a run for the Cape ... but they had told him that the French and Dutch were in possession there, so perhaps it was better to put a brave face on it, and deal with the devil he knew.

In the late afternoon of the seventeenth, the two little ships were standing up the harbour at Port Louis. They anchored not far from a heavy frigate, her lines strangely familiar—could it be the *Géographe*, and Baudin here? The frigate was dressing sails to go. He could not afford to miss her. He sent a boat to Bonnefoy for information.

No. It was not the *Géographe*. She had been anchored here for months, and had left but the night before, her commander dead.

Baudin dead! ... and the expedition over. His rivals were out of the field! Even so, that was a pity. Baudin would have been a good friend at court, in case Decaen proved difficult. These Republicans were bitterly hostile to the English. He decided to pay his respects, take in stores and water, then patch up the pumps and go.

Over the revolting greyish dirt of his under-clothing—Isabelline, he thought with a wry smile—he put on his full-dress uniform, and called the boat for the shore. The captain of the schooner, a waspish man, came with him to show him the way, or so he preferred to interpret it.

Melted slag of sunset brimmed the skies of Port Louis, and splashed over into the harbour and the streets, steeping the dirty little creole town in strange yellow light. A dark smoke of hills rolled away to the north. Swarms of negroes were crying their wares, big baskets of honey-yellow mangoes and plaintains, hot bread and freshly-roasted sucking-pig. His mouth watered. It was enough to make a sick man hungry. Curtained palanquins carried by slaves gave an Oriental flavour to the sprightly scene. He would have revelled in it under happier conditions. Ile-de-France was a green and shady place.

In a wide square, La Place des Armes, they came to the Residency, a squat stone barracks with the Tricolour floating above, at every twenty yards the sentries, each like a statue in its niche.

The schooner captain left him with the orderly at the big double gates while he went in to report. In about a quarter of an hour, he passed out, saying nothing, but a message came that the English captain must wait.

He waited on the bare, flagged veranda, a forlorn and shabby figure, restlessly pacing.

Some French naval officers were lounging round in the square, smoking and joking under the tamarind-trees. They cast curious glances in his direction. At last one of them approached and, with an exaggerated bow, asked him in English to join them. He was, he said, Lieutenant Raoul Renault.

Matthew obligingly strolled across, and found himself the pivot of an admiring circle of rather effeminate young men, all asking questions with Renault as interpreter.

"That is to say, you are come from Por' Jackson in the small skeef we 'ave seen to arrive? But it is *merveilleuse, incroyable*! We 'ave 'ear of Por' Jackson from le commodore Nicolas Baudin. You know Monsieur Baudin per'aps?"

Matthew smiled. "I knew him well. I am indeed sorry to hear he is dead."

"Ver' sad. Yourself, you are expedition of science, you say?"

"I am. My ship is the *Investigator*."

"O yess? The men of le capitaine Baudin, they speak of a Monsieur Flandare in expedition of science. Per'aps you know him?"

"What name? Flandare? I never heard of him."

"So. Where have you known then le commodore Baudin?"

"I met him on the south coast of New Holland, and again in Port Jackson, where we were very good friends. My ship has surveyed many thousand miles of the coast of that continent."

They gabbled to each other in rapid French, and their manner subtly changed. Was this too flattering attention tinctured with unbelief? He was glad to leave them, and take up his post on the balcony again.

The tropic dark came quickly. From a white belfry in the trees across the square a sweet-toned bell rang out, three notes, and three again—the Angelus, memories of Tenerifa. Never since then had he been in a Catholic country. He smiled to think that indeed they were mostly heathen. But the Angelus meant it was six o'clock. He had been waiting two long humiliating hours.

He called the orderly sharply, and demanded that his name should be taken to the governor again. The man came back to say his excellency was at dinner. He must wait.

The noisy streets grew silent and deserted … then filled again with motley crowds and the flare of torches. A stranger in a strange land, he was ill and dirty and tired.

It was nearly eight when the orderly called him to the captain-general's presence. There was a reception in one of the salons—he could hear music and laughter, and the light treble of women's voices—but he was led into a big bleak room, starkly official, its windows open to the racket of the square.

In the light of half a dozen candles, two men were standing by the table. One was a stocky and consequential person in a dinner-jacket heavily bedizened with gold lace and medallions, the other an aristocratic tall figure in dress uniform.

He was not conversant with the insignia of the French. For one moment he was uncertain. Saluting he addressed them both—"Captain Matthew Flinders—at your service."

The stocky man wheeled. Square brow, challenging eyes, unruly fair hair and a glittering row of medals, his self-importance left no further doubt.

"*Votre passeport!*" he said briskly, in the manner of one who has no time to waste.

Matthew submitted his passport, and stood in awkward silence. He was horribly conscious of his creased clothes and the aura of the *Cumberland* bugs.

The aide-de-camp stood motionless, a waxworks model. His eyes were expressionless as glass. A pencilling of black beard cleft his patrician chin.

The captain-general hitched his sword and sat down to his table, scowling in concentration. He read the passport twice through, and referred to some notes before him. Then he raised his head and glowered at Matthew with the lift of a belligerent jaw.

"Thiss *passeport*," he said, in the mechanical slow tones of very bad English, "is for sheep H.M.S. *Anvestigahtor.*"

"Yes, sir. The ship of my science expedition."

"But you are come in"—he consulted his notes—"*Gom-bair-long*, two nine tons."

Matthew paused, searching for elementary words that the general might understand, then speaking very distinctly.

"I have been shipwrecked. The *Cumberland* was given to me by the governor at Port Jackson to make the voyage to England for a new ship."

Decaen considered. "*Anvestigahtor* is sheepwreck," he stated, and was about to write it down.

"No, sir. She was condemned at Port Jackson. I was shipwrecked on my way home as passenger in H.M.S. *Porpoise*."

Decaen's eyes narrowed. H.M.S. *Porpoise* was a battle-ship.

"Your *ordre* of *embarque*?"

"It is among my papers on the *Cumberland*."

"You have *autorité* to land at this isle?" It was a snap.

A bad-tempered person. Matthew was brief.

"No. I came here for water and food."

The general rose to his inconsiderable height, thrust his right hand into his highly-ornamental vest in an imitation of the sincerest flattery that Matthew could not then appreciate, and deliberately and offensively sized him up.

"So! Captain Flinders!" His thick lips curled contempt. "The governor of Por' Jackson sends leader of expedition of science to England in small sheep two nine tons! Faugh! *C'est impossible!*"

His cheeks puffed out, his blue eyes bulged. With a sudden ferocity, he took two steps forward, pursed up his face and his fists in an accumulation of hatred, and very nearly spat. For one mad moment, Matthew thought he was going to strike him.

"*Imposteur!*" snarled the governor, flung the passport smack on the desk, and marched out of the room.

The attack was so savage, so unexpected, that Matthew stared after him amazed, almost dazed. The red surged into his cheeks as he gathered up his papers. He stood irresolute, and then turned to go.

"*Un moment, monsieur!*"

The waxwork came to life, and stalked in the wake of the governor—undoubtedly an officer of rank. He returned in a few minutes with a younger officer and Bonnefoy. It was explained that the captain-general wished to see his papers, and these were to accompany him back to his ship. Out into the streets they went, one on either side.

A long-boat, with a crew of sleepy negroes and an old French pilot, was waiting at the quay-side. The officer courteously stepped back for Matthew to precede him into the boat, and sat silently to attention through his angry denunciations to Bonnefoy of Decaen's infamous tyranny and detestable manners.

"I can't congratulate you on your new governor," he finished up. "He's a ruffian and a boor. How dare he treat me like this? I shall certainly not set foot on shore again until he has the decency to apologize."

To his surprise, the officer leant across and addressed him earnestly in English.

"Pardon, monsieur le capitaine, but no. It is true that he has the *colére*, but he is good at heart, yes. The bark is more than the bite, as you would say. This you will find."

"Neither his bark nor his bite concerns me," said Matthew loftily. "This you will find."

"Yes, monsieur, but he makes *ordre* that you return with us tonight. I think it not advantage that we compel."

"What!" cried Matthew in alarm. "You mean I am a prisoner?"

"No! No!" put in Bonnefoy soothingly. "Prisoner? No, monsieur. Guest of Port Louis, yes, for two days, three days, till your papers are arrange. You will be treat very well, and your man of affairs, he come too."

"This is iniquitous!"

Matthew looked up to the starlit heavens, a glittering court of appeal. They remained remote. Injury added to insult. What could he do? He was helpless.

To lighten his brooding, they changed the subject to the shipping in the harbour. Port Louis was of great import now, much progress, much trade.

"You see this *brigantin* we pass? That is the *Hunter*, Americain, of Baltimore, and there, monsieur, a Danish barque, that comes for vanilla and coffee. What need to go to the Indies, when Ile-de-France produce all so well? We build so much commerce with Denmark and Switzerland that there is already agents establish here from those countries. That is for the too-greedy Dutchman to put in his pipe and smoke, hein?"

Flinders scarcely listened, biting his lips on rebellion.

Arrived at the *Cumberland*, he routed out Aken and told him to make ready for the shore, leaving Elder in charge on board. While the pilot and the blacks towed the ship up the harbour, he sullenly produced his papers for the officer. He was outraged when they demanded everything—letters, maps, books, journals, everything in writing.

"Are these your orders?"

"But certainly, monsieur." Bonnefoy grew more and more bland.

He glared at these Frenchmen with smouldering anger, then took refuge in contempt. It was not their doing.

It was a long and tedious search, with several lists to be written and checked on the rough deal table in the light of the hanging lamp. They rifled his locker, and upturned the cask in the corner. Bonnefoy made out the lists, in bad English and probably just as bad French, while the officer stacked the two trunks in a nice precision. Flinders sat on his bunk, and answered in curt monosyllables.

"Three log-books only, monsieur le capitaine?"

"Yes."

"This packet of letters?"

"Not mine."

"Dispatches?"

"Yes." Was there a meaning glance between them as Bonnefoy wrote that down?

"This book—a journal?"

"Yes."

"And a folio?"

"Charts."

Not until they came to the slim little bundle of Ann's letters, in their close wrapping of sail-cloth, did he show any further interest. Then he rose very deliberately, and took them away from the man.

"These are my own—home letters," he said. "You will not require these." He held them loosely in his left hand, but his right was on the hilt of his sword.

The Frenchman did not appear to notice his emotion. Instead, he spoke quite casually.

"Our orders, monsieur le capitaine, are to take all. For the moment, I think it would be best to give, for your own sake. Such letters will, of all certainty, return."

A moment's thought, and Matthew put them down. The man was right. The merest glance would show their nature. To withhold anything at all might create a wrong impression, and he dared not make a false step now.

The checking, the packing, went on. When the trunks were full, they asked him to seal them, and handed him a duplicate in receipt. The officer then unfolded a paper written in French, spread it before him, and proffered him Bonnefoy's quill.

"You will also write your name here, pleasse?"

"What is it?"

"It is to say detaining on suspicion."

"Suspicion! Most certainly not!" Matthew was aflame again, and just as quickly contemptuous. "My passport, signed by the First Consul of your empire, places me above suspicion. His subordinates shall answer to him for this."

The officer shrugged, and folded the paper away. He clapped for the slaves, and a small procession of African giants came and carried the trunks and his cask of books, and lowered them into the boat—half-human, Madagascar men, slow-ambling like gorillas.

As they rowed away for the landing-steps, he could hear his men laughing and dicing in their black hole of a fo'c'sle. The poor wretches would have little shore leave, after all their longing for it.

It was after midnight when they came back to Port Louis, a dark night and malodorous, the streets now silent. Before the dim outlines of a two-storied house in the square, the officer called a halt and rapped on the door.

Apparently they were expected, for an obsequious gnome of a creole drew back the bolts, and with a grunt of comprehension led them through a melancholy hallway that reeked of stale wine, and up a worm-eaten stair. Their shadows, in the flare of his torch, crowded eagerly on their heels. He lit two candles in a room on the right, and with no word spoken shuffled past them to bed.

It was a large bare room, musty and fetid, the carpet worn in great gaping holes, fringed and frayed like anemones. In one dim corner a mildewed mirror was framed in blackened gilt. A flimsy furnishing of two truckle-beds, two cane chairs and a rickety table had evidently just been made, for the rest of the room was deep in dust and dry-rot.

Flinders crossed to the cobwebbed shutters, and threw them open for air. The windows were barred—the usual thing in every port of the tropics, but to-night it had a sinister aspect. Looking down obliquely, he could see the negroes and a soldier standing guard over his trunks in the streets below.

"We leave you here," said the officer, "to make yourself at home."

"This is a watch-house?" Matthew asked him sharply.

"But no!" Bonnefoy was scandalized. "This is Ile-de-France hotel, Cafe Marengo, very good. Le capitaine-général sees you shall be well looked to, Monsieur Flandare ... good night ... good rest." They clattered down the stairs.

"Well, sir," said Aken lugubriously, "here we are. I told you there'd be trouble ... right in the lion's den."

Matthew unbuckled his sword, carefully hung his uniform coat over the shoulders of a chair, turned to the raddled mirror and regarded his filthy cravat.

"Only for a few days, Aken," he said lightly enough. "When that swine of a governor sees my papers, he won't dare to keep me. But there's no hope of a ship in war-time from a man of Decaen's calibre. I dare not land at the Cape now. I'm taking no more chances. I can see nothing for it but the *Cumberland*, and ten thousand miles to go."

He sat down on his truckle-bed, and began to take off his boots. The wool of his dirty hose was stuck to the sores.

"Wait!" he went on quickly. "They said something about an American ship in the harbour—the *Hunter*, a name I couldn't forget. Now if she needs men, or whether or not, she might take us to St Helena. I'll write to the captain—I'd do it now, if I had the materials to write. *Nil desperandum*, my lad. If she won't take us, there are sure to be others that will."

There was a stealthy movement in the passage outside. In his stockinged feet he crossed to the door and flung it open.

A sentry stood there with bayonet fixed. He was indeed a prisoner.

He said nothing, but closed the door, made a motion to Aken for discretion, loosened his clothes, blew out the lights, and lay down on the creaking bed.

Hour by hour, the humid night dragged through, maddening with mosquitoes and there were no nets. Aken slept heavily enough, but he tossed and sweated the small hours through, his mind flaming in one word, impostor. The cur! The bloated French bully! He should have drawn his sword, he should have … but it was too late now. Towards dawn he dozed a little, and woke with the sentry in the room beside him. The man motioned them down with his thumb to wash at the pump in the yard, and stood over them there with his rifle. A fat negress brought them an excellent breakfast.

In the same bright sun that made the jaded room more dreary, Madame Decaen slipped through the open windows of the captain-general's bureau, home from morning mass.

An elegant Parisian *brune*, she was years younger than the general, one of the prettiest flowers that bloomed in the Ville Consulat, to be married off to its *beaux soldats*, beauty the reward of valour. Vice-regal honours weighed heavily on that preciously-curled head. She knew that the island society called them Beauty and the Beast. Had it not been for her dreams of a jewelled sovereignty in India, and the so sweetly encouraging letters of her dear friend, Madame Bonaparte, to "*ma petite soeur creole*", she would far rather serve in a Malmaison heaven than reign in a Port Louis hell.

The captain-general adored her. They had been married just one adventurous year.

"Félise!" He turned from his papers with a smile that few would credit, and fairly purred as the delicious creature perched on the arm of his chair, her silken gown falling in a soft cascade to the dainty arch of her shoe, one lace-fringed hand playing with his epaulettes..

"Oh, how this heat is frightful! If it would only rain! What are you doing, Charles?"

She leant forward to see, his eyes sensually appraising the grace of her lassitude.

"Flandare. Oh, this is the man who is come last night ... but Raoul said that he did not know Flandare, that he is English spy. Do not tell me that after all he proves to be himself."

"It is himself, it seems to me, of the expedition of science. Curses on your Raoul. He was wrong."

"So now you must let this man go?"

"Not necessarily, my dear. He has much to explain. These English are up to too many tricks. I trust none of them. You know, I believed that the English fleet had brought this fellow from India, and sent him here in this boat to spy ... but he is, in truth, come from Port Jackson."

"A marvellous voyage, Charles, in a ship so small."

"Exactly. And why? What urgent news does he carry to England? Why does he call here?"

"Well, any port in a storm, perhaps. Would you yourself not call on such a journey? Nicolas Baudin so often told us that Flandare was good friend to the French, and most amiable companion. He should be interesting. For me, I should like to meet him. Ask him to dine to-night, Charles. I shall soon tell you if he is spy."

The general laughed, and kissed the curve of her chin.

"The smile of a creature so angelic could not fail to draw him. That gives me an idea. We may learn something from him, is it not, who comes to learn from us? Well, Félise, I do not know. I shall question him first. If there is no suspicion, my wife shall have her whim, and do this fellow a kindness, an act of charity, eh?"

She threw her curly head back, framed in its ruched bonnet, and smiled at him mischievously.

"That you, old patriot, will turn to account for France ... but I die of thirst, and *déjeuner* is waiting. *Allons!*"

The wolf of a general followed her out like a lamb.

Matthew put in the morning staring into the square in black rebellion. His dinner was scarcely over when the sentry announced Colonel Monistrol.

It was the waxwork factotum of the night before, funereal still, but a little more lifelike by day. His excellency would see Captain Flinders.

Matthew hastily dressed and set off with the colonel, an interpreter in tow, not Bonnefoy, but a new man, who spoke both languages with a strong German inflection. On the way they talked of the *Géographe*, and the death of her late commander. It was not a surprise. Baudin was always unhealthy. He had been dying here for months.

"And what of the *Naturaliste*?" Flinders wanted to know.

"She has been seized by the British."

"Never!" Here was bad news. When? and where?

In the Channel, going home. The colonel could tell him nothing more.

Decaen was ensconced in his chair, preoccupied. No greeting passed between them. It was Monistrol who asked him to be seated.

The interpreter announced that Captain Flinders would be required to answer a series of questions, his replies to be set down in writing. He noticed that Dubois, his sentry from the Marengo, was on duty outside the door ... waiting for him.

The general rapped out the questions in French, his eyes on the notes before him.

"What is the captain's name?"

"Matthew Flinders."

"From what place did the *Cumberland* come?"

"Port Jackson."

"At what time?"

Matthew hesitated. "I don't recollect the exact date without reference to my log-book. I think it was the twentieth of September."

"What is the purpose of your schooner?"

"My only motive is to proceed to England as soon as possible to make a report on my voyages, and to request another ship in which to continue them."

There was a pause, broken only by the scratch of the quill and the buzzing of a wasp in the corner. Then:

"What is the reason that determined Captain Flinders to undertake a voyage in so small a vessel?"

Matthew gazed out of the window, at a squad of soldiers drilling in the sunny square, the gangs of sweating slaves, and the tranquil green beauty of the tamarind-trees. He saw only Ann's grey eyes, her lips expectant, and her shining hair. What if he were to tell these hostile Frenchmen the truth? His eyes softened into a half smile, but he recalled himself to the subject. Decaen was watching him with a curious expression.

"Er—to avoid losing two months in proceeding by way of China. Ships calling at Port Jackson all call at China."

"Port Jackson, then, offers no better opportunities for returning to Europe than a schooner of 29 tons for a journey of 16,000 miles?"

The sarcasm was irritating. His voice was a little louder, he answered with icy distinctness.

"As I have stated, there are big ships, which all call at China, and for that reason I determined not to proceed that way."

"At what place did the *Cumberland* put in?"

"At Timor, for provisions and water. I left Timor thirty-four days ago."

"What passports were required there?"

"None." He realized there was no proof of his route.

The general's tone was brusque now, but Matthew's mild enough.

"What is your motive in coming to Ile-de-France?"

"The want of water. The pumps are bad, and the vessel is very leaky."

"To what place do you intend to go from this island?"

"I have no passport for the Cape, so I shall travel past it. I may be obliged to stop at St Helena."

"What is the reason for not having your officers, naturalists, and other persons employed in this expedition with you now?"

"Two of them have remained at Port Jackson, but will join the ship I expect to obtain in England. The others have proceeded to China."

The general rose and stalked the floor, and put his hand in his waistcoat. He was about to play his trump card. He rounded on Matthew suddenly.

"Ask him why he chased a boat in sight of the island?"

"I was never here before. I was not acquainted with the harbour. Seeing a French vessel, I 'chased' her seeking a pilot, and followed her into the bay."

"Why did he make the land to leeward, when all the directories pointed the contrary route?"

"I had no chart of the island. As a matter of fact, I came to windward, but the wind shifted, and so I took the leeward."

"Why had he hoisted cartel colours?"

"Captain Baudin, coming to Port Jackson, hoisted the colours of both nations. I thought it was the custom."

"Was he informed of the war?"

"No."

"Now! Has he met with any ship either at sea or in the different ports he put into?"

"I met one ship only, to the east of Ile-de-France. I did not speak to her, though I wished to, for she passed in the night. I met with no ships at Timor."

The general laid his questionnaire on the table. He gave some directions that were not translated, yawned heavily, and without a backward glance, went out. Colonel Monistrol went with him.

The secretary asked that Captain Flinders should now give a brief account of his doings since he left the *Investigator*, and mark the place in his journals for documentary proof.

The man began writing at his dictation, slow of comprehension and slow with his pen. It was the siesta hour, and the square was quiet. The heat was insufferable, working up to a storm. Matthew was ill and fretful after the sleepless night. The first good food in five long months had nauseated him, and his bladder trouble, in weather like this, was agony. Twice he had to retire, and his sentry, Dubois, went with him, an offensive creature. Through the long pauses for writing, he sat with his head in his hands, elbows resting on the table, his fingers pressing his closed eyes.

The trunk with his papers was unsealed. He took out his third log-book and marked the passages, and it was sealed again. It was five o'clock before the work was finished, the statement duly checked and signed. His spirits were at zero when the inquisition was over. The world had gone dark. There was a sharp rattle of thunder.

"Does the captain-general require my presence further?" he asked wearily, standing erect with a quick twinge of pain.

The secretary went to inquire. He waited in the corridor, Dubois, officious, beside him.

The debonair Renault appeared, saluted, and gave him a pleasant smile.

"My respects, *monsieur le capitaine*. His excellency presents his compliments and asks that you will be his guest to dine. Dinner is served now. Will you attend, pleasse?"

Compliments! Matthew stood dumb in amazement. He could not believe his ears.

For a moment he hesitated. He looked down at his shabby uniform, his dirty linen, his salt-caked boots—then the cruel thought struck him that they were making a fool of him. A man who had called him an impostor, with no word of apology, would never ask him to dinner, unless in mockery.

"Thanks. But I've already dined."

Renault gave a little gasp, and looked round hurriedly. No one but Dubois was there, and he did not understand English. He moved a step nearer.

"Capitaine Flandare!" he said very urgently and softly. "That makes no good. It will be well, of your part, to accept."

"Shall I eat of his food, that has so grossly insulted me?"

"Then go—if only to sit at the table."

"You know little of English honour, sir. Prisoners do not sit at the governor's table." He glanced at Dubois. "Tell him that if he will set me at liberty, I shall indeed be flattered. Under present conditions, I cannot but refuse."

Renault still waited, but Matthew regarded with interest the coming storm, so he went, very slowly, to deliver the message.

There was a colourful little crowd already in attendance in the grand salon, chittering women in trailing Oriental silks and military men with sashes and decorations. Her excellency, soft and bright as a flower in a ring of brilliant uniforms, was telling of her "*brave anglais*," her hero of the sea. How thrilled she would be to meet him, just as he had come to them, through ten thousand miles of storm—*Bon Dieu*, such courage, such a sailor! They laughed and teased her.

Renault drew the captain-general aside, and spoke in a tactful undertone. His excellency, as usual, exploded tact to the winds.

"Félise!" he called to his so-charming wife. "Your English guest of honour declines your invitation." He bowed in irony. "I think we may all go in."

Madame's brown eyes flew open wide above her feather fan. There was a flutter of indignation and resentment, an emotional *chevalier* flourished his sword.

The captain-general silenced them with a scowl, and turned on Lieutenant Renault.

"Tell this Flinders that *when* he is at liberty, we shall be pleased to invite him here again."

Somebody laughed.

Matthew strode very proudly out, his sentry by his side. As an officer of His Majesty's service, he had done the right thing. He was pathetically sure of that, back in the room with Aken, pacing from the locked door to the window with iron bars.

15

The Almond-Tree

All the next day he watched the negroes in the square, the soldiers drilling in the barrack yard, and the green of the tamarind-trees.

No summons came from the Residency, no news, only the black woman with the meals.

The wet season was long overdue. The sunlight was jaundiced yellow, earth rank in the steamy heat. The sores of his scurvy were festering. He wanted to ask the negress to take his clothing to wash it, but he had no money to pay for it, and only the clothing he wore.

At night he asked for another candle and writing materials.

"For what?" Dubois was insolent.

"To communicate with your governor!"

One sheet of paper was brought him, and one seal.

It was a lofty letter, half challenge, half appeal. He demanded that his passport should be honoured, that passport to protect and encourage the sciences by which the knowledge of mankind is extended or their condition ameliorated.

Understand, then, sir, that I was chosen by that great patriarch of the Royal Society of London, and one well known by all the literate throughout the world, Sir Joseph Banks, to retrace part of the track of the immortal Captain Cook, to complete in New Holland what he had left unfinished, and to perfect the discovery of that extensive country. Does it become the French nation, irrespective of all passports, to stop the progress of such a voyage, by which the whole maritime world shall benefit?

Only the last words uncovered the anguish of his heart:

"I sought a haven. I found a prison. Judge me as a man."

The captain-general read them unmoved. "Sir Joseph Banks. Who is he?" he asked Monistrol.

The Colonel raised a polite eyebrow.

"I shall inquire, your excellency."

"No. Don't vex yourself. We prefer to remain illiterate. This Flinders is orator now at our expense. He wants his servant, and he wants a surgeon, and his books and his journals and heaven knows what. Send him the surgeon and his man-servant, but be sure he is only a man-servant."

Elder came, friend in need and Job's comforter. He washed the captain's linen at the pump, and pressed the uniform with a flat-iron, but he brought a tale of woe that meant more trouble. The men of the *Cumberland* had raided the cabin and stolen all the grog, and then made merry hell in a night ashore. They were in the common jail in Port Louis, herded with niggers and thieves, and scarcely room to breathe.

Aken should be there to keep order. Matthew called the sentry, and demanded to be taken to the governor at once, on a matter of vital importance. He must get his men out of that hole of filth and fever. The general was engaged. He sent out a message that he was quite capable of dealing with the situation.

Flinders returned to the inn. Two dreadful days dragged by, the first days of morbid inaction he could remember in his life. At the end of them he implored Decaen to "release me from my purgatory".

No answer.

The monsoon broke in pouring rain that thundered on the roof for hours, and mirrored the trees and clouds in silver pools. Elder and Aken were allowed to play billiards, but Dubois, from example, was impudent and domineering. He beckoned Matthew here and there, forbade him the billiard room, forbade him to go down to wash at the cistern in the yard. By Christmas Day he could endure it no longer. He borrowed more sheets of writing-paper and wrote his doom, in recrimination and accusation and fiery rebellion at this outrage of national faith.

The fretfulness of a sick man, the torture of inaction, and the sadness between the lines were too subtle for the general. He rapped him over the knuckles for impertinence, and told him to be silent. In three days he wrote again, this time a humble request.

Might he have his printed books, his private letters and papers, his charts and journals? So much had been ruined in shipwreck that he wished to re-compile them before the facts had faded from his memory. They would afford him better amusement than writing letters to his excellency. Matthew could not resist that final sally. He signed the letter "Your prisoner, Matthew Flinders."

Monistrol called with Bonnefoy to say he might come and select the matter he needed. The waxen colonel was unbending. He spoke with regret of the letters—a bad mistake.

An hour or two later, a palanquin pulled up at the Café Marengo, dirty and dilapidated, with a cortège of filthy negroes and mongrel dogs. With an angry flush, Flinders told them to be off. He walked to the Residency, limping badly with the pain of his scorbutic ulcers.

The trunk with his clothes, his personal possessions and his private correspondence was delivered to the inn by slaves. The other was opened for him in Monistrol's office. The first thing he did was to retrieve his naval signal book and tear it to shreds. They could punish him if they liked. His nation was not going to suffer through his indiscretion.

Now, with work to do, the hours were not so long. By daylight and by candle-light, from his mildewed journals and torn scraps of sodden paper scrawled in pencil with rough reckoning, he was compiling again the luckless chart of Carpentaria. Aken, and sometimes Elder, were cooped in the same room, good fellows, but their converse not stimulating. Pacing up and down for exercise, his mind in a prison more galling than that of his body, he wore a few more holes in the raddled carpet. Writing well into the small hours, he produced reams of grief-stricken explanation to Sir Joseph and the Admiralty, to find that ships in harbour were not allowed to carry his correspondence. He could not even stretch his legs in a walk in the twilight, when he could see nothing.

Most humiliating of all was the lack of money. He had travelled ten thousand miles without needing it—what have the winds and the waves to do with money?—but here there was not a penny for the poor little needs of the day. His crew had received no pay. They were in the naval prison at Le Flacq now, but how would they live in this foreign place when they came out? He applied for permission to sell the *Cumberland*.

No answer.

One morning Bonnefoy looked in with a cheering "*Comment ça va?*" and offered to see if he could get any one to discount a bill. He came back with good news. The old Swiss consul, M. Boand, was prepared to advance £100. Much relieved, Flinders handed over the bill, and the sentry pounced. What was the letter that had passed between them?

"A bill," said Bonnefoy innocently.

"A bill," said Flinders contemptuously.

A shout to the square, a squad of gendarmes stamping up the stair, and Bonnefoy was arrested and marched away. He came up smiling a day or two later with a pocketful of gold louis. They had questioned him and searched him, but finding nothing but the bill had let him go and cash it. The greasy, good-natured little fellow dissolved in tears of gratitude when Matthew insisted on commission. He swore eternal fidelity over a glass of Madeira, wiped his streaming eyes on his big check handkerchief at the captain's shameful plight, and trotted off with a dark hint of some mysterious "influence".

The heavy rains were over now, but the heat still sickly, and Matthew's bladder affliction was steadily worse. In a sweaty night, moths wheeling about his candle-flame, he was toiling away in his shirt-sleeves at the chart of Torres Strait when an unexpected visitor banged on the door—a French naval officer, stout and blond and free-and-easy, with a dominating manner and a seaman's stride.

"*Va-t-en!*" he scouted the sentry—"and don't you come back till you're called!"

He peered under bushy brows in the dim light.

"You're Flinders? Good. I'm Bergeret."

Matthew rose, put on his uniform coat, and cleared the books from Aken's chair. He had heard of Bergeret from the men of the *Géographe*, one of Linois's captains and a doughty one. The stranger spoke fluent English with very little accent. He was so bluff he might have been a Briton.

"I am surprised to find you here. I thought you were *hors de combat*."

"So I am!" cried Matthew. "Or I should be." He told his story freely, and with passion.

"That is not what I hear from Decaen. He believes that your voyage is more in the interests of Great Britain than of science."

"The governor falsifies facts from private spleen."

"Oh no. There's nothing personal. Purely *politique*. Tell me, what reasons have you written in your log for calling here?"

"We had only three casks of water left. I came, as I stated, for water and repairs, possibly to find a better ship."

"Mm. Have you written that you came for knowledge of the colony?"

"Yes. Of a way in, and of the periodical winds, and of what use Ile-de-France and Madagascar could be to Port Jackson."

"Exactly. In war."

"Decidedly not. I knew nothing of war when I wrote. I referred to times of peace—trade—foodstuffs. These are the nearest colonies, taking the southern route."

"Well, I believe you," said Bergeret, after a short pause. "Do you smoke?" He produced a Jamaica cigar from a gold-mounted case with a crest. That was a treat for Flinders. They watched the smoke-wreaths rise.

"There is another point," he went on. "Are you carrying dispatches?"

"Well, you could scarcely call them dispatches, but I have letters from Port Jackson to deliver in England, from Governor King and one or two others."

"Of what nature?"

"How should I know? They were sealed."

"A bad business. Your passport allows that?"

"No, possibly not. But ships are so few and far between it is pathetic, and there was no war when I left. We did not anticipate trouble."

"At all rates, King has shot you."

"What do you mean?"

"Those dispatches, my dear Flinders, were by no means neutral. They have said a little too much for your well-being. The governor is referring the whole matter to Paris, and perhaps he is justified, in time of war."

To Paris! That would mean a delay of months!

"I tell you," said Matthew piteously, "I have nothing to do with wars. Will the captain-general see me?"

Bergeret laughed. "I think not. He says that if he sees you again, he will probably have to send you to the tower. You two do not suit each other, no?"

"Because I refused his invitation to dinner, he manufactures evidence against me. I acted as any man of independent spirit who had been insulted, and unjustly deprived of his liberty. Look here, Captain Bergeret, if I swear on oath that I shall engage in no hostility to France, or Ile-de-France, that I shall disclose no knowledge I may have gained for any reasonable period he likes to name, do you think——"

"Nothing you can do or say will alter him at present. He has made his decision to send the papers to France, Oh, it will be all right for you in the long run. We know what you fellows did for Baudin, and apart from that, you have justice. Better sit down to it quietly. You'll soon be free." He looked round him with distaste at the mean and disordered room. "They might give you better quarters."

"I have received nothing but degrading and contemptuous treatment. I am penned up with my two men all day, I sleep with them at night. Apart from them, I see no one but my jailer, the man you just put in his place."

"Why haven't they sent you to the Garden Prison with the others—the English prisoners of war?"

"Because I am a spy!" said Matthew bitterly. "I cannot be trusted with my fellow-countrymen."

"Would you go?"

"Gladly. Anywhere."

"Good. I think I can arrange that. Leave it to me."

In a mutual liking they shook hands, and Bergeret left, with a parting growl to the sentry. He went back to the Residency, and in to General Decaen,

"I have just been with Flinders." He went straight to the point. "I have all the proof I want that he is no spy, and I intend to interest Linois in his case."

The general rose, his eyes as hard as agates.

"Linois to hell!" he bellowed. "He has nothing to do with me. I have no intention, Bergeret, of letting that Englishman go. He comes here in a small ship that is not the ship of his passport. He chases one of our coasters. He fails to restore our confidence under examination, and then he has the impudence to insult me—to insult my wife! I have it in his own handwriting that he landed at this island with the deliberate intent to reconnoitre our coasts, to learn what he could. He carries dispatches asking for troops at Port Jackson in British interests against us. More!" He banged the table with a pudgy fist and shouted. "The behaviour of the English government in Europe, the way she treated the ships of our expedition at Pondicherry, the seizing of the *Naturaliste*—are not these reasons enough for a just retaliation? Any man that tells me they are not is a traitor to France. Why, these brutes are out to snatch the whole trade of the Indian Ocean, Ceylon, Port Jackson, Van Diemen's Land and the Torres Strait."

"You can't blame Flinders for that."

"I know what I am doing. Flinders is one of their agents. Knowledge and science, ha! How would I be serving my country to allow this ship with no passport, and whose actions are suspicious at this time in sailing to Europe, to reveal to her government the results of her work, operations and objects, and all she has seen on this island and of our allies?"

With his arms akimbo on the table, his lower jaw thrust out above epaulettes shaking with rage, the general was the human replica of the British bull-dog he detested.

"Tell that to Linois, James Bergeret, and tell him that as captain-general of the empire of France in the South Seas, I shall do my duty to my nation as I see it, and Linois will not stop me." He sat down fuming.

"Oh, I know you have great responsibility, Charles," Bergeret smoothed him over, "and of course I don't want to interfere. But what I really came here for was to ask why don't you send this unlucky Flinders out to the Maison Despeaux. He's ill. He's fretting, like a chicken in a crate. After all, we owe him a little hospitality for Baudin's sake, you know. The least you can do is let the poor wretch join the others. You have them under lock and key, and at least he could stretch his legs and take the air."

"He can go to the Maison Despeaux," said the general ungraciously, "and I'll deal with him when I'm ready, and not before."

"He has no money."

"He'll get a captain's allowance."

"Shall I tell him?"

"Tell him what you like."

So Bergeret called at the Marengo again next morning, and told Matthew to pack. He would receive 450 francs a month to pay for his servant and his prison.

"A month! For how many?"

"Patience!" warned Bergeret. "Decaen's a headstrong man, and he'll take his own time. It's no use goading him further now, but before long he'll come to some determination about your fate."

"Will it be setting me at liberty, or putting me to death!"
Matthew managed a wan smile.

"That's the spirit, Flinders. You take life too seriously. A little exercise, and your own English people about you, bad as it is out there, you'll feel a different man. I sail to-morrow, to face the music again, but I'll be in and out of this island, and here and in India, I'll do everything I can. In the meantime, remember that patience is the password. Play a waiting game. *Au revoir.*"

His face crinkled and his blue eyes twinkled in a very kindly smile. Flinders felt better for his coming, and sighed that he had gone.

A mile away, on the outskirts of Port Louis, stood the Maison Despeaux, that the English called the Garden Prison, a ruin of one of the old plantation homes. Here, in cold comfort, Linois's hostages and Surcouf's victims taken in prizes on the high seas were kept out of harm's way till they could be exchanged for the French captured by the British in India.

Monistrol came himself in the morning to escort Flinders there. The sentry was sent packing, a consideration he valued. It saved him the public shame of appearing under arrest. Perhaps Bergeret had something to do with that. Cramped on the sandbank, cramped in the whaleboat, cramped in the *Cumberland* for five long months, and for four months shut in a room, his sad heart tired in that mile, and his lame feet faltered. The colonel kindly offered his arm, and so they arrived.

Long grass and dirty crooked paths, white-washed walls empty and echoing, the Maison Despeaux was no mansion, but there was space to walk in its ill-kept grounds, and he would have a room to himself. Monistrol helped him choose one— good light, a camp bed, a cupboard, and nothing else. Still it was his own. To be alone, to think and work, was luxury.

A shaggy head looked in at the door, with a foggy, reproachful stare. Monistrol introduced it—his jailer, Sergeant La Mêle, a gnarled old ogre with the gait of a grizzly bear, and the simple heart of the Norman peasant. The waxen colonel took his leave very stiffly, a little perturbed, perhaps, at his own melting qualities, for never again was Matthew to know him so kind—or, indeed, to know him at all.

Fussing about in dumb show, La Mêle led Matthew round the place with the aplomb of an inn-keeper, to the refectory, the swimming-pool, the remnant of an orchard, and up to the flat roof that commanded a view of the distant bay. He even produced a visitor's book, a ledger of the lost, in which the captain glumly entered his name.

The prisoners straggled in to the officers' mess at lunch hour, a baker's dozen of Englishmen, old and young, all caught in the spider's web, and all glad to meet him. They were Major Shepherd and Major Robinson, Indian Army men; Captain Matthews and Captain Lean, with Midshipmen Dale, McGraw and Seymour of the *Dédaigneuse*, that had been snatched by the British as a prize, and as smartly snatched back by the French.

There were Dansy of the *Admiral Asplin*, just brought in by Bergeret, and several officers of the Bombay Marine. One of these, second mate on the *Superb*, said that the *Bridgewater* had come in to Bombay just before he left there, with the news that the *Porpoise* had been lost with all hands. She had sailed straight out again for England. That gave him cause for troubled thought. If Palmer were lying to save his face, Annette would hear it, and believe him dead.

To walk freely and talk freely was a new experience, and their frugal board was rather a roystering one. Down at the garden gate they could buy fruit and fish and poultry from the negro pedlars, and they all clubbed in and hired a mulatto cook, so that the board was not noticeably frugal. Aken and Elder had settled in with the luggage, and doing their mile round the garden, the scurvy soon left them.

Methodical Matthew made a schedule for the day—a bathe at daybreak in the swimmimg-pool, Latin prose out in the sun till breakfast, then the *Investigator* charts and the log indoors till lunch. While the others went off to siesta he took his flute into the shade of a tall almond-tree in the farthest corner, and trilled mellifluously as the birds above. A half-hour's brisk walk round and round, and he was back to his charts till supper. In the twilight they all sat talking, of men, and manners and geography, up in the cool of the flat roof, with sometimes a game of billiards, and so to bed.

For a while he truly enjoyed the change, but some of the old comrades left, and new ones came and went, and at each leave-taking he grew more depressed and impatient. Never the news that his ordeal was nearing its end, never a recognition of his existence.

He asked the sergeant for a table to work on. It was two months before he got it. He asked for a French teacher, and that, referred to the general, was refused, though some of the others had a fencing-master. They still kept his third log-book from him. That was the fatal entry concerning Ile-de-France. He supposed he would have to do without it, though the lack of it held his work back badly. More than anything else, he longed for freedom of correspondence, that he might write and tell them at home the cruel truth of his captivity, but outgoing prisoners were searched, and it was not safe to trust any one else.

He remembered Bergeret's warning, and made no sign, each night hoping against hope for the next day … and each night Ann's letters—in their scrap of sail-cloth, bound with ship's twine and sealed now—he took beneath his pillow and fell to sleep with his lips pressed against them. It was childish but comforting. Perhaps she would feel him near.

There was a glossy young Frenchman constantly popping in and out to visit the prisoners. For some obscure reason, he showed an effusive sympathy for the Englishmen. Matthew often met him, a pile of English books and papers under his arm, a negro boy ambling in his wake with fruit from the plantations. Well-dressed and apparently wealthy, he walked with a quick effeminate gait that was almost a pirouette when he turned—a bird-like fellow, very amiable. A gift here and a word there, he brought them news of the world and the war.

He was obviously eager to be friendly, but Matthew passed him with a grave "Good morning". That super-sensitive soul shrank from any semblance of charity.

"Who is that little dandy?" he asked Lean. "Our county visitor, as it were. And how is it he has the entry here?"

"That's Thomy Pitot," Lean told him. "I suppose he is rather a fop, but all Frenchmen are, and he's worth his weight in gold, believe me. I don't know what we'd do without him. If you want any letters smuggled out, or anything smuggled in, you'd better cultivate Thomy. He's our guardian angel, the raven succouring Elijah."

"But why the anglophilia? Why should he care about us?"

"Ha! Why shouldn't he? Thomy makes more money out of us than any one else on the island, so he thinks he ought to give a little of it back. He's the junior partner in Pitot Frères."

That conveyed nothing to Matthew. "Traders in Port Louis, I presume."

"Traders? I should say so! They're the firm that sells up all our prizes, the corsairs' business agents, drat 'em. They've made a pretty penny out of it, too—must have handled a million francs in the past twelve months. Thomy comes out to the ships when that pirate of a Surcouf drags them in, and so he gets to know us, and feels sorry about us, and tries to make up with hospitality. Another thing, they're one of the old families here, and they don't like Republican manners. You can trust Thomy with everything, and it's wonderful what he can do."

Matthew was dubious. He even suspected the little man. When he heard he had approached the governor on his behalf, he was annoyed; when he heard that Thomy had been sent off with a flea in his ear, he thought that this was a ruse to get him to talk. Thomy made no headway at all in the first few months. When he did find a way to the captain's heart, it was through the Torres Strait.

On one of the drowsy days of trade-wind June, Matthew was lying under the almond-tree in the half-sleep of siesta, dreaming of Ann. His head was thrown back in the cool grass, one hand fallen upon his flute.

He dreamed that he was showing her his chart of Carpentaria, and telling her it had made him famous throughout the world, that all the great ones of the earth were seeking him and flattering him, but that he wanted only her.

"Before thee, my love, they disappear like stars before the rays of the morning sun. Without thee, dear, there is no happiness." He tried to take her lips.

But Ann shrank away from his outstretched arms, and in a frightened whisper she told him he was dead.

He laughed at her and woke to find himself looking into the pale, peaky face of Thomy Pitot, the Frenchman, down on his hands and knees beside him, and peering with a strangely tense expression.

"*Pardieu!*" stammered Thomy. "I had fear. I thought you were——"

"Dead?" said Matthew. "A curious thing, because I dreamed I was."

He sat erect. Pitot picked up the flute.

"I thought this was a——"

"Blunderbuss! And that I had shot myself?" Flinders laughed long and merrily. "And why, pray, Monsieur Pitot? A guilty conscience?—or a broken heart?"

"A broken heart!" croaked Thomy solemnly. "You look always so sad." Matthew laughed longer and louder, and Pitot joined him, his cheeks red with relief and embarrassment. He explained that a Monsieur Coutance had arrived in port, who as captain of the brig *Adèle* had known Flinders in Port Jackson. Pitot had brought him along to the prison, and he was waiting now.

They spent a lively hour or two discussing Matthew's Australia, particularly the Torres Strait. Coutance had a chart and description, but the book was too big to bring along for fear of exciting suspicion. Whenever Matthew's eye lighted on Thomy, an involuntary smile passed between them, and from then on they saw much of each other. The little Frenchman, with his live brown eyes, his quick understanding, and his love of art and music, belied all the regretted first impressions, and that was the beginning of one of the best friendships of Flinders's life.

Pitot Frères, Edouard and Thomy, took his affairs in hand. They cashed his bills without the heavy war-time discount. They very discreetly dispatched the letters to Sir Joseph Banks and the Admiralty, and influential friends all over the world, to tell them of his fate. They guarded well his sacred letters to Ann. They found him a host of French friends who were scandalized at his treatment, and all bearded Decaen in his den—to no avail whatever. He had sent the papers to Paris. The case was out of his hands.

"That man is *trop vif!*" he told Coutance. "Let him learn patience. There is plenty of time."

"Plenty of time!" groaned Matthew, when he heard it. Three lifetimes were not enough for all he wanted to do.

In the difficult months that followed, Thomy became a much more frequent visitor at the Maison Despeaux. He filled the larder with the richest fruits Ile-de-France could offer, and many a hasty errand he set out on for Flinders's sake alone. His devotion was hero-worship, and the pity that is love. He was the confidant of all the troubles, the confessor of all the tactical mistakes, the safety valve of rebellion and impatience.

He scoured the town for scientific works, and all the ships in port for information. He even scoured the native quarter, looking for Trim—poor little Trim, forsaken and lost, one of the cats of Port Louis now, but how could Thomy tell which? The *Cumberland* was rotting in the mangroves, but no Trim was there.

When things were dreariest, they played fiddle and flute together under the almond-tree, duets from Mozart and Haydn in airy rondo and graceful minuet. A musical day with Pitot could charm the cares away, and the cares were many. Had it not been for him, in the aching years that followed, Matthew Flinders could never have lived them through.

Napoleon's star was rising, and war hostility growing. The festival bells were always ringing for this or that triumph, the guns barking victory, and the negroes pelting flowers in the streets. A huge French fleet was on the way, they said, to show who was mistress of the seas.

Looking out from the flat roof on the King of England's birthday, somebody noticed the British Ensign hung with the Union downwards on the Marengo.

Insurrection smouldered at the mess table that night.

"They insult our nation!" shouted Lean, when he heard it. "Let's get into these bloody Frenchmen, and show them who we are."

"Nonsense!" said Matthew. "These valiant Gauls insult the few helpless prisoners they happen to have here. The brave fight not with words. Such things would be deserving of contempt, except that they keep alive national hostility and the flame of war."

Even so, the younger men started a brawl with the soldiers, and his own men of the *Cumberland* ran away from Le Flacq, and came to him to set him free, and knocked down the guard. Good fellows, so eager, so loyal, but he had to send them away with advice to follow the line of least resistance—just for a little while, when they would all be free, just till the answer came from France.

The governor's revenge for that night's doings was well thought out, and his punishment hard to take. The trap-door to the roof was nailed up, and all spy-glasses confiscated. They were marshalled indoors now at six instead of eight, and forbidden to walk near the garden gate, to buy poultry and fruit.

A few days after the incident, the old sergeant ambled in to Flinders, and asked him for his sword.

Absent-mindedly he looked up from his charts. "My sword. Why do you want it?"

"Le capitaine Neuville, monsieur, by his excellency's order, has come to collect all swords." He casually lifted the weapon down from the wall.

Matthew snatched it from him in a flash of white-hot anger. "That is not our tradition in England, Sergeant La Mêle. I cannot give up my sword except to an officer of equal rank, or higher. You can tell the general that from me, if he has not the grace to know it."

La Mêle backed out. Collect all swords! Flinders boiled with indignation. Was this ignorance, or deliberate humiliation? He wrote a brief note to the general, quite passionless, stating the facts.

Decaen was a rude man, but good form was his fetish. He sent Captain Neuville to apologize. It was a mistake. The captain's sword was not required, as he was not a prisoner.

"Not a prisoner! Would you be so good as to explain, what am I?"

"I understand from his excellency, monsieur, that you are but detained." Matthew laughed.

The incident had not ended. In a few weeks another popinjay turned up, a lieutenant-adjutant from the office of the Chef d'Etat Major. He had called, he said, for le capitaine Flinders's sword.

"Your captain-general——"

"The captain-general has changed his mind." The young man saw fit to explain that Colonel d'Arsonville himself had intended to come, but he was prevented at the last moment.

Why the urgency?—but better let it go. If he refused, they might take his books and papers again, and that would be a far crueller blow.

He gave up the sword with a shrug of futility, but made them wait while he wrote a label to go with it:

Farewell, my faithful companion, thou guardian of my honour, farewell. I have borne thee many a day, and but lately saved thee from ravages of shipwreck, but forced from me by those who in justice and faith and humanity ought to have been my friends, I bid thee adieu. Ah, it is the walls of a prison that echo my last farewell. The reefs of coral, so violently dashed by the wind-tossed ocean, were more merciful than they.

"*C'est la poésie! It is romance!*" cried Pitot in ecstasy, when Matthew showed him his rough copy of the screed. "Come! Let us set it to music!"

"No. Here is something more worth while," Matthew smiled at him, and handed him another sheet of paper.

"Magnetic equator." Pitot read it in mystification, in his very French accent:

Calculations and investigations taken at anchor with a spring upon the cable, azimuths taken from the shade at each end of the vane, observations upon the binnacle, the boom and the fo'c'sle.

"But this will not go to music. I do not comprehend."

"It will go further, dear Pitot, than any song to a sword. At least, I hope it will. Those are notes of my experiments in variations of the mariner's compass."

Pitot was polite, but not impressed.

The months went by on leaden feet, eight, nine, ten. A big frigate sailed into the port under cartel colours. He was quite certain she came to demand him, but his excitement was short-lived. She landed French prisoners, and carried away most of the English from the Garden Prison and Le Flacq.

Alfred Dale of the *Dédaigneuse* was left, a bright and ambitious boy. He was helping with the charts and learning navigation. That lightened the daylight hours. In the privacy of his cell in the late night, Matthew undid the parcel of Ann's letters, and savoured the bitter-sweet of love and longing.

It was surely time for dispatches to arrive from France. Not for one moment did he doubt that his passport would be honoured. Many a time they found him in the boughs of the almond-tree, the only high vantage point in the grounds, trying to glimpse between the leaves the ships in Port Louis Bay.

The leaves changed to a white magic of scented blossom. He could not see the ships, and no message came.

On 16 December 1804, the anniversary of his ill-starred landing, he begged the governor to send him to France for trial. A lone Englishman in a far-away isle, how else could he hope for justice, with the affairs of great nations weighed in the scales against him.

The general made no reply.

"Why does he persecute me like this?" he cried to Pitot. "This man is devoid of compassion and human feeling. How he must hate me!"

"He hates all Englishmen," said Pitot, "and more than ever since they chase him from Pondicherry, where he was to be big French Rajah, riding the Hindus down in his gold carriage. The English give him no chance to land. The fleet chase him out of the port, and he fly for his life. We don't want him, but if you ask me, Napoleon don't want him, too. That's why he tie him up here. The Captain-General Decaen don't like it."

"So he takes it out on me, a shipwrecked man. This thing is unprecedented in the annals of navigation. Will Bonaparte stand behind this man who dishonours Bonaparte's word?"

"Bonaparte," said Pitot, "has big fish to fry."

Thomy was right. New Year brought news that the Little Corporal was Emperor of the French, crowned by the Pope of Rome—in the previous May. So New Year was a fête day, a little belated, of the wildest revelry in Port Louis, processions and pageants, orgies of dancing and wine, and worship of Saint Napoleon, the Corsican redeemer of the world.

All day long they heard the din and the drumming. It was said that Decaen had spread the British flag in the dust of the market-place for the slaves to dance on, but outside the barracks and the square, the cries of "*Vive l'Empereur!*" were noticeably weak. The old families and the *émigrés* of Ilde-de-France were faithful still to the Bourbons.

At night the Chef d'État Major invited the prisoners of Maison Despeaux to dinner and the theatre, with the governor's permission provided they were under French escort. Thomy was away in the country, but—thoughtfulness itself—he deputed a M. Regnier to call for Matthew. M. Regnier embarrassed him with bibulous affection, sagged on his shoulder at dinner, led him to the theatre by a very devious route.

The theatre, such as it was, was tawdry with tinselled fleur-de-lis and gaudy with red, white and blue. It was so overcrowded that, craning this way and that, Matthew could scarcely see the stage, but he found plenty of entertainment in the throng of women about him in the pit.

These full-lipped, full-breasted creoles developed well and early. Their evening-gowns, or lack of them, left no doubt of that.

There was one heavily-scented and sophisticated beauty that Regnier said, with a leer, was only twelve years old. The maturer women were grossly fat, and quite as bare as the young ones, simmering with salacious laughter. They all had smooth olive complexions and well-turned ankles in silk, and great gazelle eyes that held his own, and implored, and resisted, and surrendered. Temptations of St Anthony!

What an uproar a crowd of women like this would make in an English theatre. The prudes would break their fans and cry shame, the libertines exult and clap, and the old leeches, evilly chuckling, ply their opera-glasses.

The play began with a "Danse Anglaise" that proved to be a horn-pipe, the only English dance that this African out-post had seen. Next came a harlequin show, long and childish and tedious, in which a clown in an English grouse-shooting costume was kicked in the posterior, dragged round the stage by the scruff of the neck, and pushed from pillar to post. Every time he was kicked he shouted "God dam!" to screams of hilarious applause. Ah well, it was war-time. If that were all!

After that, there was a low comedy farce of a Gascon carrying off a lady. The dialogue was much too fluent and nasal for Matthew to catch a word. His face was blank through all the japes that made the house a bedlam, and he dared not ask Regnier to translate for fear the joke should be at his expense.

During the *entr'acte* Regnier, a little more sober now, pointed to one of the boxes, where a delicately-beautiful Parisienne, in sparkling white with a tiara of diamonds, was attended by two chevaliers in full military pomp. One of them struck a familiar note—the ramrod figure of Monistrol.

"Madame Decaen!" said Regnier in a stage-whisper.

He was surprised that she should be so young and lovely. A little sadly he reflected that this radiant person might have been his hostess. Instead, she was his jailer's wife.

She turned, and noticed his intent gaze, or perhaps his foreign air, for she looked at him very directly, and he saw her speak to Monistrol. Monistrol glanced his way and bent above her. Then Madame Decaen's scrutiny became hard and haughty and inimical. Naturally. The English spy.

The curtain rose on a French play, utterly unintelligible. He was tired but polite when the gala evening was over, and Regnier delivered him back to the Maison Despeaux.

Prisoners came and went. Another summer dragged through. The swimming-pool was dry. Aken was so ill with coastal fever that at one time they thought he was dying, and Matthew's "gravelly trouble", as he called it, returned with the wet weather.

The cartel *Thetis* came in from India with another exchange of prisoners, and a request from the Marquis of Wellesley, so he heard, for his immediate liberation.

All were exchanged now save Dale and Seymour, and an old seaman named Smith with a broken leg, and Aken, and Captain Flinders … the unlucky Captain Flinders. The men of the *Cumberland* were going. To his great surprise, the doleful Elder refused point blank to go with them.

"Don't be a fool, Elder. Get out of this while you can. I'll manage well enough now," his master told him.

"It's not you, sir. It's Sir Joseph. If I desert the uniform now, what am I to tell him? I'm sure he would not approve, not here, where the climate is so—if you'll forgive me, sir—sweaty."

A smile of understanding passed between them, and Matthew rose and took his servant's hand.

In March, at the end of the long wet, Flinders wrote to Comte de Fleurieu, Councillor of State, doyen of the Institute and patron of Lapérouse.

For a fortnight a blindness most cruel came upon him, glazed eyes and swollen lids, and racking head as he groped his way about. He put it down to the chart drawing and the white walls, but the surgeon said that the root of the trouble went deeper than that. Dr Laborde, chief of the medical staff, took a keen interest in his patient, and went out of his way to inform the captain-general that Flinders's labours were calculated to assist the progress of science and be of utility to seamen.

He was curtly told to mind his own business, and he did. He promptly issued an official certificate that Aken should be invalided home by the first ship, and that Captain Matthew Flinders, after fifteen months' close confinement in grave ill-health, must be removed to a more salubrious climate to save his life.

Pitot was overjoyed. He had been agitating for this for a long time, but every application had been denied. Now the general had to grant it, whether he liked it or not.

There were so many invitations from so many unknown that Matthew was bewildered. He left it all to Thomy, who selected a new place every week, and then had to find another. For the governor delayed sanction, and would entertain none of his plans.

Pitot's own home at La Grande Rivière was too close to the English military prison, and his aunt's at Le Flacq too close to the naval one. His sister's at Poudre d'Or was too close to the bay and the shipping—so it went on. At last it was settled that Matthew might be allowed to go to the plantation of a Madame d'Arifat, well up in the hills, at Wilhelm's Plains ... but when he did not know.

In May, Aken left Port Louis on an American ship, carrying all the completed charts to Sir Joseph, with letters addressed to friends in the Seven Seas. June and July went slowly, each day with its anguish of suspense.

On 17 August, the second anniversary of his shipwreck, Dale and Seymour, the two little middies, came to say good-bye. They were off to India on a cartel, and they had heard the Garden Prison was to be closed. That looked hopeful, and the old sergeant said it was true—closed for a time, at any rate. Matthew gave young Dale a testimonial that should win him promotion anywhere in the Navy, and bade them a wistful farewell.

From the almond-tree he watched the two white-pantalooned figures disappear down the road ... back to the war and the wheel of the world. He envied them.

A figure was coming in a cloud of dust, a French courier in Navy uniform coming straight to the prison—a last-moment message for him? He was to embark on the cartel? His heart leapt up.

It was a note from Bergeret that he was back again. Admiral Linois, he said, was proud to be Flinders's champion. Was there anything that Bergeret could do?

He wrote the gallant captain to try for the restoration of his books and papers, as he was leaving for the hills—he was not sure when.

That night he spent alone in the prison with seaman Smith. The old man sat in the chimney corner, nursing his broken leg and sniffling misery. Where would he go when the place was closed in a land where he knew no one?

To cheer him up, Matthew suggested that he should come with him. Till his leg was better, he would pay for his living. So the old man forgot his grizzling, and in those dank and white-washed walls, to the flickering firelight and the crying of the wind, they lived old days for each other and sang chanties of the sea.

The next day was Sunday, a terrible day that left a scar on his memory.

He woke to a desolation he had never known before. The Maison Despeaux was silent as the grave. His diary was his only companion through the lagging hours, the lagging hours of sixty minutes each. He wrote his wandering, aimless thoughts. The writing kept him sane.

"Slipped on my shoes and morning gown, and went down to walk in the garden. Met the old sergeant and bade him *bon-jour*. The old man looked a bit melancholy at the prospect of his last prisoners leaving the house, for he will lose his situation. The dogs came round after me, and seemed more attentive than when there were more prisoners. I suppose they were a little pinched for food... .

"The grass being wet with the showers that had fallen at daybreak, I confined myself to walk at the head of the garden, where the gentlemen had cut it down. Meditated upon the extreme folly of General Decaen in keeping me prisoner here, for it can answer no good purpose, either to me or the French government, and the injury it is to me will not bear to be dwelt upon. It leads almost to madness.

"Got up into the tall almond-tree, to see if there were any ships off. None to be seen. I could have seen much further round from the top of the house, if the general had not shut it off and taken away my spyglass. The boys and the soldiers together have pretty well stripped the almond-tree before the fruit was ripe. Got down from the tree and continued my walk. General Decaen's conduct must have originated in unjust suspicion and revenge, his dignity being injured at my refusing to dine with him, and continued from obstinacy and pride, but seeing a shower coming on, hurried into the house. This rain is very extraordinary at this time of the year, but the whole year, so far, has been an uncommon one.

"Half past seven. Went up into my room, stripped myself naked, and washed from head to feet in a little tub. Called Smith for some hot water to shave. Think he walks better with his broken leg every day.

"Read five pages of Condamine's *Voyage from Quito to Peru*. Think Condamine's calculation of the level of the river at Paux being only a foot and a half higher at Pera is incorrect, for where there is a stream running downward consistently, as in a river, the rise and fall of the tide will be perceptibly much higher up the river than at the mere level at which the water rises in the sea."

Thinking over his own experiments in the rise and fall of the tides, he idly traced the map of the sunlight on the white walls, the map of the cracks in the window. At eight o'clock, he laid his lone table and brought the tea-kettle.

"Took plenty of milk in my tea, and made a good breakfast. Took three pinches of snuff while I sat thinking of my wife and friends in England. (Mem. Must not take so much snuff when I return, for it makes me spit about the rooms.) Elder returned about nine, but no answer yet to my note from Bergeret.

"Took up my flute, and played the first and second duo of Pleyel's Opera 9. It commences in the grand style, and is sweetly plaintive in some parts of it. I must purchase all Pleyel when I return to England, and Haydn and Hoffmeister and Deviennes, but the whole will be too expensive. Music is very dear in England, and indeed so is almost everything else.

"Hope Mrs Flinders will have got the better of the inflammation of one of her eyes." (Even yet it was a novelty to refer to his dear little Ann as Mrs Flinders.) "It is now fine weather in England, and she will be able to ride out. Must take a house in the country when I return, and enjoy myself two or three months before I engage in any service, but God knows it is now three years since I have heard from anybody at home, and what may have happened it is impossible to say.

"Got Elder to send my linen to the wash, and to make out a list of what is required, but not to get it yet, in case I am not allowed to go into the country.... Transcribed four pages of the log upon the state of the barometer on the different coasts of Australia. I hope Sir Joseph will be alive and well when I return, he is now advancing in years.

"Dinner at 2 p.m. The French beans are very good in this island. Drank three glasses of Madeira. Must eat more puddings and vegetables and less meat. My headache better after dinner. Think there must certainly be some large river or opening on the north-west coast of Australia. Hope the Admiralty will not give any more passports to go out on the voyage of discovery while I am still a prisoner here. Cannot conceive why there should not be any copy of Tasman's chart of that coast remaining, spoken of by Dampier. If there is an opening in the Rosemary Isles, a settlement there would be advantage to the East India Company, on account of the high tides, Spice Islands near by, a naval station and place to take in spices for China, and to counter the armaments of the French on this island.

"Would I go out as governor to the settlement there, should it be proposed to me? I cannot tell, it would depend upon my circumstances. Wish to finish the examination of the whole coast of Australia before I do anything else. If there should be any great opening on the north-west coast, it would be desirable to explore by land from the head of the great inlet on the south

366

coast, and from Port Phillip. The apes of this island would be very useful in these excursions. Must propose to Sir Joseph to touch here when I go out again, and take six apes and some fruit-trees, provided I can make sure of not being ill-treated.

"Half-past three. Find myself a little sleepy. Don't know whether to go down and play a game of billiards with the old sergeant to drive it off, or to take a nap. Determined on the latter, and lay down in bed.

"Washed. Had a headache. Looked very pale. Went down to the gate and sat down in the sentry box, looking at the people that passed by. The mulatto creoles are very thin and tall. They have pleasant countenances. The soldier talking with his comrade said that Bonaparte was only thirty-six years old when he was made emperor. Note—French soldiers talk much more than English soldiers do, and seem to be happy enough on an allowance that would scarcely keep the English soldiers from starving.

"At sunset returned upstairs and walked till Elder got tea ready, but not wishing my friend Pitot to give me more than two or three introductions to people in the country. Studied French and worked at my Voyage. Hope that Captain Bergeret will procure the remainder of my books and papers from the general. Will send off letters if he can. After tea, walked a few turns. Necessary to read over again the article in the *Britannica* for weather and wind. Am surprised at the influence that M. Noalds attributes to the moon over the waves. He supposes there are two situations in every revolution of the moon, in one or other of which all changes of weather take place. Agree with the writer of the article that the moon has little, if anything, to do with the weather.

"Went to bed about half-past nine. Lay awake considering the causes of the trade-winds and of the westerly winds, and especially upon the earth's revolution round its axis. Think they are certainly owing in some part to this cause, as well as the rarefaction of the air under the vertical sun. Must have some kind of trap set for that rat, which comes disturbing me every night, but as I am so soon to leave the house, it does not signify.

"Dropped asleep soon after ten, and waked about one by the noise of the soldiers in the guardhouse, who are playing about and running after each other like children. Wish that loud-voiced fellow had taken a dose of opium. Fell asleep again, dreamed that General Decaen was setting a lion upon me to devour me, and that he ate me up. Was surprised to find that devouring was so easy to be borne, that after death I had the consciousness of existence. Got up soon after six much agitated with a more violent headache than usual, and——"

He had written just so far when Thomy's bird-like head came round the door, Thomy, always appearing like an angel and vanishing like a sprite. He was waving the governor's permit for instant departure.

"Prepare yourself for congratulations. You are free man!"

"What! I sail with the cartel?"

Ah, the sadness! Pitot looked blank. "Well no, but you come with me to Wilhelm's Plains."

A short silence, then Matthew clasped his hand. "My good friend Thomy! How can I thank you?"

"Pack up and meet me in the bazaar at Port Louis at four this afternoon."

He was off down the garden, shouting for La Mêle.

16

Land of the Dodo

Dazed with scent and sound and colour after the myopia of the Maison Despeaux, Matthew limped through the sandy streets, focusing them with a stereoscopic interest.

Forbidding hills, blackened by some withered herb, walled in the town, now swooning with heat under pallid skies. The half-furled sails of ships becalmed on the harbour were chiselled white as a sculptor's drape, and from the flagstaff of the Residency the Tricolour hung limp. Beneath it, his arch-enemy was doubtless snoring. With such a face and such a temper, the captain-general would surely snore.

Most of the houses were wooden, two storeys and three, but ramshackle and tipsily leaning, blown down like a pack of cards in the hurricanes, patched over and propped up. A labyrinth of negro kraals ran down to the water's edge, where the mangrove marshes reeked of fever. Dusty palms stood dejected in the parched gardens of the old creole mansions. The poinciana and the frangipanni were leafless and lifeless, Japanese designs of trees in Indian ink. Only the sturdy little "shoemaker" flowers defied those etiolating rays in glossy green and scarlet. For the rest, the face of earth was drawn and grey.

In from the plains a whirlwind was dancing like a dervish in a tall spiral of sand. As Matthew watched it, the glare struck into his eyeballs like a steel knife. He crossed the road to the sharp blue shadow of a row of stores.

The booths were empty and unattended, save for humped forms steeped in noonday slumber. At one doorway a slave girl, a child of no more than eleven years, lay as though she had fallen unconscious, her full little black breast bared, and a fat negro baby tugging at it like a young pup.

As he turned in to the tavern, a Portuguese sailor reeled out of it, an ape padding behind on a chain, one of the black-faced apes of Mozambique. It wore a heavy slave collar of spiked iron, and its wicked little eyes gleamed redly. The mulatto woman brought him a glass of Madeira, and went back to her corner to squat in a doze, while he sat sipping listlessly, blinking out of the shadows into the sun.

There was a rag of a wild rose creeper on the broken pergola. Heaven knows how it came there, or why, save to carry his tortured mind back to England and Ann. A black and yellow gadfly, business-like and vindictive, was rapidly backing up hill and down dale in the sand, ignoring all obstacles, dragging an inert grey spider three times its size—General Decaen in his gaudy uniform, proud of his helpless victim. Round and round in the relentless circle went his thoughts again, a fragile hand pressed against the veins of his temple.

The angry scream of a caged macaw roused him, roused the bazaars to the cackle of petty trade. Port Louis, bewitched like the palace of the Sleeping Beauty, snatched up the threads of life just where it had left them. Half-naked donkey drivers belted and cursed their mokes, that went joggling on between the big panniers of pomelos and pomegranates, vanilla roots and coffee-beans and sugar-cane and olives, down from the plantations in the hills.

A dirty Arab with a nose like a scimitar whined his wares. Malabars from Pondicherry and Madagascar men in loin-cloths jostled each other to the meat-marts. Obese old mammies and voluptuous young negresses, their black shoulders satiny with sweat, their white teeth gleaming, swirled their vivid *pagnes* about them, settled their burdens on their highly-ornamental heads, and, with a swing of the hips, made off into the throng chattering like a horde of monkeys. Here and there stood a *gendarme*, gay as a wasp among bees, or an *habitant* in dirty white, with a cabbage-tree hat and a whip on his hip.

Palanquins borne by slaves were already making trouble in the mule-traffic. Some were richly gilt and curtained, others rickety and shabby, and all attended by a bodyguard of twenty or thirty squabbling negroes. They carried the petty nabobs back to their offices, the military back to the barracks, and the sallow creole ladies, with all their ribbons, out for a breath of fresh air that was purely auto-suggestion.

Four o'clock brought Pitot—Thomy Pitot, the ever-punctual, ever-faithful, mincing along in his dapper little boots, far too jaunty, not at all naval, and, what was worse, a Frenchman and a friend.

A raised eyebrow questioned Matthew's whimsical smile of greeting. "*Quoi donc?*" he wanted to know.

"Nothing at all. I am ready. I am most grateful. I am your man."

Together they made for the Residency, where Colonel Monistrol received them with his cool and colourless politeness, not so much freezing as frozen.

The parole was simple. Dutifully, even meekly, Matthew transcribed it at Monistrol's dictation:

His Excellency Captain-General Decaen having given me permission to reside at Wilhelm's Plains at the habitation of Madame d'Arifat, I do hereby promise upon my word of honour not to go further than the distance of two leagues from the said habitation without His Excellency's permission, and to conduct myself in that proper degree of reserve becoming an officer in a country with whom his nation is at war. I will also answer for the proper conduct of my two servants.

The official preliminaries over, they were to dine with Madame Brunet, Pitot's elder sister, where Matthew would meet his future hostess, Madame d'Arifat.

To a stately old white house that withdrew from the racket of the street into a grove of magnolias, they made their way. A negro butler ushered them in to a slightly tarnished splendour, but in mellow yellow of candle-light, the grand salon was a tin trumpet symphony of French voices. A large gathering, alas!— and the cuffs of his uniform frayed!

Indeed, it seemed that the party was for him, an unexpected honour, for there, too, were Messieurs and Mesdames Chazal and Curtat and Chevreau, neighbours-to-be out at the Tamarind River; Edouard Pitot, becoming as close a friend as his brother, and their cousin Troberville; Ravel and Bouchet and Boistel, eager young men with faintly-pencilled moustaches and a literary flavour to their converse, and quite a host of other planters from Wilhelm's Plains and the coffee lands of Mocha near by.

Thomy translated their pyrotechnic greetings. Inspired by the recent visit of the *Géographe* and her naturalists, they had formed a little *Société d'Emulation* in Ile-de-France, in a scientific fever of collecting and classifying and preserving for posterity. They earnestly hoped he would join them. He would be very happy.

In a susurrus of taffetas, and a little overpowering in propinquity and perfume, were Madame Rouillard, a Dresden blonde, Pitot's younger sister from the Gold Dust Colony; old Madame Lachaise, like a hawk, volubly adoring of seafaring men; Madame Cazeaux, shrivelled and shrill; Mademoiselle Périchon, angular and languid, and in refreshing contrast the Brunet girls and Madame d'Arifat's three daughters, nymphs in muslin.

With a sinking at the heart, Matthew could see the solitary and studious retreat he had pictured vanishing into thin air. Still, the *jeune filles* were vivacious. Their effervescence would provide light relief in his exile, and there were three brothers as well, he learned, to temper the wind. One of them might be interested in navigation. He wondered what John Franklin was doing.

Painfully self-conscious in the cachinnation of foreign tongues, he sat nervously aloof until his plump and amiable little hostess took him under her ample wing at dinner. The glitter of silver and snow-white napery, good wine and good wit, and the grace of flowers and pretty women, after the coarse bread and coarser pleasantries of the prison board, but above all the kindliness and courtesy of these friendly enemies of his, brought a warm glow of well-being. Not even the eagle eye of the *Investigator's* late commander could detect the slightest under-current of restraint, or curiosity, or ridicule.

In the hour of music that followed, all traces of his embarrassment vanished, and even his smile had lost its twist of bitterness. The gentle harmonies of Madame Chazal's harpsichord, the sweet and plaintive elegies of Pauline Brunet's singing, had charmed it away.

"You play?" demanded Madame Chazal, when an elementary and blushing "*Très bon, madame!*" had expressed his thanks and pleasure.

"I play but a sailor's instrument, the flute," he told her modestly.

"Ah, but it is excellent!" she squealed in delight. "Thomy has told me. We shall have the Pleyel quartettes, is it not? Chazal, le capitaine Flandare,'e play the flute!"

There followed an avalanche of dialogue between Madame Chazal and her long-haired *mari* with the scintillating spectacles, now and again an explosive interpolation from Pitot. The Chazals were returning to their plantation at the Tamarinds in the morning. They would be devoured to carry along Monsieur le capitaine's two servants and his baggage, and install them at Wilhelm's Plains on the way.

Madame d'Arifat was the serene dark woman with the mole on her chin, and the gracefully-waving fan. Her capacious bosom was festooned with many pearls, her grey hair chiselled to her brow. She spoke very halting English, but when the rest of the party had settled to a noisy game of La Bouillote, the rage in the island just then, she motioned Matthew to sit beside her, placed a fat ringed hand on his knee, and looked upon him with beaming approbation.

Mademoiselle d'Arifat, whose name, he noted, was Delphine, and who would have been pretty had she not been quite so pale, was a charming but not very efficient interpreter. He liked her tight little cap of burnished curls, *à l'Impèratrice*, her camellia complexion, and the curve of her full lips in pouting thoughtfulness as she switched her mind from one language to the other. There was much spontaneous laughter at their mutual misunderstandings.

The plantation, he gathered, was by no means a wealthy one, but they were content. The mountain air was good and the scenery very beautiful, 1800 feet above the fetor of the swamps. Marc and Aristide were mere schoolboys, Sophie and Lise between them and Delphine. André, the eldest brother, was a settler in Ile Bourbon. The family would return a little later, and in the meantime his pavilion was in readiness, with one for his servants. Their home was to him, and he was most truly welcome.

A happy respite was that evening, the first in three long years made blissful with music, and bright smiling faces in reassuring pantomime of friendliness. It pleased him that there was apparently no shadow of Decaen's suspicion to mar his reception among the people he must meet, no national hostility to a foreigner, an enemy to their country if they would. He was an enemy to no country, save as it opposed the honour, the interest and the happiness of his own.

It was as well that he did not overhear, and could not have understood it if he did, the whispered warning of witty Madame Rouillard of Poudre d'Or, who drew her brother aside at parting.

"You will be careful, Thomy. Your friend is our foe. The general has proof. This *anglais* has straight eyes, but they are too quick. It is said he spends all his time writing. Madame d'Arifat will not be so tranquil if it should be that she is harbouring a spy."

"But listen, my sister—" began Thomy explicitly.

"*Très bien. Nous verrons. C'est à vous!*" and Madame Rouillard disappeared into her palanquin with a wave of the hand and a frou-frou of skirts.

The two friends walked back to the Marengo arm in arm in the white moonlight patterning the dust with filigree shadow of the poinciana beans. To-morrow was a free day, for Matthew to buy a few necessaries, and to finish a paper for Sir Joseph and the Royal Society, that Pitot would forward by one of the American frigates. It was on the effects of sea winds on the barometer, and, in spheric trigonometry, operations at sea for finding the longitude. An interesting study, with some quite new deductions that would most certainly excite comment. Now, if Thomy would care to come in for a moment, and hear the beginning ...

Thomy laughed. He was not to be caught. "Enough, my friend! You shall read it, I promise you, every word, to my sister, Madame Rouillard. She is the one of the family with the analytical mind. That will be my revenge. I think it not wise we should be much together to-morrow, so till Thursday morning, and as early as you like. *A bientôt.*"

There was no Lights Out bugle to call him back to grim reality that night. The candle burned in Flinders's window till the grey hours.

Next afternoon came a merciful rain, falling heavily, invigorating and cool. On Thursday morning, astraddle on asses and under huge umbrellas, they were out into it before daybreak, three or four slaves in tow. By winding tracks across the plains, they reached the foothills.

Up and down across the steep watercourses, slipping and sliding on the wet rocks under ferns forty feet high, it was hard riding for poor prison-cramped Matthew, but his aches and apprehensions were forgotten in the stimulation of activity and the crisp hill air. He put back his shoulders and breathed deeply. Vista of gully and height, through silver veils of rain, was benediction.

Where the mule-track turned off to Mocha, they opened their lunch-baskets in the dripping shelter of a big banyan, that reminded him of the fig-trees at Port Jackson. Its pachyderm trunks made cathedral aisles of an even more lavish shade.

The sun came out in the afternoon on a world refreshed. Bright-winged parrots and blue pigeons flashed past them, monkeys scuffled in the tree-tops, and sea-birds wheeled about the crags of the mountains far inshore, a sign of bad weather.

From one jutting rock, Matthew looked down upon his beloved sea, a misty azure with showers of spray at the feet of the cliffs. On the other side lay the harbour of Port Louis, jealously guarded by Fort Blanc to the left, the battery on Ile de Tenelliers to the right, and ships of the highways and byways of the southern seas at anchor—Danish, Dutch, American, French and Spanish, brigantines from Muscat and the coasts of Coromandel, schooners from the Indies and from Africa, anything but the English.

Riding, they talked of this Ile-de-France, dream-country of Paul and Virginia, land of the dodo—a subject dear to Thomy's heart, for it was his birthplace.

A jewel of earth, a little bit of the best of Africa outflung in the Indian Ocean, it was a mighty atom of strategic importance as half-way house on the road to India. A hundred-and-fifty mile circle of coral reefs and rugged coasts, with only two or three entrances, made it impregnable, so long as the secrets were kept. There was no other defence.

Pitot knew many an aerie that had been a lookout of the pirate Arabs in the long ago. He knew the landing-places of the caravels of Tristan da Cunha and Alburquerque, when the island was Mauritius, and of the galleons of Spain, and the old stone forts of the Dutchmen. He knew well the vine-covered villa at Pamplemousses where Bernardin de Saint Pierre had written *Paul et Virginie*, the sweetest love-story in the language, in all languages indeed, its greatness its simplicity. A pity Matthew was on such a short chain. Still, they would do what they could.

Believe it, Decaen was not a bad man at heart. Anglophobe, yes; a vicious tyrant, no. Republican France was his religion, Napoleon his god. He had been sent out to make this place an eagle's nest of empire. He was fortifying the island as quickly as he could, and afraid of his schemes being known. You see, if the Dutch should become inhospitable at the Cape, or the English get hold of it again, Ile-de-France was worth its weight in gold.

This mad militarism and greed of glory were doing more harm than good, Thomy was afraid, crippling commerce, which is wealth, making France a flash in the national pan. Things had changed since the Revolution. Beggars on horseback were riding roughshod over all the old graces, here as well as at home. It would be a sad thing if, in snatching for more, they in Ile-de-France should be dispossessed.

The Dutch were a remarkable people, he said—sober, stolid, even stupid they seemed, no ecstasy, no verve, no *savoir vivre*, but what a genius for colonization. They had planted the millet, maize, rice, bananas, vanilla, cloves, nutmegs, the citrus and cinnamon groves, making Ile-de-France a spice-box. The French had added sugar-cane, olives and coffee, pepper and tobacco—all the things that make dinner worth while—and the manioc for the slaves. Most of the plantations grew everything. The hill-country was very rich. Why, with their own products and tropic fruits, they should be able to maintain themselves in a siege. A siege was surely coming.

Towards sunset, saffron-yellow after rain, they swung into a luxurious gully of palms a hundred feet high, wreathed with liana vines and garlands of agapanthus, creamy-white. Thomy said the place had been a great haunt of flamingoes in his father's youth, but now the decorative creatures had all been shot out for their plumage. Not even his grandfather had seen a dodo, nobody, in truth, since those vandal Dutch sailors who had eaten it.

That was a queer bird. A beak like a wash-jug, an eye like a boot-button, ash-coloured down. It could not run, it could not fly, it cackled like a goose.

This reminded Matthew of the struthious birds, away in his Australia, and the weird little beast he and Guthrie had found in the creek-bed in Van Diemen's Land like a duck squashed flat, with four legs and fur and quills. It laid eggs, and suckled its young.

The cassowaries Pitot had seen. Monsieur Péron of the *Géographe* had showed him two of them, cleverly stuffed, that he was carrying home as a gift to the Empress Josephine and the Boulogne Museum. Péron had found them at the Ile Decrès.

"Ile Decrès. Where was that?" questioned Matthew.

Thomy was not sure. Somewhere in the south of New Holland, he thought, west of Van Diemen's Land.

Matthew reined in his ass sharply. "Not my Kangaroo Island. It could not be, for I gave them my charts. They could not re-name it. It must be some other, but I know of no other."

Tactfully Thomy led the conversation back to the duck-bill. He was politely incredulous. He could not vision such a sleight-of-land trick in the good God's creation.

But Bligh had sketched the little nightmare. It was no Sindbad tale. The conversation that followed brought back a whiff of memory of old ships and shipmates. Where were Bligh and Tobin now? Christopher Smith, the botanist, was in Pulo Penang, and James Wiles still in Jamaica. He must write to them from this fascinating isle.

Lamplight shining through the bamboos at dusk guided them to the Pitots' country home, a deep-shuttered bungalow on the banks of La Grande Rivière, hot baths, a good dinner, an evening of Bouillote. In the morning they made an excursion to shoot hares, with M. Bayard, a judge from Port Louis, young Frederic and Robert Pitot, Thomy's nephews, and a pack of droll, bandy-legged hounds. Hares were luckily scarce—Matthew was no Nimrod—so they made a detour more to his liking, to see the waterfall where La Grande Rivière made a fifty-foot leap into the valley, and then on to Le Réduit, the governor's summer residence, a rambling old mansion now in preparation for his excellency's annual vacation.

"Spit on the doorstep!" mischievously suggested Bobby Pitot to Matthew, but he said it in French and earned no more than a questioning smile, and a box on the ears from his elder brother.

The next day they were off again, M. Bayard now of the party, goading their asses up the rough road through the ranges, and heaven all the way up.

Coffee, cloves, cinnamon groves, forests of olive and ebony, and the fields of maize and cotton were an ordered patterning on the slopes, set in a sunny glory of virgin vegetation.

Hundreds of African slaves, in blue Bengal cloth and gay kerchiefs, bent to their labours, overseers on mules riding among them. Every *habitation* they came to was hidden away in a leafy sanctuary of date-palms and papaya trees, mangoes and tamarinds, pocket-handkerchief patches of strawberries and peas about it, and the noisy cabins and kraals of its negroes.

Two thousand feet above, the slaty peaks, like poignards, pierced the skies.

The planters had heard of the distinguished young English explorer who had come thousands of miles in a midget ship to have his wings so neatly clipped by their captain-general's shears. They were intrigued to entertain such a celebrity. Monsieur Plumet, a retired Indian Army officer smoking the pipe of old campaigns on his balcony, gave them hearty greeting in passing, and so did Madame Trappée farther on. From there it was only a league and a half to Madame d'Arifat's, yet at sundown a slave with a gourd on his shoulder told them there were still two leagues to go. They had missed the way.

Heavy rain set in with the nightfall, and looking for the track they wound round in the wet of the wood for nearly an hour. They decided to go back by the road to Madame Trappée's—took the wrong road, and came to yet another *habitation*.

Slaves were chattering at the cabin door, a white man sitting among them. Ha, this was the place, and that was Elder.

"Ahoy, Elder! Here we are!"

A strange voice answered, in Irish—"An' phwat in the wurruld is the innemy doin' heerre?"

A stocky red-headed man hobbled over to where the donkeys were stamping the flies away, took out his cutty pipe, spat, and peered at Matthew curiously in the twilight. He told them they had passed Madame d'Arifat's turn-off a mile back. His name was Thomas Drouse, a sailor once, tossed up by the tides of chance on an isle as green as his own. "Poor white trash" now, perhaps, with a mulatto wife and half-breed children, but his assistance was timely, and his converse lively, as he guided them to Le Refuge, across country, through the thickets and over the streams.

A good dinner was waiting, and Elder and Smith they found already at home. At bedtime Matthew was sitting in a tapestried chair in his pleasant little garden pavilion, between a coral-tree and a date-palm, the Sistine Madonna gazing beneficently down on those precious trunks of his. Elder brought him a cup of fragrant Mocha coffee, grown on the plantation and ground for his especial benefit. His body was healthily tired, and his mind more at rest than it had been for many a long day. He could settle to good work here till the season of gales was over, and the ships called in again. Please God it would be no longer.

For a little while he stood at the doorway, listening to the ripple of the rain. A million fireflies twinkled in the wet and shadowy ferns, a tree of bats took silent flight, uncannily. No stars were visible.

A lonely heart, but a thankful one, he retired early to rest.

In the morning, Jean Barrow, a freed slave from Martinique, now on a miniature plantation with slaves of his own to flog, brought milk and fresh eggs and bacon, baskets of golden-glowing papaws, mangoes, plantains and custard apples, sweet potatoes, beans, strawberries, and the royal purple egg-fruit. His meat and other stores he must order at the bazaars at Port Louis, to be brought up by the donkey men.

Pitot and Bayard presented him to Madame Clouves and her family, the d'Arifats' nearest neighbours, and laughingly recommended him to the gentle mercies of Amélie and Aimée, two sagacious young ladies in their teens, who would show him the countryside. Then they rode back to the durance vile of court and counting-house, down in the seaport.

His first interest was a rivulet of fresh water at the back of the bungalow, where the household geese cruised in a busy flotilla, snavelling shrimps. Conscientiously he traced it to its source — that old childhood's habit still persisted — and found on the way a beautiful pool for bathing, fringed with bamboos and banana palms, silky in the sun.

In a few days of unbroken peace, he learned to love the place, played with a French grammar, practised the flute in the evenings, but for the most part walked and breathed. That in itself was redemption. With a cabbage-tree hat, a blue shirt open at the neck, knee-breeches and tough hose to keep out the burrs, not forgetting a fly-switch, he wandered in the woods and grew young. He might have been Paul himself. Oh for Virginie!

When the weather settled, he paid a courtesy visit to M. Giblot, the district commandant. M. Giblot received him in bed at eleven o'clock in the day, asked a few wide of the mark questions concerning New Holland, then dismissed him by regretting that he lived so far away, and retired into his night-cap. He had the bulbous nose and the heavy eyes of the confirmed brandy-drinker.

On the way back, he called at Plumet's, and picked up a little of the news of the world from two French travellers, from India and San Domingo. They crowed that France would soon hold Indies, East and West, with India thrown in. He did not care to argue, and started back, proud of his exploit of walking five French leagues in the day. That was an achievement for one who had lately been a cripple, doing his turn in the prison yard with scarcely the strength or heart for that.

Nearing home, he met the Clouves girls, gathering *framboises*, the wild raspberries, and all in a flutter to be caught without stockings. Gallantly Matthew assured them that most of the tropic ladies of his acquaintance went sockless and unashamed — in point of fact they dispensed with shoes, hats, and everything in between except a cowrie shell.

That broke the ice quite nicely, though, with bubbling laughter and becoming blushes, they could only pick up the gist of it in gesture. They invited the mysterious *capitaine anglais* home to tea. He came quite often, and stayed to whist.

Among the visitors there was a M. Murat, who had been captain of a merchant ship. Murat knew no English, Matthew's French was truly villainous, but together, poring over the schoolroom globe, they spoke the language of the sea. In no time Matthew was expounding, more or less coherently, his theory of the compass variation changing with the ship's head.

Conscience plucked at his sleeve. Those charts of his were waiting. Before he settled to work, he and Murat walked across to Lake Vacois, a gleam of blue in the pocket of the hills, source of all the little rivers bickering down through the ravines of the south-west. The owner of the plantation was away at the salve-market in Madagascar, but the German overseer, a gruff old chap named Charlovich, offered hospitality with guns and fishing lines. Neither appealed. With a mariner's eye, Matthew was computing the depth in the centre as from 20 to 25 fathoms. He surmised a volcanic origin, set off round the shores of the lake in an expedition of one. Finding them too muddy, he made arrangements to explore in a canoe.

They told him that the Grand Bassin was 80 fathoms deep. He must verify that, and he wanted to ascertain whether the quantity of water that flowed in equalled the quantity that flowed out. That was a matter of infinitely greater importance than the 80-pound eels that local fishermen loved to grapple. The shimmering prism of lights that played on the iridium surface of the lake, he ruthlessly reduced to degrees of atmospheric pressure and evaporation in humidity.

The stream at the home plantation still intrigued him. He followed it down till it disappeared in its own bed in Chevreau's property. He summed up all the chasms and cascades, throwing in stones to measure the height of the fall. He struck the cliff walls, pitted like honeycomb, and finding them sonorous, "I suppose them imperfect basaltis," he solemnly wrote in his journal. Rucksack on shoulder in the rain, he trudged across to the Grand Bassin, half a mile wide, completely surrounded by conical hills, and alive with little fish ornate and gleaming in many colours, known as Madame Cère. They were a new species, imported from China and Batavia. He noted the strangling vines that coiled like phythons round the trees there, "in a manner which we sailors call 'with the sun'."

Every night he wrote needle-fine reports in his diary of the day's explorations, physiographical, geographical, geological, fauna and flora complete, not omitting the wild hog tracks in the mud, the old negro woman he met catching shrimps in a handkerchief to feed to the ducks, or the myriad black and white minas that descended upon him in garrulous flocks one day at the swimming-pool. He must make an analysis of soils, particularly with regard to coffee-growing. That would be of infinite value to Britain, in her colonies in the Indies.

Would it? A chill ache of futility—the pathos of these reports! Here he was prisoned in this diminutive isle, while the last of the continents waited. Hercules was chained to the spinning-wheel of Omphale. All his knowledge and all his ambition for his country meant less to the world than the chattering of those mina-birds.

A cheering letter came from Thomy, delivered with a parcel of provisions from Port Louis. An English frigate was prisoner down there. She had chased the *Harriet*, privateer, and taken and burned a small coaster. Ah, this madness of war, this brutality of slaughter and thieving on land and sea in the name of empire!

With a heavy sigh he unpacked his log-books—and the griefs and ghosts and vain regrets were in full cry at his heels again. Like a panther ready to spring, black melancholy waited its moment.

The wind moaning through the walls of his pavilion, his head bent on his hands between the two candle-sticks, and all the shadows of the night in his heart, he was roused by the cheery hola! of Chazal. Umbrella dripping on the doorstep, his spectacles beaming bonhomie, Chazal had ridden over to spend the evening, and carry him off to Tamarinds in the morning. No denials. There was plenty of time for the log-books.

Alas, too much, thought Matthew. He strapped up the trunks again, and rode away with Chazal. The wide earth, and the sky above, the thought of the moment, the laughter of friends, the words that he must listen to and answer—these were his only escape from a mind that preyed upon itself.

As well as being the finest harpsichord virtuoso in the island—her elegant English instrument had been captured in a prize, she roguishly informed Captain Flinders—Madame Chazal was a very delightful hostess, and her husband a painter of no mean talent. Once they had lived in England for a little while—and loved it. Their thousand-acre plantation was crammed full of scenic beauty, their library of good books, and their hearts with a tactful sympathy. The Rivière des Tamarinds, with its sparkling waterfalls and the green amphitheatre of its valleys, were his to explore at any moment —and more.

Tamarinds held the secret that was to be his solace and his torment for five long years. Wandering the upper reaches of the peaked hills above Vacois, he found it quite by accident. He was climbing a cliff, for a nearer view of a wizened and grey-headed parrot that croaked to him from the bough of a dead tree, when there it was, leaf-fringed in loveliness—a distant panorama of the sea. He could see for nearly three-quarters round the compass—on a clear day, practically the whole coastline of Ile-de-France, and all its outlying islands, dots in the blue! Matthew Flinders held his breath. Could it be true? Here he could watch for the sails of his salvation. There was a white triangle on the southern horizon even now. Who knows, it might be a ship from France with dispatches for his release?

He decided to say nothing to the Chazals. If Decaen should somehow learn that the spy had found a lookout, those two poor leagues of tether would be shortened.

"Come again!" they cried to him at parting. "Come again, and we will take you to the Cascades."

"I shall indeed, my friends," he told them. "I shall come so often, I promise you, that you will tire of me."

17

Lotus Lilies and Dreams

In pelting rain the d'arifats arrived, a procession of palanquins and noisy negroes, hurly-burly of band-boxes and carpet-bags from their annual orgy of shopping in the seaport.

Madame, serene as ever, was a little reserved, he thought. Delphine greeted him with a demure nod, and told him he looked much better. Sophie and Lise, innocent of English, took refuge in pleasant smiles, while Marc and Aristide, home for the holidays, disappeared with a whoop for the great outdoors weather permitting or not.

Labauve, a half-brother by a former marriage, with curly gold moustaches and a vociferous manner, had come to manage the plantation for his mother. He seemed a bluff good sort.

"Me, I have been prisoner of war with your General Vashon," he said. "The Engliss, they have not treat me too bad."

Matthew withdrew like a hermit-crab into the seclusion of his pavilion, to give them time to settle down. From shyness, he gracefully refused an invitation to dinner. Later in the evening, Madame herself came, to inquire as to his health and his comfort, to suggest renovations and alterations, and to proffer the loan of an escritoire.

Her bearing was still very kindly, but she was not at ease. Apparently the desire, and at the same time the reluctance, to speak of something that dangled at the back of her mind, kept her dallying, her coruscating fingers busy with this and that. His quick intuition sensed some difficulty, and when, in leaving, she wheeled upon him with a direct question, he was not surprised.

"Monsieur le capitaine Flandare, you are not a spy? You seek not to know this isle to our betraying?"

A deliberate pause, and then, "Madame," he replied slowly, "I am the commander of a ship of science that seeks knowledge of all the world for the good of mankind."

She seemed pleased with the answer. "You 'ave some papers that per'aps prove to me — ?"

"I have nothing to hide."

He produced a duplicate of his passport, the second volume of his log-book lying open on the table, of which he was then making a fair copy, his charts, his diaries, all that she might wish to see. He unlocked his trunks and his sea-chest, and the private doors of his bureau. He knew that she did not read English easily. She might carry away any of his papers to the house, he said, and submit them to any friend who could translate, now or at any time. He feared no discovery.

Madame d'Arifat was not the type to be caught with chaff. She promptly packed up a goodly bundle that she gathered herself at random, taking him at his word.

"You will forgive, monsieur, this so bad hospitality, which still lives, believe me, in Ile-de-France. But I am patriot. I love my country. In Port Louis I hear what shakes not my trust, but of which I must be without doubt. You will comprehend?"

Matthew bowed his head. He understood.

The papers were returned within the hour by Alain, her *homme de confiance*. Few of them had been opened. He winced and forgot the incident. When they met, there were no longer reservations.

With a boyish enthusiasm he entered into their interests and recreations. It was the first time in years, in his whole life perhaps, that he had been free of responsibility, with the gaiety of young people about him, and time and inclination to share it.

He ate heartily, slept well, lived one day at a time, forever in hope of the freedom it might bring.

The d'Arifats were not wealthy people, and rather than baldly offer money for his board, he declined at first a standing invitation to *déjeuner* and dinner. For a month or more he ate his meals in solitary state. Prepared in the bungalow kitchen by Elder, and carried down by the blackamoors, it meant confusion and inconvenience in the wet weather. At last common sense straightened him up. He suggested to Madame that he should bring himself and 40 dollars a month to their table, for joys of association and French conversation, as well as to save time and trouble.

Madame accepted with a smile of satisfaction. She was a frugal soul.

Three cracks of old Peter Solomon's whip, calling the slaves into the fields, awakened him at daybreak, and the first eyllow sunlights slanting through the slats of the blind brought Elder with his morning coffee. A joyous plunge into his little river, a sun-bath beside it, and he was ready for breakfast with the family.

Charts and journals were a labour of love through the forenoon, French and English studies, with Delphine and Sophie and Lise—and sometimes Maman herself, nobly renouncing her siesta—in the afternoon.

Lise, with her winsome face and waddling gait, was the prettiest and most lovable of the sisters, Sophie a home-keeping heart, never so happy as when making pastries in the kitchen, lists in the pantry, or mothering the piccaninnies down at the cabins. Lise and Sophie were forever laughing, Delphine a pensive miss, with a disconcerting habit of lacing her long white hands under her chin, and fixing him with a direct and slightly-amused intentness, just when he was vainly endeavouring to reconcile to them such anomalies as "cough", "tough", "slough", "thorough" and "lough", or foundering badly, in his turn, among the French subjunctives. Those dark eyes kindled old fires.

The only one with the wanderlust, an intelligent girl was Delphine. She loved to listen to his travel stories, told, ludicrously enough, in both languages, groping with him for the right word when his French or her English failed. There was a fish-pond in the garden—his rain-guage incidentally—a stone cherub in the centre and water-lilies floating, the dry leaves sequined with raindrops in the showers. The French called them *songes*, and remote and virginal as the lilies of dreams they were. The bulbs, they said, were a deadly poison.

There they would sit occasionally, while he picked out the brighter bits and pieces from the kaleidoscope of his journeyings to entertain her, enjoying her girlish wonder and incredulity. Quite often her quick knock on the door of his pavilion, with this or that message or invitation, brought ten minutes of pleasant distraction. Always he had some small treasure to show her—the fading leaves of that prehistoric New Holland vegetation, colourless yet strangely vivid, fifteen hundred million years old yet new to botanical science, that were pressed in the back of his letter-book, the stencils of his charts, or a handful of shells he had gathered from the reef of the shipwreck.

As she bent over them so attentively, in the light of the open shutter, he noticed the copper burnish of the coils of her hair, and its tendrils on the curve of her cheek. Disturbing things, women. It made him restless at night, and deepened the "delicious misery" of remembering Ann.

He reflected that he had not told her, nor indeed any of them, that among his other griefs was a beloved wife in England, so sadly awaiting his return. He was afraid that among these emotional Frenchwomen, the scene would become too poignant, and oblige him to retire. So deeply was he indebted to them for their kindness, for their untiring efforts to beguile away his sorrows, that he had no desire to pile on the agony with sentimental interest. Besides, it was always difficult for him to speak of the things nearest and dearest to his heart.

In the lambent light of late afternoon, they all walked out together on this or that excursion through the plantation. The primitive industries of the slaves were a never-ending source of enlightenment. He watched them picking and seeding cotton, marrying by hand the male and female flowers of the vanilla orchid, crushing sugar-cane and boiling the juice to set into brown crystals, grinding the maize between two stones, sifting it, sacking the fine flour, bagging the husks for the hogs. Shelled from the soft white cobs, the creamy young corn was sent up to the house, where it made a nourishing cereal, tastier than rice with the spicy creole curries. This sweet corn, as they called it, had possibilities. He wished that he could ship a few of the blackamoors over the ocean to demonstrate the methods and the recipes in "our little colony at Port Jackson", still hungry, and so often in his thoughts.

He pitied these poor wretches of negroes, labouring in the heat at the whip's end, for a daily mess of arrowroot or rice, and meat once a week. They were penned in the cabins like animals, breeding more slaves. Some were white-headed old women, some mere children, and some strong men mutilated in the triangles, but the majority were light-hearted Samsons and Delilahs whose only sorrow was their lost homeland. New Holland, bad as it was, would never be a slave country.

One afternoon Labauve carried him off to watch them unravel the mysteries of the laundry blue-bag, one of life's commonplaces he had taken for granted. The slaves collected the indigo-plants, stalks, leaves and budding flowers, packed them into a cask and filled it up with water, two or three large stones on top to keep the plants submerged. In about twenty hours, they had fermented. The water, a sickly yellow, was drained off, and the greenery thrown away. Then the cask was washed out, the indigo water returned to it, and vigorously churned, in exactly the same way as butter. Gradually it changed to cerulean blue, growing darker and darker. A little dissolved lime segregated the particles to the bottom, while the liquid deepend from light Madeira colour to a turgid bull red—all the pigmients of a painter's palette in the leaves of one inconsiderable shrub! After draining and straining, the heavy blue mud at the bottom of the cask was put through a hair-sieve, shovelled into bags, squeezed clear of moisture in the pressing tube, and dried to a bright blue clay, ready to be cut into squares.

A simple process, it pleased Matthew. All knowledge was grist to his mill, and both the vanilla vine and the indigo shrub would grow in the north of Australia. If he were ever governor there—but what was the use of planning?

On another afternoon, he met the Clouves *en famille*, out for an airing. Aimée and Amélie sat up on asses in the vanguard, Madame and the little sisters in palanquins, with M. Boistel walking alongside. A retinue of slaves jogged after them, carrying lanthorns and umbrellas.

The two young ladies blushed between their schoolgirl plaits, frantically trying to keep their coats down over their ankles. The picturesque cavalcade delighted him, and he stood looking after it, considering it a fair specimen of the manner in which the gentry of the island paid visits.

"The girls this time had stockings on, and for what I know drawers also," Matthew remarked at supper with a twinkle in his eye, "for on their jibbing donkeys they certainly had need of them. I longed for the brush of a Hogarth to picture the droll scene."

"Do you ever," asked Mademoiselle Delphine, "regard men and women as living people, Monsieur Flandare, or are we but *illustrations scientifiques*, the natives of the country?"

His earnest brown eyes looked into hers. "Ah no!" he replied. "There are men—and women—in this world for me vitally alive."

She flashed him a coquettish glance of gratitude, but his eyes no longer held hers, and his thoughts had wandered.

He had wickedly neglected the Clouves since the d'Arifats came back, but they bore him no malice, and renewed their invitations to whist on Sundays.

The sabbath was a colourful day, mass-bells ringing in the early morning, the arrival of the dear old Abbe Flageolet from Mocha, mounted, like his Master, on an ass, with palm-leaves waving before him. He was bound for a flower-decked oratory on one or other of the plantations, leading a gay parade of planters and slaves from all the others, to the swinging of censers and the singing of hymns.

But scarcely was the odour of sanctity dissipated in that

light air, and the *curé* on his homeward way, sprinkling with holy water and blessings the woolly heads of the little black ruffians that followed him shouting, than those carefree creoles spent the rest of the day in gaiety and sport and music, and, what amused good Church of England Matthew most, cards till a rowdy midnight.

They watched the New Year in to the hollow, haunting rhythm of tambourines and tom-toms, and a wild African orgy, where Jezebels in grass skirts, their heads elaborately greased and curled, danced and sang in a saturnalia of sex the whole night long. Next morning was slaves' holiday. In a long procession they came to wish Maman *bonne année*, to receive their presents of beads and scarves and cheap rum and tobacco, and then to set out to other orgies in the hills and valleys. Some of them walked ten leagues in the day, rioted all night, and were back to answer the crack of the whip in the morning.

At home there was a festive dinner party. With a bashful courtliness, Matthew presented to each of the girls a fan, and to Maman a conch shell from Torres Strait.

In the afternoon he borrowed Labauve's horse, and set out for M. Airolle's plantation on the Bourbon road, on an excursion that was to him a pilgrimage to a shrine. For there, he had learned from M. Plumet, the Comte de Lapérouse had lived and loved thirty years before, with the beautiful Elénore Broudou, who became his comtesse only to mourn his memory.

A schooner bell hung in the pandanus by the gateway. In Matthew's hero-worship, there was a sacred peace in that beautiful old-world garden, a living presence in that quiet air. He bared his head in homage to that noble navigator, far above national enmities and emulations, who had given his life for science, and followed the light of the southern stars—into oblivion. What reef in the blue Pacific, what rude shore where savages roamed, would yield the secret of those ghostly ships, forever sailing on in the unknown?

"In this spot he once dwelt, remote from the world but happy. When he became great and celebrated, he ceased to exist." Life's irony. So ran the wistful tenor of his thoughts.

Before he left, M. Airolle, a little surprised at the Englishman's enthusiasm, promised him that he would set up a cairn of stones there to hallow the retreat for all time, to the glory of Lapérouse, of Ile-de-France, and of France.

M. Plumet was entertaining some naval visitors as he passed by. He was half-hesitant to intrude when one of the guests turned and greeted him with a salute.

Tall, bronzed and smiling, he was Charles Baudin of the *Géographe*—no, no relation to the commander, but he remembered Captain Flinders very well, remembered the meeting on the south coast of New Holland, the *Investigator*'s boats hauling them through Port Jackson heads when they came in, a stricken ship, and the brotherly love in the tents by the Farm Cove. He had been only a midshipman then. Now he was Ensign Baudin of the *Piédmontaise*.

With an unholy joy Matthew pegged him to his seat with a thousand questions. What of the *Géographe* when she sailed from Port Jackson? What had she learned? What charts had she made? Had she visited the north-west coast of New Holland? Was there an opening there, a bay or a gulf that led to an inland sea, round about the Rosemary Isles perhaps? How far north had she sailed?

Well, said Charles, it was rather a vague journeying, but they had, of course, discovered a great deal, and written the immortal names of France on five thousand miles of coast. They had spent a little time at King Island, surveying with the *Casuarina*—she was in the harbour at Port Louis still, by the way—and then they crossed to Captain Flinders's Kangaroo, and anchored in the bay on the north side, to build a shallop. After that, they made on to King George's Sound, round the Leeuwin, and up the west coast again.

It was a perfect ship-trap of coral reefs and islands, in a tumult of tides rising thirty and thirty-five feet twice a day. They had had to steer fairly clear, but for one thing it was laid down in the old charts much too far west. They had found no trace of a gulf or bight cutting the continent in two, not in either journey. Still, it might be there. There were myriads of islands, and they had never hugged a shore so dangerous.

Péron and Leschenault had done good work—the ship was a veritable hothouse and menagerie; but so far as a connected and comprehensive chart—well, Flinders would see it, for Péron and Freycinet were writing the voyage now. The only ships they saw were the praus of the Malays, down fishing trepang. Provisions were short, and the commodore very ill, so when the north-west monsoon came in they made for Timor, and so to Ile-de-France, where Baudin died, and the expedition ended.

Flinders was secretly elated. There was still time, then. He liked this Baudin well. They clasped each other's hands in the beginning of a warm friendship when he rode away into the black of a gathering storm.

That north-west coast. He must go back. For all the aching of his loneliness, for all his need of Ann, there should be no return to England till he knew. He could not leave things half done.

Discovery and his love, the old dilemma—the breath of unknown shores, or a woman's kiss, which would he choose if they set him free to-morrow? Alas, he had lost them both.

The gentleness and the green beauty of Wilhelm's Plains gave courage and a philosophic patience. He decided to try Decaen again, and wrote that night. Surely the man, if he was a man, must have his human moments. New Year was the season of French goodwill.

To His Excellency Captain-General Decaen,
        Governor in Chief, ... Ile-de-France.
Sir—

I have waited quietly and most anxiously, with hope of my situation being remembered. Grant my request to be sent to France.

The intentions with which I came to this island may have been misconstrued, but I can lay my hand on my heart and aver that I designed no injury to any nation or government or individual. It was but a relieving the present necessity, and to acquire a knowledge of the Isle of France, for the advantage of geographical and nautical knowledge, and for the benefit of those nations of miserable savages I propose hereafter to visit.

Do not, sir, deprive me of the best years of my life, ruin my hopes of advancement, and of acquiring a reputation by my labours.

Do not keep me an unlimited time from my family who for years have been looking for my return to rearrange their affairs and to console them for the loss of a father.

Think, General, it is possible that I may be innocent. What I have already suffered will then excite your regret. You will hasten to send me where, if I am found innocent, a few days will be sufficient to restore me to my family, and the continuance of my peaceful employment, and if guilty, speedy punishment would at least be the end of the anxiety, the expectation and the disappointment that my mind has been tortured with in the past twenty-seven months.

Justice speedily administered is an act of mercy even to the guilty, but how much more to the innocent? If ever, in a carelessness of prosperity, I thought lightly of this adage, the last two years of my life have most fully convinced me of its truth.

> Thy prisoner,
> MATTHEW FLINDERS.

No answer.

Floods and hurricanes lashed the island. The rivers rose. Every gully became a raging torrent. Le Refuge was cut off completely from the town highroad, and from its neighbours. Bridges and cabins were swept away, the slaves swimming for safety, and rowing across the lower fields to work. The plantation stream was a cataract, the bungalow rain-sodden through, its curtains dank with mildew, water dripping from the roofs. His little pavilion, thickly thatched with millet, was the only dry sleeping-place on the *habitation*. He offered it to Maman for the family, but she refused. They were quite used to this, she said. It happened every year.

Skies cleared, the floods went down, but the maize crops were ruined.

Crippled with rheumatism, his crutch in the corner, the whimpering Smith was fading away. As soon as the donkey-boys could get through to Port Louis, Matthew sent a letter to Monistrol, asking for the old man's release. Again the gentle Elder refused to leave.

Matthew had accomplished an enormous amount of work on his charts, finished a very rough draft of his Voyage so far as his papers allowed him, and sent more letters across the world pleading his plight. He was overdue for a little recreation when, in the first spell of fine weather, Edouard Pitot and Captain Bergeret rode up from town, and there was a general exodus from Le Refuge to a house-party at the Tamarinds.

Would he ever forget that journey, the cassias and the poinsettia yellow and red flame on the hills, the Persian lilac blue smoke in the gullies, with here and there a tall coco-nut queening it over the zamia-palms and sago-palms and fan-palms shimmering in the undergrowth?

Dwarf forests of bracken glittered like sunswept waves of the sea over height and hollow. The velvet-tree, its downy branches brushed to silver pile, breathed its cloying perfume. Ferns in the rocks were miniature trees in jade and jet, and every pool a glory of brilliant birds and butterflies, and the frail-winged *demoiselles*.

Labauve aimed at a monkey that the dogs had treed in a pittosporum. It shot clear out over the cliff, and forty feet down clutched at a white cedar, swinging for a plunge into the abyss. Matthew's shout of admiration saved the poor little ape from a second fatal shot, but Labauve was nettled.

He was even more nettled when, on a deer-stalking trip to Lake Vacois, this English captain, wool-gathering, lost him his bag. They had built a shooting-box on the shores of the Grand Bassin. Two black men were sent to circle the lake with guns and dogs, for the deer had a baffling trick of swimming off to the island in the centre when routed out. The dogs barked, the hunters holla-ed, and the quarry was away! Thrashing over the rocks they went, through the liana vines that tripped them, and clung to them, and tried to hold them back.

Labauve and Bergeret had the only horses, and Matthew on his unruly jackass was left behind. After some futile gyrations, he and Elder went back to the road. His musket propped against a stump, he was down on his hands and knees examining an ants' nest when there was a skirmish in the brush, and a splendid deer fled past them, into the forests on the other side.

Punctiliously he took up his rifle and murmured something unconvincing as Labauve, puffed red with anger and cursing his niggers, hove in sight. After hours beating round in the rain, he was outraged at such colossal carelessness, such treachery, but the jesting of the others at his expense, and a hearty meal back at the hut, soon put him in good humour.

A storm broke above them in torrents. Smoking the rank Ile-de-France tobacco, the three Frenchmen sat round the fire talking, Matthew prone on the mat at their feet, a child taking notes.

They talked of their hunting and their amours. As he knew nothing of one subject, and never made the other a topic of conversation, and besides spoke French very badly, he remained silent, contrasting their characters with those of three English men of the same class and type.

His conversation liberally bespattered with *bougers* and *sacrés* and *foutus*, Labauve bewailed the good old days before the Revolution, when the maroons and the mulatoos, hunting their meat regardless of restrictions, often brought in a buck weighing 450 pounds. The fiery breath of the Reign of Terror had blighted not only the flower of old French nobility, but the wild animals at the very ends of the earth. You never sighted such deer nowadays, with all these Republican soldiers stalking round.

Of their prowess with women, they left little to be imagined, telling their conquests and the method of them with a licentiousness and a levity that embarrassed him a little, sailor and all as he was, but after all, perhaps it was less objectionable than the sly lechery of certain countrymen of his.

Back at the *habitation*, they found the Chevreaus arrived. It was indeed a happy house-party. Tric trac and Bouillote, Blind Man's Buff and Schniff-schnoff-schnorum, all romping and *joie de vivre*, made merry the blossom-scented evenings. Music was the grace of each day's ending, Rossetti, and Haydn and Pleyel—Matthew's flute, a fluttering of sweet hollow wood-notes in tremolo and *appoggiatura* to the stately grace of Madame Chazal's harpsichord, impassioned cadenza of Pitot's violin, and Chazal plucking divine chords deep into his 'cello.

The Chevreaus had brought with them a young man named Charles Desbassayns, a visitor from Ile Bourbon, and a friend of Andrew d'Arifat. It was amazing how often, in the rollicking games, Charles managed to catch rotund little laughing Lise. He on his mare and she on her mule led all the excusions. In a weird and mysterious cave where a band of maroon bandits had been surprised and massacred, the leader's skull grinning a grisly greeting in the blackness, they were lost so long and so thoroughly that indulgent Maman was perturbed. The young man was the son of a well-to-do planter, and her Lise could hope for no marriage dot.

"That goes not," she explained to Matthew. "My little Lise must not be so foolish as to be serious."

On a dazzling morning they all set forth together, on horse and mule and donkey back, for a tour of the Cascades, in full flood and at their most impressive. Garlanded with tropic flowers, wreathed in filmy veils of glittering white, the Valley of the Tamarinds was a vision of bridal loveliness. Along the rough tracks, now winding through green grottoes velveted with moss and musical with many creeks, now perilously skirting the cliffs over a 500-foot drop, the noisy cavalcade of mules and negroes, top-hats and bobbing parasols, gradually resolved itself into twos and threes.

The lovers rode ahead. Matthew, Delphine and Edouard followed at a descreet distance. Next came Captain Bergeret, thrilling amiable Miss Sophie with the tale of his doughty deeds from Canada to Kamchatka, and then the planters, matrons and men, discussing the problems of their fields and affairs.

A good French mile off, they could hear the roar of the Grand Cascade, foaming down over the rocks for 120 feet, the great white beard of the father of waters in this playground of the dryads. Prodding with his mother's umbrella, Labauve poured forth a fountain of statistics, while Chazal guided Edouard Pitot, equipped with a brand new easel and paint-box for the occasion, to the vantage-points of an artist's delight. The lovers had taken a lover's walk into some sylvan glade.

Matthew, forever eager to explore, scrambled down over the rocks, Delphine, unasked but very welcome in his wake, taking both his hands and lightly leaping where the drop was steep, and leaning against the cliff, prettily flushed, fanning her damp curls with her hat.

An extraordinarily good companion was Delphine, possessed of a strength of mind and a degree of penetration that few men could boast—activity, industry, desire for information, she might have achieved much had she been born a man. Happy Delphine, that she did not hear the sequence of that thought. Where ignorance was bliss, her little feminine wiles were all allure.

Half-way down, deafened by the Wagnerian overture of the rapids, they found a track that diverged at a steep angle clear under the fall. It led to a wide cavern sheltered from the spray by a beetling ledge of rock.

Matthew was jubilant, Delphine apprehensive, but slipping and holding each other over the slimy stones, his strong right arm clinging to the wet lianas, they negotiated the last difficult snap in a pelting shower-bath, and climbing over a boulder, bobbed their heads and raced under the ledge to safety.

Before them now the cataract hung in a dense white curtain, translucent yet opaque, perpetual motion in seeming immobility. Delphine recklessly peered over the edge to where the dizzying vortex, seething and billowing and boiling a hundred feet below, was miraculously subdued in an instant to the tranquil silver of the river. With a word of warning, Matthew drew her back.

So deep and cool was the cave, and so thick its walls, that one could hear and speak. Here and there a fern gleamed in a chalky drift of sunlight. With childish glee in the triumph of their adventure, they sat upon the dry stony floor, hands clasped about their knees, mesmerized by the diamanté sparkle of falling waters, the play of colours in the spindrift, and the martlets fearlessly wheeling in and out to their nests in the cliff.

An ideal listener in ideal surroundings—what more could man desire? He succumbed to his pet weakness of analysis

398

and philosophy, translating the infinite into the finite, measuring the moon. He leaned back on his elbow, and narrowed his eyes in thought.

"These cascades," he said, "are a fascinating study. They have opened for me new avenues of thought. A thousand, perhaps only a hundred years ago, there was but one great cascade at the mouth of the valley, but the rush of the water through crevices of the rock has caused many a fall and flow, diminishing the height and increasing the number of the streams. As the cut of the river became steeper, as the slopes became cliffs, the mountains could not retain the vegetable earth, which was washed into the valleys to raise them.

"Thus nature proceeds," he added quaintly, "in reducing all things to a level, as well in a moral as in a physical sense. The greater the inequalities are—the higher the mountains above the valley, or kings above other men—the more is a sudden fall to be feared and dreaded."

He turned and traced a pattern in the sand. "Which leads me to the vicissitudes—the changes, mademoiselle—of my own life. I was born in the fens of Lincolnshire, where a hill is not to be seen for many miles at a distance from the sea. My family were unconnected with sea affairs or any kind of enterprise or ambition. After many fortunes and adventures, I find myself a commander of the Royal Navy, charged with an arduous expedition of discovery.

"I have visited a great variety of countries, made three times the tour of the world, found my name known in more kingdoms than that in which I was born, with some degree of credit ... at this moment I am a prisoner in a mountainous island in the Indian Ocean, lying under a cascade in a situation very romantic, meditating upon the progress which nature is continually making towards a moderate degree of equality in the physical and moral world."

Soliloquizing in English, he might have been speaking to himself. Indeed he virtually was, for Delphine, who regarded him gravely, could barely manage to follow. His whimsical smile and sudden personal interest rewarded her.

"And," he finished up brightly, sitting erect, "in company with a foreigner, a Frenchwoman, whom I call, and believe to be, my friend."

"Romantic." "My friend." That was a language Miss Delphine understood, but that, being as yet unloved, rendered her slightly nervous. She murmured a sympathetic word or two, rose to her feet, and waited, pink with anticipation.

The commander in the Royal Navy rose too. He seemed to be struggling with words unspoken. He was. He wanted to say in French "The others will be wondering where we are," and he was wondering how the French would wonder. "*Etonner*" would not do. To Delphine's mortification he remained mute, and with commonplaces they clambered up the cliffs.

Poor Delphine, dreaming her dreams of this *si triste* young English sea captain, the foe of her country, some said, so strangely come into her life, Abelard to her Héloise—Delphine was plucking the water-lilies, the *songes*, with their floating roots bitter and useless.

They joined the party under the tamarind-trees, bustling round with the lunch-baskets. For Matthew it was a pleasant day unclouded, for Delphine, fraught with the stuff of a maiden's prayers.

Her castles were rudely shaken on the eve of their leaving. The Chazals gave a ball, and the Clouves girls rode over. Matthew ventured to waltz, with Delphine, for the first time—shocked and delighted at himself, at the tempting curve of her breasts so generously revealed in the Beauharnais manner, and the high vaulting of these French dances after the mincing decorum of the English. Her nearness bewildered him a little, stimulated his pulses. After his long celibacy, the soft yielding weight of a woman in his arms was so intimate that it seemed a caress. He flushed with nervousness, and blamed the heat.

"What, then, do you think of us, dear enemy?" she asked very softly, standing beside him as he mopped his brow in the fragrant frangipanni shade, under the bright moon. "It is that we compare with your English beauties, no?"

"Ah, so truly charming," he answered, according to the book. His tone changed. "You know, mademoiselle," he continued briskly, "I have been thinking ever since I came—A great pity I cannot transport you all, you, Sophie, Lise, and the very estimable little Clouves ladies, away to my Port Jackson. There fine men with true hearts are awaiting such women as you, with wealth and honour to offer in years to come, and broad lands that will by your own. Here, in Ile-de-France, are many more women than men, but you would not long remain unmarried there, I promise you."

With a little "zut!" of dismay, she fled to the ballroom.

"Lise! Amélie!" she cried. "My partner, Captain Flinders! He would ship us all to Port Jackson, to become the wives of convicts, to be sold like a cow!"

"Over my dead body!" declaimed Charles Desbassayns, with "business" of a sword. "Lise, at least, I have saved from this terrible fate, for we would tell you. Lise and I"—taking her hand—"we are betrothed."

In the gay chorus of congratulation that followed, for all her calcium shell of wit and raillery, Mademoiselle de'Arifat was not in good humour.

They frolicked and flirted with abandon till the small hours, far more alluring and provocative than English girls would dare to be, yet next day, when Matthew and Edouard Pitot offered their escort to Delphine and Amélie riding home, it was curtly and primly refused, on the grounds of propriety.

"These same young ladies who danced with naked bosoms before the whole society, fear to be seen with two young men of their acquaintance in broad daylight!" Matthew wrinkled his brow. Truly morals were a matter of geography.

On the way back, Labauve met an old soldier from the Black River, who gave them the news that there was an English ship offshore, and others close following, across from India. There were alarming rumours that the British had taken the Cape. Decaen had marshalled two thousand black gunners, and the island would fight for its life.

18

The English Mail

No longed-for letters were waiting on his dusty pavilion table, as he had fondly hoped through all the gaiety—only a few foreign journals and a Steele's Navy List that Thomy had sent up.

He lit the candles and opened an American newspaper. Wars, rumours of wars, and a mutilated world.

Napoleon was the nightmare of Europe. He had turned the continent inside out, and scrawled his name across it in letters of blood. Frontiers had gone down like fences before the bull-rush of his armies. Crowned heads were fallen, flat and foolish as a pack of cards, and now he was handing out thrones and kingdoms to his brothers—was there a satanic humour in his madness? Louis Bonaparte was king in Holland, Jerome Prince of Westphalia, Joseph emperor of a ruined land and a starving people in Spain, Lucien lording it in the mantle of the Caesars—a family of Corsican fishermen with all the nations of the earth floundering helpless in their haul. The Pope of Rome had been whipped by the heels to Fontainebleau, and 45,000 French troops and 200,000 Turks were scourging their way into Russia. Napoleon himself was at Boulogne, planning the invasion of England. Vanity of vanities, slaughter and insanity and hate!

Matthew realized that he was not a pawn in the game. These bloody wars and devil-dances left the French government no time to consider the rights and wrongs of a solitary Englishman ten thousand miles away. His own government did not seem to care. What was an out-of-date passport with mighty empires at death-grips The world was watching one man.

He turned to Steele's List—of men and ships known and unknown to him, and sat up suddenly with an electric surprise.

H.M.S. *Investigator!* At Plymouth! What was this?

She must be a new ship. Was she coming here, in charge of Mr Fowler or his brother, that he might continue his voyage? Or would some other officer reap the rewards of his labours, while he was left to eat his heart out in prison? He called Elder and showed him the item. What could it mean?

The man shook his head blankly. "How could I tell, sir?"

Elder was more lugubrious than ever. With a dogged, lower-middle-class bigotry, he loathed the French. He had been brought up to do it, and he did it well. To him they were frogs, cold-blooded and slimy. He could never see reason. He could not even be polite to the simple people about him. His lean face was draped with the misery of toothache.

"Very well, Elder. We're sure to know in time."

The man set out his soft white shirt and homespun coat with a sniffle. They did not dress for dinner at Le Refuge, which was just as well, for Matthew's small-clothes were at the bottom of the sea, and in spite of poor Elder's care the uniform was a libel on Mr Schweitzer.

The gong rang. He went up to the bungalow and ate his meal. All the bluff camaraderie of Bergeret, Labauve and Edouard Pitot, Maman's geniality, Delphine's sallies at his expense, the eagerness of the boys to hear more of the cave of the skull, and the glowing happiness of Lise and Charles brought no more than a monosyllable. His thoughts were elsewhere.

The *Investigator*! Never the old ship. She had died in his arms, and King had signed the death certificate. No commander would risk a company in taking her home. It must be a new one. But why give it that name, unless … he would not hope yet, but Banks was powerful, and Banks was his friend. It may be that he was already free, with a new ship on the way! Still … scarcely in wartime… .

There was a dog howling on a neighbouring plantation all through the night, howling like a damned soul, impaled on a red-hot pitchfork in the kindly old abbé's incredibly fiendish hell. A howling dog, tidings of death, they said. What if Sir Joseph should die? Then would he be quite friendless at court. Or Ann? … but that way lay madness.

What was happening in England since those year-old journals were published? Had Bonaparte already landed? No. Bad news travels apace, and these hysterical Frenchmen would be crowing.

Where was Samuel? No mention of him in the Navy List. Perhaps he had never reached home. He had hoped to do so much for Sam, and the boy had fought him every step of the way. He was good at heart, but he needed guidance. That sullenness, that wall of defiance, even impudence, in his eyes, when authority galled. He had had to be harsh at times to bring him to his bearings, and Sam had taken it as humiliation. Could he not understand that it was because he loved him, wanted to see him above them all? Surely he did not resent it now, knowing his brother's fate. If he did know.

British ships round the island. Perhaps Decaen expected this from the beginning, and kept him as a hostage. What did Sir Joseph think of him?—a fiasco, a poor fool caught in a trap? Aken must have arrived by now, unless he had been shipwrecked, with all those charts and journals? For the first time in his life, he hated the sea.

The dog howled on, shrilly, spasmodically, as though it were bitten by scorpions, and Matthew tossed on a humid pillow in self-inflicted tortures no less terrible, of fears, and forebodings, and self-reproach. Wide-eyed he lay till daylight, and rest he could not find. The sun slanting on the banana-palms, the morning cool of his little river, and the merry racket of the negroes—they could be happy in their slavery and exile—

banished those adders of the darkness, gave him courage to face the day with a sigh and a smile.

Elder was as worn and haggard as he, full of maledictions. That dog, he said, was deliberately starved to make it savage, and chained there to keep the monkeys out of the corn. It was vicious cruelty, and just what you might expect. He would go over in the evening and free the miserable brute. Matthew cautioned a wiser course, and spoke to Maman. She sent a boy across with a message. The next night was silent ... and just as full of ghosts.

Bergeret had a long talk with him before he left, one leg swung lazily over the arm of his rattan chair, a pipe of peace between them in those Jamaican cigars of his that were part of the booty of a prize — "more yours, my friend, than mine," said the captain with a wink.

Bergeret scouted the self-reproaches. "Nothing to do with you personally," he said. "Fortunes of war. You must wait. The best brains of France and England are fighting your battle, men like Bougainville, Fleurieu, Linois, and Banks. It cannot be long now. Why, Fleurieu told them that the indignities you have suffered are without parallel in the nautical history of civilized nations. All we need for the order of your release is the Emperor's seal — but catch the Emperor!

"Spy? No. Not even Decaen believes that. You might know a bit too much. So far as disclosing it ... well, I'm ready to back you with my honour as a captain of the French Navy. I am leaving for France. Give me all the letters and papers you want delivered, and I'll get them across to England. If there's anything traitorous in them, I'll face the firing squad with you."

Burning the midnight oil, Matthew took him at his word. Another batch of those tragic letters was ready by morning, pleading, promising, despairing, demanding, crying for help. To Sir Joseph he expressed grave fears for his well-being — surely, otherwise, he would have written by this. The rough draft of the introduction to his Voyage was completed. He would send it along by the first conveyance, but conveyances were rare.

He was very diffident about the literary style.

It will require to be put into the hands of some skilful writer, under whose pen and with such appropriate notes and reflections in addition as would present themselves to a well-informed mind, it may become a work of interest to the public of all civilized nations. Should you not be able to do anything with it, it will remain for the few who interest themselves in my fate.

He longed to go back to the north-west coast of Australia, where the French had missed their magnificent chance of getting in before him. So keen was he for exploration for that beloved unknown land that he proposed an expedition overland, from Carpentaria to Spencer's Gulf, with a few men and five or six asses!

"That you may long live," he concluded, "a patron to science, and such of its followers who need your assistance."

How sadly did he.

To Bergeret he could not express his gratitude. "You know, my dear sir, should the account of my Voyage ever be published, one of the first impressions shall be yours."

When the three men rode away, despondency fell upon him. The war was closing in, his own people the foe, feared and hated more every day. He stayed in his little pavilion re-writing, re-calculating, trying to concentrate in the good work that lends wings to lagging hours. But so much was missing now that everywhere he came to a dead end.

The novelty had worn off the colourful plantation life. The dry season had set in, and the freshness was gone from the forests. Thomy was away in Ile Bourbon. Chazal and Chevreau he rarely saw nowadays—why?

In the Valley of the Tamarinds the music of the cascades was no more than a reedy trickle. At every possible opportunity, though it was a wearying trail there and back in the day, he slipped away to the crests of the cliffs above Vacois, to stare in a dream, eyes pale with sleeplessness, at the far-off vacant sea. Sometimes there was the joyous flash of a sail, but all his conjectures, all his hopes, were futile and unanswered. No letters came from Port Louis.

His dejection was only too apparent. The French lessons with the girls had lost their lightsomeness, because his English pride made him feel an outsider. When Delphine knocked at his shutter now, he was always busy, remote. She brought him flowers for his desk. He thanked her, and laid them aside, and went on with his work.

In the evening walks for exercise he preferred to be alone. No more they sat beside the water-lily pond. More often she was to be found in the oratory of Our Lady at the bottom of the garden, her tearful gaze fixed on his pavilion, his name on her lips in prayer. Something had come between them, she felt sure. Had she shocked him with her dancing, that night at Tamarinds? Or with her dress—but it was sweet, a model of the Empress's own, the modiste in Port Louis had said so. La Robe Joséphine, he called it, and it had cost all the money she had saved from her little allowance. Surely a naval man … but these English were so straight-laced. How she regretted that night. Perhaps she had destroyed his ideal. O Holy Virgin, restore to her his love! Had it ever been hers? Well, nearly. She was sure.

He came out on the doorstep to dry some ink in the sun. She finished her prayers in a rush, and passed him, shyly smiling. He wished her a pleasant good morning, but did not bid her stay.

One afternoon, at conversation lessons, they heard the ominous rattle of cannon far out at sea. *Sémillante* and *Bellone*, Labauve told them, attacking the British frigate *Pitt*.

More than ever, inaction galled. Matthew wrote a letter away, applying for the governor's permission to come to Port Louis for a few days, for access to certain papers. It was curtly granted, provided he took nothing away. Curtat and Troberville, of the *Société d'Emulation*, both asked him eagerly to stay with them, but Thomy wrote that he must be the guest of Madame Rouillard at Poudre d'Or—a charming place by the sea. The little lady received him affably.

The general was in the country, rejoicing at the birth of a son—there were some things in which the underling could triumph over the Emperor. It was quite true, he learned, that the British were in possession at the Cape. They had bought it, said Madame Rouillard, to persecute the French in the south. Troops under General Baird and Commander Horn Popham were in occupation there, and now four frigates, *Pitt*, *Cornwallis*, *Albion* and *Sir Francis Drake*, were cruising round Ile-de-France, a blockade. They seized and burnt the ships from France and India, even the little trading ketches from Madagascar. Her husband was not getting his official salary. The island was in a bad way. Hurricanes and floods had utterly ruined the maize and coffee crops this year. For three weeks there had been no white bread, and the slaves were starving. Wholesale famine and disaster threatened, if the tension did not lift. A bitter-sweet little hostess was Madame Rouillard, over her fine Madeira.

Colonel Monistrol kept him waiting three hours at the Residency. Of his affairs, as usual, no news. It was sixteen months since dispatches had come from France. They had had much trouble, Monistrol said casually, with prisoners of war escaping to the English ships. Ah well, fewer pensions to pay and fewer mouths to feed. They could well do without them.

Matthew glanced at him keenly. Was this a subtle suggestion? The aide-de-camp's face was more than ever a mask.

Bending over the cask of books and papers that had come from the *Cumberland*, bewailing the havoc that the rats had wrought, he pondered deeply that remark. Doubtless they thought him a dolt, so docile in his durance, when many a man less desperate had given them the slip. Or was it a trap? He could not go. He had given his word. He would never disgrace His Majesty's commission.

The next day, the excited shrieks of the servants called them all to the turret at Poudre d'Or. Just beyond the point, two English frigates were chasing a schooner from Madagascar, bringing in flour. Under close fire, she was racing dangerously near the reefs. She would break her back there, rather than be taken. Shrieks of encouragement, devout prayers for her salvation, and curses on the "*sale anglais*" were stifled into resentful whispers as they noticed the English guest among them, silent and apart.

A bark of guns, a drift of smoke, and the little ship heeled madly round the point. The tide was high, but was it high enough? For one tense moment she grounded, then scraped across, safe in deep water and gathering speed. With a parting shot, the big ships turned and swung out to sea.

"*Sauvée! Elle est sauvée!*" cried Madame Rouillard. Her glance went straight to Flinders, with a triumph she could not resist. "How, sir? No pity for those who have offered you their hospitality? Nothing for that little ship that will allow us to give you good bread to-morrow? No?"

He bowed very courteously. "Pray excuse me, madame. I am, as you know, an Englishman. Besides, famine would lead your country to capitulation, and capitulation, believe me, is abundance for all of you."

Madame Rouillard's pale blue eyes seared him through. She dropped an ironic curtsey. "Thank you, monsieur le capitaine, but we in Ile-de-France will more happily eat the manioc of the slaves."

That made it uncomfortable at Poudre d'Or. Slights, real or imagined, were too many. The weekly gazette, always left in his room, cruelly lampooned and libelled his countrymen. Open insults of the flag-wavers were no more bitter to take than the voices tactfully lowered at his approach, the subjects so obviously changed in a hurry, the *faux pas* glossed over. Sometimes he thought they were deliberately taunting him, to trick him into retaliation, and have him put away again. It was natural. Their personal regard was as warm as ever, but the undercurrent of national enmity was too strong. It seeped away his confidence and made him feel guilty and inferior.

The flat tropic life of the seaboard, its climate and its cliques, were bitter to the taste. How he disliked the languid, neurotic women who came to tea, and prattled Voltaire, lightening their *ennui* with anaemic infidelities and small scandal. There was a little Madame Malherbe, an elderly

409

coquette with red hair, a poisonous woman who made a dead set at him—fluttering fan and slanted eyes, and *risqué* stories for his ear alone. A pity she scratched herself so much and so openly. In cleanliness, at any rate, the French could not crow over the English. He had seen many a Greuze and Romney sit down to breakfast without washing her face, and where were the perfumes of yester-eve in these Port Louis suns?

A jaundiced life, it seethed with petty spite. Newcomers of the garrison and the government treated the creoles as mulattos, and the creoles, *émigrés* of the true France, looked on them as Republican rabble. Society was a veneer to cover vindictiveness. He was glad to be gone.

The only truly wholesome greeting was that of his shaggy friend, Sergeant La Mêle, out at the Maison Despeaux, who gave him news of prisoners and prizes as frankly as though he were a Frenchman. Bonnefoy had landed himself in serious trouble by smuggling papers to the English prisoners. Matthew promptly put his hand in his pocket for a substantial remembrance.

Back at Le Refuge, he fought a deepening melancholia—and lost. A quivering sensitiveness made him visibly nervous. He was afraid of what they might be going to say, and more of what they left unsaid. Physical dangers he could endure and enjoy—breakers ahead, a gale howling in the rigging, or the menace of the unknown bush—with a gay exhilaration pitting himself against the tantrums of nature; but his own kind frightened him. The slightest imagined ridicule or hostility was agony.

So he shrank from all human contacts and despised himself in that he did. The gentle overtures of the girls he ignored, invitations he refused. The most innocent conversation was full of poisoned barbs, that struck home, and went deep, and gangrened. He knew he was wrong. How little, he thought, he was fitted for a public life, or even a respectable place in society. A broken reed. All faith in himself was gone.

"Build not upon me," he wrote to Samuel. "While still a young man, misfortunes have made me old."

Peace—or death—alone could release him. Had it not been for the dear ones in England, he would have welcomed death. Above all, he wanted Ann. She would understand, and heal, this illness of the mind.

In these women's voices about him, speaking a foreign language, he heard only hers. In Sophie's blue frock, he visioned her little flitting form. In Maman's bustling motherliness, he thought of hers denied, and in Delphine's sadness—the girl seemed strangely affected by his own—again he thought of hers. Lise in love was Ann in love. How easily he could read the signs, who once had been a lover, and beloved.

If Ann were here, all sorrow were forgotten. Decaen need have no fear. If only they would set him free, he would stay with her forever, ships and the sea forgotten. In some quiet corner of sunny security, they would know "the blessedness of being little". No care now of the north-west coast. Let someone else unravel its riddles. This chimera of ambition had carried him away from all that life held dear, the comfort of her comradeship, the softness of her lips. In his mad striving, he had put the seas between them, wanting to bring her back the map of a new continent, when all his need of happiness was to take her in his arms. What was achievement, what was fame, with Ann not there to share?

No word of her in five years. The thought of Ann, in poverty, in sickness, and he unknowing, uncaring, perhaps laughing with these French people in the Valley of the Tamarinds, was unbearable. Had all his letters miscarried? Did she believe him dead?

Gusts of sheer passion racked him, that increased rather than diminished with the years. One woman alone was his need. He possessed her in dreams. There was a time between sleeping and waking when her nearness seemed almost fulfilment. He awoke with a start, and found himself angrily groping for something that had but that moment gone. He tried to recapture the dream, but he was hungry, wakeful... .

At other times, phantom lovers, they haunted the old trysting places, the Big Oak at Partney, the Essex side of the

Thames, or more often sought together in that new land some hidden curve of sunlit beauty known to him alone. He could nearly hear the words she said, and feel the little flying tendrils of her hair blown across his face as he leaned to listen, but a great sea thundered on the rocks below them, wave after wave crashing in closer and swirling to their feet, and there was dusk and danger, and a long way to travel through the maze of the darkening scrub. Haste! Haste! and a guilty secrecy.

On a bright September afternoon, as she was gathering sprays of blue plumbago and white clematis for the Virgin's altar, Madame met him returning from a solitary walk. He would speak with her, he said.

She laid aside her garden scissors, and followed to his pavilion, perturbed to notice that his clothes and his books were packed, and his charts gone from the wall. She made no comment, and ensconced her ample self in the big rattan chair.

"You will see that I am about to leave you," he began. "I have taken the disused bungalow on the Périchon estate near by. There I shall live to myself, with my man, Elder."

"But why?" demanded Maman brusquely.

"Since the term of my imprisonment is still uncertain, I should like a house and table of my own."

Maman misunderstood, and was deeply hurt.

"We 'ave done our best, Monsieur Flandare," she said sadly. "It is 'ard times. The food is poor——"

"Ah *no*!" He made a quick gesture of denial, shocked at the construction she placed on his words. "Far from ingratitude or dissatisfaction, your kindness is indelibly engraved upon my heart. The fault lies not with you, but with me."

Maman waited patiently, drumming her ringed fingers.

"My weakness," he went on with difficulty, "must be apparent to you all. I cannot face the pity and contempt that I know it deserves. My bitter fate has made me but the travesty of a man."

He bowed his head in his hands to hide the twitching of his lips.

Maman rose, and took them away, and held them warmly in hers.

"Oh my son," she said very gently, "you 'ave much wrong. Why do you grieve and grieve? We live, we love, we fight, we die, so many of us it cannot so much matter. A change will come. So surely as flows the ebb-tide follows the full. I am much older than you. For long I have watched the tides to come and go. The past and the future, they do not touch me now. I live but for the people and the *bonheur* of to-day. That is life's wiseness … no?"

He braced himself. "When I return to England, all will be well," he told her.

"Who knows that you will return to England?"

"I shall return!" His determination was fierce, challenging.

"*Bien!*" she shrugged. "Then why not remember with some happiness the time when you were with us here?"

"I assure you, I shall remember with every happiness, thanks to you all, who have done so much for me."

"No. You are a man in chains. You whip yourself with rods. Ah, you English … you strive, and strive, and do not know to live. Listen, monsieur—you are young. Life has much to give, if you will take it. Fame if you cry for it, glory if you will die for it, but the love of a woman is more. Men cannot live without that, in content of body and soul?"

"I know," he said gently, and freed his hands.

"*Voilà!* There are women in Ile-de-France."

He cleared his throat, as though about to speak, and turned, instead, to strap up a valise.

"But you do not leave us," she pleaded, "to go with that man, your Eldare! *Ciel!* he make my skin to creep! He is forever peeping, forever has fear. Thinks he we are like your cannibals, we put him in the pot? Ach, he would be but sour eating, you tell him from me. You do not live alone with that cold frog? *Frog*, we call him. *Grenouille!* Ugh!" She shuddered in comic disgust. "He has nothing insides!"

With a wan smile, he rebuked her. "For five years he has been my faithful servant, my friend."

"The dog that howls in the corn at night, he too is faithful, and better company!"

"Company I do not need. I ask for solitude."

"But, monsieur, you grow bitter, inhuman."

"On the contrary, the love of mankind was never stronger in me, for I have never quitted persons more estimable than those from whom my evil destiny now compels me to depart. I cannot dim their brightness with my melancholy lot. My gloomy presence is a shadow on them."

"Then why shall you be gloomy?" smiled Maman. "If you go, they say we 'ave made you 'ate us."

"I have chosen an *habitation* as near to you as possible, and I shall come to see you as often as my sad thoughts will allow. I tell you I am a man accursed. My way is not yours, a path of gladness."

"Hm. Not so I see…. Ah well, what shall I tell them, Delphine and the girls, to whom you are so great a hero, our friends who care for you, the others who question?"

He pressed a throbbing temple. "Tell them that I am hiding from the world and from myself. Tell them that my imprisonment has undermined my reason. Tell them the truth— *that I am going mad*!"

His voice broke on a hoarse note of agony. Maman stood aghast. With boyish contrition he clasped her hands again.

"Forgive me! I hate myself when I cause you pain. To your goodness alone can I lay bare the torture of my mind. You see now why I must go—until I am master of myself."

A silence, then "*Eh bien*, as you will have it." She gathered up the flowers, and slowly descended the step. Her uneasiness, her obvious displeasure, were coals of fire on his head. It throbbed in fever. Distracted, he looked upon the untidy room, and threw himself upon his pallet, welcoming, longing for death, the only way out.

She had not gone. He heard her voice on the threshold, talking with someone, and she tapped on the lattice again. Wearily he rose—more arguments, more anguish, but——

"For you from Port Louis," she said. "There are letters from England, that must be delivered in my presence."

She handed him a large packet addressed in Pitot's handwriting, bound and sealed. He hurriedly snapped the cord.

Half a dozen letters fell to the floor. With shining eyes, he scrabbled among them like a schoolboy, and snatched at one with a small blue seal of the "Vue Prise du Pont Neuf". Fluent writing, and a woman's. He pressed it against his burning cheek.

"My wife!" was all he said.

"Aha!" said Madame d'Arifat, and left him.

They saw nothing of him that night. When Maman sent down his dinner by one of the mammies, it was scarcely touched. The candles guttered in their sockets, sending his gigantic shadow dancing on walls and ceiling, while he sat motionless, reading over and over the pages that blurred before his tear-filled eyes.

Ann!

Every pretty flourish of her quill was as her portrait, calling up a thousand blissful memories, bringing her very close. The letter was full of news, every atom she could give him, of herself, of the family, of what she could glean of him through Sir Joseph, but there were references he did not understand. Other letters must have gone astray. This was dated October 1805, and was a year old.

His sister Betsy was long ago dead, leaving a little son.

After a pilgrimage among friends in Lincolnshire, Ann was now at Donington, looking to the welfare of his two young stepsisters, soon to return to Partney and devote herself to her own, little Isabel Tyler, always a favourite of his. The affairs of his father's estate were so far satisfactory, though they could not be finalized until his return. With his naval income added, Ann rejoiced in the ample sum of £150 a year. That set his mind at rest. He had sent her copies of Thomy's letters, and his appreciation of his French friends was reflected in her warm and loyal heart. She was learning the language that she might be more at one with him.

"I admire the French letter very much," she wrote, "and highly esteem the generous writer. I shall always regard and esteem him for his kindness to thee." He must read that to Thomy.

His case had attracted much attention in England—she enclosed cuttings from the naval journals. It seemed there was no hope of promotion, either for him or any of his men, until his release. Sir Joseph had used every ounce of his influence with the National Institute in Paris, but so far no decision had been made.

There was some trouble about Samuel, and the letter from his brother, which he probed again and again, trying to read between the lines, could not clear it up. Samuel had retired from active service on the grounds of ill-health—he was living in Lincolnshire on half pay—yet Ann said nothing of such illness. It almost seemed they had quarrelled, so brief were the references to each other. Neither mentioned the new *Investigator,* nor any plans for the continuation of his voyage. If that should come to pass, Ann must apply to Sir Joseph for a passage, and join him here. In menace of war, or if she wished it, he could take her on to Port Jackson.

How he loved that place, with its banal name and its shameful people, dragging their chains in Arcady. Whenever he visioned his ultimate happiness with Ann, it was not in the Lincolnshire of their childhood, but with the scent of the bright Australian bush about them, begetting a son who would love and hold some earth of his father's finding.

In painfully painstaking calligraphy, there was also a note from Aken, happier reefing a royal than penning a screed. But he had seen Sir Joseph, and Sir Joseph fully approved his conduct. How exactly? In making out the charts and sending them, or with regard to General Decaen?

There was no letter from Sir Joseph.

Aken said nothing of the men—they deserved much, those men of the *Cumberland*, game to challenge the winds of the world in a ship that size. Hell it had been, and purgatory at the end of it, reversing the usual order, according to these good French Catholics. He had noticed that they were caulking and coppering the *Cumberland* in Port Louis, but he dared not hope they would give her back. God, if they let him go, he would take her home alone!

In the *habitation* parlour, Maman and the girls were bent above their embroidery.

"I have discovered," said Maman out of a blue sky, "that our friend Monsieur Flandare is married."

Delphine went white to the lips.

"You know," said Lise, "I have always felt that there was something, some deeper reason that he stays alone."

"Why?" drawled Sophie.

"Because, otherwise, there would have been one of us."

"It is infamous!" burst out Delphine.

"Why?" drawled Sophie again.

"That he should not have told us."

"He does not have to tell us. We are to him, at the bottom of his heart, enemies who have surprisingly proved to be flesh and blood, rather than a background sinister to Napoleon Bonaparte, the right hand of the devil."

"To him we have been open in all things," said Delphine passionately. "He sees our lives, he keeps his own hidden. It is not just. When we have accepted him."

"A wife is there for all the world to know," put in Maman.

"Wife! Ha!" cried Delphine with extraordinary malice. They looked at her with arrested needles. "A sailor! It may be that he has another in Port Jackson. He is so much in love with that beautiful harbour." She packed up her tapestry with blazing eyes, and took herself off to bed.

"Aha!" said Maman, for the second time that night. Lise and Sophie exchanged glances. They all understood.

"Ah well," said Maman. "The tides. They come and go. It is time for supper, Sophie. Will you call Angélique?"

19

Wasps' Nest

A red flag on the signal hill in the morning—yet another enemy had been sighted offshore.

Trafalgar had gone to Britain's head. She would sweep the French from the seas. Every captain in the Navy was a Nelson unfulfilled, and whenever he saw a French ship, he primed his guns and rammed her. Now that they had the Cape as a base, they would clear the way to India, and the only obstacle in it was Ile-de-France.

No tidings of Trafalgar had trickled through the stone wall of French propaganda either at home or abroad, and Decaen, on his rocky citadel, was playing a lone hand. So long as nobody knew it was bluff, he might win through till Napoleon had England under his heel. He was all over the island at once, with stamping regiments and gangs of sweating slaves, fortifying the ports, building ramparts and bridges, spending every penny he could lay his hands on in defence, and crying for more, that never came.

There was no hope of men or money from France—the Emperor needed them both in desperation, and even if he had sent them out, they never could get through. Very few of the ships carrying dispatches made harbour at Port Louis, or got out of it far alive. Lying in wait for Linois's fleet, Pellew's cruisers were circling, pouncing, and carrying off prizes. It was much more ruinous to trade and tranquillity than the blockade of a season. It dawned on Matthew that if an order for his release had been given, it was probably burnt to cinders or sent to the bottom by his own people.

He spent the early hours unpacking, and came up to breakfast with the first real smile they had seen. Relief had brought a little content, and the suspense was gone from his face.

How charmingly they congratulated him upon his felicity, how sweetly curious they were. Was Ann dark or fair, small or tall? how long had they been married? how many children?—and how touchingly romantic they found the tale of his leaving her there as a bride. Only Delphine had nothing to say, although she listened eagerly enough. There seemed to be something mocking in her manner—but no, that surely could not be. She was his best friend of all. She left very shortly afterwards, on a visit to relatives at Le Flacq.

Both the Chazals and the Chevreaus were rejoicing in recent additions to the family—that explained their recluseness—and there was a round of innocent dissipations, in which Matthew joined with a will. Curtat carried him off to the Quartier de Saint-Louis to dine with some French soldiers at the house of M. Défait—a send-off to Flinders's very good friend, Ensign Charles Baudin, who was ordered back to France. He ate much, drank more, laughed a good deal and forgot his woes.

Out on sketching excursions with Chazal, he dabbled in art and thoroughly enjoyed himself for a while with the brush and colours. He played duets with Madame, and whist and tric trac with the boys and girls, and joined them in long walks. Exercise and exhilaration soon braced his mind for more serious studies, and if that "mortal sadness" were a dead weight on his heart, he could banish it from his countenance, and sometimes from his thoughts. But he still watched from the lookout.

The little *Société d'Emulation* was in session over at Mocha, and in this he acquired a very active interest. He wrote them a paper on the geophysical features of New Holland, and was much amused when his phrase "peaked hummocks" baffled their powers of translation and their dictionaries. Troberville was compiling a history of one Ratsimala, an ancient negro chief of Madagascar, to be sent to Paris for publication. Matthew helped him with the maps of the island, accumulating whatever knowledge he could gather for his friend, and incidentally and on principle for himself. A long letter from Charles Desbassayns, Lise's fiance, telling him that Humboldt was busy with researches in the magnetism of the earth, stimulated his own. He noted with amusement that Charles's letter, from Ile Bourbon, was addressed from "Ile Bonaparte" and dutifully he himself referred to Port Louis as "Port Napoleon". Decaen, in his idolatry, had ordered the old Royalist names to be changed.

While the young ladies were busy with the trousseau of Mademoiselle Lise, he roped in Marc and Aristide to teach them trigonometry and the science of navigation, and even found time to design original geometrical patterns, frail and dainty as a cobweb, for the girls' embroidering. Every hour fully occupied was an hour of blessed forgetfulness.

A neutral ship from Hamburg called, and carried away a big batch of home letters, to his dear one, to his brother, Aken, Sir Joseph, Sir Edward Pellew in India, James Wiles in Jamaica, Christopher Smith in Pulo Penang, and Grimes, surveyor-general in New South Wales—all via America and England, and a year at least before they could be delivered, if ever.

For his small step-sisters, Hannah and Henrietta, he commissioned Ann to invest two guineas in music, "not songs only, but the best." There was a missive enclosed for Miss Isabel, a playful reproach in English and French telling her that

There is a report among the whales of the Indian Ocean that a letter from you had passed by for Port Jackson, and a flying fish in the Pacific even says that he saw it, but there is no believing these travellers.

If you will take the trouble to give it to me under your own hand, I will then believe that you have written to me … As I have a fund of

420

justice which will not permit me to exact from others what I would not perform myself, I do hereby certify that I have this day addressed a letter to my well-beloved sister Isabella Tyler, spinster, in which letter I do desire for her all manner of blessings, spiritual and temporal; that she may speedily obtain a husband six feet high, if it so pleases her, with the wishing-cap of Fortunatus.

A gay whimsical letter, written in heartbreak to interest and delight a little girl, Miss Isabel kept it forever, as well she might.

Ann's own epistles, he told her, marked the greatest epochs in his monotonous life. "I sigh for them as the most desired of blessings." With impassioned longing he sealed the envelope.

Happy letter! Happy seal! They will be received by thee with joy, perhaps receive a kiss. O that I were freed from the bond of my parole, and could as easily be transported to thee. Still, my beloved, entertain hope. Misfortunes must sometime have end, and what happiness will be ours when they shall cease.

That parole troubled him more than ever. There were so many opportunities now, were he not bound by a promise.

If some change does not take place before the end of next May, I must and will attempt something. Great risks must be run and sacrifices made [they certainly would clamp him back in the Garden Prison] but my honour shall remain unstained. No captain of His Majesty's Navy will have to blush at calling me a fellow-officer.

Vigorous exhortations went to Samuel—the elder brother again—deploring his unemployment, lecturing, advising, urging him on. "When out of use, like metals, we become rusted and unfit for service." What could be the matter with that boy?

Another New Year came and went. He spent it at Port Louis with Thomy and his friends. A pathetic reminder of his claims upon the *Cumberland*, he sent to Colonel Monistrol a few pairs of shells gathered on the reef where he was shipwrecked, with regrets that his more valuable relics had been taken from him. A formal note of thanks. No more.

Once again the anger of heaven descended on Ile-de-France in squalls and cyclones. Since his arrival drought, flood and disaster had reduced the island to pitiful distress. Matthew liked to think that God was punishing the captain-general for his obstinate injustice to him. Maize was six and ten dollars a hundred pounds, and food for the slaves, grown in the fields, four times the ordinary price. The poor wretches were starved to skin and bone. The English fleet now had the island hermetically sealed.

Another cruel blow fell from between the pages of Steele's List.

It was Whiplash Kent, his friend, who had brought the *Investigator* home. No other on earth could have done it. Kent had received promotion. So that name signified no new ship for his voyage of discovery, but the old one he had—abandoned, were they saying? If Kent had been honoured, it followed that he was censured.

Again he was stung to frantic and futile action. Through the Danish merchantman, Kerjean, who had the captain-general's ear, he implored to be sent to France, even as a close prisoner, to stand his trial there, with whatever results. That would at least be near England, that he might know of what he was accused, and state his case.

Decaen refused. He implored an interview. The captain-general had no time. Kerjean told him that he had been infuriated by a letter he received from Governor King about ten months before, enclosing, in support of his statements, one that Matthew had smuggled away to him! Decaen's ire had cooled by this, but he would not see Flinders. It was a waste of time. The case would be dealt with in Paris.

Brooding over his wrongs, utterly powerless to gain a hearing in Port Louis, in France, or in England, he turned his steps to the hills again, the only home he knew.

Delphine was at home, and the French lessons went on, but she had subtly changed. Whenever he spoke of his wife, as heaven knows he did now often enough, while the others were full of sympathy, her attitude was hard and cynical, or she yawned and left the room.

One day, when he had been carefully copying some French verses to send for Ann's translation, and discoursing with much pride upon her sparkling intellectuality, her wit, her wisdom, her verve, and—

"And her fidelity?" Delphine cut in. "Penelope, she spins her web, *mon Ulysse*, all the time for you? Six years is a long time."

The unexpected shaft went deep.

"Her letters to me are as the dew of heaven to the traveller in the barren desert."

"That is very charming. She tells you all things, without doubt?"

"She tells me all I wish to know, which is just what she wishes to tell me. I am not one of those suspicious husbands who think of their wives as forever doing wrong when they have anything they desire to keep to themselves. My confidence is as complete and illimitable as hers."

"You resemble not most men, monsieur. They would be lord and master, and be sure of it."

As usual intrigued by theories, Matthew was launched. "There is a medium between petticoat government and tyranny on the part of the husband, that I think to be very attainable and the sum of happiness in the married state." He felt he was being sententious. His voice lowered, and his tone changed.

"You see," he went on, almost reverently, "Ann is to me not only my beloved wife, but my most true and intimate friend, as I hope to be to her. If we find failings, we shall look upon them with kindness and compassion, and in each other's merits take pride and delight to dwell upon them. Thus will we realize, as far as may be, the happiness of heaven upon this earth."

His face was alight with such tender emotion, such radiant idealism, that Delphine was a little ashamed.

"Madame Flinders is very fortunate," she remarked.

Matthew was annoyed at the turn the conversation had taken—uncovering their hearts to a stranger—but he liked the sentiments so much that he promptly wrote them to Ann, and good little Thomy Pitot found a Swiss merchantman to carry the missive of love and trust, straight as a homing gull.

A second letter came from her—only six months between them. It told him that Samuel was back under Admiral Collingwood at Cape Finisterre—how he hoped the boy would find a chance to distinguish himself—and broke the news of Susanna's marriage to an artist, a Mr George Pearson, "without consultation of friends". What was the world coming to? As head of the family, he was perturbed. This sort of thing might do much harm in society, and should be opposed. He wrote in mild indignation:

She may say that if she married without her father's consent, so did I, but independent of the difference between a man of twenty-six and a girl of twenty-two, perhaps she did not know that when I spoke to my father of my affection for thee, he acknowledged that thou wert a most worthy young lady, and that he upheld that inclination, and even the will made in thy favour, and the circumstances of my voyage allowed no time to take the advice of friends.

She may not have realized that I have always loved her most tenderly, and that on my return to England she and her dear little family shall be among the first objects I shall be most anxious to see.

Sue married, with a baby daughter! There was a handful of tiny pink corals in his sea-chest, that he had picked up on Wreck Reef, going to quite a lot of trouble to find the right size and shade in his haste, dreaming that—no, he would send them home to Susanna now, for her little one. He scarcely liked to ask Delphine to thread them, but Sophie was delighted.

If Matthew had settled down to a more or less philosophic resignation, Elder had not. The man was retreating like a snail farther and farther into a hard shell of hatred and resentment of the French. One night he was openly abusive to Labauve.

Labauve shouted "Get out, you English cur!—no offence," he said to Matthew, "but that man of yours is imbecile. You would do better without him."

It was true. The faithful servant and companion of all his dangers and misfortune for six years past had fallen into a mental and physical misery. Matthew had fears for his sanity, even that he might take his life. He suffered from hallucinations. He refused to eat for fear of being poisoned. Every slave on the plantation was a potential murderer in the pay of the French, and the negroes, he said, would stop at nothing. In every copy of the *Port Napoleon Gazette*—full of vituperation against the English, but quite harmless, as a barking lizard—Elder found personal libels and covert threats against his master, and pointed them out, trembling with rage and fear. If he saw two of their friends talking together, they were plotting against them, their kindness a cover to their designs. If they laughed, it was ridicule. His mind was unhinged.

This was all the more troubling because Matthew had been conning over a scheme to send Elder home with his most valuable books and papers, then demand back his parole from Decaen, and escape, if he had to swim for it. He realized that, in Elder's deranged state, it would be dangerous to trust anything to him, and that if he were not made to leave, he would die of hypochondria or starve himself to death.

So he made application for Elder's liberation on the grounds of his grave ill-health. To his surprise it was granted, with a passage on the next out-going ship. The man would be reasonably safe, and Matthew impressed upon him he would help him far more by going. His health and normality improved so much from that moment that Matthew determined to take a chance with the papers. He gave him an excellent reference as gentleman's man, steward, copying clerk or storeman, and letters of introduction to captains of His Majesty's ships. Also, he gave him a written list of instructions.

If on a French ship captured by the British, he was to ask for a passage to the Cape or to St Helena, and so make for England; if on an American ship, to ask the British consul at New York for a passage to London, take the trunk to the agent Standert, open it and check it in his presence, and see that it was delivered straightway to the Admiralty. Then he was to go, at Matthew's expense, to Lincolnshire with letters—to Mrs Matthew Flinders at Partney, to Miss Henrietta Flinders at Spalding, and to the Franklins at Spilsby.

Elder packed his sea-chest singing, in a voice grown raucous with disuse, but with anguish of foreboding and prayers for its safety Matthew stacked the trunk. The bill of contents he made out with three signed copies.

There were two invaluable parcels for the Admiralty, the first and second volumes of the *Investigator* log—Decaen had the third; charts of the north coast of Australia, and the *Lady Nelson's* track along the east coast; the *Investigator's* journal, saved from the wreck; five quires of the *Norfolk* journey; five quires of the *Francis* expedition; ten yellow charts of the *Investigator's* discovery; all his public letters received at Ile-de-France, and a rough introduction to the writing of his Voyage.

If these should be lost, he may as well not have been born.

There were his will; Cook's time-keeper that Sir Joseph had given him—a poignant memory of a faith, in a cruel fate, forsaken; various charts of his own, and others lent; the pillows, sheets and table-cloths that had been his sop to civilization on the evil-smelling *Cumberland*; his second laced uniform coat, a waistcoat, and two epaulettes—they might be relics, he cynically reflected; three silver table-spoons, a gravy spoon and five tea-spoons; and seven new long-cloth shirts that would fit Samuel if he never claimed them. There was also a collection of books, ranging from the *Endeavour* log-book to Knight's *Worship of Priapus*.

He bade Elder farewell with a grip of friendship that knew no class distinction, told him casually that he would see him later in London, and watched him out of sight, a black servant carrying the trunk. Then he walked slowly back to the pavilion, alone indeed. It was 1 July, 1807. Lagging years, lagging footsteps.

Maman sent down a negro boy called Toussaint, with a wide white smile and a secret admiration of the captain, of whom he soon copied every mannerism, and became a walking replica in ebony. The gap that those papers left in Matthew's heart was greater than the loss of Elder, his last countryman in exile. Ah well. He had promised Marc a lesson in middle latitude sailing. He rode over to the Tamarinds for music at night.

There was a moment when his flute lay listless on his knee, and his thoughts went wandering seven thousand miles of perilous ocean, in war-time, with Elder and the battered tin trunk. He came back to earth to find Chazal sketching him in pencil, on the back of a sonata, on the lid of the harpsichord.

"A living picture of your English 'Amlet," said Chazal with a mischievous smile, and showed him the woe-begone caricature. "But seriously, you will let me paint you? The subject, if not the execution, will then reserve to me a place on Olympus."

Here was a chance to send his likeness to Ann. He agreed with a graciousness that surprised them, and the next day the sittings began.

"You know," remarked Chazal, gently tilting his chin into position, and buttoning blue coat on white cravat, "it is very possible that now comes the captain-general's pardon. Always I lose my models when I am most enthusiast, for me an unfinished canvas. This is the way in life."

"If it were only so!" said Matthew, smiling. "My wife would have the substance instead of the shadow. There would be no complaint."

Three weeks went by. One Sunday they went for a picnic down to the Bay of Tamarinds, and even out upon it in a pirogue. An old creole fisherman camped in a grove told them a mystifying piece of news. Yesterday a big English warship passed close inshore, but *oui monsieur*, with English colours, to Port Louis, and there had been no red flag, no guns. They thought she must be bringing French prisoners from India, under a flag of truce, to exchange for the British in the island. Had her mission anything to do with him, Matthew wondered? Banish these hopes deferred!

There passed another sunny, silent week. He learned that the ship was indeed H.M.S. *Greyhound* from India, under a flag of truce come and gone, but not with prisoners. A cartel was following for them. Captain Troubridge, her commander, had

had an audience with the captain-general. Troubridge!—if only he had known!

On 22 July, Labauve was to be initiated into the Freemasons' Lodge at Mocha, and Matthew rode over to officiate. Coming back, he met a courier, with letters for him from Colonel Monistrol.

From Sir Edward Pellew! His eye flashed down the written page. *Cumberland*—Council of State—Admiral Decrès. Madly, joyously, he set his mule to a gallop.

Vivre l'Empéreur! Napoleon had set him free!

Sir Edward wrote that one of his frigates had captured a ship with dispatches for Decaen. Among them was the order for his release. Pellew now delivered it to the captain-general, told Flinders to embark at once on the *Greyhound*.

But the *Greyhound* had been gone two days! His face fell, a bitter disappointment. He might have been in England for Christmas.

The flagellation of these terrible years had left its mark. He must still be meek. He sent Toussaint with an urgent letter to the governor, imploring him to confirm or deny the news, to tell him if these letters received had buoyed his heart in vain. He watched the Port Louis track for a week. At last, at the governor's pleasure, the answer came, a copy of the order.

The Council of State is of the opinion that the Captain-General of Ile-de-France had sufficient reason for detaining there Captain Flinders and his schooner, but by reason of the interest that the misfortunes of Captain Flinders have inspired, he seems to deserve that His Majesty should authorize the Minister of Marine and the Colonies to restore to him his liberty and his ship.

Approuvé au Palace des Tuileries, le onze mars, 1806.

and signed by the world's most celebrated, most notorious signature

NAPOLEON.

All he had asked was justice in an outrage of national rights, but Napoleon, ever romantic, was inspired, not by his achievements, but by his misfortunes. What did it matter, so long as he was free?

Restore his liberty and his ship—his love—the life-blood in his veins—Discovery!

The smiling landscapes of Ile-de-France were a thousand times more beautiful. It seemed that a cloud had passed from the face of the sun.

A brief covering note in Decaen's own handwriting drew attention to Napoleon's noble and generous gesture, and informed him that as soon as circumstances would permit, he should fully enjoy the favour of His Majesty the Emperor and King.

"Dès que les circonstances le permettent ... "

What were these circumstances? How long——? He asked permission to come to Port Louis. That was refused. He asked for the return of his books and papers, so that he could put them in order from the confusion of shipwreck, and sell the *Cumberland*.

No reply.

So the cat still played with the mouse ... for a while. It would not dare for long.

Gladly he radiated the news to the four quarters of the globe. "I may arrive as soon as this letter," he announced gleefully to Ann.

He sent an order post-haste, through Pitot to India, for his home-coming gifts, though they would arrive long after him—one piece of black China silk, three pieces of finest plain muslin, three plain handsome veils and fine threads to broider them, delightfully vague in a man's imagining of feminine glory, but Ann and his stepmother, Henrietta and Susanna, would know all the love and gladness that came with them.

The cartel *Wellesley* was at Port Louis, he heard, with 230 French prisoners from Madras to be exchanged for the English at Grande Rivière. Perhaps he was to be sent to India by her—but it she were detained, the fleet from India would have sailed, and that would mean the loss of three months. Decaen seemed determined to make him drink the cup of bitterness to the very dregs. The black pack of doubts and fears was on his tracks again.

Towards the end of August, he received permission to come to the town for access to his papers. It was glorious weather for his farewell. The dear French people about him brought him many presents. They arranged little *soirées* and the last of the happy quartettes, and Chazal shed mimic tears for his portrait unfinished, even as he had said.

Delphine, so sullen and aloof for so long, thawed into wistful sweetness at the end. Sophie brought him a copy of her brother André's translation of *Le Marquis de Carabas* into the negro-French of the creole tongue, *Puss in Boots*, only a fairy story, but its language, at least, a curio, and it would help him to remember them. Could he ever forget?

All four kissed him on both cheeks, and the plantation darkies shouted a rousing *bon voyage!*

By some cynical intuition he left his trunks and his personal effects till he should send for them.

In Port Louis, he found that the *Actaeon* had just sailed for France, but the *Wellesley* and the *Waldemar* were in the bay. Decaen refused to let the prisoners board the *Wellesley* till he had prepared his dispatches.

The captain-general prepared his dispatches for the next three months.

Matthew put his papers in order—those that the rats had left him. Then he went back to the plantation because there was nothing else to do. Anti-climax. Humiliation. Day after day he strained his eyes along the Port Louis road.

"It is inconceivable, the animosity of this barbarian!" he cried to Madame d'Arifat. "Will he never be wearied of tormenting me? In all this island, I have but one enemy, and that one, alas! your governor."

Marc and Aristide went on with their navigation lessons. They could calculate the variation of the compass by azimuth and amplitude now. Reading and writing in fluent French,

Matthew put in the rest of the time on a chart of the north of Madagascar. How dared Decaen flout an order of the Council of State—and what could be his reason?

The thought of that invitation to dinner came back to haunt him again. On what little pegs of circumstance hung a man's destiny. Perhaps the object of this vicious delay was to taunt him into recriminaton and rebellion. He tried hard to be dumb and docile, but at the end of October his patience snapped. He wrote a letter to the captain of the cartel, and sent it down by Toussaint to Pitot for delivery, as the officers of the *Wellesley* were not allowed contact with the shore.

Le Capitaine-Général Decaen, hero of Hohenlinden, friend of the Emperor, and monarch of all that France surveyed in the South Seas, lounged on his balcony in lowering mood, glaring at the glare of the market-place. The sweltering heat and the buzzing of the flies had ruined his siesta, and made him savagely irritable. Worse still, the captain-general had been thinking, and it did not agree with him.

A lot of water had run under the bridges of the Seine and the Somme and the Loire since he had been sent out as Governor-General of India, had ended up, like a bear in a bear-pit, in this accursed island. The First Consul had become an emperor, the Emperor of Europe. Popes came and went at his beck and call, and crowns he juggled at whim. Had Jena and Austerlitz dazzled away all memory of Marengo? Why should he, Decaen, be exiled and forgotten, left to the mercy of these wolves, the English, while men who had been cadets with him—Ney, Joubert, Murat—were Grands Maréchals of France and glory?

Empire du Sud! The Tricolour on top of the world; Poh! Canada was gone. India was gone. An island or two in the West Indies, a rotten patch of swamp in Guiana, and this malodorous rock. A southern Gibraltar, they called it. Then why could they not give him arms and men to keep it? No. He was to shoulder the shame, the helpless scapegoat of their naval weakness. His only defences by sea had been taken away. They were frightened of the ghost of that one-eyed cocksparrow of a Nelson. He was left with a few poverty-stricken planters, and not one of them Republicans at heart, *emigrés*, provincials, peasants; a handful of soldiers, scarcely enough to defend Fort Blanc; a herd of niggers who would fight only at the whip's end, and then could not fight. How could he hold the place … and if he did, what was it worth to him? The Légion d'Honneur, the knighthood of a self-crowned king, a medal and a ribbon to titivate the whipper-snappers. Bah! He did not want it—but he had not got it.

From these sour sediments of reflection the captain-general was finding solace in a snatch of slumber when he was rudely recalled to them by a loud knocking on the wooden door of Pitot Frères, Négociants across the square. He rose to curse the hill-negro making the confounded row … it dawned upon him he had seen that particular nigger before, and a not-so-idle curiosity prompted him to inquire the slave's business.

An orderly returned with the news that the boy came from Madame d'Arifat's at Wilhelm's Plains. He carried a letter from the English captain there to be given to Monsieur Thomy.

"Bring him here," said the captain-general, "and bring me the letter."

He ripped it open. His ruddy colour deepened as he read:

Dear Captain le Blanc,

Mr Boand tells me that you have not any information as to the time when the governor will give you his dispatches for India. Surely he does not intend to keep you as well as me here until the peace… .

Over me he has absolute power, but over you he has none … suffer him no longer to trifle with you. I would give him a certain time, suppose a fortnight, and unless he assigned a good reason for remaining a few days longer, I would sail, unless a shot from the forts stopped me… .

Nothing pleases such Frenchmen as him so much as to play the English at the end of a line, like a trout… . It amuses them and gratifies their vanity to show the nations how easily a proud Englishman may be trifled with.

If I did not love my country, and esteem you, I should not tell you my opinion so freely… . What is the selling of a little corvette or petty merchant-ship to a ship like yourself? Surely three months, or even a week, are sufficient for him to deliberate his intentions.... The other inhabitants cry shame on his conduct.

Notwithstanding this haughty general's pride, I think he will hardly proceed to atrocities with you ... not being aware to what lengths this man is capable of pushing his malignity so long as he finds we give way to him, you have perhaps not proceeded further ... you will gather my opinion from what I have said.

I have to thank you for your attention in having prepared a convenient cabin for me on the Wellesley. Would to God that I may inhabit it, and that both you and I may one day soon be out of the power of a man who knows so little of justice or humanity or national faith, or the true interests of those whom he is appointed to govern.

It is hardly necessary for me to ask you to destroy this letter—

Your faithful humble servant,

MATTHEW FLINDERS.

"Any others?" rapped out the haughty general.

A colloquy in creole.

"Yes, excellency. A packet for M. Boand, on the *Waldemar*. She sails to-morrow. That is already delivered."

"Good. He can go."

Toussaint went, accelerated by a kick in the rear. The captain-general resumed his shattered siesta. He was not visibly cast down. In fact, he looked more cheerful, and a few minutes later his thick mouth opened in a tranquil doze.

That night an armed guard descended on Mr Boand as he lay inoffensively smoking in his cabin, with a warrant to search his papers. They found a neat packet, wrapped in waxed cloth to safeguard it in shipwreck, and addressed to Standert, in London.

"*Bien des remerciments*." This was all they wanted. They bowed their apologies for disturbing him, and left Mr Boand fuming in earnest.

There were letters to Ann, to Sir Joseph, to Sir Edward Pellew, to Governor King and John Palmer at Port Jackson, and what the captain-general learned of himself from these letters sent him into a righteous rage of anglophobia. He was glad to know that in his reply to the Minister of State, written a month ago but still there among his dispatches for the *Wellesley*, he had written of the lowering storm, the changed conditions in Ile-de-France, that made it foolhardy to let this Englishman, "always dangerous", go. He had sometimes thought of changing his mind. Let it be.

So Chazal finished the portrait, and Matthew started in on the *comédies* of Molière.

His feet had worn a track up the hills of Vacois to the crow's-nest lookout. In Port Louis he had carefully noted the ships and their positions. One morning there was a vacant space where the *Wellesley* had been. A carefully casual inquiry told him that the prisoners at Grande Rivière had gone.

For the third time he was the only Englishman left in the island.

His days were spent in vague uncertain plans, his nights in despair. In that brief cessation of hostilities, brigs, frigates, sloops and cartels swarmed into the port, all noted by the watcher on the hill. He began his vigil at daydawn, and lingered till the last light faded from sea and sky. Every strange sail brought anguish of uncertainty. Perhaps it was the white wing of peace. How glorious it would be to achieve his liberty in peace, with no shadow of obligation, and in spite of the tyrant.

New Year brought blossom-time again, and all the gaiety of Lise's wedding. Under scarlet canopies of poinciana and a field of the cloth of gold of the cassia, came the bridegroom from Bourbon with the eldest brother André, and the old Abbé Flageolet, beaming and puffing on his donkey. The marriage was celebrated out of doors. Our Lady's grotto in the garden was a kaleidoscope of tropic flowers. Palanquins were arriving at every moment, decked with greenery and laden with gifts.

Labauve in his element as best man, and Maman with her bevy of shouting mammies, were apoplectic with excitement. Sophie and Delphine, butterflies of bridesmaids, rustled their taffetas everywhere, flushed with laughter and greeting. All the slaves of the Plains plantations were assembled, dressed in their gaudy best, the girls carrying vivid garlands of fast-fading blooms.

Before the ceremony began, the worthy abbé took time by the forelock, and received into the all-embracing arms of Mother Church no less than seven of the smallest heathen. Pouring holy water and benedictions in sonorous Latin on their krinkly heads, he frightened them out of their voodoo-haunted wits.

A silver gong rang out. The scent of incense blended with the scent of blossoms. To the deep-throated chanting of negro choirs in a joyous *Kyrie* came Lise on the arm of André, leading the bridal party—an angelic figure in virginal white, beaming into the huge bouquet of waxen oleanders that deepened the blush rose of her radiant little face. There was no trace of the familiar comfortable waddle that day. Treading on air, Lise might have been a lesson in deportment to the Empress Josephine herself.

The feast was held in a big marquee, while the slave kraals echoed with tom-toms and fireworks and the din of revelry. Matthew was chosen to propose the toast of the bride.

With what graceful and self-deprecating smiles he wreathed her glowing countenance! With what brotherly affection he dwelt upon her never-failing gentleness, her sunny nature, and her homely virtues.

He turned to Charles—"To wish you happiness would be to doubt it, therefore I do not wish it"—and very slowly and distinctly he concluded with a well-loved quotation in English, the words that a poet had written of Lady Banks's sister, the famous beauty, Lady Knatchbull—"Grace in her steps, heaven in her eyes, and in all her actions dignity and love."

There was a storm of applause, for even those who knew no English could not but understand, and in any case they knew they were safe.

The only shadow on the brightness of the day was Delphine's extraordinary curtness. She refused to dance with him, in front of Charles, and sailed abruptly away with Ravel.

"Miss Delphine," said Matthew, "is not yet recovered from the state of sadness in which you left her, Charles. I believe she

435

sheds many tears in secret. She has changed to me. She has changed for more than twelve months. It is evident that I no longer possess any place in her friendship. That has been one of the bitterest ingredients in my chalice."

"Women," remarked Charles with a new-found air of authority, "are enigma. They go by contraries. Where they hate most, they often love most. Perhaps you will find the answer in that."

Matthew considered. "Impossible! She knows that I am married."

"*Quand même!* To love is not always to marry."

Matthew laughed outright. "Your wedding has gone to your head. If Delphine's heart is broken, 'tis you I suspect."

"And for that she is angry with you? *Mon Dieu*, how you English are—*thick*. Very well. Perhaps it is for the best."

Matthew had better luck with kind, sensible Sophie, who billowed away on his arm to the lilt of the harp, but that night, with his head on his pillow, he pondered Charles's flippant suggestion, set it out in mathematical equation, added and subtracted, then wearily laid it aside.

Love of women … and great was his need of it. Other men had their *affaires de coeur*. Perhaps in this, as in all else, he had seemed to them an ineffectual fool. There might have been an episode charming to look back on in this perfect setting of love … but it would only have meant more heartache, for whatever he did, in life and in love, he would have to do well. There would be a pathetic parting, a shadowed meeting with his wife after the long years. And then came back the intimate thought of Ann. No. Life's small compromises were not for such as he. He was of those who take the farce too seriously.

Lise and Charles set out for Bourbon, the palanquins departed, and humdrum reigned again. Swallows were wheeling for the long flight northward, and with the south-west wind came restlessness unbearable.

Pitot had seen Monistrol, and Monistrol had given not an atom of hope. So Matthew decided to take things into his own hands, demand back his parole at all costs, leave everything, and watch for a chance of escape. Others had found it. There were documents and the dispatches from King, important letters from Macarthur and Grimes and Paterson among his possessions. He did not want to desert the trust, but there was no other way.

With great discretion, he began to plan, saying not one word to his friends for fear of implicating them. A farewell letter was already written to Thomy, enclosed with some sheets of music he was returning, to be received when he was well away. It assured him that there was as little hostility in Matthew's leaving the island as there had been in his coming, that his friendship for these good souls would never change. It offered all the help in times to come that was in his power to give.

That letter was never sent, for they found him packing once again, and Thomy was hastily called to a little council of war. Chazal and Chevreau attended, and Maman in mock despair.

His back against the wall, Flinders was grimly determined.

"You have been too long witness to my sufferings," he cried, "to be surprised. I shall deliver myself into the hands of this man who has so long persecuted me, and then when I am free of parole, let him do his worst. I shall defy him. I shall outwit him. I *shall* be free!"

"But you are free!" shouted Thomy. "Go if you must, but do not surrender to Decaen. On the Emperor's word, through the Council of State, you are a free man. Shall our *capitaine-général* dictate to the mightiest monarch of the known world? Never! Your powerful friends of France and England—will they take this in silence? Pellew is near by. We know it to our cost. What is he doing? What of the citizens of this island? We shall make a petition at once. If that fails—but no. On no account surrender. In prison again you will die. Stay with us! Patience a little longer."

In patience he was growing old. A free man? Tell the bird in the cage it is free.

However, they dissuaded him. Tamely back to his charts and his vigil he went, read Saint-Pierre's *Nature Studies*, and wept for the too highly-coloured soul of the author of *Paul et Virginie*.

Nothing changed. No letter from Sir Joseph, no more letters from Ann.

Thomy spent a whole month with him in winter at the Tamarinds—music and laughter, gay companions and gentle, understanding friends. While he was there the *Venus* came in with Hamelin in command, his rugged old Port Jackson friend, Hamelin of the *Naturaliste*, who had nailed his post to the north-west coast of Australia, and Matthew envied him that.

Thomy arranged a dinner at Chazal's, and Hamelin told him that Péron's voyage of the *Naturaliste* was written, and about to appear. The Emperor had given 200,000 francs from his private purse towards the publication and the engraving of charts, for beauty of the atlas and good production.

"It will be very interesting, Captain Hamelin," said Flinders quietly, "to read what your people will write of me, and to contrast my treatment here with that you received at Port Jackson. That chapter will require a little good management in handling, a little—juggling, shall we say?—for the honour of France."

"The circumstances here, monsieur," growled Hamelin, "are unfortunately beyond our control."

The French captain knew all that was happening in Port Jackson—what agents had they left there? Matthew wondered—and he came to light with one diverting scrap of news. After unending trouble and strife in overproof battles with the Rum Corps, Governor King had gone home in disgust. His successor was none other than—Bligh.

Bligh, it seemed, was back to his *Bounty* form. With a wry, but affectionate, smile Matthew learned that on the voyage out to New Holland with the new *Porpoise* and a convict fleet, he had fought with the convoy captain all the way. He forged on in the flagship, ignoring all signals and sailing orders, until Short, the captain, fired a shot across his bows. There was nearly a battle. Short was scouted and flouted, and ordered to give right of way on the high seas. Heaven help those who fell foul of Mr Bligh when his blood was up. Things were going to happen to Macarthur and the Rum Corps now.

The fierce hand-to-hand fighting of the nations began again. Guns were barking offshore in the night, rumours were rife by day. The crippled *Caroline* slunk into the bay with an English frigate and a Portuguese merchantman on a leash behind her, both prizes, but at a price. Her death-roll had been heavy, and hovering between life and death aboard her was Ensign Charles Baudin, Charles the gay, the debonair—he might not live the week.

However, he did, and down to Port Louis, as soon as he could get permission, rode Matthew in haste, bought up the whole stock-in-trade of an orange stall, and waited on the doorstep of the hospital for hours, only to be told by the white-robed nuns to return on the following day.

An orderly sergeant fell into step behind him as he moved away, shadowed him everywhere, slept in the room above him. When questioned, the man replied that it was by the captain-general's orders. So he was virtually under arrest. What did it matter? When one is ten feet under the water, another inch makes no difference.

In the morning he sent in a request for permission to board one of the ships in harbour, to make a few vital experiments for his thesis on the variation of the compass. It was curtly refused. Monistrol kept out of his way.

The walls of the hospital, clammy and white, smelt sickeningly of lime and echoed the groans of the dying.

"Ohé! friend Flinders!" piped Charles, with the wraith of a grin. His lips were bloodless, and his wan face beneath the bandages drawn with pain. His right arm was gone, and he was "shot to pieces amidships", he proudly informed Matthew. "But don't forget, we beat them. We always shall. *Vive la France!* How are the national rights?"

Flinders bent his head in a very real shame. Here was a brother in war's misfortune, a far crueller misfortune than his. A sleeve that hung limp was a wrong that could never be righted. Liberty was more easily restored than a missing limb.

They talked freely and cheerfully of many things, and Charles promised to visit him at Wilhelm's Plains as soon as he was convalescent.

"At any rate," said Matthew, as he rose to go at the sister's nod, "you can thank God your fighting days are over."

"*Pardieu*, not by a long way," laughed the patient. He pointed to his empty sleeve. "I see myself the Admiral Nelson of France."

"Never! Henceforward we work together, you and I, for the knowledge and the happiness of man. Ah, Charles, how often have I regretted that you, with all your eagerness and bright perceptions so well calculated to pursue scientific researches, should be deflected into this bloody business, that brings the world nothing but woe. Newton and Cook were benefactors of mankind. Alexander and Caesar—don't be afraid, I shall come no nearer home—desolated it to their own ends. Oh, that our two nations were convinced of this truth. Then might we hope that the unreasoning hatred that makes it a duty for man to kill his fellow-man would become an honourable emulation for excellence in the universal arts and sciences.

"We should strive and battle—yes!—but in achievement, and in good calculating print of measured words. We should seek in the lands and seas of the globe not gain, but an empire of beauty and knowledge and truth—the explorers, the scientists, the English philosopher and the *savant français*, each in emulation for honours of his country, the envy not the jealousy of his rival, the homage of posterity and the benefit of mankind. That would be a conflict worth while."

"A dream," Baudin interrupted, impatiently.

Striding the room, his head in the clouds, Matthew glanced out of the barred window, and saw his sergeant waiting below, in a sunny side-street.

"A dream," he echoed sadly, "that in human nature, it seems, will never come true. But you and I will be faithful."

"My country is my faith," replied the invalid, a little testily. "While there is one ounce of me left, it shall fight to the death for France."

Matthew swung round upon him. "You are wrong! Let us fight—to the life! Lapérouse, I tell you, has done more for the glory of France than any military seaman. What is the honour of the Portuguese? Columbus and Vasco da Gama stand far above all the captains and admirals the nations that employed them have produced. To take my own nation, Newton and Cook are as the light of the sun, Nelson as a flambeau, brilliant indeed for a time, but in half a century he will scarcely be remembered.

"Charles Baudin, let us follow not Nelson and Napoleon, but Laperouse and Cook. In you I should have a friend and rival whose energy would be my stimulus to efforts worthy to obtain me a place in the annals of navigation, in the list of those who have contributed to our knowledge of the globe and the blessings of civilization. Like two satellites following the movements of the great illuminary and archetype of navigators, we would each receive the reflected light of the other. Our bright courses would be concentric circles of harmony, our emulation would be that of brothers, eager to serve the cause of the common family of which we are members, the people of this earth!"

His pitying gaze fell on the wounded man, a little wearied by his eloquence.

"Think of it, Charles," he added very gently. "A ball launched by my own hand might, perhaps, have been the destruction of you whom I hold so dear. No, my friend, I cannot contemplate without horror the waste of human life to serve the cause of restless ambition. Never shall my hands be voluntarily stained with blood, unless it be in the defence of my country, my loved ones, and my home. In such a case, every other sentiment vanishes."

"I shall remember that, friend Flinders," said Baudin, smiling, "when I meet you in battle on the sea. For no sooner will you be free than the flag you love will call you. You do not think so now, but we shall see."

Spurred anew with the old thoughts, Matthew rode back to Wilhelm's Plains—to busy himself in learning chess in time for Baudin's coming.

And Baudin never came. It was only another of the bitter little disappointments he learned to expect, so sure as the sun rose. The gallant young lieutenant wrote that he was leaving immediately for France, invalided home, and with the Legion d'Honneur—but there was a chance. He was in high favour. He would have the ear of authority. Let him carry Flinders's "Memorials", and be his advocate, knowing the truth and loving his foeman friend.

20

The Cordon Closes In

The maize was ripening to another meagre harvest. In the shade of the coral-tree, Matthew sat writing to Ann:

It is still from this fatal island, my dearest friend, and I know not what power will make this inexorable general let me depart, for no sentiments of honour, of justice, of humanity, or even the orders of his government are sufficient.

More than a year has passed, and I have again tried to learn his intentions. Nothing short of a peace will set me free, and the ploughshares of England and France have become swords of destruction.

The little path I had traced out for myself by which to arrive at some distinction had nothing to recommend it but its philanthropic principles, its general utility to commerce, and the extension of geographical and nautical knowledge. They are become antiquated themes, and the misfortunes of one who had the folly to dedicate his life and labour to them are scarcely worthy of attention.

He stopped to listen to the hollow rhythm of a tom-tom, the nasal whine of an African chant near by. What was the use? Would the letter ever reach her? So shadowy had his love become in these foreign, fleeting years.

No American ships were calling and neutrals were not safe. Napoleon had declared any nation an enemy that traded in British ports. He did not know if Elder had arrived with the trunk, or what had happened to his men of the *Investigator* and the *Cumberland*. He did not know if his wife's maintenance were still secure, for no report of financial matters had ever reached him from the agent Standert. By chance he had learned—for Pitot would never have told him—that there had been difficulty here lately in discounting his bills.

Troberville and most of his *Société* friends had enlisted, and Pitot Frères were facing almost certain ruin. The firm was in disgrace with the government owing to its association with the English, and particularly with him, and Surcouf could no longer bring his prizes through the cordon to sell their gold and spices. Loyal little Thomy! His friendship was deeper than thought of repayment. His own recent appeals to the French minister had been smuggled out on ships promptly seized by the British. Doubtless they had been thrown overboard.

But this letter—what could he say that might be cheering? Cousin Henrietta came into his thoughts, with her aged parents at Spalding, and Susanna, struggling with her little family. He wrote on:

To know how deeply the love of country and family are embedded in the human heart, it is necessary to be kept for some years from them. It is a consuming fire, capable of destroying the human frame when hope is lost.

Bergeret and Baudin would have arrived in France, and the letters they carried must have reached their goal. Decaen was afraid to let him go, lest he should tell the truth. But it was too late for his precautions.

If he thinks that, so long as he can keep me here, my voice will not be heard, he is mistaken. A memorial I have written will be read in France, and the injustice and inhumanity with which I have been treated will not be wholly unknown in either nation. I think the steps I am taking will obtain an order, at least to send me to France, that he will not be able to resist without risking his head.

Surely such men as the Wellesleys, Bougainville, Pellew, Banks, Fleurieu, Minto, and the members of *L'Institut* and the British and French State governments might intrigue the Emperor to some purpose now. Might. That groove of thought had left a scar in his mind.

Do not hope. Do not despair. Put thy trust in God, who has protected me through dangers and preserved my health through a trial that has not its parallel in history.

The love that ever fills the heart of thy

MATTHEW FLINDERS.

He laid aside the letter, and idly took a fresh sheet. If he could only recapture the old brisk energy—but who cared about his work?

"Attraction and repulsion of the poles," he wrote, and for a few moments was deep in the problem, but the drowsiness of the afternoon was upon him. He packed up his papers and retired to his pavilion. A half-written sheet had blown unnoticed into the thicket of bamboos at the water's edge.

Home in the dusk from lawn tennis at Clouves', Delphine found it. The angular handwriting she knew well, the English words, at first glance, were significant. "Attraction ... repulsion ... magnetism ... if I succeed as I hope ... oscillation," she read.

"*Regardez*," she whispered mischievously to Sophie, "what it is. A love-letter. Oscillation–it is the English word for *baiser*. Now for your English captain. Have I not told you? They are all the same. We shall translate, and know that which he hides so carefully. Never you tell me a sailor has one love."

A little ashamed, but curious, they carried it in to the candlelight in Sophie's bedroom, and an English dictionary. "Pole," they read with disgust.

It is the power of one pole over the other that makes the deep incline towards the north and the south. The square of the number of the oscillations—

How Sophie laughed, for whatever they were, they certainly were not kisses—

made by the same needle in a given time. If I succeed as I hope, the place of the poles will be allocated, and an important step made in illustrating the magnetism of the earth.

Hélas! Just science. The science of his writing, night and day.

"Delphine, you are wrong about Monsieur Flandare," said Sophie. "He is not as the men we know, just flesh and blood, and fire for women. The whole earth is his love, and he cannot love so much in small measure who loves in great. We are no more than dolls to him. Just in the pleasantness of every day we help him. Will you not make friends again? This manner of yours so cold, I know it grieves him, and he will soon be going. We should be good friends for the ending."

"I showed him I cared for him," said Delphine, too carelessly. "That was the trouble. They do not care when they know."

"My dear, he has not even seen. He is so kind, he would be the last. He would be filled with pity."

"Pity! I would not have his pity!" she flashed.

"Oh, this love!" said Sophie laughing. "I will have none of it. The chickens and the piccaninnies will do for me, they are no heartache."

To Matthew's surprise and pleasure, Delphine came shyly back into the picture of their daily life. He wondered vaguely what it was that changed her, but never asked and seemed content that all was well again.

It was she who brought him the news that the petition to the governor, of all his friends in the island and many who had never seen him, had been fruitless. A week later there was a curt note from Decaen that he had communicated to the Minister of the Marine good and sufficient reason for delaying the departure, and was again awaiting instructions from France.

This after eighteen months of agony since the release.

Another interchange of prisoners was at hand, and a cartel expected. Open enemies taken in battle, after maiming and killing Frenchmen, were restored to their country. Without a trial, he who had been innocent even of patriotic militarism, was condemned to eternal exile. Why?

"From the bottom of my heart I speak," he said to Maman. "There is no other reason than that I refused to dine with a man who had called me an impostor. None but myself can know all that he has made me suffer for that."

Madame d'Arifat had her own troubles. Lise was expecting a baby, and she wanted her mother to be near. In a mad race across the Strait for Bourbon, Maman must take the chances of war and brave the English guns. She might be taken prisoner, and find herself at the Cape, or in India, or even in England. What could she do?

The news strangely moved Matthew. He never ceased to wonder at the miracle of procreation, and new little people in the world seemed ever a matter for rejoicing, a sad business though the world might be. He wished that Lise's child might be a boy.

"I don't suppose," he humbly suggested, "that, being a heretic, you could let me be godfather, but if you ever thought of educating him in England, would you trust him to me? Perhaps you would ask that his third, or fourth, or even fifth name might be Flinders? These two are indeed dear to me. Their son shall be as mine, and the name a memorial of our friendship."

Maman, laughing, promised that Lise and Charles would do their best. She was amused and gratified at this rather premature adoption. It did not occur to her that beneath it was the wistfulness of fatherhood denied.

A review of Baudin's *Voyage de Déscouvertes*, written by Péron and just published, came to hand from Thomy — an active volcano! For the south coast of Terra Australis was Terre Napoléon. St Vincent's Gulf and Spencer's Gulf were Golfe Napoléon and Golfe Joséphine. Surely enough, his Kangaroo Island was Ile Decrès, and the north coast of Van Diemen's Land

Terre de Géographe. From what he read, Freycinet's charts were genius. The Frenchmen had given to the world the first full map of New Holland.

So. While he was kept here a prisoner, they had pilfered his honour, stolen his credit among scientists for all time, filched an empire from his country. The thoughts burnt like live coals. Who was the barefaced pirate? Baudin was dead. Hamelin had no part in it. Surely not Péron and Freycinet, who knew so well the truth? Napoleon himself then? The man was crazed with vanity, but not a sneak thief. Was it a spider-web of intrigue and deliberate national perfidy? He was utterly powerless, in a world that was deaf, dumb and blind to any cry from him. What he had gained for Britain, he had lost. This was the cruellest stroke of all, yet, strangely, it did not penetrate nearly so deeply as it might have done two or three years ago. Self-torture had left him numb. Or was it that he had expected this, dreaded it all the time?

Of the crowning sorrow he said very little. "The wise man knows how to submit himself to imperious necessity, and to find in his own heart and useful occupation wherewith to defeat the injustice of men and the severity of fortune," he wrote calmly in his diary.

A crustacean shell of philosophy, his secret communion with his lost love, and his work, were a bulwark against the slings and arrows. Again they heard the plaintive notes of his flute in the evenings, a mournful phrasing lightening now and then to inconsequent little trills of gaiety as Mozart and Haydn wiled away his loneliness. He slept a great deal at this time, and when Sophie chided him that one so vigorous, so virile, should have become a sluggard, "Sleep, that sweet charmer of human woes, is my great resource," he told her simply. "Therefore I sleep much."

He played chess, and fingered the pieces absently. Somebody lent him a copy of Burney's *Discoveries in the South Seas*. He mislaid it here and there, and forgot it. Down by the old stone bridge at the Lataniers River lived a dear little girl of about eleven years old, Noémi Sauvejet. She found the quiet, dark-eyed English *capitaine*, slightly stooped and far gentler than he should have been for his years, a delightful companion.

Noémi came fishing and exploring with the two boys. Their toy skiffs sailed the still pools of the mountain streams under expert nautical direction. On one exciting day, they calculated their latitude by an eclipse of the sun.

Matthew started in as a breeder of stock. He bought a cow, calf and heifer, and solemnly believed that he was leaving the germ of a fortune that might one day be considerable. The capital should double itself in three or four years. The d'Arifats prophesied that he would be a planter among them yet. There was an idea. Why not? Forget the tang of the wind and the dirge of the surf, the scent and sight of new lands, forget the clamorous beating of his very heart for knowledge—take what God sends. With Ann. She could surely love this tropic isle with all its beauty, these friends, with all their kindness, and already they loved her. Until the peace, they could be happy here, and with her in his *habitation*, let it be a Seventy Years' War. He would not care ... or perhaps, when fate was kind, he might finish the north-west coast, and come back.

So now he made application to the Chef d'État Major, asking, if safe conduct for his wife could be arranged, and if she were to present herself before the port, that she might be admitted. The Chef d'État Major referred the matter to Captain-General Decaen, and there was no reply.

Name of a dog, would this Flinders never be still? One thing after another, with his endless plaints and pining. If that were all! Let him be silent!

An unlucky incident happened about this time, that upset Matthew's philosophy badly, and shaved his wings still closer.

Through Pitot he was more or less in touch with the English prisoners at the port. He was an unseen host, as it were, from his long residence on the island, doing the honours with letters of introduction, favours of fruit and plantation produce, books and papers to lighten the hours in the Garden Prison, and tentative invitations that were never sanctioned. On the other hand, for the French people with sons, husbands, lovers in the enemy's toils, he

449

used every ounce of his influence to procure their freedom and return, or at least their comfort at the Cape and India, and at home.

Towards the end of June, a midshipman named Brereton on the captive *Seaflower* wrote to him claiming relationship, suggesting that he should run away and join him. Flinders, interested at first, traced the genealogical tree into all branches and buds, and could not place the boy, but he strongly vetoed the suggestion for fear of suspicion and for his friends' sake.

A week or so later, visiting the Tamarinds, he heard that Brereton was at a neighbouring plantation, and invited the youngster to Chazal's to dinner. A fair little fellow with a shiftiness in his pale blue eyes, and a neatness in evading direct answers, he had no connexion whatever with the Flinders family. His own came from the South of England. He had no written permission to come into the country, but that was quite in order, he assured Matthew. He asked for money, and with a slight frown of uncertainty, Flinders gave him a promissory note for an advance from Pitot. He soon regretted it. The boy landed himself in trouble in the gambling-dens of Port Louis, airily bandied his patron's name about, and the immediate result was a rap over the knuckles from Decaen. He was not paying a pension to be squandered around by ne'er-do-wells. Let Captain Flinders mind his own affairs, and confine himself in future to the d'Arifat plantation.

This was the last straw. Matthew looked at himself in the glass—the crisp dark hair silvered at the temples, the wistful eyes, that once had been a sailor's. From the paralysis of inaction, his features had grown vague. His chin had dropped, and sharpened. The upward curve of the lips was lost, straightened to bitterness. Chazal's caricature had told the cruel truth. These empty years had sapped his blood, and left him but a wraith. An officer and a gentleman—the words rang hollow. One lives but one life, and half of his was gone.

Not in any high temperature of rebellion—the day was long past for that—but from sheer weariness of a mean-spirited persecution, of futile struggling and torturing thoughts, he would take the quick way out. This nice little sense of honour of his was a pearl before a swine. His submission was taken for subservience, his meekness for weakness. While ever it persisted, the world could do without him.

There was another young Englishman in the Garden Prison, two in fact, Wolcombe and Lynne, who had attracted more than his passing attention. Naval captains who had the bad luck to be caught, they had cooled their heels in Port Louis for nearly a year, and were to be released in the next exchange of prisoners. Ridiculous of the captain-general to pretend to be afraid of disclosures. These two knew far more than he did, and would have no scruples in reporting it.

Lynne was a likeable young fellow, betrothed to the daughter of Admiral Bertie, commander at the Cape. More than once he expressed surprise at Flinders's resignation, with a hint of deeper meaning between the lines.

One word from Matthew, and his good wishes were good intentions. He resolved to send it. The cruising squadron had repeatedly sent requests, demands, for his liberty. Let them help him to snatch it.

But the sense of honour still raised its prickly little head. He spent much time over a diplomatic letter to Decaen, written in French so that there would be no accusation of misrepresentation, announcing that he considered himself a free man, no longer on parole. More than that he dare not say, but if the captain-general had any sense, he would know what it meant.

In the meantime, quietly, he prepared his plans. The English were about all the time, now smuggling water at Le Flacq in the night-time, now waiting for a fair wind in the Bay of Tamarinds, or standing guard at Port Northwest, where nothing could get in, and the *Bellone* and *Gazelle* could not get out.

A deep-laid plot was set afoot. Thomy and Maman willing conspirators. It was arranged that Lynne should smuggle away all his possessions with his own, and hold them for him at the Cape. As soon as he arrived there, he would arrange with Admiral Bertie to send a ship to pick up Flinders in the Bay of Tamarinds. She was to cruise off the signal mountain for the greater part of the day after the full or after the new moon, carrying her pennant forward. When lying to, it should be with the fore-topsail to the mast, and under sail, with the main-t'gallant or royal set, and the fore-t'gallant or royal in. So Flinders would know her. He would stand on the lookout, wearing black, waving a handkerchief in the left hand.

At sunset she was to make sail out of the bay, and return on the second night after, under cover of dark, or in the quiet hours before dawn if it were moonlight. An armed six-oared boat could be put off for him—and he would be there. Nothing would stop him.

There was only one shallow opening in the reef, on the north side of the bay, where the waves foamed in to the head. A boat could easily make it, and land a hundred yards from the inner end of the long white beach. If a negro prisoner could be found at the Cape to show the way through the reefs, so much the better. Words must be few and the oars muffled. The English language was watchword enough.

The cartel duly arrived and sailed, Lynne and the others aboard her. She had brought a new commissioner of prisoners in place of old Stock, a sprightly young man named Hugh Hope. Thomy said that was prophetic, but Matthew merely smiled. He spent the time now cutting a track for easy riding to his lookout—well out of bounds, but what did he care?—and was about to take up his stand with a white handkerchief in his left hand, when events in his own life and the nation's began to move.

News came that Ile Bourbon was British.

A black courier running through the plantation sent him hurrying to the bungalow, to find Maman in tears. There was no hope of her going to Lise in her hour of travail—indeed, she could not know that Lise was safe. For the tidings were of the fall of St Paul, of fortresses taken, and ships sunk, and a revolution of the slaves. At the head of 700 men, de Brûly, the governor, marched to resist the English, but the planters implored him, for the sake of their lives and property, to surrender. He hesitated, and was lost. He surrendered, and then shot himself. Two hundred thousand dollars' worth of indigo had been seized from ships in the harbour, the forts and magazines of the Baie de St Pierre were blown to pieces, and the negroes were burning and killing.

The captain-general called every man in Ile-de-France to arms. With two thousand black gunners, he would defy the whole British Navy. His bluff had been called, and he knew it.

The general was a broken man, his dreams of empire faded, his little tropic kingdom surely lost. In his silences these days was more than a tinge of bitterness. He had played for the honour and glory of France, and France had let him down. Too shrewd to be sanguine, he was playing a losing game, though neither friend nor enemy knew it. He was made of sterner stuff. The Tricolour would wave in Ile-de-France till the British tore it to shreds.

It was on a steamy evening in March that Mr Hope, the new commissioner of prisoners, approached him with the latest list of exchanges. The cartel *La Mouche* had crept in from the Cape, dispatches from France aboard her, and Hope was making his plans for her return.

He found the general morose and listless, a sheaf of documents from Paris before him, his brows meeting in an absent-minded frown. Mr Hope had found the general extraordinarily amenable lately in the matter of prisoners, signing recommendations with scarcely a question, his volcanic splutter and his angry bellow a thing of the past. He could not know, as Decaen did, that the gold of Napoleon's crown was turning to brass. Mr Hope put it down to his own particular charm of manner, and became emboldened with success.

"There is one other matter before I leave, your excellency," he suggested pleasantly. "The case of Captain Flinders, at Wilhelm's Plains."

The general turned and faced him, with a cold stare of dull resentment.

"This is a particularly tragic case, your excellency. I find that the captain, through no fault of his own, has been a prisoner of war here for the past six and a half years—a cruel exile to an innocent man. Never, never I say, has he been a militant enemy to Ile-de-France or to France. His career has been blighted, for science is his life. The highest idealism, the desire, not for naval honours, but for the undying fame of great exploration——"

"Spare me your eloquence, Hope," cut in the general sharply. "I know this man, much better than you can tell me."

Hope stared that cold resentment in the eye.

"And yet you refuse to him the freedom you give to those who in truth deserve the fate of enemy and spy?"

"Have I refused it? Have you asked it?"

"Then, general——" Hope rose in delighted surprise.

"Ach. What does it matter. Let him go."

"A thousand thanks, your excellency."

"I want no thanks. The man means nothing to me. He will sign a paper that he will not engage himself in warfare against this nation during the present war, that he will not disclose the knowledge he has gained in this island—and let him, in future, acquire a proper respect for the officers of His Napoleonic Majesty's command."

The news reached Matthew the next afternoon, a letter from Hope to say that he might sail in the cartel immediately for India—the "full enjoyment of the favour" that he had been granted three years ago.

No shade of emotion, no ray of brightness, crossed his care-lined face.

"Another false dawn?" he said briefly to Maman, handing her over the note.

"Ah, no, you must believe this time."

"I have believed so often."

"Things are changed. I believe it now—unless you will not sign."

"I will sign anything, provided they do not forbid the publication of my discoveries, or challenge my honour."

No word from Monistrol confirmed it as yet—Monistrol, the ghost man, the living shadow of perfect politeness and nothing more. He could do without it. He wished for contact with none of them. If it were true, let Hope take charge of it all. He went back to his game of tric trac.

But next day came the official confirmation. He was to embark in the India cartel on the following Saturday.

For all his doubts, it brought a rosy glow of expectation to his face, a light into his eyes.

21

Blue Water

It was on 20 March in 1810 that Flinders rode for the last time to his lookout.

Cloud-races flecked the rippled mirror of Vacois in fleeting sun and shadow. The valleys sparkled in the sun-showers, and the cascades were singing.

Six years in paradise, six years in hell.

Never a day that he had not wakened to anguished hoping, never a night that his last thoughts were not of bitter despair.

Now that the time had come for leave-taking—surely he need not doubt it—a wistfulness came over him for all his unwisdom of grieving. He was almost sorry to go. *Partir, c'est à mourir un peu* ...his fretfulness, his melancholy, would leave a poor memory. They, too, had had their troubles that he might have lightened, and now, perhaps, they were to be evicted, and by his people. How generous they had been, how deep their understanding. Enemies—for six years his only friends.

Time and again he halted Labauve's pony, to look back on the nestling roofs of bungalows in the green, the familiar patchwork of the plantations, above them the ramparts of the hills. The hills would stand sentinel to horror. A grim and terrible thought, the vision of shellfire in this happy valley. Slaughter and the sword, the wreckage of homes, the fruitful earth torn and gaping, littered with dead. Whichever triumphed, heaven protect his friends.

For him, England again, and what would he find there? Sir Joseph aged, no doubt. Ann, perhaps, aged. Involuntarily his hand flew to his brow, the deep grooves of the wrinkles of thought, the tell-tale silvered hair. He had been young and gay when last he kissed her. Could they grow young together again, forgetting the years between? Might yet the name of Matthew Flinders rank beneath that of Cook? His voyage, his country, and his love—these three. Fate yet might smile upon him. The story is written for us. Who can tell?

As the pony scrambled and reared to the heights, a sudden fear came over him. What if Decaen should ask him to dinner again? Heaven forbid. He would die a prisoner rather than eat of humble pie at that man's table. A puny consideration—he knew it. Nevertheless his cheeks grew hot.

Ile-de-France—a shining prize for Britain. It lay at his feet in beauty, encircled by the sea, but the clouds were dark to westward. What was that black speck? A ship! And another … and behind her a fleet! If he only had his spyglass! What pennant flew at the masthead of the flagship? Red, white and blue it must be, but which red, white and blue? That men should foolishly fight to the death beneath the same colours! They had swung to anchor far off the Coin de Mire. His eyes grew blurred with watching, but through the morning none of them moved.

He told them the news at home, and their faces lengthened. It could but be the English. The dark hour was come. They listened for shellfire during the night, but heard no sound.

With most of his baggage gone before for the daredevil escape he had planned, preparations were easy and simple. His shirts, jackets and uniform were soon packed, his charts and chessmen with a few personal trifles, and a pretty little tric-trac board, the gift of the family, presented by Labauve.

"To you, and to Madame," said Labauve, "and when you play together in the happy future, you will perhaps sometimes remember the players of the past."

For his part, he had sent to the Cape for two cases of the best Constantia wine, that they might drink to him *bon voyage*, but not, please, this time, till he was on the high seas.

Farewells were quiet and very restrained when it came to the moment of parting. Suspense lay heavily on their hearts, and Matthew was not happy.

"Strange our reactions," he said to Maman. "Now that I am fairly certain of going, so much of my joy has vanished. My heart is oppressed with the idea of leaving you all, at such a time, and perhaps forever."

"Ach, but you do not speak so. We shall see you among us when peace has made us one."

"A thousand times yes, with my good ship's company, and my brother, and my wife. Then you will meet as friends, for friends we shall be always, whatever betide. I shall call at Ile-de-France to refit, and I shall tell them of all the wonderful products you have for the advantage of Australia. Not forgetting my little friends, Marc and Aristide? They come too, as midshipmen, is it not? Oh, let us hope that it will not be long—just time for your captain-general to be out of my way."

Maman dimpled in laughter. "He is to you *bête noire*."

"I take no more chances with him, Maman, no—not even for you."

"May we write to you in England, no?"

"I think so, if you word your letters with caution. Remember that you have made me not of France, but of Ile-de-France."

"Then let it be *au revoir,* and not *adieu*."

"Never *adieu*."

They kissed him, Delphine with a gentle gravity, a little self-conscious, Sophie with a jest, Maman with tears and a smile.

"Blessings, my son."

"May God in his infinite mercy preserve you and yours," he said simply. A hand-clasp to Labauve, and he was gone, at last, along the Port Louis track.

Toussaint carried his sea-chest down to the seaport, where Hope told him he was to board the cartel *Harriet*, bound for Bengal, but not yet. He would give the word. The English fleet was all about them—the lid was screwed down tight—cruising so near the forts that shots had been fired to warn them to safe distance. The cartel must wait her chance to slip away.

He need not have worried about a vice-regal invitation to dinner. The masque of Monistrol melted into kindly congratulation but the captain-general kept well out of his way. Hugh Hope was his host, and Pitot his constant companion. They made the most of the few brief hours that might be left to them.

An inquiry concerning his papers met with a brusque rebuff. The general had given no orders. Let him apply to the Imperial Government in Paris. When he considered a formal demand for the third copy of his log-book, Hope strongly advised against it.

"Sleeping dogs," he cautioned. "You are lucky enough to get away. Be quiet, and be careful what you write."

Three weeks went by in Port Louis. Always on tenterhooks, waiting for the signal, he spent it in a round of farewells. La Mêle, the old sergeant, clapped him on the shoulder in rough but sincere affection, introduced him to all his new English prisoners as an exhibit he was proud of, and wished him good luck. The Brunets gave another dinner party of pleasant reunions, but many were the gaps among his acquaintances—fighting for France or taken prisoner. Mothers and wives, old and young, known and unknown, tapped on the lattice every day to tell a tearful story, to ask him to do his best for missing boys. Gladly he promised. No name would be forgotten. He kept a special notebook for persons, places and pleas.

Permission was given him to visit the Pitots' country house at Grande Rivière, and some of Sergeant La Mêle's English were invited, a Mr Hunter, old Mr and Mrs Scott, and a Miss McCary, who were to be fellow-passengers in the cartel. In a grand procession of chaises, palanquins and ponies they arrived, enemy guests of honour! French and English made merry opponents in the excitement of the games, with the best-loved songs of both, and all singing.

Many a toast went the rounds of the company, and Matthew's health over and over. When Thomy, taking advantage of the long friendship, raised his glass "To a wife who waits in England—our loss is her gain—Madame Flinders!" the loving-cup was full and brimming. A few of the Frenchwomen wept as the story was whispered. They surged about him, and kissed him in soulful good-bye.

Matthew rose and cleared his throat, and there was expectant silence. In fluent French he thanked them for their never-failing kindness, that had saved him from despair. Of Thomy he had so much to say that Thomy went pink with embarrassment, trying to hide his beaming smiles under his cravat. Thanks to the associations of Ile-de-Freance, his sorrows never without sympathy, the French people would be his friends forever.

"*Après la guerre!*" he cried. "Before this year is ended, may our two nations, France and England, stand as united as we."

They cheered him to the echo.

On the way back, as they passed the old stone bridge at the Lantaniers River, the palanquin was stopped by a familiar little figure with boyish brown curls. It was Noémi, come to bid her dear captain adieu, with a fragrant bouquet of La France roses, that she had grown with great pride in this rank tropic isle.

At the end of that week he received a message to board the cartel at once. The first warm breath of the trade-wind was drying the streets of Port Louis as, with a few shouted instructions to Toussaint out in the courtyard, he hurried to the office of Pitot Frères, *Négociants*.

Hemmed in by dusty files and barred windows, Thomy was looking blankly at the square, day-dreaming. Edouard was away at the war.

Thomy was sad and glad to hear the news. He would miss Matthew, but *hélas!* their little circle was so much broken that it was but another good one gone. Thomy was not so glossy these days. He had not the heart—nor the money. The firm was well bankrupt, but so was the rest of Port Louis. Things could not be worse. There was no trade in the pirates' loot. The English got all that. But soon they, too, would be Great Britain, was it not?—the ghost of an ironic smile.

Thomy clapped on his hat, and walked down to the landing-steps with him, while Toussaint carried the luggage to where the *Harriet's* boat was waiting. It was their last farewell. The general would not allow departing prisoners contact with the shore, and Thomy would certainly not be allowed on board.

With his head bent, as he walked in silence beside the young Frenchman, Matthew realized all he had done. When he was a stranger among them friendless and dishonoured and penniless, Pitot had come to him. When he was hopeless and ill, Pitot had been there. When others branded him a spy, Pitot had trusted. From the shadow of the prison walls, where he was like to die, his friend had redeemed him to live in a land of loveliness, with those who would ever be dear. The carefully-guarded letters that had stated his case in England and in France, and at last had won him his freedom, the letters that told his loved ones that he still lived, and set his distracted mind at rest about them, the money matters smoothed over without a shadow of surety, and the faithful championship with the captain-general of this colony that had saved him from ruin and ruined his benefactor—all these he owed to Pitot. Whatever he could do in a life-time was not sufficient to repay this man for the blessing of a friend in need.

Thomy was prattling of this and that, in false animation. With Toussaint and the baggage in the prow, the boat was waiting.

"Good-bye, my dear friend," said Matthew brokenly, "which means, in our old-time English, God be with thee. I shall not try to thank you. Believe me, should you ever be cast up by ill-luck upon some English or other land in the same condition as myself, do not place confidence in many marks of friendship. There is much treachery in the world. It will indeed be a great wonder if you should ever meet one like yourself."

"God's blessing," replied Pitot. For once his volubility failed. His eyes were full of tears, and even English Matthew blinked as the long-boat pulled out … and that dapper little figure alone on the landing-stage merged into the blue of the houses and the hills, even as the tall figure of Doctor George had faded into the headland long ago.

Deck of a ship again, echoing his footsteps. An old salt in a Turk's cap, bowling along with a bucket, and the wide harbour about him, dazzled with afternoon sun. The years fell away. Would they sail at sundown. Nobody knew. The captain was ashore, and the master's mate knew nothing except that a servant was here for him, an English seaman named Hermon from the *Seaflower*. He was called to take the luggage from Toussaint.

In great haste, Matthew scribbled a note to Maman, and gave it to Toussaint with a silver dollar. The African tore his woolly hair, and bawled like a baby. He ended up by grovelling at his master's feet and imploring him to let him be a stowaway. The only way to get him ashore was a promise to take him as ship's boy when he came back. The new *Investigator* was filling up nicely with a very diversified crew.

No anchor was weighed that night, nor for many days — April, May, June, and in June they heard the guns of joy for the marriage of Napoleon to Marie Louise of Austria. A little frigate had slipped through the lines with dispatches and the news. Matthew played whist day after day with Mr and Mrs Scott and Miss McCary. He was sick unto death of the outline of the hills. From a coloured sailor he took lessons in Malay, to prepare for the north-west coast.

On 7 June, a Monsieur Francis sought him out, bringing his parole.

I, the undersigned, captain in his Britannic Majesty's Navy, having obtained leave of his excellency, the captain-general, to return to my country by way of Bengal, promise on my heart and honour not to act in any service that might be considered as directly or indirectly hostile to France or its allies during the course of the present war.

MATTHEW FLINDERS,

Port Napoleon,

I. de F.

They returned his sword, wrapped up like a parcel, but not his spy-glasses, and never a further word of his papers and log-books. The next day the captain-general's man-servant came on deck—a moment of expectation—but he was bringing only a little conservatory of plants in tin pots from Madame Decaen, consigned to a friend in India.

At dawn on the thirteenth, he woke to find the ship under way. There was a white flag at her masthead, and the landing-steps were receding from view. Someone was waving there. Wildly he waved back. Ten minutes later they were aground on a sandbank in the middle of Port Louis Bay. In those slow tropic tides, it was four o'clock in the afternoon before they hauled her off, and turning for the entrance they met a cutter from the British fleet, sailing in under a flag of truce.

What now? A demand on Decaen to surrender, a threat of attack? Not yet were they out of his talons. They clapped on sail, and sheered the forts so closely that they could hear the rowdy voices in the canteen. A few minutes more—blue water.

Another chapter in Matthew's life had ended. The island was a dark blur against the early stars, and all its sadder memories a dark blur in his mind. Six years, five months and twenty-seven days.... At last he was going home.

Lights on the port now, and at nine o'clock that night they came up with the British, the squadron cruising under Commodore Rowley. They signalled the flagship with lanterns. No answer, and she tacked out of their way. It was an hour before they caught her up—to learn that the cutter they had sent in had promised they would not speak the cartel if Decaen would let it go. They assured Rowley that his promise had not arrived when they left.

Ah! The commodore's compliments to Captain Flinders. The corvette *Otter* had just arrived from India, and Rowley was sending her on at dawn to the Cape. He would be happy to accommodate with a passage. In view of acceptance, might they have the pleasure of his company at dinner?

Straight to the Cape, cutting out the long roundabout to India and back!

Hurriedly he changed into full-dress uniform, that venerable uniform from Messrs Schweitzer and Davidson, its great days not yet gone. As his foot touched the deck of the flagship, he was hailed with a salute of three long lines of British tars.

Monsieur Flandare was Captain Matthew Flinders again.

He dined that night in the rollicking company of six officers of his own forgotten rank, hearing the epic stories of Trafalgar. The *Otter* sailed for the Cape at daylight. Ile-de-France was a fragrant whiff of vanilla on the morning air.

Halcyon days of whipping the white-caps at sea, and the Sugarloaf and Table Mountain swam into sight. The *Otter* put into Simon's Bay, and Captain Tomkinson went ashore with dispatches, taking Flinders to call on Colonel Butler. He found in port a whaler from the Derwent River in Van Diemen's Land, heard of the death of his old friend, Captain Collins, and a sensational tale of Captain Bligh, returning to England after a revolution.

He was just on board after a hot and weary morning when the semaphore called him back. Colonel Butler had learned that the India packet was leaving Table Bay that day. Flinders might take the wagon as far as Nuremburg, with horses from there for a 22-mile ride. He was joyously off, leaving instructions for Hermon and the luggage to follow when they might.

The slow jolting of the old Dutch wagon through the white dust was torment, but after a breakneck ride he came into Capetown—to see vanishing sails on the rim of the dusk.

Three vessels had left for England within the week, and nobody knew when to expect another. Stiff with riding and sore at heart, he turned back into the traffic of the ox-carts with a lump of disappointment in his throat. Somebody touched him on the shoulder—Harry Lynne. Lynne found him a lodging with an old vrau at 86 dollars a month. She offered to make it 46 dollars a fortnight, and he finished up by paying her 120 for six weeks.

He dined with Lord Caledon and General Grey, Commander of the Forces, much interested in his charts, and with Admiral Bertie, Harry's father-in-law.

"You are aware, Mr Flinders," said the Admiral after dinner, "that we are waiting the wind of the word to strike at Ile-de-France. A chart at the moment will be helpful, and all the information you could give."

"I shall do what I can, sir—a map of the ports and so on—but I prefer to disclose nothing vital that I might have learned privately against the safety of the island. I have given my parole."

"After your experience, you could hardly be expected to keep it. I doubt that Decaen expects you to. These French are our mortal enemies."

"To me, with one exception, sir, they have proved the best of friends. Then again, a parole is a word of honour."

Admiral Bertie looked at him queerly. He was not so welcome after that—indeed, Bertie became so openly hostile that finally Flinders stopped calling.

Bathing in the cascades of the hills, driving to the vineyards of Wynberg and Constantia, he cooled his heels in Capetown, always afraid to go out of sight lest a ship should come and go. The colony had made miraculous progress since his first visit with Bligh—the population quadrupled, and the slopes of Table Mountain a glory of waving corn.

For the rest of the time he sat in his room, reading English newspapers, or restlessly rambled the quays.

Lord Caledon gave a ball on the Prince of Wales's birthday, and ruefully he realized that Sir Joseph's uniform was scarcely up to that. He appeared in boots and round hat, but his excellency was graciously amused, and the romance of his story spread. He certainly was no clumsier than his rolling Dutch partners, slow-footed and sure of speech. Capetown beauties were cabbages to lilies compared with the lissom demoiselles of enemy Ile-de-France.

Regimental dinners and military parades lightened the tedium a little, but he was reduced to a tapping impatience by the first week of August when the *Olympia* cutter put in to the harbour from India, England-bound.

For six weeks they beat the Atlantic behind them, via the Cape Verde Islands, and with heaven within reach were caught in a gale that threatened to toss them to the tender mercies of the coastguards on the rocks of France. Out of the frying-pan into the fire!

Matthew Flinders fought that gale as he never fought before, and—shades of William Kent!—he won.

22

Homing

It was gusty October when the *Olympia* ran the gauntlet of guerilla warfare in the Channel, snavelled a little prize for herself in passing Brest, and came in to the docks at Spithead.

A figure in naval uniform was waving from the landing-stage, and Matthew's heart gave a bound. Samuel! They knew, then, of his coming.

But as they drew closer, he saw that it was not Samuel. That stalwart form, that purposeful stride—surely not little Mr Tycho Brahe!

John Franklin it was, grown to manhood. The *Olympia* was moored, and they clasped hands.

"John!"

"Captain Matthew!"

"How you have changed!"

"And you!"

"Do the others know?"

"Yes, sir. I have told them. Just back from South America, I heard the news of your coming."

"And my wife—?"

"Is in London, waiting."

To hide his flushed face, that twitching of his cheek that would betray emotion, Matthew hurried away to find his servant.

Franklin stood embarrassed. Was this slight, nervous man the sturdy hero of his boyhood, the figurehead of adventure and achievement that had guided his own youth to its fulfilment? He must show no sign of noticing the ravage of the years.

Sir Roger Curtis was in command of the home fleet, and Flinders hurried to him to ask if there were any chance of quick conveyance to London. Not that Sir Roger knew. They must wait for the mail-coach. The malicious little gods of delay and frustration were still tantalizing.

While Hermon went to book their seats, they found a tavern by the dockside, where a sonsy wench brought them a jug of steaming coffee, her coquetry worthy of a better cause.

Flinders was distrait, trying to pick up the broken threads with a thousand random questions.

The first was for the *Investigator* and her men.

All home safely, and scattered in war. Brown was Sir Joseph's librarian. Elder was with Hollowell in the Mediterranean.

George Bass was gone, it seemed forever. When he left Port Jackson in 1803, he sailed into oblivion. There was a mystery about that. King knew more than he told, and King was dead.

King dead?

Aye, in London a couple of years ago, scarce lived to reach home. Some said that Doctor George had been gun-running, or privateering … or it might be looking out a harbour for His Majesty, or helping on a revolution in the interests of the Union Jack. Doctor George had so many schemes, and all of them so hopeful, "until," he wrote, "one hears that I am digging gold in Peru."

A bad place to dig for gold, under the thonged whips of the Spaniards. It was not gold he dug, but silver, if reports were true. The captain of the brig *Harrington*, across from there the next year, told King that Doctor George and Scott, his mate, with the *Venus* and twenty-five men, had been taken prisoner, and sent to the silver mines out from Quito or Valparaiso, or it might have been Valdivia. He had called at all three, and could never remember which. That was a pity, for they might have found him, and the information "of public advantage" that King promised their lordships.

A long silence.

"Tell me, what happened to the *Bridgewater*? I learned that at Bombay she reported us lost."

"She left Bombay and was never heard of again."

"Lost with all hands?"

"So it seems."

"God's justice. Kent?"

"Is dead. Died on the *Agincourt* in May—off Toulon, and buried at sea."

"He brought the *Investigator* home?"

"Aye, and said she was the craziest hulk he ever fought for. She swept right past the Channel over to Denmark. He couldn't bring her in, and when they dragged her she fell to pieces. Brown will tell you the hell of that journey. He chanced his luck with her, and Sir Joseph's garden."

Matthew winced.

"Paterson's gone too, did you know? Mild little Paterson, died in a gale off the Horn, couldn't stand the shaking. And Shortland, the madcap hero of the Mediterranean. Drank the King's health on top of Pompey's Pillar at Alexandria, and then went off to the coast of America, and waded into four fighting Frenchmen with a 40-gun ship, the *Junon*. They smashed him to atoms, only his head left whole, and buried him with full military honours, as a little Nelson, at Guadeloupe."

Flinders felt like a wandering soul, come back to a world of his own long empty. "Thank God you're here, John."

"A close shave at Trafalgar with the *Bellerophon*," laughed Franklin. "I'm one of four out of fifty-eight on her quarter-deck left alive."

"You were in the *Bellerophon*?"

"Aye, signal midshipman. But better than that. I was signal midshipman with Dance, in the *Earl Camden*, coming home from China, after we left you in the *Rolla*."

"What was that?"

"You haven't heard! The Battle of the Painted Fleet!"

"I have heard nothing."

"We left China with the merchant fleet, sixteen in company, with a fortune in tea and silks, Nathaniel Dance in command in the *Earl Camden*. Only thirty-six light guns we carried, but our hulls were bedizened with gun-ports and muzzles, painted on in Chinese lacquers. From a distance we looked like line-of-battle. Linois was hiding in the straits of Malacca. He pounced on us at dusk—Linois in the *Marengo*, with a full-strength squadron of war. All we had was pot and brush, but we puffed up our feathers like fighting-cocks, and the Frenchman wasn't sure.

"At dawn he came after us, to cut off our rear. We turned and faced him. I sent up the flags, 'Bear down in line ahead and engage the enemy.' The gunners stood to the painted guns, every man of 'em grinning. The *Marengo* alone, with eighty-four, could have blown us out of the water. There was a lot of sharp shooting, and powder and smoke—we hit nothing, but they hit one of our men—and then Linois turned tail and ran. We chased them for two hours, and cleared them right off the route—sixteen poor little merchantment chased a French squadron of war. Paris laughed, and Napoleon frowned, and Linois nearly lost his head. Dance is a commodore now, and a knight of the realm. The signal's as much a proverb as Nelson's—and I took Nelson's too, when it ran up on the *Victory*.

"After that, they sent me to Rio, taking the Portuguese king and queen out of Napoleon's reach. I've been out there for a couple of years, acting-lieutenant in the *Bedford*, and I've just come home in time to welcome you."

Matthew smiled. "Now tell me of the family."

Thomas was dead. James was a clerk with the Company in India, and Willingham was in town, a Fellow of Oriel College, Oxford, but thinking of applying for the office of judge in Madras.

"And Samuel?"

"In Devonshire. On half pay. Some trouble. He was in command of the *Bloodhound* under Collingwood, but lost it for some reason."

"A court martial?"

"I believe so. He will tell you. I've heard only gossip."

"Not scandal?" Matthew's searching eyes demanded the truth.

"Oh no, merely gossip. You know what the Navy is. Nothing serious."

Of New Holland Franklin knew nothing. "A curious thing," he said, "your loyalty to that dreary and uncultivated place. There's little future there, unless I'm much mistaken."

"You're mistaken, my boy." The captain of the *Investigator* was back in command. "You were the veriest child there, with little discrimination. In a continent as wide as that, there surely must be something. God doesn't make three million square miles for nothing. Lost, I grant you—too far away. Uncultivated, I grant you. How could it be otherwise? But it's young. Earth uncluttered by the mould of the dead. Give me the new thoughts, the breath of new earth—and it's there. If I could go back—to know what there is to know!"

The bleak wind doubled him up as they jogged up to London in the stage-coach, and a chill of sadness and apprehension was at the bottom of his heart. He was trembling. Franklin noticed.

"A drab welcome our England gives to her wandering boys from the tropics," he said very kindly. "For me, I like the cold, but you need fattening. You'd better go back to Lincolnshire for some of our gooseberry fool."

A wan smile came over the face of the shadow of Flinders beside him.

London was ten years shabbier, ten years older, scarcely changed. The old do not change. The tenement houses leaning, the blur of the streets and the people seemed but the soiled drop-scene in a fifth-rate playhouse, all so familiar, yet nothing friendly, to smile recognition to the exile. His dream. Would it fail him? "Beware of the day when your dreams come true." Who had said that?

He tried to speak of Ann, but her name would not be uttered. Now he could understand the natives of New Holland, who never would mention the name of the dead. But Ann was living, was here! Was his sanity seeping away?

Almost a panic came over him. Now that the meeting had come, the joy he had lived for, he was afraid to face it. He longed for time, an hour, a day, that he might brace himself to the ordeal. Ordeal! How strange, how strange is the human heart.

"Ann," said Franklin suddenly, in answer to his thoughts, "is staying with our cousin, Mrs Proctor, in Whitecross Street. I thought you might prefer—er—a more private place of meeting. Where are you going to stay?"

"At the old address—the Norfolk Hotel in the Strand."

Franklin looked at him keenly. Was he remembering, trying to recall the past?

"I want to be near the Admiralty," Matthew explained awkwardly, "and my agent Standert. There will be much business to transact."

The coach pulled up at the Bull and Crown at Hammersmith, and they hired a fly to take them to the city.

St Paul's in the same place, and London Bridge. The Norfolk Hotel had changed hands, and nobody knew him. A meek man with ceremonious whiskers showed him to a cheerless room on the first floor. It was not the room that he had shared with Ann. Franklin left him, and rattled away in the fly.

Mechanically he poured water from the ewer, and washed and dressed with exactitude—in Mr Schweitzer's uniform, so stained and worn, its gold epaulettes frayed. He drew a chair to the window, looking out on the dismal street with lack-lustre eyes. Autumn—where once it was spring. The falling leaves.

How young they had been, the Matthew and Ann that this place had known ... so ignorant, trusting life. Ann, with her clear grey eyes and curly hair, and all her little furbelows and her laughter, sitting by the window with Trim in her lap, and that bronzed young captain, the youngest in the Navy, kneeling beside her, mapping tracks round the world and building castles in the air. Ah well. Perhaps they could begin from there again.

Franklin would be an hour or more. Inaction now was

unnerving, he was restless. There was time for a hasty call at the Admiralty, no more than to report that he was back in London—back it seemed, from the grave. He put on his wet-weather coat, and went out and battled the wind.

Mr Yorke and Mr Barrow received him with open arms, clapped him on the back with loud congratulations. Promotion was a foregone conclusion, said Mr Yorke. Now they could go on with the matter. A visitor there was his old friend Pearce of the *Providence*. Mr Bligh was back in London, *and* Mr Macarthur. They all laughed heartily at yet another mutiny. Sir Joseph was expected in town from Heston Grove within the next few days. Obviously they were pleased with him. His fears had proved phantoms. Absence had made their hearts so fond it was difficult to leave.

With a lighter step he hurried away as Bow Bells chimed noon, hurried through the racing hackneys and the clockwork crowds—home. Drumming of the redcoats, drumming of the waves on the reef, drumming of quickened blood to his heart ... in the rapids of time he was whirling down to the moment that must come.

In the half-dark at the top of the stairs he paused, hearing voices. One was a woman's. She was there.

With seeing eyes he looked at the closed door ... the door in the dark void that led him to sanity and love. The wandering sickness was over. He had been lost in a phantom world where friends were forgone and forgotten, fretting in fever of ambition, fighting the eternal sea, and dancing in the web of relentless fate. Delirium had fallen from him like an evil dream of faces in the clouds—foreign faces, half-witted men flogging each other, the rambling sailor, the exile, the accursed. Masts of ships swaying in the vortex had become the steady spires of England. He who had forgotten his own language was safe home in the thoughts of his own people ... free to hold the woman he loved, the woman of his dreaming. She was his peace of mind, his purpose, his wisdom and his life. He would know the kindness of her hands, the kindness of her lips, warm as the trade-wind, quiet as low tide.

He opened the door and stood silent. The woman sitting in the chair he had left rose to her feet with a little nervous cry. Rather a small woman. Her back was to the light, and he could not see her face, but she was dressed in brown. There was someone else in the room—of course, Franklin.

All three seemed strangers, actors in an unfamiliar play.

"It's you, Annette," he said very quietly. "Yes ... I knew you were ... waiting."

The woman covered her face with her hands.

He went forward swiftly, and put his arms about her— sombre brown against the faded blue. With cold hands he lifted her face to his.

This sober little body his lovely, laughing Ann. They kissed, and the kiss seemed formal, empty.

Then in long shivering sobs she clung to him, the helpless tears staining the shoulder of his frayed uniform coat. Haggard eyes looking out on the grey, he might have been a man of fifty years.

Were these lips really hers, too thin and too colourless for the kisses of his dreams ... such slight stooping shoulders, her wood-brown curls no longer wilful. Gently he lifted the elderly little bonnet, and put it on the bed, then impulsively, half angrily, drew her nearer, and closed his eyes and laid his cheek on hers.

Her convulsive crying ceased. A sense of comfort came from the warmth of their bodies. He closed her eyes in kisses, and with the salt of her tears on his, he took her lips ... and the depth of their love was heaven on earth, and their need of each other unchanged. Franklin had gone, neither of them knew when.

All through that dreary afternoon they sat there, clasped in their joy and sorrow, now and again to find dear remembered caresses of reawakening love, telling the sad litany of their loneliness, feeling their way, as a blind man feels, back across the years. The lights of London were a faint sprinkle in the grey when the servant brought candles.

Ann wore a rose-pink frock that night, with a deep fichu of cream lace, her hair in high-piled ringlets—and love and the candle-light were very kindly. How often he caught her hands at dinner, bending forward, his heart in his eyes, uncaring that all the world should know them lovers. Shamelessly her head nestled in to his shoulder as they went upstairs together. And at some gay nonsense Matthew Flinders was laughing like a boy.

Wan moonlight slanting above them in the quiet inn room, she was passionately, compassionately his... .

"But the question is," he said in the morning, "what about this promotion?" His hair was tousled, his eyes were bright, and he said it purely in whimsy.

"Oh, 'tis quite sure that 'twill be from the date of thy imprisonment," said Ann, very practical.

"Imprisonment. When was that?" he asked. "While you are near, there is no past, Annette." His arms were about her again, and his lips on hers in hunger.

"Dull skies and rain," he wrote in his diary joyously. Many things now to think of, but first to call upon Lord Spencer.

"Gracious mercy, no!" said Ann firmly. "The first of them all, good Captain Flinders, is to have thy hair cut, and a new uniform, and present thyself to the Lords of the Admiralty looking less like one of thy New Holland kangaroos."

"Australian," he corrected her, smiling. It was strange to have someone to notice his French, flowing hair.

In a hired chariot they set out to have Matthew measured for a new suit. The wet breath of the fog was freshness and fun and mystery, radiant as a remembered spring of ten years ago. London was friendly now, Ann's warm hand in his in her little fur muff.

Lord Spencer was not at home. Captain Flinders left his card.

No sooner were they back at the hotel than Mr Gold of the *Naval Chronicle* came for material to write a leading article, and then Admiral Hunter. A warm Scots handshake, and a burring welcome home. Hearty as ever, his hair brushed back and the neat white curls on top, Admiral Hunter was wearing well—but Admiral Pasley was dead.

This was the beginning of a horde of friends from all voyages, to breakfast, dinner, and tea. Willingham Franklin came, Sam was on his way from Devonshire—and Surveyor Grimes and Surgeon Jamieson, Mrs Paterson and Mrs King arrived, all in a bevy, from New South Wales. The ladies were majestic in widows' weeds, and Mrs King brought young Phillip, a midshipman now, eager to shine in exploration.

The bugles danced on Mrs King's bonnet, and Mrs Paterson's aquiline nose grew sharper as they told of the utter rout of Captain Bligh. Bligh was not to be tolerated, but Macarthur was a menace: a black and bitter man. He was in England, too, awaiting his court martial, for daring to turn the tables on Bligh, to put him in prison! to chase him under a bed! Macarthur had filched half the colony with his money from rum and his pretence of sheep.

"Madame, I don't agree," said Grimes. "Those sheep are doing well. There is method in Macarthur's madness, for all the man's faults."

"But tell me about Bligh," Matthew said. "An impossible man, but I like the old bully well."

They told him. Rum and rampage and nearly murder. Had it been a century earlier, it would have been "off with his head!" There was a clattering of tongues and excitement, contradictions, scandal, and very righteous wrath. They all had been in the thick of it.

What saddening tales of that lost, lovely country they brought him, hunger and strife in the sunlight and peace—no progress, just madness and misery, and the convicts were still being flogged.

Ann, the stranger to their Port Jackson, was sweetly detached, pouring tea. From what she could gather, Macarthur, whoever he was, had steeped the colony in rum, carried escaped convicts on his schooner, defied the judges, refused to pay fines, and when Governor Bligh tried to arrest him, marched his soldiers on Government House, seized the governor, and bundled him into prison. She was rather shocked that Matthew should laugh at such doings.

That Sweet William was found under a bed when the soldiery came to arrest him, his senior midshipman Flinders refused to believe. Under a bed he might have been, for his own obscure reasons, hiding papers, perhaps—but Bligh hiding? Never.

The next day Samuel arrived, genuinely glad at his elder brother's homecoming, but, after the first three hours or so, sullen and difficult still. Strange that the years so little change us, when all is said and done.

Sam had been in and out of trouble all the time, quarrelling with his commanding officers. Now he declined employment, smarting under real or imagined wrongs. He promised Matthew that he would send all papers that he could sift the case. Matthew was proud of that confidence, and only too hopeful that he might take his brother's part.

Bustling about in heavy weather with a light heart, Ann found them very pleasant lodgings with a Mrs Major, at 16 King Street, Soho. For the first time in their ten years' marriage, now she could care for her dear captain with loving hands, like Martha, troubled with many things, to Matthew's loving amusement. If he suddenly took those hands and held them captive, and held her to him in his need of love, she was, in passionate surrender, the woman he had dreamed.

For him, in the prosaic moments, there were long sessions with Standert the agent, to put his father's affairs in order, the oft-told tale of his adventures with the French to naval cronies, and thrashing thither and yon to look up Ile-de-France prisoners.

Mr Yorke at the Admiralty, had noticeably cooled, and it was slightly disturbing to note that Lord Spencer, though in London, was not yet at home. Matthew wrote him a crisp note, drawing his attention to the fact that his card was unacknowledged. Then it was regretted that Lord Spencer had left town.

A letter arrived from the Admiralty stating that he was promoted to the rank of post-captain as from 20 September 1810, the date of his leaving the Cape. Surely there was some mistake. He hurried round to see them.

Yorke received him blandly. He quite agreed that in ordinary circumstances the promotion should have been conferred in 1804, but Flinders had not been a prisoner of war, and so there

477

was no precedent. An Order-in-Council would be necessary for this particular case, and His August Majesty was not meeting the Council now. For reasons that might be obvious if he did.

"So the achievements of science are to be overlooked in the eternal glorification of war?"

Mr Yorke thought that might be so.

"For my six years' imprisonment, I shall be paid at less than £100 a year?"

"I doubt that, under the circumstances, we can offer any more. You were not, I think, engaged in useful service."

Matthew flushed scarlet. "Then the value of my explorations are as nothing?"

"Of that, Mr Flinders," said Yorke very coldly, "I am in no position to judge."

The snub direct. Could Banks know?

A week of suspense, and he was bidden to breakfast at Sir Joseph's.

The door of 32 Soho Square was open. The Sun of Science, in all his splendour, was shining on his satellites as of old.

Sir Joseph had changed very little—his smile, perhaps, more set, his presence more consequential. He took Flinders's hand in his with affection and warm congratulation—but very much the *bon viveur*, with a substratum, or did Matthew imagine it, of steel … perhaps indifference. There were too many others present, too many sycophants scavenging the crumbs of Dives' table. The great man's condescension was kindly to them all, but carefully non-committal.

He presented Flinders to the company with a sympathetic smile.

"Poor Flinders! He put in to the Ile-de-France for water, and was detained as prisoner, and treated as a spy!"

It sounded rather a jest.

Poor Flinders. So that was it.

The charts he had received, very fine, very fine. Oh yes, he had written, via America, several times in fact. Yes, of course, there was the writing of the Voyage. They might go into that to-morrow, at this hour perhaps—that is, if Flinders had the time.

Was that irony? For this interview he had lived in anguish for years.

"Ah yes," said Sir Joseph kindly. "A gruelling experience. Extraordinarily merciless the French. No? You found them most kindly? Well that's interesting too. I'm quite looking forward to hearing all about it. Now all's well that ends well, so make yourself at home."

Matthew took his hat to hurry away. In the hall a courtly lady stopped him.

"I know your face!" she said, in a deep bass voice and almost smiled.

"Miss Sarah Sophia. How well I remember. My name is Matthew Flinders."

"Flinders? Oh yes, of course. But that was a long time ago."

"Ten years."

"Oh dear, I must be growing old. Quite well I hope?"

"Quite well, I thank you."

"Flinders! Yes of course." With another stone of stateliness to carry, Miss Sophia passed on.

He was moody and silent with Ann that day, distracted with misgivings. What if they did not want his work, now that the Frenchmen had stolen it? Were all the years of effort and grief a mockery?

His spirits were brighter when he woke, with thoughts of her tenderness, in the morning, and brighter still when they ushered him in to the big luxurious coffee-room, and a booming welcome from none other than Bully Bligh. At least there was sincere good fellowship in that beefy hand-clasp. The enemy of so many was Matthew Flinders's friend.

Sir Joseph himself, without the crowd, seemed much less superficial. Sitting behind the coffee-urn, gravely judicial in a slant of sun, he heard the long, long story, so often and so sadly told. There were times when he disconcerted Matthew with a glance of shrewd appraisement. His comments were few, in contrast to Bligh's running fire of oaths. He seemed not hostile—Sir Joseph could never be hostile—but undoubtedly reserving judgment. Once or twice his fine eyes narrowed when the condition of the *Investigator* was mentioned.

After breakfast, the charts were spread out, and Flinders forgot his self-consciousness. Now, while Banks watched him more closely still, he was utterly oblivious. The old fire burned brightly. He argued with Bligh, he expounded to Sir Joseph, his cheeks rosy with excitement, his eyes clear, and unafraid, and young.

What did it matter what the Frenchmen had stolen, for the simple reason they were wrong, they were lying. Fifty leagues of the poorest country in Australia, that was all they could lay claim to. Thank God he had come home again, that he might give Britain the truth.

"Which brings us," said Sir Joseph, "to the writing of your Voyage. I have certain manuscripts here, and you, no doubt, have others."

"I have all except my third log-book, and that Decaen has stolen."

"Well, perhaps we can get it, if we make the right representations. This work of exploration must be written."

"If only to damn the Frenchmen," put in Bligh. "They can't touch this man. I taught him what he knows. The impudence, the impudence, sir, of Terre Napolèon!"

"You doubtless enlist with the fleet when your leave is over?" inquired Sir Joseph.

"By no means. I have given parole not to act in any service hostile to France in the present war."

"Ah, good. A parole that serves us very well. Then we can make our plans without delay."

"With regard to the writing, Sir Joseph, I am more than a little diffident. Authorship sits awkwardly upon me. Like Dampier, I am no more than a seaman. The Admiralty, I take it, will engage a literary man for the narrative."

"Literary man to hell!" roared Bligh. "It was one of those bloody land-lubbers that made a fool of Cook. You know the alphabet. You know the facts. Write 'em."

Sir Joseph set the tips of his fingers together.

"No," he reflected. "I don't really see that the Admiralty could find a better man than you. You write quite well, Flinders. Don't trouble yourself about literary style. Leave that to the *Robinson Crusoe* artists. As Bligh says, we want facts."

"Not sunsets," said Bligh with a grin.

Matthew's smile was as merry as the one in Van Diemen's Land, twenty years ago.

"Well," went on Sir Joseph, "that's settled, and I myself will supervise the work. Arrowsmith will do the charts, and Westall's drawings—I've seen them all—are excellent illustrations. When can you begin, Flinders? What are your arrangements?"

"Before anything else, sir, if I may, my home in Lincolnshire. I have not seen my mother and sisters since my father's death."

"The New Year then, and as early as you like."

When Bligh had taken himself off, with congratulations for good work done and Mrs Major's address in his pocket, Sir Joseph Banks and Captain Matthew Flinders, patron and protégé, sat face to face in silence for a moment. There was restraint between them. For Banks, Flinders had failed. For Flinders, Banks.

"I had hoped, Sir Joseph, that my promised promotion to the rank of post-captain would date from the period of my imprisonment—a catastrophe, I assure you sir, that was no fault of mine. I understand from the Navy Office that it dates from my liberation."

"Is that the case?" Sir Joseph proffered snuff.

"This seems unjust."

"It is apparently in order."

"Then could it not be dated from my release, signed by the French Emperor in 1807?"

"I cannot tell you that, Flinders. I have no right to interfere in purely naval matters."

"If I am to write the Voyage, it means such a difference in circumstances. I shall have to remain in London for reference to charts, books and papers. I doubt that, on my present income that is possible. I shall be on Navy half-pay, the limbo of the unwanted, not being engaged in the war."

"Mm. I'm sorry to hear that." Sir Joseph was genuinely sorry. "We might make a memorial, to the King in Council. I'll map out the skeleton, and you can fill it in. But in any case, the Admiralty should make you a grant for the writing of the Voyage. I'll see what I can do, and let you know."

"My thanks, Sir Joseph."

Strangely disheartened, Matthew rose to go.

"By the way, Flinders," Sir Joseph spoke very quietly, "you know, I take it, that the *Investigator* came home."

"I do, sir. Captain Kent brought her."

"Exactly. After she had been a store-ship at Port Jackson for a little over two years."

"You have Governor King's report, Sir Joseph, on the *Investigator* as I left her."

"I have. I perused those quite early, with your letters, and could, at that time, see your point of view."

"My fears were not for myself, sir, as I think my record will show. They were for my men aboard her. Captain Kent is dead. I knew him well. All I can say is that England will see few greater seamen."

Sir Joseph rang the bell for his man.

"A fine seaman indeed. He brought the *Investigator* round the Horn, in winter. Brown will tell you about it—you'll find him in the library. He came home with an excellent collection after all, to add to my box of seeds that you sent with your brother on the *Rolla*. Well, good-bye till I see you ready for the work, and the best of good fortune, Flinders."

Matthew came back to Ann in their lodgings with tragedy written in his eyes.

"What is it? No success? Has Sir Joseph failed us?"

"Sir Joseph," he told her quietly, "is invariably kind."

23

A Voyage to Australia

Frosting of moonlit silver on city roofs, the first snow he had seen in ten years was friendly enchantment as they hurried through the dim streets of November dawn. A cockney boy, feet stained with the slime of London, trundled their trunks to the White Horse Inn in Fetter Lane, but the coach was five minutes gone.

"Tike a 'eckney 'n' y'll kitch it hup 't Fower Swans 'n Bishopsgite!" the urchin yelled for a cab as he bit his florin.

The hackney lurched them through chasms of drab sleeping houses, grimy strands in the great cobweb of London. Through the thick reek of a tanning factory they were rolling down to the Four Swans, and there was the Cambridge coach, still jerking and bustling outside it. Another florin to the sweating hackney driver, Ann's trousseau bumped to the roof, cry of ostlers, crack of whips, and they were off for the counties.

The odours of the big slums, manure, tanning factory, gin-palaces, and stagnant humanity were soon lost in the scented breath of spreading meadows. Smoke o' London fell behind, a drop-curtain to the flying green of Cambridge fields.

Burnt umber and smouldering blue of New Holland … crystal vistas of Ile-de-France … the spires and the shires of his own England passed in a pastel of mist. How little he knew of it save this London-Lincoln road, and then forever in haste.

Fifty-one joggling miles in the day, they came to the old university town in the early winter dusk. It was too late for sight-seeing round the cathedral and colleges, so they sat round the ingle of the Blue Tower Inn, regaling their fellow-travellers with Matthew's Sindbad tales of riverless lands and rocs' eggs. Next day, on the postchaise for Wisbech, was opaque and clammy with rain. Nameless inns, nameless towns in a vague litany behind them, they changed at five in the evening for a chill night on rough roads to the goblin dance of a lantern.

At daybreak, bruised by the black angular seats, they crawled to the flapping sign of a "Rose and Crown". Cold eggs and frozen ale, they were off down the ruts to Tydd ... and the senator oaks of Lincolnshire lashed by the wind of the North Sea.

A grey fog veiled the Fenlands as the wanderer came home. All the little villages and farms and hedgerows were snooded down in snow, a phantom shape looming above them. Boston Stump! Soon the blue lintels of the bluff spire were racing over the foreground hedges, and those Gothic arches rose higher and higher to the scudding clouds.

But the shepherd's staff of St Botolph enfolded a stranger people. Hooded and shrouded in their dark cloaks, heads bent to the whipping wind, they seemed a procession of mourners. Where were the lads and lasses who danced "Left Hand and Right"?

The frail smiling shadow of Cousin Henrietta came to meet them at Spalding, and Grandfather Flinders, hearty at eighty, his white beard, down to his knees, a landmark. They dined together at the gabled old White Hart, and then the postchaise clattered them north through the dreary afternoon to Boston. A fitful sleet swept the cathedral. The same old trawlers were painted at the quays. The old salts were weather-bound in the inns.

At nightfall the bridge by the musty, homely Corn Exchange, and Donington ... Bodycoat, Odling, Hopper, Blanchard, Tagg,

Hiley, Cawkwell, the shop-signs of the High Street just the same, but the green of the ivy was gone from the house in Market Square, and gone the slate where he had written his love of the sea. Never again would a little doctor come bouncing out in his gig.

Elizabeth Flinders met them in the doorway, the lamplight shining on her thin grey hair, a greeting less of smiles than tears. She had just come from Spilsby, from Aunt Franklin's burial.

Ann's mother was waiting in the prim little sitting-room with its Otaheitian mats and tropic shells, and Susanna was there, tranquil, full bosomed matron, a small, shy Susan by her side. The curly-headed mite turned to him with a rehearsed curtsey, her baby fingers in the corals he had sent from Ile-de-France—"Welcome, dear Uncle Mattie, and I do thank thee for the pretty pink beads." There were two tall, graceful girls, his step-sisters. Young James Harvey, Betsy's bright, intelligent boy, slept in his own old corner under the eaves.

Which was harder—missing the dear lost faces, or learning to love the new? He smiled on them from the doorway, a thin, braided figure, dark eyes too bright, lips set in too straight a smile. The grandfather clock watched him quizzically from the perished plush curtains.... "It's the boy!" The carpet was in tatters on the stairs ..."Did thy cousin Willingham admire my new rose bonnet?"

He turned to Ann, seeking the comfort of her warm, living hand.

But the little doctor was with them at the big dining-table that night, and George Bass was there, laughing across to black-haired Betsy.

He talked alone with his stepmother where once all were laughing together. Times had been hard for the Franklins since father and eldest son were gone. The Spilsby bank that Thomas founded had failed, the business and the big house were sold. Some of the girls were married, the others lived on with their mother on what Willingham could spare them as a poor lawyer in London, and John, out of a sub-lieutenant's pay. Doctor

485

Flinders had left £600, which in nine years had steadily dwindled. Perhaps, now that Matthew was home, the properties might be sold—or perhaps he and Ann would come to live here?

He sadly told her he must go back to London, to write his Voyage for Sir Joseph.

New faces everywhere among the bankers on the Fens, the townsfolk scarcely remembering, he felt more foreign among his own people than with the enemy French. Goody Cawkwell, sweetshop-marm of merry childhood days, was a shrill little skeleton in a shawl and a wheel chair.

"Eh? Eh?" she screeched. "Ou aye! Matt Flinders ... used to be da-octor's boy!" She squinted up at him curiously, and for an unconscionable time went on wagging her head.

Flax-fields, mills and maltings deep in charcoal of fog ... St Mary's of the Holy Rood and Boston Bells tolling the generations by.

All round the Fen country in dark weather trundled Ann and Matthew in a dog-cart, to uncles, cousins, aunts, druggists, clergymen, shopkeepers, tutors, descendants all of the old Nottingham lacemaker, eager to hear of isles of wonder on the under side of the earth. Their world stopped short with the Witham and the Wash, but their hearts and their peat-fires glowed warmth and pride, and in the end the homecoming was happy.

One evening Matthew walked back through the snow from a silent, reproachful Revesby, his eyes on the white-shrouded Stump, his thoughts of the boy who had travelled this road when the bells rang Enderby. One day he and Ann drove over to Partney, to the little brown rectory shivering in the wind and the Great Oak weighted white with its thousand years.... They held each other close and kissed there, but—dare he admit it to himself—he felt a little foolish that the villagers should see them, elderly people love-making in a flurry of rain and sleet, spectres peering after the past. On the way home, Ann suffered a sick headache.

Nurses and servants, bobbing curtseys, were everywhere remembered. Mr and Mrs Shinglar called, and Mr and Mrs

Lound, delighted with their old pupil who had changed the map of the world that hung on the schoolroom wall.

"A new Archimedes, a new Ptolemy," mumbled Mr Shinglar. "Have I not told thy father long ago?"

Two of the school-fellows brought sons who yearned for the sea. He mapped out their course of studies by Robertson and Hamilton Moore, remembering Uncle John, and promised to find them a ship with his friends if he should not go again … why should he have said that, he wondered. There were officers in the Navy twice his age. Why should he feel so old?

After holly and hilarity of Christmastide, they made north through Lincoln to Hull, where Matthew was interested to find Mr Watt's miracle steam engine, now known at the other end of England, raising the Humber in millions of gallons for the town's water supply. There were ridiculous rumours that they were fitting it into a wagon that would travel without horses at fifteen miles an hour for the mad creatures who cared to risk their necks in it. On the packet-boat for Barton, Ann lost her bandbox with the new honeymoon finery, and fretted for it all the way down.

Dinner at Lincoln, supper at Falkingham, breakfast at Stilton, dinner at Baldock, and London at ten o'clock at night—the world was certainly gathering speed. After thirty-four bone-shaking hours of misery in the coach, and a hot bath that cost him four shillings, he called on Sir Joseph early next morning, ready to begin the great work.

Sir Joseph had thought no more about it. A heavily-bandaged foot on a stool, an occasional frown of pain, he was in the throes of a vicious attack of gout. Lightly he twirled his globe of the world to the unfinished outline of the Great South Land sketched in ink on the blue of the Great South Sea—nine thousand miles of swinging arcs of coast in a mighty half-circle, where once had been but the hazy dotted line of Cook's New South Wales.

"Great work in truth, Flinders. I am mortified to neglect it. Let us get your voyage under way. I shall be honoured to supervise production in all its branches. To-day I shall consult with Barrow at the Admiralty. If you can call to-morrow, I shall have him here."

They sat in the big coffee-room, a Major Rennell present and Captain Bligh, a volcano in action, still spouting fire and brimstone at Macarthur.

Flinders ran his finger round the well-known coastline he had drawn with so delicate a brush.

"Sir Joseph, I have a suggestion. Now that New Holland and New South Wales, except for the merest shadow of doubt, are known to form one land, I feel there should be a general name to embrace it. For some years I myself have referred to it as Australia—more musical, more apt than Terra Australis, a fitting name for a fifth continent, I hope you will agree. I should like to entitle the work 'A Voyage to Australia'."

"Australia."

Sir Joseph savoured the word, as though testing one of his own fine wines. "Europe, Asia, Africa, America, Australia. Mm. What do you think, gentlemen? It sounds pleasant and appropriate to me.'

"A happy thought," said affable Major Rennell.

"Better than New Holland," growled Bligh, "or the cock-shy of Terre Napoléon."

"That reminds me." Sir Joseph took down an elegant volume from a shelf within reach. He handed it over with a crooked smile.

"*Voyage de Déscouvertes aux Terres Australes* by Monsieur François Péron—but don't take it seriously, Flinders. Don't let it perturb you. Sir John Barrow and I have long ago vindicated your discoveries and your name with articles I shall show you from the *Quarterly Review*. They may take a little time to penetrate to Paris, but have no fear. The charts you sent me from Ile-de-France will stand forever in history."

Matthew studied that elegant volume well into the small hours.

Nymphs, scrolls, sea-lions, flying fish and flying Mercuries, Protée and Poseidon, Aeolian harps and fantastic *kangouroux*— M. Péron, like M. Perrault, had written fairytale. Commodore

Baudin's poor fifty leagues he had stretched to a round three thousand, in fantasy of a land, till the French found it, *entièrement inconnue*. There were myriad French names to prove it, from Baie Talleyrand—Murray's Port Phillip—to Ile Lucas, in the far north-west, named for the sniper in the shrouds who shot Nelson down on the deck of the *Victory*.

In poetry and drama, M. Péron described discoveries he had never seen. Freycinet's charts, so far as they went, were very good indeed, but they went very wide of the mark, like Commodore Baudin's. By some extraordinary oversight, Baudin was never mentioned. Terre Napoléon, in one majestic sweep, embraced the south coast of Australia from Bass Strait to the Leeuwin—in words, not in maps. The Flinders charts were quoted but not stolen. Decaen, for all his malevolence, had not robbed Britain to pay France.

With Napoleon's purse behind it, production was superb ... but through those flowery and heroic chapters, Flinders could smell the sickening reek of the *Géographe*, could see her laggard sails, her squalid decks, the suppurating sores and the dragging limbs of her men. In discovery, as in war, it seemed, the horror was best forgotten. He felt no anger, no animosity. His work, unchallenged, would stand as his own, and now François Péron himself—one of three of Baudin's twenty-three scientists who had lived to return to France—was dead. *Vanitas vanitatem*. Why will men steal, and strive with each other, and hate?

Next morning Sir Joseph was business-like, Sir John Barrow bland. Not to be outdone by Napoleon, the Admiralty had agreed to pay for the reproduction of charts, Westall's engravings, and Bauer's excellent plates of birds, animals and botanical treasures. All they expected of Flinders was that the general sale of the work should defray the cost of printing and paper.

So the author must pay the piper—and the author, as he modestly pointed out to them again, was no literary light to draw the crowd.

"I am a man of figures, not letters," he said. "I doubt that I can combine science with sales."

"Oh nonsense," said Sir Joseph. "Whatever you do, you do well. So now there's nothing but to begin."

Flinders flushed.

"Gentlemen ... it may not have occurred to you that, not being in the service of war, I am at present on half pay. Were it not for this work, I could live in the country contented, but for reference to many authorities, first of all you, Sir Joseph, and the Astronomer-Royal and the Admiralty, I must live in London. Living in London is beyond my present means. I cannot be employed during the time in any other way. Is the work of sufficient importance for me to be rated at full pay?"

Sir Joseph referred to Sir John, and Sir John looked grave.

"The trouble is, we have no precedent," he said. "Such an arrangement, so far as I know, has never been made before. If you can find one, Flinders, submit it, and we shall be pleased to consider."

Flinders was silent for the sake of the work. If he persisted, they might postpone it till after the war. His time and labour, then, must be given in the limbo of half pay.

That night, a little ashamed, he discussed his means with Ann. She was sweetly understanding, and they selected another lodging—No. 7, Naussau Street, Soho, £2 10s. a week, nicely furnished, over Hyde the jeweller, and the landlord found fires. Mr Watt's new steam-engines had made coal a luxury in England—O for the reef seven miles long that Doctor George had touched with his hand on the coast of New South Wales.

A Voyage to Australia—that week it was begun.

On 25 January, the anniversary of his captain's commission, Brown, Bauer and Westall came to dine ... in a terrace house with a number in a dull city street, but as they quaffed the last of Matthew's Constantia port, the *Investigator*'s sails swelled white above them, the yellow sands of Lilliput loomed up on the port bow.

Westall was an R.A. In leather jerkin and impressive cut gilt lettering, Dr Brown's *Prodromus*, a heavy Latin tome, had just been published—*Prodromus Floriae Novae Hollandae, a* genealogical tree of the world's botany back to the Stone Age continent, an exhaustive dissection of every green leaf in that wide brown land. Beaming behind his spectacles, ever-genial Ferdinand Bauer basked in the shade of its fame. Their work was accomplished ... and Flinders was ten years behind. So much to do, so little done.

Ann was in bed with a sick headache next morning.

He went out in the drizzling rain to see Arrowsmith, and Nicol, the King's bookseller, then down to Greenwich by coach to the Astronomer-Royal, but Dr Maskelyne was now so withered, so querulous, so hermetically deaf that he made little headway there. He came home late at night via Sir Joseph's library, where Brown was installed in the seat of Solander as chief librarian, with tomes of antique exploration sheltered under his coat. Alone in the melancholy lamplight, he propped them beside him on the scratched oak dining-table, and sat there making notes for an historical introduction till the clock in the hall croaked three.

Most of the days that followed he sat writing, cramped in the cold, and most of the nights by the landlord's niggardly fires. His writing was stilted as a schoolboy's essay, and he knew it. He read it over unsatisfied, and began it again and again. Of the charts that were stained with sea-water, nibbled by Port Louis rats, riddled and creased from so long packing in casks and trunks, he started what he fondly hoped were the final fair copies. Patiently, silently, he bent to his work for hours. Even on Sundays, Ann, gently reproachful, went to church alone.

"There is so little time," he excused himself.

"My dear Matthew,"—she paused in tying her bonnet strings—"why this fevered urgency, this anguish of haste? You are still a young man."

"I will soon complete my thirty-sixth year. Seven were lost to me, a gap in my life that must be bridged before I live again. Thank God that after all my sorrowing and my fears, thou shouldst be near to help me. My dark star."

His arms about her in happy realization, he laid his head on her breast a moment, then kissed her away to service—quick

491

step, pretty frou-frou of skirts, and a backward wave of her hand as she turned the corner ... Ann grown young in womanhood since her love had come back from his gypsy lover, the sea.

The sixteenth of March was bleak and dirty in thaw, but Annette sang gaily at the household tasks, and all morning Matthew worked by the window, perfecting the great discoveries of Doctor George's brief career, so familiar to him, so new to the world. In grey square of parchment he could see the eternal grey surges herding west in the twilight to where seal cities flourished in the cold archipelagoes. He could see the tanned forehead of Doctor George wrinkled in some problem of titanic tides, see the muscles rigid in those strong young arms as he hauled on the *Norfolk's* mainsail, shouting above the shouting of the gale.

"'Twas Christmas week, so westward singing carols ... swing and crash of a big strait down there... ." The boy who found it was a wraith of the seas that had called him from his home in the Fens. The quill of Matthew Flinders scratched in its Gothic curves memorial to his friend, that cepheid star, George Bass.

By noon the chart was faultless, even to his searching eye. As they stood together conning it over in the wan light of the window, Ann admiring the tiny figures and quaint design of the soundings, came a peal of the bells of victory and a faint throaty cheering from over Westminster way. He hurried out to hear what the criers were calling.

Ile-de-France had fallen! The wasps' nest was broken in the south. The sea road to India was Britain's right-of-way.

At the Navy Office he read the dispatches—Decaen had fought like a wild-cat, and Hamelin with him on the sea. No sooner had he himself left the island than Keating and Rowley landed troops at Roderiguez, while the fleet from the Cape under Bertie followed and closed in. The British had snatched the forts at La Passe—to be whipped out of them by the French in three days' vicious battle.

Till November the Tricolour waved defiance, but then the gallant little game was up. With the Cape fleet storming the western coast, the Bombay squadron hove in sight—70 sail, 11,000 European troops, 2000 marines, and nearly 3000 Sepoys. Resistance was mad, but Decaen was mad. He whipped his negroes, rallied his creoles, and set the island ablaze ... but on 1 December, Abercrombie was marching his regiments from Pamplemousse, down through the blackened hills into Port Louis. Decaen struck colours from the Residency flagstaff, and invited his conquerors to dine. Poetic justice! they clapped him into the Garden Prison, to be sent to France by cartel.

Flinders listened with a philosophic smile. Fellow feeling might teach a tyrant to be kind.

The English ships brought letters from Thomy Pitot and Labauve—letters that echoed the lightning and thunder of war—and one from Ann, sent back to him, written five years ago.

"I shall answer it now, my love." ... They put the work away for a gay day at Kensington Gardens. At night he brought out Labauve's little board, and taught her ladyship tric trac, with memories of Tamarinds and Wilhelm's Plains, and all the calls—and all the endearments—in French.

Scores of requests now came from enemy prisoners, seeking his influence for passages home ... it meant long trudgings across London in the rain, so often to find that the people he sought were out. Admiral Hunter was a frequent caller with friends homing from New South Wales, and Bligh, from his home in Lambeth, came to rant about Macarthur for hours on end. James Wiles from Jamaica, and Job Lound from Lincolnshire wrote that they were sending their sons to be naval cadets in the new Portsmouth College. Would Flinders see to their wardrobe and well-being?

These things took sorry toll of the precious hours, but by the end of April he had completed the charts of Van Diemen's Land, with the Derwent River, and the Tamar at Port Dalrymple.

"Why do we never see you," Brown asked him one day, "at the Sunday night conversations?"

"Sir Joseph has never invited me, Robert. I have lost the open sesame of friendship I enjoyed in 1801. I have no desire to intrude where I am not sure of welcome."

"Oh nonsense. An oversight. You are never a stranger at Soho Square."

Next week came a lackey with a standing invitation, also an embossed card requesting that Captain Matthew Flinders should be guest of honour at a Royal Society dinner.

He accepted with pleasure, and swept the Royal Society to its feet in pompous applause with his eloquent descriptions of New Holland. Sir Joseph presided, the ribbon of the Bath on his breast swelling with paternal pride, his public praise a glowing reassurance ... but Matthew wished the thought had been spontaneous, and not so obviously a "by the way" of Brown. Sir Joseph's attitude nowadays was not easy to explain.... Came a voice from the long ago, the voice of old Tom Pasley, "Thou couldst come with a cargo of rubies, but without the sprouts he'd never forgive thee." Peter's garden awash in reefy seas—Sighing, he went back to his work.

Sam had agreed to stay in London to see the reckonings through, but he constantly moaned for his cheaper lodgings in Plymouth. At the Admiralty their old friend Mr Crossley, as near to the sea on his high stool as he ever wanted to be, gave them the worn volumes of the *Investigator*'s time-charts, and a copy of the new Nautical Almanac.

One evening as they sat together over the mathematics of an eclipse of the sun, a sinister difference in figures crept into the calculations. It grew until the threads of the chart were ravelled, the longitudes all awry. An hour of logarithms, and the terrible truth was plain. Since the *Investigator's* journey, the lunar time-tables had been revised and altered. By the new Greenwich reckonings, the sun and the moon were slanted.... So the maps made at the masthead in three years of travail, and in an island prison of sickness and sadness, were all to do again.

In silence Flinders looked at his brother, his face haggard in the shadow above the lamp. Years of Sisyphus ... an endless labour wasted. He took up his compass and set-square, and made no complaint.

All through the gentle spring and summer he worked, his time broken by loving attendance on Ann, for her headaches were more severe and much more frequent. Two or three days in the week she lay in a darkened room, patient but in pain, cold cloths on her head, taking the foxglove concoctions of a friendly but futile Doctor Dale. On fine Sundays, they went to the Abbey and Museum, or to an exhibition at Somerset House, but those blinding headaches spoiled most of the pleasure. Matthew decided they came from the porter she drank with Sunday dinner, and, when she gave up taking it and the headaches still persisted, to the bugs that kept them awake at night.

At last his Annette became such a confirmed invalid that Isabel Tyler was sent for, the same dear girl and a ray of gaiety in their quiet home. They had little outings to Vauxhall to entertain her, and driving to Kew over Richmond Hill, back to Chelsea by water.

On one memorable Saturday they went to Hackney to see a Mr Sadler go up in a balloon, which he did in good style before a crowd of 200,000 picnicking in the fields, and roosting like pigeons on the house-tops. A truly startling age! They heard at night that the aeronauts had come down at Tilbury Fort, and as they were returning to town met the coach with the collapsed balloon, a mountain of silk, piled on top. Seeing is believing. Matthew thought it possible that some day there would be aerial mariners guiding their craft in the sky. Ann was afraid it was wickedness—a dare-devil challenge to Providence. To Isabel, it was just a thrilling show.

Torrents of excited letters came from Ile-de-France now that shipping was free—more causes to plead, more prisoners of war to visit. Thomy Pitot had a court case pending with the Admiralty over a prize, and asked Matthew to represent him in London. That meant four days of legal parley, a lot of time and thought spent running between the lawyers and the Admiralty, but a slight return it was for unbounded kindness. There was a letter from Edouard that he joyously read to Ann. Edouard, in the National Guard, had been thrown into prison by the British. One day he wrote to his wife, and General Abercrombie sent for him.

"Your name is Pitot? Well, Monsieur Pitot, our couriers have more to do than to play post-boy to you. You can take this letter and deliver it yourself."

Edouard had stared, uncomprehending. The general thawed in a smile. "This name is passport with us for your kindness to an Englishman, Captain Flinders. You may go, Monsieur Pitot. You are free."

Money vanishes like spray on the wave when one is a public personality with no means to uphold it. Dining with naval men and scientific celebrities, coach fares hither and yon, even the postage of a heavy correspondence became a very real problem. In autumn Matthew and Ann found a lodging much more moderate, in Mary Street off the New Road. They saw so little of Sir Joseph nowadays that it scarcely seemed necessary to be near him. The place was clean and airy, on the rim of the fields, with an enjoyable walk on Sundays by the Chalk Farm to St James's Chapel at Hampstead. The carpenter made a movable case for Matthew's books and maps, and carting and arrangement lasted a week.

Then Ann became so unwell that Adams, the apothecary, was called. In the days of her illness, with potions and poultices at all hours, there was still no time for the charts and writing, but at last things were tranquil, and with her to care for him again, he could settle to the re-calculations.

Postman's rap! An angry letter from Captain Burney at Portsmouth. Junior-cadets Wiles and Loud had run away from school. Alarums and excursions! The two young reprobates turned up that afternoon on Matthew's doorstep. Cross-examinations and lectures, he promptly packed them back, with a letter to Captain Burney promising they would never do it again.

"You will adopt other people's sons, sir," laughed Ann when he came home for the third time that day, wet through, after seeing the youngsters away on the Portsmouth coach.

He was sitting in the firelight, weary, his coffee-cup forgotten on his knee. She slipped to the hassock beside him, and he put a hand on her head.

"There are times, Annette," he said slowly, "when I have fears that I may not finish my work. While Napoleon rides in Europe, how can we be free to dream of humanity's future? What hope have I of a ship when ships are built only for slaughter? Therefore I have thought of adopting a promising boy, to follow if I fail. Of my brother I cannot be sure. John Franklin, yes, but he is gone from me, into his own life. It may be that one of these little chaps will some day turn to science. If so, I could help him along the way,"—he finished a little bitterly—" 'a sure and safe one though thy master missed it'."

Ann looked up at him, her eyes unusually bright.

"It has never occurred to Captain Flinders that there may be a son?"

There was silence. She nervously fingered her boot-buttons, then "Matthew,"—hastily, shyly—"it was not the porter."

He frowned at her, utterly mystified, until she laughed outright.

"I mean those headaches … Doctor Dale is convinced now that there will be a child."

For so long he looked at her, his lips half-smiling, his eyes so intensely dark and so strangely absent, that she felt discomfited, as one outside his thought. Then he slipped to his knees beside her, and in the light of boyish gladness in his face, the passionless reverence of his kisses, she knew that for Matthew Flinders the world had changed.

Next day's mail brought a letter from Aken, stationed at Jamaica. Someone was slandering him. Would Captain Flinders use his personal influence immediately to set the matter right? He went to the Navy Office to do it. When he came home, there was a long and unnecessary screed from Samuel, full of spleen and self-justification and self-pity. Sam was in a serious scrape. Would Matthew come at once and guarantee him in a debt of honour? Honour! He went again into the city. So it went on. His work was at the mercy of every wind that blew.

Studying antique charts, building his own again, writing and rewriting, little by little the manuscript grew deeper. In October he submitted the unfinished introduction to Sir Joseph and Lord Liverpool. He modestly asked Sir Joseph if the allowance of a marine surveyor might be added to naval half pay, only for the period of the writing of the book. Sir Joseph approached the Admiralty, and wrote that they had granted an imprest of £200, to be carried to the debit of the Voyage. In a word, they would lend him £200, an advance on public sales.

With many misgivings, he read his chapters through. Was the general interest wide enough to carry the sales to £200? Incentive to achieve was stronger now than it had ever been in his life. The fag end of the year was dreary travail of superhuman striving. He bought a ticket in a lottery—a one-eighth share. Who knows—heaven might unexpectedly smile.

Samuel was coming to spend the Christmas season and New Year, and Matthew planned for a few clear days for the calculations. Sam's airy, affectionate greeting little prepared him for a blow.

Sam was still in trouble with the Navy Board. He had had good chances and lost them. His too-sensitive nature made him vindictive and reckless, and he left a sour impression with his commanders. Some said that only his brother's reputation and influence kept the younger Flinders afloat. Now he was demanding not only reinstatement, but promotion.

This was refused. Very well. He knew what to do.

"I have written to the Astronomer-Royal," he told Matthew, as they sat at their port and cigars after the Christmas dinner, "withdrawing myself and all my books from the *Investigator* Voyage. Why should I give them my work? I'll get nothing out of it, and you little enough."

"You have *what*?" Matthew was appalled.

"You heard what I said. I have withdrawn my astronomical books, and refused to go on with the business. Let 'em fish." Sam blew a casual smoke-ring.

A flame of sudden anger leapt up in Matthew's cheek.

"You have already done this? Without my knowledge?"

"I'm capable of deciding my own affairs."

"How dare you involve me?"

"You have nothing to do with it. You're not my commander now."

"Those books were given you in trust for a national purpose. You will produce them immediately. They do not belong to you."

"They're my books—my handwriting to prove it."

"Are you mad? You not only cripple my work. You write your own death warrant in the Navy."

"Glad to be out of it. Let them do their worst."

Matthew rose.

"But this is incredible! You, my brother, have withdrawn from my use the astronomical records of my ship, the work for which I myself obtained your promotion, which I myself taught you, and which I supervised? Strange conduct in a brother!"

"Look at the way they're treating me. Let them pay me for it."

"You have already been paid your *Investigator* salary."

"And docked on half pay most of the time since. They gave me command of the *Bloodhound*, then took it away."

"That, from what I gather, you might have deserved."

"You said yourself, when you saw my papers, that I had a good case."

"As a trusting brother, yes, anxious to plead your cause and see you reinstated. I find that your conduct appears to most people in a very different light. But enough of this. If you persist, I certainly shall not shield you. I shall tell Sir Joseph the truth."

"You can tell Sir Joseph what you damned well like. What is Sir Joseph to me?"

Ann came to the door in alarm, hearing the angry voices.

"Very well," Matthew spoke quietly now. "If that is your attitude, go."

Sam took up his cocked hat and gloves with a contemptuous smile. "A beautiful brotherly spirit, to turn me out because I won't knuckle down to injustice and persecution. For all your sheepish loyalty to your fine friends, they do little enough for you." He bowed most gallantly to Ann—and savagely banged the door.

After a sleepless night, Matthew wrote to Crossley at Greenwich to bring the remaining books, to see how far he might go. He learned that Lieutenant Flinders was in possession of all the Investi*gator's* record books in which he had written, wholly or in part. He wrote again, demanding their instant return. Sam replied, with a fraternal flourish of condescension, that he would hand them over if Matthew asked it as a brother. As a matter of right and wrong, he must refuse point blank. Crossley had already reported the affair, and when Matthew called at Soho Square, Sir Joseph was dryly displeased.

"No cause for alarm, or even delay, my dear Flinders," he said briefly. "The Board of Longitude will take immediate action in prosecution for recovery, and your brother's name will be removed from the list of lieutenants."

Trudging homeward up to the knees in snow, lanterns of the gigs and carriages bobbing gaily about him in New Year revelry, the grief and shame of this sorry business weighed heavily on Matthew's heart. Samuel's name removed from the list of lieutenants … his young brother that he had taken to sea, promising the little doctor to guide him to success. This insane defiance meant ruin to them both. It meant the end of all things, failure, humiliation, the Flinders name a byword in the Navy, the *Investigator* journey a jest … no hope of honour in discovery, nor of future discovery together, nor of knowledge of the new land to the world. It could not be. It could not, must not, be.

He wheeled and went back in his tracks to find Sam's lodging. It was a mean and dingy rooming-house not far from Temple Bar. A blowsy woman from a downstairs gin-party smartly answered his knock, and, finding he was not an expected guest, carelessly waved him upstairs to a door at the back.

The room was shiftless and unlit. Samuel sprawled on a truckle-bed, nursing a black eye and a swollen jaw. He had been knocked down by robbers, he said, and all his money stolen on Saturday night.

Matthew accepted the explanation without comment. He removed some clothing from a rickety chair and sat.

"You have seen fit to tell me, Samuel, that I am no longer your commander. Very well. I come to you as a brother. My belief in you, my faith in you, what I have done in years past I do not wish to stress. I ask you now, for the sake of our future, to do something for me. We are together in a hostile world, with too much to battle now without fighting each other. Give me back the books of my Voyage, on your own terms."

A slant of lamplight from the street wavered across his face—Chazal's cartoon of cynical sadness, but still the resolute lips.

Sam slumped to a sitting position, and covered his battered countenance with his hand. In the fitful light of the dirty room, he cut a poor figure.

"If I do," he said, "I'm giving them back my only weapon against them."

"And using it on me. Deny them now, and my whole life's work is lost."

"Well, if you put it that way ... but I still don't see why my labour should go for nothing. It's insult to injury, how they're treating me."

"Return the books and I can do without you. If you care to help with the reckonings, I shall pay whatever you ask, but I have no doubt that the Admiralty will reimburse your expenses. A matter of money, Sam? Then money you shall have, theirs or mine."

Samuel groped about and lit a candle. He produced the worn old volumes of the *Investigator* books, after all their adventures, hidden in a pack of soiled linen. Matthew conned them over and counted them.

"They are all here?"

"All I had."

"I thank you. As we are talking of money, I suppose at the moment you are short ... having been robbed."

A faint emphasis of irony, Sam missed it. He obviously brightened as Matthew counted out a guinea, and put it down by the candle-stick, with "Don't bother to consider this a loan." In fact, he was even lofty.

"You understand, Matt, it's only for you I'm giving up these books. I don't want to injure you. You've had enough. When you ask for old sake's sake, well take them and good luck. I'll be along when I'm fit to go out, and see what I can do." He slouched his hand out of his dressing-gown pocket.

Matthew left it hanging in the air.

A scream of bawdy laughter and stamping of songs greeted him from the stair. He thought of the corroborees of New Holland … he preferred them of the good earth, out in the open air.

New Year's Day, and the snows of yesteryear still on the ground. He made up his annual accounts. Expenses £447, income £350. There was nothing else for it, they would have to move again. If it were not so vitally necessary to stay in London, they could have lived happily in Lincolnshire on £5 a week.

Young Henry Wiles was on vacation from Portsmouth. The lad had no friends in England, and James, away in Jamaica, would take it for granted that Matthew would ask him to stay. But Isabel Tyler was coming to care for Ann, and at such a time it was impossible, even if there had been room.

He happened to mention the problem to John Franklin in a letter. John nobly came to the rescue, and offered to take the boy with him as midshipmite on the *Bedford*, anchored in the Downs. So Matthew gave young Henry a day in London, bought him his kit, and waved him away to start life in the Navy, his arms full of gifts. Sam came along for supper that night with a voluble Monsieur Stuart, who wasted a good evening for them in small talk, the clock ticking in a malicious little tt … tt … tt …

Ann was too frail and too precious now to share the weary search for lodgings. Every penny was needed for her coming travail, and those lodgings must be cheap. This time Matthew found them, with a respectable family in Fitzroy Square—a family too prolific to be other than respectable, a hang-dog cottage in a swarming quarter, but £15 less a year.

He unpacked his books with a sigh of resignation, forgetting the discoloured walls and the reek of cabbage in the charts of the south coast of Australia. Outside, the whining street-cries and the screaming of children at play ... but for him the double-bass of the southern ocean rollers, green, green, rumbling in to a crescent of snow-white sand, and the scent of sun-swept grasses on a solitary shore.

Isabel came, with boxes of cheese and Lusby hams in her luggage. Matthew hurried to Charing Cross in a flurry of mud to meet her, to find that she had given him the slip, and gone all the way to Mary Street, not knowing they had moved. He followed her up, missed her again, and found her, all dimples and reproaches, on his doorstep, her freckled nose in the air with disgust at the inquisitive small rabble about her.

"I don't like this, Matt. Whatever hath made thee bring Ann here?"

"Needs must, little Miss Dignity, when the devil drives. 'Tis but for a while, my dear, for her sake." He answered her lightly enough, but there was shame in his eyes.

All through the years he had been awaiting a chance to verify his theories regarding the fact of iron in the ship affecting the variation of the compass. Now that Ann had Isabel's companionship and care, he could snatch a few days' leave. In a weeping thaw of early March, he crossed by boat from Chatham to Sheerness, and arrived at the Fountain Inn in a bitter midnight ... the window looking on the road to Bluetown, where he had watched Nelson go by.

Next morning, brisk with anticipation, he called on Admiral Sir Tom Williams for permission to board one of the ships. The admiral was indisposed. Would he please call later?

Waiting ... he sauntered round the dockyard, fretting at the eternal wasted time, hearing the ticking of imaginary clocks, thinking of the appointments broken, the fruitless journeys, the little foxes eating away the vines. However, the blank day ended with his dining with the admiral and his lady, forgetting clocks and remembering far coasts in their cheerful drawing-room. At daylight, he boarded the *Helder* at the Nore.

Plunging like a porpoise in a boisterous northerly, the brig made experiments impossible. He could not use the vane of the azimuth compass. The deductions of three chill and tireless days were rough and inconclusive. In the wild weather, he had to give it up and go home. Frustration every step of the way—circumstance against him.

There were hours of suspense now, watching Ann.... On 1 April his child was born. A daughter.

The baby was christened at St Giles-in-the-Fields, and they called her Anne. After the ceremony, they sent the nurse and baby home and went the rounds of a modest little celebration—a "poppy show" of the Nile and Trafalgar, the Natural History Museum at the Pantherion, Sir Joshua Reynold's new pictures at the Gallery, and tea at an eating-house in town.

Ann—pale, anxious Ann—knew that he had longed for a son, but no shadow of disappointment clouded her Matthew's brow. He worked noticeably harder, he fretted more for the hours lost. A young and delicate child accounted for many.

A permit came from the Admiralty to pursue his compass experiments at Portsmouth, and down there he met his old *Providence* friend, Captain Portlock. They raised a sailor's glass to the waving palms of Otaheite before Flinders boarded the vessel allotted to him, *La Loire*, a French prize lying in the stream. Taking the dips of the needle with the ship's head east, he found that the guns on both sides were surely drawing that needle to the horizontal line. On the fo'c'sle the dip was greater still, undoubtedly owing to the greater quantity of other iron there.

A stranger to captains and crews, all over the dirty decks, and now in a lighter alongside, he was overlooked in the officers' messes, left without food for ten hours at a time. But he proved his point—that iron in the ship was responsible for the changes in compass variation. John Thistle's "wee knife in ma powk" was the answer to the riddle after all. He came back to London eager, thin and triumphant, wrote his treatise with infinite care, and picked up the threads of the Voyage.

In that, it seemed, there never could be a concentration of thought. The compass variations discovery electrified maritime England, bringing showers of excited correspondence from all over the British Isles. In the midst of it all, Desbassayns and his wife arrived from Ile-de-France. It was Matthew who scoured the streets to find them board and lodging. They brought news of Madame d'Arifat's death—sad thoughts, sad letters to send.

Sam's friend, Monsieur Stuart, had acquired the habit of calling round in the evenings—a well-meaning, pleasant fellow, and the courteous Flinders could not tell him, in good round terms, to go. Navy friends in need of a pound breezily hailed him as brother. Sailors who wanted berths on whalers, and French prisoners who wanted their freedom or passages home, were a daily procession.

William Bligh, Admiral of the Blue, rapped for congratulations—Matthew's best wine, Ann's best supper, and a sigh for the Voyage neglected; but my Lord Admiral, rotund and affable, breathed benediction on the household, informed Matthew loftily that he might dedicate the result of his labours to him, and carried him off in the next fortnight to dine with the Duke of Clarence. The royal sailor, thanks to Bligh, desired to see his charts—"right in line for the throne, my lad, and a King comes in handy."

That meant a new uniform, at princely cost, for Mr Schweitzer's old soldier had gone beyond recall. Then the Navy Club invited Captain Flinders to dinner at St Alban's. That meant a guinea subscription, and an injudicious £1 8s. spent on the dinner alone. These shameful extravagances—or puny little economies—hurt.

Now Mr Wilberforce, in a friendly morning call, asked for a lengthy dissertation on horrors of the slave trade, and the Admiralty for an authoritative chart of the Isle of Madagascar. Curtat sent for a presentation snuff-box of specified design, and a young man bound for the Feejee Isles called for sailing directions.

The little foxes, eating away the vines.

Pitot Frères were restored to comparative prosperity in a free port, and the faithful Thomy—how could he know?—was always well in the picture. He commissioned Matthew to handle all his negotiations with Admiralty concerning prizes, and finally sent along eighty pounds of silver in ingots to be sold over the counter at the best possible price. So Matthew trudged the rainy streets, laden with treasure of Aladdin's cave, to silversmith after silversmith to be sure of a good deal. Thomy he could never repay.

Westall brought along the plans of his drawings for approval, Crossley came for long sessions to check the completed charts, and all the time the baby cried, and the shoddy little rooming-house was bedlam.

"This day I have done nothing at my work... ." How often the patient slanted writing in the diary showed the depressing entry.

A *Voyage to Australia* limped along. In the small hours, when the house and the streets were quiet, he tried to blend letters and figures in one, to marry fact and fancy, to unveil his new continent to a careless world and make its story live.

There was much joy in these chapters. Poring over his log-books and his logarithms, he lived the magic past—smell of the wet decks in the grey of daybreak, swelling fathoms cushioning the keel in the swing of the south-east trade, first faint shadow of a coast unknown, viridian of shoal water and cobalt blue of the deep, or his men shouting on a turtle hunt on some tropic beach by moonlight—sharp breath of memory to carry him on, and the new land calling. He lived when all the others were asleep.

Another New Year found him "employed as yesterday on rough drafts and re-writing". His accounts were again £150 on the wrong side of the ledger. He sounded the Admiralty trying to find some supplementary work.

Mr Pearce, that good "Navy whisperer", told him that Captain Gifford was resigning his position as Lieutenant-Governor of the Royal College at Portsmouth. The ideal thing—he built academies in the air. Times had changed since his young day, when naval cadets were thrashed to sea from some rotten old tub in the Thames. As tutor and inspiration of youth he could be very happy, and the duties allowed ample time for completion of the Voyage. He wrote to Lord Melville, now First Lord, and hurried to consult Sir Joseph.

Sir Joseph was benign, even delighted.

"I know no person better fitted for the situation," he said. "I trust Lord Melville will refer to me, and I shall certainly tell him so" ... no suggestion that Sir Joseph would refer to Lord Melville. Ah well.

There was gay anticipation in the family at Fitzroy Square, yet the letter to the First Lord remained day after day unanswered. When Flinders attended his levee, hoping to see him personally, he was only one of a surging social crowd. Some weeks later, a brief response dashed hopes.

DEAR CAPTAIN FLINDERS,

I have caused a note to be made of your wishes, and of the pretentions you urge, to which I am no stranger, but there is no probability of Captain Gifford's retirement at present.

For the rest there was nothing, in the iron-bound confines of the Articles of War. Philip Desbassayns told him that Decaen had been amazed he had not rejoined the fighting Navy.

"But my parole! Did he not believe that I would honour my word?"

Philip, as Decaen had done, shrugged.

He had promised, in the present campaign, never to fight the French, and if there was a cruel little coterie that dubbed him "French Flinders", let them talk. Forced into a narrowing groove of introspection and retrospection, he was constantly meeting once-junior officers whom war had exalted, senior officers who looked upon his failure with tolerance and pity. He wrote to the Admiralty a ringing appeal for the dying cause of science, but it was too busy to answer—answering Napoleon's guns.

John Franklin was in financial difficulties, so Standert advanced Matthew money to lend him from his father's estate. By March they were looking for cheaper lodgings still, and took a place at 45 Upper John Street. It proved to be a rackety house, besieged by creditors by day and revellers by night, the door-knocker never silent.

So there was yet another packing up of the baby, the books and the charts to 7 Upper Fitzroy Street—£100 a year, but newly-furnished and quiet, and they were ready to pay anything now for cleanliness and peace.

Ann's bilious headaches had come back. The period of her motherhood and nursing the child had been only a brief respite. Still, she was always her dear bright self, a smiling dragon trying to guard him from the endless intrusions, checking over fair copies and observations with him, bringing him cups of China tea and scraps of gay gossip to lift the tedium of imprisonment, sitting still. His little girl Anne, though she was very fragile, alarming them with severe spasms of illness, was a quaint and sweet diversion in the odd moments when he could play with her. She touched the deep furrows in her papa's brow with rose-leaf fingers, wondering about them with eyes as dark, as earnest, as his own. A grave little girl, and thoughtful. Ann said she would be clever. With wistfulness for the lost years, he was still far away from those two dear ones, the beloved of his long-ago dreams. When this gruelling labour was over, as it soon would be, he would indeed be theirs.

So from the first gleam of morning through the crescendo of day till the sounds of the city were hushed, he never left his chair. Apprehension was whipping him on, and a yearning to be free. London was killing him, stifling body and mind in its fog of fetid living—the dead horizons of tenement roofs, the humans grinding their lives away in a petty roundabout of penny trading, millions breeding millions in a musty cocoon of some infernal spinning. His eyes had seen the glory, "the scene of Thy splendour". He had gone down to the sea, to men as God made them, heirs of the earth and the sun. The last words of his book written, he would be out of it all, he cared not where. Through spring and summer he sat to his work unmoving, "all day and evening as before".

By July, Jacob Arrowsmith was piecing together the mosaic of the Great South Land in his first temple of cartography. That was a shrine that Flinders loved to enter, the bearded old man bending above his spherometers, high-priest of scroll and folio, the spherical light of the globes playing on the dusty colours of the Magellanic maps, and in text of the wall-charts shining the diphthonged letters of antique Dutch script. His profile of the stranger continent was now almost completed, decisive copper etching of a broken parallelogram coming clear through the chaos of the blowing winds and thrusting waves. The blurred vision of Cook and the Dutchmen was in perfect focus on the parchment of his own faultless charts. Arrowsmith pursed his thin lips and said nothing … he had never copied better.

In August, the title-page was called for.

A
VOYAGE
TO
AUSTRALIA

Undertaken for the purpose of completing the discovery of that vast country, and persecuted in the years 1801, 1802, and 1803.

In His Majesty's Ship Investigator, and subsequently in the Armed Vessel *Porpoise* and *Cumberland*, schooner.

With an account of the shipwreck of the Porpoise, arrival of the Cumberland at Mauritius, and imprisonment of the Commander during six years and a half in that island.

BY MATTHEW FLINDERS
Commander of the *Investigator*

In Two Volumes with an Atlas.

Printed by W. Bulmer and Co. and Published by
G. and W. Nicol, Publishers to His Majesty.

Australia—new rhythm to the music of the sphere. Science and sales were subtly married in that title-page—history for the blue-stocking, discovery for the savant, charts for the mariner, the imprisonment for fireside pathos, shipwreck for sensation—the Robinson Crusoe writers could do no better. Sure of approval, he sent it to Sir Joseph, and turned to a forest of press sheets, and the chart of Timor Sea.

The Sun of Science had withdrawn the light of his countenance from satellites and sycophants in London. He was at one of his country seats, Spring Grove near Heston, nursing his Chinese camellias and his gout in the magnificent gardens of another, nearer, Revesby. To the "able but unfortunate" Flinders he was benign, as ever, but remote. The title-page returned promptly. He had made but one alteration—the only one that counted. The word "Australia", in its careful Caxton characters, he had carelessly scrabbled out, and in his free flowing hand was written "Terra Australis".

"Old names, outworn ... this is a new world, a world for youth to conquer ... archipelago or continent, I call the whole land Australia." Was that name forbidden?

Anxious letters flew to Spring Grove, to Bligh, to Major Rennell, to the Admiralty. Sir Joseph had so often agreed—they had always referred to the country as Australia—had he forgotten? Sir Robert Peel made no protest, nor Lord Liverpool, Secretary of State.

Sir Joseph, in reply, was pleasantly vague about such recollections, and quite as pleasantly determined that Terra Australis it should be. Arrowsmith had pointed out to him that Flinders's innovation would quite upset the sequence of existing charts. Considering that all Arrowsmith's previous charts had carried title "New Holland" or "New South Wales", Flinders, with spirit, could challenge that point, but the tone of Sir Joseph's letters left no more to be said. The scribe who copied the charts would take precedence of the discoverer who made them. The honour of naming his Great South Land was snatched out of his hands.

With the cruel old sense of frustration upon him, he went on with the final chapters of the book—his life in Ile-de-France. Decaen still kept the fatal third log-book. Paris disclaimed all knowledge, and Decaen was lost in the mill of Napoleon's madness somewhere between Moscow and Marseilles. For these significant chapters he was wholly dependent on his journal, his letter books, and rough foundation notes, but from his landfall to his leave-taking the vitriol of humiliation had scarred every outrage, every kindness, only too deep in his memory. Page by page of those meticulous diaries brought emotions flashing that flamed in the old futile anger—soldiers drilling in the sunny square under the tamarind-trees, the bitter-sweet of magnolias in the moonlight ... lagging days of blindness in the white walls of the Maison Despeaux ... the shimmering mirror of Vacois, and the lookout above it where year after year he scanned the empty sea.

The mental torture brought back the physical pain. In the first melancholy nights of 1813 winter, his old enemy "the gravel!" was upon him, the disease of the bladder that came of the damp and the long sitting still.

The lodging-house grew dark—too dark to write. It reeked of human mould. Ann was ill, and the baby always coughing, all three in the hands of that blissfully ignorant bedside humbug, Doctor Dale, who prescribed gum arabic to clog Flinders's complaint, and opium pills and a baked raven for his child—medicine was witchery still in England. In November they packed up once again, and moved to number 14, London Street, Fitzroy Square. They were seeking a slant of grey light instead of candles by day, and a fresher draught of third-storey air. The work went patiently on, nearing the end.

Samuel, thanks to his mildness in rendering unto Caesar and helping with the re-calculations, had been given a post as lieutenant on H.M.S. *Success*. Home on leave at Christmastide, he raced through to Lincolnshire with a "Hail and farewell!" and a word of concern for a family so sorrowful and so lean.

Matthew reassured him that the travail was nearly over, that high summer, from alien London, would see the exiles home ... to the hawthorn lanes and the meadowsweet that blows by

Fenland rivers, the thatched houses and the hayricks in the wind-rippled brown of the flax-farms, Lusby hams and gooseberry wine, the churches snugged down in the trees.

O! 'tis my delight on a shining night in the season of the year! ...

in minor chords of weariness and longing.

Visitors were few now. The prisoners had mostly gone home, casual friends could scarcely keep up with this paperchase of moving, and the dearest respected the urgency of his work. He had neither the health nor the time to seek them. John Franklin and the *Bedford* were fighting off the Americans and French in the Channel. Willingham had applied for a post as judge in India, and gone out to Madras. Brown, Westall and Crossley were the only regular callers, with Sam's Monsieur Stuart an occasional nuisance. Charts, proofs, engravers, preparing quires for the binder, the long months of winter were all too swiftly gone.

Always his "gravel" complaint had left him in the warm, dry weather, but April came—and sharper suffering than he had ever known before. He realized that Dale knew less than nothing—that fat and fatuous little man lived on his leeches, and pocketed the guineas of the dead.

The nights were a burning torture of this obstruction in the bladder. Sluggish yellow crystals were appearing, some secret chemical formula of the body that he tried to analyse, a scientist turning the microscope in a terrible precision upon himself.

From his slight bio-chemical knowledge, acquired in the *Reliance* days from Doctor George for the purposes of exploration, he identified the crystals as muriatic acid—"single crystals with some whitish earth, apparently phosphate of lime." He took 22 drops of neutralizing alkaline, and "passed a good deal of gravel, which proved to be the same triple phosphate as before, amongst it pieces which have evidently been broken off from the larger body, hollowed out on one side and ribbed smooth on the other, whence I conclude there are two or more calcules in the bladder." So dreadfully impersonal, written side by side with titles for the views of headlands, it might have been the geological analysis of rock-soils in New Holland.

"Taking gum arabic in barley water. Worked at the examination of the drawing of the General Chart as long as I could, but the leaning forward seemed to bring the rough calcule in contact with the neck of the bladder, and take off the mucus which forms there for its defence. I consequently suffered a good deal in the evening, and a little blood came away... .

"Crystals imperfect, with flesh attached.

"Unceasing dull, heavy pain and sharp spasms.

"At half-past one the pain ceased, and I was able to work at the examination of the General Chart... .

"Got through this day with no particular suffering. Occupied in correcting errata throughout the book."

The hot China tea was soothing. Ann brought it to him at all hours of day and night, her red dressing-gown caught up by her hand at her throat, lending colour to her weary little face. He did not speak to her of the horrors of his illness, the mystery there in the microscope of the dull yellow crystals, his tragic research to dissolve them.

"By means of a cushion made hollow I was able to sit up and do a little.

"In the afternoon a little more easy unexpectedly, correcting proofs and examining for errata ... a shivering fit. Difficult to sit on one haunch... ."

Eighteen and twenty times he rose from bed in the night, lacerated as with jagged knives. Lack of sleep and loss of appetite wasted his flesh, made him haggard and listless, but the work must be done before he could rest. The cushion was constantly changed and bolstered to alleviate the lightning-streaks of pain. Ann's tempting little invalid dishes were scarcely noticed on the table, as through those recurrent agonies of his writing, he sat with his head on his hands, fingers pressing his closed eyes. Then back to the amendments to the General Chart, the final labour of Hercules... . "Make the dot larger ... delete three points of the dotted line." It was returned to Arrowsmith with ninety-two corrections.

In a blithe morning of early June, harlequin summer dancing down from tenement roofs in diamonds of yellow sun and blue half-moons of shadow, London sparrows twittering alegretto, the last words of his book were written. They were a wistful appeal to France to make restitution of an Englishman's work for humanity.

Years of Sisyphus were over.

The superb charts of the unknown were in perfect reproduction. The navigation tables were in page-proof— Ptolemaic pillars of hieroglyph indelible to harness the stars of heaven, shackle the winds, and guide the mariner of the new continent through its mazes of reefy seas. The natural history plates, in clumsy Bauer's delicate penmanship, were acquainting the world with the world's weirdest fauna— "animiles the like you'll never see, Master says they were on earth before Adam." Now the narrative was away to the printer, the long unfinished story told.

The cushion was laid aside. Ann helped him to his couch.

"Brown came to see me for two hours while I lay on the sofa. Up at eleven, and to bed in the afternoon."

Rest brought no respite as Dale had promised. Babbling his platitudes, the leech-man was sent away, and the surgeon Hayes called in. Onion water, seltzer water and *uva urse* were his stock-in-trade for the "kidney-troubles" of his airy diagnosis. When all three failed of any effect, Ann sought the services of Dr Marcet, the fashionable emigré specialist from Paris, a charlatan whose minuets had made his reputation. In an ode to Morpheus he prescribed a course of opium pills, and diagnosed an abscess in the right side, to be fomented with poppy heads.

The sleeper woke to a keener, crueller torture.

"Slow fever and temperature at 110. Dry mouth still continues, as does the want of appetite."

The spectre of Matthew Flinders lay in the wan light of the window, watching other skies. High-piled clouds of summer were sails to a fair wind, the street-cries the screaming of sea-

514

gulls about the sheer brownstone cliffs, and the passing carriage wheels the creak of cordage. Sea-faring cares forgotten troubled his fitful dreams. His giddiness was the dizzying swing of the maintop in a gale. For the first time in ten years the diary was a log, prefacing the terrible data of his disease with tally of wind and weather.

"*Warm with thunder showers*. Have had no motion since yesterday. Sucked the remaining half of an orange. Rose at one o'clock.

"*Dull and windy*. Enema, three hours passage, much relief. Mr Brown came in the evening to say that he had obtained from Mr Nicol a copy of the Atlas to put on Sir Joseph Banks's table this evening." There was no copy of the Atlas for the maker of charts, Matthew Flinders.

"*Moist with east grind*. Miss Tyler came to assist Mrs Flinders in caring for me and our little Anne who has the measles. Some days I rise and shave. Arrowsmith brought me a set of the proofs of all the charts of the Atlas, and I gave him a note expressing my approbation of the engravings. Uneasy. I lie on my back for soreness of the lower bones of the side.

"*Warm and fine*. Hired an easy chair and took out the cushion bottom to relieve my bones. Moistening my mouth with jelly and orange water. My brother called and took my half pay affidavit to the Navy Office to see if they would make it effective.

"10 July. Did not rise until two, being, I think, rather weaker than before… ."

Blind in a spasm of agony, he laid the book aside.

The *Investigator* had sailed from Spithead on 19 July.

24

Colours

Steady ticking of a clock, the sound of a horse trotting ... the relentless little scythes of time cutting away the years.

Day and night no longer in division ... faces seen through a red mist of pain, no more than faces in the clouds or a ravel of foam on the wave.

An Otaheitian girl with her ripe veined breasts and feet dragging flowers... .

The Jew tailor, Schweitzer, cringing at Sir Joseph's knee... .

John Thistle, with his bristled brows and red right arm upraised, challenging a grey-headed eagle... .

One-eyed Péron... .

Timothy Wanjon, his little ebony wife squatting behind him on the floor-mats under the flag of Orange... .

A ragged woman in sunny wilderness wandering the road to China... .

Admirals of England grouped on a blood-smeared quarter-deck in the light of the horn lanterns, Nelson, Hood, Collingwood and Howe, Black Dick Howe with snowy ruffles at his throat and the chiselled calm of a Red Indian... .

A Prince of Wales bespangled like a rose and grinning like an idiot—Bongree, naked and black, grinning his fidelity... .

Haytime in Lincolnshire, the gaffers sitting outside the inns like Toby jugs.... .

Whiplash Kent, whipped under to drown, defying the victorious sea.

Design—the shuttle and thread—eternal weaving and changing—a lacemaker's pattern of figures and faces that girdles a globe of the world.

Two volumes and an atlas. They came from Bulmer the printer, the bluff brown books that held his life within their weighty covers, so heavy for Ann's arms. She brought them to him trembling, and smiling through her tears.... In twisted preoccupation, the red mist of pain, he searched her face with his eyes, and did not see.

Sobbing, she set them on the bed, and laid his hand upon them—that thin hand white as a woman's that had thrown filaments to Fomalhaut and guided ships to the future. In troubled endeavour it made the motion of writing ... the never-ending writing of a Voyage ended.

On her knees with her arms close round him, she pressed her quivering cheek to his, and cried in her broken sobs "Come back!"

Bells. He turned to listen. A flight of bells ... the Brides of Enderby. At the top of the stairs a little white figure ...."Thee did come back, Mattie! I knew thee would come back!"

Still the Brides ringing. Someone was lost on the marshes in the high tide of the year ... and then a man's voice, slowly and bitterly saying, "Stay clear of the sea, I tell thee, a lone mad thing, a gypsy. 'Twill twist thy soul and make thee but a manikin of a man, up in the yards dancing to the fiddle of the winds."

The bells were tolling now.... Angelus bells of Ile-de-France, the tamarind-trees stained saffron in sunset. The streets were all silent and empty, and he was beating madly at an old old house with doors and window barred.

"My papers!"

A hoarse shout of anguish. He sat rigid, and beat the air, and fell back spent and sleeping.

The long London twilight ... street-cries eerie as the cry of seabirds ... the woman kneeling by his bed, his left hand warm with her convulsed lips and blinding passionate tears, his right lying listless on those bluff brown volumes that held his life within their heavy covers.

Discovery and his love.

As the lamps twinkled out one by one in the vague city below, John Franklin came and found them there together.

Grey of morning brought Sunday. It was 19 July.

His ship must sail at nightfall with the land-breeze. A slant of sun in the cabin—the sun that had slanted on Ann's wood-brown hair. Empty sun.

Watchful, wakeful day. Sometimes he stirred and smiled, dark eyes bright with fever.

"It grows late, boys. Let us dismiss!" he said once very clearly.

His wife was there. His baby played by his bedside, the quaint small Anne with her tight, tawny curls, her long skirts and her laughter ... but he was with the phantom love that he possessed in dreams. Her light hands touched the wave of his hair, his lips slipped from the kindness of hers to the pulsing of her throat ... but a great sea thundered on the rocks below them, wave after wave crashing in closer, and there was dusk and danger, and a long way to travel across the years.

"Write me volumes, dearest love. Tell me the dress that thou wearest, tell me thy dreams.... When thou art sitting at thy needle and alone... ."

The bells again. Ship's bells. Chorus of fo'c'sle voices full-throated on the wind.

The hours whispering by—with no division.

Quiet.

Will-o'-the-wisp of evening colours watering away. Men stand in silent ranks. The stained jersey of the seaman at attention at the prow is soft in the rays of a setting sun on steamy, pitchy teak. Pastel smoke ripples the meniscus of tropic water.

Red cross on the white field is misty purple, a drape of gauze against the vapid sky. Notes of a bugle die like fading lights.

Curve and sway of the decks of ships, heads bowed as Colours fall ...

fall from a world through darkening veils.

25

The Dead Awakes

If the plan of a voyage of discovery were to be read over my grave, I would rise up, awakened from the dead.

—MATTHEW FLINDERS.

Of the ever-restless thousands flocking beneath the Flinders statues in Australia's cities, few indeed there are who know the tragic life and love story of the young explorer deathless in bronze—last of the great navigators of the unknown, the man who mapped, and named, the fifth continent.

A hundred years forgotten, to-day the *Encyclopaedia Britannica* honours him as the most exact and accomplished of the cartographers of all time, a genius in navigation.

Seven years ago I knew as much about him as the average Australian—that Bass and Flinders sailed the coast of New South Wales when its history began in an heroic little tub, *Tom Thumb*; that Bass discovered Bass Strait, and in a whaleboat; that Flinders made other explorations, creditable but vague. Which was Bass and which Flinders was not quite clear in my mind. For all our educational systems, we learn too little at school.

It was when I sailed Carpentaria, a thousand miles from Thursday Island to the rim of Arnhem Land, tossing about in a little black lugger in that windy, desolate Gulf, that I began to take note. With a Torres Strait islander at the masthead, and swinging the lead for every fathom by tropic isles and rivers, "Have you no chart?" I asked the doughty skipper.

"Not since the one Flinders made," he answered, "in 1802."

By a hurricane lamp swinging on the deck at night I pored over that chart—its pathetic recording of vanished sandhills and mangroves, the "smokes" so punctiliously marked that an Englishman may have thought were permanent "Indian villages" instead of the casual camp-fires of the nomad, the neat figures of meticulous soundings that the big tides sweep to chaos in a day.

Here he had cried his failure. "I had hoped to make such records that there would be no need for any man to follow, but in such a ship I know not how it may be achieved." Yet here was his reward. One hundred and forty years have passed, and to that lone little lugger, the only traveller of Carpentaria's wide and wind-swept waters, the last chart of his making is still the guide.

Matthew Flinders, long dead, became to me as a friend. In my frequent researches, of this and that, in the libraries of Australia, I snatched a few minutes for him now and then in the busy days. As the history was pieced together in jig-saw fragments of manuscript and memoir, my eyes opened in wonder. The figure of a woman came into the picture, a childhood sweetheart lost in long roving, a beloved young wife renounced through the lonely years. Their reunion was but the final chapter of supreme sadness, for to his life's work the lover gave his life.

Through the rack of much journalistic work and the writing of other books, those graceful shades of the past were ever with me. I hoped some day to write the story never yet told in full— not in stark biographical form, but that Australia might see it in living character, and hear the spoken word in voices from the dead.

Scenes and situations are created from written records. Not in any instance have I played with history. Logs, journals, letters and treasured private diaries are my authority. Dialogue is founded on fact.

The character of Ann Chappell is lightly sketched, through Flinders's eyes. Apart from his unending labours in science and seamanship, in the logs, charts, treatises, books and journals, perhaps no man has set down in black and white more of his environment, associations, friends, impressions and work, but one does not write in indelible official record the things closest to the heart. His passionate letters to Ann are poetry.

That she was a woman of great intellect, charm and vivacity, and that she valued her lover's work for the world above her anguished need of him, and endured a ten years' parting with unfailing faith and evotion we do know. Her only enjoyment of "the delight of my eyes" was limited to a few brief weeks of love-making in the autumn 1795, of honeymoon in the spring 1801, and the four years of tribulation and sickness in London that preceded his early death.

It was Flinders's expressed desire to be with us in Australia. Had it not been for his death in youth, we would have honoured his children here for generations. I have had the pleasure of meeting descendants of the family in South Australia and West.

Mr F. Pilgrim of Adelaide, grandson of his sister Susanna, treasures relics of the great navigator—an original copy of *Terra Australis* inscribed by his wife, a set of buttons from his uniform, a pocket compass and sundial combined that Flinders always carried, and the set of pink corals from Wreck Reef that are a circumstance in my story.

He also has two chests of letters from Mrs Flinders to his mother, who was her favourite niece. Here are typical letters from Ann's very lively pen, written at Woolwich Common in 1843, and sealed with her blue French seal:

I think I told you some time ago that Sir John Franklin had caused to be erected a monument in South Australia to the memory of my dear husband. This was effected through the permission of Colonel Gawler, the governor of the colony.

About three or four months ago Colonel Gawler and his family came to reside in Woolwich. As a matter of course Anne called upon them. The announcement of her name struck them with astonishment.

The name of Captain Flinders was very familiar to them, and held in high estimation, but they were not in the least aware that he had left either widow or child—so that we seemed to them like people risen from the dead or some fossil remains just dug up.

Colonel Gawler, when here, asked me if we had any friends in Adelaide. On my replying in the negative, he said "Then I can tell you you have a great many there, and that if you were to go thither they would not know how to make enough of you."

I thought this little account would please you, as it did us, for it is truly gratifying to find that there are some who appreciate the services of your dear uncle. They seem to be forgotten in England, but in the scenes of his discoveries those services stand out in bold relief, and will long be remembered.

Colonel Gawler has given the name of Flinders to a range of mountains. There is also a river called after him, as likewise several islands and a street in Adelaide.

Colonel Gawler was very gallant. There is a later letter, Ann's mittened hand held up in concern:

Should you visit Melbourne, you will perhaps hear of two young men of the name of Newsham, or Newsome, who have represented themselves as nephews of Captain Flinders, and have in consequence obtained from the authorities there good situations.

Now let Mr P. seek out the matter. You well know that your uncle never had any nephews of that name, and such shameful cheats ought to be put down. Your uncle's name is in such high repute in Melbourne and Adelaide that anyone related to him would be noticed.

Colonel Gawler told me that if either Anne or myself were to go to the latter, we should have a deputation to meet us, and be chaired, if we liked.

I understand Henry Chambers intends o avail himself of Captain Flinders' name. I hope he will not disgrace it.

Anne, my pen-mender, is from home, and the steel pen writes as it likes.

Your affectionate aunt,

A. FLINDERS.

There is but one reference of deeper import, in quaint philosophy of second marriage.

> I am no friend to second marriages, being persuaded that they are seldom productive of much comfort, particularly when the first has been a very happy one ...
>
> Respecting my union with my beloved Captain Flinders, I think I may say that during the period we were permitted to live together, not a cloud cast a shadow over the sunshine of our affections, and each day seemed to rivet the attachment more firmly.
>
> After such a union, to seek another would be the height of folly.

The Pilgrims were among the early colonists of South Australia. Charles Edward Flinders and Sergeant John Franklin Flinders, personalities and historians of Kimberley in the far north-west, are of another branch of the family.

The magnitude of Matthew Flinders's work for Australia was too long in finding recognition. Such is the fate of genius.

Sir John Franklin, when he was governor of Tasmania in 1841, first raised a monument to his memory in the quiet bush at Port Lincoln, South Australia. It was unveiled there in the silence by the beautiful and brilliant Lady Franklin, immortalized in the tragedy of the North-west Passage and the song "Where Swallows Build". She crossed the stormy Bass Strait to bring that 25-foot monolith in the little barque *Abeona*, and travelled 500 miles with it through a scarcely habited wilderness. It was Franklin's dedication of the land they found together to his leader, his kinsman, his teacher, his inspiration and his friend.

Captain Matthew Flinders, R.N., was buried at St James, Hampstead. Of this his daughter was written:

> Many years afterwards my aunt Tyler went to look for his grave, but found the churchyard remodelled, and quantities of tombstones and graves with their contents carted away as rubbish, among them that of my unfortunate father, thus pursued by disaster after death as in life.

His will, in which he left a keeper ring to his French friend, Thomy Pitot, was, for all his genius of exactitude, the will of a dreamer. Imagined assets in cold reality were few.

Somehow the little family battled on the pension of a post-captain's widow, between Lincolnshire and London, keeping their lodgings and their lives as bright, as thoughtful, and as happy as he could have wished. Representations made to the British Government, on the grounds that Mrs James Cook had been so generously provided for that some recognition might be made of the epic work of his successor, found British Government in unresponsive mood.

It was not until 1852 that the colonial States of New South Wales and Victoria, then radiating the wealth and optimism of gold, recalled a pathfinder of early years and the name he had chosen for the island continent he circled—Australia. In a belated gesture of gratitude, they offered to Ann Flinders and her daughter Anne an annual grant from each State of £100.

There is in the archives a graceful acknowledgment from Anne, regretting the recent death of her mother before she could know of this deeply-valued appreciation, and saying that she herself would gladly accept it to educate her son "in a manner worthy of the name he bears, Matthew Flinders Petrie".

The son of Flinders's dreams had come, into a world he was to leave the wiser.

Doctor of Laws, of Literature, of Science and Philosophy, author, musician, and the greatest archaeologist of the ages, Sir William Matthew Flinders Petrie needs no introduction. For him the Chair of Egyptology at London University was endowed. After a lifetime's invaluable research and excavation of buried cities, the resurrection of forgotten languages and forgotten kingdoms from the desert sands, at the age of eighty-seven years, he greets the sons of Australia in Palestine to-day. His first antique collections in childhood were a pocketful of Roman coins that the boy Matthew had found on the Lincolnshire fens. Well has this son of his, of the second generation, justified the education that it was the privilege of Australia to provide in his name, a gift from the dead.

Matthew Flinders's fame has grown steadily brighter with the passing years. The boyish escapade of *Tom Thumb* endeared him to seafaring youth, his friendship with George Bass is ever a David and Jonathan story. The map-making miracles of the *Francis* and *Norfolk* still confound the mariners of to-day.

His charts and navigations are the foundation of all our geography and all our sailing directions, charts as near to perfection in their time as human hand and eye could make them, and forever a model of cartography. Charles Darwin built the foundations of a new world of scientific thought on his knowledge. His observations of the barometer in land and sea-breezes are still a seaman's textbook. His discovery that the deviation of compass variations was due to the presence of iron in the ship revolutionized nautical science, stabilized the latitudes and longitudes of the globe. The Flinders Bar now keeps the compass true on every ship that puts to sea.

It is a fact that, with George Bass, he was the virtual discoverer of coal at Port Kembla on the South Coast of New South Wales in the *Tom Thumb* journey. Of all the harbours of our capitals and larger ports of commerce, with the exception of Sydney and Fremantle, he made the first authentic survey. From the masthead, he selected and recommended for settlement much of our richest agricultural country, including the hills and valleys of Albany, Hobart, Launceston, Illawarra, and Brisbane, the pageant of the Melbourne and Adelaide plains, the principal ports of Queensland.

His was the first suggestion of a settlement in North Australia, and the new Lincolnshire he wrote in his map of the south is a county in its own right to-day.

He sailed with Kent and Waterhouse when they introduced to the world's greatest wool-country its first merino sheep.

Of this, John Macarthur has written:

By these sea-captains, I was favoured with five ewes and three rams, of the Escurial flocks of the King of Spain presented to the Dutch Government at the Cape. The remainder were distributed among different individuals who did not take the necessary precautions to preserve the pure breed.

Mine were guarded against any impure mixtures, and increased in numbers, and improved in quality of their wool. A year or two after, I had the opportunity of augmenting my flocks by purchase from Colonel Foveaux of 1200 sheep of the common Cape breed. Results soon made themselves manifest.

In 1801 I took to England specimens of wool of the pure merino and of the best of the cross-bred, and having submitted them to an inspection of manufacturers, they reported that the merino wool was equal to any Spanish, and the cross-bred of considerable value.

Thus encouraged, I purchased 9 rams and one ewe from the Royal flocks at Kew, and returned to this country determined to devote my attention to the improvement of the whole of my flocks.

There is the origin of Australia's wool industry in a nutshell. To "Whiplash" Kent, first to vision the future of the merino in the rank river-flats of wilderness, we must give the credit as "the man before Macarthur".

The scene I have painted of the naming of the continent on the sands of King George's Sound is not a direct paraphrase of written history, but by the time he reached Port Lincoln in the *Investigator*, in February 1802, Flinders was writing familiarly of the natives as "these Australians". This is the first use of the word I can find. Through all his subsequent journals and letters, his name for the new land most frequntly appears — occasionally, in clarity, he may revert to the antique New Holland, for those not acquainted with the change.

There is a sentence in *A Voyage to Terra Australis*, written in 1813, when Sir Joseph Banks had denied his right to rechristen the great island. It preserves his claim to that honour for all time.

Had I permitted myself any innovation upon the original term, it would have been to convert it into "Australia", as being more agreeable to the ear, and an assimilation of the names of the other great parts of the earth.

For all Sir Joseph's excessive care, Australia was a well-known country in England from 1820 onward, and never anything else to its own people. The name was not formally adopted by statute until 1855.

Flinders sailed with Bligh of the *Bounty* when he established the first oak-trees, apple-trees and potatoes in Tasmania, the first oranges in Tahiti. He introduced the berry fruits to Australia. He helped Wilberforce to abolish the slave trade. Of his men of the *Investigator*, three attained to transcendent fame, Robert Brown, greatest of English botanists, Charles Wesall, R.A., and Sir John Franklin.

A valuable *Life of Matthew Flinders* was written by the late Professor Ernest Scott, from wide research and all data then available, in 1914. It was eight years later that Sir W. M. Flinders Petrie offered his grandfather's intimate diaries and letter-books to the archives of the first Australian State that would have the grace to perpetuate his memory in the erection of a statue. By this time we were "Flinders-conscious", and competition was keen. New South Wales, in the interests of the Mitchell Library, storehouse of the nation's history, promplty produced an expensive effigy with more haste than thought. The bronze figure purporting to be Flinders that guards its portals to-day is a poor presentation of a great sailor.

Not to be outdone, the other States followed. Melbourne, in an imaginative conception by the sculptor Web Gilbert, accorded him pride of place in the city, beside St Paul's Cathedral, in contemplation of the vast railway station that bears his name. It was unveiled to an oratorio composed for the occasion, "Let Us Praise Famous Men".

In Adelaide, a more lifelike commemoration of "the indefatigable Flinders", a sturdy young Lincolnshire sea-captain, his eyes a-dream of "the vacant spaces of the map", was erected by public subscription, convened by the late Sir Frank Moulden, Mr A. S. Diamond and the late Fred Johns. Lord Tennyson, at one time Governor of South Australia, was a grandson of Flinders, and son of Alfred Tennyson, poet laureate of England.

The fatal Third Log-book, confiscated by Decaen, for which Flinders fretted to the end of his days, was lost for nearly 130 years. Its facts and fabric have gone to the making of this book. It was discovered in the London Records Office in 1927 by Miss Ida Leeson, Mitchell Librarian, in a miscellany of old mariners' manuscripts unclassified.

In all probability, it had been restored by the french Government to the British at the time when Phillip Parker King, who was to complete Flinders's unfinished work on the north and north-west coasts, made application for it in 1818. Recognized as a treasure, it was not generously presented to Miss Leeson by the Records Office, though the originals of the *Investigator*'s first and second log-books are among the most carefully-guarded manuscripts of the Mitchell Library. Her share of the discovery she had made was a photostat copy.

Poring over the old letter-books and diaries—so much of emotion, so much of thought in the faded copper-plate hand-writing of one who so loved the world—has been to me one of the rarest pleasures of the writing. Flinders forever lives in those sea-stained pages, the ink bronzed and burnished by time, of his own written word.

On his map of the new continent, on which he had inscribed a thousand names for friendship, for association, and in his humorous fancy, he claimed nothing for himself. The years between have given him tribute. Those who followed could never forget him.

From Cape Leeuwin nine thousand miles to the Wessel Islands, both commemorating the valiant Dutch sailors drifting down in olden day, from Flinders Bay in the south-west to Flinders River in Carpentaria, all the explorers since have paid him his due respect. Islands, headlands, inlets, and lighthouses innumerable hold memory of his epic work, notable among them the Flinders Passage, the channel he found in his nine days' travail through the Great Barrier Reef. The Flinders Ranges in South Australia, 300 miles from south to north, their colourful peaks majestic against the desert sky, are worthy monument. The tufted yellow *Flindersia*, that blows all over the continent, is one of the richest fodder grasses of a mighty pastoral land.

His name is a household word in our five capital cities, each of them having conferred it on one of the principal streets. The little towns are legion where you will find it. Australia's great naval training school in Victoria is the Flinders Base. Flinders Column, the tall white monolith on Mount Lofty, visible for sixty miles by day and night, is one of our great southern aviation lights, in this century a beacon to navigators of aerial seas. The most modern locomotive of Commonwealth railways, that glossy green giant, stream-lined in its strength, that swings the Spirit of Progress nightly between Melbourne and Sydney at seventy miles an hour, is the *Matthew Flinders*.

Even the blacks immortalized his memory. At the Wessel Islands, where he left the survey off the coast of Arnhem Land, there are caves with crude drawings of Stone Age Man, Old Masters in red ochre and pipe-clay depicting his redcoat marines with their white cross-bands. Mrs Daisy Bates, the famous "White Mother of a Black Race", assures me that in her wanderings among the Bibbulmun aboriginal tribes of the south-west of Australia, an ancient native named Nebinyan danced for her the "Kurranup" dance of Flinders's men, when he drilled them to amuse a simple, savage people of the woods of King George's Sound. That corroboree of the "white brothers" had survived five generations.

In the windy solitudes of the Gulf of Carpentaria, on the brown crest of Observation Island, where, limping with illness, oppressed with fever and the knowledge that his ship was breaking, he discovered that his time-keepers were three degrees out of reckoning, I stood beside a little cairn of stones. It was erected there by Commander Bennett of H.M.A.S *Geranium* in 1925, dedicated to Matthew Flinders's memory. As I travelled his ship-tracks all round Australia, visioning a new land through his eyes, I have noted no monument, no recognition, that would be dearer to him than that rough cairn of stones, where no ships pass to-day.

Still stands that chart of Carpentaria, the original lost in shipwreck, the duplicate compiled from stray notes and a genius of mathematic memory, as the only existing documentary knowledge of too-long-neglected shores.

For the rest, our one hundred and fifty years have seen a miracle of change. Leviathan ships of the world follow the track of *Tom Thumb* through Sydney Heads, to carry away thousands of Australia's sons fighting for Britain's empire.

Now the sandhills where he wandered, theodolite on shoulder, look down on pulsing cities and prosperous towns. Rarely did his instinct fail him in visions of the future. From Albany in the far south-west, to Cape York, the apex of the continent, a chain of great ports and happy havens was of his finding.

The one blind spot in his eye was for Australia's rivers. It is a curious fact that Flinders found none. He missed the mouth of the Murray, one of the earth's greatest, though, as I have told in "Fleur-de-Lis", its tumbled breakers were sighted. He missed the broad stream of the Clarence—though he anchored in its harbour—and passed unseeing, two thousand miles to the Roper, all the rich waterways of the west and the north coast that swing down from the Great Dividing Range to slink through sand-flats and sandhills into the sea. As one who knew only the free English rivers, he could not be prepared for such deception. But he was to circumnavigate Australia again after this preliminary survey. Let us remember that he left his work unfinished when he was only twenty-eight years old.

That was the most poignant sadness of his life.

In our brotherhood with America, Great Britain's eldest child, it is a fact too long forgotten that we claim the same birthplace. The square tower of Boston Stump looked down on the little ships that sailed to great beginnings; that low coast of East Anglia has mothered two great nations.

From there the Pilgrim Fathers buffeted the lonely sea in quest of God and freedom. From there the Whitby collier *Endeavour* followed a star of destiny to strange adventure. Banks, Bass, Flinders and Franklin dreamed of the Unknown in those tranquil Fenland villages, all within the throb of Boston bells.

And the greatest of these is Flinders, "that obscure name", as he wrote to Sir Joseph, at last a "ray of glory". The map of Australia is his memorial. For his consuming love of this country, his great achievement when it was a shapeless bulk in the minds of men, unlucky and unwanted, he will some day be crowned our national hero.

The soul of Matthew Flinders lives in every boy who points the prow of his little skiff to sea.

As the life's work of his illustrious grandson leads back across the age-old past to earth's beginning, so his life's work rolls as a crested wave to the triumphs of the timeless future.

While the old order crumbles in Europe, in the new world that we shall build, Australia, continent of his naming, faces the dawn.

Addenda

Charles Daley, Esq., for twelve years secretary and a past president of Melbourne Historical Society, contributes the following valuable notes:

With regard to the gravestone of Flinders, about ten years ago Rev. Hewton of Launceston, Tasmania, while visiting England, at St Thomas's Church, Maryon Road, London, saw a tablet commemorating Flinders. He stated that the tomb at St James's Church had been destroyed or removed before 1854. Mr Hewton found the stone in the churchyard, in a dilapidated state, and on return to Victoria suggested that steps should be taken for its preservation. Sir James Barrett, then President of the Flinders Statue Committee, wrote to the Prime Minister, Right Hon. S. M. Bruce, to endeavour through the offices of Sir Granville Ryrie, then High Commissioenr for Australia, to have this historical stone rehabilitated. I understand that through Australia House this was affected.

About a year afterwards, Mr Harry Kitchen, a native of Donington, wrote to me stating that on a visit to his home town, after thirty years in Australia, he had designed, and prepared for casting in bronze, a tablet which had been affixed to the birthplace of Matthew Flinders, bearing the following inscription:

CAPTAIN MATTHEW FLINDERS, R.N.
THE EXPLORER,
BORN ON THIS SITE, MARCH 16, 1774

Apropos of Flinders memorials, there is a cairn erected to the memory of George Bass at Rhyll, Phillip Island.

In 1912 a bronze tablet was erected on a granite boulder on the summit of Station (or Flinders) Peak, from which excellent viewpoint Flinders looked upon the future site of Melbourne.

In 1914, at Dromana on the Bluff at Arthur's Seat, a cairn was erected at the place to which Flinders had ascended, and which was identified by Sir John Franklin on a second visit in 1844. On the badly-defaced inscription, Lieutenant Murray, discoverer of Port Phillip, and John Franklin are mentioned in addition to Flinders.

At Indented Head, near Portarlington, a tall cairn was raised a few years ago to mark the landing of Flinders there, and also John Batman's coming in 1835.

To show the personal regard that Flinders has won for himself from the Australian people, I might mention that some years ago a Melbourne lawyer notified me that by a client's will the sum of £600 was bequeathed to the Historical Society of Victoria for the purpose of erecting a memorial to Matthew Flinders at Mornington, the vicinity of which he reached in his long-boat before striking westward to Indented Head. The bequest is to become operative on the death of lagatees.

Angus McMillan, explorer of Gippsland, in a letter describing his journeys (1839–41), writes: "I had no guide but a compass and *a chart of Flinders*."

Count Strzelecki (1840), a close friend of Governor Franklin in Tasmania, also carried a chart of Flinders in his extensive explorations.

The prophet who had such scant honour in his own country is, without doubt, honoured and esteemed in the land for which he did such valuable service.

Acknowledgments

In the writing and compiling of this book my thanks and most grateful acknowledgments are due to:

The Commonwealth Literary Board of the Prime Minister's Department, which, in 1940, accorded me a Fellowship to complete the work;

Dame Mary Gilmore, for her friendship and encouragement throughout;

Dr G. A. Mackaness of Sydney, who as historian-author of valuable contemporary studies of *William Bligh*, *Governor Phillip* and *Sir Joseph Banks* has spurred me to completion of the task with kindred historical spirit;

Captain C. H. Peters, of Messrs Robertson and Mullens, Melbourne; Lloyd Dumas, Esq., Editor of *The Advertiser*, Adelaide, and S. H. Deamer, Editor *A.B.C. Weekly*, for their helpful interest;

The late Professor Ernest Scott, whose documentary *Life of Matthew Flinders* has been a storehouse of information;

Mitchell Librarian, Sydney, and officers of public libraries and archives throughout Australia, who made available all *Flinders Papers* in their possession, including intimate diaries and letters never yet published;

Mr F. Pilgrim, of Adelaide, who allowed me access to a number of Mrs Flinders's letters, treasured in the family;

Miss Edith Abbott, who aided me with research in Melbourne;

My son Robert, whose knowledge and vivid conceptions of sea-life in the eighteenth century, whose admiration of Flinders and zest of expression, in flagging hours of labour, have helped me to carry the burden of my "young man of the sea".

ERNESTINE HILL
1941

www.ingramcontent.com/pod-product-compliance
Ingram Content Group Australia Pty Ltd
76 Discovery Rd, Dandenong South VIC 3175, AU
AUHW021257051225
420544AU00010B/110